SYMPH

DEVIL

BOOK II IN THE BLACKMOORE LEGACY

Marcus James

Candiano Books

Symphony for the Devil
Book II in the Blackmoore Legacy
Marcus James

Also by Marcus James
Following the Kaehees
Blackmoore
In God's Eyes
Symphony for the Devil
Rise of the Nephilim
Fall of the Nephilim
Instructions in Flesh
Ghosts of Blood and Bone

Featured short story anthologies
Ultimate Undies: Erotic Stories About Underwear and Lingerie
Best Gay Love Stories: New York City
Ultimate Gay Erotica 2007
Dorm Porn 2
Travelrotica 2
Best Gay Love Stories: Summer Flings
Island Boys
Frat Sex 2
Best Gay Love Stories 2009

Acknowledgments

*This book is dedicated to My amazing editor, Evanne Freeman-
Casey, my amazing cover designer Elise Ortega, and my husband
David Potterton for putting up with me typing and reading for
hours upon hours on end. To Shelly Alexandre, as always.
To the readers, for waiting so long for the return of the Black-
moores.*

*In loving memory of Blair Cameron. Thank you for all of those
early morning talks when I was growing up. Thank you for always
believing in me and encouraging me to pursue writing as you had
done. You will always be loved and never forgotten.*

*Finally, to myself. It took me a decade to write, and there were
times I never thought there would be a completion. But there was,
and the tears were bitter-sweet.*

DIANA WAS NOT KNOWN to the witches and spirits, the fairies and elves who dwell in desert place, the goblins, as their mother; she hid herself in humility and was a mortal, but by her will she rose again above it all. She had such passion for witchcraft, and became so powerful therein, that her greatness could not be hidden.

And thus it came to pass one night, at the meeting of the sorceresses and fairies, she declared that she would darken the heavens and turn all the stars into mice. All those who were present said "if thou canst do such a strange thing, having risen to such power, though shalt be our queen."

—Aradia, or The Gospel of the Witches

Prologue

TREVOR HATED CEMETERIES. There was no way around that fact, and yet here he was, standing with Braxton and the rest of his family, all of them clutching black umbrellas and listening to the priest give last rites.

Three weeks ago, everything had changed. He and Braxton had found out that their entire lives had been orchestrated, that their destinies had been planned out hundreds of years before, denying them any say on the matter. The fabled evil that had plagued the Blackmoores had returned upon him and Braxton's union, and as a result his cousin Brighton Blackmoore was dead.

It was the first weekend of January and the rain came down slowly, tapping on nylon, slipping down the ribs of the numerous umbrellas. Trevor's hazel eyes surveyed the faces around him—all of them worn out, the melancholy of their truth taking a physical toll on their bodies. His mother Kathryn stood silent, not a tear to be found on her lovely face.

The last time she had cried was on that doomed Christmas Eve night. Her auburn hair was smooth and clipped back behind her. Gentle strands hung down, framing the sides of her face. She wore a simple black dress and knee-high leather boots, her body kept warm by a long black wool coat.

The rest of the women looked no different. The coven had grown since their arrival. Mary-Margaret and Natalie, the twins, stood with cool green eyes and the same dark red, almost-burgundy hair as Trevor's. Their little brother Sean clutched Natalie's hand. Trevor hadn't even known there was a little brother until a week before they had arrived in Ireland. Their father Seamus stood behind his two daughters, his salt-and-pepper hair cut short, and his eyes that same cool green.

Adamo and Francesca held tightly to their father Malachey, Seamus's brother. Adamo was originally going to give the last rites, but in the end was too grief-stricken to proceed. Mitchell stood with Maria, Brighton's daughter. She was alone now. There was no one. Her husband had been lost to the Legacy, her son Jason had been killed in a drug deal, and now she was burying her father.

Trevor knew that there would be more deaths, that this was only the beginning. The ancient Dark God of the Wood, not too far from this place, was calling its agents while it waited and gathered strength. Yes, there would be more.

Magdalene, Queen Mab, and her mother Fiona stood with Darbi and John—all of them obviously reflecting on the last time they had all been here in the parish of Kilcommon, County Mayo, for Darbi's mother Mona Blackmoore's funeral.

"Are you okay?" It took him a moment to register the words, to recognize the voice. It was all foreign to him now, everything. He felt as if he were Ebenezer Scrooge, looking upon the shadows of his own past. There seemed no logic to any of it, and since the night of his eighteenth birthday, everything had begun to seem even more unreal.

"Yeah...." He looked into Braxton's large onyx-brown eyes, so soulful and so all-consuming; it made him grin. Braxton was wearing that same black-and-blue pinstripe suit that he had worn the night of J.T. Oliver's party, though it no longer seemed to hold the same festive air that it once had.

Ever since finding out that they were it—that he and Braxton were the chosen ones, that Braxton carried Blackmoore blood—things between them had changed. Not in distance, but in closeness. It was a security that their being together was meant to be, that they were made for one another and no one else. They never had to worry about anything coming in and changing things around.

When the priest was finished, Mitchell, Adamo, Darbi, Jeffery, Marcel, John, Trevor, and Braxton stepped forward, gripping the handles on the coffin and lifting it up, preparing to put him in the Blackmoore Mausoleum. It was a mammoth thing made of limestone in a Greco-Roman design, set in the ground with a slated roof.

Strong wrought-iron gates granted them entrance, six steps descending into this man-made pit. The columns of the tomb had been weathered over countless years, when the first Sarafeene and Malachey Blackmoore were laid to rest in the gravesite, newly constructed by Tristan after his daughter Katy had paid the family off in exchange for being left alone.

Here Brighton would remain, with Mona and the rest of the Blackmoores, waiting for those still living to join them.

Night's Black Agents

The evil angels had sown the seeds of that strange art among men and had introduced every kind of sorcery and magic among them.
—*Eusebius* from the *Praeparatio Evangelica*

Millions of spiritual creatures walk the earth
Unseen, both when we wake and when we sleep.
—John Milton

Chapter: One

HE DIDN'T THINK THAT he could run any faster. The earth was kicking up beneath his feet as he navigated through thick dark, the air chilly and the fertile soil evident of the rain that had just fallen. He knew where he was; he recognized the thick monuments which stood like silent guards watching him pass. The sweat beaded down his face, staining the neck of his thin white tee, acting as a sponge and soaking up his perspiration.

This was Bayview; this was where Christian Vasquez and Greg Sheer lay beneath the earth, being devoured by worms and maggots. The fog was thick and the air was crisp as he ran, knowing that if he stopped, they would catch up. He turned and spied numerous burning orbs moving towards him in succession, like fairies in the Halloween night: desperate to lure a weary traveler or awaken the slumbering dead.

There was a dull hum as he moved, slipping past trees and headstones. He was trying to outwit the burning prisms that slipped through the mist. He stopped, caught off-guard by the darkened figure of a cloaked woman, her face covered by a hood, paying him no mind. She moved apart from the present, and he knew that she was one of the dead. Not ever an entity that lived a life, but one that was made up of thousands of lifetimes. She was an essence formed from the very pieces of the hundreds that lay beneath the earth.

She was Bayview's guardian. She watched over the souls; her business was not the living, except for only when they trespassed—and at night, a human being's presence was certainly that.

His skin crawled as he watched her, forgetting those ominous, burning orbs that glided through the mist—wondering only about this shadowed woman, and what she may or may not do. His foot gave, his knee popping his leg straight, a lone twig snapping beneath his foot. He turned and came face-to-face with a quick black form: the face withered, the nose narrow, the mouth rotting away. From beneath her hood, her yarn-like, purple-silver hair billowed, but it was those empty sockets—black and endless, hollow in her skull—that took him by surprise and sent him into darkness.

TREVOR BLACKMOORE'S eyes popped open, staring up at the darkened ceiling of Braxton's room, trying to regain composure. His hair and shirt were damp with sweat, and his cheeks felt hot, flushed from the nightmare. He sat up and looked to his right side, seeing Braxton sound asleep in the bed, his chest bare and his hair slightly disheveled. The signs of stubble lined his face, and it seemed to Trevor that he was grinning.

"I'm glad someone's sleeping." He looked around the quiet room. Bright moonlight shone pale blue through the windows, illuminating the floor and glistening on the quiet waters of Lake Samish. There were boxes everywhere. Though they had spent the remainder of their senior year living in the Volaverunt house, Braxton had no wish to remain in it, and simply moving away wasn't enough. He needed the comfort of knowing that it no longer existed, that it was no longer standing as a testament to his father's death.

'*Trevor....*' His name fell out like a hiss, and it drew his attention to the foot of the bed. There, standing in front of the white maple armoire, was a handsome young man with chestnut hair, disheveled brown knickers, and a dirty white oxford. His eyes were black, and his flesh like marble. Trevor knew that it was a spirit and that it was somehow connected to him, not simply a lone soul lost and looking for a guiding light.

"Who are you?"

The being's arm lifted slowly and stretched out firm, pointing an accusing finger at Trevor. He felt the air turn cold, as if the warmth were being sucked out, taken in by this being. *'You will soon see, and you will soon understand....'*

Before Trevor could ask more, the entity departed, fading into nothing—leaving him alone in the silent early morning, his worried face and hazel eyes illuminated by the glow of the moon.

In a few hours the movers would arrive, and soon all of the boxes would be loaded up into the trucks on their way to Seattle, where Trevor and Braxton would be residing. He was relieved now more than ever to be leaving, hoping that some of the darkness that had been haunting them would stay behind in Bellingham, and not follow them to the big metropolis.

Trevor had been accepted to the University of Washington, and Braxton's band, The Spit Monkeys, had signed on with Arcadia Records. Though they both battled with the idea of leaving, the two decided that in the end it would be better for them to get out and try to live their lives in a new environment, far away from all of the pain of the previous school year.

Along with them would be J.T. Oliver and Cheri Hannifin, who had also been accepted to U.W. Trevor hadn't been sure at first how Cheri would feel about them rekindling a friendship after what had happened to her on Christmas Eve, when she was almost murdered by the resurrected Tom Preston, and all of the unexplainable and otherworldly events that she had witnessed—but to his surprise, she hardly batted an eye.

Trevor was worried about leaving his mother, but she had Queen Mab, and for the time being, Francesca was staying with her. Though she said it was for Kathryn, Trevor had a feeling that it was more for her own peace of mind than anyone else's. He knew that he needed to sleep, that they were going to have a big day ahead of them, but the early morning's visitation had his mind racing and his eyes curious.

He sighed and took a look at Braxton, seeing that peaceful face, and knew that the last thing he wanted to do was wake him. Unlike Trevor, who could handle little sleep, Braxton was different, and he was a terrible driver if he wasn't rested. The two of them would be driving their cars up, so there would be no one to take turns at the wheel.

Quietly he padded across the floor, cracking the door open and moving out into the hall, maneuvering in the dark. There were pictures still on the walls and furniture that would be left behind, to be sent off to charity before it was all destroyed by the demolition crew as soon as their belongings were packed up and ready to go. It wasn't like they needed the furniture. They were moving into his family's penthouse in downtown Seattle. It included a study and was already furnished. Still, he wondered if this wasn't more coming from Braxton's need to purge himself of the loss that had been suffered inside of these walls.

Trevor sighed and slipped through the front room, making his way to the long front hall with the numerous windows that had been replaced three days after Christmas, before Brighton's funeral in Ireland. They never went to the late Eric Volaverunt's office at the end of the hall, and yet Trevor was finding himself being drawn to it now, seeing that solid door with its steel handle beckoning to him with the gleam of moonlight. He moved to it quietly, seeing the dark stain of blood still pooled on the wood, unable to be removed. They had tried everything possible and hired as many different cleaning services as possible, but still the blood of Eric Volaverunt refused to go away.

Why am I doing this? he questioned, wanting to turn back, to tuck himself under the covers with his boyfriend—yet even as he contemplated turning away, his hand was already twisting the handle. The door jutted open and the coldest rush of air welcomed him, slipping around his body and spreading into the rest of the house.

The room was dark but even still, Trevor could make out a clutter of things all over the walls. It was unsettling to be surrounded by all of this memory—these shadows that Braxton wished to avoid, so that he could deny their existence and do away with them as quickly as possible.

He searched around and knocked his thigh into the corner of the desk, feeling for the lamp and pulling its cord. His breath caught in his throat as he surveyed the numerous eyes that stared down at him, the constant images of Braxton's mother smiling and laughing. All of these snapshots of Tammy had been caught in candid moments, and she appeared slightly uncomfortable with having her photo taken by her husband or whoever had taken these pictures. Eric had really loved his wife, and so now his grief, more than ever, was understandable.

I need to get out of here. He flipped off the lamp and slipped back out into the hall, closing the door behind him, not turning until he heard it latch into place. He spund around and stood, stunned, feeling everything inside of him freeze. His blood seemed to become ice, and his legs were like blocks as he witnessed the vision that played before him.

'Goodbye, Braxton!' A frail Eric Volaverunt lifted a pistol to Braxton's head, pointing it between his kid's eyes. The man's pajamas were soiled and his body was frail, sickly—just as Braxton had always described his father in the past. His dark hair greasy and unkempt.

"Braxton!" Trevor yelled, and yet neither of them took notice. Braxton was dressed in those loose Jnco's and a black shirt, his chocolate eyes wide and his cheeks flushed red, bits of shattered glass everywhere.

'*No!*' Braxton yelled, and Eric dropped the gun, convulsing suddenly while the blood began to ebb from his ears, his breath sputtering before stopping—choking on his own blood, which was blubbering out of his mouth. He hit the floor with a dull thud, and Braxton was racing to his father in tears.

Trevor closed his eyes and hit the floor, feeling the immensity of pain that seemed to take over, fermenting in the air around him. He could feel Eric's death, the pain that his body was going through as everything was shutting down—as his lungs seemed to be collapsing as if he were underwater, and the anguish of his blood vessels in his brain bursting due to the sudden aneurysm.

He sobbed and rocked himself, trying to end the vision, trying to end the terrible flood of memories that were playing—memories that stained this house, just like Eric's blood stained the floor.

"Trevor?" He heard his name, but it seemed distant, as if it were just another memory, and now Trevor was suddenly afraid that everything in his life was just a series of shadows of a time that no longer was. "Trevor, baby...." He felt those familiar hands take hold of him, those fingers curl into his flesh, and the scent of salt and iron that lingered beneath skin. Trevor opened his eyes and saw Braxton staring at him, his face kind, his lips moist and slightly pouty, and accentuated by a subtle under-bite. He was so beautiful that Trevor thought again that Braxton would make a great model.

"Sorry... I was just...."

Braxton shook his head and pulled Trevor into him, supporting his weight, his firm body and semi-hard cock clothed in black American Apparel boxer-briefs with white piping and stitch. "Shh... it's okay. We'll be away from this place tomorrow; we'll be far away from all of these ghosts."

He nodded. He knew that just because they left didn't mean that they were going to be able to escape the truth of their lives, the ghosts of their pasts. But, he figured, that distance might help give them time to be like other eighteen-year-olds, ready to make it out on their own as adults.

"It was so real..." Trevor managed against Braxton's chest, his lips pressing against the soft of his skin. The mild hard-on that tented his boyfriend's underwear was a comfort in this place that, at the moment, seemed void of any real emotion other than anger.

"NO, MOM, YOU REALLY don't need to come down here... yes, the movers are already here." Trevor grinned at Braxton, who winked at him while carrying a handful of boxes to Trevor's Jaguar, setting them down in the backseat. "All right, fine, we'll see you in a few minutes." He hung up his cell phone and walked over to Braxton, who was standing in a pair of jeans and a forest-green Burberry polo, the classic nova-check design on the hem of the sleeves and on the neckline.

"Is she coming?"

Trevor slipped his sunglasses on his face and nodded, taking his place at Braxton's side, and he slipped his hand into Trevor's. "Yeah, she is... she wants to see us off." He nodded and grinned, leaning down and placing a gentle kiss on his cheek. "What was that for?" he asked Braxton.

"For loving me like you do." There wasn't a moment when Trevor didn't. Throughout the past several months, things be-tween them were just getting better. Now they could pick up on each other's thoughts and feel the connection between them as though it were solid and protective, sheltering them from danger. Their blood was strong; they could sense it reflecting in one another as if they were each other's mirror, and this made Trevor happy in a way that he had never dreamt possible before he and Braxton had gotten together.

"I think the crew is here," Braxton said, forcing Trevor to turn his attention to the drive—seeing the collection of workers pull up along with the wrecking ball and bulldozers, their faces eager to level the sprawling lakefront home.

Trevor gave the movers a check and thanked them for clearing out all of the furniture—which was being donated to the Salvation Army as well as the Goodwill—knowing that Braxton had wanted nothing of his past except for those few personal things that would go in their cars, that Trevor felt shouldn't go to waste. Though, if it had been solely up to Braxton, he would have left them in the house as more offerings to the carnage that was going to take place.

"I'm pretty sure my mother was already on her way when she called me."

Braxton turned to him and looked at him inquisitively. "She's already here." Braxton turned back towards the drive to see Jared, the driver who had replaced Miles after he passed, open the back door to the Lexus GS-450 limousine and reach his hand out, helping Kathryn Blackmoore get to her feet. She was dressed in a black skirt-suit with luminescent black pinstripes, her three-tiered pearl necklace resting in her neckline, a pair of large Chanel sunglasses on her face. Her auburn hair was pulled back, and she had a black sun hat on her head.

"Mom." Trevor walked up to his mother, who was making her way down the walk like a model on the runway, her feet tapping on the stone in her usual Manolo Blahniks.

"Hello, darling." She clutched her checkboard Louis Vuitton handbag, her nails painted in their usual deep crimson.

"I don't know why you insisted on coming down here, and dressed like that. Ever hear of jeans and a t-shirt?"

Kathryn chuckled. "I came down because I wanted to see you two off, and secondly, I have to go down to the old cannery and lumber yard. The contractor is coming to take estimates on the cost of converting it into a market and shopping pavilion." It had taken years for them to get all of the companies that they had wanted to agree to move into the new shopping center, especially since they were so far removed from the big city that was Seattle.

"So it's really happening?"

Kathryn nodded. "It's going to rival Pier 39 in San Francisco and Pike Place Market in Seattle. We got Coach, Louis Vuitton, Burberry, Marc Jacobs, Kitson, Sephora, and Ben Sherman. We also got many fine restaurants, a café, Starbucks of course, Banana Republic, The Melting Pot, an Imax theater, plus an indoor roller coaster. Two nightclubs, a full-service gourmet market, fresh seafood, plus several other shops as well as a bakery, and yeah...." All of this she had counted off continuously with her fingers.

"This will be really good for the city."

She nodded. "A lot more jobs, of course, which the mayor seems to be thrilled about. What he's not thrilled about, though, is the fact that I have to build up on the cannery."

"How up?"

"Two more stories."

He looked at his mother, completely stunned. "But it's already four stories."

"Yes, but how else do you expect everything to fit?" They both glanced over at Braxton, watching him discuss the plans of the demolition with the supervisor, their voices inaudible.

"And what about the mill and shipping yard?" Trevor asked, bringing their attentions back to the discussion.

"Well, in the old shipping yard we're going to construct an aquarium, and the mill is going to be turned into luxury apartments for all of the employees of the new... I don't even know what to call it. The first people we're going to offer jobs to are the homeless teens and homeless families." It seemed to Trevor that whenever he thought he had his mother pegged, she always seemed to do something to blow those notions right out of the water.

"That's really great of you...." He said it without really meaning to, and Kathryn only looked at him as if perplexed by his observation.

"So, are you two ready for this big step?" Trevor nodded, his eyes watching the summer sun glisten on the water. A speedboat raced along, tearing into the cool water, creating streams of white. He wondered if any of the families picnicking on the shore across from them would be startled and curious when the wrecking ball came crashing through that ceiling, sending large amounts of wood and concrete into the air, hindering the tranquility of this late August morning.

"As ready as a person ever can be when leaving your home for someplace entirely different." His mother nodded, and her face moved into a warm smile as she watched Braxton jog up to them both.

"Kathryn, you look lovely." She blushed, and Braxton kissed her politely on the cheek. "Thanks again for letting us move into the apartment." She shook her head. The truth was, she was happy that it would finally be occupied, since the last time she had been there had been with Tom—who had completely remodeled it behind her back, stripping the home of any inkling of Sheffield.

"Not a problem... at least it's getting some use now." Braxton loved that whisky voice, and could not help but think on that morning when he had felt the press of Kathryn's body against his own and the taste of her lips on his, that invigorating slip of tongue.

He turned and his gaze met with Trevor's. He seemed to be aware of something going on, something that Braxton figured he may very well now know. He knew that he couldn't deny the attraction he felt for the great Kathryn Blackmoore—nor could any other man in the city.

She was sex. She walked with Aphrodite; hell, she *was* Aphrodite, but he also knew that her charms meant nothing. Especially not when it came down to Trevor, who had bewitched him from that day long ago back in the seventh grade.

"Well, are we ready?"

Braxton grinned at Trevor. "Yeah, we just need to pull our cars out of the way."

Trevor nodded, and Kathryn stepped to the side to allow the two boys to pull their cars out onto the side of the road, making way for the heavy machinery.

"This should be exciting!" Kathryn's tone was genuinely joyous, and it was slightly unnerving for Trevor, who didn't quite think that this event was going to be something that Braxton would take to be happy.

"It's a new start." Braxton wrapped his arm around Trevor's waist and planted his lips on his forehead as they watched the crew get revved up, turning on the wrecking ball. The three of them observed as it made its way to the side in a slight turn before coming back around, that large ball of destruction slamming through the roof and sailing through the wall.

Trevor winced as he watched it come back round again, erupting through the windows of the front room, a cascade of wood and glass showering down. The home was becoming more and more of a ruined battlement. He saw the confident grin on Braxton's face and the excited smile on his mother's, and he couldn't help but feel out of place, like this wasn't someplace that he belonged. He seemed to be the only one who wasn't indifferent to the chaos.

It took no more than a few minutes to have the Volaverunt home reduced to nothing more than scraps and lumber. It made Trevor cringe, and yet it seemed that still Braxton appeared unaffected.

"Well, that's that." He gave his hands a slap and a rub before making his way back up the drive to their cars. He was ready to go; there was no hesitation or pause about that. Kathryn and Trevor looked at one another as they watched him get further and further away, already leaving this place—his entire past—behind.

"Don't even think about it."

Trevor looked at his mother. "What?"

She narrowed her glasses and looked at him. "Oh, please; you know what. Look, I know that you don't understand it, but maybe you should count yourself fortunate. Braxton has nothing. Sure, he has us, but everything he's known, since the day of his birth into this world, is now gone. It doesn't exist, and in both instances it ended because of us, because of Blackmoore blood. He just needs to see it gone, no longer able to haunt him."

Trevor did understand. Not to the same extent, but he got it. He felt the same way with Christian, and though he would never tell it to Braxton, he was still on occasion haunted by his dead lover's shadow. "I just want to know that he'll be okay."

His mother frowned and took him by the arm, drawing him close to her. She smelled like flowers and cotton candy; it was obviously her Burberry perfume, but he had grown to associate that with her, and now he was finally feeling the first pangs of sadness. "He will be... and so will you; it's not like you're in another state." His mother had read his mind, though she would never admit to it even if asked.

"So, where's Francesca?"

"She's already at the cannery."

"And Queen Mab?"

"That old bat is getting one of the rooms prepared for Mary-Margaret." Trevor looked up at her inquisitively as they made their walk up the drive.

"Didn't I tell you? Anyway, she's coming to teach a course on music theory or something like that at Fairhaven University for the year, so she's staying with Queen Mab." Trevor nodded in a very casual way, interested enough to know but not enough to care. "But don't you worry about any of us up here; you're going to have a whole new life ahead of you down in Seattle... but Trevor?"

He looked up at his mother and saw the grim shadow that had taken over her face. "Yeah?"

"Don't forget, either one of you... Braxton, are you listening?" He nodded and drew in closer. "The darkness is not gone, and the evil of the old moor is not dead, only asleep. Its agents could come for you at any moment, and though I do not want you to think that everyone is really out to get you, I still want you to be wary of those whose paths you cross.

"I want the two of you to be happy and have a great time in Seattle; after all, you have a great home and an unlimited bank account. You can do anything, but don't let this freedom blind you. You are the chosen ones; you are the two that *It* is after."

"We know, Mom... we know." She kissed them both and they stood hand-in-hand, watching as Kathryn slipped back into her car and pulled out of the drive, the young Jared navigating the car away, back into the city.

"So, babe?"

"Yeah, stud?" Trevor responded playfully.

"You ready to go home?"

Trevor looked around them one more time, seeing everything that they had ever known, and realized that it was no more than a distant pin stuck in a map on a corkboard. "Let's go home."

Braxton gripped Trevor and dipped him in that old Hollywood way, planting a sweet kiss on his lips. It was powerful, and Trevor felt that mild kinetic twinge and knew that Braxton had gotten some sort of flash, some sort of insight. "Wow... I liked that!" he said with a grin.

"What?"

Braxton's brows arched playfully. "Now I'm really ready to get to Seattle, so we can try out our new bed!"

They kissed one more time and got into their vehicles: Trevor into his Jaguar Roadster convertible that had originally belonged to his father, and Braxton climbed into a black Mercedes-Benz 320 Kompressor he had purchased after selling his Acura.

It had been easier than they both had thought. Braxton knew that the only will that had ever existed had been in Eric's office, and that he himself had no representation. John and Braxton went before the judge and explained that Eric had been manic and had smashed all of the windows in the house. When Braxton went to check on his father, he had just arrived when his father began having his aneurysm. There was nothing that could be done.

In the end, everything was given to Braxton. He inherited great sums of money-the details of which were explained to him by John and the other lawyers, though he had barely paid attention-as well as the house and any of the other properties owned by the American Volaverunts.

He didn't want any of it, except for the money. It was hard enough now that they both knew the truth. There was no escaping what their bloodline was, and because of that Braxton could never leave the Volaverunts behind, because they were in fact Blackmoores.

They were eighteen and as rich as kings. Trevor didn't really like the idea of that, namely because he didn't trust himself and Braxton enough—but he also knew that they had grown up with money their entire lives, and so were raised to treat it like anything else. It was there if you needed it, but not for the hell of it.

Kathryn had told him that off-and-on as he got older, and Tammy had apparently been the same way with Braxton, though she had not come from money like Eric. But it was that humbleness that kept Braxton from turning into many of the kids that they had went to high school with, the ones who lived on Edgemoore in their mega-mansions.

As they made their way out of Bellingham, Trevor leading the way and Braxton right behind, their cars racing along the freeway, he felt a great weight lift—as if being thrown off and left along the side of the road. It was invigorating. He knew that his mother's warnings would heed true, but with the warm summer air wisping through his hair and the stretch of land ahead of him, he realized that for now he didn't care. For now, Trevor Blackmoore was just like everyone else.

Chapter: Two

THE SLEEK SILVER ROLLS Royce passed through downtown Seattle, the gleam of the sun slipping along the car's body, cutting through the road like a knife, maneuvering around other vehicles and pedestrians, making its way to One Pacific Tower at 2000 First Avenue. It crept into the private garage under the sprawling citadel, all of its eight private parking spaces filled with BMWs and Porsches. The front door opened, and the female driver stepped out, her stilettos spiking the concrete.

She was five-foot-ten, and her black hair hung past her breasts in curly tendrils, her eyes covered by large sunglasses. Her slender frame was clothed in a powder-blue sleeveless skirt, her hands clutching a leather date book; her French-tipped nails were long and glossy. With a commanding walk she made her way to the elevator and slipped inside, pressing her finger into the button for the twenty-seventh floor. It rose up quickly, and within seconds it came to a stop, the door sliding open and revealing a lone foyer with peach-colored walls and white molding. A chandelier glistened above her, dripping with expensive crystals.

She walked up to the massive double doors and stuck her key in the slot, giving the gold handle a turn, pushing it open. Light glistened on the Venetian-plastered walls, and the marble floors gleamed. She passed through the long hall. Various pieces of rare art hung on either side, spotlighted with tract lights, giving the feeling of a gallery.

The great room was bright with a long wall of glass, the French doors in the center opening up onto an expansive balcony with unobstructed views of downtown Seattle and Puget Sound. The walls that surrounded the white marble fireplace at the left were covered in maple paneling that reached from the floor to the ceiling, and matching beams crossed above this in deep squares above.

There were two beige couches and two chairs with cream stripes. A table stood behind the couch, facing the entrance. Two gold lamps with black shades stood on either end, and a giant vase with dozens of roses added a striking bit of color to a space that was nearly devoid of it. To the right of this was a grand piano and two more armchairs. A short but long bookcase separated the seating area from the dining room table, which had chairs seated for ten, but could be extended as needed to seat up to twenty.

"I'm home!" she called out, only now seeing her brother out on the balcony drinking a cup of tea, his short black hair glossy in the sun.

"Out here!" his tenor voice sounded back, and she grinned. She sat her date book and classic black YSL bag on one of the striped chairs, finding that one of the glass doors was cracked open.

"Elisabeth, how was your meeting?"

She looked over at her brother and sighed. His icy blue eyes were covered with his Gucci sunglasses, their thin frame sitting graciously on his slender and handsome face, his lips full and moist, his six-foot-two frame clothed in black slacks and a black polo.

"That bad, huh?"

She nodded and looked over his shoulder to see their butler Maurice standing stoically in his black suit and matching tie.

"Maurice, can you please make me a Bloody Mary?" He nodded and walked back into the house silently.

Joshua's iPhone began to buzz, and he quickly picked it up and put it to his ear. "Joshua Dianaca."

He stood and walked away from the table, sounding muffled, but still Elisabeth was able to overhear most of what was being said. Maurice returned and handed Elisabeth her drink. She thanked him and turned her attention back to the Sound, the water glistening blue and the numerous yachts and sailboats moved calmly through the bay.

"Is everything all right?" she asked her brother.

He nodded and sat back down. "Yeah... but it just seems that our cousin is more concerned with her classes than with making sure that everything is set up and ready to go come October."

Elisabeth groaned and rolled her eyes. "Well, that's pretty ridiculous, but I still think that everything will be fine and that she'll do her part. I just hope we're not wasting our time."

Joshua looked at her as if she were stupid to even question his sources. "We're not. I've even confirmed with the Dean. Mary-Margaret Blackmoore will be arriving this afternoon, in fact. She's going to be staying with her aunt Mabel."

She didn't like that bit of news. If this cousin from Ireland was going to be residing with one of the most powerful Blackmoores, then there was a chance they would never get to her. "Should I be worried?"

Joshua laughed. "No. This will all go according to plan. And then, not only will we have our revenge, but we will also be rewarded." It was then that they heard the tapping of a child's shoes, followed by the sluggish shuffles of a worn-out adult.

"Alex, my love!" Elisabeth called out, her arms stretched open for a hug. Eleven-year-old Alex Baker stepped out onto the balcony with a smile on his face. His large blue eyes were like midnight waters, and his brown hair seemed like hazelnut. He wore a pair of jean shorts and flip-flops, as well as a blue-and-white striped tee.

"Hi!" They hugged, and she kissed him on the cheek. It was always strange for them to hear his American accent, when everyone in the house spoke as if they had just arrived from England.

"And how was the aquarium?"

He looked back at his cousin Basil, who seemed completely exhausted. He was twenty-eight and very handsome, like Joshua, but with silver-bullet hair and the same crisp blue eyes. He was wearing a green Lacoste polo with that familiar alligator on the left breast, and a pair of white slacks looped with a brown leather belt.

"We saw sharks and we had fish and chips at Ivar's."

Elisabeth gave his hair a pet. "Good, and was your cousin Basil on his best behavior?" Alex turned around and nodded. "Well, that's fantastic... I'm glad you had such a lovely time; I'm only sorry that I had to miss it." Elisabeth would have loved nothing more than to go to the waterfront with her family, but other obligations kept her busy.

"Me too." She hated to hear the disappointment in his voice, but she also knew that there really wasn't anything that she could do about it.

"So, do I get a hug?" Joshua asked with a smile in his voice. Alex ran to him and wrapped his arms around his neck, smiling when Joshua kissed him lightly on the cheek. It was then that the winds moved through the air, bringing with it a strange feeling—one that Elisabeth caught right away, locking eyes with her brothers.

"Alex, come here." He walked over to his cousin, and she placed her hands on his shoulders gently. "Why don't you have

Maurice make you a sandwich, and then when you're finished how about Joshua and I take you out for some chocolate, and we'll go to the amusement park?" He grinned and kissed her on the cheek, slipping back inside the penthouse.

"What is it?" Basil asked her, stepping closer.

"There are Blackmoores here in Seattle." They all looked at one another, the contempt evident on their faces, their annoyance thick in the air.

TREVOR AND BRAXTON moved down Fourth Avenue, turning around the corner of the old Seaboard building, sitting on the corner of the street and extending on either side. They turned into the alley and Trevor typed in the code for the black gate of the underground garage, waiting for just a moment as it pulled open.

After parking, they grabbed as much as they could carry from their cars and rode the elevator up to the tenth floor, both of them eager to get into their new home. The door opened up directly onto the apartment, the hardwood floors leading them from the long hall and into the main living area, gleaming in the light.

"Wow, this is nice," Braxton said. The building had been constructed in 1909 and featured a granite fireplace with gracious double columns on either side of the hearth. The walls were gray, and two large beams extended overhead. To the right and wrapping around at an angle was the kitchen. The counters featured slab granite, and the appliances were all stainless steel. The cabinets were made of cherry-wood, and above the island were three decorative yellow-orange ceramic lights. On the other side were three tall stools painted black. Across from this was a round table with four white upholstered wingback chairs. Two chocolate-brown chairs faced one another, and across from the fireplace was a rather formal beige sofa.

Between the three of these was a black coffee table with a glass top. The windows were large and reached to the white ceiling, its views looking out on downtown and Westlake Center. An abstract painting hung above the fireplace mantel, and there was recessed lighting throughout the penthouse, as well as numerous pieces of Asian inspired furniture.

"You can say that again," Trevor responded.

"You've never been here before?" Braxton asked him, but Trevor only shrugged.

"Yeah, I think maybe once when I was really little, but I don't remember it. My mom and Tom came out here once or twice, but I never went with them."

Braxton sat down his collection of boxes and walked over to his boyfriend, gripping him tightly and drawing him to his lips. "Well, let's break this place in, shall we?" He grinned seductively, biting his bottom lip before kissing Trevor, his tongue moving deep into his mouth.

His hands began to search his body, slipping up underneath the hem of his shirt, running along his soft flesh and twisting his nipple playfully. It didn't take them long to find the massive master bedroom at the end of the long hall. The blue four-post bed was like a box, and the headboard was upholstered with tan canvas. All around them were windows facing the city and French doors leading out onto a large enclosed balcony.

"God, you're fucking hot!" Braxton said with an exasperated breath. Trevor blushed and leaned back on the bed, unbuttoning his jeans and kicking off his shoes. Braxton gripped the legs of his pants and pulled them off, staring eagerly at Trevor's erection, which was tenting gray briefs.

"I love you..." Trevor said with a smile. Braxton curled his fingers up under his polo and revealed that strong chest and stomach, that thin trail of black hair—just as tempting to Trevor as ever before. Braxton slipped off his own jeans, wearing blue boxer-briefs with white trim, his cock hard and eager for Trevor's touch.

Trevor lay out and Braxton moved on top of him, their cocks rubbing together, ignited by the cotton of their underwear and causing them to drip with pre-cum.

"You're my everything, you know that?"

Trevor nodded and closed his eyes, slipping his hand between Braxton's legs and tugging on his hard-on. It didn't take them long to get through the foreplay, to have each other in their mouths, sucking on one another and cumming, drinking each other down without fear of killing the other person.

Trevor's legs were thrown over Braxton's shoulders as he fucked him, moving into him slowly and taking him to other places. He was seeing past the ceiling, past the sky and to the stars. There were planets and constellations unknown, and he knew that Braxton was having his own visions, seeing things that were unique and completely unto himself. Nothing felt more sacred than this, and it charged them with a need to see more—to push beyond everything and get to the heart of it. To reach the gods and learn the secrets of everything they were, to learn the very origins of the world itself.

"TWO HOURS! WE HAD SEX for two hours!" Braxton said with a chuckle, staring up at the ceiling. Trevor was resting against his chest, their hair damp with sweat. The windows were open, and the gray curtains moved with the breeze. The sounds of the city and the scent of the sea filled the room, and it felt good against their flesh.

"I know, isn't it great?"

Braxton nodded and gripped his boyfriend's hand, kissing it gently. "Great? I'd say it's fantastic."

They fell asleep there, knowing that they still had more boxes to bring up, but for the moment that could all wait. They were together in a new place, starting a new chapter of their life. Nothing could have seemed better than this moment—and yet there was something else, something that lurked in the background.

Trevor had tried to ignore it, had tried to deny that it was there. But ever since they had arrived in the city he had felt something, something dark and menacing that seemed to have its grip over the city. Something that had been aware of their presence, and was not happy about it.

If he closed his eyes and listened intently he felt that he could pick it out, that he could pinpoint its presence in the air, its invisible form lingering just beyond the veil. He knew that he would have to say something to Braxton about it. He was going to have to bring it up; after all, their lives depended on it, but for now he would sleep and suffer uneasy dreams. It was better than worrying over something that for the moment they could do nothing about.

THE OLD BLACKMOORE cannery was in disrepair. Many of the windows that lined the forty-foot ceiling were broken, and the beams that supported the structure were fragile and threatening to collapse. There were some hints of its former life still visible: the bins where the fish would have been deposited, the old canning machine, as well as the conveyor belt which still resided in the middle of the room. The concrete floor was spotted with paint stains and bird droppings, and Kathryn could tell by the look on Francesca's face that she didn't like being here.

"Kathryn... well, this is it, huh?" She nodded. Francesca Blackmoore was dressed in a strapless black leather dress and matching stilettos. Her hair was dyed cherry red and cascaded down her back in loose, curly tendrils. Her accent was still just as prevalent as ever, that mix of Irish and Italian curling off of her tongue.

"Have the contractors arrived yet?"

Francesca nodded. "Yeah, they're in the back right now or something. I don't know; it didn't seem that they were too hopeful."

Kathryn didn't like the idea of them telling her "no," and if she had to resort to other means to get this accomplished, then so be it. "Well, I'm sure that it will be fine." There was no reason for her to fret about it. If they told her that it wasn't feasible, then she would make it so. She was Kathryn Blackmoore, after all, and she could do anything that she wished.

They stood there in silence. Jared, her driver, was staring at her with lust in his brown eyes. She liked him; that was one of the reasons why she had hired him after Miles had died. But there was that fear. She knew that if something were to happen, she would never have to worry about killing him. The Legacy was over, its power broken by Braxton and Trevor—but just because they were suddenly handed a pass, it didn't necessarily mean that she was going to be able to use it. Things were different now; this was true, but old habits had a tendency to die hard, and age-old fears never seemed to pass on completely. Instead, they lingered there just beyond the horizon.

She flashed him a casual glance, scanning him up and down quickly—long enough to grab his attention, but not long enough to seem desperate. She had seen him once without a shirt on. He had been washing the car, and the water slipped down olive skin, dark nipples that were erect—tempting Kathryn in a way that she hadn't felt in such a long time. She had loved watching him stretch out his arm over the roof of the Lexus. The flash of black hair in the pit of his arm was invigorating, and the sweat in his dark brown hair was tempting. It made her want to walk out there and run her fingers through it, to have him take her right there on the hood of the car, for everyone to see.

"Miss Blackmoore?" She turned to see an older gentleman with balding white hair and a slight paunch staring up at her. He was slightly shorter than her, but for Kathryn that wasn't too surprising; after all, she was taller than most men.

"Yes, I'm Kathryn."

He nodded. "Well, aside from structural wear and tear, everything seems fine, and I think we can proceed with the plan. Now, I take it we will be knocking out the ceiling and opening it all up?"

She shook her head. "No. The ceiling is coming down, that's true, but only to be replaced with another two-story structure. That's where the nightclubs are going to be."

He nodded, and Kathryn and Francesca looked at one another, grinning. Things were definitely coming together as planned, and soon the city would have a waterfront hot-spot that would not only generate more money into the city and provide numerous jobs for people unable to obtain work at the moment, but it would also put the Blackmoore name back on the map.

As they continued to walk through the structure, discussing the look, possible fixtures and floor plans, Kathryn felt her heart suddenly quicken, and her knees seemed as if they would suddenly buckle and bring her to the floor. Perhaps it was the anxiety that she felt about Trevor being far away, or perhaps the arrival of Mary-Margaret—but she could not shake it, and it turned her stomach into knots.

The air was hot and lovely, and though they were in such a ruined place, the sound of cawing seagulls and the lapping sea brought her a welcoming comfort to all of it. Earlier in the day Kathryn had received news that Detective Randy Kit was now former Detective, and this had given her a reason to find joy in a day where she would have to be saying goodbye to her one and only child.

She had warned him on Christmas Eve that she was going to make him pay for the trouble that he had caused all of them, but she had figured that perhaps he had thought that she wouldn't—that she would somehow have a change of heart. He hadn't obviously known as much about her as he had thought, or else he would have done the honorable thing and resigned before she had had the chance to get to him herself. But still, the vengeance had been just as sweet as she had thought about it being.

As they continued to saunter through, moving casually in the usual lazy summer way, it seemed that perhaps for now things would be okay, that her son and his boyfriend would have a chance at a normal life... at least for a little while. The darkness was always going to be there, but Kathryn figured that for now they could ignore it. Mabel would tell her "no" if she presented this hypothesis to the matriarch of the Blackmoores, but she would never do that. For now, she wanted to live in this ignorance for as long as possible—and she wanted the same for Trevor and Braxton. After all, their time would come soon enough, and then everything would change.

Chapter: Three

WHEN THE CAR HAD DROPPED her off at the home on Sixteenth Street, Mary-Margaret had been taken aback by the immensity of the sprawling Queen Anne Victorian. The flower beds that lined each side of the concrete steps bloomed with roses, and their perfume mixed with the saltiness of the bay. The deep purple siding and pink-and-white trim of the home seemed to glisten in the sunlight, and the lace curtains of the bay windows made her think of her home back in Dublin. She felt odd here, without her twin, Natalie. It was as if a piece of her was missing, and she knew where to find it but had no way of getting back to retrieve it.

The teaching job had not been offered to the both of them. Though she hadn't wanted to take it, her sister told her that she must. She knew the way of the fates, and if the universe saw fit to request her presence in Bellingham, then that was where she needed to be.

The wind moved through her hair, long red strands thick and layered, feathered at the ends. She wore her favorite emerald green spaghetti-strapped dress, which split open in the middle and looked like the petals of a flower. She wore heeled sandals and a simple gold cross around her neck, as well as a delicate gold bracelet on her right hand. In the other she clung to the case of her two-hundred-and-ninety-one-year-old Stradivarius, knowing that without it in hand she would certainly have had a panic attack.

"Mary, be with me," she said, calling on her patron saint. The driver followed her up calmly as she made her way from the sidewalk and up to the long concrete walk of the front, looking at the great picture window that overlooked the porch and the front yard, its bamboo blinds pulled shut so that she didn't have even the smallest glimpse of what awaited her inside.

The old wood creaked beneath her feet, and as she came closer to the large oak door with its glass window, she felt everything inside of her tighten up. If this fear was based on any kind of intuition, then perhaps it would be best if she got a hotel room.

"I guess you just have to knock," the gentleman said to her, and she nodded. But as she lifted her hand, she spotted a doorbell and decided on this method instead. It sounded out like a church bell, and she heard the shuffling of feet on floorboards. She stepped back, trying to stop her heart from beating so fast. The door opened, and Mary swallowed her breath.

"You're here, I see." Mabel Blackmoore stood taller than she was, if only by a couple of inches. Her hair was now whiter than what it had been at Brighton's funeral, and yet her gray eyes were just as crisp as ever before. Her face was stern and her lips were rouged in scarlet. She wore a plum slip dress with a matching velvet coat, which draped the floor.

"Sorry; I know I was supposed to be in sooner, but my plane got delayed in Boston." Mabel nodded and stepped aside, telling the driver to take her things up to the second door on the left on the second floor.

"Don't worry about it. When one comes by planes, you must expect delays." The humor of this proverb made her ease up, and she felt better about staying with this cousin. "Now, come in." She nodded, and they stepped inside. She was immediately taken by the sweeping grand staircase and the high ceilings. The gold walls and white crown molding brought her a comfort. The details of such an old home made her think of her townhouse in Ireland.

"You have such a lovely home."

Mabel nodded and gave the driver a check, which he took kindly and slipped out of the house, closing the door behind him.

"Now, my dear, I must tell you, I am not accustomed to a lot of noise, and I like to go to bed early. Now, during the week I do give readings from one to four in the afternoon, and so I would prefer it if you would not be around then—though I am sure that you will be working at that time."

She nodded. "Um, what do you mean by readings?" There was a slight tinge of fear in her voice.

Mabel turned around and looked at her, her expression stunned. "What do you think I mean?" She stepped into the music room, which was off the front parlor, and pointed to the table with her candles and her tarot deck already laid out as if she were in the middle of a reading when she had arrived.

"Oh… right." She noticed the violin sitting in the corner, along with a pedestal and opened sheet music. She had never heard anything about Mabel playing the violin ever in her life, but perhaps there were things about her American relatives that she just wasn't aware of.

"No, dear, I don't play."

She turned and looked at her, her green eyes pressing. "Did you read my thoughts?"

Mabel grinned. "Well, not on purpose… surely you know about this family?"

Mary sighed and took a seat in the chair opposite the bookshelf. "Of course I do… I mean, I know enough. I know that we're not cursed anymore. I also know that supposedly this great devil or whatever is going to rise up and kill us… but it's just legend."

Mabel's face grew stern. "Just a legend? My dear, how do you think Brighton died? What do you think had happened up here at Christmastime?" She shrugged. "The great evil; that's what happened. God, have you all been so far removed from the rest of us? I mean, Francesca and Adamo knew, and they both live in Europe."

"It wasn't really ever talked about. It wasn't part of our lives in Ireland." She shook her head.

"You can do things, can't you?" Mary knew where she was leading—and for a moment she wasn't sure if she was going to confess it, or if she would deny it.

"Well, yeah. I mean, my sister and I can do things when we're together, like talk to the dead and cause storms when we're angry... but I would never try to use it, to commit such sin. To give in to the devil."

Mabel could not believe the lack of information her young cousin had. "My dear, we can all do things, and it has nothing to do with the devil." There was something about all of this that was making her uneasy, and on impulse Mary clutched her cross.

"We were raised to believe that that stuff was evil. It was one thing to have it in your blood, which you couldn't control. But to live a pure and good life, to never summon it at will, to never use it—then you were safe. I'm sorry to have to say this, but we were taught to believe that whatever evil befell this family would be exacted on the American Blackmoores. After all, your entire history since arriving here has been one of witchcraft."

Mabel reached for a cigarette and lit it up, exhaling a puff of blue-gray smoke. "Jesus Christ. Let me tell you, my dear, our 'witchcraft,' as you say, has been in this family since before arriving in America. Every Blackmoore can see beyond the veil of the living and peer into the place of the dead; every Blackmoore can affect the structure of the physical world and bend it to their will. It's not from the devil, child, but from something ancient and beautiful... something that deserves *respect*." She stood and walked away, her feet clicking on the hardwood as she made her way down the long hall to the back of the house.

In a few minutes, Mary-Margaret had managed to offend her cousin, and now they were going to have to exist under one roof. *Great... good going.* She stood and froze for just a moment as she glimpsed a black form move quickly in the corner of her eye. She whipped around, and just as she expected, she found the room empty. There was something here—another presence besides her and Mabel.

She knew that it would do her good to avoid it and to stay away from the house as much as possible. She felt now as if she were trespassing, and the last thing she wanted to do was be in anybody's way. Still, she knew that if she did stay away, she could do more harm by seeming like she was avoiding her family entirely.

Slowly she crept up the stairs, seeing the cool blue shadow on the landing. A portrait of a soldier in a gold hat seemed to be watching her, and another portrait of an angel in early twentieth century illumination watched over the three wise men. It was a picture that struck unease inside of her, one that went beyond the peace of mind that such a painting should have brought her. This was not her home and she was in another land, one far away from anything that she had ever known before.

The top floor moved in a half-circle, and four doors faced her. She saw that only one door was open, and the light of the two narrow windows greeted her. The blue-and white floral wallpaper seemed inviting. She came closer to it and was relieved to see her belongings on the great mahogany bed. The room was bare save for a matching dresser and an antique satin armchair that was positioned in front of the windows. Another window on the left looked out on the side of the house, and she could smell the perfume of roses in bloom, as well as hear the humming of her elderly cousin.

"Well, this isn't so bad." She plopped down on the mattress and placed her head on the pillow, allowing her eyes to fall shut and her breathing to slow. She was beginning to drift now, and she knew that if she wanted to she could rise up out of her body and go to her sister just by thinking on it—but not now. For the moment, Mary-Margaret had had enough of flying; for now, she just wanted to sleep the afternoon away.

THERE WAS A KNOCK ON the bedroom door, and Mary-Margaret opened her eyes slowly, her lids fluttering like moths' wings, adjusting to the near-dark of the setting sun. She had dreamed of rolling hilltops along Ireland's coast and the crashing of the waves along the shore below, foaming violently over rocks and their jagged edges.

"Mary-Margaret, are you awake?" It was Mabel, and her aged voice seemed sweet and full of genuine care.

"Yes, I'm up." She rolled over and looked up at the ceiling, seeing it in ink-blue shadow.

"Well, that's good. Listen, we are going out to dinner with Kathryn and Francesca in fifteen minutes, so meet me downstairs when you've changed." She made a sound of compliance and was met with the pitter-patter of the old woman's feet moving down the steps.

"I think what I have on is just fine." She walked over to the door and opened it, seeing the open second floor cast in an almost purple hue, darker than the room she was in, and it forced her to cringe just a little. She turned and grabbed her handstitched purse that she had purchased in Spain while on tour with her cousin a month before. She had fallen in love with it, and took it with her everywhere she went, and tonight would be no exception.

At thirty, she felt that she knew enough about the world—but upon her arrival in Bellingham and meeting her American family on their turf, she suddenly felt that this place was exotic and filled with mystery that was different from Ireland, and it held just as many secrets beneath its earth.

"Shit!" she screamed when she had turned around. Though she never fully trusted her eyes when it came to shadows she knew that she had seen a young man standing outside of her door, staring at her. It hadn't lasted long, just enough for her to get a good look at him, because in the blink of an eye the upstairs was once again empty—but she knew that he had been there. On instinct Mary crossed herself, and decided then to leave one of the Tiffany lamps on, if only so that she was guided in the dark when she returned home.

"SO HOW WAS YOUR TRIP from Ireland?" Kathryn asked her. They were seated at *Le Chat Noir*; its dimly-lit room and ancient bricked walls seemed familiar to Mary, who felt like she was sitting in one of the old pubs of Ireland.

"Tiring. I mean, it was just long, you know." They all nodded. "It just takes a while to get over the jet-lag." She had forgotten how beautiful Kathryn was, as well as Francesca. It seemed to her that these women possessed something that she never would, no matter how hard she tried.

"Well, when do you start at Fairhaven?" Francesca asked her, taking another drink from her glass.

"Oh, well, the quarter starts soon, but I need to be there next week—you know, to give myself a chance to prepare, and get everything the way I want it in my room." She couldn't help but think about the wisp of a person that she had seen in Mabel's home in the afternoon, nor could she stop thinking about the man that she had caught staring at her from outside her bedroom door. She had a feeling that they were one in the same, and she wanted to question Mabel about it—but knew that after what she had said earlier in the day, perhaps that wasn't such a good idea.

"So, where is Trevor?"

Kathryn seemed to grow sullen at the mention of her son's name, but just as suddenly as it had come it had gone. "He moved up to Seattle today with Braxton. He'll be going to school at the University of Washington."

Braxton. She remembered the very attractive young man who had come to the funeral, and was apparently their distant cousin. It seemed strange to her, and she had also had a very uneasy feeling about the two of them—as if they had been a couple.

"That's because they are." She looked up to see Kathryn staring into her, her icy eyes like daggers.

"But isn't he related?" Kathryn nodded. "That's perverted." The air suddenly seemed to harden, to chill, as if a bitter cold front had set in on the entire restaurant.

"First of all, my dear..." Kathryn began, her tone calm. "They had fallen in love and gotten together before they discovered the truth. Secondly, he is not related to us enough to really consider it incest. He has but a tiny traceable drop of our blood left in him, but it's enough to make him one of us.

"And thirdly—and, now, this is the most important—if it wasn't for the two of them getting together, we would still be burying lovers. So you remember that when you decide to get married and have a child. Because of them, you won't ever have to carry the burden of killing your husband. Not like us; not like your father with your mother."

She should have known that that was going to come, but she hadn't planned on it. Now she was scorned, and wanted to make sure that the next thing she said would carry a sting.

"But still, even with that, the homosexuality... I mean, it's sinful. He will certainly be damned for it." That was the thing to do it. Kathryn's mouth gaped open, looking to Mabel and Francesca, who also had similar looks on their faces. Mary felt dirty, and knew that she had crossed a line that she might not be able to come back from.

"I think that that's the first time in history that a Blackmoore has ever—and I mean, ever—said something like that!" Mabel said, more stunned than appalled.

"Why? We all have our beliefs; I was raised Catholic —"

"And so were we!" Francesca interjected.

Mary sighed. "A true Catholic, not like the rest of you, and we were taught that such behavior is an affront to God."

Kathryn made a scoff that sounded more like a snarl, and downed the rest of her wine. "Let me tell you something, my dear. There have been more queers in this family than can be counted on one hand. And my son is perfect. He is exactly how God made him." Her eyes were now beginning to well with tears.

"I didn't mean to —"

"No! My son has had to spend his entire life shunned and hated for who he is. And I'm not talking about his being a Blackmoore. He grew up teased, ostracized. He lost some of his closest friends when they all found out. He is the most special person in this family, and the most normal. I don't care what anyone says; he is who he was always meant to be, and I wouldn't have him any other way." She was choking on her words now, trying to keep her composure—but when it came to her son, the stoic, hard Kathryn melted away, becoming just as vulnerable as any mother when defending the honor of her child.

"Why would you say something like that?" Francesca asked. Her voice was steady, but an equaled anger crept beneath the surface.

"I don't know... I guess I just don't understand how someone could choose to live that life when it's so wrong." Kathryn snatched up her purse and stalked outside, clutching her pack of cigarettes.

"My darling," Mabel began, placing her hand gently over Mary's. "Do you really think Trevor would have chosen to be gay? I mean, really. He's going to have to go through life with people telling him every day that he's less than, that he is somehow not equal to straight people, that he is somehow inadequate. Each of us, in life, live with the cards we're dealt, and we try to do the best with what we can.

"God is not the church, and you cannot find him in there. God is in each and every single one of us, and if you believe that God is perfect and that God doesn't make mistakes, then you have to believe that each and every single person on this planet is exactly how God planned them to be."

Her words churned over in her mind, telling her truths that she knew deep down, but through childhood obligation to her faith she had constantly disregarded. Her sister Natalie was different. Natalie was a self-proclaimed atheist, and had argued with her on more than one occasion about the humanity of gay people. Part of her wondered if perhaps she held on to these things because they had been so important to her mother Frances—that if she allowed herself to let go of them, then that would mean she was letting go of her mother.

"No, Mary, you would not be... your mother now resides in a place where who people sleep with or what others do is of no importance. She is in a place full of love and light; she's constantly enveloped in it. The fact that you may let go of some of those old dogmas means nothing." Mary wiped tears from her glistening eyes, seeing through the watery haze that Kathryn had returned.

"Kathryn, I —"

She held up her hand in protest. "I don't need an apology. You have your beliefs, no matter how narrow, and I have to respect that. You're my family; my love for you is unlimited, and if this is true, then I have to accept you. All of you, not just certain parts. A person can't pick and choose; I couldn't with my son, and I can't with you." Kathryn leaned in and pointed her finger at her face. "But you have to understand that with Trevor, you take all of him or you take none of him. He didn't change for anyone else, and he won't change for you."

"You're right. The damage is done and I can't fix it; I can't take it back. I have my prejudices, and I need to let them go. I want to know my family—all of them—and if I don't let this go, it's going to stand in my way." She didn't know if Kathryn believed her. She couldn't blame her if she didn't, and all she could do was hope that in time she could prove to her that her words were true, and that she would never do it again.

Chapter: Four

THE CITY WAS OPENED to them: its bustling streets, its Technicolor illumination, the conversations and the cigarette smoke that floated like the wisps of ghosts along the sidewalks. Braxton and Trevor loved it, loved basking in it, and even more thrilled that their friends were with them to enjoy it.

They were sitting in the intimate comfort of *The Melting Pot*, a fondue chain restaurant in downtown, a candle burning on the table that surrounded their semi-circle booth. Cheri Hannifin sat, talking about their upcoming orientation day. Trevor watched with mild amusement as her scarlet-colored lips curled into a sly grin as she took notice of the fact that J.T. Oliver was hanging on her every word with bewilderment.

He had cut his hair and wore it in a faux-hawk, his frame having bulked up over the past few months. Cheri, on the other hand, was just as petite as she had always been—wearing a snug spaghetti-strapped white dress falling just short of her knees, with pink flowers on it, purchased at Banana Republic earlier that day; a white gold chain with tiny diamonds strung around her neck.

"So, is it weird being in a city where people don't know who you are just by looking at you?" J.T. asked, his eyes only briefly falling on Trevor.

"No, not really weird, more like... freeing." He nodded with a smile and turned to Braxton. "So, what time is that meeting with Arcadia on Friday?"

Braxton shook his head and chuckled. "What?"

"I have a feeling I'm always going to be your personal date book." He rolled up his cloth napkin and tossed it at Braxton.

"Hey!" They laughed, and Braxton leaned down and gently kissed Trevor on the cheek. "It's at one-thirty."

"A record deal... that's so cool," Cheri said, and J.T. looked at her seductive face. Trevor and Braxton both knew that he was falling for the young debutante.

"Yeah, well, it's not a big surprise to us... we've always known that we were meant for it."

"Speak for yourself." J.T. looked at Braxton. After what had happened at Christmas, Braxton assumed that his future would consist of nothing more than he and Trevor fighting for their lives and the lives of the entire Blackmoore family. Cheri glanced at him with knowing eyes. Trevor had told her everything, and though it worried her more often than she liked to admit, the truth about him in itself didn't scare her. It was the possibility of his demise that frightened her.

"Well, whatever; the point is, it's happened!"

Trevor nodded and looked at the hot melting cheese, already finished with their bread dippers and other things, and it was soon time for the main course.

"And the new place, how's that working out?" Cheri asked.

Trevor shrugged. "It's fine. I mean, it's beautiful, but I'm hoping that eventually we'll put our own touches on the apartment. And you?"

Cheri moved her hands in a dismissing way. "Well, good I guess. But the place that was chosen was more for my mom, I think, than for me. It wasn't the building I wanted, and it's further from school than I wanted. I wanted an older building—I guess because it reminds me of back home—but my mother chose The Meridian Tower, which is really nothing but walls of glass... completely modern." They all understood it—except for perhaps J.T., who had not grown up in the antique manors of South Hill, but instead the newer Edgemoore.

"But don't you have your own money? I mean, I'm sure you had a trust fund," Braxton said.

Cheri rolled her eyes. "Yes, but I needed a co-signer, and so in the end where I lived was up to my mother. It's really stupid to be upset about it; I know that. It's just that it feels so sterile, without any kind of life—you know, any kind of history."

Trevor took hold of his sprite and gave it a drink. "As opposed to the ghosts that we grew up with?" A memory moved across the surface of Cheri's mind, thinking about what at the time she had thought was Christian's ghost decaying in front of her in her kitchen while she cowered against the cabinets along the floor. She shot Trevor an annoyed glare.

"Let's not," Braxton stated, sticking his arm out across the table, signaling them both to not go down that road.

"Are you guys ever going to tell me what in the hell went on back at Christmas?" J.T. asked, completely perturbed at being left out in the dark.

"Trust me, it's not important," Trevor responded. He liked being with his friends, and he especially enjoyed being curled up next to his boyfriend in the booth, his hand between his legs, keeping warm and teasing Braxton all at the same time.

"I just think that eventually you're going to have to tell me. I kinda feel betrayed, like I can't be trusted." They immediately began to tell him that that wasn't the case and that he was just being paranoid, but he didn't want to hear it.

"Fine, you really want to know?" Trevor asked. Cheri shot him a "don't you dare" glance, and Braxton squeezed his hand tightly.

Don't worry, he won't believe me, Trevor said in his mind, hoping that Braxton would hear it—and by the loosening of the hand and the slight nod, he knew that he had.

"Yes, I do."

"I'm a witch."

His lips curled into a smile.

"No, J.T., it's true. I am, and so is Braxton. And there is this great and ancient evil that has been stalking my family for hundreds of years, and now it's been released but it isn't strong enough to come for us yet. My mother killed my stepfather, but he came back from the dead and killed Teri Jules and Greg Sheer—though Greg had been possessed by this ghost named Jonathan Marker, and killed my uncle Brighton with a shot gun. Then Tom, my stepfather, almost killed Cheri." He looked over at her, and she grinned and waved uncomfortably. "Oh, yeah, and Braxton's a Blackmoore."

He had said it all, trying very hard to stop it from summoning up painful memories, but it didn't work and they could all see his face grow dark.

"Ha, ha; yeah, right." It was over before it had begun, and Trevor's head was hanging low.

"C'mon," Cheri said, slipping out of the booth and gripping him by the hand, pulling Trevor out of the booth and dragging him outside for a smoke.

THEY WERE OUT FRONT, both of them sparking their lighters and inhaling their Nat Shermans and smelling the crisp salt water air.

"Sorry..." Trevor said sullenly.

Cheri shook her head. "Why did you do that? Not tell him the witch part, I mean, but why what happened—especially when you knew that it was going to bring up things that you're not over yet?"

Trevor shrugged, staring at the burning cherry of his cigarette. "I guess I thought that if I told him the abridged version, it wouldn't do as much harm. Stupid, though, 'cause now I can't stop thinking about Christian."

She sighed in understanding. "It's been eight months; you need to let him go. I know you don't say anything about it to Braxton, but I see it: you're still holding onto Christian."

Trevor's eyes seemed to spark with tears, glistening even in the dark, catching in the orange glow of streetlight. "The problem is, I can't escape him. I don't think I ever told you, but after he died, Christian came to see me—more than once, in fact—and he told me that he would always be with me. I thought that perhaps with all that had happened, with the revelation of everything, he would move on. But the truth is I still feel him near me, though he doesn't reach out anymore... it makes me sad."

Cheri took hold of his hand, squeezing it gently and with reassurance. "Maybe he hasn't gone away yet because he wants to make sure that you get through this okay."

Trevor nodded. He knew that that was the reason why his dead lover hung around, but it still didn't lessen the pain and it didn't quell the longing.

"I just don't know how I'm supposed to get on with my life with him over my shoulder all of the time... it's bad enough I have to walk around always fearing for my life." It seemed then that words hung between the two of them, things that couldn't be said. Cheri wanted to tell him then that she worried for him too, that she spent almost every other moment knowing about a world that seemed to be out of terrifying childhood stories, a world set out to take her best friend away from her.

"Don't worry, Cheri, it won't." She looked at him and saw by the expression on his face that he hadn't even realized that he had heard her thoughts, and so she kept it to herself.

MARY-MARGARET AWOKE with a start. At first she thought that she had been dreaming, that perhaps she had been remembering a time when she and her sister were playing a concert—sometime in the past, a moment only half-real. It was there, creeping in the back of her mind as all memories do, but when she heard the music with her eyes open, she knew that it was not from a moment in slumber, but from within the house.

"Jesus...." She swung her feet from off the bed and padded barefoot across the floor, making her way out into the upstairs hall. It was a sad song, crying from the violin with its own heartbeat. She didn't recognize the song as anything that she had ever heard before, but she also knew that she could not avoid it. The house creaked as she tiptoed down the stairs, trying to be discreet and not interrupt whoever it was that was playing inside the home.

The moon shone through the glass, its silver light making everything illuminated, the old photographs of dead Blackmoores staring at her in what seemed to be silent judgment. If she had been smarter, she would have taken this as a sign to turn around and go back to her room instead of acting brave and pressing forward. The music grew louder as she touched down into the foyer, the furniture in the front parlor seeming monstrous in the thick. The temperature seemed to drop as if it were the middle of winter, and her breath began to form in front of her face.

"Mary, protect me." Out of habit, she crossed herself as she neared the pocket door to the music room; her plain white cotton nightgown was skirting across the floorboards and catching under the balls of her feet. She nearly tripped on more than one occasion, but she let it pass and pressed on, swallowing hard before gripping the door's handle and pulling it open.

She wasn't sure what it was that she had been expecting, but an empty room was not one of them. It left her feeling all the more unnerved as she observed the empty space. The antique mirror reflected her and the silence. The table that Mabel used for readings and whatever else was alone, save for the deck kept in purple velvet. The shelves with their numerous volumes of books seemed like hundreds of stone blocks arming a fortress. The home seemed terrifying then, as if it would come to life and swallow her whole. It was as if it were the inner labyrinth of hell and she had no idea how to escape, no way of knowing how to save her own immortal soul.

Wood creaked above her, as if someone was walking the floor. In fearing that it would be Mabel, she turned around and tiptoed back towards the stairs, making her way back up to her room, trying to shrug off the eerie events that had awoken her in the first place.

Chapter: Five

HE SHOULDN'T HAVE BROUGHT up what he did about Christian the night before at the Melting Pot. He had known that it would summon feelings and memories that he wasn't ready to deal with—but then again, maybe that was his problem. He wasn't talking about it—not to Cheri, not to his mother, and certainly not Braxton. He kept his thoughts within his own troubled mind, not wanting to feel like he was burdening anyone, and not wanting to give Braxton the impression that he was still in love with his dead former.

Trevor had thought that perhaps if he left those ghosts of his past alone, then eventually they would go away; eventually they would leave him be. But unfortunately this was not the case, and now it seemed that it only got worse and worse. In his dreams he saw Christian as he was before the accident that killed him, that accident that he had caused when his witchcraft got the best of him.

Christian spoke with a grin on his face; he ran in the grass in shorts and a plain white tee, kicking around a soccer ball, the light of the sun glistening on his short black hair. There were moments where the two of them sat atop a grassy knoll of some unknown park, Trevor leaning against his chest, Christian's arm curled around Trevor's shoulder, bringing him in close for one of the sweetest kisses imaginable. But as with all dreams, Trevor had to eventually wake up and remember once again that Christian was dead and gone, nothing more than slowing decay beneath the earth.

He sat in the study, curled up in a leather armchair, his knees drawn up to his chest, a cigarette between his fingers, staring at the blue-gray smoke, which curled about his head in delicate ribbons. Sleepless nights were becoming a habit, something that was getting really old really fast. And yet nothing seemed to help, not sleeping pills or massages from Braxton, which only put him to rest for a couple of hours—before he was brought back to life by one of these torturous dreams.

Braxton knew that something was going on, and yet he never questioned him about it. In truth, Trevor didn't really want him to. He knew that everything between he and Braxton was fine, that they couldn't be closer... but to his boyfriend's frustration his wall did not come down, and sometimes Braxton would just sit and stare, trying to figure Trevor out.

He liked this time the most, when the early morning began to creep in ever so slightly, lighting the sky from its inky blue to a softer, almost ethereal white hew. The curtains moved with the push of the cool breeze which invaded through the open widows. The sounds of Westlake Center were filled only with the noise of delivery trucks and people returning from a long and adventurous night out on the town. He wondered how long this could go on for, and why he was suffering it in the first place. If this was the way it was going to be from now on, well, he didn't want any part of it.

'Trevor....' His name came in a whisper on the wind, like a whistle, and it seemed to stop his heart in its place, keeping it frozen in mid-beat. He lifted his eyes first, trying to survey beneath the curtain of his wine red hair, feeling the air around him thin and chill like winter.

'Trevor....'

It came again, and this time he cocked his head, bringing his attention to the bookcases in front of him. It was that same boy from before, the one who had met him at the foot of Braxton's bed, the one who had pointed the accusing finger at his face, giving him its ominous warning.

"What do you want?" he asked the specter, attempting to keep his voice steady, staring into those thick black eyes.

'They're coming... and with them may be your ruin, with them shall come their worst reckoning....' Just like Jonathan, like with all spirits, his words moved without a question mark, without a lapse in thought—just a stating of the facts that left more questions than answers.

"Who are you talking about?"

The dead boy shook his head. *'An ancient feud is drawing to its close....'* And just as before, the specter faded, slipping into the ether. There was a horn honking in the distance, and it drew Trevor out of the semi-trance that he was in, seeing the room and the sky brighter than it had been before. The sudden tapping of rain drops on the window and the hardwood floor beneath the sill stirred him with a sort of ease that he hadn't thought possible; it was a calming of his soul.

He felt weighted and he placed his hands to his temples, wishing to slip his fingers beneath his flesh, through the protection of his skull, and massage the sticky membrane itself, to ease his weary brain. Something was coming. Something out of the deep dark was reaching out for them all yet again, and he wished that he could understand what it was. He wished that he could comprehend the full extent of the evil that he was feeling in the air. A noise stirred in the apartment, but it seemed distant to him—perhaps the opening of the door, and the creak of the floorboards. It scared him.

"Trevor?" He looked to see Braxton standing in front of him, his hair messy and his lids heavy, black lashes almost touching each other, his stance heavy with the lethargy of sleep.

"Oh, hey; sorry if I woke you up."

Braxton grinned and shook his head. "It's okay... don't worry about it."

He liked seeing the curves of his naked skin, the shape of his muscles, the bulk of his chest, the firmness of his arms. It seemed that the both of them always had sex on their brains, as if the hunger inside of them was never quelled, and they were always starving for one another.

"I need to tell you something. I wanted to put it off; I had hoped that it wasn't going to happen again, but it has, and you need to know."

Braxton's eyes grew wide, those dark chocolate orbs which seemed to absorb him, to consume him and take him captive, never letting go. "Baby, what is it?" He moved closer to him now, leaning down in front of him, before bending his knees and taking Trevor's hands into his own, staring up into his hazel eyes.

"The dead have come again." Braxton's jaw dropped. "This boy—I don't know who he is; I've never seen him before—but he's come to me twice now. The first time was the other night at your house, and now, just now, not moments before you woke up, he came again... warning me."

Braxton shook his head, trying to wrap his head around what it was that was going on, trying to understand what it could possibly mean. "Well, what does he say?"

"That they're here, that we're in danger." Braxton stood up and walked to the window, the pale gray morning light illuminating his flesh, reflecting off of his round, naked buttocks, his long cock grazing the sheer linen curtains, hardening slightly at the contact. He folded his arms across his chest, his nipples erect from the cold, his eyes wide with worry.

"I know... I've felt it too. When we first came into Seattle yesterday, and since then, at the slightest moments, when I'm not really thinking about anything else... I've felt it." Trevor sighed and rose to his feet, wanting only one thing—and it wasn't to talk about the ghosts and devils that had begun their mission in killing the Blackmoores.

"Let's not think about it now." Trevor placed his hand on his shoulder, running his fingers along his soft skin. Silently he placed his lips to the back of his neck and began to kiss him, dragging his tongue slightly along the shoulder blades, tasting the salt of his flesh.

Braxton reached out for him, but Trevor moved his hand out of the way and pushed Braxton against the window, his bare ass visible to anyone on the street who decided to look up.

Erratically he made his way down his body, dragging his lips and tongue down the middle of his chest, getting lower and lower, feeling the press of Braxton's stiff cock against his chest, then to his neck. Finally he was on his knees, at level with it, seeing the slick of pre-cum trail out of the head.

He grinned and put Braxton inside, tasting him, hearing him groan in pleasure. His hands were sifting through Trevor's hair as he worked him hard and fast—hearing his boyfriend's exasperated breath as he forced him to orgasm, slamming his head and backside against the window over and over again, shooting his load in Trevor's mouth, feeling it stick to the back of his throat before making its way down inside of him slowly. If there were any worries for either of them, they were gone at this moment: lost on a sea of each other.

"SO, HOW WAS EVERYTHING last night; did you have another dream about Christian?" He looked at Cheri and nodded. They were walking around downtown. The rain had gone by 9:00am and it was warm and sunny once again, with a bright blue sky and soft white puffy clouds above them.

"Yeah... but I don't really remember any of it, which I guess is a good thing." Cheri was dressed in a black thigh-length slip dress with a soft three-quarter-inch sleeved powder-blue cardigan, left open, a white gold necklace with a diamond Celtic cross hanging in her cleavage, her black Marc Jacobs stilettos tapping on the pavement.

"Well, personally I think it's a really shitty thing if Christian is really coming to you still and it's not just dreams. He needs to leave you alone."

Trevor sighed and shook his head. He pulled on the bottom hem of his black polo and looked at his denim skinny jeans, seeing a stain of blood from a couple of years ago when he had gotten a bloody nose one day in gym class. He was still unable to get it out, though it had been washed hundreds of times since then.

"I know, Cheri, but what am I supposed to do?" She looked at him and rolled her eyes. "What?"

"Oh, please, Trevor; you have the ability to command spirits. You don't think that if you really wanted him to move on, you could make him do so?"

He opened his mouth, but no sound came out. He didn't like what she was accusing him of: that he was purposefully subjecting himself to Christian and his unwavering presence. This had to end, and the truth was that he had begged Christian to leave him be, to pass on and begin again, to start another life or to exist as part of the whole that surrounded and joined them all. But he would not let go—not of Trevor, no matter how much he pleaded. He would simply not let Trevor be.

"Cheri, believe it or not, I do not like my dead ex hanging around, and I have tried to get him to move on, but he simply won't. I thought after Tom, after Jonathan, I thought that after those two, that Christian would go with them. Obviously he has another purpose, and until it's completed he won't be going anywhere."

Cheri started to lead him into Abercrombie & Fitch. She felt that he needed a little cheering up, and walls covered in nearly-naked men would get his mind occupied with something other than a world of witchcraft, ghosts, demons, and hexes.

Trevor's world was scary, and one that she chose to be a part of, even though it had brought her undeniably closer to death. It was something she chose to align herself with but she could walk away anytime. She could leave it and live a life where the only things that go bump in the night are the monsters of a child's imagination, not the realized beings of another world.

She felt bad for Trevor; unlike her, he had no option to leave. This was his life, whether he liked it or not. This was his situation, his destiny, and it couldn't be avoided. No matter how hard he fought to live a normal life, he never could—and what was worse, he knew it. He knew that his future was laid out before him, that it was the turning of the universe, the well-mapped destiny of God that decided his fate. In the end—one way or the other—this world of his would kill him.

Chapter: Six

FAIRHAVEN UNIVERSITY was nestled within a thick of mammoth evergreens, sitting high atop a hill that overlooked Bellingham Bay and the street of North Garden. Its older buildings were made of aged stone and wrapped in a plethora of English ivy, the newer buildings absorbing the sun with their deep red.

She stood next to an enormous metal sculpture, its pieces looking like branches stacked atop one another, as if getting ready to be lit on fire. The air smelled fresh, crisp, with that gentle hint of saltwater clinging to the air, attached to invisible currents.

Mary was anxious, waiting for the head of the music department, who was meeting with her to show her the room in which she would be teaching for the year. Strangers moved past her, paying her no mind—though the occasional pedestrian would look at her with a gaze that made Mary uneasy.

She had been feeling off ever since her encounter from the other night with the spirit that was playing that haunting melody, that phantom violin. She didn't feel threatened by the entity, only startled. Though the voice of her mother echoed in the back of her mind, telling her not to pursue the spirit, not to engage her witchcraft, she also knew that her curiosity was going to win out in the end, and she couldn't avoid the temptation. And in the end, Mary wasn't sure if she wanted to.

"Miss Blackmoore?" She cocked her head to see a distinguished older man looking at her—a slight paunch to his stomach, his eyes bespectacled with wire rim frames, and his hair a shocking silver that reflected the light harshly.

"Yes." She extended her hand to him and he took it, giving her a weary shake. He looked her up and down, taking in the sight of her petite frame, dressed in her black Diane Von Furstenberg wrap dress and a pair of simple black heels on her feet.

"I'm Cedric Rippner, head of the music department." She smiled and averted her gaze for a moment, blushing in her ignorance of not recognizing him by the faculty photo that was on the school's website.

"Yes, of course; how are you?"

He nodded casually, obviously charmed by the melody of her accent. "I'm fine; um, right this way."

He seemed to keep a distance between them, and as they entered into the massive building, walking down the dimly-lit corridor, Mary was even more aware of the distance that separated her and Cedric. There was uneasiness in his gaze; he gauged their distance as if he needed to be wary of the possibility of attack. She didn't like it, and by the time they got to the door of the music room she had had enough.

"Excuse me, Cedric." He looked at her. "Is there something I'm not aware of here? Am I disturbing you?"

Cedric swallowed hard and opened the door, ushering her into the room quickly. The lights came on, igniting the room in white illumination. It was ridiculous, really, this sudden secrecy. "It's just, well...." He was finding it hard to speak, his eyes moving frantically. He seemed to be reviewing everything he was about to say, as if he were reading them from the pages of a book.

Mary sighed and moved to one of the chairs, taking a seat and staring at him as he leaned against the podium. "Mr. Rippner, please...."

He nodded and sighed. "You must be aware of the reputation of the Blackmoore name here in Bellingham." She nodded. "Right; well, anyways, you see, people are aware of your arrival. As soon as the faculty found out, everyone was in a panic. You see, no Blackmoore has ever attended the school. In fact, this school has seen to that for over one hundred years."

Mary rolled her eyes. "Well, then, how is it that I'm here? Why was I permitted to teach here; why was the job offered to me?"

Cedric adjusted the collar of his shirt and looked to the door, as if trying to see through the wood, see if there might be someone on the other side listening in. "Because I invited you. You see, Ms. Blackmoore —"

"Please, Cedric, call me Mary."

He nodded. "All right. Mary. You see, I wanted the best for my students; I wanted them to understand music theory and form in a way that they've never considered. And in order for that to happen, you need to expose them to the best; you need them to learn from the best.

"I've lived in this city for my entire life. I went to school with your cousin Kathryn, and I must admit that for a long time—like most everyone else—I was afraid of her."

Mary didn't say anything right away. She understood his fear of Kathryn; she had experienced that same fear, but she was eager for him to finish. "So, what happened?"

"Quite simply, your cousin saved my life." Mary nodded, but it was stiff, still questioning where he was going with everything. "Most of the faculty do not want you here; they are afraid of what will happen to the school if you teach here."

Mary stood, her arms now folded tightly across her chest. "Well, then, as far as I can see it, there is no reason for me to remain here—and furthermore, no reason for me not to return to Ireland." She began to make her way to the door, when Cedric reached out and gripped her arm. She turned on him and he released her at once.

"You're witches." Mary fumbled for words, feeling caught off-guard. "I know it because of your cousin; it was her...uh... witchcraft that saved my life. I've told no one, but you must know that the school has been collecting information on your family for decades!"

Now Mary was growing uncomfortable, and she started to feel as if she were walking into something far more sinister than anything she had ever known.

"Why are you telling me all this?"

Cedric shook his head, as if he were growing frustrated with the fact that she couldn't figure it out on her own.

"I just want you to be aware of what it is that you will be facing. Many of the students here have lived here all of their lives, and many of them are wary of Blackmoores, and the staff may be hostile towards you. I just want you to be careful; that's all. There are many that are excited to meet you and learn from you, but you may encounter others who may not be so nice. I just want you to understand that."

She nodded, but followed it up with another question. "Why is the school collecting information on my family?"

Cedric paused, not sure if he should tell her. "I don't want to offend you, but you're part of a course on Northwest folklore and superstition."

She was offended. She couldn't understand why they were part of some curriculum, and it made her furious. "My family is not just some novelty. We're real people and we deserve privacy, not to have rumors continuously spread about the Blackmoore name!"

Cedric nodded. "It really isn't like that. Rebecca Tramer is a fine teacher, and an even better anthropologist. The information fell into her lap; it was her decision to teach the material. But the information in itself has been at this school long before Rebecca ever arrived."

Mary wanted to meet this woman, wanted to question her; in fact, she wanted to see the material for herself. "Can you set up a meeting with her?"

Cedric nodded. "I can set it up for next week."

Mary smiled politely and made her way to the door. She turned briefly to see him staring at her. "Oh, Cedric?" He nodded. "Thanks for the warning, but why were you so secretive?"

"Because, my dear, I may owe my life to a Blackmoore, but I guess, in the end, I'm still just as scared of you as anyone else would be." She turned, pivoting on her heel and walking out of that classroom as quickly as possible and finally out into the open air, feeling as if for the past fifteen minutes she had not taken a single breath.

FRANCESCA STOOD ON the rocky shore of Marine Park, listening to the waters lap calmly against the earth, its bottle-green water reflecting the pink, orange, and yellow hues of the setting sun, falling behind the San Juan's slowly, and yet dropping at distinct intervals. She thought that perhaps the distance between herself and Paris would be enough to make the loss of Lucas hurt a little bit less, and that those terrible memories could subside themselves and quit with their full-on assault.

Her thick red hair moved gently with the summer breeze, warm but cooling as dusk turned to the first hints of twilight.

She was spending much more time alone, which Kathryn was more than willing to leave her to; if it bothered her, her cousin was masterfully skilled at hiding it.

She caught the sound of laughing children and turned to see two girls and three boys ride into the park, dropping from their bicycles and going to the giant rocks. She hadn't told Kathryn—or anyone else, for that matter—that she had been four months pregnant, that she was going to have a little girl that she would name Tabitha. But the attack from those witches, the attack that led to Lucas's death, had also caused her to miscarry.

In her deepest dreams, she sometimes felt that Tabitha was calling out to her, a sweet musical voice giggling and calling her Mommy. Francesca wiped a tear from her eye and swallowed hard, closing her lids for just a moment and summoning the strength to carry her through and reserve herself to the stoicism that she carried—that they all carried.

All, that was, except for Trevor.

Francesca knew he was a different breed. He gave in to his emotions; he allowed himself to feel them, and he acted on his emotions. They were not like that. Trevor had never shown the iciness that the others had mastered, of which Kathryn Blackmoore was the undisputed queen. They feared for Trevor, wondered if perhaps he would be able to do what was destined for him.

Braxton was a person who felt—like Trevor—but had this raw strength, this fierce machismo that could step in, could take control and push all of the other things aside. Trevor didn't have that. He was sensitive, emotional, and raw. Often he seemed like a wound refusing to heal itself, denying the blood of its ability to clot and begin scabbing the wound until at last fresh skin could form and the scab could be removed.

What scared her even more was that Trevor was the most powerful Blackmoore in this coven, though he could not yet master his gifts like the rest of them. He had it brewing inside of him, moving around his insides like a cyclone waiting to be released. Emotions were a double-edged sword when it came to the witchcraft of the family. If in danger, you could expect an explosion, but in times of personal conflict, you could also expect an explosion—and the endangerment of everyone present.

What she feared greatly for Trevor was the moment he was to be in danger: his own fear, his own hesitation, could stifle that witchcraft, and as a result he could end up dead. His emotions were a gamble, but his head was tethered to his heart, and no one saw that severing anytime soon.

Francesca sighed and turned from the water, making her way back to the street, her black Chanel boots and her Christian Dior black A-line dress absorbing the last bits of heat from the nearly vanished sun.

The streetlamps along Harris Avenue sparked to life. Many nodded kindly as they passed; others, especially teenage boys, could not help but look her up and down, or turn back around for a double-take. She knew what they saw; she knew what thoughts crept into their minds when looking at her. That thick and stylish cherry-red hair, the smooth silkiness of her olive skin, and the absorbent Irish blue eyes.

Francesca used to pride herself in this: her exotic beauty, the sway of her hips, and the curves of her body—which were in all of the right places—her sly grin and confident walk. She was used to men wanting her, sometimes relishing in it—but now, since Lucas, it seemed to not matter anymore. Men were just faceless entities, phantoms that moved along, glancing at her and trying to commune with her.

She looked to see families gathering in the emerald lawn behind Village Books, getting ready to watch some old movie on the painted movie screen on the back of an adjacent building. She and Kathryn had come here a couple of times with Mabel, who delighted in some of the old films that she could recall from her youth. Though now in her eighties, she still moved with the strength of a woman in her early fifties.

While she had stopped to look at the crowd, she noticed that her Chloé bag was buzzing. She debated whether or not she should answer her phone, but in the end she figured it to be Kathryn, and caught it at the last ring.

"Hello?"

"Francesca?" It was Kathryn.

"Yes, Kathryn?" She saw a child throw a ball into the air and grinned.

"Where are you?"

Francesca looked to her boots. "I'm down in Fairhaven, near Village Books."

"I just walked in; you should join me upstairs for a glass of wine." Francesca told her she would and hung up the phone, making her way down the concrete lane towards the lower level of the bookstore.

She stood in the elevator, climbing up the floors and hoping that she wouldn't have to be joined by anyone else; fortunately for her, she wasn't. She arrived on the second floor and looked around, the heels of her boots tapping on the polished wood floor—perhaps cedar, or oak; she couldn't be certain. Tract lights hung above them, and she moved behind her to see the counter. A display of pastries, an espresso machine, plus a menu of assorted foods and wines loomed above her.

"Francesca!" She looked to the left to see Kathryn sitting at a table beneath large windows, that setting sun still burning in the sky. Perhaps it had just been where she was standing on the beach that had made it seem farther gone than it really was.

"Hello, Kathryn; what are you doing down here?" Unlike Francesca's absorbing light blue eyes, Kathryn's were icy, almost gray, and they were reflective constantly, as if they refused to let anything in. All of Kathryn was a wall, and nothing could penetrate it, not even her own family.

"Oh—Trevor; he needed a few books for school and he didn't want to deal with the student bookstore." Francesca nodded. A young woman walked over to them, carrying two glasses of rosé, the pink blush sparkling on the wood table.

"A rosé?" Francesca asked, while bringing the glass up to her lips and taking a drink.

"I figured something light and sweet for a summer's evening." Kathryn's gaze was distant, and her voice was tinged with sadness.

"What is it? You're thinking about Trevor, aren't you?" Kathryn looked at her, startled, but her face calmed and she nodded.

"Yes." She flipped that thick auburn hair from her face and hugged herself lightly. "I can't deny that I miss him terribly. I have never been without him, and I had hoped that he would have stayed here and gone to Fairhaven."

Francesca thought about it for a moment and shook her head. "But Kathryn, you didn't even attend the university, and he's only an hour and a half away, depending on traffic."

She nodded. "I know that. I had just hoped that he would have stayed here." She didn't like the vulnerability in Kathryn's voice; it was so uncharacteristic of her that it seemed psychotic.

"Did you not tell me over the phone years ago that they wouldn't admit you, and even though they claimed it as simple capacity issues, you knew that it was because of the fact that you were a Blackmoore?"

Kathryn nodded and averted her gaze. "Yes, I just... I just thought that with Mary-Margaret on staff this year, he would have been able to attend." These were the dying pleas of a mother having to let go. Francesca may never know that feeling, though she had often thought about it when she was carrying Tabitha inside of herself.

"Well, if I remember correctly, you left for L.A. alone after your split with Sheffield, to get him back. If anything, he is following in your footsteps and leaving home." Francesca pointed sternly at Kathryn.

"And that's what scares me...." Her words trailed off, and they both drank from their glasses.

"Kathryn, the Legacy is over. Cheri and Trevor are friends once again; they have nothing to worry about from each other. In fact, the only thing they need to worry about is what we all have to worry about."

Kathryn's eyes glittered with tears, tears that she was simply ready to extinguish before they fell. Francesca was silently relieved; she didn't know what she would have done if Kathryn had actually started crying.

"I'm afraid that they will meet with danger and not even see it. And I'm not there to watch over him, Braxton, or anyone else." She was used to being in control—and now, with her son miles away for college, living his life without his family, it seemed that she was filled with anxiety. Perhaps not so much of the absence of Trevor himself, but with nothing to do to keep her busy, to keep her mind off of other things.

"C'mon, Queen Mab has invited us over for dinner tonight. I think it would be good for us to go; besides, we need to make Mary-Margaret feel more welcome."

Kathryn shot her a wicked glare before giving out a grunt. "She's a sweet enough girl, but my God, does she consider half the shit that comes out of her mouth?"

Francesca gave her a scolding grin. "That was her first night; we haven't spent any time with her since she arrived. I think there is much more to her than all of that. Let's just consider it a bad trial run." Kathryn rolled her eyes again. She removed her large Chanel sunglasses from her purse and slipped them on her face, throwing the leather straps of her handbag over her shoulder and standing, downing the rest of her drink and waiting for Francesca to join her.

She was wearing wide-leg black slacks, pointed Jimmy Choos, a black off-the-shoulder cashmere sweater, and that usual three-tiered pearl necklace dripping delicately. "Coming?" she asked.

Francesca nodded and stood.

"Kathryn?" They were walking towards the elevator, the sun still out somewhere and casting the street in front of the bookstore in a cool shadowed blue hue.

"Hmm?" she responded casually.

"You're such a MILF!" They laughed. It was good to laugh. Laughing had seemed to be something that occurred less and less since last Christmas, and a bit of witty banter even caused them a little pain in their sides. It felt good, and for the moment they moved on to lighter subjects. Shopping, especially shoes, the possibility of a movie later in the week, or a drive to Canada for the weekend. For the moment, the bad things of their lives had crept away, returning to the shadows of their minds.

THEY WERE SITTING AT the table in the kitchen, its ceiling high and covered in a scattering of different prints of paper. Behind the table against the wall was a giant antique wood cabinet with glass windows in the doors, the countertops wrapping around from the fridge and towards the door to the formal dining room. Next to the fridge was the old Aga, which Mabel was hovering over, moving between it and the sink directly across from the table. The window was framed with chili-pepper lights, which were illuminated red and reflecting in the dark glass. All around the kitchen was Mabel's collection of antique dolls and figurines of black girls, and several elaborate drinking glasses.

They could smell bourbon mixing with the hearty broth of the stew that was simmering in the pot, and fresh cornbread baking away, a slight perfume of clover honey emanating from them. A surprise to them all was the fact that Mary-Margaret was drinking a glass of merlot, seeming to have dropped her walls.

"So, did you have a tour of the campus?" Kathryn asked.

Mary sighed. "I walked around it a little on my own, but what I was officially shown was the room I will be teaching in."

They all nodded. Mabel moved to the window and popped it open, allowing the perfume of the summer night to creep in. She lit a cigarette, and offered one to the others. Mary Margaret shook her head, along with Francesca—but Kathryn took one and walked to the window to join their aunt.

"Well, I suppose that's all you really need to know," Kathryn said, her voice lyrical and smoky.

"Yeah, except the head of the music department said that you saved his life, which was really interesting—and kind of odd for him to simply tell me." They turned their eyes on Kathryn.

She seemed to think about it for a moment before speaking, as if trying to pull the memory out of the fog of her mind. "Oh, yes," she said, giving a gentle nod. "Cedric Rippner. That's right; I suppose I did." She took another drag from her cigarette.

"What happened?" Francesca asked. Kathryn was about to answer when Mabel spoke up instead.

"In 1979 there was a guy running around killing high school students. They called him The Campus Slasher. It was terrible: in the end, ten teens were found dead, throats cut open, genitalia removed. It was bizarre." She took a drink from her wine.

Kathryn rolled her eyes away from her aunt and continued the story. "Yes, I happened to be leaving from a study session. In those days we were allowed to remain at the school for a lot longer than kids can now. I remember that I was cutting through campus, heading towards the back, when I saw Cedric running up from the field. He seemed terrified. He kept looking over his shoulder. I saw him trip and hit the ground hard. I ran over to him, and as I did I saw a large black figure moving towards him—this guy was like a wall, really—and I remember that long blade that he held in his hand.

"He wore a skeleton mask, one of those shiny plastic things on string, one of those 50¢ things. I grabbed Cedric's arm and tried to pull him up, but he just kept screaming, and that man kept coming closer."

She had drifted now. She was seeing it again, as if it were happening all over again, as if she had stepped into the past and was battling it all over again. "He swiped at me. I fell back trying to get away from it, and he shoved the knife into Cedric's leg and pulled it out again, prepared to give him the final fatal blow."

Mary gasped. "What did you do?" she asked in breathless wonder.

"I looked at him and focused all of that witchcraft on him. I felt it move through my body like a tingling cyclone, and I sent it out, and he flew back through the air, so far that he crashed through a set of steel doors.

"An alarm went off and soon the police came, but he had gone. I can remember Cedric thanking me over and over again for saving his life, and apologizing for everything he ever said about me. It was... well, it was strange." They nodded, no one really knowing what to say or if they needed to say anything.

"Was he ever caught?" Francesca asked, pouring herself another glass of wine while she did so.

"No." They looked at one another, feeling that slight terror creep in, when you think that someone might still be out there.

"Oh, shit; why not?" Francesca asked again.

"Because I killed him."

Mary-Margaret let out a tiny gasp, but was quick to extinguish it with the gulping down of her wine.

"He had been following me after that night. He thought me to be something of importance; he was a Satanist or something like that. He believed that if he killed me, he would gain the power I possessed. He came to my home one weekend. My mother was in New Orleans visiting Fiona, and he broke in. He came close to killing Sheffield, but in the end, as with Tom, he never succeeded."

Mary had heard all about Tom Preston; everyone had. His assault on the manor, the near-killing of Trevor and Braxton. It had been the thing to start it all: the realization and slight paranoia over the oncoming danger that was descending on the family. They all waited for Kathryn to elaborate on the tale that seemed fresh from the screen of a horror film, but she did not. After a few moments, Mary decided to change the subject to something more intriguing and immediate.

"So, I learned something very interesting today while at the university." They all looked at her, only slight interest in their eyes. "A professor—her name is Rebecca Tramer—is teaching a course called Northwest Folklore and Superstition, and apparently there's a whole syllabus about our family." Now she had their attention. It felt good to feel as if, for the first time, she was a part of this family—that whatever had transpired the other night no longer seemed to divide them.

"Really?"

Mary nodded. "And what's even more interesting is the fact that the university has had lots of information on our family for a very long time. Apparently the information sort of fell into Ms. Tramer's lap, and she organized it into a curriculum." Mabel and Kathryn seemed to instinctively exchange concerned glances, and Mary wondered if perhaps she had done the wrong thing in telling them.

"Maybe there is a reason why you were brought here," Mabel said gravely.

She wanted to tell them that her sister had said the same thing, but for some reason she felt that that would not have been okay.

They spent the rest of the night talking about many mundane and trivial things. It was simple, and they all spent the time laughing and enjoying the food that Mabel had cooked. It was a lamb stew with bourbon, rosemary, thyme, baby new potatoes, celery, pearl onions, carrot, and caramelized fennel. It made Mary think of the stews that she could find in the pubs back home in Dublin. It warmed her to be surrounded with family, and yet the sickness for home lingered in the back of her mind. And she knew that she had to fight against it, or else she would be crying right there at the table for everyone to see.

Chapter: Seven

TREVOR SAT AT THE DINING room table, going through his course book for the first semester. The sounds of Westlake Center poured through the open windows, and the nighttime sky was inky blue. The glow of streetlights, like tiny orange-and-white orbs hovering in the air, added a distinct feeling of coziness.

He liked that he was able to sit here alone and sort things out, afforded this solitude thanks to Braxton and J.T. going out to meet with Tim Roth, who had left Fairhaven University to move to Seattle and be with the band. He and J.T. were going to be sharing a house together, and Trevor figured that they would probably be spending the night drinking beers and talking about how they were going to be famous.

He was plagued with thoughts of that phantom boy, wondering who he was and what he wanted. He was warning him, but of what? What dangers could there be waiting somewhere just around the corner? He didn't like it. He never liked when the dead came to him. Though it had been something that he had dealt with since his childhood, he still found them unnerving and terrifying.

He heard a wisp of air coming from one of the windows, and it made him turn his gaze towards it. There, in the corner, was Christian. He was dressed in a white tee and a pair of jeans, with a Mariner High School track jacket covering his bare arms. Those black eyes stared at him like liquid, immaculate against his brown skin, and his cushion lips were frowning. That little patch of black hair under his lip was still seductive, even in death. Trevor closed his eyes quickly, and when he opened them again Christian was gone, as if he had never been there, just the slight billow of the drapes. He ran his fingers through his wine-red hair and sighed. He couldn't handle two ghosts. Hell, he couldn't even handle one, and he was a mess with what he was supposed to do.

"Leave me alone, Christian..." he whispered. The front door unlocked and he heard Braxton's familiar steps, firm and strong, come walking into the apartment.

"Hey, baby." He turned to him and grinned. He could tell right away that Braxton knew by the struggle to smile that something was wrong. Trevor turned away from him and averted his gaze to the papers before him, still gripping the ballpoint pen that he held loosely between the fingers of his left hand. "What's wrong?" Braxton asked, wrapping his arms around him from behind and resting his chin on the crown of his head.

"Nothing; it's just all of this school stuff."

Braxton sighed. "You know what might make you feel better?"

Trevor smiled and tilted his head gently. "What?" He brought his hand up and clasped it over Braxton's wrist.

"Letting me take you out to dinner at Capitol Cider."

He shook his head and laughed. "Oh, yeah?"

Braxton nodded and moved his head to the side of Trevor's face, bringing his lips near his ear. "Yeah," he said in a sweet, kid-like voice. "That's why I came home early. Especially since our fake I.D.'s just came in. J.T. brought them into the studio today."

Trevor giggled, while Braxton kissed his cheek. "Really?"

"Yup. So I wanted to take you out, just the two of us." He kissed him on the cheek again and stood, slipping his hands away slowly and giving him two gentle pats just below his shoulder. "So c'mon."

Trevor nodded and rose sluggishly from the dining room table. "I'm so exhausted."

Braxton laughed. "Do you need me to carry you?" Trevor shook his head. "Yeah, I think you need me to carry you." He slipped his arm up under Trevor's waist and flipped him over his shoulder like a firefighter carrying a hose.

He raced out of the apartment with Trevor draped over him, keeping him like that all the way to his Mercedes down in the parking garage.

THEY SAT AT A TABLE in front of large windows that looked out on the corner of Pike and Broadway on Capitol Hill, which was the city's known queer neighborhood, much like the Castro in San Francisco or Boystown in Chicago.

"So, I bet Tim is excited," Trevor said, sticking his fork in a brussels sprout while Braxton took a bite out of his burger.

"Yeah, but he knows that he can't be a flake like he's been in the past. This isn't like local gigs back home; this is a $100,000.00 deal. I just hope he doesn't start to think of himself as a carefree rock star and fuck it up for us." Trevor hoped not either. It wasn't like they were in need of the money, but this was Braxton and J.T.'s dream, and the last thing he wanted to see was it all being taken from them by Tim's recklessness.

"I think it'll be fine." Trevor took a sip from his wine and looked out onto the street. Everyone seemed so normal, so happy; none of them having to be concerned with things that go bump in the night.

"So, how about you and Cheri; you guys ready for classes to start?" Braxton asked this with a tone that suggested there were things that Trevor and Cheri spoke about together that he wasn't privileged to know.

"I think so. I mean, I don't know really how to answer that. We talk about school; we have some of the same classes. I don't know if it'll be at the same time, but I think that we'll be okay. We know that if we have any problems, we can tell each other about them. Hopefully it won't be so overwhelming."

Braxton nodded and reached out, taking hold of Trevor's hand and massaging the back of it with his thumb. "And you have me, Trevor; you know you can tell me anything, right?"

Trevor nodded. He wanted to tell Braxton about Christian haunting him, the fact that his dead lover wouldn't leave him alone, and yet he knew that this would not be the smartest thing to do.

He was afraid that Braxton would be able to use his psychometry to divine what it was that was going on inside of his head. Braxton had learned from Queen Mab how to control his power, which was good in the sense that he wouldn't be assaulted with visions at spontaneous moments of touching people or objects—but at the same time, it meant that he could use it at his discretion.

Braxton hadn't had an outburst of fatal power since his father. Causing an aneurysm and blowing out windows was a far more dangerous gift than simply knowing things by touching people. It made Trevor wary whenever he got pissed off or if they argued—which was next to never, but when it did occur, he could not help but worry in the back of his mind that Braxton might lose control and kill him.

"So, I was thinking," Braxton began, looking at him and smirking.

"Uh-huh?" Trevor responded suspiciously.

"What if we go out Friday night?" Trevor arched an eyebrow. "Yeah, we could go to Neighbors. It's a gay club here in Seattle, a nightclub." Trevor thought about it. The idea of going out to a club made him uneasy. He wasn't certain why, but he had never had a desire to go to these places, and he didn't think that would ever change.

If it weren't for the eager look in Braxton's eyes, he would have said no. "All right."

Braxton looked shocked. "Yeah?"

Trevor nodded. "Yeah, I'm down." Braxton seemed happy about this—extremely happy, as if he had been planning to do this for a very long time.

They finished their meal, discussing all of the things they could do in Seattle, the new life that they would have for themselves, and all the things they wanted to get to add to the penthouse so it would have their own personal touches.

They both wanted to bring up what it was that could be coming for them; they wanted to talk about the mysterious boy and his warnings, but neither one did. They didn't want to break the momentary peace that they were having in their lives; they didn't want to tear away from the fact that they were able to discuss trivial and mundane things. Mostly, they didn't want to step away from the illusion that they were normal. That they had lives just as uneventful as everyone else. They did not want to have to remember that they were the other, that they were simply masqueraders in this world, that they were nothing more than shadows clinging to the feet of normal people.

CHERI HAD NEVER GONE grocery shopping before in her life. Perhaps it was a true observation of the spoiled Daddy's girl life that she grew up in—but now, here at the Broadway Market, she felt more than slightly freaked out.

She was pushing the cart through QFC and trying to look as if she had done this a thousand times. She wanted to cook dinner for herself, get acquainted with her seemingly thousand-window apartment. Most importantly, she wanted to prove that she didn't have to whip out the plastic every day for every little thing.

She went through, pushing the cart but unsure where she should start and what she was looking for. She felt as if she were not dressed appropriately for grocery shopping, her brown hair thick and long, cascading down her back and over her shoulders, spiraling in loose curly tendrils that stopped at her breasts. Her petite body was dressed in a pink Lacoste polo, tight and hugging her waist, followed with a tight white pencil skirt, and her soft, hairless legs ending with strappy Manolo Blahnik sandals.

She listened to the sound of her heels clicking on the concrete floor and gave a displeased sigh. This wasn't going how it should have—at least, how she thought it should have gone. She had just maneuvered down an aisle of canned goods when her cell phone went off, bringing her to a halt.

"Trevor!" she exclaimed.

"Hey, what ya doing?"

"Grocery shopping, groan!" They laughed and exchanged witty banter about how Cheri didn't know how to shop for groceries, and that Trevor was surprised that she even knew where to go to start. "Hey, hey, I don't wanna hear it; you can't grocery shop either."

Trevor laughed. "Hey, I can too."

Cheri snickered. "Really, now?"

"Really—if I have Braxton write a list, pick everything out, and most importantly, let me sit in the cart!"

Cheri smiled and stomped her foot on the ground. "You can't be serious; you ride in the shopping cart?"

"Yes, my heinous one, I do, until we need more room in the cart. I seriously cannot stand around for the hour and a half that Braxton likes to shop for." She had to agree with that; she was the only one here, and she was wishing that she could climb into the cart and push herself around.

"So, what's up?" she asked him. She grabbed a can of cream corn. She wasn't certain she even needed it or would like it, but she felt that she needed to put something in her empty gathering vehicle, as she decided to name it.

"Braxton wants to go to Neighbors Friday night." Cheri gave a slight sound that told him that she had no idea what he was talking about. "Neighbors; it's a gay nightclub."

"That sounds like fun..." Cheri remarked, standing there and staring once again at her can of cream corn, trying to figure it out. "Hey, do you know what to do with cream corn?"

Trevor went silent for just a moment. "What? No, of course I don't know anything about cream corn. I didn't even know it was real; I thought it was a myth, like Santa or the Easter bunny. Cheri, we're talking about a nightclub here!"

"Trevor, it's a nightclub; I'm sure you'll have a great time!"

"Okay, you're only half listening to me. Just meet me at the Market tomorrow for breakfast—say nine?" She agreed, and they hung up the phone. Cheri continued to walk, scanning the shelves and not coming any closer to a decision. She rounded a corner, and that's when she glimpsed someone in the next aisle following her.

She moved and stopped, and so did the guy, his brown eyes scanning her from between the products sharing shelves. Her heart began to pound, thinking of Tom Preston and fearing that something like him could be coming for her again. She had to get away and call Trevor to warn him. She was not sleeping by herself tonight, and she hoped that Trevor and Braxton would be willing to give up their guest room for her.

Cheri moved frantically, glancing continuously over her shoulder, thinking perhaps that she looked like a freak, but that was better than ending up dead with your heart torn out, or something even worse.

"Cheri!"

She screamed and looked to see J.T. Oliver standing in front of her. He was grinning and looking sexy; even in her panic, she couldn't deny that.

"Jesus, was that you following me?" He averted his gaze and shamefully nodded his head. "Jesus Christ, that scared the shit out of me!"

He looked at her, confused. "Sorry, I figured I would surprise you. I didn't expect for you to start taking off as if you were running from Leatherface."

She gave a slightly relieved and annoyed laugh. "Yeah, well, single girl in the city, grocery shopping at night, you never know," she lied. The truth was, after Tom, Cheri had enrolled in kickboxing and weapons classes as well as a defensive assault class, usually attended by female victims of muggings and survivors of rape. She couldn't say that the reason she was there was because some intelligent zombie thing had tried to rip her heart out. She wasn't concerned with someone on the street; she could handle herself. Homicidal corpses with super-strength... that she wasn't too sure about.

"I see. So, grocery shopping?"

Cheri shook her head and blinked, as if returning to her senses, and gave a nod. "Trying to, anyways."

He grinned and stuck one strong arm into her cart, as if he even needed to. "Let's see; well, you've gotten your obligatory can of cream corn, which will sit in your pantry till the day you die because you can't really use it for anything." Cheri and J.T. shared a laugh and then averted their gazes, giving each other a sheepish grin. "But I'm certain that we can find more useful things for you to have here."

They wandered through the market for nearly an hour, conversing about the Spit Monkeys' record deal and their impending meeting with the studio heads. They talked about Cheri and Trevor's first day of university, which was just beyond the horizon, all the while getting Cheri everything she would need for her kitchen. She hadn't much considered J.T. Oliver in high school—but now, far away from the social obligations of Mariner, Cheri was finding herself becoming more and more captivated by the rebelliously handsome young man.

THEY REACHED HER LAVISH apartment, which was on Terry Avenue on First Hill, near the Convention Center. Geographically speaking, in a metropolitan sense, Cheri was considered Braxton and Trevor's neighbor. When she had told them at dinner a few nights before that it was a luxury fortress of glass walls, she hadn't been exaggerating.

It was a lavish expanse of polished oak floors, with a mustard-colored satin couch and arm chairs, slick mahogany end tables, coffee table, and in the dining area behind the living room sat a matching dining table that seated four. From the floor to the ceiling was glass with pocket windows and a lanky yet narrow balcony. The city was bright all around them, a mess of skyscrapers and illuminated windows, and instead of switching on the tract lights, Cheri opted instead to switch on two lamps, which gave a soft glow that added warmth to an otherwise cold space.

"Do you like Billie Holiday?" Cheri asked. She flashed him a gentle smirk, and her brown eyes caught the light in a way that made J.T. shuffle his feet and nod dumbly. "Great." She went to her stereo system beneath her television that she had gotten nearly a year earlier from her father for an early Christmas gift; in fact, it had been on the same set that she had watched the revelation of Christian's death.

They stood in the kitchen, beneath recessed lights, listening to the late jazz singer croon softly in the background, and put the groceries away. They brushed up against one another discreetly, and the both of them were trying to keep their thoughts focused on the task at hand—and not travel to fantasies best kept behind the bedroom door.

"Are you hungry?" J.T. nodded. "Well, if you help me cook I'll let you stay for dinner."

He moved closer to her, keeping a respectful air between them, like a string lay out to mark their territories. "I think you got yourself a deal."

THEY SAT AT THE TABLE, with two vanilla candles burning between them; the candlelight glistened in their liquid eyes, and neither one could stop their feet from casually touching the other. The air was perfumed with salmon grilled with lemongrass and a balsamic reduction of ginger, garlic, and cumin. They sipped gently on their glasses of white wine and hardly touched their salad of baby greens, spinach, and ringlets of red onion, which was accentuated with crumbled feta and drizzled in raspberry vinaigrette.

There was a desire brewing between them, and not since Greg had Cheri been with a man, and never with someone that she felt such innocent passion for. It made her squeeze her thighs together and try and stifle the yearning she felt between her legs. She guessed by his constant squirming that J.T. was having the same problem.

"If I tell you something, promise to be gentle when you shoot me down?" Cheri nodded. "I really want to kiss you right now."

She grinned and blushed, averting her gaze for just a moment, weighing the gravity of her want with what she felt was responsible, and turned her eyes back on him. "I've been sitting here wondering if I had lost my chance."

They leaned forward, brushing their plates aside and taking hold of the backs of each other's necks, locking lips and pressing tongue against tongue, allowing their eyes to close and let go of analyzing what was happening between them.

They rose from the table and J.T. took hold of her thighs, lifting her and pulling her legs around his waist. They continued to kiss as they maneuvered into the bedroom. The whole thing was fevered: the fumbling of fingers in the sparkling dark, the heat of their flesh as he removed her top, followed with her bra, slipping his lips between her breasts, pressing them against her firm nipples, rolling his tongue along their surface.

Cheri curled her fingers under the hem of his shirt and pulled it up off of his head. She imagined for one brief moment that she could see his heart beating beneath his chest, and she was eager for his cock, feeling his hard-on pressing against her. *Screw foreplay*, she thought to herself, *I want to get fucked.*

Soon they were undressed and atop her comforter, his cock thrusting inside of her, making her wet, the sweat slipping down their faces, glistening on their bare flesh as he pumped inside of her. Their speed increased, and in that moment her bedroom became something else. It was a temple to desire, a shrine to pleasure, and Cheri felt like herself again. A piece of that calculating master seductress was still resting beneath her flesh. She wasn't dead, just lying dormant in her skin—and now she was alive, but no longer serpentine. Now she was cunning yet demure, and skittish like a fox.

They fucked several times before finally giving in to the lethargy of sleep, and that night, lying there against J.T.'s chest, the sound of his murmuring heart easing her to sleep, Cheri did not dream of dead friends and hands gripping hearts through torn chests. That night she dreamt of sunlit backyards and four children chasing one another with outstretched hands, and laughing without the slightest care in the world.

Chapter: Eight

IT WAS RAINING, THE first signs of autumn being read like tea leaves in the gray sky, and they sat at a table in a restaurant called the Athenian on the top floor of Pike Place Market, looking out on the cold waters of the sound, seeing ferries move slowly along the surface. The restaurant had been made famous as one of the shooting locations for *Sleepless in Seattle*.

Cheri ate a bagel with butter and strawberry jam with a side of hash browns, while Trevor ate a plate of eggs benedict. Cheri was dressed in low-cut jeans and a petite black hoodie with nothing underneath, zipped up to her chest, and likewise Trevor too wore jeans and a hoodie with nothing underneath. It made Cheri wonder if he had read her thoughts when he woke up that morning. It made her smirk.

"You got laid, didn't you?" Trevor asked.

Cheri looked at him and blushed. "Are you reading my thoughts?"

He shook his head. "I don't have to; it's written all over your face." He returned her grin. "Who was it?" She shrugged. "Either you picked up a hooker, or...." She grew wide-eyed and chuckled. "Oh my God, you fucked J.T.!" She cupped her head in her hand and nodded.

"I know; God, what in the hell was I thinking?"

Trevor cut into his English muffin, which was bathing in golden yoke and velvety Hollandaise sauce, and laughed. "It's obvious you two like each other; I think it's great."

Hearing his honest approval did something for her that she hadn't expected; it somehow validated that she wasn't wrong in feeling something pure and genuine for another person. "You do, really?"

Trevor nodded. "Cheri, you deserve to be happy; you always have."

Hearing this sent a mild tremor throughout her body. She didn't understand why Trevor Blackmoore had such unending love for her, especially after the five years of hell she had put him through. She thanked the universe then for its preservation of his innocence—that despite everything, his bleeding heart hadn't been corked, that he had not shut down and lost his generous light. She knew that she had Braxton to thank for that.

"Well, my love, enough about my harlot ways. Tell me about you and that dangerously gorgeous boyfriend of yours."

Trevor's face grew dark, and he shifted in his seat. He took a sip of his coffee and folded his arms across the old wood table. "Well, he wants to go out to the club, to Neighbors. Which is fine, I guess, but I don't want to go... all of those people," he shuddered.

"What are you afraid of?" Trevor shook his head, telling her it was stupid. "No; now, you're going to tell me. What kind of fag hag would I be if I didn't listen?"

Trevor smiled. "I'm afraid of all of the hot guys that will be there; I'm afraid that —"

"That he'll be attracted to them?" Trevor nodded. "Babe, you are all that Braxton can see of tomorrow. I honestly don't think anyone else registers on his radar—and so what if one or two of them catch his eye? It'll all be surface, and nothing would ever come of it; if anything, it'll just make him want you more." She could tell by his weary nod that he was trying to believe it.

"Just the same, will you and J.T. come along?"

Cheri smiled and placed her hand over his. "I've already been thinking of an outfit."

ARCADIA RECORDS was located within the heart of downtown Seattle; it took up the last five floors of an eight-story building. Braxton, J.T., and Tim sat on a giant burgundy sofa, all of them equally tense and tapping their feet erratically. A door swung open and in walked two men. One was a scruffy white guy covered in tattoos, with jet-black hair and five o'clock shadow; his charcoal tee was tight and scattered with holes.

The other was in his early thirties, a beautiful face, and Braxton's height. His eyes were icy, like Kathryn's, his hair black and short, spiked in the front. He wore a black fitted blazer and dark blue denim jeans, with a white and black check shirt underneath with a black and white striped bowtie and he reminded Braxton of the actor Jonathan Rhys Meyers.

"Gentlemen, I am Joshua Dianaca, president of Arcadia Records, and this is Jeffery Waterson, one of the foremost producers in the industry. He is going to help you really tighten your sound and get your record ready for the public." His words moved in the air with a melodic grace; there was something gentle in it. Braxton guessed it was because he was English. The last name made him think of the famed Dianacas of South Hill, but he shrugged it off as mere coincidence. They had lived in the states for more than a century, after all, and this man was clearly not from these shores.

When they shook hands, something passed between the young men, something that sent a mild wave of shock down Braxton's spine and titillated him all the same. At that moment, he wanted nothing more than to get away from the studio and get back to Trevor.

For the rest of the meeting Joshua went over the terms of the working contract once again, stipulating the hours dedicated to studio time, the expected time frame for the production of their first album, and booking the first showcases for the press —such as The Stranger and the Seattle Weekly. Every now and then Braxton would feel those icy eyes of Joshua Dianaca on him, and the heat began to rise on the back of his neck and his heart drummed in his ears.

The meeting was brief, only an hour, and yet it felt like the longest hour of his life. Every single minute seemed to tick by at a snail pace, and he was only half-listening. He could sense another presence, as if it was inside of him, as if someone else were moving into the deepest parts of himself and looking around. *Stop*, he said to the force inside. *This can't be real; just stop.*

He looked up from the contract that he hadn't really been looking over, half-expecting to see Joshua staring at him—but he wasn't. *I'm imagining this*, he concluded and smiled nervously, giving his head a shake and dismissing the notion completely. Perhaps, he figured, he was just nervous about the record deal, and worried that the implications of their schedule would interfere with his time with Trevor.

"Does that all work for you?" Joshua asked. Braxton nodded, along with the rest of the band. He had already read the contract and knew the details—and if there was anything he missed, at this point he didn't care. He just wanted to get back home and see Trevor's face and kiss his lips, and forget everything that he had felt in the past hour.

"I NEVER THOUGHT IN a million years that I would be going to a gay cabaret," J.T. said, holding Cheri's hand. The four of them were standing outside of the entrance of Julia's, which was located on Broadway. They had already purchased their tickets earlier in the day and were taken to their tables by the host, who sat them near the stage and handed them menus.

Trevor was aware of the eyes that moved over Braxton, scanning him up and down, taking in the unquestionable beauty of his form. It made him nervous and slightly nauseous. "This should be fun," Braxton said with a smirk. They kissed and he took hold of Trevor's hand, giving him a gentle and reassuring squeeze.

They had ordered drinks and their dinner and watched the show, the drag caberet featuring one of the stars of Ru Paul's Drag Race's many seasons. When the show broke for an intermission, J.T. and Cheri both excused themselves for the restroom, and Braxton leaned over to Trevor.

"J.T. told me that he and Cheri hooked up; did you know that?" Braxton looked at Trevor, and he gave an assuming nod. "Of course you knew that," he concluded with a sigh.

"So, how did your meeting with Arcadia go?" Trevor asked him, his voice rising over the music.

Braxton thought of Joshua and his English charm and fierce eyes; he was shaming himself immediately. "Tedious, but good." He averted his gaze from Trevor, letting them fall on the crowd around them. He felt Trevor's eyes exploring his face, as if he could see that shameful lust written all over him.

"Well, that's good, as long as it went well," Trevor responded. In the end Braxton concluded that Trevor must have recognized nothing, which was good because the last thing he needed was for Trevor to worry over infidelities that would never take place. "I want to have a smoke." Braxton nodded and followed Trevor out; Cheri and J.T. did the same as they returned from the bathrooms.

They stood outside, laughing and talking about incidental things, while Cheri and J.T. were wrapped up in one another as all new couples are. It put a smile on Trevor's face to see this—to see Cheri happy and with a guy that was good and would treat her well and respect her for the person that she was, and not demand her to be anything other than herself.

He had long since been aware of Greg and Cheri's dangerous liaison, and he knew that it had scarred her in a way that could have had lasting implications—but to his relief, the opposite had been true.

They walked back into the restaurant, thinking of nothing of particular importance, when Trevor was brought to a standstill, his knees buckling and threatening to bring him to the floor.

"Trevor, what is it?" Braxton asked, but no words could pass his quivering lips. "Babe?" Braxton closed his eyes and summoned his witchcraft, feeling that familiar buzzing, that heat rising throughout his body, the sensation of a thousand tiny needles running along the back of his brain. He connected with Trevor, seeing what he saw.

Standing by their table, completely apart from the rest of the crowd, was Christian and another young man similar in build by his side, a white light coming from someplace without a source shining down on them. Their phantom arms were outstretched and their fingers pointing at Trevor, their eyes empty, black endless pools without life, without any spark. He pulled away.

"We need to go." He shot Cheri a knowing look, secret and something understood by her—something that created confusion in J.T. and made him nervous.

"What, why? The show isn't over yet!"

Braxton shook his head. "Trevor's not feeling well; he's got a bad fever."

He was sweating, but if J.T. had felt him, he would have gotten the sensation of touching a bag of ice. Something was happening, something bad. Cheri knew it, and yet she wasn't sure if she wanted to know. There was only so much of this that she could take, only so much of this that she could handle. And if she was going to become privy to the knowledge that Trevor may be in life-threatening danger once again... well, this was just a secret that she may have to pass on to J.T. Because keeping these things to herself—this knowledge of this other, more frightening and mysterious world—was beginning to weigh on her. She was the only normal person in this world of the supernatural. She was helpless, without any abilities, any powers to keep herself or her loved ones safe.

She felt alone in a lot of ways, and wished that she could tell the new guy in her life, so the secrecy could end and she could have someone else who understood—and who could worry and feel as helpless as she did. She knew it was selfish and wrong to want to bring someone else into all of this, to possibly put that person's life in danger... but she felt if there was just one more thing, one more terrible dark thing, she would be pushed too far over the edge to care.

Chapter: Nine

"TREVOR, WHAT IS GOING on; how long has Christian been visiting you?" Braxton was in a panic, his words revealing a kind of distress that he had never heard before—not even that time last winter, when he had told Trevor that he had killed his father.

"I don't know...." His gaze fell away from him, and he began to shuffle his feet on the floorboards. He couldn't look at him—wouldn't look at him; it was as if he were being questioned about an affair.

"How long, Trevor?" Braxton was bracing the backs of two stools at the island, his grip tight and his muscles constricting. His brown eyes, which were always gentle, seemed to express a cold hostility.

"Since his death."

"Goddamn it!" Braxton threw the stools away from him, which caused Trevor to flinch as they hit the floor with a *CLAP*. "And you just conveniently forgot to tell me, after all of this fucking time!" Braxton and Trevor stood bare in their underwear, having prepared for bed like any other night—and now it had turned to this.

"I didn't say anything because for a while it had stopped, and I thought that he had crossed over. I didn't say anything because I didn't want it to be concluded to one thing or the other, especially since I have no idea what it means. I didn't say anything because I wanted to avoid *this*!" Trevor fired back, his voice now just as enraged. He couldn't believe Braxton; he could not understand why he was freaking out like this. It was stupid, childish, and he could not understand what Braxton could possibly be worrying about.

"Avoid what? Me being upset that your dead boyfriend has been having little rendezvous with you, rendezvous which you have decided not to tell me about?—which only leads me to believe that you have something to hide!"

"Like what?" Trevor began, locking his gaze with Braxton's, the both of them now staring the other person down. "Like that I am having some kind of paranormal affair?" Trevor could sense that the next thing to come out of Braxton's mouth was going to be sharp and cut deep, but he couldn't see how deep.

"If I recall, it wouldn't be the first time," Braxton hissed. Trevor's jaw dropped and his eyes began to well with tears, feeling a rage so strong, so fierce, that he wanted to pick up something—anything, really, that was around—and hurl it with all the force he had at Braxton's head.

"Fuck you, you bastard!" Trevor spirited past him and disappeared into the bedroom, slamming the door behind him. Braxton knew not to follow, and what was worse, he knew that he had sliced Trevor wide open. And what was an even worse revelation was that in that moment, he was glad he did.

THE SUN WAS SETTING, deep orange light filtering through parted satin drapes, the color a nice merlot, tied back by gold cord with elegant tassels that glistened on mustard walls. Freshly-clipped lilacs seemed to bloom from a porcelain vase resting on a wood pedestal of polished mahogany. The reflection of the violet blossoms seemed like a painting in the oval mirror, with its silver frame made prominent with its decorated Athena faces.

The young violist stood there, occasionally opening his eyes to spy his surroundings, the double parlor divided by a pocket door. Behind him was a brick fireplace, the hearth occupied by a wicker basket filled with logs left over from the harsh winter, and yet still on hand for any cool spring nights. There was a piano in the corner to his right, fixed between two windows both looking out to the lush orchard at the back of the house. The window behind him faced the side courtyard, which was laid with flagstone and featured a two-tiered fountain in the center. A young mermaid spat water from bow-tie lips, its sound unnoticed in the day but rather noisy in the dark of night.

The young violinist fell into his music, swaying back and forth, losing himself entirely in the rhythm of his bow on the strings, the dozens of white horse hairs giving little resistance to the demand of his fingers.

At seventeen, they considered him to be a prodigy, having played since the age of three—but he never saw it, wishing only to play for the sake of playing alone. He stood at a height of five foot ten inches; his body was lean but fit from all of the hours spent standing, and keeping himself poised like a statue yet moving his arms, inadvertently working the muscles in the biceps and torso. His skin was fair and aside from a few discreet moles there was not a blemish to be found.

His jaw was distinct but not overt, and his lips were soft and his eyes were gentle and brown, giving him a sharp contrast to his chocolate hair, which was parted down the middle. Strands reached to half an inch above his eyebrows, which were thin and gentle, and the tops of his cheeks were nearly kissed by long black lashes. His ears were that perfect shape with that slight point at the ends, and the sides of his hair were shaved—but not enough to reveal any flesh.

He was dressed in black knickers that reached just past his knees, and black stockings made of wool protected the rest of his legs.

He had polished black shoes on his feet and a black jacket, which was over a starch white oxford and black vest, and his neck was wrapped with a black silk tie. His lids fluttered erratically. He went with the rhythm of the finale to Tchaikovsky's Violin Concerto in D Op. Thirty-five, *knowing every pull, every demand of every note like he knew his own name.*

His fingers pressed tightly onto each individual string, lifting some and stressing others, hardly concerned with the sheet music before him, resting on the iron easel with its elaborate ivy design. His feet tapped on fresh hardwood floors, unhindered by the many feet that have walked across it.

Three settees lay about the room, all made with sturdy oak frames, the cushions made of lush red velvet. There were tiny round tables in front of each settee that were set with empty tea trays. His mother's usual crowd of The Fairhaven Women's Society *was missing, though due the following afternoon for a fresh performance: something that he loathed. He did not have the courage to play for others, but his mother Claudette and his father Jasper were insistent that he should play for the sake of others—that if he did anything less, then there was no point in playing at all. To them, there was no such thing as playing for the sake of playing.*

"Excuse me, Master Donovan." It was the maid, Nellie, twenty-five years of age and plump around the thighs. She had a kind face, hindered by sad brown eyes, her hair's color and length unknown to anyone in the house due to the white bonnet that was required of her by his mother. Her long skirt was a forest green, with a black apron wrapped around her waist; the color was so as not to reveal any stains that she may have collected throughout her workday.

"Master Donovan?"

"For God's sakes, what is it?" he replied. He slammed his bow on the music stand, and his eyes were exquisite and looked on her with contempt.

"The Misses says that she is needing to stop by the American Theatre, and that you are to handle dinner orders."

He looked at her, perplexed, his lips parting slightly, expressing words lost in sudden thought. *"Did she not leave a list?"*

Nellie shook her head, standing in front of the large picture window that faced out onto Sixteenth Street. The lane of dirt was dry, and for once missing its usual puddles. Bellingham Bay glistened with the setting of the April sun, unhindered by the steam ships that moved across it.

Nellie glanced up to the grand staircase, its banister made of rich fir, which swept down from the second floor, meeting briefly at the landing with its two narrow windows and tiny bench, before spilling down to the foyer, greeting the front door with its glass front and crystal knob. To its left was the dining room with its bay windows and distinct fireplace, and a portrait of Queen Victoria hung oppressively above its mantle. The walls were papered with prints of fruits. The cherry-wood dining table was long and hosted fourteen chairs and was occupied with fine china, silently awaiting a grand meal: a meal which now fell on his shoulders.

"We'll have lamb and potatoes." Nellie nodded, and he returned it, watching her move back to the kitchen, disappearing down the narrow hall that led to the back gardens, as well as the lavatory with its windows of stained glass. Opposite the lavatory were the steps that led down to Nellie's room, which was the basement. It was the coldest room in the manor, and once he had asked that she be allowed to sleep upstairs in one of the available rooms. But his parents had only scoffed at the idea and said, *"Oh, what the neighbors might say."*

MARY'S EYES POPPED open, needing a moment to adjust to the dark. What had she dreamt? She knew that it was this house, but who was the young man? The Violinist. Was he the specter that she had seen in this very house, where the walls seemed to breathe and the portraits and statues gave off the impression that they were watching your every move with guarded interest?

She stood and grabbed a pale pink silk shawl that was draped over the post at the foot of the bed, throwing it over her and clutching it tightly across her breasts with her right hand. She felt the compulsion to go out into the house; it was some unknown force that was pulling her, guiding her now through the thick dark. She opened the door and stepped out into the open hall of the second floor, hearing Mabel's quiet snoring in the room next to hers. She feared that her bare feet padding across the creaking hardwood would awaken her elderly cousin, but to her relief she did not stir.

The air seemed to change, the temperature not altering in any way, yet it seemed as if she were maneuvering through gelatin. Silver light from the moon filtered through the low-resting windows on the landing, and the painting of the soldier with the gold helmet that hung on the wall seemed threatening, causing Mary to avert her gaze from it quickly and move downstairs.

She watched the first floor grow in size as she neared the mouth of the grand stairs, feeling out of place now, awkward, as if she should not be down here at this hour—that in the twilight of early morning, the house was reserved for other occupants. Her heart slammed in her chest, hearing the blood pump in her ears and she could feel that familiar tingle, that spark of power within her, switch on as if buzzing dimly inside of her, moving in swirls through her bloodstream.

She thought to go to the music room once again—but now, she found her feet taking her in the opposite direction, forcing her hand to the brass handle of the pocket doors to the dining room. She wanted to stop herself; she wanted to turn around and go upstairs, but she found that she could not, that her limbs would not listen to the command of her thoughts. There was something else going on here, something else that was in control, and there was no way that she could avoid it. There was no way that she was going to escape whatever it was that was awaiting her on the other side of those doors.

The fire burned orange-red in the brick hearth, and standing before it, liquid black eyes intent on those flames but reflecting nothing, was the young man from her dream, The Violinist. He was dressed in black trousers, a white shirt, and a black jacket. His skin was immaculate and white like marble; in a way, he seemed to be plucked from a silent film and placed in a world where everything was in color but him, save for his glossy chocolate hair.

Her beautiful voice trembled as she attempted to summon the courage to speak with the phantom. "Mi-Mi-Michael?" He turned and looked at her, his black pools falling over her there at the white doors, the glow of the fire splashing across her fair skin and casting the side of her face in shadow. He gave a half-nod.

Mary pulled the door closed behind her and attempted to speak once again. "Ha-have you been trying to reach out to me?" The same slight nod. "Why?" She didn't know what to expect. She didn't know if he would speak, if he could speak, and would she want to hear the words that would come from his phantasmal lips? In that moment, confronted with a ghost for the first time in her life, she found herself questioning the very existence of everything she had been raised to believe.

'Because this family is in grave danger....' It seemed then that her heart ceased to beat, and the sweat began to bead down her forehead. His voice was soft, gentle, and his words flowed out

in a whisper, a steady stream which seemed to somehow envelop her and slip through the pores of her skin and mix with her cellular structure.

"But why? How? Please tell me!"

Michael closed his eyes and shook his head. *'The time is not now. You will know; when the clock chimes thirteen, you will then be ready....'*

The fire was out and the spirit was gone, leaving her alone in the dining room, where the light of dawn was slipping delicately through the lace of the bay windows. Time had moved like water, and what had once been 3:00am was now 6:00, and she could hear Mabel moving one floor above her.

Chapter: Ten

TREVOR DIDN'T WANT to get out of bed. He didn't want to move, couldn't move even if he had the will to do so. He just wanted to lie in the bed and rot. In three days' time he would be starting his first year of college, and now he didn't care. He didn't really care about anything. It had been a restless night, with him tossing and turning and feeling as if he could sense Braxton's own uneasy sleep in the apartment—aware of the fact that he had stayed up in the library the entire night, flipping through pages and looking for God knows what in all of those books.

Things seemed to be unraveling now. Their life, which had seemed to be going so well, was now crumbling around him. What was he supposed to do? He knew that he had done wrong in not telling Braxton, but he had thought that he was doing the right thing—that he was protecting the man that he loved more than anything else in the world.

He contemplated going to him, wrapping his arms around him and whispering apologies in his ear. But whenever that urge to do so would come, he would recall Braxton's accusations and his backhanded attack in mentioning his past with Jonathan Marker, and he would become upset all over again and refuse to offer any apologies until Braxton did so first.

It was all so petty, and yet it seemed to tap into something very human that resided in both of them, something that even their own witchcraft couldn't obliterate: simple mortal jealousy. He had thought by now that Braxton had understood how much

Trevor loved him, how much he worshipped him, and could not exist without him.

They were entwined together, bound not just by their hearts, but also by their very genetics. They were made for one another at the cellular as well as spiritual level. It was where the soul meets body; together they made one complete being, one perfect person, and yet Braxton had expressed doubts in all of it. If it was so easy for him to jump to the idea that Trevor could so easily sever himself from that, then it made Trevor question how well Braxton really knew and understood him at all.

He knew that there were bigger things going on, things that went completely beyond them, and yet had everything to do with them and their being together—but he could not bring himself to worry about any of it. He didn't care about some great evil that craved their blood; he didn't care about unnatural things that may be waiting for them just around the corner, or lurking within the shadows of their own home. At this moment, the only thing that mattered was what was going to happen with him and Braxton. The only thing that seemed to exist to him was this relationship and its sudden rupture.

BRAXTON HAD SPENT THE night flipping through books upon books about spirits, incantations to get rid of them, and ways to decipher their purposes here on this plane. He wanted to set Trevor free from Christian Vasquez; he also wanted to free himself. He had never told Trevor about all the nights he had sat up and watched him sleep, spending those nights as if he could do nothing, wasting hours waiting for the world to end. The thought that there were things out there that he did not have the ability to see, things that Trevor could not help but see, filled him with an indescribable fear that those things that were invisible to him would somehow be able to take Trevor away from him.

He had spent so many nights watching Trevor toss and turn in his sleep, dreaming terrors that he could not keep him safe from. It was as if in those moments in the still dark, he was being told not to wake at night to watch him sleep. Because in the end he would always lose; shadows seemed to be murmuring Trevor away from him. Every time Trevor shifted in the bed, Braxton would find his eyes popping open and his head turning immediately to Trevor, as if prepared to reach out for him and make sure that he was still there.

He didn't trust spirits. They seemed to do nothing but lie and manipulate the living. In the dark world of the dead, Trevor seemed to be a shining light in that darkness, and in hoards they seemed to approach. Since they had gotten together, Braxton had spent so many times in one day watching Trevor recoil in the middle of a sidewalk because a spirit had moved past them—and it seemed in those moments, especially in crowds where the dead mixed with the living, Trevor seemed to be thrust into immobility.

If Christian was hanging around, he figured that it couldn't be for anything good, and if spirits become jealous of the living, then perhaps Christian's real motives were to find a way to claim him once again. Though Christian had had possession of Trevor's heart for many years, he had never valued it; he had never cherished it. In fact, he had spent those years exploiting that love and manipulating it to his advantage; it wasn't until the very last moments of his life that Christian had come through. But in Braxton's eyes, that still did not redeem the dead soccer star of any of his past sins.

Trevor may have found it within him to forgive Christian, but Braxton could not and would not. He was going to find a way to get rid of the dead teen, no matter how arcane the ritual or how grave the consequence. He wasn't giving up Trevor that easily, and it was time that Trevor learned how to give up the ghost.

He was tired, his vision blurring, and he knew that he needed to sleep. He could very easily crawl into the bed in the guest room, but he knew that what he needed to do was swallow his pride and go to Trevor. He needed to be in his own bed, and he needed to mend the tear that last night's argument had caused.

He stood and shuffled down the hall, moving sluggishly towards the bedroom door, his heart pounding in his ears, hesitant to open it and walk in. He wanted to reach inside his own chest; he wanted to slip in through the flesh and break his ribs to get to his heart. He wished nothing more than to grasp that bloody, pumping muscle and rip it from his body, and offer it up to Trevor on a silver platter. He would do anything to make things right, and he needed Trevor to know that.

He turned the handle and pushed the door open, hearing it skirt across the floor. The room was shadowed in early morning blue. It was cold, as if any kind of joy that had once resided in their bedroom had been forced out and replaced with a kind of apathy that he could not avoid. His breath caught in his throat and his lids grew heavy as he took in the sight of Trevor there on the bed, unmoving, unflinching, his eyes wide open and staring out towards the windows with their drawn curtains.

He stood with one arm folded across his chest; the other he ran through his black hair, taking a deep breath before bringing himself to approach him—to step over the invisible divide that seemed to be drawn between them.

"Trevor..." he said, sitting down on the bed, reaching his hand out for him, running it through that soft head of burgundy. The tears welled in those hazel eyes, and his cheeks flushed red.

"Trevor, I'm sorry." He shook his head. "Please...." Braxton brought his head down on Trevor's chest slowly, listening to his heart beat in his ear.

He drew his arm across Trevor and felt how cold he was, as if he were clinging to a corpse. A memory flashed across his mind, seeing his father there on the floor, stained with shit and that blood that had slipped from his ears, nose, mouth, and eyes. He shuddered and forced it away.

"I don't know what to say..." Trevor responded, his voice muffled with tears. Braxton shook his head, knowing that it was not the time for Trevor to speak. This was Braxton's moment; it was his duty to offer up remorse, not Trevor's.

"I was stupid. Jealous, really. It's just that I am always so afraid of losing you; I live with that threat every single minute. There isn't a moment that goes by that I don't think about you being taken from me, that some dark force will come in and bring an end to everything that we have.

"I try not to think about it. I try to believe that everything will be okay, but we've already faced this evil once before. We've seen what can happen when spirits get involved, and to think about the fact that lives have already been lost and others have been ruined because of us.... I just don't want to walk around with that much responsibility, especially if it will one day mean that I have to carry the burden of losing you.

"I don't trust Christian. I don't know why he's here or what he really wants from you, but you need to consider the fact that Christian could have moved on if he was finished, but it seems like his only unfinished business is with you. And if it was simply to make things right, to make amends for the sins that he spent years committing against you... well, then, he would have already done it. Which leads me to believe that there is something more going on here, something that we need to know about. It just seems like he is tormenting you for a reason."

Trevor placed his hand on Braxton's head, petting his hair gently and releasing a sigh. "I know."

"I want you to know one thing, Trevor. I love you. I love you more than I have ever loved anyone in my entire life, and not only am I going to find out what that reason is, but I am going to stop him, one way or the other."

He couldn't be certain, but in that moment he thought that he felt Trevor shudder beneath his chest, and somewhere in the unseeable distance he thought he heard a familiar, arrogant chuckle. It made Braxton's entire body tense.

They fell asleep together, lying against one another, dreaming of someplace familiar burning down around them, streets covered in bodies and skies smoldering with black smoke. They could taste the charred flesh in the air, and the screams of pain were deafening. When they woke, neither one felt the desire to share it.

KATHRYN STOOD IN HER kitchen, sipping a glass of chardonnay, the sun setting behind her, the tract lights illuminating her in a dim halo. She was wearing a black sheer blouse and a tight black skirt with translucent black stripes, her wedding band to Sheffield glittering in the light, as well as a loose gold chain-link bracelet on her left wrist. She could hear Jared moving through the house, his steps coming down the hall, drawing ever so closely towards her. Her heart was beating and her pulse racing. She wanted him. She knew that she could no longer contain the need for him, the desire to be with him, to feel him inside of her, and she didn't know how much longer she could control herself.

"Is there anything else you'd like me to do before I go?" he asked her. His eyes were gentle, his face handsome, kind, and yet his body seemed to express a certain lust that perhaps he wasn't even aware of.

"Um, no... that's it, I think." He nodded, grinning at her as she moved to cut him his monthly check. She felt her cheeks flush and she turned from him to write out the check, hoping that with her back to him she could stop herself from thinking the things that always went through her head whenever she was around him.

She could feel him coming closer, could smell his cologne in the air, and it sent a shiver down her spine and caused her to swell between her legs. "You know," he began, his voice soft, "you don't have to pay me so much." She turned to look at him, her eyes meeting his, her lips parting, wanting to say something but not knowing what.

There are moments when you act, and others when you think things through—and she knew that this was not one of those times. She attacked his mouth, their lips meeting, their tongues tangling, hands sifting through hair, moving beneath the fabric of shirts, feeling skin against skin. He gripped her and lifted her off the floor, laying her atop the island. Kathryn reached down and took hold of his slacks, pulling them open and gripping his hard-on, which was tenting his boxer-briefs.

His breath was hot, his mouth moist, and he wasted no time in hiking up her skirt and tearing her panties open. She needed him, wanted him, and with her own animal strength she tore open his white oxford, seeing that firm, chiseled body, his flat torso and perfectly defined chest.

He tore her blouse open and undid her bra, cupping her breasts and laying her down on the granite countertop, shoving his cock inside of her, feeling how warm and wet she was inside, the both of them moaning and grunting, hearing it echo off of the walls.

She could feel her mind spinning, thoughts like cyclones, and cautions like bombs going off in her head, but for once not caring. He fucked her hard, and she loved it. Kathryn felt as if something inside of her was coming back to life, as if the woman that she had once been and had since thought was gone had stepped back in and was taking control.

She knew that this could have consequences, but she didn't care. She knew that perhaps she was breaking so many rules, that perhaps the passion that she was feeling—passion that she had never felt with Tom Preston—was somehow violating her vows to Sheffield, but in that moment she didn't care. After all, the truth was that Sheffield was dead, and for the first time since his passing, Kathryn realized that she was still very much alive.

"WE SHOULD PROBABLY get out of bed," Trevor said, lying against Braxton's chest, kissing the right pectoral and tasting the salt of his skin on his lips. Braxton had his arms draped around him, running his fingers along his arms.

"No," he responded. Trevor looked up at him, their eyes meeting and the both of them grinning.

"No?"

Braxton shook his head again. "Nope, I think we should stay right here and do nothing until you have to go to school."

Trevor laughed and began to pull himself up from the bed, but Braxton grabbed him tight and pulled him back down against him, wrestling with him, the two of them laughing erratically.

"Where do you think you're going, huh?" Braxton snickered.

"Nowhere —"

"That's right, nowhere!" He was warm. That's what Trevor liked best about Braxton—the fact that he was always warm. It was comforting to him, and if he could, he would never leave his side. They fit together, like two pieces of a puzzle. There was no other person in the world that Trevor could fit so perfectly with, and he knew that the same could be said for Braxton. "I love you more than anything; you know that, right?"

Trevor nodded. "You know that nothing, not even Christian, could take me away from you? I just don't ever want you to question that," Trevor said to him in response. He was playing with Braxton's fingers, entwining them together, feeling their pulse beneath their fingertips. The sun had long since set, and the only light was from a single bedside lamp that was glowing from beneath a black shade.

"I know, and I'm sorry if I did. It's just that everything is so uncertain right now; we don't even know how to keep ourselves safe from whatever it is that is coming for us."

Trevor nodded, understanding the concern in his voice. "We were able to stop Tom."

Braxton sighed. "That was only because we had that spell to stop him, and that was only because it was a counter one to a spell you had already done."

Trevor didn't like to think back on that. He didn't like to remember that the whole reason Tom had come back was from a spell that Trevor had done to bring Christian's spirit back from the dead—a spell that had worked, but had inadvertently brought the wrong person back to life.

"We'll be fine, Braxton; I really —" The lamp went out suddenly, causing them both to sit up with a start.

"What the fuck was that?" Braxton asked.

"I dunno...."

"A power outage?" Trevor looked to the foot of the bed and let out a yelp. That boy, that mysterious boy, was standing before him, cast in soft blue light, those inky black wells large and endless. The air seemed to grow cold around them, and though he knew Braxton could not see him, he could tell by the sudden outbreak of gooseflesh that he could feel his presence.

'They are gathering....' Trevor tried to summon the courage to speak, but found his words falling short in the presence of the dead boy. *'It is happening again; they are coming!'* Trevor was shaking now, and somewhere in the distance he could hear Braxton screaming his name, wanting him to tell him what was going on. But it seemed in that moment that the only thing that mattered, the only thing that was real, was he and this boy, and the rest of the world was nothing but thick black shadow.

"Who?" he finally managed, unaware of how loud he was screaming.

'The Soul Wanderers....' As his words trailed off, so did he, and soon the world returned to normal, and the lamp flickered back to life.

"Trevor, what happened?" He was shaking him, trying to get him to look at him, but he could not tear his eyes away from the spot where the ghost had stood in front of the fireplace. "Trevor!" He jumped and turned to face him, trying to summon his voice to articulate the message from the dead boy.

"He said they're coming: the Soul Wanderers —"

"What the fuck is that?"

Trevor gave his head a shake. "I don't know...."

MARY-MARGARET STOOD in front of her class, her syllabus before her, seeing their wide eyes, each one of them staring at the white board, their copies of Form in Music before them.

Here goes nothing, she said to herself and took in a deep, calming breath.

"I am seeking always... the coherent and living expression of my musical ideas-Rodger Sessions." It was written in red behind her, and yet she felt that it would hold more power if said aloud. She stood before them in a pinstripe skirt suit, the jacket left open, revealing a silk lilac blouse with a low-cut collar. Her red hair was pulled back in a tight bun, and her long legs were accentuated with a pair of Marc Jacobs stilettos.

"In this class we will not be playing music, but studying it—its philosophy, so to speak. We will strive to understand its personality, its structure, and its body. Music lives like we do; it beats with its own heart and exists with its own soul, and we will spend the semester trying to decipher its genetic code."

She had thought that perhaps it would have been harder than it was, that much more skill would be needed, skill that she felt she did not possess. And yet as she explored the smaller structural units of Motive, Figure, Common Cadence, Phrase, Repetition, Period, Tonality, Enlargement of the single Period, Double Period, Polyphony, and so on, as she coursed through examples of Brahms, Mozart, Beethoven, and Tchaikovsky, she realized that it wasn't going to be as difficult as she had anticipated.

They wanted to ask her questions about her own illustrious career, her sister, and how old they had been when they started playing, but she had surprisingly been able to keep the fifty or so students on track. She kept herself on track, and neither side of the classroom veered off course. By the end of the two hours, they seemed halfway eager for their first assignment.

"Write each of the following—at least the melody, with appropriate cadential harmonies indicated below the melody line: a four-measure phrase, a five-measure phrase, an eight-measure period with a half-cadence at the middle, a ten-measure period with the second phrase extended, a twelve-measure period with two antecedent phrases, a double period, and any of the other types of small structural units discussed."

They seemed relieved when she had taken a pause; oh, how she was going to dash their hopes in one fell swoop.

"And one more thing." They stopped in their tracks, and she was certain that a few of them had groaned. "Develop an analysis of the first twenty-four measures of Beethoven's *Sonata in E minor, Op. Ninety*. Do you feel that the half-cadence at measure sixteen is a period division? Classify the cadences and identify the key levels. What elements of symmetry do you observe? Would you describe the passage as a phrase group or an enlarged period?"

She hoped that she had talked slow enough that they all had been able to write it down; she also hoped that her accent had not gotten in the way of them understanding the homework. Though it seemed like a lot of work, they had an entire week to complete it, and surely that was enough time for these scholars of sound to bring her answers that were thoroughly thought-out and brilliant.

As soon as the students filed out, Mary was met with the applause of Cedric Rippner, who was looking at her, his face beaming. "Bravo!"

She collapsed in her chair and rolled her eyes. "I was certain that I had lost them. I mean, I'm not much older than they are."

He shook his head. "No worries; you did a fine job. Would you care to join me for lunch?" The invitation was nice, polite, and she couldn't help but feel relieved—especially when she realized that she hadn't eaten since the previous evening.

"I'd love to." She stood and grabbed her large Louis Vuitton bag.

"Great." They were walking out into the hall. "I hope you don't mind, but we will be sharing a table for three." Mary looked at him, and Cedric grinned.

THEY ARRIVED AT THE *Colophon Café* in Fairhaven, Cedric telling her that it used to be joined with Village Books, but had since separated, and now both establishments enjoyed their own buildings. They neared a table where a young woman stood—no more than thirty, though she looked to be twenty-five at the oldest. She had a wave of curly black hair, which was short and reached to her jaw. Her eyes were a gentle blue, and her skin was milky and soft like satin. She was dressed in a black pantsuit with a modest silk blouse of deep blue. She was elegant, with delicate makeup, as if she weren't wearing any at all—and there was something about her that made Mary-Margaret blush.

"Rebecca Tramer, this is Mary-Margaret Blackmoore." The two women looked at one another and grinned.

"It's a pleasure to meet you," Mary said.

"Charmed, I'm sure." They took to their seats and ordered a bottle of wine. The two women said nothing at first, nothing that went beyond the pale of cordial conversation, but soon Rebecca was telling her all that she knew of Mary's American counterparts.

"Before the arrival of the Blackmoores from New Orleans in 1897, the fishing port of Fairhaven flourished under the business of the Donovans, who owned most of the properties along the waterfront. Canneries, shipyards, fishing vessels, all of it owned by the Donovans. The Blackmoores hadn't really intended to ever make a name for themselves within the village.

"The Spiritualist movement of the Victorian age had swept through the town like a plague and showed no signs of dying off.

The church was concerned, but felt there to be little threat. Then in January of 1910, the Donovans, ruined over the loss of their son Michael, sold all of their properties, including their home on Sixteenth Street, where your cousin Mabel now resides. It was a much larger property back then. Lush gardens and blossoming orchards—prime land, really.

"The village had now joined with the greater city of Bellingham, and yet in the two-year lapse of enthusiasm from the Donovans, the city's economy had begun to suffer. But then the Blackmoores took over and did more than just revive it; they dominated the export of goods and the building of vessels for the entire west coast.

"Another thing happened that took them beyond infamy and made them legendary. It was the arrival of a teenage Fiona Blackmoore. She rose to mythic proportions within the spiritualist movement in her early adulthood, and surged its growth to a level that took the church beyond mere concern, and sent them into a frenzied battle for the souls of Bellingham itself."

"Incredible!" Mary let out, entranced by Rebecca's knowledge. She seemed to smile bashfully at Mary's exclamation, and she suddenly felt self-conscious of her praise for the scholar.

"For years the University's local vital records department, so to speak, has been collecting information on your family, ever since it was known as the Washington State Normal School. And when I came here three years ago, I was putting my syllabus together for my first semester, and I just fell in love with the history. There was just so much Victorian gothic beauty, which was not only a fantastic read, but it also seemed to be the underlining life force of this city. In all honesty, Bellingham may be in a state not unlike many of those depressed automobile cities if it wasn't for the Blackmoores sustaining it and keeping it going.

"This city owes so much to your family. It's just such a shame that most of the people here demonize them and give in to rumors and superstition that really have no place outside of Salem of 1692."

Mary nodded and took a bite from the salmon spread they shared between the three of them. "Well, if I'm not mistaken, isn't most of the city's population of Irish, Scandinavian, and Dutch descent?" Rebecca nodded. "Well, that explains it."

"What do you mean?"

"You see, Rebecca, the Irish very much believe in the supernatural. For the Irish, the spiritual world is not above you or below you; those are just metaphors to separate the good from the bad. For the Irish, the spirit world is right next to you. In a lot of ways, the Irish fear witches and fairies more than any devil." The two women shared a grin, a grin that carried something else, something secret.

"And are you a witch?" Rebecca asked.

Mary grinned, flashing her sharp eyes on her. "You're the expert; you tell me."

SWARMS OF YOUNG PEOPLE moved around them both, brushing against their shoulders and nearly knocking them over. Students clutching book bags and reading over numerous flyers announcing this or that event, party, or organization—everyone too busy with what they needed to do or where they needed to go to pay attention to anything else around them.

"This campus is huge!" Cheri let out, wearing dark True Religion jeans with a pair of black Prada heels on her feet, a black pinstripe oxford under a tight black cardigan, and a string of pearls around her neck. She clutched tightly to her black

Givenchy bag and appeared to Trevor in no way someone who was starting her freshman year of university.

Trevor sighed and nodded. "Yeah, yeah... I have my Gay Lit class in like twenty minutes, though I have no idea how to find it." Trevor had his hands tucked in the pockets of his skinny jeans, looking similar to Cheri with a white oxford under a black v-neck sweater, a pair of black Valentino sunglasses on his face, his hair spiked messy with hair gel, which had a glossy sheen in the sunlight.

"Isn't that a coincidence? I have my Women's Lit class right now, too." They laughed and proceeded to walk with languished strides through the campus, passing great gothic structures, many of which appeared to be elaborate cathedrals, places in which you could go to worship at the altar of academia.

"Do you think we're ready for this? I mean, couldn't we just avoid growing up?"

Trevor smiled at her. "Don't say that, Wendy; we'll never grow up!"

They laughed and continued to make their way through the campus, walking towards the first moment of a new stage of their lives. They parted, hugging and agreeing to meet for lunch, the both of them taking several glances at one another as they continued to walk towards their classes. Trevor and Cheri both felt as if they were going to throw up.

He made it to his first class. It took him an additional twenty minutes of searching, and by the time he walked through the door, the students were already seated and the professor was giving his introductions. Eyes seemed to fall on him, the majority of the students being young men who seemed to have paired off by deciding which guy they most likely wanted to blow. The professor, a man in his late thirties with a curtain of dusty brown hair and a groomed beard, with wire-rimmed glasses on his face and a tweed suit, looked at Trevor with mild interest.

"Yes?" he asked, staring at Trevor with one hand clutched to his waist.

"Um, Trevor Blackmoore; I got lost...." A flush of whispers came over the class.

"Then perhaps a map, young Blackmoore. I assume you are familiar with them, just as we are all familiar with you." Trevor averted his gaze and nodded. "I'm Dr. Greene." Trevor managed a smile, though he could feel a hundred eyes burning into him.

"Um, where should I sit?"

He looked around the room and grinned before returning his attention back to Trevor. "Sit next to the boy you think is the cutest." Trevor's cheeks flushed as he heard the class erupt into nervous and anxious chuckles. "Quiet!" Doctor Greene shouted. "Let him make his decision." Trevor's eyes searched the room and felt uneasy as many of the young men looked him up and down, raised their eyebrows suggestively, and motioned for him to come sit next to them. He thought about how nice it would have been if Braxton had enrolled at the University and signed up for the same class, because then he would have had no problem finding a place to sit.

Four rows up, in the middle of the room, was a young man with shaggy, neck-length dirty blond hair. His skin was a warm olive, and his eyes seemed like two polished orbs of amber. He wore a tight black tee with two Griffins on it, printed in red, and a navy blue hoodie. They looked at one another, and he offered Trevor a smile—which he returned, trying to think about anything other than how much he liked that smile.

"Mr. Reese!" The young man sitting next to the guy with the amber eyes popped his head up. "Find another seat." The guy grunted and shook his head, gathering his things and stalking away, Trevor waiting till he had sat down before proceeding towards his new seat.

It felt like one of the longest walks he had ever taken, and as he neared the chair next to the young man with the amber eyes, he couldn't help but feel his pulse begin to race and his ears begin to turn red.

"So, I'm the lucky guy, huh?" he said with a smile, meeting Trevor's gaze. He nodded and sat down, removing his notebook and a pen from his black suede Kenneth Cole messenger bag.

"You just seemed like the least possible candidate for homicidal maniac."

He snickered. "Good to know."

"As I was saying," Doctor Greene began, "in this course we will be examining the origins of queer literature, and examining some of the most historic works and its authors. We will discuss what affects these writers and their stories had on the G.R.M., as well as the awareness of the AIDS epidemic. I want you all to keep your eyes open, use your minds to really absorb the stories these writers are trying to communicate, the messages that they want you to walk away with from their stories."

The young man with the amber eyes began to speak, pulling Trevor's attention from the instructor, tuning him out instantly. "My name's Ben Tramer." He extended his hand and Trevor took it, giving it a shake.

"Trevor Blackmoore."

"I remember." Trevor blushed despite himself. "So, are you one of *The Blackmoores*?"

Trevor hesitated before nodding. "Yeah, yeah... I'm one of *those* Blackmoores."

Ben's eyes grew wide. "That's so cool. So, are you like a cousin or something, or from the immediate line?"

Trevor felt anxious, his palms beginning to sweat, and he found himself worrying about what any of this had to do with Ben. "Um, I really don't know what you mean by *immediate line*."

"I mean that you are directly descended from Sarafeene and Malachey Blackmoore." This conversation was getting suspiciously uncomfortable, and yet Trevor didn't feel the need to lie. "Yeah, I am."

"So, you're directly related to Kathryn Blackmoore?" There was so much eagerness in his voice, and he could not help but feel uncomfortable with the sudden mention of his mother's name.

"Um, she's my mother." Ben seemed to get extremely excited, and yet there was nothing threatening about him, only his questions that seemed to throw things askew.

"My turn. Why do you know so much about my family? Particularly my mother, and how did you know about my ancestors?" He tried to sound as casual as he could about it; he didn't want it to come across like an interrogation, but he figured that if it did come across like that, then so be it. After all, Ben had opened that door.

"Oh, God," he began, blushing and covering his face with his hand. "I feel so embarrassed; I must have come across as a total freak." Trevor nodded. "I'm not, and I'm not like a stalker or anything. It's just that my sister-older sister-teaches up at Fairhaven University. She teaches a class about Northwest Myth and Folklore, and she has a particular interest in the stuff about your family."

"Oh...."

"Yeah. For the past three years she's done nothing except regale me with all the stories and legends about the Blackmoores, as well as the savvy businesswoman that your mother has turned out to be. In fact, my sister refers to your mother as a real feminist in the corporate world."

Trevor nodded, offering a slight grin, but trying to hide his uneasiness with the conversation. "That's pretty cool, I guess." There was an innocent attraction between them; Trevor could feel it, and he was certain that Ben could too. He felt bad about it, and he felt as if he was doing something wrong—but he reminded himself that attraction is attraction. It is chemical, and nothing more. If he actually was able to convince himself of that, he wasn't completely certain.

"So, do you want to get some coffee with me after we get outta here?" Trevor wanted to say yes; he could feel himself about to say yes. But he remembered Cheri and he thought of Braxton, and he knew that he had to decline.

"Sorry, I am meeting up with my best friend for lunch."

Ben leaned in close, his gaze gentle but not lacking with intensity. "Oh, well, some other time. You'll find I'm very determined." He grinned, and Trevor grinned back.

"I'm sure," he said, focusing his attention back on Dr. Greene, trying to expel any thoughts of Benjamin Tramer from his brain, feeling what he considered to be the sin of carnal desire and hoping to escape it.

BRAXTON SHUFFLED OUT of the studio, desperate for a cigarette. He didn't like being close to Joshua Dianaca, hated being in the same room with him because he summoned a whirlwind of conflicting emotions that were starting to drive him mad. He was aware of the fact that he was attracted to the young studio mogul, and if he were a lesser, more primal man, he would certainly give in to those desires and violate the sanctity of his relationship. But he wasn't a lesser man, and he could not separate his heart from his desires, and his passion burned for Trevor. Yet the very thought of feeling something, no matter how basic and carnal, for another person, was enough to make Braxton feel as if he were being unfaithful.

He didn't understand what was happening. For five years, ever since he first laid eyes on Trevor, Braxton had never looked at another person, had never felt any kind of passion—not even a mild sense of attraction—burn for another; and now, now that they were here in Seattle, away from all of Bellingham's torments, he was suddenly feeling his pulse race at being in the presence of someone else.

"Yo, Brax, you coming back in or what?" J.T. asked, poking his head out of the door. Braxton turned to him and nodded, throwing the cigarette to the ground. "Hey, man, is everything okay?" He wasn't sure if he should tell his best friend about what was troubling him. He feared that J.T. would chastise him for it—or worse yet, tell him to jump into that car and take it for a test drive.

Braxton sighed. "Yeah, I'm good." He slipped past J.T. and walked back inside, prepared to make music and stare Joshua in the eyes for the next five hours. He was paying them a lot of money to make music, and he couldn't let the band down—though the fact of the matter was that Braxton would have walked away from it in a heartbeat if it meant never having to suffer this torture again.

CHERI AND TREVOR MADE their way back to Capitol Hill and decided on lunch at Deluxe, a bistro-style diner that made an amazing three-cheese macaroni and their signature veggie burger, which Trevor had come to love even though he wasn't a vegetarian. They walked in, looking at the almost-empty restaurant, and were directed by a young man with a slender frame, light brown hair and eyes, and who moved with a swish in his step to the booth closest to the front of the door.

They looked at one another, and he could tell that Cheri was trying to search his face and eyes for any indication of anything that he may have been hiding.

"What are you looking for?" he asked.

She averted her eyes to the menu, wrapping her hand around the back of her neck and giving it a rub. "Nothing." He didn't believe her. Was he being obvious that a possible indiscretion occurred with Ben? No, that couldn't have been it. How could she know anything?

"I think I'm getting the veggie burger," Trevor stated, trying to get everything back on track with their afternoon.

"Me too." She smiled at him, and he returned it. "I think I want to go to Nordstrom's. There's this Givenchy skirt and matching blouse I just have to have—oh, and these Burberry ankle boots with a stiletto heel." He nodded. "What about you? Do you need to pick up anything?"

He thought about it. There wasn't really anything that he wanted, but he thought suddenly about picking something up for Braxton. Was it guilt that was making him decide to buy something for his boyfriend? He didn't really want to think about it, and he knew that he'd just tie his stomach up in knots if he did. After all, he hadn't done anything, and if he wanted to get a gift for his boyfriend, it didn't necessarily mean that it was because he had done something wrong. Braxton was his partner, and that's what you do for people that you love.

"Sounds like a plan. It's getting cold anyways, and Braxton could use a new coat."

They placed their orders and minutes later their veggie burgers and their martinis arrived, and they toasted to their friendship and their first year of college. Trevor sipped it and smiled, trying to shrug off the ominous feeling that was moving inside of him. Something wasn't right; something wasn't adding up in the universe. He knew that darker things were coming, were already here—and it was like he could sense their vibrations in the air, coiling around him and leaving him cold on the inside.

He took a gulp this time and shuddered.

THEY RODE DOWN THE escalator to the men's department. Trevor didn't like it down here so much; it was much darker, and the fact that it was beneath the department store and not upstairs with windows and bright lights made him feel subdued, and not really in the mood to shop.

Cheri had known exactly what she wanted, where it was, and to pay for it quickly. She never got side-tracked with anything. Trevor felt a sense of relief as he too, like Cheri, disdained people who just wandered aimlessly for hours in stores and malls—or in the case of Seattle, in Pike Place Market—not really having any plan, purpose, or direction, but simply a need to pass the time.

"So, what do you think he'd like?" They were wandering through the collection of Rag & Bone and Viktor & Rolf, but nothing seemed right; nothing popped out at him. Perhaps it was the reason he was looking to buy something for Braxton in the first place, because he knew there was an unwavering sense of guilt that lingered behind it.

"I dunno...." His fingers dragged across the various sweaters and jackets. "I guess I'll know it when I see it."

"I think J.T. and I are going out later to dinner at Etta's on Western; do you and Braxton want to come?" Cheri ran her fingers through her hair and looked at the ends.

"Found it!" Trevor called out, not answering her question about dinner. He pulled out a refined charcoal wool trench by Dolce & Gabbana. It was definitely a Braxton-type coat, and one that he would wear often enough. "Though I suppose I could just get something at H&M."

Cheri shook her head. "You know I love H&M, but come on, it doesn't hurt once in a while to splurge. It's not like you can't afford it."

Trevor nodded. It was true, he could afford it, and it wasn't like he was buying high-end all the time. And it wasn't like he was buying it for himself anyways. He was doing something nice for the guy he loved, and there was nothing wrong with that.

"You're right. You're right, and I so don't have any excuses not to!" They laughed and proceeded to the customer service counter to pay for it.

As they walked back out onto Pine Street, Cheri took hold of his arm and leaned into his ear as they made their way to Fourth Avenue, where they would part ways and walk in opposite directions towards their downtown citadels. "Babe, you never answered my question about dinner tonight."

Trevor looked at her and gave out a sigh before nodding. "I'll let Braxton know. Just text me the time." They smiled and kissed one another on the cheek before letting go and walking to their homes.

Trevor clutched tight to his shopping bag and readjusted the strap of his messenger bag with his other hand as he walked into the lobby of the Seaboard Building. The doorman nodded politely at him and Trevor returned it, making his way to the Private Residences lift, pressing the button and waiting for it to arrive and open its doors. He really wanted to see Braxton. He just wanted to hold his hand, to smell him, to feel the heat beneath his skin, his absorbent eyes. Everything about him was a comfort, a comfort that Trevor so desperately needed to feel.

BRAXTON WALKED DOWN Pike, trying to shake away the face of Joshua Dianaca. His piercing blue eyes seemed to be burned deep into his brain, as if he were looking at him now, as if he were standing right in front of him, whispering to him. He couldn't shake it, and he didn't like how it was making him feel.

What was wrong with him? Never in all the years since he had first laid eyes on Trevor, had he ever once noticed another. Never once had he been tempted by desires that were not for Trevor, and now here it was, happening, at this very moment.

He looked at his reflection in store windows and contemplated dropping the band right then and there. He rolled his thumb along the scroll ball of his Blackberry, ready to pull it out of his pocket and call J.T. and tell him that it was over, that he would have to find another bassist. The problem with this was that he'd be letting a lot of people down—including Trevor, not to mention himself.

"This fucking sucks!" he spat out, not caring if people heard him or not. He neared the Seaboard building and sighed, trying to keep his shoulders straight and his head up, but he felt weighted by what had occurred at the studio. And he was afraid that with Trevor's skills, he would be able to see it all as soon as they looked at each other.

HE OPENED THE FRONT door and walked in, seeing a white box with black ribbon on the glass tabletop. He walked over to it and looked at the crisp white note card with his name penned on it. He gently removed the ribbon from the box and was just about to lift it open, when he heard the door in the bedroom open and shoes tap down the hall towards him.

"Braxton, babe, is that you?" He looked to see Trevor round the corner, smiling wide. His eyes were large and bright, and he wore a black Ben Sherman polo with red-and-white trim on the collar and sleeves. He could feel all of that love he had inside for Trevor flowing through him, erasing the lust he had suffered for Joshua—and yet the guilt magnified.

He averted his gaze to the box, unable to watch Trevor come closer to him any longer. He opened the lid and unfolded the tissue paper, finding a wool trench inside.

"Do you like it?" Trevor asked him, setting his hand on the table and leaning into Braxton. He could smell him, the citrus scent of his cologne, the silk-like feeling of his skin. He looked at him and nodded, trying to smile but feeling the tears welling up inside of him, catching in his throat and making him unable to speak.

"I saw it at Nordstrom's and I couldn't resist getting it for you. I know it's a lot, but I figured it was an investment piece, you know?" Braxton nodded, and just as the tears began to spill, he took hold of Trevor and pulled him tightly against him.

He just needed to hold him, to feel him, to smell him. He just needed to be as close as he could possibly be. He wanted to crawl inside of Trevor, to feel his organs, the warmth of his pumping heart. He wanted to touch it.

"Are you okay, Braxton?" His breath was warm against his chest, and his voice reverberated inside of him. He didn't need words, didn't want words; he only wanted the silence.

"I'm fine..." he said at last with his eyes shut tight. "I'm fine."

Chapter: Eleven

"ARE YOU SURE ABOUT this?"

Kathryn looked at Francesca and nodded. She was standing in her dressing room, which was the size of the largest guest room. The recessed lights illuminated on the hardwood floors and gleamed on her jewelry and various shoes, bags, and dresses. She had chosen a tight black BCBG sleeveless cocktail dress that stopped just above the knees and a tight thigh-length black sheer long-sleeve blouse, the neck wide and exposing her shoulders. She had just stepped into her black satin Dior pumps with the stiletto heel and was clasping her pearls around her neck when her cousin walked in, hugging her waist with one arm and holding a glass of scotch in the other.

"Stop worrying. I haven't dated in such a long time, and now Scott Maler, founder and CEO of Maler Investment Corporation, has requested me specifically for a date while he's in town on business!" Francesca could hear the excitement in Kathryn's voice, an excitement that she would conceal from Scott by the time he arrived.

"Yeah, and he's also a notorious womanizer. I mean, really, Kathryn?" They were facing one another now, Kathryn holding her waist and popping her hip. Francesca knew this was the "this conversation is about to be over" stance, but she didn't care. She knew that it was mostly the scotch giving her the nerve to confront Kathryn on what she saw as a possibly bad decision, and she was too buzzed to care about Kathryn's indignation.

"What, Francesca?" She raised her perfectly groomed brow and rolled her eyes.

"Kathryn, I love you; we're like sisters, which is why I'm telling you this. I know the Legacy is over. I know you want to get back out there, but this guy is known for making women feel like whores after spending the night with him."

Kathryn smirked and shook her head. "Why do you think I'm doing this, Francesca? I'm going out with him to flirt, seduce, and get him to pump hundreds of thousands of dollars into Blackmoore World Corp. I have a meeting at the Manhattan office in a month, and I want to make sure that when I present the board with his fine contribution, the non-family members will feel more confident in our plans for the waterfront."

Francesca took a drink from her scotch and shook her head. "You're already President and CEO, and half of the board is family; I don't see why you'd need to bring this guy's money in anyways. Besides, B.W.C. has more money than Maler Investments."

Kathryn walked over to her giant art deco vanity table and grabbed the martini that was sitting there, grinning at her own reflection as she took a drink. "Because," she sighed. "It would seem someone—I don't know who, and it isn't family, obviously..."—Francesca nodded in agreement—"but someone is trying to interest non-Blackmoore members in voting against it. They think it's too risky and is not a viable plan for a city like Bellingham. They don't think the city brings in enough tourist dollars to earn back the expense."

Francesca threw back her cherry curls and shook her head. "I didn't hear anything about this."

Kathryn nodded. "I know; no one has. I picked it out of the brain of Carolyn Maxwell when she politely called to remind me of the monthly board meeting. So, I need to arrive in a few weeks with the rarest steak those jackals can get their teeth on, so to speak."

"He's here," Francesca said, seeing a vision of a sleek black limo approach. Just then, they heard a vehicle pull up in front of the gate.

"I know." Kathryn downed the rest of her martini and grabbed her cream-colored Chanel satin trench, which hugged her waist perfectly and bloomed out delicately. "I saw it two minutes ago." With that, she was out of her room, the sound of her heels fading in the quiet.

Francesca shook her head and finished her scotch. "I'm going out," she proclaimed to no one—except for perhaps the ghosts.

"RESERVATIONS ARE DEFINITELY a good thing," J.T. said with a grin. He looked amazing in his black Penguin polo with the white trim around the sleeves, collar, and the buttons of the shirt. The white bird for which the company was named was stitched above his left breast, and his dark denim-wash Levi 5'11s clung to his muscular legs. One arm was draped with his navy pea coat, and the other was holding Cheri's hand.

"I've always been a fan." She smiled and J.T. returned it, leaning down and giving her cheek a peck. She looked stunning, and she knew it, clothed in a gold-and-silver button-front dress with belt and collar from Burberry, a flower brooch between the collar, and blue-and-white platform heels with white laces on her feet.

Her hair had been trimmed lightly and made lustrous with honey highlights, which she had done at Seven after parting with Trevor. She knew the women in Tom Douglas' famous restaurant were envious of her, and all the straight men wanted to be with her. It came with being Cheri Hannifin, and it didn't bother her at all. She was with J.T. Oliver, and that was the only thing that mattered to her.

"Follow me," the hostess said with a grin at J.T. and a glare at Cheri, as she led them to their table. She carried four menus and walked as if it was her restaurant. "Here you are...." The table was in the center of the room, as if they were being spotlighted. The tourists walked in herds down Western Avenue on the other side of the glass. It made her think of a zoo.

"I hope they get here soon; I'm starved."

Cheri nodded slowly in agreement and looked away. She could sense that there had been something wrong with Trevor, but he wouldn't tell her. It was giving her a sick feeling inside. Could it be more beasts from the pits of hell that he didn't want her to know about?

She didn't like secrets, not when it came to these things. She had faced Tom Preston as a heart-devouring zombie, and the ghost of her childhood friend. She had had to bury both Christian and Greg, as well as her best girlfriend Teri; if there was something happening that threatened their lives, then she felt she had the right to know it.

"Okay, what's wrong, babe?" Cheri looked at J.T. There was concern in his eyes, and she softened immediately and smiled.

"Nothing, it was just a long first day at school and I'm glad it's over; that's all." He nodded, and his eyes widened as he looked over her shoulder towards the entrance. Cheri turned around to see Trevor and Braxton walking in, hands clasped and grins on their faces.

Heads turned to watch them move. They had a presence, something that sparked in the air and alerted everyone around them. They were Blackmoores, after all. Cheri understood this; they were powerful witches, and that witchcraft seemed to give their skin a slight luster. After Trevor, Braxton, and the rest of the Blackmoores, Cheri had deduced that something about being a witch made them genetically beautiful. Their power, their blood, made them something other than human. They were beings of another world, a world that wasn't visible to everyone.

It was said in legends and myths that witches could seduce anyone, bewitch them into fawning over them and bending to their will. Well, Cheri knew it wasn't the result of any spell spoken or any incantation worked. It was the power they possessed inside; it made them irresistible. It made them dangerous.

She smiled at them and watched them move through the dimly-lit restaurant, in the same awe and bewilderment as everyone else. Trevor was dressed in a pair of black skinny slacks, white collared shirt, black skinny tie, black cardigan, and his midnight-blue iridescent trench with the cinched and belted waist, cuffs, and collar. His burgundy hair glistened in the lights they passed, and his eyes seemed to spark in the shadows.

Likewise, Braxton was just as amazing. His dark bangs draped the left side of his face, shaved in the back and sides behind the ears, and the rest of the hair falling forward. His tall, broad frame was clothed in a white-and-black check button shirt, a skinny black tie, and a sweater vest with a solid black back and a black-and-gray diamond-print front, over which he wore his black Bond Mac with the button front, belted cuffs and collar, and his skinny jeans made his large and muscular quads stand out even more.

The two looked at one another and grinned, and with perfect timing they released their hands and took turns hugging Cheri and J.T.

"God, you guys, like, make everyone—with the exception of Cheri—pale in comparison!" J.T. said. Braxton and Trevor looked at one another with oblivious eyes and shrugged.

"No, it's true," she added. With anyone else she would have never dared to confirm such a thing, concerned of inflating egos, but she loved them both so completely and knew that neither one of them would fully accept the fact to let it go to their heads.

"Eh, they were probably just freaking out because we were holding hands," Braxton said with a grin. "Now I just gotta get this guy to kiss me." Trevor grinned, and they leaned into one another and kissed sweetly—not concerned in the slightest with who was watching or who would care.

"Aw... thank you, baby," Braxton said with a smirk.

"You're welcome."

"Can I get any drinks for you guys?" their server asked them. He was a young man in his mid-twenties, with short and spiky black hair and narrow brown eyes. He looked at them, and Cheri was happy that it wasn't the girl who escorted them to their table when they had first arrived at Etta's.

"I'll have a whisky sour, and he'll have a Manhattan—right, babe?" Braxton rubbed Trevor's knee and looked at him with a smile. Trevor blushed and nodded. "Yeah, he'll have a Manhattan."

"And I'll have a vodka tonic with Grey Goose, please," Cheri requested, not even bothering to look up from her menu.

"And I'll also have a whisky sour." Their server nodded, not even bothering to write down their order.

"If I could just see your IDs, please...?" They all nodded and removed their fakes one by one, and there was nothing to distinguish them from authentic Washington State Driver's Licenses. "All right," he smiled, and handed them back. "Thank you so much, and I'll have those drinks right out for you."

They nodded, and snickered at one another after he left.

"So," Cheri began, looking up from her menu and eying both J.T. and Braxton. "How has everything in the studio been going?" Braxton's eyes widened, and Cheri took note of this, while J.T. grinned.

"It was awesome, like I always imagined—right, dude?" He cocked his head to Braxton, who brushed the hair from his face.

"Yeah, it was pretty cool." He sounded less than enthusiastic, and Cheri shot a glance to Trevor, who seemed to also note the lack of excitement in his voice.

"More than cool; c'mon, man. And that Joshua dude, he was, like, really nice, and he was really into Braxton's skills on the bass." Braxton shifted uncomfortably in his seat and cleared his throat.

Trevor turned to him and looked at him briefly before averting his gaze. "Really; should I be worried?" He was trying to make it come off as a joke, but Cheri could hear the anxiety in his voice.

"Oh, please; everyone pales in comparison to you, Trevor." His black eyes flashed on Trevor, and Cheri could see the love glistening in them, but there was something sad and almost deceptive in them—and she wondered if Trevor could see it too.

"Here are your drinks." Their server sat their glasses in front of them and Braxton took to his immediately, as if he had been wandering the desert parched from thirst. "Have you guys decided on anything?"

Braxton cleared his throat and spoke. "Can we start out with the mini Dungeness crab cakes, the spicy shrimp and ginger spring rolls, the wild gulf prawns, and the halibut ceviche?" No one said anything, Braxton having ordered an assortment off the menu that they would share. "And two bottles of Dom for the table." Their server nodded and walked away.

"That's a lot of food..." Trevor said, taking a generous sip of his Manhattan.

What was going on? Cheri wondered. She wanted to pull Trevor aside and ask him, but knew that there was much more of a chance that he wouldn't tell her.

"Well, it's a special night," J.T. added, jumping in to back up his best friend. "You guys started at university, and we've been killing it in the studio. We should be indulging!" He lifted his drink in a toast, and they all followed suit.

There was an awkward vibe that seemed to hover around their table, and they concentrated more on their meals than anything else. "Can I have a bite of that?" Trevor asked, looking at Braxton's Coho salmon. He nodded and tore a piece of the delicately-cooked fish with his fork and fed it to him.

The food was good, the champagne even better. They went through the bottles like they were water, enjoying them with their two orders of the cheese plate and crème brulée for dessert. It was good, and offered a distraction to the weird feeling that they all seemed to be having. When the bill arrived, Braxton didn't even bat an eye when he took it and removed his black American Express card from his wallet, and placed it in the receipt book.

Their server took it eagerly and hurried to run it through. "Well, that was a great dinner," he said, taking hold of Trevor's hand and giving it a squeeze.

Trevor nodded. "Yeah." He looked at Cheri and offered a weary smile. She returned it and frowned as she placed her hand comfortingly on his thigh. "I have a lot of homework to do," he added, standing up and slipping his arms into his trench.

Braxton nodded. "I should really get him home; besides, I'm really tired."

Cheri and J.T. exchanged glances, and it seemed to her that J.T. was finally catching on to the fact that there was definitely something amiss with the golden couple.

They said goodbye and watched silently as the two young men walked back out into the dark street, making their way hand in hand back into the market and towards their home.

"Well, that was...."

"Weird," Cheri finished for him.

"I MUST SAY, I'M SURPRISED you agreed to go out with me."

Kathryn looked at Scott Maler and smiled. "Why's that?"

He grinned. "Because you're notorious for being a bitch; that's why." She liked his bluntness. He was a handsome man of thirty-six years with dark hair trimmed and messy, and with more product than she had ever seen her son use on his own head of hair. He had broad shoulders with a very fit body, clothed in a simple gray three-piece suit with a merlot tie. His tan skin was natural and not something baked in a bed—or worse yet, a spray bottle—and he smelled good.

"They're right," she remarked with all seriousness. The limo sped down the road to the docks and Kathryn looked out the tinted window, watching the world pass them by as they neared the water. "And where are you taking me?

Scott grinned and shook his head. "Uh-uh; it's a surprise."

Kathryn hated surprises, and loathed anyone who thought they could impress her with them. They stopped, and Kathryn waited as the driver walked over and opened her door, offering her his hand as she stepped out. The air was crisp and smelled as if it would rain, and the only sound to penetrate the silence was the lapping of the waters.

Scott strutted confidently towards her and offered his arm—which she looked at briefly, dismissing his gesture. "Follow me," he said, only mildly insulted, but mostly impressed with the fact that she did not instantly swoon over his charms. Kathryn followed him to a sleek family-sized yacht with black windows. Its aerodynamic shape was indicative of the speed she was sure it could achieve.

"Are we going to go fast?" she asked him.

"I hope so."

She rolled her eyes and chuckled. She had already walked into his mind as soon as he had watched her emerge from her front door. Sex was the only thing on his mind, and if she was going to give it to him, he was going to have to work for it. He assisted her on board, and led her down below deck.

"I'm assuming you have someone else driving this thing?" she asked, allowing him to remove her coat as she slipped seamlessly into the white suede couch.

He looked her up and down and nodded. "Of course." He directed her gaze to the Cristal that was on ice on the table in front of them. Kathryn looked at it with passing interest. "Does nothing impress you?" he asked her.

Kathryn shrugged. "I have a fleet of yachts at my disposal, ones much bigger than this—and on New Year's, or any other parties I may throw, I have an industrial fridge loaded with Cristal. So no, this doesn't really impress me, and if you're hoping to get between my legs tonight, it's going to take a lot more than this."

He let out a *guaff* and shook his head, acting appalled at her insinuation that he only wanted to bed her. "I can't believe you would think —"

Kathryn waved her hand. "Oh, please; you think I haven't done my homework on you, Scott Maler? Well, I have." She looked at her nails in fake boredom. "More than you know." He nodded and began to stand, but Kathryn stopped him, putting her hand on his chest and pressing him back down.

"But," she began, reaching out for the bottle. "That doesn't mean we can't start with this, and see where the night takes us."

FRANCESCA SAT AT HER table holding her glass of chardonnay in her right hand, swirling the pale gold liquid in her glass. She still hadn't touched her salmon tartar on its bed of fennel, lemon grass, and thinly-cut bamboo shoots.

She gazed into the void of her thoughts, seemingly unaware of her own beauty. Her slender frame was clothed in a sleeveless black Helmut Lang cocktail dress and white satin stiletto Christian Louboutin sandals on her feet, accentuating her long legs. Around her slender neck was an Ioselliani three-tier necklace with tiny pearls, silver, and charms of swords dipping between her breasts.

She felt burdened. She admired Kathryn for her ability to jump into dating; exploring the freedom in knowing that their curse, the mystical poison that had existed inside of them was over, that no one would die from loving a Blackmoore. But Kathryn had lived without Sheffield for so long now, while Francesca still felt herself attached to the shadow of her deceased fiancé.

She tried hard not to think of Lucas, tried so often to keep herself occupied so she couldn't feel him hovering over her shoulder, whispering in her ear. Francesca wasn't certain if it was really his ghost or just the thick fog of memories, refusing to give her peace.

Kathryn had always been the strongest, the ice queen, the stoic Athena, the beautiful Diana. She was the war goddess, the huntress. She had always been the one to act! The one to refuse her emotions any power over her. She was a woman many other women longed to be like, but always found themselves falling short. Francesca was one of them.

Maybe it was her Italian blood; at least that's what she could blame it on, with all of that intensity and passion that restrained her and refused to let her be free.

"More wine?" Francesca shook her head and blinked, looking up to see the petite blonde server girl staring down at her and smiling. Francesca swigged back the rest of the chardonnay and sat the glass back down, nodding as she sighed and closed her eyes, running her hands through her thick hair, which she had straightened earlier that evening.

"Yes, thank you." The girl offered her a sympathetic smile and refilled her glass.

"Let me know if you need anything else," the girl said to her gently before walking away.

"How about a shooting..." she whispered, listening to the curl of her accent, the blend of Italian and an Irish lilt. *I know I should stop wearing this...* she thought, looking at her Tiffany's engagement ring. It had been every girl's dream, Lucas had told her; all girls wanted a ring from Tiffany's. She had never been one of those girls, but when he took her into the landmark store—made legendary by Audrey Hepburn in *Breakfast at Tiffany's*—on their last trip to Manhattan, it had instantly become her dream as well.

Now that dream was dead, along with Lucas, deep beneath the earth in Paris, rotting in maggots, worms, and stink. A lone tear slipped from her eye and she wiped it away quickly, taking another swig from her glass.

'The devil shall come....' She heard the icy, damp voice, felt the air turn cold around her. *'The devil shall come for his witches....'* She looked up, finding everything inside of her tightening, her limbs like bags of sand, and she could not find the strength to

move. She was helpless and stared unblinking as Lucas came towards her, emerging from the shadowed back wall near the entrance.

He stumbled as his right leg hung limp, dragged across the floor, creating a scraping sound on the old wood floorboards of Le Chat Noir. His khakis were dirty and full of holes, his black oxford ripped and exposing the cavity of his chest, which bore the holes of flesh that had been eaten away. His ribs were visible, and maggots fell from those holes.

She watched, disgusted, as his face came into the light, patches of hair missing, the dishwater blond dark with earth, sticking out from the top of his head like scattered brush in the deserts of Texas.

The skin clung to his bones like elastic, gray and cold. His eyes seemed to bulge, and yet they were black as ink. She attempted a gasp when she beheld the hole where his nose should have been, and part of his jaw was exposed from the flesh that was rotted away.

This isn't real! She tried to tell herself, but still Lucas kept coming.

'*...And he shall move through them all, one by one, until the one is found....*' He was coming closer, and she wondered who else could see him.

He was there. She could smell the stink of him, putrid, and those maggots and roaches spilled out of his chest and mouth and landed on the table.

'*Give us a kiss...*' he sputtered out, hissing like a serpent.

"No!" Francesca shot out of her chair, knocking it to the floor and shaking her table. She looked around at all the perplexed faces that stared back at her in wonder. "I'm sorry...." She tried to calm her heart as she grabbed her blood-red Dior handbag, the letter charms clinking like little bells. She pulled out her matching wallet and threw cash on the table, knowing it was more than what her bill was, but she didn't care; the girl would be getting a nice tip.

She sent a text message to Jared as she raced down the stairs of the Harris building, and by the time she emerged outside, the limo had pulled up and she opened the door, not bothering to wait for him to do it.

"Home, Ms. Blackmoore?"

Francesca started typing a text to Kathryn.

"No," she began, looking up briefly to see his handsome face smiling at her lustfully. "Take me to Sea-Tac." He nodded, and she raised the back window, enclosing herself inside. By the time Kathryn read her text, Francesca would already be up in the air, making her way back to France. There was something she needed to do, and Paris was the only place she could do it. She only hoped there was still time.

THE AIR WAS FERMENTED with the perfume of patchouli, apples sweetened from rot, and cinnamon sticks which smoldered slowly in the hearth. The light from the tiffany lamp illuminated the gold walls, and the rains moved in, sliding down the panes of glass and blacking out the garden and the fountain with the statue of the mermaid spilling water from her cupid lips.

Mabel sat at the round table covered in velvet, her wise eyes sharp and gray, scanning over her ancient deck of tarot cards, passed down to her from her mother, who had received them from her mother and so on down the line—originating from Sarafeene, who by legend had been given the deck in New Orleans by a voodoo priestess upon she and Malachey's arrival back in 1788.

"This is bad..." she said aloud, slightly startled by her own voice. She leaned back in her old wooden chair, folding her long, spidery fingers in her lap. She was draped in a white silk Pucci caftan, her long three-tier amber beads glistening in the light.

She sighed, her aged face still beautiful and surprisingly youthful, despite her near century of life. Danger was close, and it was already taking steps to infiltrate the coven, but the fates kept giving cockeyed answers, and when it came to pin-pointing the identity of these threats, the cards cast dead, revealing no tangible answer—nothing that was clear and insightful.

'You have to go back to the beginning....' Mabel raised her eyes to acknowledge Michael. His eerily beautiful and marble face looked back at her with inky wells of black that were always shockingly expressive.

"What are you talking about, Michael? What beginning?"

He shook his head and seemed to blink at her without blinking. *'It's all at the beginning....'*

Mabel heard a sharp scream, male and pained, tortured, but the sound was coming from within her—and yet it was not hers, and she could feel it. It reverberated through her limbs, shook her nerves and attacked her brain. It surged up through her spinal cord and forced her to put her hands to her head, trying to bring an end to the torment.

"Stop!" Her voice broke into a sob, and the tears slipped down her flushed cheeks. *1908* flashed in her mind. Was it an amount? Was it a year, or a code? She wanted to ask the spirit but could not find words, could not form a stream of thought that could make a question. It didn't matter, though, because when she opened her eyes to steady her spinning mind, Michael was gone. Not even the faint echo of his violin remained to tell her he still haunted the halls and rooms of the Blackmoore estate.

"WHAT'S GOING ON?" TREVOR asked, his eyes burning into Braxton, seeking him out and looking to penetrate his mind.

"Get out!" Braxton shouted at him, throwing his hand up at Trevor. It was like getting pushed back, the invisible force that emanated from him, knocking him against the dining room table.

"You're hiding something; I know it." Trevor tried to stop the tears from welling in his eyes.

"Don't go looking for things." Braxton looked up at him, meeting his gaze, and his face was full of hurt and guilt. "Please, baby, there's nothing for you to worry about, nothing for you to have to find."

Trevor curled his fingers into his hands and began to squeeze, digging his nails into his palms. "Cheri could see it; J.T. could see it. What are you hiding? There's something. You look like you've done something, something you shouldn't have."

Braxton brushed the bangs from his face and shook his head. "Maybe I just don't feel like I do enough for you. Did you ever think of that?" He shouted the question, slamming his fist against his knee. Trevor didn't believe it.

"I want to know, Braxton." They locked eyes and Trevor summoned his power, power that he knew Braxton could never challenge because unlike Braxton, Trevor had been raised with the full knowledge of his power, of the strength that burned inside of him.

He let it fill him, locking Braxton in his sight, and Braxton became helpless. "Please, don't do this Trevor...." He could plead, he could beg until he was blue in the face, but he could not move. Braxton watched as those hazel eyes began to spark to life, their color intensifying, until they were like smoldering emeralds. They were the most lustrous green he had ever seen, and as this was taking place—this shift, this green inferno—he could feel himself, his mind, rip open.

Trevor saw the face, the ice-blue eyes and the stylish hair, the beautiful face, sexy like a model for Burberry or Ben Sherman. Trevor let go, detaching himself from Braxton's mind.

"I'm sorry..." he muffled in sobs.

"I'm going to bed." Trevor pivoted on his heel and began to walk down the hall. "Don't follow me."

HE LAY IN BED WITH the curtains drawn, refusing to move. Had Braxton actually cheated, or was he just having lustful thoughts? He didn't know how to move. He didn't know what to think about or what to believe in. There was suddenly an alien logic in functioning, in moving, and this logic was now unknown to him.

The night, the day, they had all passed. He never spoke to Braxton, never looked at him, and Braxton never bothered him. He heard him run the shower in the bathroom attached to one of the guest rooms; he listened to him shuffle through the penthouse. He held his breath when he stood outside the door. Was he checking to hear for any sound, some breathing, maybe hoping that Trevor would call to him?

That face, which was the source of Braxton's guilt, made him want to dig deeper; he wanted to know who this face belonged to, and he wanted him dead. When Braxton left, Trevor knew that he needed to get up and go to school; it was the second day, and yet moving was just impossible. He didn't want to be here; he didn't want to exist. He only wanted to rot in his bed. He wanted to melt into the sheets, to become a part of the fabric and never be seen by anyone again.

It had seemed that Seattle had brought a strain to their relationship. It was a strain that seemed to be tearing them apart. He had felt, believed, thought, that nothing could sever them—and yet there was this danger, this threat. And what of Benjamin Tramer, the guy he had met the previous morning in his G.L. class? He had felt an attraction to him as well, and yet it seemed that he did not feel it once he had left that classroom. All that mattered once again was Braxton—and Ben's face, no matter how beautiful, would not sit on his brain.

But Braxton was something else, always had been. He had been a primal boy, driven by his testosterone. There was something in the way that Braxton had always moved through the world: with this sense of ownership and a hidden, yet still prevalent, predatory nature. Trevor was always secretly envious of it.

Braxton was unaware of it—unlike Christian, who had always known the power he had had—and that had been part of his problem. The thing that had caused him so much pain in his life for so long, was what everyone detected from him, and what he had embraced, trapping himself in a corner that he could never get out of.

Cheri had had it too, and she had to lose everything to climb herself out of that place.

Trevor wasn't like them, could never be like that, and he wondered if maybe now—now that they were in the city, with new temptations and the whole world suddenly at their feet—Braxton was wanting something else, something more like himself.

Limbs had to move; he needed to force them to move, and yet what was the point? It seemed that any functioning, any movement in this world, was just bringing more and more damage to his relationship with Braxton. And he couldn't allow that; he had to find a way to stop it from happening.

The witch in him, the part of him that was his mother's son, wanted him to cast a love spell, to simply invoke the gods and force Braxton to him, to bind his heart to him. But he knew this was not right, that stripping Braxton's free will was wrong—and not only wrong, but they were one and the same. They shared the same blood, the same power, and what could happen if he did such a thing? What wrongs could be committed in the universe itself if he did such a thing?

No. He could not do this. He had to trust his boyfriend. He had to refuse the urge to condemn him for simply finding himself physically attracted to someone who wasn't Trevor. But that was not what haunted Trevor about it; that was not what shook him to the core. It was the fact that Braxton carried so much guilt over it, as if he had really wanted to do something wrong—or worse, that he actually had.

In the end, Trevor concluded, there was nothing he could do about it either way, and the best thing he could do was just keep going. With a sigh Trevor climbed out of bed and made his way to the bathroom, determined to get to campus and make it through the day. Whatever else there was to deal with, he'd deal with it later.

MARY-MARGARET STOOD in front of her students, their eyes only half-eager to hear what she had to say. Some of the men were too busy staring at her long legs, strapped in her Chanel slingbacks, to listen to anything about Chopin, and when the class ended she was too exhausted to assign any homework.

She walked to her desk and sat down, straightening out her black skirt and crossing her ankles. She was relieved to be finished, and wanted nothing more than to get back to the manor and take a long bath. She couldn't stop thinking about her encounter with the ghost, Michael, and his ominous message of doom for the Blackmoores. Six months ago she would have grabbed her rosary and spent hours praying, spinning those beads one by one between her fingers and begging for the divine mother to intercede; but that was then. She didn't know what to do now, or how to find her answers. Everything seemed to be called into question with that one simple encounter, and now she had no idea what she was supposed to do.

"Excuse me, Professor Blackmoore?" She looked up to see a nineteen-year-old girl staring down at her. She had an English accent, which was complimented by her straight, neck-length brown hair, stylishly layered with bangs that hung over her left eye. She wore a black sweater and matching skirt, the neck wide and brought down over her shoulders, revealing her collarbone. She was pretty, but the black eyeshadow and eyeliner seemed to be a little too excessive.

"Mary, please."

The young girl nodded. "All right, Mary." She grinned. "I'm Victoria Dianaca; I sit in the fifth row." Mary nodded, urging the girl to get to the point. "Anyways, I was wondering if you could meet with me sometime to discuss Tchaikovsky's Violin Concerto in D Op. Thirty-five?" Her head cocked and their eyes met, and in the moment it was like a bucket of ice water had been thrown in Mary's face.

"Tchaikovsky's Violin Concerto...."

Victoria nodded. "Yeah. See, I am having a bit of a problem with it, and I figured that since you're obviously well-versed with the violin, I'm guessing it means that you have a very good understanding of music made for the instrument, which means that you could help me."

Mary's mind went blank. She knew that that was what Michael was playing in her dream—or was it his memory?

Could it be a coincidence that this girl was talking with her about the same piece of music? "I'll take a look at my schedule and I'll let you know."

Victoria offered a smile and slipped out of the class, clutching her books to her breasts. Mary watched her go and then released a great shudder. This was just getting to be too much. Two different worlds that still coexisted with one another seemed now to be merging into one new force right before her eyes, and she didn't have the slightest clue how to deal with it.

"Working hard or hardly working?" Mary looked to the door to see Rebecca standing in the frame, a warm smile spread across her face, and in that moment all of those worries seemed to be replaced with something else: a kind of unexplainable calm. She knew that she could not think on it too much, for fear of ruining it all with her analyzations.

"Working a little too hard," she responded. Rebecca offered a playful frown and walked towards her, her stilettos clicking on the tiled floor, and even the harsh bright fluorescent lights could not take away from her uncompromising beauty.

"Well, then, how about you and I go out for some drinks tonight? Say around eight?" Mary struggled to nod. She didn't know what was going on, but suddenly she was nervous and excited all at once. "Great," Rebecca said, turning on her heel and walking out of her door, looking back only once before she turned the corner, offering Mary a playful smile.

BRAXTON TRIED TO WRITE out the lyrics to the new song that they were working on for their album, but what had happened with Trevor was bothering him, refusing to let him concentrate or focus on anything else. He wanted to talk to J.T. He wanted to tell his best friend what had happened, to get advice on how to make it right, but what would he say? *So my boyfriend used his powers to walk into my mind and find out that I was popping wood for another guy?*

No. There was nothing that he could say, and there was perhaps no way of working this out. He needed to, though. He wasn't going to lose Trevor—and yet it seemed to him that since arriving in Seattle, some strange undercurrent was moving through the city, something mystical and yet unable to be pinpointed. He wanted to try to put his hands to the ground, to try to focus on it—whatever it was—and tune in, to become one with it and allow it to seep through his fingertips and move up his arms and into his brain, allowing him to see what strange darkness permeated this city.

"You seem troubled." He looked up, hearing that familiar English accent. There, standing in the doorframe, was Joshua, his blue eyes crisp, like ice glittering like a frozen lake. His face was too perfect; it wasn't natural for someone to have a face like that, and he looked irresistible in his Chip & Pepper jeans and black deep-V tee. There was something strangely familiar about him—not like he knew him from somewhere, just something about his aura that seemed familiar. Something he had felt before, but could not recall when it was that he had first felt it.

"Boyfriend issues." He felt instant relief in stating this. He was mentioning Trevor aloud, in front of the person who had given him so much vexation. He hoped that perhaps, in doing this, it would somehow bring him peace.

"What's wrong with him? Not like you?" Joshua stepped closer to him. There was a confidence in his stance; it was calculated. All of his movements seemed calculated. All of his words seemed as if they were well thought-out ahead of time, and that he had even come up with possible responses to anything that Braxton could say.

"No, that's not it. I mean, we are different... but the same where it counts the most." Joshua nodded, but he seemed skeptical. Like Braxton gave a shit. They *were* exactly the same where it counted, the parts inside that mattered the most.

"Well, then..." he grinned, "I wish you all the best that it'll work itself out." There was mock sincerity in his voice. "But if it doesn't, I'm sure you'll have no trouble finding ways to move on."

I need to get home to Trevor.

He threw his stuff in his Chrome bag and snapped it shut, throwing it over his shoulder and walking out the door. He buttoned the new coat Trevor had given to him the night before and walked to his car, not minding the rain. It was nice, and it was another sign that summer was finally ending and that this was a new time, a new year, and a new beginning; and no matter what, he and Trevor were going to make it through together.

Chapter: Twelve

FRANCESCA MOVED THROUGH her lavish apartment on the *Avenue Montaigne*, famed as one of the world's most expensive streets. She hated this place now. It was cold, and the curtains were drawn. She felt like nothing here was right, but that wasn't the point of coming here. She wasn't trying to walk through rooms that held only pain; she didn't want to look into faces behind glass in frames that recalled happier times—times she would never have again.

She sat her purse down and walked quickly into her bedroom, passing the bed and going straight for the second closet—Lucas' closet. She took a deep breath, brushed the hair from her face, and gripped the gold knobs and turned them, throwing open the cream French doors and grabbing what had been his favorite sweater. An old black cashmere thing he had gotten at a second-hand shop years before they had met.

She smelled it briefly and was overcome with the thought of his smile, his eyes, so blue and gentle, like the Mediterranean. "Damn you..." she said aloud. It wasn't meant for him, and yet she feared that if his spirit lingered and could hear her, he would be injured by her condemnation.

She hated having to do what she knew she needed to, and opening those wounds would be the worst thing she could put herself through—and yet it had to be done.

Being a Blackmoore had always meant sacrifice. Sacrifice of the people around you; sacrifice of your heart, and of yourself.

It meant setting aside your own selfish concerns and doing what needed to be done for the good of the coven, for the good of the world.

Sometimes it was like listening underwater, and there was no getting around that. There was no way to decipher anything clearly. Every action had a reaction. She had learnt that in science, and she had learnt that in witchcraft. Common sense was the voice above you; logic was the thing yelling at you above the water, but you couldn't hear it because you were too busy swimming beneath the surface.

Her heels clicked on the parquet floorboards as she walked back out into the main room, grabbing her Dior bag and walking back towards the elevator. No need to lock it up. No one could come up here without the code that had to be punched into the elevator.

She needed a coat. It was raining and she lived close to every store that she loved, and they all knew her by name. When she emerged outside, it was cold and coming down hard. The streets were busy, the noise distracting, and yet she paid it little mind and moved apart from it. She was not one of the masses, and they sensed it, felt it in the air when she passed them. They saw it in her eyes; they smelled it in her skin.

It was what made witches so dangerous: they could lure in anyone; all they had to do was look at them and command it.

She walked into Chanel, and they all whispered in quick French. They knew the rules: not to approach, not to suggest anything. To just let her shop and ring her up at the end. She didn't like to be bothered, and every time she was, it meant less and less that she would be buying.

She sifted quickly through the coats, grabbing a black herringbone long coat in tweed and walked to the register, setting it down along with her credit card. "I want to wear it out," she told the expressionless woman in French. She nodded and went to work removing the tags as soon as she had charged her card, and handed it back to her.

Francesca gave a nod and walked back out into the damp, gray world, refusing to let the awful sense of dread take over.

SHE SAT AT THE CAFÉ, waiting for the dark to set in. The night needed to come and envelop the city of lights, to cast it in a wave of black. She sipped her wine and looked at the people who passed her. The men looked at her and she could feel their eyes inside of her, burning into her. They lusted for her; they took her apart and tried to get so deep inside of her. They wanted to know all they could about her, just through the glance of their eyes.

They were hoping to penetrate her mystery, but there was nothing to see, and nothing to find. She could feel it. There was an emptiness that was swelling inside of her. It was eating away at her insides, leaving her feeling empty, leaving her heart cold.

She wanted to scream at them, to tell them to go, to banish them to their wives, their girlfriends—or to whatever desperate and lonely woman they picked up in a bar or disco later that night. She was not there for them to inspect, she was not there for them to examine, to explore.

"Another," she said to the young waiter. He nodded and quickly left to retrieve the bottle of merlot, which he promptly refilled for her. Francesca nodded and wiped away the tears. She could smell Lucas' shirt in her bag. And she tried so hard to ignore it, but she could feel him calling out to her, whispering love to her from that bag, and all she could do was say that she was sorry. How could she correct what had happened? How could she make right the wrongs that she had done? There was no way, not when those wrongs had resulted in a death.

"For the coven..." she said to herself, trying to resolve what she must do. She clung to that family obligation for strength, for that thing that would carry her through. This was where it had to come from. This was what needed to be.

She knew that she was risking her sanity in doing what she was about to do, but she knew that there was so much more at stake, the lives of her family being the thing that sat at the top of that list.

She hated Paris. She didn't want to be here. All it did was remind her of Lucas. She saw him on every street corner, recalled memories of them holding hands as they emerged from shops, smiling and throwing their heads back in laughter. She wanted to feel that again, but without Lucas—without him there to tell her a joke, or make some cynical comment about someone or something they saw—the laughter simply became pointless.

She watched as the sky grew darker, and the air became colder. She waited until every streetlamp was on and people were hurrying to cafés and bistros for dinner before she stood, placing money on the table top, and began to make the walk to the *Père-Lachaise*, one of the most famous cemeteries in the world. She hated this, hated walking amongst the dead. She knew Trevor did it all the time, and yet she knew that it was something she could never get used to.

She had never been tormented by spirits as a child. When her mother passed she had come to Francesca only once, and she was bathed in light. If she had believed in the Bible she would have been certain that her mother had been an angel, but that was not the reason for the light, and she knew this. It was just her brilliant aura transformed by the letting go of the flesh.

Her mother would not become a wandering soul, cold, with black eyes and unable to move on. Her mother was clear and magical, and she had been at peace. But the souls that wandered lost, cold, unable to move on, those spirits she feared. As she moved through those monuments and gravestones, she prayed that Lucas would not come to her in this way.

It didn't take her long to find his grave, unassuming as it was, beneath a willow tree. *Lucas Le Remière: For the dead travel fast*, read his epitaph. It had been his favorite quote from *Dracula* by Bram Stoker.

"Hi, Lucas." She could already feel the cries catching her throat, and her eyes filled with tears, their delicate sheen misting before slipping down her face. "I hope you can forgive me." She reached into her bag and removed the shirt.

"Oh, God...." She closed her eyes and smelled it. "Please forgive me." She stepped forward and bent down gingerly, placing the shirt on top of his grave. Francesca looked around once more, listening to the night, waiting to see if there was anyone else around who could hear her or see her.

There was no one, and with a beating heart she began. "The gods of the underworld and the demons, those untimely carried off.

"Men, women, youths and maidens, year by year, month by month, day by day, hour by hour, I conjure you, all demons assembled here, to assist me, and awaken him at my command!" The wind began to stir instantly, angry and violent, and a thick fog began to come forward, coming from nowhere, it seemed, and yet was now quickly consuming the cemetery—curling around her legs, hiding everything from view, making it all a thick haze.

"Whoever you may be, male or female. Betake yourself to *that* place and *that* street and *that* house and bring him hither, and bind him!" A wail, haunting and sad, moved through the air around her, and then in haze she watched as Lucas emerged, wearing the black Hugo Boss suit that he had been buried in. His face was soft, handsome, his jaw strong, his lips full and wide, and his eyes as brilliant and blue as ever. He did not look as the apparition had in the restaurant. He was vibrant, and looked fresh, happy. He looked alive.

"There is nothing to forgive." His voice did not come out like the haunting whisper that accompanied the others; his was thick, emotional, and expressive, like it had been in life.

"I'm so sorry!" She ran to him and he opened his arms. She fell into him and he was warm and strong, as solid as he had ever been in life.

"Shh..." he purred in her ear, as he rocked her and stroked her head. "I'm always with you, Francesca; I'm always watching."

She looked up at him and saw the love in his eyes. It warmed her and broke her heart all at once. "At the restaurant?"

Lucas shook his head. "No, that was not me. That was evil. That was a messenger." She nodded. Of course. It could have never been Lucas; she had to know that deep down. She had to trust in the love she had with him.

"Walk with me..." he said. He took her hand in his and brought it to his lips. He kissed it and his lips were warm, moist, and she cried and laughed.

"I've been so empty without you..." she managed.

Lucas nodded. "I know." He kissed the back of her hand once again. "But you need to allow yourself the strength to move on, to recover. I will always be by your side, and I will never feel betrayed."

They moved between gravestones. She felt for the first time that everything would be all right, that there was no evil, and that no one had died, that everything would be okay.

"It's just so hard...." She looked down, taking note of his hand. She had never forgotten how perfectly large his was compared to her own.

"Well, one day, it'll happen—and when it does, I want you to allow yourself to feel it, and to do so without guilt." They stopped, and he turned to her, his eyes piercing her.

"The Blackmoores are in great danger, and Trevor is in the greatest danger of all. You must get back to Bellingham; you must get back to Kathryn and Mabel and tell them. Whatever Trevor intends to do, it will alert the Conclave."

Francesca stopped and looked up at him, her eyes wide and full of shock. "The Conclave."

Lucas nodded and bent to kiss her fiercely on the lips. "Our time has ended, and I must go."

Francesca nodded, even as the tears spilled. "I know."

He smiled and slipped his finger under her chin. "I love you."

He turned and walked away, drifting into that fog, and as his form became a haze and then that haze became nothing, the mist began to withdraw, evaporating into the air until she stood alone at the front gate. The only sound was that of the city on the other side.

"TREVOR!" BRAXTON CALLED, slamming the door behind him and tossing his keys on the table. "Trevor, you here?" He was frantic, checking all of the rooms in the penthouse and finding them empty. He reached into the back pocket of his jeans and pulled out his BlackBerry, scrolling through his address book and stopping at Trevor's name.

"Hey, you've reached Trevor; at the beep, you know what to do!" Braxton hung up, not bothering to leave a message. He knew Trevor, and his boyfriend never checked his voicemail.

"Where could he be...?" Braxton went back into his address book and dialed Cheri, praying that she would pick up.

She did. "Hey, what's up?" She was outside; he could hear a cluster of inaudible voices in the background.

"Is Trevor with you?"

"No, I haven't seen him since dinner last night." Braxton's brows furrowed, and he adjusted his broad shoulders. "What's going on with you two?" There was annoyance in her voice, and Braxton smirked, finding humor in the tiny hint of the horrible bitch that she used to be.

"Nothing. Uh, thanks." He hung up the phone and took a seat in the club chair in the far corner, listening to the rain and the traffic along Pike and Fourth. He was going to just sit here and wait, with his eyes fixed on the door.

"SO, DO YOU MISS IRELAND?" Rebecca asked her from across the table, the candlelight glittering in her eyes. They were sitting at *Nimbus Bar & Grill*, the city lights sparkling beneath them.

"Sometimes, but mostly I just miss my sister." Rebecca nodded. Mary wasn't sure what was going on, if this meant any-thing—and the truth was she didn't know how to ask, or if she should. Whatever was going on, she realized that in regards to her cousin Trevor, she was beginning to seem like a hypocrite.

"What about you? Where are you from?"

Rebecca took a sip of her wine and tucked her hair behind her ear. "Seattle. My family has a home out there, a really gor-geous house that looks out on the water. They were very adamant about me teaching at Fairhaven." Mary gave a "huh" and took a sip from her drink. "What?" Rebecca asked.

"Nothing. It just seems that you'd think that if they wanted you to teach at a University, it would be a much more prestigious one, that's all."

Rebecca laughed. "Yeah, but my family used to live out here and many of them studied here, and they felt that it was one of the most esteemed universities to receive an education from, and they thought that this would be a good place for me to teach. Besides, I've had such an interest in Northwest folklore that it seemed right to just teach up here."

Mary couldn't argue that; besides, if it was asked of her why she was here, she knew that she would have to make up an answer—one that didn't involve witches, ghosts, or the end of the world.

"So, how about the seafood platter to start?" Rebecca suggested, holding the menu and scanning it casually. Mary liked the way Rebecca looked, dressed in a black spaghetti-strapped dress, with a black shawl with delicate fringe draped loosely around her shoulders and knotted under her arms at the small of her back. She liked the richness and body of her hair, and the sweet perfume of apricots and lavender that seemed to simply emanate from her pores. There was something enticing about Rebecca, something that made her stomach knot up and her pulse begin to race.

"Sounds good." Rebecca gave a giggle. "What is it?"

Again, she laughed. "Nothing, it's just your accent; it's charming."

Mary covered her mouth with her fingers, shaking her head and blushing, finding herself averting her eyes from Rebecca's intense gaze. "I'm serious, and your eyes," she reached out, brushing those red bangs from her face. "They're so gentle...."

Mary's breath caught in her throat, and she looked up to meet that hand which still lingered on her face, and those fingers, which now brushed the soft of her cheek. "I —"

Rebecca shook her head. "Maybe we should just skip dinner and get straight to dessert."

Mary wanted to say no. She wanted to say the she didn't think that that was such a good idea, but when she felt the soft of Rebecca's bare leg brush against her own, she knew that she was never going to be able to say anything ever again.

"YOU KNOW, YOU MISSED it; turns out we have World Mythology together too." Trevor looked at Benjamin and grinned. He knew that he was doing something he shouldn't, but if Braxton was going to tread the line, then why not try it as well?

Trevor was wearing a bright green-and-black check Ben Sherman button-up with a black cardigan over it, the same green running lengthwise down both sides of the chest, along with a stripe of red and navy. His Cartier watch glistened in the light of the Starbucks they were sitting in. "Interesting..." Trevor replied with a smirk.

Benjamin was wearing a gray deep V-tee with a long Burberry scarf draped over his neck. His shaggy blond hair was pulled back from his face in a bun. His amber eyes were gentle and clear, and his smile was infectious.

"So, I'm curious," Benjamin began, taking a sip from his chai latte. "Why did you ask to go with me to coffee; I thought you weren't interested?"

Trevor looked away, trying to search for the answer, trying to find an answer that would both suit his desire and ease his guilt. "I just figured that if we were going to be sitting next to one another in class, well, we should probably get to know each other."

Benjamin nodded, but he seemed skeptical. "And that's it?"

Trevor nodded. "That's it."

This was getting slightly ridiculous, but there was no way around the facts. Despite what he was feeling for Benjamin—the draw, the attraction—it didn't lessen his love for Braxton, and as far as he was concerned, Braxton was still the only thing he could see of tomorrow.

"Then let me ask you another question." Trevor nodded slowly. Benjamin looked at him with intensity. His eyes seemed to be trying to pierce right through him, as if trying to figure out all of his secrets, all of the things that he didn't want anyone to know about himself.

"Do you like being a witch?"

Trevor nearly choked on his mocha, coughing and covering his mouth. "What are you talking about?" His face was flushed, and he was wiping away the tears from his eyes.

"The Blackmoores, witchcraft, Ireland, New Orleans voodoo... you know what I mean."

Trevor sat his cup down and shook his head. "I don't. I mean, I do, but I'm not a witch; I'm just me. That's all superstition."

Benjamin laughed. It was confident, yet gentle, expressing not a single ounce of cruelty. "I don't think so. Trevor Blackmoore, you're a witch. You know it and I know it. Why do you think everyone reacted to you the way they did yesterday in class? All of them wanting to sit with you, hoping that you'd pick them... you're a witch, and you bewitched them."

"That's ridiculous..." Trevor said, trying not to give himself away. How did Benjamin know so much about him? Beyond what his sister had told him? He knew it was fact. He knew that Trevor Blackmoore was a witch—that he wasn't human, that he was something other than. It was unnerving, and yet even though he knew he should get up and leave, he couldn't do it. There was something in Benjamin Tramer that was making him stay right where he was.

Benjamin leaned back in his chair and placed his left arm around the back of his head. "Say whatever you want, Trevor, but I could see it in your eyes, and I could see how everyone acted when around you. You did something to all of them. You may not have meant to, but it doesn't mean it didn't happen."

Trevor felt something strange pass from those golden eyes of Benjamin's, something that stirred that familiar buzz, that cyclone of power: the humming, the thing that had grown and moved out of him—that thing that had driven Christian Vasquez blind. It was the power that had killed his childhood love.

"I should go..." Trevor replied. He stood up and put his coat back on, and slipped his glasses over his face.

"Yeah," he said with a nod and a disappointed grin. "Before all of your secrets start spilling out."

Trevor rolled his eyes and shoved his hands in his pockets. "See you in class." There was nothing else he could say, and nothing else that he wanted to say. It was all just... pointless.

KATHRYN HAD BEEN STANDING in her kitchen, drinking a martini and leaning back against the counter, her eyes fixed on the island where she had had sex with her driver.

She didn't like the sense of guilt that was sitting in the back of her mind for doing what she had done, especially since she had no reason to feel bad for it. She had done nothing wrong, and Sheffield had been gone for so many years now. She could no longer pass on the deadly curse of the Legacy, and in that she was free to do whatever she pleased. But there was a weighted emptiness, and it seemed to come down around her.

She looked at her wedding ring, the one Sheffield had given her, and she thought with a heavy heart that she should finally take it off and put it in the safety deposit box, never to be worn again—not until it was her time to be put deep in the dark of the Mausoleum.

Her Samsung began to vibrate and Kathryn was going to let it ring on into voicemail, but she glanced at Francesca's name on the screen and knew that she needed to answer it.

"Francesca, what is it? Where did you go?"

"I came to Paris." Her voice seemed rushed.

"Oh, sweetie...."

"I'm fine, Kathryn, but you need to listen to me... Kathryn, Trevor's going to do something that is going to alert the Conclave." Kathryn's heart seemed to stop, just for a second, and she braced her free hand on the island for support.

"The Conclave? What is he going to do?"

Francesca sighed. "I don't know. I really have no idea, but we can't let that happen."

Trevor didn't even know about the Conclave, had no knowledge of it, and she realized that having skipped over that piece of information, a piece of information that was extremely crucial, may have sentenced her son to a terrible punishment.

"Didn't you tell him about the rules? About the Conclave?"

Kathryn sighed, cursing herself for her mistake. "No. No, I didn't, Francesca; obviously we've had so many other things going on, that all of those things kind of slipped my mind."

"Well, call him and tell him, or something, before all of this goes to hell."

Kathryn hung up the phone and dialed her son's number, and just as anticipated, it went straight to voicemail.

"Shit!"

REBECCA HAD LED HER into the bathroom, down the narrow stairs from Nimbus. She looked around casually to see if the coast was clear and then she pulled Mary in, throwing her against one of the stall doors and drawing her lips to hers. Mary's head was spinning, and she felt as if she were going on autopilot, allowing Rebecca to take the lead.

Their lips parted, passing hot breath at first, then finally tongues meeting. One of Rebecca's hands gripped Mary's face, while the other slipped down her stomach and moved up under her powder-blue slip dress, her soft fingers finding their way between her legs, slipping between her lips and entering inside.

"I've never —"

"Shh..." Rebecca purred, kissing her and trailing her tongue along her neck, while Mary writhed at her touch. She was fucking her with an intensity that she had never known, and her body was slamming against the metal door, hearing it echo off of the walls of white tile, moaning out as she felt herself getting wetter and wetter, feeling herself swell around Rebecca's fingers.

"I'm going to —" Rebecca silenced her with her lips, and then brought her mouth to her ear, dragging her tongue along her lobe, biting on it while continuing to fuck her.

"You're beautiful," Rebecca let out. It was then that she came, her juices hot and spilling over her fingers, her hair damp with sweat, and her heart racing madly beneath her chest. "Are you okay?" Rebecca asked her when she was finished. Mary nodded and pulled her close, kissing her hard on the mouth.

"Brilliant," she responded with a smile. She allowed Rebecca to lead her out of the bathroom, their hands clasped as they made their way to the elevators. She wasn't certain then what any of this meant, and if she would regret it come the morning—but at that moment, she simply didn't care.

Chapter: Thirteen

TREVOR OPENED THE FRONT door and walked in, finding Braxton sitting there in the chair, his eyes locked on the door, a glass of scotch in his hand, swiveling it around.

"Hey." He sat his coat and bag on the counter and walked towards Braxton. His dark eyes were like garnet, and they seemed to be unreadable.

"Where were you at? I came home and you weren't here." The question was not accusatory, but pained. It seemed to express a sense of worry, a fear of losing something: of losing Trevor.

"I met up with one of my classmates; we were going over notes for World Mythology." Braxton nodded. Trevor looked at him and could not decipher what it was that was going through Braxton's mind, what it was that he was thinking—and even though he had the power to walk into his thoughts, he felt that this would be a violation.

"I called you and your phone was off."

Trevor nodded. "Yeah, my phone died. I should have called you from a pay phone; I'm sorry, but these days it's, like, really hard to find one." Braxton nodded once again and stood, walking towards him. He looked at those broad shoulders, that curtain of dark hair, his height, and the strength he emanated. He was like a wall, Trevor's wall, and nothing could harm him while he was with him.

"I love you," Trevor let out, and Braxton sighed, opening his arms and crushing Trevor against him.

Trevor breathed in the smell of him, his Old Spice deodorant, and absorbed the heat that he radiated. He kept his head rested against his chest, listening to his heartbeat. The rhythm was soothing; the sense of safety he felt with Braxton's strong arms around him was unmatched by anything else.

"I love you too...." His lips crushed against Trevor's forehead, and they rocked gently from side to side. "I know the sun rises because you bring it to me." Trevor looked up at him and smiled wide, as soon as he saw that grin of his.

"You're my life, my entire world... my love, forever." And Trevor once again knew it the moment he said it, that there were no other arms he wanted to be wrapped in, no other lips he wanted to kiss, no other eyes he wanted to look into, and no other heartbeats he wanted to hear fill his ears.

This was where he belonged, and he wasn't going to let anything take that away from him. No one would lure him away from Braxton, no matter what he had to do to make sure that happened.

"Things haven't been okay with us lately."

Trevor pulled back from Braxton and looked at him. He had spoken words that finally pointed to the elephant in the room. "I know."

They searched each other for answers, and for the first time, they were afraid to use their witchcraft to dip inside of the other to see the truth. They didn't want to know the truth. There was something that threatened to tear them apart, and they didn't want to acknowledge that it existed. It could mean too much if they did. It could rock foundations and split the sky in two.

"I don't want to lose you. The fear of that hurts my heart; it sickens me and twists my stomach." Braxton hung his head while saying this, as if he was afraid this admission would somehow not be felt by Trevor. It was like everything they had known and trusted in each other—the love, the obsessive love and dedication—would no longer hold true in the other person.

"I feel the same way." Trevor bent his head down and craned his neck slightly to meet with those heavy eyes, guiding his head back up with his gaze. "Braxton, don't you get it? You are every single part of me; you are every piece of substance that makes up my existence. If I lost you, I don't know who I would be. I don't know where I would go or what I would do. You own everything that I am.

"Without you I'd die." He reached his hand out and placed his open palm on his chest, letting that heart beat into his flesh. He could feel it through his hand, through his arm, and connect with his own beating heart.

"God, Trevor, I'm afraid to face the world without you in it. To exist in it without you; I couldn't do it. I'd shit myself if I lost you, and I'd hide myself away if I had to face the day knowing you weren't by my side."

They embraced once again and closed their eyes, never wanting to let go, not knowing how to let go. They began and ended with each other. It was so precise and entangled that they didn't know where the other person began and where the other ended. They had been made for each other, in every conceivable way. They were each other's other half, their perfect counter-part. If a world without the other ever happened, they both secretly knew that that wasn't a world worth living in.

"Let's go to bed," Braxton suggested, and Trevor nodded, allowing his boyfriend—his soulmate—to lead him down the hall and to their room.

"HOW WAS YOUR TRIP?" Kathryn asked. She sipped her wine and leaned against the counter in the kitchen. A spread of artisan cheeses, crisp-bread, and assorted fruits on a cutting board sat on the island, the open bottle next to it like a flag at a golf course.

"How do you think it was?" Francesca kept her hand to her hip and stared at her, the look of worry over her dead lover's warning written across her face. "I'm certainly worn out from flying to Paris and back on two red-eyes. Did you get ahold of Trevor?"

Kathryn closed her eyes slowly and breathed deeply, shaking her head and taking another sip of her wine. "No. I have tried and tried. He's not returning my calls. I don't think it's on purpose; it's probably just him being preoccupied with school. But it doesn't change the fact that the longer he goes without getting back to me or answering when I call, the more worried I get."

Francesca nodded and reached up to pull a wine glass down from the overhead of the island. She poured herself a glass of chardonnay and sighed. "Do you think whatever it is that he's going to do, he's already done it?"

Kathryn thought for a moment, furrowing her brows and then shook her head. "No, I don't. If the Conclave's attention had been alerted, we would have been made aware of it. It's just a matter of preventing him from doing it. Though, not knowing what it is, how are we supposed to do that?"

Kathryn didn't like being in a situation where she couldn't control it, predict it, understand its movements, determine its course, and know instinctively how to divert it. She knew that she should have told Trevor about the Conclave, their history, their purpose, the Blackmoores' involvement. All of it had just required time, and with everything else that had been going on, she had allowed it to escape her thoughts.

"I am leaving for Manhattan in a few weeks to appear before the board, and find out who it is that is trying to undermine me —"

"So, your tryst with that Maler guy went well, I take it?"

Kathryn rolled her eyes and gave her cousin a grin. "Yes, we had a great time—and not only did he scratch my itch, but he agreed to invest in the waterfront development."

"Well," Francesca began, pouring herself a gin and tonic, "Here's to you." She laughed warmly and took a drink, savoring the woodsy flavor of the juniper contrasting with the fresh citrus of the lime juice she had added.

"Thanks!" Kathryn responded, echoing her salute. "Anyways, I will leave a little earlier and stop by the penthouse on the way to the airport, and hope to catch Trevor in the morning."

Francesca picked up a piece of smoked Havarti and a crisp and took a bite, noting the flavors of sea salt and cracked pepper in the little cracker. "Well, we know the family won't vote against you."

"That's not what I'm worried about."

"I know." Francesca reached out for another piece of cheese, not realizing how famished she actually had been. "You're worried about the fact that the board was purposely set up to have ten family members on the board, and ten non-family members to keep it fair."

Kathryn nodded. "I just wonder if now, looking back in retrospect, if the family hadn't fucked up big time in setting it up that way."

In theory it had always seemed like a great idea, made Blackmoore World Corp. more trusting for other companies to do business with them because it stood outside of simple family interests. But a Blackmoore had always been at the helm, and the idea that someone outside of the clan would even try to undermine the President—given the fact that the Blackmoores had managed to make countless others rich—was completely inconceivable at the time of the company's expansion back in the Sixties.

"There's nothing that can be done about it now; I just have to deal with it. I need to pow-wow with the rest of the family on the board first and come up with a plan of attack, and then proceed from there."

"And Trevor?"

They locked eyes and held each other's gaze for several seconds before Kathryn finally spoke.

"If I don't get ahold of him till then, then I just need to pray he doesn't do anything between now and when I leave for New York."

Chapter: Fourteen

MARY-MARGARET WAS RIDING high on an elation she had never known before. Her time with Rebecca was opening new doors and allowing her to accept parts of herself she had always kept locked away. Her witchcraft, her power, her beauty—things she had reserved, things she had put away due to her upbringing, were now glistening brightly, shining like the sun even in all the gray that surrounded her.

Her students were actually enthusiastic about coming into class, about learning from her, understanding music, its structure, and its own strange spirituality. They listened intently as she spoke of music's power to transcend languages and cultures, to speak something universal and all its own.

Now, a month in, there was nothing they didn't seem to want to know of her, her talent, her career, and her life. They wanted Mary-Margaret to be an open book, something they could explore and take in. They wanted her keen sense of understanding of the musical form to wash over them for their pores to absorb, for their cells to attach to and be mutated by.

"So, if the rumors are true... does that mean you and your sister play so well because you were given the power of the violin by the devil himself?" She hadn't expected the question, but it caught her off-guard nonetheless and forced her to whip around from the board and face her classroom, seeing the hundreds of eyes who stared back at her in confusion and a subtle fear.

"Who said that?" she asked, her sharp green eyes sweeping over them, focusing in on them. She locked eyes quickly with a petite, caramel-skinned girl with a thick mane of chocolate curls, her brown eyes large and absorbent.

"I did." She stood, her petite body clothed in a lacy black top and gray suede skirt, a pair of knee-high Dior boots on her feet. An earring made of quail feathers hung from her left ear, and a string of black and white Chanel pearls hung from her neck.

"And who are you?" Mary-Margaret asked, placing her hand to her hip and hardening her gaze.

"Melanie. My name is Melanie Porter." They seemed to be locked in a stare-down, and neither woman was willing to break it.

"And what, Miss Porter, would incite you to ask such a question?"

The girl seemed to grin without actually grinning. "Well, you're a Blackmoore, and your family's history is known all over the world, and found in many history books. It's rumored that Elijah Blackmoore made a pact with the devil in 1830 that his direct offspring would be musical geniuses, since he himself had failed at the Irish fiddle, and wished to redeem his family's name till the end of time."

Mary-Margaret sighed, but refused to avert her gaze. She had to stand her ground against this girl who wished to stir superstition and controversy in her classroom.

"And your branch of the Blackmoore clan is a direct line to Elijah Blackmoore."

"That's enough, Miss Porter. Take your seat, and if you interrupt my lecture again without raising your hand first and waiting to be called upon, I will have you removed; do you understand?"

The girl grinned and sat back down, not at all embarrassed or sorry for her outburst.

"And to answer your question... no. My sister and I started lessons and training when we were three years of age. We're only as accomplished as we are because of years of dedication and five hours of training a day, from the very beginning."

"What method did you learn by?" a young man with a narrow face and thick black glasses asked her.

"We learned by the Suzuki Method—which we will be learning about next week, actually."

What she negated from all of this was that though this was true, and the hours of training and hard work did play a factor in their accomplishment, the violin had also spoken to the girls. It had called to them, had whispered to them how to play their father's instrument before they had ever picked it up, and when they did, the bow and violin only controlled them and moved them. It had been the same violin that had belonged to Elijah and that had been passed down to his own son.

"I'M REALLY NOT SURE about this, Braxton...." They were walking up Pike Street, crossing Boylston, hands gripping tightly to one another as they got closer and closer to Broadway. Trevor looked across the street, seeing as they passed The Honey Hole, a gourmet sandwich shop, and Edge of the Circle Books, an all-purpose occult shop in the city.

"You'll be fine, babe," Braxton responded, bending his head down and placing a quick kiss on the top of his head and giving him a reassuring squeeze.

"I guess I'll be okay when Cheri and J.T. meet us." Braxton nodded. The truth was, he wanted it to be a night for just him and Trevor, but he knew that Trevor needed a support system to be in a gay nightclub. It had taken a month to finally convince

Trevor to finally agree to go out, ever since the first failed attempt at Julia's weeks before.

Braxton figured they'd both probably not care for it in the end. They both listened to punk, hardcore, metal, and alternative music. He was trying to recall if they had even one dance song on their iTunes or in their CD collection, and he couldn't recall a single one, not even a Lady Gaga song.

It was cold out. The temperature had dropped dramatically since the sun had gone down, and they were clutching to one another's hands, feeding each other warmth, though Trevor seemed to be sucking the body heat right out of him.

The throngs of young men and women were building up in an alley, and Braxton remembered being told by one of the mixers at the studio, that the entrance to Neighbors was in the back alley. "C'mon." He guided Trevor into the alley. The men in tight jeans and shirts, overly groomed and looking to impress, turned their attention to the two of them. They winked, smiled; one guy even said hello while placing his hand on Braxton's arm, without any concern of Trevor's presence, letting his hand begin to drag down his arm.

"Hi, but I'm not interested." Braxton was polite enough, but he knew that this was unnerving Trevor. He was looking around the alley, anxious, and he seemed to fidget when removing his I.D. from his wallet.

Braxton followed suit, and within moments they were walking inside the darkened club.

"Ten bucks, please," said a young Asian man with spikey black hair, looking them both up and down, though his attentions were more focused on Braxton than Trevor. But Braxton planted a kiss on Trevor's cheek as he handed the guy a twenty.

"Thanks." Braxton led Trevor into the dark club. The space opened up around them, and bodies moved, some half-naked,

under strobe lights and Technicolor. To their left and right were
bars, though the one on the left was larger, and they looked up to
see that the club had a second story and two catwalks on either
side of the dance floor.

"I need a drink!" Trevor shouted. Braxton nodded, and they
walked towards the bartender, who was standing there in nothing more than a pair of black boxer-briefs.

"Hey there, sexy! What can I get you?" the bartender asked,
his green eyes falling on Braxton and giving the young man a
grin.

"Two Jack and cokes!" Braxton replied, not paying any attention to the flirtatious compliment.

He could see that the bartender was bothered by this lack
of acknowledgment, which Braxton ignored. He looked over at
Trevor to see him shifting uncomfortably, and instinctively he
reached out and took hold of his hand, squeezing it reassuringly
before reaching for his wallet to hand him his credit card.

"Just keep it open!" They took their drinks and walked away,
moving back into the throng of bodies gyrating on the dance
floor. Trevor was anxious for Cheri and J.T. to show up; Braxton
could see that plainly. He didn't need his sight to divine that.

"Should we go upstairs?"

Braxton shook his head. "Why don't we just stay here?"
Braxton grinned, and Trevor could not help but feel himself
melting slightly. Those black eyes of his, sharp and cunning, reflected the glint of the strobes. He reached out to push those
thick dark bangs away from his face, looking deeper into those
eyes.

"We can do that too." They drank from their glasses and
started dancing, mindful not to spill and holding tight to one
another, moving to the beat. They could not break away from
one another's gazes, and the grins on their faces would not sub-

side. There was a certain magic in this moment. There was something about the music, the feel in the air, the darkness and the sudden flashes of multi-colored lights that seemed to thrill them both.

They were letting go. They were allowing their minds to let go of all of the fear, the impending doom—whatever that would turn out to be—and allowed themselves to simply be. They could exist in this moment and simply live.

For the moment there were no demons, no witchcraft, and no dead boyfriends. Fathers did not die at the mercy of their child's power, teenagers did not rot before their time, and there was no fear of a life that would end before the journey was fulfilled.

"Are you happy at this moment?" Braxton asked him, having to shout over the music.

Trevor looked up at him and felt himself being pulled into those inky black pools. He smiled. His smile was slow, as if lethargic, being pulled into a swoon. Trevor was feeling everything inside of him begin to detach, wanting to go to him, wanting to move out of his body and lose himself into those black wells that rested in Braxton's sockets.

"Yes..." he let out. He couldn't believe it, and if he looked around him once again and took a critical eye to what he was seeing, he may once again have felt differently. He didn't want to feel differently. He wanted to feel that everything was perfect, that they were perfect, and that there couldn't be any other way to feel. He couldn't think of a feeling more terrible than the opposite of what he was feeling right now.

He curled his arms around Braxton's neck and pulled himself in, placing his head against his shoulder and closing his eyes. "What's going on?" Braxton asked, bringing his lips close to Trevor's ear.

"Nothing," Trevor said. "I just want to stay, right here in this moment. I don't want anything to come and take it away." Braxton could hear it in his voice. It was a certain sense of desperation, a need, a yearning, as if through the sound of his words, the way he said it, he was trying to hold onto something that he felt was already in danger of leaving him.

"Trevor, everything's okay, I promise." He pulled Trevor back from him gently and slipped his index finger under his chin, tilting his head up so that Trevor could look into his eyes. "Use your powers if you need to look, if you need to see inside of me like I can do to you. But believe my words when I tell you, nothing, and I mean nothing, will ever tear us apart."

"I know. I know you're right, you're right." Trevor did believe him; there was nothing in his mind or in his heart that doubted what Braxton was saying to him.

"Hey!" They were startled by a loud voice, not connecting it to who it was immediately, but they looked up to see that face and let it all register; it was Cheri Hannifin. "We made it!" she added with a grin.

"Good," Braxton replied. "Where's J.T.?" Cheri nodded and tilted her head to the bar, the same bar where the shirtless bartender stood, the same shirtless bartender who was now shamelessly flirting with J.T.

"Careful," Braxton began, using his eyes to direct her over to see what he was seeing. "Don't wanna lose your boyfriend," he said with a grin.

Cheri returned it. "No worries; if that bartender takes him from me, I'm sure I can find another boyfriend by the end of the night," she responded with a wink.

"So, did you have a problem finding the place?" Trevor asked her, taking her in. She was wearing skinny black Marc Jacobs pants with zippers that moved up the back of both heels and stopped just above the ankle. On her feet she wore what looked like to be a new pair of Christian Louboutin platform heels, and she wore a heather gray draped tee, with a five-tier brass chain necklace woven with natural river pearls around her neck.

"No, not really, though we did try coming in at the Broadway entrance in the beginning. But then I remembered that you had shot me a text telling me that it was through the alley earlier today." She looked over at J.T. getting drinks and shook her head. "You know, I asked him to find out where coat check was, and of course he's getting booze instead. Men!" she snickered and shook her head.

"Come on, I'll go with you."

Cheri nodded and they took each other's arms, walking away just as J.T. arrived with drinks, looking at Braxton. "Did I do something? Do I smell?" Braxton chuckled and shook his head.

"Are you okay?" Cheri asked as they made their way through the crowd of sweaty, nearly-naked flesh that surrounded them, flesh that glistened under neon and strobe lights.

Trevor nodded. "For the moment, yeah, I think I am. How about you?"

Cheri grinned and tousled her chestnut hair with her hand. "I couldn't be happier, Trevor. I mean, really, J.T. is amazing in every single way."

"Good, I'm glad." They arrived at coat check, and Cheri handed the young man with the spiked hair behind the counter her leather-paneled wool Theory jacket. He looked at it for a moment, taking in the olive-colored fabric with the chocolate leather trim, and the details of the Mandarin collar.

"Hot jacket," he said.

"Thank you." Cheri handed him a five-dollar bill and she and Trevor walked back to their boyfriends, who were standing in the middle of the dance floor, simply talking and not moving.

"You'd think maybe they'd try to dance—maybe not together, but at least move in place or something—or at least have the courtesy to get off the dance floor," Trevor observed with a chuckle.

"Yeah, you'd think that, wouldn't you?" They laughed and slid up next to Braxton and J.T.

"Sorry about forgetting coat check, babe."

Cheri shook her head and kissed him on the cheek. "Don't worry about it; I was just teasing you. It's no big deal."

J.T. nodded. He was wearing the long-sleeve gray Henley she had purchased for him the other day. He had one hand tucked into his black John Varvatos jeans, and the colored lights glimmered in his eyes.

She adored looking at him: his faux-hawk, his green eyes, everything about him, the smell of his skin mixed with the scents of Old Spice and his Burberry Brit cologne. Everything about J.T. Oliver kept her captivated, and helped her momentarily forget about the situation that had been she and Greg Sheer.

They danced and moved. They grinned and smiled. Cheri and Trevor had the better ability to move with the music in a way that J.T. and Braxton found to be challenging, but neither she nor Trevor minded. Often they looked to one another and smiled, a silent knowing, a silent bond of confirmation that existed between them, a wordless conversation that could only be because of the nearly twenty years that they had known each other.

Bows and Arrows by Immoor played, remixed and made a lot longer than it should have been, but it was okay. They all loved the song and could ignore the fact that it was a dance remix, especially grateful that it wasn't another Katy Perry song.

"I'm going to step out for a smoke," Trevor said. Cheri looked at him, and he brought his fingers to his lips. "Smoke.

I'm going to go have one." Cheri nodded. Trevor kissed Braxton on the lips and walked over to the coat check. He suddenly felt something cold take hold. It stopped him in his tracks, and whatever it was, he knew it wasn't right. He shook his head and likened it to a sudden wave of insecurity, which he could ignore.

He was handed his dark green Dolce & Gabbana shoulder patch jacket, pulling out the pack of Marlboro Smooths from the slit pocket on the contoured waist seam. He slipped his jacket on as he made his way to the door, skirting past the bouncer and exiting out to the alley. He walked over to the smokers' section, which was across the alley and roped off. He couldn't help but feel like a cow being rounded up, but he could shrug it off.

He lit his cigarette and exhaled. He felt relaxed, and he looked around him, seeing guys dressed in a casual hip way, juxtaposed with people who didn't seem to know how to dress at all. Seattle was so different from what he knew. It confounded him and made him weary of the city itself, and the people on Capitol Hill perplexed him. He didn't understand it at all.

Trevor knew that a lot of this had to do with where he came from, the world that he had grown up in. It was different from this. A world of old money and schools of prestige, neighborhoods filled with homes that had been around for nearly two hundred years, and the families that lived in them having been around for the same length of time.

There were etiquette classes and Deb Balls. These were rites of passage and cocktail parties with cellists and violinists. Ties, collared shirts, Mass at Sacred Heart, and brunch at Skylark's on Sundays. He wanted to be able to feel as carefree as the crowd around him and those in the club, but he felt prevented from doing so. He also knew that a lot of it had to do with sex, wanting sex, needing sex, not seeking love.

There was an iciness to the people in Seattle. A surface politeness which didn't last for very long and they seemed, through his observations, to be able to exchange sex like a handshake. And yet when it came to simple human interaction and connection, when it came to letting someone in and being vulnerable, they simply couldn't do it.

But sex, sex was a different story entirely, and they dressed for it, wearing clothes that seemed to tighten in the places they wanted. They wore jeans that were snug around the crotch, shirts that clung to their chests and showed off how toned they were or how thin. The more butch men wore tees that hung loosely off of their pectorals and sleeves that clung to their biceps. Sex was the main goal of the night for the majority of these people, and though it was cold out—and everyone could feel it—he seemed to be the only person who was actually being smart and keeping warm.

"So, having a good time?" He looked to see a guy with short blond hair and hazel eyes smiling at him, looking him up and down for a moment.

"Uh, yeah, I suppose I am." Trevor gave him a polite nod.

"Here alone?" the guy asked, wearing a white V-neck tee. He slid along the brick wall, closer to Trevor.

"No, actually, I'm here with a couple of friends and my boyfriend. I should be getting back to him." Trevor offered a polite and genuine smile, flattered that someone was actually hitting on him for a change—though he knew that if Braxton had come out to join him, that would not have been the case.

He stepped on his cigarette and made his way into the club, flashing his stamped wrist to the doorman and once again entering the din of pulsating beats, body heat, perspiration, sex, and darkness.

It happened again. That wave of cold, of dread, something that seemed out of place. He tried to grapple with it, to continue to move, but it only seemed to hold him in place.

The sound seemed to drown out, as if he were underwater, and the club was suddenly empty: there were no bodies, just an empty dance floor and empty bars. He looked around, feeling himself moving slowly, though he wasn't meaning to. And then he connected with those panic-stricken black eyes, that mocha skin, the blood ebbing from the top of his head, sticky in his hair and drying on his face. His shirt was bloody at the abdomen, and he was pointing a bloody finger at him.

Christian Vasquez seemed to be speaking, yet no sound seemed to be coming out of his mouth, and his lips were moving rapidly. Trevor started moving closer to him, his eyes squinting reflexively as humans do; as if it would somehow help him better decipher what was being said.

Christian suddenly stopped and then opened his mouth once again, and this time it was audible. This time he could understand it; this time the voice moved into him, curled through his body and shook his nerves.

'*The Soul Wanderers are coming for you, and they will rip you apart....*' Trevor screamed and closed his eyes, and when he opened them again everything was back to normal and everyone in the club was staring at him.

"Trevor!" Braxton was shouting, holding tight to his shoulders and giving him a shake. "Trevor!" he shouted again. He looked into those eyes, those eyes that indicated that he was using his psychometry and looking into him. Those eyes told him that Braxton was seeing everything that he had just seen, and his face was cast in a grave shadow.

"What's happened?" Cheri asked.

"I need to get him home. Right now."

"DO YOU THINK HE'S GOING to be okay?" J.T. asked
Cheri as they walked out of the Seaboard Building and back
out on to Westlake Center along Fourth Avenue. She swung her
purse in her left hand, the gold hardware details and the gold
lock embellishment gleaming in the street lights. Her right hand
was entwined with J.T.'s, and her heels sounded out on the concrete.

"I don't know...." He could tell she was troubled, that she
knew something that he didn't, something that she was keeping
him in the dark about—that everyone was keeping him in the
dark about.

"What's going on, Cheri?" She shook her head. She wanted
to tell him, but she knew that he wouldn't believe her—that, or
he would simply think that she was crazy.

"Nothing; don't worry about it." They walked up Pike and
made their way to First Hill, where Cheri lived, with her view of
the Convention Center and all of downtown.

"Well, I am worried. I can't help it, and I feel like you are
all hiding something from me, and I just don't understand why."
There was a deep sense of frustration in his voice. She wanted to
calm his nerves, to reassure him that there was nothing wrong,
but she didn't know how to do that.

"What if..." she began, trying to find the words to satisfy him
without breaking any bonds of trust. "What if you knew something, something that affected a lot of things and a lot of people... what if you knew this thing and wanted to tell but couldn't,
not even the person that you love, because it wasn't your secret to
tell, and you didn't know what could happen if you did tell it?"

She contemplated waving down a cab, but she knew this
conversation merited a walk, that if there was going to be any

point of a cool-down, then it had to come through the absent-minded journey of the walk.

"Well," J.T. began, releasing a deep sigh. "I guess I would find some way of making that person understand, though I would say that this burden is not fair to the person whose secret it isn't. I mean, suddenly it becomes this person's secret—this person who I'm assuming is you, and this secret that I'm assuming is Trevor's."

Cheri hung her head. She could already tell that she had explained this wrong, because the way that J.T. was speaking, it was turning Trevor into the bad guy. "The thing is, it's not even really a secret, and I mean, you already know it. The thing is, I can't go revealing it, and it's not something that Trevor told me and made it my secret. It was something I found out on my own, and it inadvertently became my secret as well."

J.T. seemed to perk up to this. "So then, if it inadvertently became your secret, then that means you can tell me what it is." She had trapped herself without meaning to, but she did have to give props where props were due to J.T. for being clever enough to trap her. Greg was never that clever.

"It's only my secret because I now hold it, but it's still not my secret to tell, because it has nothing to do with me other than I know." She wasn't being truthful. It did have something to do with her. It had something to do with everyone in South Hill, for that matter, in one way or another. It was the dark current that built South Hill's foundations and she had known it her whole life, and part of that came with the knowledge that it wasn't shared with outsiders.

"Besides, it's also Braxton's secret. You want to know, ask him. It's not just Trevor, and it's not just me."

J.T. didn't like that and she knew it, but it wasn't her concern either way. She wanted one part of her life that was normal, that had nothing to do with the truth about the Blackmoores, about witchcraft and demons, dead boys and secret loves and teenage apathy being quelled by booze and secret bulimia.

"Wait," J.T. said, stopping a block away from her building on Terry Avenue.

"What is it, J.T.?" She tried to keep herself steady and not get frustrated with him, or use an angry tone.

"Did you tell me you loved me in that little scenario of yours?"

She grinned. "I could have." She kissed him on the cheek, letting out a sigh of relief and they continued to walk, holding tight to each other in comfortable silence.

It felt good to Cheri. It felt normal.

Chapter: Fifteen

"ALL RIGHT, CLASS, WHO can tell me what was the first reference to same-sex love in literature?" The sound of his professor drowned out immediately as Trevor began to drift, thinking about the night before. Braxton had been pissed about Christian Vasquez appearing once again, but this time, his anger was not directed at Trevor, as it had been previously. This time, his anger was directed at the former Mariner deity, and he was happy for that; what he wasn't happy about was the presence of the spirit, and why he wouldn't let Trevor move on.

"I take it you don't really care about any of this?"

Trevor shook his head and turned his gaze to find Benjamin grinning at him. "No, it's not that. I just didn't get much sleep last night." He didn't like the disbelieving look that Benjamin was giving him, but he wasn't going to attempt to even convince him of this. There wasn't any point, especially given the fact that whether Benjamin believed him or not was of no consequence to him. He knew that he needed to concentrate on what was going on in his class, but there was so much more on his mind, so many other pressing things—things that were much more crucial and immediate.

"Well, maybe you should consider investing in some sleeping pills."

Trevor grinned awkwardly and nodded. "I suppose maybe I should." There was a glimmer in those amber eyes, and the way they looked at him was distracting, and caused his nerves to become uneasy. He didn't like this.

"Who is that talking?" Benjamin and Trevor both stopped speaking and looked around the rest of the room, just as everyone else was doing, trying to seek out the culprit, knowing that they were the guilty party. Dr. Greene did too.

"Mr. Blackmoore, Mr. Tramer, perhaps the two of you would like to finish your conversation outside. The two of you can return to class when you both feel prepared to learn. Now get out." Trevor's face was flushed with embarrassment, and he was shocked and agitated with the fact that Benjamin seemed to find it amusing. The grin on his face spoke volumes, and Trevor really wanted to smack that smirk right off of him.

"Well, at least we have free time before our next class."

Trevor looked at him hard. He was pissed off, and he wasn't going to hide it. "You know, I actually want to take this class. I actually do want to learn and do well, and perhaps get on the Dean's list. I actually do have ambitions of higher learning!"

Benjamin snickered. "I'm sorry, dude...." He reached out his hand, perhaps to place it on Trevor's arm, but he tore himself away from him and rolled his eyes.

"Yeah, I bet you are. It seems like you've made me your fucking pet project or something! I don't get it; I don't understand it. All I do know is that you're making it a lot harder for me to do anything, to even focus lately!" Benjamin smiled, and Trevor shut his mouth and looked away from him quickly.

"I'm distracting, huh?" Trevor knew he had said the wrong thing and was giving away too much, and only fueling Benjamin's desire.

"I meant that your constant questioning—your fixation on me—is really unnerving and bothering me." Trevor looked all around him, everywhere but at Benjamin. He didn't want to see those brilliant eyes or that knowing smirk. He didn't want Benjamin to think that he stood a chance.

"Whatever you say, Trevor Blackmoore... whatever you say." Trevor stoically watched Benjamin pivot on his heel and walk away confidently down the concrete path. He watched him and his stomach turned as this uneasy feeling began to take hold, twisting in his gut, as if his intestines were wrapping around his spine.

"I need to end this. I need to end this for good," Trevor decided. He knew what he needed to do, and he knew where he needed to go. He wanted his life back. He wanted to be able to get through school without any more distractions, and he needed to make sure there were no more temptations getting in the way of him and Braxton.

They had a lot more dangerous and horrible things to worry about. Petty human things were the last thing they needed to deal with, and were easy enough to get rid of, and so he was going to handle it for the sake of his relationship, and for the sake of the coven.

MARY-MARGARET AND REBECCA sat at Brandywine Kitchen on Commercial Street in Downtown. It was one of Rebecca's favorite places, and she couldn't wait to take her there for lunch. Mary-Margaret liked the concept of the quaint restaurant with its dark woods, yellow and brick walls, supporting sustainable, locally-grown produce and farm-fresh meats and cheeses.

They sat in a booth near the back of the restaurant, a pitcher of cider from the bar between them. They both had a green salad with balsamic beets, orange-marinated radishes that were drizzled with rosemary-balsamic dressing. Along with this they ordered the quinoa salmon cakes, served with sliced avocado and cucumber with a tomato roasted red-pepper aioli.

They couldn't help but grin at one another, and every word that passed their lips sounded like raindrops made of liquid gold. "You're so beautiful," Rebecca said to her. Mary-Margaret blushed and looked down at the table briefly.

"And so are you." She picked up Rebecca's hand and brought it to her lips.

"So, you didn't tell me how classes went today."

Mary-Margaret shook her head. "Two of the girls in my class seem to want to get under my skin." She shrugged and gave a sigh. "Maybe it's some entitlement thing or something... I don't know."

Rebecca's brows furrowed, and a shadow of concern seemed to pass over her face. "Which girls?"

"Oh, I don't know if you'd even know them; Melanie Porter and Victoria Dianaca."

Rebecca's eyes widened and it was apparent the girls' names struck something in her, but she was quick to compose herself. "I'm familiar with them; they like to cause trouble. Just don't pay them any mind. They're just spoiled bitches, that's all."

Mary-Margaret nodded and tried to ignore the look on Rebecca's face, but she couldn't. There was something very wrong with those two girls; she was certain of it, and Rebecca was confirming it. Whether she meant to or not.

BRAXTON SAT AT ONE of the many benches that lined the fountain at Cal Anderson Park in the middle of Capitol Hill, listening to the water spilling down the large stone fountain-head. His hands were tucked inside the pocket of his Bond Mac, and his bangs poked out of the black Ben Sherman fedora on top of his head. His dark eyes were fixed on that water, unblinking, the entirety of his life since Trevor Blackmoore first walked into it racing through his brain.

He thought of Tom Preston, of Christian Vasquez, and his father. He thought of that day in the locker room after he had kneed Christian in the groin and when Trevor had come to him, telling him all about Christian and how happy he was that Christian had confessed his love for the young man. Times he hated to think on, times when he didn't exist for Trevor as anything other than just a friend. The memories were excruciating, and even now, still stirred in him an indescribable anger: an anger that seemed would never die, not as long as the dead boy's spirit kept coming to torment his boyfriend.

"Why won't you just leave him alone?" The question passed his lips aloud, and he recognized immediately the desperate frustration to his tone. It seemed like they would never be released of their past, that Mariner High School and South Hill would forever hold on to them, and that those old ghosts would haunt them no matter how far they went.

He wanted to take Trevor away from all of it, as far as they could go. To Europe, to the Mediterranean, Asia—but he knew that no matter how far they went, those ghosts could find them anywhere.

He contemplated calling Kathryn or Queen Mab to ask for advice, to tell them what was going on. But he figured that that would be the wrong move, the wrong thing to do at this moment: that not only would it upset them, but that it would agitate Trevor, who had just started school and was trying so hard to try to live a normal enough life for as long as they could before everything came to a head and the big bad—whatever that was—would come for them and perhaps take it all away.

The thing that he was seeing, the thing that it seemed Trevor was all too ready to ignore, was that the big bad was already here, that it was already coming for them.

"Fuck." He shook his head and stood, slipping on his Wayfarers, and began to walk down the gravel path back towards Pine Street. He looked at his watch and saw he still had some time before Trevor thought he would be home.

Braxton had called J.T. and lied about not feeling well; the last thing he wanted to do was be in the studio and deal with Joshua Dianaca. He needed time to himself, and that situation was another mess of things that he didn't have the patience to deal with. He was afraid it would cause him to act out, and inadvertently cause them to lose their record deal.

He crossed the street and headed towards *Oddfellows Café and Bar*, located in the historic Oddfellows building, on the other side of *Molly Moon's Ice Cream* and beneath *Century Ballroom*. The only thing he wanted was a good IPA and a smoke. The rest of it—Joshua and the band—those things could be put off for another day.

TREVOR WALKED INTO the penthouse, knowing that Braxton wouldn't be done with the studio for another hour, which was plenty of time to do what needed to be done. He took his shopping bag and made his way to the study, sliding open the pocket doors and walking into the room with its ornate desk and floor-to-ceiling shelves lined with books.

He walked over to the shelf nearest to the window on the left hand side, scanning all of the titles carefully. They were all there, books on spirits and histories on witchcraft. After a few moments of searching through the titles, he found it: *Le Grimoire Blackmoore*.

Sarafeene Blackmoore had penned four copies, all identical, all bound in the same leather and written on the same papyrus, a year before her death in the early nineteenth century. Copies were left in the possession of his mother, as well as Queen Mab, Magdalene, and this last had been given to him on his eighteenth birthday, upon vanquishing Tom Preston and the family familiar, Jonathan Marker.

He flipped it open and began searching through the pages until he found what he was looking for.

"To turn passion into indifference." He walked back over to his shopping bag and began pulling out the items needed. His feet creaked on the floorboards as he walked, listening to it echo off the walls of the silent apartment. First he removed two black male-shaped candles and a black satin ribbon, then a vial containing raven's blood, a long needle, and a bundle of raven feathers; lastly, he pulled out a suede pouch containing powdered wormwood and another containing black snake root.

"I need a cauldron... seriously?" Trevor ran his hand through his hair and chuckled. "Should I get a conical hat and a broom too?" He looked around the room and spied a black cast-iron bowl filled with potpourri, and shrugged. "This'll do." He dumped it out in the stainless steel bin.

He rolled up the Persian rug and moved it to the side of the room, and then proceeded to close the crimson satin drapes—which had been left open by the housekeeper and were flooding the room with the sounds of Westlake Center and Pike Street beneath him—and then returned to the center of the room.

With a deep breath he began setting up, placing the bowl before him in the center of the room. Grabbing the pouch of wormwood, he began dumping it around him counter-clockwise in a circle, followed with the black snake root, which he traced along the powdered wormwood, chanting in a whisper repeatedly while doing so: "Papa Legba, *ouvrez le barrier por moi passer.*" The air around him was shifting; he could feel it, and his fingers and hands began to tingle and get hot. He could feel that familiar power—that witchcraft—begin to rise within him.

Upon returning to his place before the bowl, he opened the vial and dipped the needle in the blood, and then began carving his name into the first candle, followed by Benjamin's in the second.

"To anoint and assign." Then with each ribbon, he took the candles and placed them back to back, and secured them together with the ribbon. "To seal the spell and keep it in place." He then placed a few of the feathers on either side of the bowl and struck the match, lighting the bound candles. Lastly he scattered the remaining feathers around the bowl and candles, creating a smaller circle.

Finally, he dumped the remaining black snake root and wormwood into the bowl and tossed another lit match in, watching as the herbs began to burn and the smoke began to rise up in a cyclone towards the ceiling—but not spreading out of the boundary of the circle.

"What was passion, I now turn to disdain. Goddess Inanna Ishtar, I invoke your name. Break temptation, turn lust to indifference, and send it away on ravens' wings." Trevor lifted the bound candles and tossed them into the bowl. "Banish the desires forbidden and wrong; into the dark abyss it shall now remain!"

It was then that the winds stirred and rushed into the room, like a great, powerful, concentrated hurricane—causing the herbs cast around him to rise, along with the feathers, and the flames from the candles to quickly ignite, consuming the contents of the bowl and turning them to ash.

Trevor watched as the smoke and ash were carried out of the study and through the window, and over the rooftops of downtown Seattle. He grabbed the bowl and walked over to the window, dumping out the melted wax onto the street beneath him, making sure it didn't land on anyone below.

"Babe, you home?" he heard Braxton call out. He quickly grabbed the book and returned it to the shelf.

"Yeah, in the study!" He pushed the drapes back open and raced to grab the supplies off of the floor, and shoved them in the lower desk drawer.

"What are you doing?" Braxton asked, as he pushed the doors open.

"Nothing, really. I was going to sweep up in here, since the housekeeper doesn't come in again for another two days, but I got sidetracked looking at all of the books on the shelf."

"Uh-huh..." Braxton said with skepticism. He walked over to Trevor and placed his arms on his shoulders. He looked deep into his eyes and placed his lips to his forehead. "So I was thinking..."

"Oh, now I have to be skeptical," he said with a grin.

Braxton laughed and rolled his eyes. "I was thinking we should have a house-warming party."

Trevor felt uneasy about the idea. "Okay... when?"

Braxton's eyes squinted, and he began to make a face like someone had just stepped on his foot. "I was thinking tonight."

Trevor's mouth dropped open. "Tonight? Are you serious?! Tonight?"

Braxton nodded. "Yeah, I already told Cheri and the band, and Cheri already invited some people from your school."

Trevor shook his head and walked over to the bar in the corner of the study. He removed a glass and poured himself a scotch, throwing it back in one swig and pouring himself another.

"I barely know anyone at school; it's only been a few weeks, and I'm so not prepared for this. I haven't planned a menu; how am I going to cook everything? And what about booze?" His mind was swimming. He deduced right away that this was meant to be a surprise, which explained why he hadn't heard from Cheri all day. The only way Cheri could keep a surprise a surprise was if she avoided everyone all day.

"Baby, don't worry," Braxton said, wrapping his arms around Trevor's waist. "I've taken care of everything. Purple is catering, and I've got cases of booze coming, and bartenders. The band is coming over to move all of the furniture in here to our bedroom, along with all of the uh, important books, which of course we will have to move ourselves, and it'll all be locked up. I have a deejay coming, and the study will be the dance floor. It'll be great!"

Trevor felt nauseous and fell into the love seat.

"I even invited Mary-Margaret, and she apparently has a date," Braxton added with a smirk.

He rolled his hazel eyes and sighed. "Oh, great; that should be interesting."

CHERI STOOD IN HER walk-in closet, the walls lined with clothes on satin hangers and lit with recessed lights, staring at her clothes and hundreds of heels and boots, and sighed. She had her hands on her hips, wearing a violet La Perla bra and matching panties, trying to figure out what to wear. She knew Trevor hated surprises, and she feared how pissed he would be about this party. She hoped that Braxton would be able to charm him into submission, and that he would be in a good mood by the time she got there.

"What the hell am I going to wear?" Her phone buzzed, and she read the text from J.T. telling her that they were there setting up, and that Trevor was sitting in the corner of the living room, not saying anything. "Great." She shook it away and ran her fingers through her chestnut hair. She grabbed a pair of her skinny dark denim Seven's, a sheer cream Marc by Marc Jacobs short-sleeve blouse, Burberry stiletto boots, and her black-and-white pearl Chanel necklace. After dressing, she wrapped a black-and-white Chanel scarf loosely around her neck and slipped on her black tweed jacket.

I should pick up a couple of bottles of Veuve on the way, she decided, while slipping on her Dior sunglasses and grabbing her handbag. As she walked out of her room and back out into the living room, she looked out on the city, already growing dark, and there was a sudden unease that seemed to take over her. It was brief, and she couldn't determine its source or what it was about, but she shrugged it off and figured it was just anxiousness over the influx of new people that would be at the apartment.

She had invited people from Trevor's gay lit class, and a few classmates from Art History. She thought it would be a great opportunity for them to be a part of something. To continue building a normal life for themselves—especially for Trevor, who had never had the chance to be part of anything while they were growing up.

There was also a part of her, something she would never admit to anyone but herself, that missed being the young socialite who threw the best parties and knew all of the right people. There was a part of her that wanted to be that girl again. She was young, had a fortune at her disposal, and she wanted something that was hers: something that had nothing to do with evil entities, dark secrets, and witchcraft. A sense of an ordinary life, a life she knew Trevor so desperately wanted to have as much as she did.

Chapter: Sixteen

AN EVEN MORE DANCE-driven version of Kylie Minogue's *Speakerphone* blared from the study and out into the rest of the penthouse, and the apartment was filling up fast with young people. The island and dining table were filled with exquisite finger-foods from *Purple Café & Wine Bar*.

Trevor found himself especially addicted to the sweet peppadew peppers filled with salmon mousse, and the baked brie filled with caramelized onions and wrapped in phyllo dough, covered with sliced purple grapes and served with crisp, sweet flatbread that was covered in coarse sea salt. If he looked like a greedy pig, well, Trevor just didn't care.

The drinks were flowing with top-shelf liquor, and as more and more people began to show up, the more relaxed Trevor began to feel, despite the fact that he didn't know anyone there. Several classmates from his Gay Lit course were there, and they had brought their own friends with them.

Trevor wore black skinny slacks and a fitted white Prada oxford and matching fitted blazer, with a black skinny tie and black Burberry motorcycle boots on his feet, and a chunky black leather Burberry watch. He smiled at people as he made his way through the penthouse, sipping a sidecar and searching for Braxton, who he eventually found, talking to J.T. and chatting with a couple of girls who seemed to be hanging on every word they said.

They locked eyes and Trevor blushed, feeling as if he were sixteen again, overwhelmed with reticence and taken aback by the devilishly beautiful young man with his dark hair and eyes. Braxton was dressed in dark denim 511's and a mod fit black-and-blue short-sleeve checkered Ben Sherman button-up, with a silver-and-black checkered skinny tie.

His large arms were folded across his chest, and he could tell one of the girls was fixed on the tattoo sleeve on his left arm, which he had started work on a month earlier and had just now finished—save for an image of a sunflower that still needed shading and coloring.

"And this is the love of my life," Braxton said, reaching out for him and pulling him close.

"O-M-G! You guys are the cutest couple!" the girl who had been staring at his sleeve said. He could see the mild jealousy in her eyes, but he shook it off.

"Thanks." Trevor blushed and downed the rest of his drink. He was definitely going to need more booze. "Are you guys classmates of Cheri's?" The girls nodded, and Trevor quickly noticed the other girl was making eyes at J.T. He pulled out his phone and sent a text to Cheri, telling her she needed to get there as quickly as possible.

"Where is she?" Braxton asked. Just then, Trevor heard the elevator open and Cheri walked in, looking as amazing as ever and carrying two bottles of *Veuve Clicquot* in her hands. She strutted confidently towards them, a grin on her face as soon as she and Trevor locked eyes.

"Hey, sexy pants!" she said, handing the bottles to both he and Braxton.

"Hey yourself, hot stuff!" They laughed and hugged, kissing each other on the cheeks. "You look fierce!"

She smiled and rolled her eyes. "I know." She looked over at the two girls in their American Apparel leggings, heels, and co-ordinated thigh-length deep-V tees, and offered a polite smile. "Hey, Christina and Becca, I'm glad you guys made it!" she said, while slipping into J.T.'s arm.

"Thanks for inviting us; it's an awesome party!" Becca, the girl who had been eyeing J.T. said, and looked away, making Trevor smirk at the entire display of passive-aggressive jealousy.

"I wonder when Mary-Margaret is getting here."

Cheri looked at Trevor, surprised. "She's coming?"

He nodded. "Yeah, apparently Braxton invited her."

Cheri's brows rose. "I know; you don't even need to say it, and supposedly she has a date."

Cheri gave a slight nod. "I think we need drinks."

"I couldn't agree more," Trevor replied, and they excused themselves, walking arm in arm down the hall and back out to the living room.

MARY-MARGARET AND REBECCA stood in the elevator, their hands locked together as they each held a bottle of *Veuve*, which Kathryn had told her was Trevor's favorite champagne, and waited for the door to open. Rebecca was dressed in a black knee-length Gucci dress with matching heels, and Mary-Margaret had gone with a fuchsia Betsy Johnson cocktail dress with a little three-quarter-sleeve sequin purple jacket. The door opened to the private foyer, and the front door was wide open. *Hurt You* by The Sounds was pouring out of the room, and the bright lights and mass of young people drew them inside.

Kathryn had stressed repeatedly that she needed to make sure that Trevor called as soon as he could. "Are you ready for this?" Rebecca asked her.

She nodded, and they entered hand-in-hand. Mary had never had the chance growing up to go to parties with people her own age, and now here she was, a girl in her late twenties, mixing with people her own age. It excited her to think that she would be able to let go and be young for once. Not a famous violinist who had traveled the world twice over and not a teacher at a university. Here she was an equal to everyone else and she was overcome with a sudden elation.

She had not anticipated this excitement, but there it was amongst all of these people who were laughing, dancing, and throwing back drinks, and engaging in heated debates while smoking cigarettes or passing glass pipes. She had only seen these things in movies or television shows, when she had time to watch them. The thought that she would ever step into what she saw on the screen had been as foreign to her as the idea of never playing the violin again.

"IS THAT MARY-MARGARET?" Cheri asked, directing Trevor's eyes to the two stylish young women walking towards them and holding hands. It took him a moment, but those brilliant green eyes and ethereally silky red hair told him that it was, and he realized quickly that his cousin was dating another woman. There was a part of him enraged by the sudden hypocrisy, but in the end he shrugged it away.

"Hey, cousin, you look amazing!"

Mary blushed and looked away. "Thank you, Trevor... this is Rebecca. She's my...." The two women looked at one another, and Rebecca gave her a reassuring nod. "She's my girlfriend."

Trevor offered a smile and noticed that there was something about Rebecca that seemed oddly familiar, though he couldn't place his fingers on it.

"It's really great to meet you." He extended his hand, and they shook. He felt a slight charge, like an electric shock, when their hands touched, and he was sure she could feel it too.

"You too."

"Well, there's plenty of food and booze, and there's a deejay down the hall."

The two women nodded and smiled wide. "I'm going to grab us a couple of drinks," Rebecca said, kissing Mary on the cheek.

"I'll follow you," Cheri said. As soon as the two girls walked away, Trevor turned to Mary.

"So, a girlfriend?"

She nodded. "Yeah, and I owe you an apology. I gave some narrow-minded opinions about you and Braxton...."

Trevor nodded. "I'm aware."

Mary hung her head. "I'm really sorry. Perhaps I was uncomfortable with it because I sensed something inside of myself that I wanted to avoid."

Trevor took a sip from his glass and shook his head. "It's okay. I'm glad you have someone, and I'm glad you came."

Mary seemed genuinely surprised by this. "Really?"

He nodded. "Yeah, I am. Now, c'mon." He took hold of her hand. "Let's dance, and show these people what a couple of witches can do!"

"SO HOW LONG HAVE YOU and Trevor been friends?" Rebecca asked, sipping from her glass of Chambord and sour. Cheri looked around the room briefly to see J.T. and Braxton talking with a group of guys she didn't recognize, all of them throwing back Pyramid Amber Ales. She was trying to fight back the complicated string of memories, the history of she and Trevor that Rebecca's question had summoned.

"Um, well, we grew up together. Our parents were friends... so, really, all of our lives, give or take a few years in between." She tried to fight back those moments where she had called Trevor names in the hallways of Mariner, the times she had made fun of his quiet tenor voice when he spoke in class. She knew she would never be able to forgive herself for those years, even though she knew that Trevor already had—so long ago, it seemed. There was nothing she could do to take it back, and though she knew the reasons behind it—the hold that Greg and Christian had had on her—it still did not excuse her lack of courage to stand up to them, and stand by her best friend's side when he needed her most.

"And what of the whole witchcraft thing?"

Cheri nearly choked on her drink, coughing and trying to clear her throat. "Excuse me?"

"Oh, I'm sure you know."

Cheri shrugged. "It's just rumors—lies, really. There's no such thing as witches."

Rebecca brushed her hair over her shoulders, the diamond tennis bracelet catching the light and shimmering as her hand moved. "Whatever you say...."

And with that, Rebecca smiled and walked away, back down the hall towards the kitchen.

MAKE-UP SEX by The Clear Static began to play as Braxton walked into the study, seeing a cluster of young bodies gyrating to the beat. It didn't take him long for those dark eyes to land on Trevor and Mary-Margaret dancing in the center of the room. He smirked as he watched his boyfriend move, the two witches entrancing everyone else around them, and he laughed to himself at the fact that they both were so unaware of it.

Sometimes he found himself staring at Trevor as if he were a mysterious stranger, an ethereal being, the cunning witch who had spelled him as well, and it was this that he found so endearing and so charming about Trevor Blackmoore—that he was so completely oblivious to the power he held and the sheer beauty that existed with in him.

"Hey..." Cheri said, leaning against him.

"Hey yourself, lady." Braxton smiled at her, and she returned it. It never ceased to amaze him that for such a long time he had hated this girl so much, and now, he'd do anything for her. He'd die for her, he'd kill for her, and he knew that she felt exactly the same for him.

"Care to dance, stud?" She stuck out her hand, and he nodded.

"I've been waiting for you to ask me all night." They stepped into the room and made their way to Trevor and Mary-Margaret. It was this moment, this simple moment that reminded Braxton that he was alive, that the compounding loss of his parents did not stifle him. His life did not die along with his father; on the contrary, it was the day that his life really began. He wouldn't stop living and enjoying his life; no matter the difficulty, he wouldn't surrender to any feelings of defeat.

THE NIGHT CARRIED ON, and even at a quarter till midnight, people were still arriving: a never-ending cycle of people. He felt normal. He wasn't Trevor Blackmoore, the witch from the cursed and infamous family; he was just Trevor, the carefree college freshman who was living a normal life, and doing all of the things that people his age were supposed to do.

There was no responsibility, no obligation—nothing other than classes, his degree, and the life he was building with his boyfriend. He had never dared to dream that he would have a life like this. He had never thought that he'd have friends or have a boyfriend whom he loved and who he would be sharing a life and a home with.

In this moment, happiness had hit him like a train on a track, and he couldn't move and there was no turning back. There was only this moment and this life, and no matter how long he had to be this young, to be this carefree, he was going to hold on to it as tightly as he could, and just enjoy the night.

He leaned against the fireplace mantle and observed the room, nodding to his classmates, raising his glass to people as they came by, sipping on his sidecar and taking it all in. The elevator chimed, and he craned his neck to the front door to see Benjamin walk into the penthouse, wearing a pair of gray skinnies and a red-and-black flannel shirt.

"Fuck, this is just what I need." He shook his head and rolled his eyes, making his way towards the hall to try to slip past him, to get to Braxton before Benjamin got to him.

As he walked he caught sight of Rebecca, who stood steadfast and locked eyes with Benjamin. It was brief—so brief that if he had not been so acutely aware of him, he may have missed it—but it seemed that Rebecca and Benjamin knew each other, though they spoke not a word and Benjamin hurried past her as if he was avoiding her.

Weird. He kept walking, trying to get around a cluster of boys and girls talking in a tight circle.

"Hey, there." A hand fell on his shoulder, and he whipped around to see Benjamin staring at him; an uneasy smile was spread across his face.

"Hi."

He quickly removed his hand from Trevor, as if he suddenly couldn't touch him. "Great party." Benjamin seemed disoriented, and the sweat began to bead down his face.

"Thanks, glad you could make it." He offered Benjamin a smile, which he seemed to struggle to return.

"Really?" he asked in disbelief.

"Sure; are you feeling okay?"

"Uh, I don't know." Benjamin rubbed the back of his head and then looked at his open palm, studying the sweat that had rubbed off from his hair. "Maybe I should get a drink."

Trevor shrugged. "Yeah, maybe."

Benjamin once again tried to offer him a smile before walking away. Trevor rolled his eyes as he watched him go, glad to know that one way or another he was no longer going to be burdened with Benjamin Tramer, and he hoped it would last for the rest of the night.

"YOU DON'T LOOK SO GOOD," Rebecca said, making her way up to the bar to order two more drinks for herself and Mary-Margaret.

Benjamin looked over at her and rolled his eyes. "Sis, what are you doing here?"

Rebecca laughed. "I think the better question is, what are you doing here?"

Benjamin ordered a scotch on the rocks and took a sip. "What I'm supposed to do, and you?"

Rebecca looked down absentmindedly at the ends of her hair and sighed. "I was invited."

Benjamin furrowed his brows in suspicion. "By who?"

Rebecca locked eyes with Mary-Margaret and waved at her. "By my girlfriend."

Benjamin looked at the alabaster redhead talking to Trevor and Braxton, and shook his head. "You can't be fucking serious! Since when?"

Rebecca dropped five dollars into the brandy snifter and grabbed her drinks. "It's none of your business... and you're telling me you're not here stirring up trouble?"

"I'm doing my job, sis, and that's it. We have a mission, which you seem to have forgotten."

Rebecca began to tap her heel on the floor and gave an annoyed sigh. "Really? Because it looks like when you walked in here, you bee-lined for Trevor and tried to stir something up... and if I know you at all, dear brother, you have your own personal motives that have nothing to do with *the mission*."

Benjamin rolled his eyes and took another drink of his scotch. "I have no idea what you're talking about."

Rebecca didn't believe him, and he knew it; he also didn't care. "You like him, don't you?"

It was an accusation and not a question, one he didn't feel like answering. "Not at all."

"Don't lie to me. You'd fuck anything that walks. Stay away from Trevor. You want to do your job, your mission, then go ahead. I'm not. I want no part of it. I don't have the same loyalties that you do. But I'm telling you: don't try to get between Trevor and Braxton. They love each other; they're good together, and if you try, you're only going to get hurt."

Rebecca gave on last disapproving glare and pivoted on her heel, making her way, drinks in hand, back to her girlfriend.

"DO YOU KNOW THAT GUY?" Mary-Margaret asked.

Rebecca handed Mary-Margaret her drink and shook her head. "No, we were just making small talk while we were waiting for our drinks. What did I miss?"

"Well, apparently Braxton's band is having a show in a couple of weeks at The Comet, and we've been invited to come."

"Really?"

Braxton swigged his beer and nodded. "Yeah, it's a Halloween show. I'm really excited."

Trevor stood with his hand around Braxton's waist, and looked over at Cheri, who was angling her eyes and cocking her head towards the direction of the back hall.

"Hey, babe, Cheri and I are going to go have a smoke." Braxton nodded and gave Trevor a peck on the cheek as they made their way towards the back hall, Trevor grabbing a bottle of champagne on their way.

THEY WERE IN THE BATHROOM in the master bedroom, the both of them sitting opposite of one another in the giant porcelain tub, the bathroom floor and walls covered in pale pink Venetian marble, and the recessed lights shone down on them. Trevor had locked the bedroom door behind them, and the entire bedroom had been overtaken by the contents of the study, so the bathroom ended up being the only place that they could sit comfortably.

"I feel like we're teenagers hiding out at some bad house party," Cheri said. The two of them nodded and laughed as they smoked their cigarettes and passed the bottle back and forth.

"So, what's going on?" Trevor asked, swigging back some champagne. He loved champagne; if he could drink it and nothing else, he would. He would bathe in it if he could, and he reckoned, in his slightly drunken state, that maybe one day soon he would in fact bathe in it, in the very tub they were now lounging in.

"Well, first, are you enjoying your party?"

Trevor gave a drunken grin and dragged from his cigarette. "You know, I am... I feel like Holly Golightly! All I need is a long cigarette holder."

Cheri giggled and took her turn with the bottle. "That's because you are, my darling! You are Holly Golightly! Cheers!" She handed the bottle back, and Trevor took another swig.

"Okay, onto the serious stuff. What's up?"

Cheri didn't want to alarm him or ruin his party, but she knew she needed to say something. "All right, so earlier, I was getting a drink with your cousin's girlfriend, and she started asking about you."

Trevor passed the bottle slowly and dragged his smoke to his lips, his eyes filled with a suspicious questioning. "How so?"

"Well," Cheri began, putting out her smoke and lighting another. "She first just asked how long you and I had been friends, but then she started asking me about you being a witch. It was very strange."

Trevor nodded slowly, his thoughts obviously turning. "Peculiar... peculiar indeed."

"SO, WHERE DID TREVOR and Cheri go?" Rebecca asked Braxton. He rubbed the back of his head with his hand and looked around the apartment.

"Eh, J.T. and I have learned not to question; they're off doing the whole fag/fag-hag thing. It's what they do."

"I see; so, have you always known you were gay?" Rebecca asked him.

Braxton took another swig from his beer and shook his head. "Oh, I'm not gay."

"I thought that you and Trev–"

He laughed and nodded. "Oh, yeah we are... I don't know how I can explain this. I've never been attracted to other guys before; actually, I was never really attracted to anyone, except for Trevor. I don't actually know what it's like to be interested in anyone else... Trevor and I were kind of made for each other."

Mary-Margaret cleared her throat, and she and Braxton exchanged quick and knowing glances. "And your last name is Volaverunt...?"

"Yeah, why?"

"Oh, nothing. It's just interesting. Your last name means 'to fly' or 'has flown.' It's also the name of a famous painting by Goya of a witch."

Braxton took a long, slower swig from his bottle. "Interesting."

"Yes, it is. It's also rumored that the Volaverunts of Madrid are descended from witches, and that they have some relation to other witch families."

"SO, WHO WAS THAT GUY that stopped you outside, the one who was talking to Rebecca?" They were halfway through the bottle of champagne, and were both almost through their packs of cigarettes.

"Oh, God, Benjamin Tramer... he's in my Gay Lit and World Mythology classes. He's also a total pain in my ass."

Cheri let out a laugh and passed the bottle. "It looked like there was a lot more going on there."

Trevor rolled his eyes. "I don't know; hopefully I took care of that problem... I think he likes me—actually, I more than think. He's made it very obvious."

Cheri's eyes grew wide as she dragged from her cigarette. "And what about you; do you like him?"

Trevor began to chug the champagne, not stopping until he nearly choked on it. "Fuck, kinda... I've had thoughts. Fuck, I dunno. I can't even be talking about this right now. If Braxton touches me, he could get all witchy on me and find out, and then I'll be in major trouble!"

The tears began to slip down his face, and Cheri hated seeing him in this much pain. She didn't want to see him so distraught. "Look, let's grab lunch tomorrow after class and talk about this—away from school, away from our boyfriends—and just get back to the party."

Trevor nodded wiped the tears from his face. "Okay," he sniffled.

"And let's hide these tears; the last thing Braxton needs to see is that you've been crying."

"Thanks." They stood and walked out of the room and back out to the party. *Hang Me Up to Dry* by Cold War Kids was playing loudly, and a couple of girls seemed to be sloppily attempting the Charleston on the dance floor.

KATHRYN LAY IN BED, unable to sleep. She had been tired all day, and had spent the entire day preparing for her impending trip to New York. Yet despite all of that, she could not find sleep. She knew she needed to rest, and she knew she needed to speak to her son, to warn him about The Conclave and everything that went along with that. It had been her fault for neglecting for so long to warn him, to tell him the rules—and yet she had kept putting it off. She had wanted for so long, since he had first lost his childhood friends in middle school, for him to just have a normal life with a relationship and friends, that she had kept thinking that she would have all the time in the world—and now it would seem that that time was running out.

"Oh, Sheffield...." She looked at her wedding band in the dark and sighed. She wondered if, now that the Legacy had been broken, that her departed love—her soulmate—had finally found the peace he had not had in so long. She thought on those times, their life before the Legacy took him from her.

It was her marriage that had allowed she and Trevor to have friends, and feel as if they were part of the South Hill community. It was her marriage that had allowed Trevor a normal childhood, and it was his death at the hands of the family curse that had taken all of that away.

Since Christian's death, she and Lila Vasquez had rekindled their friendship—though it hadn't been easy in the beginning, and sometimes it still felt like a struggle. Kitty Hannifin, on the other hand, had been a different story; even though Cheri and Trevor were as inseparable as perhaps they had ever been before the initial falling-out, Kitty Hannifin didn't want anything to do with any of them. She had never really attempted to have friends, and now, it seemed, she had come to the conclusion that even acquaintances were too much of an effort.

"Shit!" Kathryn let out as her phone rang. She searched the night stand with her hand and took hold of the phone, lazily placing it to her ear. "Hello?"

"Kathryn." It was Magdalene.

"Is everything okay?" She could hear the panic in her voice as she spoke her name.

"The Conclave; they've been alerted." It was then that Kathryn heard a loud *clap!* on the floorboards out in the hall. "Kathryn?"

"Broom fell... someone's coming." She hung up the phone and sat up in bed, praying that Trevor would call. And if she hadn't heard from him by mid-morning, she would call him—and she wouldn't stop until he picked up the phone.

TREVOR AND BRAXTON laid in bed, having said good-night to everyone, and feeling relieved to finally have their home back to normal. They were drifting in a drunken haze, breathing in the scents of one another. Their pores were leaking out the mixed scents of cologne, nicotine, pot, and alcohol.

"Did you have a great time?" Braxton asked in a murmur, his fingers running absent-mindedly through Trevor's hair.

"I did."

"Am I forgiven?"

Trevor yawned and clung to him tightly. "For what?" he asked in the dark.

"For everything."

Trevor heard the slight break in his voice, and what he was certain was the catching of tears in his throat. It split Trevor's heart in two, and he hated to know that Braxton was feeling so much pain, that he had harbored so much guilt. He thought on the spell and hoped that it would work. He hoped that it would keep Benjamin at a distance, and that he and Braxton could return to the closeness that they had always possessed.

"You don't have to be forgiven. Everything you do will always be perfect, Braxton... you're everything to me."

Braxton chuckled and bent down and kissed the top of his head, breathing him in and caressing his arm. "And you're all I can see of tomorrow."

Chapter: Seventeen

CULTIVATE was the closest restaurant that they could find near campus that could appease their refined appetites. A campus eatery located in Elm Hall, it was focused on elevated Pacific Northwest cuisine with locally-sourced ingredients, offering an upscale dining experience to students, staff and faculty. It had a sleek modern setting, with deep mahogany varnish and retro white rain-drop lanterns that seemed to drip from the ceiling.

Cheri and Trevor sat across from one another at a rustic wood table in front of two large corner windows. The sun slipped through the glass in such a soft way that it was as if this too were nothing more than a painting or subtle light installation.

"So what? You had a completely empty, lust-filled attraction to another guy. You would never act on it, and that's what matters." Cheri sipped her fresh raspberry iced tea, which was filled with macerated raspberries floating in the sweet brew.

"I know that I would never act on it. It just scares me. I mean, I know I haven't exactly been a saint when it comes to the men in my life. I mean, Jesus, while in love with Christian, I fell in love with Braxton. Then when I was with Christian, I was still lusting after Braxton, and not wanting to give up Christian, and during all of that I was messing around with a fucking dead guy."

He could see the quick wash of horror come over Cheri's face, but like any well-taught South Hill debutante, she quickly dismissed it. "And when did all of that stop?"

"When I got with Braxton."

Cheri smiled and nodded in a way that said: *well, duh.* "Don't you see that's the point? You and Braxton got together, and none of that mattered anymore. Granted, you and Christian had split up..." *and died,* she wanted to say, but bit her lip. "And I don't think that will change. You two weren't just meant for each other, you were made for each other. You'll be fine."

He really wanted to believe that, but at this moment he wasn't so certain. "And what about you? How are things with you and Mr. Oliver?"

Cheri grinned and blushed, tucking her hair behind her ear and nodding. "Um, we're good, really good. I mean, it's all still new and every day is a fresh discovery; I just hope I don't fuck it up."

Trevor rolled his eyes and shook his head. "Why do you think you would? I mean, really, I don't think you have anything to worry about; that boy is hooked on the Hannifin train. I think that perhaps you have a little witchcraft yourself, girly."

Cheri laughed and shrugged. "Well I mean, look at *my* fucking track record. So far, the only experience I've had in a relationship was with Greg Sheer, and look what that was like. I mean, he was insane and abusive, and on top of that he got his ass possessed by a fucking ghost. I mean, Jesus Christ. I sometimes feel like I fucked him up. I was such a plotting-detached-conniving-bitch –"

"Stop it." Trevor placed his hand over hers. "You were hurting. No one could see it; no one ever looked, not even you. You carried so much for so long, trying to stay one step ahead of the rest of them, just so you wouldn't be thrown away like they threw me away. It must have been so exhausting."

It had been, but Cheri felt that nothing would make up for the things that she had done, the kind of person that she had been. For years, she was the reigning queen of South Hill's world of privileged, decadent youth—and in order to keep her throne, she had had to destroy many reputations and lives to simply survive. Nothing was going to be able to take that away, not even Trevor's forgiveness.

"Thank you."

Trevor smiled and kissed her fingers. "Everything will be all right, I promise."

It was then that they noticed something happening, something that began to stir the attentions of everyone in the restaurant and out on the streets. It had started subtly enough—a casting of shadow—but then it became much more dramatic, and soon Cheri and Trevor noticed the lanterns were burning brighter, and Trevor's skin began to spread with gooseflesh.

"What's going on?" Cheri asked, looking out of the window.

"We need to leave," Trevor responded with trembling words. "Now."

KATHRYN AND FRANCESCA Blackmoore stepped outside of Gary's department store, clutching matching Marc Jacobs hand bags and being followed by a female store assistant who carried their shopping bags to the town car, when they both felt the blood in their veins run cold. The sight of the sudden crowds gathering out along Holly filled them with dread. People in vehicles began stopping in the middle of the street to get out of their cars and simply stare at the sky, completely dumbfounded.

"The sun; it's..." Francesca began, finding her words falling short in the sudden and unnatural dark.

"Gone," Kathryn finished. They could both feel that there was something otherworldly about all of this, but never had their world spilled so dramatically into everyone else's. She knew she had to get to Trevor and Braxton. There was no question.

"I WANT YOU TO GET INSIDE your apartment and I want you to stay there. Don't leave until I call and say it's okay!" Trevor was shouting to Cheri as he dropped her off outside of her building. It had taken more than an hour through the traffic to get back to downtown from the other side of Lake Washington and in that time they had scanned the radios for some kind of explanation as to this sudden and unpredicted eclipse.

It was just confusion and reports began to come from all over that a sudden wave of panic and chaos was setting in-a fight or flight response-making everyone lose it. The streets were in pandemonium and riot teams were being dispatched everywhere.

"I don't understand!" Cheri shouted back, her voice and body trembling. "I don't want to leave you alone!" Trevor shook his head, looking around at the people beginning to lose all sense of control. Like the blackout of New York City in the Seventies, chaos was slowly mounting in the downtown streets.

A trash can was sent through the windows of a *GNC* by way of two reckless teenage boys, and others raced down the street to avoid the bicycle cops. Crowds were gathering in droves, some to take part in the growing mayhem and others to observe it with a mix of titillation and horror.

"Cheri, I need you safe and inside right now!"

She shook her head. "I'm not leaving you!"

Trevor was going to respond when he caught sight of another trash can being hurled in her direction by some idiot who had removed his shirt and stumbled, inebriated, while yelling belligerently about the end of the world.

"Cheri!" Trevor shouted. He summoned his witchcraft; if it was going to ever work for him when he wanted it to, then now was the time. Like the scope of a bird of prey he seemed to lock the trashcan in his gaze, seeing it and nothing else. He commanded it to stop and it did, then he ushered his head back towards the drunk man and the trashcan followed, slamming into him and knocking him back many paces. His head hit against the concrete wall of a building and he slipped to the ground, with the trashcan rolling down his legs and back onto the street.

Trevor climbed out of the Jag and ushered Cheri to the door of her building. A group of guys came rushing towards them, and just beyond them was the door. They, like the other guy, were obviously intoxicated. Trevor could only imagine what they would do to him and Cheri if they got ahold of them. He could feel that witchcraft stirring in his veins, like a humming, and that familiar sensation of tiny pinpricks raced along his spinal cord and surged through his brain.

Trevor shot his hand out and began to clutch his fingers together, inching them closer and closer. As he did, the five men began to choke and gasp for air before dropping to their knees and rolling onto the sidewalk, struggling for breath.

"Jesus!" Cheri let out, her brown eyes wide and her jaw hanging open.

Trevor got her to the door and kissed her on the cheek. "Don't leave this place until I call you!"

She nodded and raced inside. Trevor walked fast towards his car; he casually looked at the men choking on the ground and held out his hand, giving it a relaxed wave. "You're fine," he said to them without the slightest sound of concern for their well-being.

He got in his car and sped away from the curb and down the street, attempting to make his way through all of the people in one piece. There were just too many of them, and in the ensuing chaos the police were called in—hundreds of them, it seemed, all of them decked out in riot gear and lining up into the streets.

Police on horses followed in behind them, but by now so many had filled the streets and trash cans burned with great orange flames, and broken glass glittered on the streets all around them. It made Trevor think of the W.T.O. Riots of 1999. Even then it had terrified him: that swell of people losing control and police risking the boundaries of what they could and could not do, all in an effort to keep the peace. It made him think of what Abraham Van Helsing of *Dracula* once said: "We've all become God's madmen."

"Shit! I just need to fucking get home!" His cell phone was blaring and Trevor picked it up, hoping that it would be Braxton, but just as relieved when he saw that it was his mother. He wasn't certain if he was going to answer it, if that was even a wise decision, but it was her perspective that he needed. Braxton would be just as blind as he was to what was happening, but his mother wouldn't. Kathryn Blackmoore was always one step ahead of the game.

"Mom!" he shouted, answering the phone. "Mom, what's going on?" Someone lunged for his car and Trevor shot his hand out, forcing the unknown assailant through the air.

"Where are you?" she asked.

"I'm driving; I'm trying to get home. Mom, what the fuck is going on?" More people began to swell in numbers on the streets, and Trevor decided to keep his hand out and his eyes focused.

"Listen to me, listen carefully. Francesca and I are on our way; I want you to get home, lock your doors, and get into the study." He was trying to focus on what she was saying, but there was so much going on, and Trevor could feel the consternation rise in his veins. His heartbeats became erratic and he feared that he would never see his family, Braxton, or his friends ever again. "Trevor! Are you listening?"

"Uh-huh...." Two people this time, a boy and a girl clutching crowbars and running out into the middle of the street, nearly colliding with his car.

"There's that chest in the corner near the window. I want you to open it and remove two white candles and two black, then I want you to put them in a circle around you, the black to the north and south, the white in the east and west. There's a protection spell written by hand on a piece of parchment framed on the wall above the chest. Take it down, get in the circle, light the candles and say the spell—and don't leave that circle until I get there. Piss your pants if you fucking have to, but don't leave that circle!" The other end of the line cut off, and Trevor repeated "hello?" a few times before cursing at his phone and tossing it on the passenger seat

Almost home, he told himself with weary thoughts as he got closer to his building. *Almost home.*

CHERI WATCHED THE EVER-growing chaos from her apartment windows; with glass walls all around her, she had a perfect view of the destruction that was taking place in the streets. She was trying to process everything that she had seen. Trevor's knowledge that this was not natural, the fact that she herself could feel that this was something else—something darker, and speaking to all of those things that she had hoped would have been left behind in Bellingham.

She kept replaying what Trevor had done over and over again; it was a film that wouldn't stop. The way in which he had prevented that trashcan from hitting her, the power that he exuded over those men down on the street outside of her building. That power, whatever it was, was strong inside of him, and it had seemed as if it had taken over. He had nearly killed those men, closing their throats like that, as if he were strangling them all at the same time. She knew she had nothing to fear from him, but she worried that in the end he would have to fear himself.

There was a pounding on her front door, and Cheri jumped and cried out in alarm. She wasn't certain who it could be on the other side—or what was worse, what it could be. She thought of Greg after he had been possessed by Jonathan Marker: clutching to that shotgun, looking crazed—or how Jonathan had come to her in the form of Christian Vasquez, his head and side ebbing with blood, his flesh rotting before her terrified face. The door pounded again and she walked towards it cautiously, fearing that perhaps Tom Preston had once again returned from hell, seeking to finish what he had started.

"Who-who is it?" she called out, her words trembling with fear.

"Cheri, its J.T. Open up!" he demanded from the other side. Cheri smiled, relieved, and ran to the door, quickly turning the dead bolt and unlocking the doorknob. She threw it open, and he came in. He was like a glowing white knight: his broad shoulders and wide, concerned eyes. He opened his arms and she ran into them, clutching to him as if her life depended on it—and in a strange way, it seemed as if it did.

"Oh, thank God!" she let out, breathing in the scent of his skin and cologne, which perfumed his chest.

"Baby, it's okay," he began, petting her hair and kissing her forehead. "What the hell is going on out there?" Cheri shook her head. The truth was, she didn't know. She knew more than he did about it, of course, but she knew she couldn't tell him—and that he wouldn't believe it even if she did.

"I don't know; I don't know...." It was the only thing she could say. Though only half past two in the afternoon, it might as well have been two in the morning. Streetlights were now glowing around them, and the sun still refused to shine. They looked at it, seeing its white fire burn like a ring around the dark of the moon. It seemed as if hell had decided to open up and swallow the city whole.

BENJAMIN TRAMER STOOD on the terrace of his family's sprawling three-story, 9,410-square-foot mansion in the Highlands, overlooking Puget Sound and the Olympic mountains. Its aged white brick was draped in tiers of English ivy, and the ground beneath him was covered in rustic slate.

He sipped his scotch and looked out on the usually-glittering blue Olympic-size swimming pool, reached by a sweeping staircase of stone. Beyond the pool was the pool house, with its flat black roof and two chimneys on either side of it. Its white siding and glass walls showed its modern design with a set of retro black leather chairs and a sleek, massive table of glass.

The lights of the estate were on, gleaming like gems in the thick black. He could not help but think about how the dark of an eclipse was so much different from the dark of night, where the sky was draped in inky blue with twinkling stars. This was different; this was like a jar of black ink, thick and unseeable. It had taken over everything and thrown the entire city into a netherworld.

"The first move has been made." He turned, seeing his grandmother walk out, clutching to her cane, her aged face cracked with a smile. She wore a rotting wedding dress, the same she had worn since her intended husband had left her the morning of her wedding, never to meet her at the church, never to return to her again.

Her long, white-wire hair was pulled back and held together by the jeweled clip of her tattered veil. Her eyes were clear, like glass, the palest gray ever possible—though still, even to Benjamin, they seemed unnatural. "Have you yet chosen a side?"

Benjamin rolled his eyes and shook his head. "No, Grandma."

She nodded. "No, of course you haven't. But you will...." She began to chuckle, turning around and walking back into the mansion. "You will!" she repeated with a cackle, continuing like the warnings of Jacob Marley to Ebenezer Scrooge, haunting Benjamin though her presence had long ago faded.

He downed the rest of his scotch and shook down the burn of the alcohol. He could hear the chaos—far from the Highlands, but still, it carried. As he watched the sky fill with the sudden presence of clouds, he knew that strong magics were being worked and he needed to get back inside, far away from the devil's reach.

"OUT OF THE DEPTHS, I summon thee! Out of the darkest hells, I invoke thee!" Elisabeth Dianaca stood on her balcony, arms outstretched, and her brown curls billowing around her. A great fire blazed in the chic fire pit, to the left of the back doors overlooking downtown Seattle and Pike Place Market. Her black Marc Jacobs satin cocktail dress blew around her, and the fire reflected in her blue eyes with an intensity that would have chilled anyone's blood in a heartbeat.

"Great Set, hear me, oh exiled one, bringer of storms and chaos, I call to you to take advantage of this dark time; I petition your holy darkness!" She bent down and picked up an ancient

Egyptian urn, removing the lid and raising it high into the dark sky above the flames. "I offer to you the blood of a donkey, your sacred animal; its blood shall be offered up to you for your swift work!"

Elisabeth tipped the urn, watching the flames illuminate the faded design of the shirtless man with the crocodile head. It poured out, thick and crimson, spilling into the flames. The clouds filled the sky quickly, adding to the thick black.

Lightning flashed in the heavens like bursts of fire in the sky, and the boats and waves crashed against one another in the marina. "Bring forth the torments of their blood, bring forth the despair of their Legacy, and show the horrors of their dynasty! Obey me, Set! Obey me!"

The wind howled and the rains came, pouring down around her hard; like needles they tapped against her soft skin. The fire roared and ignited into a burst of flame, and then was gone. Elisabeth grinned triumphantly and walked back into the penthouse, dripping wet and her dress clinging tight to her sumptuous form, hoping that tonight the Blackmoores would fall and that she would be rewarded by the hellish god who wished to eradicate them.

TREVOR STEPPED THROUGH his front door, slamming it shut and locking it behind him. The windows were open, and he heard the commotion from the streets below: people screaming, police shouting, and tear gas fogging the streets in thick, noxious clouds. He wanted to be done with it; he wanted to be away from all of it.

Get to the library. He heard his mother's orders run again and again in his head. He dropped his bag to the floor and raced past the kitchen and down the hall, throwing open the doors and stepping inside. It was cold, cold in a way that was unnatural, and he watched his breath plume in front of him. He felt his veins constrict and his limbs begin to ache at the chill that seemed to envelop the room.

'Trevor....' He heard the whisper. It was around him, above him, beneath him. It was everywhere that he was, and yet nowhere at all. It was ominous and threatening; it was everything a whisper should never be. And he knew then that he was with unnatural things—evil things, things that had only one goal in mind: to kill him.

"Leave me alone!" he shouted to the empty walls, to shadows he knew were not lifeless. He spotted the chest in the corner and ran to it, hopping over the coffee table and nearly tripping on his own feet.

'Trevor....' It was closer now, though he wasn't certain how he knew this. He just knew that it was. He could sense it; he could feel its fingers on him, caressing him, as if it were a butcher and he was the rabbit being stroked before the blade came down swiftly on the neck, severing head from spine and spilling blood on the block. He ignored it and flipped the trunk open, finding an assortment of occult items waiting to be used. He sifted through the collection of candles and found the four that he needed, clutching onto them for dear life.

He stood and closed the lid to the trunk, seeing the spell framed on old parchment on the wall, just as his mother had said. Trevor breathed a sigh of relief as he reached for it, curling his fingers underneath the black frame and beginning to lift it from off the hook in the wall.

He felt a firm, cold hand grasp the back of his neck, and those icy fingers seemed to be burning into his flesh, reaching into the jugular itself.

'I don't think so, faggot!' He turned and locked eyes with Greg Sheer, rotting and stinking behind him. His eyes yellowed and bulging from his sockets, his skin gray-blue and pustular, his right cheek eaten away, and his buzzed golden hair was dull and there were exposed crevices in his skull.

Trevor only managed the first half of a gasp before he was tossed across the room, dropping the candles with a thud but still clutching to the spell.

He collided with the table, cracking the back of his skull on the sharp corner. He didn't have time to worry about that because Greg was on him, moving towards him like a lion about to kill a wounded gazelle.

"Shit!" Trevor stood and ran towards the door, only to watch it slam shut and Christian Vasquez step out from behind it. He too was rotting, putrid, and just like Greg, there was the lust for blood in his eyes.

'You know I wanted you to be a part of me always, and now you can be...' the spirit said with a grin, running his tongue across the top of his lip.

"No...." Trevor backed away, watching both Greg and Christian advance on him. He shoved his hand in his pocket, the other still holding the spell. He pulled out his lighter and charged Greg. Trevor dropped to the floor and slid between Greg's legs and made his way towards the candles, which lay in a bundle on the ground.

They both turned and looked at him, these two former gods of Mariner, now rotting demons from hell. All that he had ever thought they had been was now nothing more than ghosts of his past life—and with all ghosts, eventually you give them up. He moved the candles around him and lit the flames, followed with a piece of his hair, which he tore from his head and spread about him.

They were only inches away, the flames glowing bright in those black pools. "By the water that flows to the air that blows, by the fire that burns to the earth that grows, this circle is formed, its protection is sewn!" Christian and Greg stopped at the candles. They attempted to reach for him, but their rotting hands could not move past the flames.

'You think you can hide from us?' They began laughing, their eyes burning into him. Trevor whimpered and slid away from them, clutching his knees with his arms.

'We are your past, your present, and your future. We are all that you are; our existence is all that you will ever be, and your soul already bears our names!' The tears slipped down Trevor's face, and he closed his eyes as tight as he could and tried to shake the sound of their voices from his ears.

"Stop it, please; God, STOP IT!" It was then that he heard a laugh. It was sinister, and yet familiar. It was a laugh that he never thought he would have to hear again.

'All in due time, my son....' Trevor looked into Tom Preston's corpse-like demonic face and screamed.

HE HEARD IT BY THE time he reached the door. It was Trevor's scream. Nothing in the world could shake him more; nothing else in the world could trigger the rush of adrenaline like that could, and his hand was on the door, turning the key quickly. It was then that he saw it in one quick vision. He saw Trevor inside the apartment, hiding in the study, surrounded by candles which burned brightly. In his sixth sight he could see the energy that surrounded him: glistening rings of red, white fire acting as a barrier that pulsated from the floor to the ceiling, keeping three figures at bay.

He gasped when in this clarity he saw the faces of Greg, Tom, and Christian surrounding him, though he could see in this vision that they were wraiths, familiars, demon spawns that only took their forms. "Trevor, I'm coming!" His brows furrowed and he threw the door open, racing down the hall towards the library. It would not open. "The door; it won't budge!" He heard laughter on the other side.

"Braxton!" Trevor yelled.

He threw his hands against the door and concentrated, summoning that power, power he had not exerted since the death of his father. It was a chilling reunion with his witchcraft, but at the moment he could not worry about these memories. They were only shadows, and they vanished once they were faced with the light.

He felt the mild pulse move through his hands like a burst of electricity, and the door imploded from its center. Those monsters faced him, and past their glowering faces was Trevor, keeping his eyes closed and paying no mind to the tears that moved down his face.

"Get away from him!" he commanded.

They grinned, and then he heard laughter from behind. It was familiar, an echo of his own. No, not an echo; it was the originator. It was where his laughter came from; it was his father's laugh.

He turned, his eyes widening, his heart pumping blood at an erratic pace. Braxton tried to tell himself that it wasn't real, that his father did not stand before him, rotting away. He was trying to stay grounded, telling himself that these were evil spirits working for some greater-evil force, a force that could take many forms and devour them from beneath.

'Don't you have a hug for Daddy?' Braxton stepped back, forgetting about those beings that stood behind him, almost forget-

ting Trevor. Almost. He heard him whisper his name: *come back to me*, he had said.

"NO!" Braxton sung behind him, taking Greg by surprise; his hand went right through the thing. It laughed, and the being guised as Greg returned the punch and was able to connect with Braxton's face. The blow sent him to his knees. He stumbled, shook his head, and tasted the blood from his split lip.

He maneuvered around them, knowing that all he had to do was get into the circle that he could pass— and their spirit forms, no matter how corporeal, would not allow them to cross that barrier.

Braxton focused on what he was doing and he moved, racing artfully towards Trevor.

So close, he said to himself, *so close.*

It was then, in that moment when his foot crossed the threshold, that he felt that firm, icy grip on the back of his head, pulling on his hair and threatening to tear it from his skull.

He let out a grunt, and was hurled into the bookcase. The strength with which he was thrown was substantial, the muscles so controlled, backed by so much speed, that when he collided with the bookcase it cracked, and two of the shelves broke as books cascaded to the hardwood alongside of him.

"Braxton!" He didn't budge. Trevor didn't think about it; he didn't consider what he was risking. He abandoned the circle and raced to Braxton's side. He placed his hands on him and closed his eyes. He could feel the pain inside of his body; it was evident in the way his muscles tensed, the way in which he bit his lip and struggled to speak.

He turned to look in Trevor's eyes, and in those eyes Trevor saw everything that he could ever be, everything that he had ever been. In Braxton's eyes was his past, his present, and his future: a future that he needed to protect.

"Only spirits..." Braxton forced out.

"What?"

Braxton fought for the words again. "They're only spirits."

Trevor was trying to register, and then he was understanding. They were spirits. It didn't matter who they were; it didn't matter what form they took, if they were really who they looked like or not. It didn't matter if they came from heaven or hell, if they were demons or fairies; none of that mattered. In the end, they were shadows of the other world, and Trevor could talk to shadows.

They were close, their eyes bloodthirsty, but Trevor no longer seemed to notice. He closed his eyes and took a deep breath. He could feel the current move through him, the power, and he lifted his eyes slowly, looking at them but not seeing them. He was seeing through them, as if they no longer mattered.

"No," he said. They laughed and continued to move towards the two boys. "Stay still." They stopped and laughed. They attempted to move again, but they could not. "Stay where you are," he commanded once more, and the entities were frozen.

He turned his attention back to Braxton who was still on the floor, but breathing. "Good job," he said.

Trevor's eyes were misted with tears. "Oh, are you okay?"

Braxton grinned and nodded. "Never better, stud." He buried his head quickly in Braxton's chest and wiped his tears on his breast. "It's okay, I promise; help me sit up."

Trevor nodded and reached out for him, noting absentmindedly that his skin was just as soft but paler than his boyfriend's, as if for the first time seeing that Braxton was tanned.

He propped his leg up and stretched out the other, resting his arm across his knee. He stared into Trevor with those large dark eyes, his snug red tee damp with sweat. His forehead glistened, and his black hair was wet as well. "You okay, kid?"

Trevor nodded. "You?"

Braxton chuckled and nodded as well. "Just spiffy!" He turned and looked at those things, at how they did not move. He sighed. "What about them?"

Trevor shook his head. "They're not going anywhere," he grinned devilishly. "No, sir."

The flames of the candles still burned and Braxton looked at them, widening his lids ever so slightly, and as he did, that force pulsed from him ever so slightly, and the flames were extinguished. "I think I could get used to this."

A terrifying sound moved from the throat of the monster guised as Christian Vasquez, as if it knew that of all of them to speak, this one would be the most unsettling.

'It is not over. The darkness shall persist, and the city shall be chaos, and then the world. All of this shall be our reckoning.'

Trevor rolled his eyes, still luminescent from tears, still sniffling from the crying. "Where did you come from?" Trevor asked, seeing the spirits attempt to defy him, trying to use their will to overpower his own.

'We're yours....'

Trevor gasped and lost his concentration, losing his control over them the second he heard that voice, that voice that had stayed with him in the secret places of his heart. It was the voice of his father.

"No!" Trevor began to shake, seeing Sheffield Burges come into view from somewhere in the shadows. The lightning flashed and the fires from the streets began to grow, bathing everything in orange. The entities laughed and began to advance on them.

"Trevor, it's not real!" Braxton shouted, gripping him, trying to get him to look away. "Trevor, focus!" Nothing. Trevor's eyes were locked on the rotting face of his father, smelling his decay, seeing the skin that had rotted away in the cheek, exposing the bone and teeth. "Fuck!" He took hold of Trevor and tried to move him, but it was too late.

'Stay a while...' Greg said, moving too fast for Braxton to see. His open hand shot out and sent Braxton into the wall, splitting him from Trevor.

'It's time to come with us, Trevor; you've been a very, very naughty little boy...' Sheffield said to him. All of them began to circle Trevor, moving closer and closer to him. Braxton's eyes grew wide, his bangs falling in his face, dripping with sweat, his muscles tensing. He closed his eyes and charged at them, throwing his arms up and tucking them in front of his chest, barreling into Eric and Christian, breaking their chain and taking hold of Trevor.

"We're getting out of here now!" Trevor was disoriented, and Braxton knelt down in front of him. Trevor wrapped his arms around his neck and fixed his legs around his waist. Braxton slipped his arms under Trevor's knees, piggy-backing him as he charged down the hall and towards the living room, seeing the kitchen and the table in front of them. Just beyond them was the front door.

It happened so fast. First there was the form of Greg Sheer coming around the corner, then the kick in his backside. The force of it was strong, super-human, and it sent Braxton and Trevor through the air and into the dining table. Braxton went through the table, and Trevor went someplace else, someplace far away from his reach. In that same distance, he heard the sound of glass breaking. He was battered, bruised, and bloody. He was finding it hard to move, to get his hands and feet to work; it seemed that everything ached.

'Who knew the chosen ones would be so easy to kill...?' Tom said, as Christian stepped over Braxton, placing his boot on his arm and stepping on it, forcing the bones to separate.

"FUCK!" Braxton wailed, and Christian laughed, taking hold of Braxton's hair and yanking his head up.

'You're going to watch him die first....' He pointed to Trevor, who lay amongst broken glass and pooling blood. He had fallen through the coffee table; the glass that he had heard breaking was from the tabletop. Sheffield and Greg were nearing Trevor. What was left of their faces was contorted into grins, and every step made Braxton's heart quicken. *'The heavens shall bleed tonight....'*

"Get away from my fucking son!"

Braxton closed his eyes, and the tears slipped down his face when he heard Kathryn's voice. The spirits guised as Greg and her dead husband were sent through the air. He summoned his last leg of strength to get himself to his feet, ignoring the pain that inflamed him, using it instead to drive him, to get himself out of Christian's grasp and back away. He looked to see Kathryn and Francesca standing there, immaculate as always, and their eyes seemed to burn with intensity, and the two women reached out and clasped hands.

They were someplace far away, someplace ancient, someplace that flowed with the power of their bloodline, tapping into a power that he and Trevor had never touched; perhaps they didn't even have access to it.

"Ancients, come forth, open the gates and collect these wraiths, expel them, and send them away."

Braxton watched the entities begin to tremble, but not from fear. It was something else, as if an electric current had begun to course through their bodies.

"Nameless of the named, damndest of the damned, soul-eaters, tormentors, the coldest of the cold, we command you, we compel you. Collect these demons, remove them from our sight, expel the darkness and return the light!"

The spirits cried out; it broke the windows and the glass of the cabinets. Everything fragile exploded, and they were gone, as if they had never been there in the first place, their only indication being the destruction that remained in their wake.

"Trevor!" Braxton shouted, racing to his boyfriend. He was covered in cuts, and there was blood, a lot of blood. "Oh, God!" He could see Trevor's eyes flicker in and out of consciousness, and he was gasping for breath.

"It's cold," he managed. Braxton rolled him over and found a shard of glass sticking in his side.

"Trevor; please, babe, stay with me!"

Francesca was calling for an ambulance and arguing with them on the phone, her voice panicked.

"Trevor, please!" Kathryn pleaded; the tears were spilling down her face. "Honey, stay with us; don't close your eyes."

"Mama..." he managed, trying to keep his eyes open.

"I'm here, baby." She ran her fingers through his hair. "I'm here."

Braxton held tight to his hand and brought it to his face. "Trevor, don't leave me, please! Trevor, I'll die without you!"

"Damn it!" Francesca threw the phone across the room. "The ambulance," she began, pushing her hair from her face. "They said they can't get anyone out here, not with everything that's going on!"

"Then we'll fucking take him!" Kathryn said. "But first, we need to get that out of him and get him bandaged up!" She stood, and Braxton let go of Trevor long enough to wipe the tears from his eyes. His arm was at the very least dislocated, but it didn't matter; he ignored the pain and slipped his arms under Trevor, lifting him carefully off the ground and holding him close.

"All right, this is going to hurt, but I need you to be brave, okay?"

Trevor gave a groan, and Braxton shook his head and then counted to three. He gripped the glass and pulled it from Trevor's side. A guttural cry escaped his throat, and the blood began to pour out of him like a fount.

"Shh, it's okay; it'll be okay," Kathryn said to her son as she placed a towel to the wound and applied pressure. Francesca raced from the bathroom holding surgical tape from the First Aid kit, which they quickly wrapped tightly around him.

Kathryn stood and wiped the tears from her eyes, smearing her son's blood across her face. "Let's go!"

They raced down to the garage, Braxton tossing the key of Trevor's Jag to Kathryn. Braxton raced over to his Mercedes and managed to get the door unlocked. He put Trevor in first and then raced over to the driver's side. With his injured hand he gripped the wheel, and the other he kept on Trevor. They sped out of the garage quickly, and though there were rioters and police on horses in the streets, Braxton didn't care. He would run them all down if he had to. He needed to get to Swedish Medical Center; he needed to get Trevor fixed up. He needed to save him, and everyone else could go to hell.

"Stay with me, babe, stay with me!" He honked his horn and sped, moving up the streets, getting closer and closer to Broadway.

"I'm so cold..." he responded. His body was trembling, and his lips were turning blue. Braxton tried to ignore the fact that touching Trevor's skin was like touching ice. He tried to focus on what was ahead of him, but it seemed that even now that he was reaching 110, it still wasn't fast enough, and the chaos around them only grew.

"Remember when we danced together in your room before homecoming in the eleventh grade? I know I said it was practice for my date, but it wasn't; I just wanted to dance with you. The truth is, I didn't take anyone to the dance with me, I stayed home too."

Trevor managed to open his eyes ever so slightly.

"You never knew this, but I used to follow you home every day in the seventh grade, just to make sure that Greg and all of those other assholes wouldn't hurt you. Just to make sure you got home safely." Trevor managed a slight, almost untraceable smile.

He was now at 140, and it took him a second to realize why he hadn't hit anyone; it was because Kathryn and Francesca were forcing people out of the way as they kept behind him. He reached the emergency vehicle entrance of the hospital and braked it. The tires screeched, but the car came to a smooth halt.

"We're here," Braxton said to Trevor.

He hopped out of the car and raced over to Trevor, taking hold of him once again and carrying him quickly towards the entrance. He shouted to Francesca, telling her that he left the keys in the ignition and to park his car. She yelled "okay," but he didn't hear her; all he could hear was his own thundering heart.

"Help us!" he cried out, looking at all of the faces around him, all of those eyes that returned his frantic gaze with shock and horror. "Someone help us!" he called again, sobbing, his knees beginning to buckle. A nurse raced over to him, calling for a gurney and an I.V., and for other things that he didn't understand.

"What happened?" the young man asked.

"We were trying to get home; we live downtown. Everything happened so quickly. I was trying to protect him from rioters, but we were attacked. I got thrown into a bench, and he went through a window; I think my arm is broken." He laid Trevor on the gurney and watched them begin to attend to him, his eyes moving erratically.

"Please save him!" He watched them take him away, crowding him, moving him beyond his reach. He followed him to another set of double-doors, but he could go no further. Then there was nothing. Time didn't matter; his pain didn't matter. The faces around him contained no life, and the words that came from those mouths were just sound, inaudible and annoying.

"Trevor! Trevor!" Braxton turned to see Kathryn and Francesca enter the waiting room. Kathryn's face and hands were covered in her son's blood, the crimson like a mess of paint on her milky skin, both women's eyes searching, wide and darting around the waiting room.

"They took him in the back already," Braxton said, holding himself and the tears staining his face. The only places that were free of the blood were the places where his tears had streaked his cheeks.

"And they haven't attended to you yet?" Francesca asked.

He shook his head. "Not yet." The place was bedlam as more people injured from the riots came in.

"We should be back there. You should be back there!" Kathryn said. She was about to walk up to the admitting window when a short Asian nurse came out from the doors that led to the emergency room and approached them.

"Did you come with the patient?"

They all looked at her and nodded. "Yes, my son. Trevor."

The nurse nodded. "He's lost a lot of blood. We're going to do some blood work now, but he needs a transfusion. What's his blood type?"

Braxton shook his head, and they all looked at Kathryn. "He's A-positive."

"Okay," the nurse said. She turned her attention back to Braxton. "And you—you need to come with me so we can get you in for x-rays and get you fixed up." Braxton nodded and began to follow them.

"Wait!" Kathryn shouted. They turned and looked at her.

"Yes?" the nurse asked.

"Braxton and my son should not be alone. Let us come back there."

"Not right now. You need to wait out here. We need to stabilize your son and get him stitched up." Kathryn felt helpless, and they could see it plainly on her face. Braxton didn't care at this point. He just wanted to get back there and get to Trevor, to be as close to him as possible.

"But—" Francesca began, but the nurse gave an adamant shake of her head.

"Right now it's critical that we get him the blood he needs. We can't have anyone back there right now who isn't a patient. It's chaos. Please, just stay here."

Braxton looked at Kathryn and Francesca and shook his head in defeat. There was no point in arguing anymore. He understood where they were coming from—especially Kathryn, who was so used to being in control and fixing everything. But there was no time for any of that.

"All right." Kathryn threw her hands up in the air, and she and her cousin watched as Braxton disappeared behind those doors. They kept their eyes on him through the glass in the doors as they watched him vanish down the harshly-lit corridor.

Braxton looked at the blood on his hands, the blood that stained his shirt, and he continued to sob. There he was: his boyfriend, his other half, his best friend, his family, all over him in bright red. He was covered in that blood—blood that was his own—blood that in so many ways was so powerful, but was now nothing more than the symbol of the life that may be lost for good.

Though people screamed in pain and begged for drugs and mercy, it was all growing distant. He couldn't hear any of it anymore. There were just his thoughts, and the replaying of everything that had happened in the apartment.

For now, everything was quiet.

Chapter: Eighteen

MABEL HAD BEEN SOMEPLACE else. Mary was certain that the old woman was still in the manor, but there was no sign of her in any of the rooms. She had been watching the news all day. She hadn't thought about her drive home with Rebecca from the party the night before, or the strange, preoccupied silence that seemed to take over her for the rest of the night. She had woken up in Rebecca's bed, smelling those curls and feeling the soft skin against her. She had slipped out of the condo quickly and quietly and raced home, calling in to the university and requesting a personal day.

She had had a dream of the world growing dark, of the ground opening and the fires of hell raging, consuming everything that lived. She didn't know why this had been as unsettling as it was, not until the sun was eclipsed and the city of Seattle began to burn.

She thought of Trevor and Braxton, thought about what they meant to the family, to things that for the longest time she had separated herself from, which she had seen as an American Blackmoore problem—that if she ignored it, then it would not touch her. But the truth was that it was her problem. It was the problem of anyone who carried Blackmoore blood, no matter how small the amount.

She wanted to talk to Mabel, to Kathryn or Francesca. She wanted to talk to any of these women who understood their witchcraft with more clarity than she could ever give it, because she had ignored it for so long, hoping to pray it away.

She sat curled up on the couch in the front parlor, in a knitted gray sweater-dress. Her hair was pulled back from her face, and her green eyes began to drift from the television to the music room. The pocket door was cracked enough that she could see the aged violin sitting against the armchair. She thought of that spirit Michael, the spirit that she knew was somewhere in this house, somewhere in its cracks and crevices.

She felt that if anything had the answers to what could be going on, then perhaps it would be this spirit, this boy who had made himself known to her, trusting her to show himself. Part of her told her that this was wrong. It was a sin to commune with the dead, an even bigger sin to summon them on your own, but she knew that she needed to ignore that logic. She was a witch; this was her birthright, and this was in her blood.

She took a deep breath and rose from the couch, creeping up on that door and poking her head in, pushing it aside slowly, as if afraid that she were going to be interrupting someone on the other side of the door. She tiptoed in, glancing at her reflection in the mirror. For a second she thought she saw the white face and the black liquid sockets of the boy, but when she looked again it was just her own mousy face that stared back at her.

"Get yourself together." She sighed and pulled her hair back behind her in frustration. "How the hell am I even supposed to do this?"

She stared down at that violin, and it seemed to be singing to her. It was humming, calling out to her as her own instrument had always done. It stirred her blood and it seemed that every piece of her being, every cell, was becoming alive, rising and coursing through her. She could feel the pull and the need, and she found herself drawing ever so closer to the thing.

She paused and looked at her own reflection once again in that ornate mirror, seeing the wide eyed terror look back at her. She noted that it seemed as if her hands were shaking, but when she looked at them they were steady at her side.

What's happening? She could feel what seemed to be tremors, electrical pulses moving through her hands, and yet they remained still. It was the same sensation she always felt when she played.

The darkness that had overtaken the city had not subsided, and though midday, it seemed as if it were midnight, and her dream would not let go of her. She knew, though she wasn't certain how, that this violin and the dead boy who haunted this house all held keys to this occurrence. As her steps drew closer she could feel it pulling her, as if she had no choice. She told herself to turn around, to close the pocket door and leave it alone to sit in the silence of the music room, but she could not. With every step, her blood began to sing and that tingling, that heat in her hands, only seemed to increase the closer to the instrument she came.

"What am I doing?" she asked aloud, hearing her own voice echo off the walls and return to her. She heard the spitting fountain out in the courtyard and looked to it, seeing the water gleam in what little light radiated from the sun's ring around that black moon, and the great darkness began to impress upon her the importance of this task. She was a Blackmoore, a witch from a line of powerful witches, and it was her blood, her inheritance which commanded her now. She understood that she had an obligation, a duty, to see this through.

She picked up the bow with her right hand, and slipped the dark cherry-wood instrument under her chin. There was no turning back. She closed her eyes and laid bow to strings, beginning the Allegro Moderato, and as she played it her cells seemed to awaken. The power she felt, the hum stirring inside of her, the heat rising in her, the familiar heat that always seemed to move through her when she played, now felt stronger, as if the clear intent of her witchcraft, the place she had always known it had come from, was now growing to a fever pitch—and she was playing like she had never played before.

Not in all the years that she had commanded the violin, not in all the practices, the concerts with her sister Natalie; this was something new, something untapped, and the violin felt hot, as if the strings were burning. As she reached the song's pinnacle, that heat forced her eyes open, and it rushed out of her in one great wave of force.

One by one the lamps blinked out, until she was lit with nothing more than the great chandelier above her, which then blinked out as well, and the clock began to chime. "Saints above, protect me," she whispered.

There was a strange sound, as if something were cracking. She searched around frantically, until her eyes fell on the window and she found its source. To her disbelief, the waters pouring from the fountain began to harden, to freeze, until it was all ice, and the air around her became thin and grew cold.

"What have I done?" She crossed herself and reached into her pocket for her rosary, which she brought to her lips, closing her eyes and beginning to back out towards the front parlor.

She sat the bow and violin down in the chair in front of the ornate circular table in the middle of the room, watching as her breath began to form in front of her, and the last chime rang at thirteen.

She turned around and felt her knees buckle, and no sound escaped her lips as her heart raced and her blood ran cold. There before her was the spirit, the young Michael Donovan staring back at her. His liquid black eyes, endless and yet gentle, looked on her, and his alabaster skin seemed luminescent, and yet he was real enough to touch. He was dressed in black trousers with a matching jacket; the white shirt with its propped collar and black silk tie, popular in the early part of the twentieth century, made him look all the more out-of-place.

Mary couldn't believe it. She had summoned his spirit, the boy from her dreams. The boy, whose music flowed with an ethereal mastery that not even she could ever hope to produce, was now before her. He had sought her out; she knew this. This was all meant to be. There was something the boy needed to say, and she was the only one who could understand the message, because it was in the music that he could reveal his secrets.

"What do you want with me?" she managed to ask, her voice quivering with excitement and fear.

The spirit did not blink, and he seemed as if he were made of stone, and when he began to move his lips to speak, it was as if they were not moving at all.

'Much....'

BRAXTON AND TREVOR *walked through the hallway locked hand in hand, Braxton's eyes always* en garde, *daring anyone to say anything in regards to them. They had returned from winter break a confirmed couple, to the shock of everyone at Mariner, who were still reeling from the deaths of Christian Vasquez, Teri Jules, and Greg Sheer. Overnight the two of them, along with Cheri, had become the talk of the school as the foundations of the Mariner hierarchy seemed to be cracking beneath everyone's feet.*

The students had all assumed that as Queen Bee, no longer shrouded by Christian's shadow, she would take her rightful place, and rule the school with the ferocity and calculated, cruel determination that everyone had come to expect from Cheri—but she was having none of it. When they had returned to the school after the New Year, everything had changed; the one person who they had expected to pick up the pieces and dictate through example how everyone else was to behave, was not doing so.

Cheri spent her time with Trevor and Braxton, and rarely breathed a word to anyone else. She was Vice President of the Student Body, and yet when the time came to assume the position left empty by the deceased Vasquez, she had declined it and dropped out of Student Council altogether. She had moved like a ghost—all three of them had, for the first few weeks of the new semester—and it left everything that had stood as the legacy of Mariner High School in complete disarray. But by spring everything had seemed to return to a sense of normalcy, and a certain ease had seemed to spread throughout the halls. Everyone was relaxed, even the three of them.

"They still talk about us, you know?"

Braxton looked at Trevor and nodded. "I know. I don't care, though; do you?"

Braxton was wearing a navy deep-V tee with a gray knit cap on his head. There was a Tiffany's diamond-encrusted key hanging from his neck. It had been a gift from Trevor for Christmas, which he had forgotten about and didn't remember to give him until they were on the plane, returning home from Brighton's funeral. His quads were big and strong and looked good the way his black 5'11's clung to them, and he smelled of Old Spice and Burberry Brit.

Trevor glanced down at the floor and shrugged. "Sometimes; not really for what they have to say about me. I mean, I'm used to being talked about behind my back, but in regards to you, yeah."

Braxton gave him an exaggerated pout, and his dark puppy dog eyes caused Trevor to grin. "Well, then, I think we should really give them something to talk about!"

Trevor playfully protested as Braxton put his arms around him and lifted him off the ground. He pressed his lips to Trevor's and kissed him deeply. Trevor felt the blood stir in his veins, and it seemed that the entire hallway began to spin. When he touched back down, he still felt as if he were floating.

"You, sir, are a devil!" Trevor laughed, and punched Braxton casually on the chest.

"Only because you bring it out of me," he replied with a grin, kissing him once again on the cheek. They both heard the chorus of whispers that followed, but neither one cared. They had a lot more important things to worry about besides a bunch of narrow-minded teenagers.

"So, you wanna go to that?" Trevor asked.

"To what?"

Trevor cocked his head in the direction of the wall. "To that." There on the wall was an advertisement for the Senior Ball, which was going to be held at the History Museum in downtown.

"Why? You know I don't go to those things."

"Because I'm going to go. Cheri made a commitment to help with the dance committee. Apparently Student Council still needed her assistance, and she asked me to help her with it, so I'll be there. Besides, you went last year with that Michelle girl...."

Braxton gave an understanding nod, which then slowly gave way to a slow shake of the head. "Yeah, no, still not going to go." Trevor frowned and dropped his head. "Gotta get to class!"

"But –"

"We'll talk later!" Braxton pecked him quickly on the cheek and ran off down the hall to European History, grinning to himself.

TREVOR HADN'T SPOKEN to him for days. After spending the better part of two weeks trying to plead and beg him to go to the

dance, he had finally given up, and no longer answered his phone or came to the door. Braxton sighed, looking at his phone, displaying only missed calls from J.T., Becky, and other friends—but none from Trevor. He knew that in a short matter of time everything would be better again, and they'd be back to the way they always were. He knew that what he was doing was going to make Trevor extremely happy, but it still didn't change the fact that even his best intentions were still fucking everything up.

He walked into the museum. The former Courthouse with its tall red spires and numerous floors didn't seem like the place for a dance, and yet as he walked up the steps and handed the girl at the table his student I.D. and ticket, he could see the dance taking shape in front of him.

Classmates and their dates, all dressed in their best formalwear moved throughout the main floor, dancing slowly to chasing Cars *by Snow Patrol. He walked in, wearing his new Ben Sherman suit and a boutonniere. He searched the museum-turned-dance floor nervously, his dark eyes falling over everything as he made his way to the room on the left, near the stage where the deejay was set up.*

He saw J.T. spinning Cheri on the dance floor. The light caught in the diamond Harry Winston tiara and matching tennis bracelet, and her custom plum satin Versace gown made her look like a princess. As J.T. dipped her, Braxton's eyes caught with hers, and she looked him up and down and smiled, and pointed one perfectly-plum fingernail over towards the corner by the deejay booth.

Braxton looked over and saw Trevor standing there, his arms folded across his chest. His short wine-red hair shone in the light, and Braxton thought he looked beautiful in the black Burberry tux and bow-tie that he had dragged Braxton with him to pick up three weeks before.

He smiled and mouthed "thank you" to Cheri as he made his way over to Trevor, who was swaying slowly to the music. Braxton grinned as he drew closer, noting how amazing he looked. He felt his heart race as if he were about to speak to Trevor for the first time ever, as if they had never exchanged a single word before. His smile quickly faded as soon as he saw the tears in his hazel eyes, making them look like brilliant liquid emeralds.

Trevor leaned himself against the wall and turned to face the corner of the room, putting his back to everyone at the dance. He felt bad. He knew that Trevor was regretting having come at all.

Fuck.... Braxton moved closer to him, knowing that Trevor was either missing him desperately, or cursing him as hard as he could in his head.

"I hope you saved me a dance." Trevor whipped around, and their eyes met. Braxton felt his heart dropping in his gut as he looked into those tear-filled eyes, their green reflecting in the colored lights that danced around them and shone on oil paintings of the Northwest and the early foundations of Bellingham.

"What are you doing here?" Trevor asked, sniffling and attempting to wipe the tears from his face.

"It's my failed attempt at a surprise." He dropped his head towards the ground, and lifted his eyes back up to meet Trevor's tear-stained face.

"What?"

Braxton nodded. "Yeah, I planned this all along... since, you know, I had you practice-dance with me last year, and then I took Michelle whatever-her-name-is to the Spring Ball... I wanted to surprise you."

Trevor chuckled and wiped away more tears. "I really hate surprises."

Braxton smiled and removed the plastic container with the boutonniere inside. "I got this for you." He lifted it to Trevor's face, before opening it up and pulling out the tulip with the darkest of purple petals. "It's a black tulip."

Trevor nodded and grinned as he allowed Braxton to pin it to his jacket. "It's my favorite flower...."

The tears came again, and Braxton was quick to bring his hand to his face and brush the saline away from his eyes gently with his thumbs.

"I know, baby." He pulled Trevor into him, bringing his lips to his forehead and then his cheek. "I know."

"I never thought you'd come," Trevor let out, clutching tightly to Braxton and smelling him and caressing the back of his head.

"So, if I remember correctly, I still owe you a dance."

Trevor laughed and nodded, allowing Braxton to lead him out to the middle of the dance floor. "You owe me about a hundred."

"Yeah." Braxton put his arms tightly around him, and Trevor rested his head against his shoulder. They moved in silence, listening to the music as Chasing Cars played on. Braxton never wanted this moment to end. He didn't want to return to any life where they were in danger; he just wanted them to stand in this spot forever, moving to the music.

"You know, Trevor, you're not like other boys..." he said softly. Trevor looked up at him, and their eyes met for just a moment as he smiled, before drawing his face back to his shoulder.

"Yes, I am," he whispered back. In that moment, he realized that perhaps Trevor was. If he could take away the spirits and the witchcraft, all that would remain was this gentle young man with a fragile heart.

"No," Braxton began, drawing Trevor's face towards his own. "You're better."

They kissed and Braxton spun him around, clutching to him tightly, both boys' eyes shut, with serene looks on their faces. They kept dancing on, as if they were the only ones and no one else. It was just the music, the dim lights, and the paintings that surrounded them; for Braxton, in this moment, nothing could be greater.

"HEY, I FIGURED YOU could use some coffee." Braxton looked up and rubbed his eyes, offering a grateful smile to Cheri as she handed him the *Caffé Vita* cup. "I got you a latte with an extra shot." She smiled back. Braxton could see the pain in her eyes as her gaze drifted from his face over to Trevor, who was lying in the hospital bed, his scars now bandaged up. His face looked peaceful, though Braxton figured that everyone in a coma looked this way.

"Thank you." He sat with his leg propped up in the chair by Trevor's bedside, listening to the steady *beep* of the heart monitor.

"Any changes?" she asked, setting her Louis Vuitton canvas bag down on the bedside table. She was dressed in a black Diane von Furstenberg wrap dress and a Cartier necklace, made of white gold, diamonds, emeralds, and black onyx, with a pendant of a panther, resting between her breasts. He smiled to himself that even in times of crises, Cheri still managed to look immaculate.

"None. I keep waiting for him to wake up, to just open his eyes and tell me he's not moving until he gets some coffee. They say right now it's touch-and-go." Braxton thought again of the memory of the Senior Ball and laughed, while fighting back the tears that threatened to come. "You know, I was just remembering how much Trevor really hates surprises." He and Cheri smiled, and she removed the large Chanel sunglasses from her face, revealing her bloodshot eyes.

"Oh, yeah, the Senior Ball...."

Braxton nodded. "At least this time with the housewarming party, he enjoyed it in the end." Trevor's private suite rose high above First Hill, and the large picture windows looked out onto the city around them, the windows of skyscrapers lit brightly, penetrating the never-ending darkness that had overtaken them.

"God, I can't believe it's 3:30 in the afternoon and it looks like the middle of the night," Cheri observed.

"I know... how bad is it out there?" he asked, turning his attention briefly to the window.

"A few riots, some looting here and there. Of course, every gay bar on The Hill is throwing a party based around the eclipse; trust the gays to make even the end of the world into a party."

"It's hardly the end of the world, dear." Kathryn's seductive whiskey voice sounded cheerful, in an oddly sarcastic manner which Cheri assumed was due to her perpetual intoxication. "Someone's gotta keep the bars in business," Kathryn said aloud, obviously having heard her thoughts.

"Hi, Kathryn," Cheri replied with a smile, kissing Trevor's mother on the cheek. She looked stunning in her sleeveless day dress in classic Valentino red, and her blue plaid Valentino coat draped over her left arm.

"Cheri, you look beautiful today."

"Thanks." They smiled briefly, though they quickly faded as soon as they looked down at Trevor's unconscious and fragile body. "Then if it's not the end of the world, what is it?"

Kathryn looked at her and sighed. "The truth is, it's something else, something I should have told Trevor and Braxton about months ago."

Braxton looked up at her, his eyes wide and rimmed with dark circles from lack of sleep. He hadn't shaved, and he looked as if he were going to break down at any moment. He had avoided J.T., who had started asking too many questions about the eclipse, the riots, and what had happened to him and Trevor.

His arm had been fractured in three places, and yet he seemed to not even notice the pain, and had refused all of the pain killers that had been offered to him. "What are you talking about, Kathryn?"

She averted her gaze back to her son, and the tears began to well in his eyes. "I was hoping to avoid all of this; I just didn't think... I thought I would have had a lot more time. I didn't think that there would be any danger, so soon...." Her words trailed off, and he let out a frustrated sigh.

"Again, what are you talking about, Kathryn? No offense, but just get to the point."

She wiped the tears from her face and nodded. "It's the Conclave."

"What the hell is the Conclave?" Braxton asked her. He was exhausted. He was on edge and shaky. He shook his head and rolled his eyes, snorting in disgust over the entire situation.

"It's an organization– a Tribunal, really, made up of thirteen representatives from each witch family. You see, in the world there are twelve other families like ours. There were rules that were established in the eleventh century, just as the Crusades began. All the families agreed upon them, and it was determined that every thirteen years it would circulate, and one family would be in charge of enforcing the rules upon the twelve other families, for the entire time they rule."

"So who is in charge now?" Cheri asked.

Kathryn sighed. "No one knows. It was established to protect each family from attacks from other witches while they reigned. The laws of the Conclave ensure that the member of each family who represents the ruling coven would be called in secret and the power would be passed automatically, heralded by the spirits just like the angels blowing their trumpets—to call that member of the next ruling family to the throne, so to speak. There are thousands of witches on the planet, but they all come from these thirteen families."

"And they did this? They did this to Trevor?"

Kathryn shook her head. "That I do not know. I know that what is going on out there, what has occurred, is because of the Conclave, that it has something to do with something Trevor did. That he must have used magic against a member of the current reigning family."

Braxton looked at her, frustrated and puzzled. "Trevor hasn't performed any witchcraft... except for the goddamned spell you told him to do!"

Kathryn put her hand to her waist and looked at him. She was pissed and injured that he would raise his voice to her, that he would even think of speaking to her in such a manner. But she had to reserve herself to the fact that the young man he loved, her little boy, the boy who had grown inside of her for nine months, the boy who had been made for Braxton, was lying in a coma he might never wake from.

"Francesca was told about this a few weeks ago... she warned me about it. I was just never able to get a hold of Trevor. I tried calling –"

"Then why didn't you call me?!" Braxton fired back.

"Braxton!" Cheri spat at him.

"No." Kathryn raised her hand. "It's all right." She directed her attention back to Braxton and walked towards him, stopping at the foot of Trevor's bed and playing delicately with his fingers. "My son has always thought impulsively with his witchcraft... but that's my fault, and you're right. I spent so much time trying to protect him from it—and later, you as well—that I kept putting things off that I shouldn't have, and now this...."

Braxton wanted to apologize; he wanted to reassure her, but the fact was that he could not. He was just too damned tired, too damned worn out to deal with anything at the moment.

"We need to solve this; we need to get to the bottom of this," Braxton said with a defeated sigh.

Kathryn nodded and put her hand to her head and began massaging her forehead, wishing she could reach through the skin, wishing that she could move through her skull, penetrate the bone and touch that fleshy membrane, and ease her troubled thoughts.

"I know. And we will... we will." They looked to the door to see Francesca walk in. She glanced out into the hall behind her, and then proceeded to close the door.

"What is it?" Braxton asked.

Kathryn sighed. "We have a more immediate problem to deal with at the moment."

"What's that?" Cheri asked.

"We need to get Trevor's blood."

Braxton and Cheri looked at her, stunned. "What? Why?" Cheri asked. There was a look of horror on her face.

"I know," Braxton began. "Our blood is different. Regardless if the Legacy or whatever is over. We're genetically different."

Francesca nodded. "That's right. We don't donate blood, and we don't get sick. A Blackmoore—well, any witch—never gets sick, and we never go to the hospital."

"If Trevor's blood were to get looked at, if it were to fall in the wrong hands, he'd be quarantined and most likely dissected."

"But by who?" Cheri asked. They could tell she was at her breaking point.

"My dear," Kathryn began, walking over to the windows and looking out on the fires that burned red-orange in downtown. "It's not just other witches that are a threat, or any other supernatural thing.

"Witches are known. People with abilities... there are programs out there, scientists who may not call us witches, but other things—maybe mutants—who would want to prove that there are people out there with extraordinary skills, and who would love to put us to work.

"And there are other, more religiously-driven organizations that are always seeking us and hunting us, and looking to wipe us out. It can't be risked."

"Every time I think I've grasped this, every time I think that I've come to terms with this, it just keeps getting bigger and more complicated!" Braxton shouted. He took his seat back in the chair at Trevor's bedside, careful not to irritate the splint that was secured to his arm.

"So what do we do? We can't just go take his blood. They would know that it was missing."

"We need blood. A male's blood." They all looked at each other; their faces were weary and their eyes were heavy.

"Where the hell are we going to get that? And how?" Francesca shook her head, and Kathryn shrugged her shoulders and let out a great long sigh.

Then Cheri, who had been resting her hand on her chin, gave a sudden nod. "I know where. You guys just figure out the rest."

J.T. STOOD IN THE ELEVATOR, knocking his phone against his leg. He hadn't heard from anyone for twenty-four hours—not since Cheri got a phone call from Braxton and raced out of the apartment, telling him that she had to go and that she would call him later. He had sat on her sofa, anxious, calling and getting sent to voicemail. And now here he was; he had run the few blocks from her building as soon as she had called him and told him where she was.

"What the hell is happening?" He shook his head and looked as the screen showed the various floors they were passing.

Finally, the elevator stopped and the doors slid open. Cheri was standing out in the hall, waiting for him. Her brown eyes seemed dim, and her body seemed to be heavy.

"Hi," she said to him. She wrapped her arms around him and kissed him. The kiss made any agitation that he had been feeling towards her wash away.

"What's going on?"

She shook her head and began to lead him down the hall. "Not here," she responded. "Wait till we get to the room."

He hated hospitals. He was convinced that nothing good ever happened in them. The only time he had ever gone to hospitals was when someone he knew was going to die. He had a feeling that this time wasn't going to be any different.

They walked into the room, and the first thing he saw was Braxton sitting in a chair with his head in his hands and his left arm in a blue sling, and two women—one he knew to be Trevor's mother Kathryn, standing against the wall with the look of exhaustion and defeat on her face. Next to her was a beautiful woman in her late twenties or early thirties, with dyed cherry-red hair that was long and thick and cascaded down her back, with that same look on her face.

Her skin was a dark olive and her fit and slender body was dressed in a black tank-top with a black pencil-skirt, and shiny black pumps on her feet. Though he didn't know shoes, he knew by the high heel and the bright red under the shoes that they were designer.

Lastly he looked down at the body in the bed, the body they were all holding vigil over, and his heart sank. He had never seen Trevor look so diminutive, so fragile, so like a small child. His face and arms were covered in bandages, and the heart monitor beeped above him. There were two I.V. bags hanging, and he guessed that one was fluid and the other was morphine.

"What the hell happened?" He walked over to the other side of Trevor, and took hold of his motionless fingers with his own. He held them there and was saddened when there was no response, no acknowledgment to his touch. "Is he asleep?" He looked down at Braxton, who only now lifted his head to meet his friend's gaze.

"No. No, he's not," Braxton responded. J.T. hadn't seen Braxton like this since his mother Tammy died. He hadn't even been this distraught when his father was found dead—but then, in a lot of ways, Eric Volaverunt had been dead for many years before he had actually passed.

"Coma?"

Braxton nodded. "Yeah, we got injured in the riots."

"Shit." J.T. walked around the bed and placed his hand on his best friend's shoulder. "I'm so sorry."

"Yeah, I know."

"I wish there was something I could do...." J.T. felt defeated. He wanted to make everything better for Braxton; he wanted to do something to make everything better for Trevor. He didn't believe in God or prayers, and he wasn't going to start now. It was pointless.

"There is." He turned to look at Cheri. They all looked at her, and that's when it dawned on him that he had been called for more than support.

"What are you talking about?" They all sighed. Braxton shook his head, and Cheri walked over to him. She attempted a smile and took hold of his hand, walking him over towards the bathroom door. "What do you mean?"

Cheri placed her hands on his shoulders and stood on her toes, bringing her lips close to his ears. "We need your blood."

J.T. looked at her and shook his head. "You mean like a transfusion?"

Cheri sighed. "No. We need your blood to switch with Trevor's." His eyes grew wide, and the look on his face was a mix of shock and horror.

"What do you mean, switch his blood? What the hell is going on here?" Braxton stood, but kept his free hand locked around Trevor's.

"They can't test his blood. If they do, they'll send it out to others and everything will just get worse from there!" Cheri said to him. Her eyes were filling with tears. She was close to begging. He could see it.

"What do you mean, everything will get worse? What the hell are you guys into?" He looked at all of them for answers, and finally settled on Braxton. "What is it, drugs?" He walked over to Braxton and stared him dead in the eyes.

"What do you want me to say?" Braxton asked him. He hung his shoulders and looked away from J.T.'s face.

"What do you think?" He looked at Cheri, who slapped her face with her hands and wiped the tears from her face. "I want the truth! You're asking me to commit a crime in order for you to hide your boyfriend's blood!"

"I know," Braxton sighed. "I know, and I'm sorry. It's not drugs. I promise it's not drugs. I just need you to do this for us."

"Why don't you do it?" Braxton looked at him but said nothing. He didn't flinch; he didn't blink. He just stared at him. "Oh, 'cause you can't. 'Cause whatever Trevor's into, you're into, and your blood isn't any good either."

Braxton shook his head.

"Is that why you've been all quiet and half-gone when we're at the studio? Is it drugs? Are you shooting shit up into your veins?" He had injured Braxton with his accusations. He knew it. He could see it all over his face. He had cut him deep with his words, and there was a look of shock across his face, as if he couldn't believe that J.T. would ever think that of him.

"J.T.!" Cheri shouted. She ran over to him and yanked on his arm, pulling him back from Braxton.

"I want to know what the hell is going on. Is this why you guys are always so fucking secretive? Is it because you guys have a drug habit and you've got my girlfriend covering up for you?"

Cheri looked over to Francesca and Kathryn. Their faces were unexpressive, and yet their eyes seemed to emanate with a silent rage.

"That's enough!" Kathryn commanded.

"What? You think that because you're a Blackmoore, you can just get people to do whatever you want? Oh, just go ahead and break the law, who gives a shit?!"

"It's not even like that, dude," Braxton said to him. Kathryn had moved on J.T., but stopped as soon as Braxton spoke up.

"Then tell me, please, what is it like?"

"There are things that you are better off not knowing," Cheri said to him, forcing J.T. to look at her. "Things that if you knew, would just make your life way more complicated than it needs to be. But trust me, please, just trust me when I tell you it has nothing to do with drugs, and we need your help."

He looked into Cheri's face and felt his heart break. He loved her so deeply that it consumed him, but he suddenly realized that he wasn't sure if he trusted her. He looked over at Braxton and saw the desperation in his eyes, the helplessness and exhaustion, and realized that for the first time ever, he was wondering if he knew his friend at all. If all of these years together, playing in their band, nights going to parties, nights getting drunk and hoping they didn't get caught, all those classes skipped and bowls smoked... if all of it was meaningless.

Everywhere he looked there were secrets. Deceptions that were being committed by the two people he trusted the most, and the third one was lying on that hospital bed in a coma, and they were asking him to give up his blood to replace it with Trevor's—to pass it off as his.

But then he thought about something bad happening to him, something that could possibly take Trevor away from Braxton, and the idea of it—the idea of even more happening to them, after all that they had lost, all of the friends and parents and now, possibly each other—softened his heart enough for him to give in.

"All right. I'll do it, but after this is done, I want you to tell me what the hell is going on. I don't want lies; I don't want half-truths or riddles. I want the truth!"

They all looked at each other, and then finally Braxton sighed and gave a slow nod. "I will. Everything. I promise."

"Let's get this over with."

Francesca had slipped out of the room, and when she returned she had the plastic tubes and the syringe, and was wearing a lab coat. Cheri was holding his hand while Kathryn sterilized his arm with the iodine and tied the elastic tourniquet around his forearm just above his elbow. He didn't look at any of them, with the exception of Braxton, who was standing in front of him. Their eyes were locked, and when the needle went in he barely felt it.

There was only a boiling rage beneath the surface. He wanted to get up and punch Braxton across the face. He wanted to knock him down to the ground and kick him over and over again, until he was bloody and his bones were broken and his organs were bruised. He wanted to pound all of the rage he felt into his friend.

It seemed to him that Braxton somehow knew this. There were no words said, but a look in those dark eyes—a knowing, coupled with a slight nod—seemed to acknowledge exactly what he was feeling, as if he had said it out loud.

"There we go." Francesca stood and looked at the six vials in her hand, all of them with different colored lids: one green, three purple, and two that were like yellow mustard.

"And those are the right ones?" Cheri asked.

Francesca nodded. "I checked when I slipped into the lab. Hopefully it'll be empty again, and I can get the labels switched."

"And if it's not?" Braxton asked her.

"Then, well, I'll deal with it when the time comes."

FRANCESCA WALKED CONFIDENTLY down the hall, hoping that no one would look at her long enough to realize that she was wearing a pencil skirt and Christian Louboutin pumps on her feet. She kept the vials of blood in the pockets of the lab coat, and nodded casually to the other nurses and doctors that she passed.

She turned the corner into the lab and cursed when she saw two lab technicians staring at her. They were both males in their late thirties. One was a handsome and fit black man with a thin moustache and shaved head of hair, wearing magenta scrubs. The other guy was white and larger—much larger, and his choice of mint-green scrubs did nothing to help hide his portliness.

"Can I help you?" the black technician asked her.

"Well, I was hoping this wouldn't happen," she responded.

"Excuse me?" the portly one asked her. "I've never seen you here before."

"And, I'm sorry, but you never will again." Francesca raised her hand and summoned her witchcraft. It hummed through her body, and the back of her neck became hot. "Take a nap," she said with a wave.

The two men looked at her and then began to look at one another just as their eyes closed. Their bodies collided with one another and stood for just a second with their heads on each other's shoulders, before they slid to the linoleum floor.

Francesca stepped over them and went to work, going through all of the samples on the desk. It took her a moment, but she found them, and pulled out the sheet of labels that had been left on the side-table when they had first admitted Trevor into the room.

"Done and done," she said when she was finished.

Francesca slipped the vials of her cousin's blood into her pockets and made her way back out into the hall, stepping over the two technicians. She stopped and looked at them and smirked as she opened the door.

"You know, I'd thank you guys, but when you wake up, you won't remember any of this."

She waved and stepped out into the hall, closing the door behind her. She made her way quickly down the corridor towards Trevor's room, hoping that no one else had seen her.

She knew her skills weren't as great as Kathryn's, and that if they woke and did remember what had happened, then it would only add more problems to the mess that they were already dealing with.

AS SOON AS FRANCESCA slipped back into the room, giving a nod of confirmation that the switch had been successful, J.T. looked at Braxton, and his face was filled with a determination and a hardness that Braxton had never seen in his friend before. "All right, now you're gonna tell me what the fuck this was all about."

Braxton looked at Kathryn and Francesca and Cheri. They all seemed to be searching for something to say. "I can't," he finally replied.

"You have to. You promised. You either tell me right now, or, Braxton, I swear to God, I will go out there right now and tell them what we did. I will go out there and tell them that you guys are mixed up with drugs or whatever the fuck is going on, and that I agreed to switch my blood with Trevor's. I will blow the lid off of this whole thing!"

"Babe..." Cheri began, placing her hand on his arm.

J.T. yanked it away. "No! I want you to tell me what I did this for! I want you to tell me why you guys just had me commit a crime—a federal crime, mind you—and risk going to jail!"

They all said nothing. J.T. was so angry that he was shaking. He had never felt this much pure rage before, rage that was mixed with so much heartache and disappointment.

"Fine!"

J.T. made his way to the door, unable to look at any of them. He grabbed the handle and threw it open, beginning to make his way out into the hall, when the door suddenly tore out of his hand and slammed shut.

"Stop," Braxton said behind him. J.T. went to open the door again, but it wouldn't budge. It was as if it were locked, though it wasn't, and no matter how much he pulled on it, it was as if the door had been sealed shut with cement.

"What the fuck is going on here?" he asked, still trying to pry the door open.

"We're witches," Braxton said to him. J.T. rolled his eyes and turned to look at him. He ran his hands through his hair, and looked at his best friend and his girlfriend, and his friends' family, and they all returned his gaze without the faintest hint of humor.

"Yeah, right." J.T. shook his head. "Open the fucking door. I don't have time for this shit." He turned around again to try the door once more.

"Sit down!" Kathryn said to him. He rolled his eyes and was about to tell her off when he heard something scratch across the linoleum floor. He turned around just in time to see a chair move towards him and nearly hit him in the legs.

"What the hell –"

"I said, sit!" As if he had lost all will of his own—all control over his motor functions—J.T. found his knees bending and his body taking a seat in the chair that had moved with what appeared to be a will of its own.

"No, not its will, *my* will," Kathryn said to him.

"I don't understand."

"You wanted the truth; well, now you're going to get the truth," Kathryn said to him, pulling out a cigarette and placing it between her lips.

"You can't smoke in here," he said to her.

She looked at him, and he watched as her eyes narrowed to look at the cigarette, and as she did, the tip lit up red and she dragged the first puff from the tobacco.

"I don't care. I'm Kathryn Blackmoore. I can smoke anywhere." Another drag. "Now, you're going to sit there and listen to your best friend, and you're not going to say a damned thing. I appreciate what you've done for my son, but now, now you've threatened to put him in more danger, and my patience is about running thin. So you're going to listen to Braxton, and then you can do whatever you want to do."

He nodded.

"And if you threaten to tell after, I'll make it so that the only thing you remember is where you live and how to spell your own name. Got it?!"

"Got it!"

"Good!" Kathryn hissed. "Because we have more important things to deal with than someone who can't keep their mouth shut."

THEY STARED AT EACH other: Mary-Margaret and the boy who did not blink, who did not flinch, and who seemed to be made of stone. "You're Michael Donovan, aren't you?"

The spirit gave a slow and assuring nod. *'I am....'*

She could feel the hairs along her arms and neck stand on end, and her skin spread with gooseflesh. "And you know what's happening? You know why the world's dark?"

The spirit nodded again. *'I do....'*

Mary looked down at the violin in her hands and thought she should play it again, as if it would be the only way to pull his knowledge, his other-worldly wisdom, from out of him.

"Then tell me, what is this? What is going on here?" Michael said nothing. He stared at her for several seconds and she could feel her courage, her strength, waning. "Why? Why come to me, then, if you will not tell me? What is it, spirit that you feel you can keep this from me? I thought your loyalty was to this family!"

The spirit shook his head.

'My loyalty is not to the family. It is to this place; it is to this house. The family is the reason why I cannot leave it. Why I shall never move on and see my own family....'

She heard the sadness in his words, and it saddened her in return. She felt her heart drop inside of her chest, and in this moment she wanted to cry out, to shed the tears she was trying so hard to fight back.

"I just want to understand."

The spirit pointed to the violin in her hand. *'To understand the present—to prepare for the future—one must go back to where it all started.... Play... play and listen to the music, and you will understand it all....'*

Mary looked down at the instrument once again and let out a deep sigh. It was a moment's courage, a single act, and then it would be done. There was no going back from this, no returning to the woman she was before this. She knew that if she did as the spirit instructed, if she gave in and began to play—to finally give in to her witchcraft, to do so with an open and willful heart and eager spirit—then she would come out of it a different being altogether. In the end she would reemerge on the other side, changed forever. She would be initiated into this coven she called family. In the end, she would be a witch.

She closed her eyes, put it to her chin, and she began to play.

The Tale of Michael Donovan

Zig, zig, zig, Death in cadence,
Striking a tomb with his heel,
Death at midnight plays a dance-tune,
Zig, zig, zag, on his violin.
The winter wind blows, and the night is dark;
Moans are heard in the linden trees.
White skeletons pass through the gloom,
Running and leaping in their shrouds.
-—HENRI CAZALIS FROM *Danse Macabre*, opus 40 by
Camille Saint-Saens

I

HE WAS STEADY AND SILENT, focused only on the music, focused on the zinging of the horse hairs on the strings that were crying out in beautiful poetry: poetry without words. There was nothing that couldn't be done, nothing that couldn't be accomplished through the music. He could play for hours; he was convinced he could play for days if only his mother would let him, if only he could abandon his academics and move into the music room. If only he could stand in this place, perfectly positioned, playing *The Meditation* from *Thais* for as long as possible, playing until it carried him away on its sonic sea.

He listened to the rain tap on the glass, sliding down the windowpanes and distorting the view of the lush apple orchard beyond the garden. He could smell the scents of a roast being cooked by Nellie and the other cook in the kitchen, and the sounds of china, silverware, and glasses being set at the table. His parents were having guests over for dinner. He was going to be expected to play for them, to entertain them, as he was always made to do. He hated it, but he could hide in the music and forget the eyes watching him, eyes gathered and fixed on him in the front parlor. He didn't play for the sake of others; he didn't play for their enlightenment or awakening. He played for himself. He played for the music and what it deserved. He played for his violin.

His beautiful Stradivarius; it was his confidant, his loyal friend, his familiar in the alchemy of music. It helped him with his incantations of sheet music, those beautiful notes that when played could paint pictures with sound, could stir the blood, could manipulate emotions. His Stradivarius allowed him to incite sudden rage, heartbroken tears of misery, bursts of indescribable joy and elation. With his Stradivarius, Michael could do anything.

He wondered how long he could hide in this room, and he tried not to think about when it would be dinner. He didn't want to think about having to leave this sanctuary and be the wind-up monkey for his parents and their friends. He just wanted to play. He wanted to play until the world melted away; he wanted to play until he could see God. He knew that God was in the music, that the Violin was really the only way to pray to him. The proper way. It was the violin that spoke the language of angels and whispered the Aramaic of Christ. If the Christ even existed.

He was never certain of divinity, of heaven and hell, of God and the Devil, unless he was playing the music. It was only then, in those moments, that he believed. But when the music stopped and he had to exist with others, then he no longer knew if he believed in anything.

Music was his religion, and if anything, he was certain that the violin was his God. No. It was not the violin; the violin was only the invoker, and the sheet music was the ancient scripture. His gods were Mozart, Tchaikovsky, Paganini, and Beethoven. His gods were those who crafted the scripture and put it to paper. Or perhaps, he sometimes pondered, were they just the prophets?

He never asked these things when he wasn't playing. There was never any point, when the world was moving and changing around him. There were automobiles; there were moving pictures and silent films, expeditions to the North Pole, and oil in a country called Iran. The President, who was affectionately known as "Teddy," was conserving natural areas as wildlife preserves, and had just ended his term and was succeeded by Taft. There was so much going on in the day-to-day that the idea of divinity was a moot point.

There was a knock on the door. Michael stopped and sighed in frustration. "Michael, darling..." his mother Claudette called out from the other side of the pocket door.

"Yes, what is it?" His voice was tense, his tone was sharp and his words short.

"Darling," she began again as she slid the door open. "Go get cleaned up, my dearest. The Larrabees, the Bennets, and the Bloedels will be here in an hour for dinner, and I need you to be presentable."

Michael rolled his eyes and sat down his Violin. "Whatever you say...." He ran his hands through his short dark hair and kissed his mother on the cheek. She had her raven hair up in a style that almost resembled a cushion, and her slender frame was dressed in a floor-length blue satin gown that covered her all the way up most of her throat. Often Michael wondered when looking at her, how could she possibly breathe dressed like that? How could any woman, for that matter?

He stomped up the grand oak staircase, making sure that his disdain was made known to everyone in the house. Though the Queen Anne Victorian was a mansion just like all the others on his street, he liked the narrowness of it. It allowed for his tantrums to be felt and heard by every occupant of the home.

Michael reached the landing and began to make his way up the rest of the way to the second floor, when he thought he saw someone—a gentleman, perhaps—move into the library. "Hello?" he called out. It was at that moment that he was certain the now rather gaunt-looking figure had stopped. "Is someone there?" Michael waited, but there was no response.

"If someone's there, then you must answer me, please." He could feel his heart begin to race in his chest, as if slamming against the breast plate. He took a deep breath and made his way up the rest of the steps, and summoned up whatever ounce of courage he had inside of him to walk over to the library and confront whoever it was that was hiding in there and refusing to acknowledge him.

He could feel his knees buckle as he walked, and the floorboards creaked beneath his feet. The house was only seventeen years old, a year older than him, and yet it seemed it had already existed from some time much longer than that, the way the floorboards often cried out. He shook away the small amount of apprehension and fear, and forced himself to the library, telling himself that it was just one of the servants and that, for whatever reason, they couldn't hear him.

"Hello?" he called out as he pushed the door wide open.

He could hardly breathe. It caught in his throat like a giant lump, and he wasn't sure what it was that he was seeing. It was nothing but an empty room. Just two tables with oil lamps and walls filled with books, and the twilight spilling through the one large window. He thought of crossing himself, but decided against it at the last minute.

"Nonsense and superstition!" he spat out, and rolled his eyes. He slammed the door shut behind him as he pivoted on his heel and made his way to his bedroom. He opened the door and slipped inside, slamming it behind him and taking a deep breath. He looked at the blue floral wallpaper, and the two windows facing the bay, and the ornate mahogany desk in front of it with the Venetian armchair spread with golden fabric. There was his matching sleigh bed to the left against the wall, and a matching armoire which kept his coats and suit jackets. Atop of his dresser, against the wall by the door, was his phonograph, and he went to this now, putting on Chopin's *Nocturne*, and stared at himself in his giant mirror. He took note of his eyes, those blue eyes which were sharp and alert, almost erratic—and he worried that he looked mad. He thought he did, that he looked absolutely crazed, but he shrugged it off and attributed it to fatigue.

He had been trying to keep up on his studies and his violin practice. He was being groomed for Yale, and in two years that was where he was expected to go. The thing that plagued him, the thing that added more stress and exhaustion to his life over everything else, was that he did not want to go to Yale. He wanted to escape to Paris. He wanted to run away and leave all of it behind. Michael Donovan wanted to fade away and leave the person he had spent the past sixteen years being in Fairhaven. He wanted to leave him in South Hill and never deal with any of it again. He wanted to create another person entirely, and begin a new life in the cafés and salons of Europe. He wanted to leave with his beloved Stradivarius and never return.

If only it were possible, he thought to himself. *If only I really could get away from all of this. To never return, to never see this place—any of this suffocation—ever again. If only.* He wasn't sure how long he had been standing there. He didn't really even notice the light of day growing dimmer and dimmer, and the inky blue dark filling his room more and more with its ever-expanding shadows. He thought perhaps he had missed the whole affair. He smiled, entertaining that idea, but then he looked at the clock atop his nightstand and realized that he still had a half an hour before everyone was expected to arrive.

"This is never going to end, is it?" he breathed out. "I'm going to be a little wind-up toy in this house until the day I die, aren't I?" He wasn't even sure he ever needed to question that. He knew he was expected to return after graduation and take on the family business with his father and his uncle, John-Joseph, who was co-founder of the Skagit River Coal Mines, Lake Whatcom Logging Company, and the Bloedel-Donovan Lumber Mills, along with Julius H. Bloedel, who was the president of Fairhaven National Bank.

"It's all just planned out for me, from start to finish. I'm never going to have a life, not one of my own. I'm never going to get to do any of the things that I want to do, and I'll probably stop playing the violin altogether. I wouldn't be surprised; isn't that how things like this always go?" He gave a sigh and sat down, defeated, on his bed. "Fulfilling what everyone else wants at the price of your own soul, and the sacrifice of your truest self."

He found the more he thought about it, the more paralyzed with fear he became. The future was what frightened him, nothing else. He knew that growing up meant the death of dreams, the separation from his true self, from the existence that he felt he had been destined for by the universe—and that his parents were taking it away from him, that they were going to strip him of everything that made him who he was. By the time he graduated from college and returned home, he knew that everything that Michael Donovan had ever been would be gone, and all that would be left would be an empty shell, waiting to be filled with his father's hopes, dreams, and expectations.

"Michael! Are you ready yet?" his father called out from the landing. He rolled his eyes and walked over to his closet, looking at the assortment of pressed white shirts waiting to be worn.

"It's always the same...." He gave another sigh and pulled out a shirt, which he laid out on his bed, then, moving over to the armoire, he removed a navy blue dinner jacket, and from the top drawer from beneath the rack, he removed a matching silk tie and laid it out on the bed, followed with black trousers from the second drawer.

He wanted to delay all of this as long as possible, but also knew that in doing so, he would incite the wrath of his father, which could often mean being lashed by his belt. He walked over to the table near the window and lit the oil lamp. Their home was one of the first in Fairhaven to have electricity, but he couldn't stand how bright the light from his ceiling was, and how much it gave him a migraine. Dim lighting was better; it was easier to deal with and didn't feel so oppressive.

"There's never any goddamned time...." Michael walked back to the door and opened it. He walked out into the hall and made his way back down the stairs.

"What are you doing?" his father, Jasper Donovan, asked him, sitting on the sofa in the front parlor facing the fireplace, with his eyes scanning the paper in front of him. His glasses were sitting on the bridge of his nose, and his salt-and-pepper hair was slicked back neatly. His arms were strong and large—unlike Michael's, which were lean and by comparison to Jasper's, petite and effeminate.

"Going to the shower." His father didn't even bother to look up from his paper. He didn't even bother to turn his head to the side to face his one and only son, who was still standing on the stairs.

"Very well, then." Michael gave an irritated nod and began to make his way down the hall and towards the restroom at the back of the house. "Make it quick," his father said. He could hear the click of his pocket watch, and knew that, as usual, his father was counting down every single second that ticked away.

"Yes, sir." He walked into the restroom with its stained-glass-plated windows of red and blue, and turned his attention to the claw-footed tub, pushing back the shower curtain and turning the faucet on for the water. It came out fast and hot, steaming up the bathroom almost immediately. He undressed slowly, looking at the lean build of his chest and the pale nipples which began to grow hard as he brushed his thumb across them. Then he allowed his hand to drift down to the buttons of his knickers, removing them slowly and standing there in his BVDs.

He stared at his own crotch, focusing his eyes on the bulge between his legs, the bulge that began to grow as he imagined it belonged to someone else, another man who was standing before him, waiting for him eagerly to reach out and touch it.

Michael let his left hand drift over his growing bulge, and he began to rub it gently, feeling the sensation and staring in the mirror, imagining he was touching someone else, another who wanted him just as badly. He began to swoon, to give into the sensation of this, when just as quickly he stopped himself and shook it away, banishing the thought along the mist of tears that had lined his eyes without his knowing.

"You can't think those things! You just can't!" he said again. He finished undressing and hopped into the shower, pulling the curtain shut behind him and pushing himself beneath the water, allowing it to soothe him and wash it all away, every dark erotic thought.

THEY WERE ALL SITTING around the large oak dining table, glasses clinking, the roast almost completely devoured, and they had already gone through two bottles of wine. Michael was bored, listening to Charles Larrabee and his wife Frances discussing the recent Model-T Ford that they had purchased the other day, along with the new mink coat he had gotten his wife. His mother made some comment about wishing that her husband would be so thoughtful. They all laughed, but he could see by the slight cloud of disappointment that his mother wasn't joking, no matter how she had said it.

It seemed Frances Larrabee and Mina Louise Prentice, Julius's wife, understood exactly the sentiment underlying her comment.

"Well, who has the time to think of such things, when so much work needs to be done?" Jasper asked rhetorically. He was always working. Money and the accumulation of more money seemed to be the only thing that his father ever considered.

"And what of Jeremiah Blackmoore's offer to come in on the lumber mills? Have you given that any more thought, Jasper?" Julius asked, taking a sip of wine. The look in his eyes was hinting at something else, something suspect and cynical.

"What about it?" Jasper asked.

"Well, can you imagine the capital? I mean, we were looking to expand south of the bay, towards Seattle. That would definitely provide us the leverage to do so to push the others out."

Jasper looked over at Julius and shook his head. "My brother and I have discussed it, and we both feel that we don't need that money. The stupidest thing we could possibly do is bring Blackmoore money into the equation."

The Blackmoores had moved to Fairhaven in 1904, and had purchased a shotgun-style single-story home along Knox, just across the street from the Maylands and next to Dianaca Castle, the large plum three-story mansion on the corner between Knox and Fifteenth Street. They had started a firestorm of gossip within two weeks of their arrival, as soon as it started to spread that Aria Blackmoore—Jeremiah's sister—was creating a spiritualist church and hosting séances out of their home.

"Oh, you don't really believe all of that witch nonsense, do you, Jasper?" Mina asked him with a smirk.

"That is irrelevant, and why not? I'm a God-fearing man, I go to Mass, and we've been warned. But that really isn't the point, is it? The point is that no matter what, having their name attached to anything is bad for business. And we are in the business of making money, are we not?" Charles gave a cough, and Julius shook his head. "Exactly," his father concluded.

"Well then, moving on. Michael?" He looked up from his plate and met Charles' eyes. "Are you going to entertain us with your Stradivarius this evening?" Before he could answer, before he could decline, his father interrupted him, telling them all that of course he would be playing. Tonight would be no different from any other night.

"I'll go get my violin...." His voice was low, and he hung his head slightly as he excused himself and made his way towards the music room. He wasn't certain, but Charles had seemed to know that he didn't want to play, whereas his parents lived in a cloud of self-imposed denial to everything he did or expressed; and it had seemed, as he had stood to leave the table, that Charles had a look of regret in his eyes for having asked the question.

He grabbed his violin and thought for a moment that he saw that same figure standing outside of the narrow side window directly in front of him, but when he tried to focus his eyes to really see, there was nothing—only his own reflection in the glass.

He knew that he could tell himself that it was only his reflection and nothing else, but somehow he knew that this wasn't correct. He knew that there had been someone out there at that moment, looking in at him and connecting with his eyes, just as he had known that that same person had been upstairs moving through the rooms. He also knew better than to go chasing after it.

He turned around to make his way back out of the music room, and there the party had gathered in the front room, facing him. He pushed the pocket door all the way into the slot in the wall and took a deep breath, closing his eyes and securing the instrument beneath his chin. He lifted his left hand, bow secure, and placed it against the strings. He began to play the *Carmen Fantasy, Opus twenty-five*. He was summoning that music, drifting into it. The power of it, the cry of the strings, and the music in all of its tragedy swayed him. The room disappeared, his parents and their guests. They didn't exist; nothing existed but the music.

If he could just find himself in the place of the music, in the land of sound. If he could just escape and become part of the sound itself. In his mind he saw so clearly the Austria of Marie Antoinette, the palaces of Vienna and the guests in all of their pageantry dancing the Viennese Waltz. He saw polished dance floors and gilded walls and burning chandeliers above them—above him. He was in this palace. He was far away, crossing time and space and existing in another century altogether. There was beauty all around him. Faces covered in elaborate masks, women and men dressed in their finest velvets and satins. Bright colors engulfed him.

The faster he played, the faster they danced. He was the prodigy, the star; he was the violinist that the Crown-Heads of Europe came to see. They traveled far and wide for him. He was a virtuoso of melody, the maestro of song. None were like him; none could exist as he existed. He opened his eyes, and they were still there: these faces of nobility, dancing in the regality of his talent.

Women in corseted gowns held in polite hand with gentlemen of refinement. Their smiles expressed the joy he filled them with; it was intoxicating. They seemed to move closer to him, like the tide on the shores coming in, they neared him, and Michael was the shore. He was the sand and the rocks that they crashed against. Faster and faster he played, the cadence rising, the thrill growing, their steps quickening, and that's when he saw him. The man. He was beautiful. Tall and lean, a chiseled jaw with white skin as smooth as milk, wearing a Mephistophelian mask of red and black. Tiny horns, like two antennas pointing in defiance towards heaven, protruded from the corners above his brow.

He was dressed in black velvet, with gold buttons on the jacket. Elaborate gold vines wrapped around the sleeves and moved along the sides of the jacket, working their way up to the collar. He moved closer and closer to Michael, keeping mysterious black eyes locked with his. Black fires burned in his sockets, spinning with one beautiful woman after another, drawing closer to him. Michael played faster, feeling his heart begin to quicken; his pulse raced and his body swayed. The melody carried him, and his eyes stayed fixed on those black orbs.

His black hair was sleek and pulled back, tied with a gold ribbon of satin. Closer and closer he came, until they were face to face. Michael's eyes grew wide and his mouth fell open, but no sound came out as the man took hold of him and spun him around. His bow slid hard and fast against the string. It broke, whipping him in the face and lacerating his cheek.

"Goddamn it!" he cried out. He shut his eyes, and when he opened them again it was all gone. He was standing there in his home once again. The guests seemed startled, a look of shock on his mother's face and silent rage on his father's. His heart raced and his eyes moved erratically as he looked at his violin. It was broken and the bow was hot, emanating smoke. He threw it to the floor and stared at it in disbelief.

"Michael!" his father shouted, as his mother ran to him and placed his face between her hands, trying to look at the wound.

"I... I don't know what happened...." He was trying to make sense of all of it, trying to understand what had just occurred.

"Darling, are you all right?" his mother asked him.

He jerked his head away from her and shrugged out of her grasp. "I'm fine."

"Let me see it." She reached for him once again, and again, Michael shook her off.

"I said, I'm fine!" he fired at her, instantly regretting it as soon as he registered her pain-stricken face.

"Upstairs, Michael, now!" his father commanded.

"But Father..."

"Now!" Michael closed his eyes and bowed in defeat. He gathered his Stradivarius and bow from off the floor and made his way silently up the stairs.

"I DON'T UNDERSTAND..." Michael said to his violin, as if he could coax an answer from it. He was in his navy blue silk pajamas, laid out on his side, one arm propped up under his head as he stared at the broken strings and the singed horse-hairs of his bow. It smelled burnt, with broken tips distorted by fire.

He thought of the vision. The mysteriously haunting and terrifying man, who seemed to draw him in and seduce him all at the same time; what did it all mean? He was certain it was the same apparition that he had glimpsed in his home. Though he had only appeared as shadow, he was certain that it was he.

He sighed and climbed off of his bed, padding barefoot across the hardwood floor. He reached the window and pushed open the curtains, looking out on the bay in the distance. He saw the lights of a steam ship getting ready to undock and make its journey to some far-off place. He wished with all of his heart that he could be on that ship, going someplace foreign and far from his father's reach.

Being dismissed to his room was as much punishment as he would receive, and yet he would have rather preferred the belt to his father's refusal to acknowledge his existence. The belt was only dealt for the most severe cases of insubordination, but fumbling on a performance was just considered an embarrassment and shame that needed to be dismissed and excused for.

He thought again of those black irises that stood out against the whites of the man's eyes. In truth, he hadn't stopped thinking about those eyes since they had first met with his in that trance. They haunted him now; they were burned deep into the surface of the flesh of his brain. They wouldn't leave him alone, and they would not let him sleep. Michael knew that something was going on; something was happening that he would not be able to avoid.

It was something terrible, something dark that would never let go. He understood this, and could not figure out what he could do to get rid of it.

MICHAEL AROSE FROM a dreamless sleep. His eyelids fluttered like moths' wings, fighting against the morning light. It irritated his eyes and made them water as he rubbed the sleep from them and yawned. He sat up and looked around his room, the cool bluish hue of morning shadow and the blue sky beyond the window. He was glad for a pristine morning and not another dreary Washington day.

He moved out of bed and walked over to his armoire and threw it open, removing black cotton slacks and a crisp white shirt, followed with a black tweed vest and black jacket, followed with his ankle garters, socks, and polished black shoes. After throwing on a fresh pair of white BVDs and dressing, he opened his tie drawer and removed a black silk tie, which he finished with a pearl pin.

He looked in the mirror and brushed his hair neatly to the right and walked down stairs, fastening his sterling silver Tiffany's wrist watch as he did. He looked at the painting of Saint Sebastian that hung on the wall of the landing and kissed the nearly-naked and sensuously exposed saint on the lips, wishing he could remove those arrows that stuck from him as he stood there bound in wistful agony to a tree. He wished that he could move his fingers through those auburn ringlets and caress his smooth body, allow his hand to drift down his chest and sternum until he reached the rag of white that covered his pubic nest and that organ that seemed to Michael must have been stiffening as he died, looking towards God and being filled with His grace.

Michael shook the thoughts from his mind again and made the rest of the way down into the house, instinctively moving into the dining room. His mother sat there, cracking open a soft-boiled egg. She smiled kindly at him as she tore a piece of toast and dipped it into the golden yoke.

"Good morning, my sweet," she said to him, as he walked over to her and kissed her kindly on the cheek.

"Morning." He looked around the dining room, which was governed by a portrait of Queen Victoria, who hung over the fireplace mantel in her staunch and prudish judgment. "Where's Father?" he asked, looking at the head of the table where he usually sat, reading his paper and drinking his morning coffee.

"Oh, he left early, some meeting. You know how he is."

"Yeah." He knew exactly how his father was, and he knew that his absence was due to his frustration with his accident with the violin the night before.

"Now, sit, have some breakfast!" She motioned to the chair across from her, and he did so, looking out on the street outside the large bay windows. Nellie walked in from the kitchen, which faced him on the other side of the dining room.

He placed his white linen napkin in his lap as she set down his usual plate of toast, eggs over-easy, and apple slices from the orchard. "Thank you," he said to her with a smile. She nodded and poured him a cup of coffee.

"So, any exams today?" his mother asked.

He shook his head as he split into the eggs with his knife and fork. The yoke, like golden blood, pooled out all over the plate. "No, not until tomorrow, but I've already studied up on everything." A sip of coffee and another bite of egg. "What about you? What are you doing today?"

His mother sipped fresh orange juice. "The ladies are coming over for a game of bridge and tea this afternoon, but other than that, I have no commitments."

She averted her eyes and Michael suspected that she was hiding something, but he didn't feel the need to press it. "Well, that should be fun."

His mother smirked and rolled her eyes. "You know how that Eslie Churchill gets. She practically absorbs all of the air in the room with her witless gossip."

Michael laughed as he ran his toast through the yoke, sopping it up and sticking it in his mouth. "That is true."

They continued to talk and eat. He loved his mother, and loved these times with her, without the shadow of his father's expectations lingering over them. When he was home, mornings were conducted in near silence, as he felt it was rude to converse during meals unless one was entertaining guests.

He wished, in these moments, that it was just he and his mother, imagining a life in which his father had abandoned them with money and the house, choosing a life of business and money, and not the responsibilities of familial obligations. It was these moments, few and far between, that Michael felt no resentment to his home life, or towards his parents for birthing him in the first place. He knew that he shouldn't spend his thoughts wishing he had never been born, but when it came to the pressures of high-brow society and parental demands, he couldn't fathom any other alternative.

The walk to Fairhaven High School took him through the village, past the pharmacy and the shoe shop. The sun was glistening on the water, making the green bay look like crisp blue with glitters of gold. The air smelled of saltwater and the seagulls cried above him. He crossed the dirt road, just as the trolley rolled by, its bell chiming, and Model-T's traveled alongside horse-drawn buggies.

He kept his books in a distressed brown leather Brooks Brothers satchel, and for the first time, he was without his violin. He hung his head and sighed as he tried to shake the sensation of a phantom limb in his left hand where his Stradivarius was usually clutched, like a weapon against any beast that wished to challenge him.

He crossed the bridge over a creek and made his way to the three-story stone citadel of Fairhaven High School. The path on the corner of the street, which led to the front step of the school, was marked by two ten-foot stone pillars which supported a sign, which arched over the path with the school's name.

Students sat on the grass chatting, and boys tossed a football to one another. They were all soaking up the sun, enjoying this beautiful morning, and on days like this, most classes were taught outside. Michael loved days like this, and he wished that every single day could be like this.

"Right at you!" Richard Larrabee shouted, just as the football came towards him. He jumped out of the way and found himself colliding with the grass.

"Damn it!" he spat out as he righted himself and brushed the grass off of him furiously.

"I'm really sorry," Richard said to him as he ran up to check on him. He was dressed in white trousers, and his white collared shirt was untucked, with his vest open and his waistcoat discarded on the grass. He had milk-chocolate hair that looked as soft and delicate as silk in the sun. His face was strong, with just the lingering hint of baby-fat, with olive skin that was unusual for Washington, and penny-colored eyes that glistened in the sun.

The sleeves on his shirt were rolled up to the elbows on his strong, tan arms, and his chest was firm and lean. Michael had to avert his gaze from the sight of the exposed neck and crown of his chest, which was decorated with a sparse scattering of black hairs.

"It's fine; I'm fine!" he replied defensively. Richard furrowed his brow, and Michael wished instantly that he could have taken it back. "I mean, I'm okay. I didn't mean to snap at you like that."

Richard nodded. "It's okay; honestly, though, it was an accident." Michael blushed as soon as Richard smiled at him. "Say, don't you usually have a violin with you?"

Michael frowned. "Yeah, there was an accident last night at dinner when your parents were over."

"I heard." Richard placed his hands on his hip and looked down at his shoes, which were now dirty. "I'm sorry about that." Michael shrugged in response. "Well, I should get back to my game; Carter and the others are waiting for me to get the ball." Michael nodded and bent down, retrieving the ball from the grass and handing it back to him.

Their fingers touched; they lingered there for a moment as he accepted the ball from Michael, his fingers sliding along the tops of Michael's. "You know, it's good to see you get a little dirty, Michael," he said with a grin.

"It is?"

"Yeah." He began to trot backwards, still facing him. "You should do it more often!" He grinned and turned, jogging back to his friends. Michael watched him hand the ball to his neighbor, Carter Mayland, who was asking him what had taken so long—or so Michael imagined.

He could feel the heat rise on the back of his neck and spread to his ears. His legs shook ever-so slightly, and his hands began to fidget. He grinned and tried to shake it away as he once again made his way back into the school, excited to see Richard Larrabee in class. He hoped that it would be conducted outside, so he could stealthily admire the sun glittering in his eyes once again.

II

THE LAST THING MICHAEL Donovan cared about was the Mexican-American war, and the battle of the Alamo. History wasn't thrilling to him, and he found his mind drifting to his interaction with Richard Larrabee. The way he had looked at him, the way their fingers had lingered, and the sensation in his body that followed.

He couldn't ignore his growing desires for men. He knew it was wrong; he knew that it was a road that led straight to hell. But writers like Oscar Wilde told him that it wasn't wrong, that the desire wasn't shameful, and the world of the ancient Greeks and Romans expressed an idea that it was natural.

But these things were rarely touched upon in class, if mentioned at all. He reached beside his desk for his violin, only to be saddened by the reminder that it had been ruined and was not there to comfort him with its touch. He wondered what would happen if he gave in. Would the ground beneath his feet crack open and swallow him whole? That's what they taught in church, and who was he to argue the word of God? Who was he to challenge the teachings of the priest?

His teacher, Mr. Upton, seemed nothing more than a vague shadow in the periphery of his vision, and his voice seemed like an inaudible hum. Nothing was really there at the moment to register anything of significance to him. All that existed for Michael at that moment was Richard Larrabee's smile.

He sighed and moved his head lazily towards the window. He looked out on the field one floor beneath him—the sun on the emerald grass, the stately evergreens—and he wished that he could be out there, lingering in that sun with nothing to distract him or occupy his mind.

Michael closed his eyes and yawned, and when he opened them again he was startled to find that he was being watched out there on that field. It was the same man; he was certain of it. He was far out in the field, and the black hair was short and neat. Not long and tied with a golden ribbon. He stood there in a navy waistcoat with matching vest and trousers. He held a bowler hat in his hands, which lingered over his crotch, and his face was turned up in his direction. The features couldn't be made out, and even though he was without a mask, Michael was certain it was him.

He looked away and shook his head, and when he looked again, the gentleman was gone, as if he had never been there. Any other person may have thought himself mad, or close to it, but he knew better. He knew that this man, whoever he was, was real and had a keen interest in him, and him alone. There was no doubting that. Michael knew he was sane; he just needed to find a way to prove to himself that this man was just as flesh and blood as he was, as all of the other people in his classroom.

"What is happening?" he whispered to himself, rubbing his forehead with his fingers, attempting somehow to ease his troubled thoughts. People just didn't appear and disappear. But he knew that this man, this thing, whatever he was, had the ability to do just that.

When the class ended, Michael hurriedly stuffed his notebook into his satchel, along with his pencil, and swung it quickly over his shoulder, pushing his way ahead of the other students, who seemed to be taking their time to get out of class.

MICHAEL MADE HIS WAY to the dining hall. It was a large space towards the back of the school, with several rows of oak tables and matching chairs which stood on the Douglas fir floorboards. The walls were lined on either side with large cathedral-style windows, and rich fir beams stretched out above them.

He took a seat towards the back of the hall, opening his satchel and removing a tin lunchbox, which held a sandwich made with the roast from the night before, a thermos filled with fresh milk, and a smaller thermos containing vegetable broth. He never dined with anyone; though the tables he sat at were always filled with other students, they rarely spoke to him, and he liked it that way.

He didn't have the patience for most other people his age, as most of the things they talked about hardly interested him, and when his thoughts were most often occupied only with the music, he knew that he had nothing else to offer.

"Did you see what she was wearing? It came straight from Paris!" one girl, Kaitlin Fairchild said, dressed in a calf-length white cotton dress belted at the waist and covering her entire chest and neck. Her copper hair was gathered tightly at the top of her head, and her green eyes were as sharp as a blade of grass and aligned with the sharpness of her tongue.

"I wish my parents would get me a dress from Paris," another girl, Esther Smith, responded. She pushed the long strands of her wheat-blonde hair behind her shoulder. She wore an almost identical dress to Kaitlin, except hers was burgundy in color, with gold buttons on the sleeves and down the front of her chest to the waist.

"My mother told me not to speak to her. Her family are heretics."

Esther gasped and shook her head. "Witches, is what my mother says."

Kaitlin laughed. "We need to watch out for her. She doesn't belong here; they're not Christians."

Michael was curious, and though he rarely spoke to these girls—or with anyone—he couldn't help himself. He needed to know who it was that they were speaking about.

"Um," he began; they looked at him and widened their eyes with annoyance at his interruption.

"What is it?" Kaitlin asked, her tone clipped.

"I really don't mean to bother you, and I didn't mean to listen to your conversation, but, uh—who are you talking about?"

The girls looked at each other, and their lips spread in mischievous smirks. "Fiona Blackmoore."

"Blackmoore?"

The girls nodded. "Yeah, she just transferred here from the Redemptionist School; apparently her family wanted her closer to home," said Esther.

"Yeah, most likely so they can further their mission." Michael looked at them quizzically and shook his head. "Their mission to aid Satan in the takeover of our souls. The souls of everyone in Fairhaven! Then I'm certain they'll extend their reach to Bellingham!"

There was a sudden chill in the air, as if it had become winter outside instead of spring, as if it had dropped from sixty-seven degrees to thirty-five.

"Actually...." They all looked up, startled, turning their heads to the right of the table. Michael suppressed a smirk when he saw the girls' eyes widen in shock. "If you don't remember, Fairhaven incorporated with Bellingham five years ago in 1903." Michael snickered, and the young girl caught this. She was beautiful, ethereally so, and there was an indescribable sensation that seemed to emanate from her and wash over him like a warm bath. He no longer felt the cold, though Kaitlin and Esther continued to shiver.

Her large topaz eyes of blue and green were accentuated with long red lashes, and her auburn tendrils cascaded down her back and over her shoulders, as perfect as a doll's. Her cheeks were peach and her lips pink like a rose. Her skin was porcelain white, and she was dressed in a plum satin short-sleeve gown with a high waist.

Unlike the other girls, she appeared much more slim and graceful, and the neck and collar-bone were exposed, along with the top of her breasts, showing the hint of her cleavage. Wrapped twice around her neck was a string of peridots which gleamed in the light and enhanced her irises.

"I'm Fiona," she said to Michael, extending her hand to him and ignoring the other girls, who huffed in disgust and got up from the table, stalking away in defiance.

"Hi, I'm Michael –"

"Donovan; I know," she interjected with a smile. "Do you mind if I sit with you?" He smiled and shook his head. No one had asked to sit with him before.

"Please." She sat down and bit into an apple that he hadn't noticed had been in her other hand. "How did you know my name?"

She shrugged. "Everyone knows the Donovans. My uncle is trying to get into business with your father."

He nodded and took another bite of his sandwich. "I'm sorry about those girls; they're not exactly friendly."

Fiona smirked. "Most people here aren't very friendly."

He nodded in agreement. "Yeah, that's very true. People aren't too fond of newcomers in South Hill." Michael looked around the dining hall to see several students staring at them.

"You want to go outside?" Fiona asked him. Michael didn't even have to think twice. He put his food back into his lunchbox, shoving it quickly into his bag as they stood, and he adjusted his tie.

WHEN THEY GOT OUTSIDE, it seemed as if every single head turned in their direction, and as they walked across the lawn, some students crossed themselves and averted their eyes before risking eye contact with the young Blackmoore.

"Are they always so curious?" she asked him. She didn't seem the least bit annoyed by the staring; it seemed to him that she found it entertaining.

"Honestly? They think you're a witch or something like that."

Fiona threw her head back and laughed. It had the sound of a sweet silver bell. "Of course they do."

"Well, doesn't your mother conduct séances?" Fiona tilted her head to the side, as if uncertain of how to answer.

"Like most teenagers, I don't really pay attention to what my mother does. I just want to have fun." As they walked, Michael looked around and caught sight of Richard waiting for another boy, who Michael didn't know, to pass the football. He let his head roll to the side and rubbed the sweat off of his face with his shirt. There was a hint of navel and dark hairs leading to the place beneath his trousers, which he had rolled up to his knees, exposing his strong calves.

Their eyes connected, and he smiled at him. Michael gasped and averted his gaze. "You can talk to him if you want to." He looked at Fiona, and was instantly struck by the kindness in her smile.

"Oh, I... um, I wasn't looking at him."

She put her left hand on her svelte waist and laughed. "Okay."

"So, um, your first day at Fairhaven, huh?" She nodded. "Why did you leave Redemptionist?"

Fiona stopped mid-step and turned to face him. "I was kicked out. Too wild or something. I was tired of private school anyways. Part of me probably acted up on purpose so I would be dismissed."

That seemed an honest enough answer, and one that Michael was willing to accept. "Well, hopefully you'll make some friends here."

Fiona smiled and slipped her arm into his, and led him again through the grassy field. "I already have."

She continued to smile, and Michael returned it. Though he had never sought friends before, as he couldn't be bothered with even the idea of anything other than the music, he knew that now, with Fiona Blackmoore, it was different entirely.

III

IT TURNED OUT, TO MICHAEL and Fiona's pleasure, that they were both in the same class. They arrived in the classroom on the third floor, facing out on the front of the school. There was a framed portrait of Charles Dickens and another of William Shakespeare hanging on the walls on either side of the blackboard behind Mr. Upton's desk.

They took a seat towards the back of the class and talked of the complexity of Beethoven's work as the students filed in—including Richard Larrabee, who had cleaned himself up again, having rolled his pant-legs back down and tucked his shirt back in. His vest was buttoned back up and his black tie was secure around his high collar. He kept his waistcoat draped over his right arm.

He smiled and gave a throated laugh as he spoke with Carter Mayland, who was equally handsome with chestnut hair that fell in his eyes, and an equally lean frame, with light peach skin, and blue eyes that fell on Fiona and stayed there.

She looked at him only briefly before turning her attentions back to Michael. "Hi, there." Michael and Fiona looked up to see that Carter was standing in front of them, one hand balled into a fist and resting on his waist, the other outstretched to take her hand. She looked at it, and then looked back at him without accepting.

"Hello," she said.

"I'm Carter Mayland." She only looked at him. "Uh, Ca-Carter; I'm Carter." He was stuttering, seemed to have lost himself on her disinterested gaze.

"I know," she smiled. "You already said that." She turned from him and brought her attentions back to their conversation, as if Carter Mayland hadn't interrupted them at all.

"All right, my young absorbent minds! *Faust* by Johann Wolfgang von Goethe! It's the book we'll be reading. Everyone pass out a copy and follow me outside!" The kids clapped, and the portly teacher with his usual charcoal tweed trousers and matching vest, sans waistcoat, pushed his wire-frame glasses up on his face and ran a hand over his slicked-back ashen hair. He handed out stacks of the novel, which were being passed back to the other end of the classroom.

"But before we go out, I want to announce that we have a new student joining us today. Miss Fiona Blackmoore." He extended his hand in Fiona's direction. She offered a gracious smile. "Please, tell us a little about yourself."

She stood and placed her hands behind her back. "Well," she began, not bothering to pay any attention to the eyes that stared up at her. "I was born in New Orleans, sent to boarding school in Bordeaux, France from the age of ten till I was fourteen. Then joined my family here and attended the Redemptionist School until two days ago, and now I'm here."

"Where now you can worship Lucifer with the rest of your family," Marjorie Hampton said. Like all the other girls, she wore her blonde hair down with the bangs tied back with a ribbon. She wore a white calf-length dress that looked like all of the other dresses worn, and she had black leather boots on her feet.

"Miss Hampton, that's an infraction!" The girl huffed and folded her arms across her chest. Michael turned his attention back to Fiona to gauge her reaction, but she only yawned and checked her fingernails and the emerald ring in the sunlight. She stood with the rest of the class and Michael followed suit, clutching his copy of Faust as if it were a life preserver.

OUT ON THE LAWN THEY sat in a disjoined circle, taking turns reading from the epic play. Michael instantly felt as if he could relate to the embittered alchemist, and his desire to acquire pleasure and knowledge that he would sell his soul for it. It was an idea that, if possible, he would never do himself, but he could understand it. Perhaps it was his own wish to escape, and often contemplating what price he would pay in exchange for that escape, that made him sympathetic to the doctor.

"You know, their family sold their soul to the Devil," Marjorie whispered to another girl. "Father Kieran spoke about it the other day at church. I mean, he didn't outright say the Blackmoores, but you knew who he was speaking about."

"Really?" the girl asked her. Michael was trying to ignore it, and kept his back to the girls, hoping that he could distract Fiona, but she only rolled her eyes and shook her head.

"Of course. Father Kieran is from the same County in Ireland where the Blackmoores came from. They were wild—gypsies or something heathen like that—they would dance naked in the woods for the Devil... and then...." She whispered the rest to her friend, who gasped and snickered all at the same time.

"I'm sorry," Michael offered.

"Don't be. It's not like this is a singular occurrence." He nodded, but offered nothing else. She didn't want pity. He could see that on her beautifully serene face and in those topaz eyes that glittered in the sun. "You only care about what other people think and say if they're true, and you are embarrassed. Nothing they say is the truth, so I have nothing to be bothered about.

"I know what's true and what isn't, and that's all that matters." She picked a large lilac-colored honeysuckle off of the ground and began to pluck its petals.

"Besides, she'll learn soon enough that to spread lies and to perpetuate fictions as truth about others will only lead to her own loneliness, when everyone else finally sees her on the outside for the ugly thing she is on the inside."

Michael looked at her, perplexed, but shrugged it off with a slow nod, returning to his book, when they both felt the sensation of bodies behind them. Michael and Fiona looked at one another and then over their shoulders, squinting as they faced the direction of the sun. Richard and Carter had moved behind them from where they had been sitting, a few feet away. They had been too focused on their conversation to notice that the young men had left the spot where they had been sitting to make their way towards them.

"Hi, Michael." Richard grinned and looked at him briefly before averting his gaze.

"Oh, um, how are you, Richard?"

Richard looked back up at him, and this time it was Michael's turn to avert his eyes. "I'm swell."

"Uh, hi, Fiona," Carter managed, though his voice still seemed to be quaking with panic at how she may or may not greet him.

"Hello, Carter." This time she offered him a smile, and it seemed upon seeing this that Carter almost fell over.

"I hope you don't mind if we join you?" Richard asked, not taking his eyes off of Michael the entire time, except for when Michael returned his gaze to the athlete. "It's just that you two have managed to get all of the sun, and we've been sitting in shade." Michael picked at a few blades of grass and tossed them away at his side.

"Well, then, you must join us! Michael and I insist!" Michael looked at her and raised his brows, and his eyes grew wide. She smiled and nodded at him.

"Thanks!" Carter said, taking a seat next to Fiona on the grass. Richard still sat with his buttocks resting on the back of his feet, as he stayed kneeled on the ground.

"Well, I will if Michael doesn't mind. I know he's very particular about his company." Michael looked at him and at first wasn't sure if the comment had been a pointed jab at his expense, but at the sight of Richard's effortlessly genuine smile and the quick wink—a wink that was meant only for him—Michael had to quickly avert his gaze back to the ground.

"No, not at all, please."

"Thank you."

The four of them sat there, not speaking, and yet there seemed to be something developing between them, something that was growing around them, connecting the four of them through the earth. Like roots, like vines, it was an energy that made its way out of their fingers and spread, forming another, smaller circle entirely.

He wasn't sure if Richard or Carter could feel it, but he was certain that Fiona could. Her eyes told him that she could, the way that she was breathing and her elated smile. He knew that whatever this was, it was binding the four of them in this moment, though he wasn't certain why, and for what purpose. But it made his heart quicken, and he felt as if he were on a swing, propelling himself higher and higher each and every single time.

There was no end, and this power—this energy, this force, whatever it was—it was going to send him straight to the moon, past the stars, into God's face himself. He hadn't felt anything like this except for when he played his Stradivarius. He had worried that he would never feel it again, but here it was, and it wasn't letting go.

"So, class, what have we learned thus far about Faus –" A scream came out from the circle, cutting through Mr. Upton's words, splitting through the trees and causing the birds to take flight from the trees that were near them.

"My hair!" They all turned to look at Marjorie Hampton, who was pulling out strands upon strands of hair from her head. Her scalp was bleeding, and the tears were spilling down her face.

"Oh, my..." their teacher said.

"What's happening?" she cried, getting up and trying to keep her hands on her head, as if she could prevent it from falling out, but it just wouldn't stop. It just kept coming out, golden strand upon golden strand, glistening in the light. Students looked at her in shock. Everyone's mouths hung open as she continued to cry.

"Rebecca," Mr. Upton said to the girl who had been sitting with Marjorie. "Take her to the infirmary, please." The girl nodded and sat up, rushing her friend back towards the building.

"Okay, class, calm down, calm down. Let's get back to the room." The kids began to sit up, and to his surprise, Carter and Richard both extended their hands, helping he and Fiona off of the lawn. Michael and Richard's grasp lingered for a moment, and they looked into one another's eyes and blushed, and dropped their hands quickly.

"Uh, thanks," he said.

Richard nodded. "You're welcome."

"I wonder what the hell happened?" Carter said to them. They all shook their heads.

"I don't know..." Fiona responded. Her eyes seemed to hint at something, and the smile that started on the side of her face was brief, but Michael had caught it. He wanted to ask her what it meant, but knew that with all of the other students around, it wasn't a good time. He figured, since they lived on the same street, he would ask her after school on the walk home.

MICHAEL AND FIONA HAD made a plan to meet at the sign at the base of the walkway after school, and he stood there thinking over and over again about what had happened to Marjorie, trying to find an explanation for the mystery. He believed in science and logical explanations, but try as he might, there was nothing that he could conceive of, nothing that he could come up with, to explain what had taken place.

He looked up towards the sun and closed his eyes, taking in its warmth, soaking up the vitamin D through his skin, and wishing that he did not have to return home. He didn't see the point, after all, now that his beloved violin was broken.

"Waiting long?" he heard Fiona ask. The strangest sensation had occurred before he had heard her voice announce her presence. He had felt her. Standing there, eyes closed in the sun, he had felt her presence. It had been drawing nearer to him. This pulsating, vibrating warmth that he had known was her, and he didn't understand it, couldn't fathom how it was possible that he knew it was her. But he did, and he wasn't the least bit surprised when he heard her voice.

He opened his eyes and she was smiling a knowing smile, as if she had known he could feel her, and that she could feel him too.

"Not at all," he replied.

"Good." They began to make their way in serene silence, crossing over the bridge and making their way back into the village. Automobile horns honked. It was a strange sound, like a squawking goose in a field. He wasn't sure if he'd ever get used to the sound.

"So, what's on your mind, Michael?" Fiona asked, gripping her books to her chest. Her movements were like liquid, as graceful as the movements of a prima ballerina on the stage. "Are you thinking about what happened to that Hampton girl?"

Michael looked at her, startled, but then regulated it to nothing more than a really good assumption. "It just doesn't make any sense how it happened, you know?"

She shook her head and followed it with a dismissive shrug. "It's probably just a health condition." Michael gave a "hmm" of consideration and continued to walk without another word. They finally reached Knox and made their way up the hill, passing the Church of the Sacred Heart. They both looked up at the sun glistening on the stained glass, and their eyes followed up to the top of the single spire.

"Did you do it?" he asked matter-of-factly.

Fiona stopped, dropping her books to her side and looked at him. "What an odd question." She didn't appear to be offended, but he wasn't certain what to think.

"I'm sorry," he offered, just in case his question had bothered her and she was just too polite to show it. They were standing in front of Dianaca Castle, the mammoth behemoth of a mansion with its English lattice panes. Various Grecian statues lingered over the property, and two menacing Poseidons with their sharp iron tridents stood *en garde* at the front gate.

"Don't be. With everything that gets said about my family, it's a fair question." She stopped there, not denying it nor confirming it.

"I mean, did you? I wouldn't be bothered in the slightest if you somehow did. But I just can't see, in such a rational world, how anything like that could be possible."

Fiona laughed and shook her head. "Oh, Michael." She placed her hand gently on his arm. "There is so much more to the world than can be comprehended or explained by the rationale of men. But I will tell you this...." She looked at him directly in the eye, with a concern that was so deeply felt that he had no words to explain it, as no one had ever shown such care and concern for him before.

"You have nothing to fear or worry about from me, or my family. We're not evil in any way; it's that family you have to worry about." She cocked her head to the Dianaca estate, and Michael looked at the pristine mansion and shook his head with perplexity.

"The Dianacas?"

Fiona gave a slow nod, and a grave shadow seemed to befall her face. "If any evil exists in this city, with the most diabolical intentions to somehow possess the souls of this place, it's the Dianacas. I will never let them get you. But you must avoid them. Promise me!" The urgency in her voice seemed to stop his heart and make his blood run cold. "Please, promise me!" Michael nodded furiously.

Satisfied, it seemed, she smiled and slipped her arm back into his, and they continued their stroll to her home, which faced his block on Sixteenth Street. "Escort me to school tomorrow morning?" she asked him.

Michael grinned sheepishly and nodded. "It would be my pleasure."

Fiona smiled and pulled him close, kissing him quickly on the cheek. "I know we're going to be the best of friends!" she said, before running inside.

Michael grinned and made his way down the street back to his house. The Blackmoores were mysterious; there was no doubt about that, and he knew that behind their walls were esoteric mysteries that may never be discovered. But he wanted to know them, and he hoped that his friendship with Fiona would only continue to deepen to the point that she trusted him with those mysteries.

He had never thought about having a friend before, but now that he did, he felt everything would simply get better. That the stress, the pressures, the ever-present expectations would no longer feel so heavy and burden him into a pit of despair. It was this joy, this elation that kept his lips spread in a smile all the way to his front door.

"MOTHER, I'M HOME!" Michael called out as he opened the mahogany door with its glass window in the center, covered by a lace curtain. He stood in the front foyer, where the grand staircase greeted him and the blue hue of afternoon shadow spilled in from the window on the landing. He looked into the dining room on his left and found it empty, and the dining table cleared and untouched.

"Hello, my sweet, how was school?" Michael turned to face the front room and found his mother sitting on the sofa with a smile on her face, and a strange man he had never met before sitting beside her. He was beautiful in a way that he had never seen anyone, with the exception of Fiona Blackmoore, before. His face was like that of the painting of Saint Sebastian at the top of the stairs on the landing, and his eyes were the darkest brown he had ever seen. He felt they were familiar, but he couldn't think how.

His lips were like soft cushions, and his black hair was short and parted on the left, like his own. He wore charcoal trousers, and a blue waistcoat that was so dark it reminded him of the night sky itself. He wore a matching silk tie, and kept his hands clasped in his lap. There was a tea set on the table with cucumber sandwiches cut into neat circles, and an assortment of biscuits on the tea tray.

"Uh, fine. I'm sorry," he said, turning his attention to the strange man. "You are?" He smiled and looked to his mother.

"This is Marsilio Merrin; he's your new violin instructor." Michael could feel the hot rage burn inside of him, and he balled his fingers into a fist and kept them at his sides.

"My new music teacher?" he asked, his tone visibly offended.

"Err, yes," he confirmed, standing up and stretching his hand. Michael only looked at it. "Your mother tells me you're a virtuoso, a prodigy. And everyone in the city has raved about you."

"Then you know that I don't need instructing."

Marsilio hung his head and turned his attentions to Claudette, who stood and held a new violin in her hand. It had a black bow tied around it, and it was made of a wood he had never seen. It would have appeared entirely black as ink if it wasn't for the varnish of red that seemed to be going through it.

"Darling, he's here to simply help you discipline your bow so you have a better command of the music, that is all." Jasper nodded in agreement.

"So you can control the music, instead of it controlling you. I'm not here to treat you as a novice. I promise." He looked back at his mother.

"He came highly recommended by Jonathan Marker, the tutor for the Mayland boy." Jasper smiled and nodded.

"Was this Father's idea?" His mother nodded her head.

"Yes, and I'm sure it's a good one."

"Meaning," Michael concluded, "there's no option for discussion." He sighed and directed his gaze to the large picture window, looking out on the sun and the water, wishing that he was still outside with Fiona. "Very well, then."

"Fantastic!" his mother said. She stood and smoothed out her dress. "I'll let you two get acquainted. If you'll excuse me." Marsilio Merrin bowed, and she kissed Michael on the cheek as she handed him the violin.

He had never felt anything so light, as if it were made of air. The strings, along with those on the brand new bow, made of that same wood, seemed to glisten in the light as if they were made of silken strands of silver. "Please," Marsilio said, motioning to the instrument. "Give it a try. You'll find there's no need to tune it."

Michael looked at him, puzzled, but shrugged and did so anyways, removing the satin ribbon and placing it under his chin, closing his eyes and lifting the bow to the strings.

He began to play one of his favorite pieces, the *Allegro Moderato*, starting somewhere in the middle. He had never felt something like this before: it played fast and furious, and sang like a choir of the Italian Castrati. He could feel it pour out of him with such speed and clarity that he had never imagined an instrument could create such perfect and pristine sound.

There was that electricity, that ocean, and he felt as if his hand would never tire, as if the music would never stop, and he could stand there in place, playing until time came to an end. "That's enough," Marsilio said to him. But it wasn't enough; he didn't want to stop. He couldn't imagine that he ever could.

"All right, Michael," Marsilio said again. But he couldn't. The music wouldn't allow it; the violin wouldn't allow it. The strings refused: they weren't done singing. "Enough," Marsilio said again, taking hold of his hands and bringing him to a halt. The bow slid sharp against the strings, but they did not break, and they seemed to spark in the sunlight.

"Where did this come from?" Michael asked, staring at the violin as if it were truly alive—a living, sentient being that understood him, and drew its own captivating breaths.

"It was specially crafted in Ireland. You're the first to play it."

Michael studied it. "And the wood?"

"It's called black mahogany. It is a tree that grows only in one special part of the country."

He had never heard of such a wood before. "And you're giving this to me?"

Marsilio smiled, and those dark eyes seemed to gleam. "You do not have an instrument, and an instrument so unique and beautiful should be played by a musician worthy of its beauty, should it not?"

Michael gave a slow, agreeing nod. They continued to stand there, Marsilio's hands still gripping his wrists gently. The smell of him, sweet and yet woody, like the burning hearth of chimney smoke, filled his nostrils and stirred in him the very desires he had been trying to ignore.

He cleared his throat and moved his hand to his side, out of Marsilio's grasp. "Um, thank you. I have to go."

Marsilio bowed low, crossing his right arm across his stomach. "Till next time."

Michael kept his eyes to the floor, nodding and making his way to the stairs. He moved quickly up the steps, trying to keep his feet steady. He reached the landing and bolted up the rest of the way, running across the second floor to his room, slamming the door behind him and throwing his back against it.

His breath was quick to come, and his heart slammed in his chest as the sweat began to bead down. His armpits were soaking through his shirt; he could feel it so keenly, and he unbuttoned his jacket and removed it furiously, throwing it to the floor.

He felt the fear rise fast inside of him, along with the titillation between his legs. He could feel his groin swell, and he was desperate to pray it away. To invoke other, benign thoughts, thoughts that were not tinged with lust. The eyes of Marsilio, the tanned strong arm that belonged to Richard Larrabee, his smile... the touch of both men seemed to ignite his hands and fingers with memory.

It was taking him over, working through every synapse of the brain, every part of him was on fire with these thoughts, these desires to know that flesh, to kiss those lips, to gaze forever in those eyes. Richard and Marsilio became one at this moment. He could not differentiate between the two, could not separate them into their own individual forms. The desire he felt for both men ravaged him.

IV

VISIONS OF DEMONS DANCING in time, playing vicious violins and moving in a sabbatical circle around a body burning on a pyre, but he could not recall the face. There was something that he understood in this, something that seemed all too familiar, as if it was calling to him to be a part of the vision.

Black robes everywhere, garments as black as ink covering these lithe bodies dancing around the burning body. Their faces were covered by loose fabric that hung from the conical crowns on their heads. They moved in unison, in circles, to rhythms of drums and those ghastly violins that screamed hellish melody. They could not be stopped, as frantic as they moved, casting this circle and chanting.

What was it that they were saying? He couldn't make it out and he didn't want to watch, but Michael was unable to turn away. The smell of that putrid flesh burning filled his nostrils and went down into his lungs so that he was choking on it. It was the most horrendous thing that had ever occurred; it was the worst feeling, this flesh in his lungs, and he was gasping for air. It was burning his eyes so much so that he began to cry, to try to eradicate what was infecting them, this flesh of the deceased that was making its way in.

Was it trying to consume him, the spirit of the body that was burning? Was it trying to find a new home in a new body? Was it pushing his soul out and taking its place? Michael felt as if he were being forced out and this, the intoxicating scene, would not let loose its grasp. It seemed as if the earth around them began to bleed, as thick tar-like liquid oozed up from each crevice, between each mosey patch of grass. And they continued to dance faster and faster as the demons played. Their pointed ears, their naked bodies with long claw-like hands, and their monstrous faces and horns that were thrown back with maniacal laughter as they played, and these shadow figures danced around the burning body.

"Oh, dear God!" he cried out as this black river made its way out from the roots of that central pyre and flowed around them, so that they were all ankle-deep in a midnight river. It continued to flow, to make its way towards Michael, and soon it had. No matter how he tried to back away from it—to find his footing and get freedom, to will his limbs to move and to run back into the thicket and get away from this sabbat—he could not, and this thick black river took hold around him and kept him in place.

His eyes grew wide and his mouth fell open in fear as he watched in horrified silence as a dark figure, tall and lean, rose up from the black river.

At first this figure was covered in it, his body shiny and slick as it reflected in those burning flames—but that water, that black oil, slipped off of him slowly, and the figure began to take form. His eyes were inky wells that gleamed, his coat of black velvet and silver buttons, bejeweled in garnet. Like the rest of the demons, his hands were home to long, clawed fingers which held onto a dark violin, not unlike the one that Marsilio had given him.

He tried not to look into the eyes, those eyes that were beset in a handsome face. Between them was a narrow, somewhat pointed nose, a strong angular jaw and dimpled chin, his hair long and black, framing his face. He seemed to play with a fury and passion that Michael had never seen with anyone, a form and passion and skill that was rumored to belong to Paganini himself.

He was in awe of this devil that commanded this rabble and matched his rhythm to the fury of their heartbeats—or was it the other way around? Was this devil commanding the beating of their hearts?

"Please, let me go!" *he pleaded, but they all seemed not to hear him.* "Please, let me go home!" *And then the maestro, with his long pointed bow, turned it on him at the same time that those fierce eyes acknowledged him, and he smiled.*

The grin cut straight through him like a hot blade, a blade that had been sharpened to a quick and placed into that pit of flames and carcass before being shoved through his chest, sliding through him like butter that had become soft in the sun.

"Stop!"

MICHAEL AWOKE, BATHED in sweat. The moonlight shone through his window and onto the floorboards and the papered walls of his room. It was quiet, and he was safe.

He looked to the armchair in the left of his room in front of that window, and saw the case to that new violin sitting there like some silent specter, beckoning him. He wanted nothing to do with the instrument—the one that was so like the thing that soloist from hell seemed to be playing—and yet its allure was consuming. It seemed to radiate with a kind of energy that moved from the case and seeped into every crevice—every pore of flesh, his nose, his eyes—and get inside of him. It seemed to fill him up and try to move him from his bed.

He wiped the sweat and shook his head, trying to fight it, to refuse it. But he could not.

Michael put his feet to the floor and stood, steps moving cautiously across the cold boards as he reached the instrument. He could feel his heart race as some surge, not unlike that moment before orgasm, moved through his legs and made him shudder throughout, and his cock quivered in his sleeping pants as he reached for it.

It was as if it was saying, *'Yes, take me out, feel me, stroke me, pluck me. Feel the strength of me in your hands, how hard I am, how stiff and thick, just as you've always wanted to touch, to taste. I am that thing; I am what you hunger for.'*

And so he gave in. Michael sighed and felt the tears slip down his face as he realized he was giving in to it. The guilt he felt, this thing that seemed so wrong, and that he could not ignore. He undid the latches and threw open the case, looking at the black beast shine in the moonlight. He held it in his hands, caressing it, looking at it, stroking its neck as he rubbed its back against his growing erection.

This was ecstasy; this was pleasure and pain. He wanted it. Nothing else could mean as much to him—no person, and no god. This was his god. This was the religion of his soul. This was the only scripture he needed to follow.

It was then, with a great sigh and his eyes closed, letting the tears slip down his face, that he placed it under his chin and began to play in the night. Not caring who heard, who he woke. He would play for the night; he would play for that moon. He would play for his soul and his desires. He would play for the young Larrabee who had touched his hand so gracefully and carefully.

He would play for Fiona Blackmoore.

He would play for them all. He would play for the darkened world. He would call those demons and those witches to his performance. He would call them from the land of the dead, invisible and out there across the bay.

He would play for it all. He would give them everything he had inside of himself at this moment. And it would be glorious and forbidden, dangerous and dark. It would be the song that the violin wanted to play. For in this moment, the instrument was the master, and he was nothing more than the zombie that did its bidding.

"ROUGH NIGHT?" FIONA asked him. She had just come out of her house, holding onto her books and wearing a navy satin dress, and her cheeks were lightly rouged with powder. The sun was bright in her eyes, and her smile seemed to fade as she took a look at him.

"I didn't sleep well," he said to her, his leather satchel in front of his knees, the handles being clutched by both hands.

"No offense, but it looks that way." Her smile returned as she placed her hand on his arm. "Come on, tell me what troubles you." They began to make their way down Knox and into Fairhaven, the water glistening brightly in that sun.

"I got a violin instructor. I haven't had one in ages; I haven't needed one in forever, but now, now my parents feel that I need to work on my control, and I guess he's the guy to do it."

"Hmm.. and what's his name? This instructor of yours that seems to be bothering you so much."

"Marsilio Merrin. I think he's Italian."

"What about all of this bothers you? Aside from feeling you don't need an instructor?" Michael thought about it for a moment. The truth was he hadn't been certain, he hadn't really thought on what, beyond feeling he didn't need a teacher, that unnerved him so. But then he thought of those absorbent dark eyes and that beautiful face, and he realized there was something far more sinister to him.

"He just... I don't know. He seems so mysterious, and he brought me the most beautiful violin. I had never seen anything like it before, and it just seemed so strange to me that he would gift me something that is obviously so expensive. Perhaps my feelings will change once I actually work with him."

Fiona nodded in understanding. "Well, that was very kind of him. Maybe he knew that of anyone, you, Michael Donovan, are beyond formal instruction, and he was trying to make peace with you before your lessons begin. Take it as a token of his respect for you."

He considered her words and allowed them to rest there on the surface of his brain. Perhaps that's all it was. He felt the sudden urge to tell his new friend about the dream, and the calling of the violin last night, but he dismissed this quickly. He didn't want to scare away his new friend, though he knew that if he did tell her, she would not run. She would not cast him aside or think him mad, but there was just something about all of it that made it seem difficult to confess out loud. Perhaps because he came closer to a deeper truth, a truth that he had never wanted to confess or to even touch on.

As they walked, passing the shops that were beginning to open, the doormen nodded to them as they passed the Fairhaven Hotel with its numerous turrets and spires. He thought of Richard Larrabee, his kind copper eyes, and he grinned. They crossed the bridge and approached the campus, and he hoped that they would cross his path, that once again he and the young Larrabee would look at one another, and he would smile at him and that smile would warm him.

The closer they got, the more the torments of the night and the new violin back in his room seemed to drift, to move far away from him, as if those things could not hold onto him this far from home.

It seemed suddenly at school he was safe.

"Another day of learning and whispers..." Fiona said with a sigh, as they moved up the walk towards the front entrance of the school with its large double doors. Michael hadn't taken notice at first, but as they walked he saw the numerous eyes on them, and the hands cupped to ears in whispered comment.

"They don't matter, right?"

She looked at him and nodded. "You're right. I just wish they'd find something more interesting to discuss than me. I'm really not that interesting."

Michael knew this wasn't true, though he would never voice it to her. She was a Blackmoore. She was from that family, a family that held so much mystery in their world. She was the first Blackmoore that was their own age, a Blackmoore that they could get close to, have access to. No longer were they simply a family that their parents went on and on about in the front parlors of their homes or in church. This was a real life Blackmoore that was right in front of them all.

"It'll die down, I'm sure of it. Give it a couple of weeks and they'll see how normal you are, how utterly just like them you are, and they won't care."

"Well, in any event," Fiona said with a sigh, "I'm glad you don't."

He smiled as she slipped her arm into his and squeezed him close. He had never had a friend like this, not someone who cared for him and valued him. He had never known that it was possible for people to become fast friends, but he knew that he and Fiona were like partners in crime. It was the two of them against the world. He would do anything for her. He would do anything to protect her. He would face down any army to keep her safe. He hadn't known that he had this capacity, but it turned out he did, and he was all the better for it.

"And I would do the same for you. And we're both the better for it." He didn't bother to look at her, and he was only taken aback for just a moment. But he knew then that she had read his thoughts, and he didn't care. In that moment, it was comforting. Maybe he wouldn't have to confess anything to her aloud because she would just know, and that knowing would make all the difference.

"Hey!" They stopped to see Richard Larrabee waving at them and jogging towards them with Carter Mayland in tow. They seemed to move effortlessly, as if gliding, and as they came closer Michael's heart began to race, and the blood moved quickly throughout his body.

Their eyes were locked to one another, and he tried to suppress his grin. He tried to hide his joy and his excitement, but there was nothing he could do about it. His grin grew into a smile as Richard came to a stop right in front of them.

He was so beautiful in his black trousers and jacket. His black silk tie seemed to reflect in those eyes, and his smile seemed only for Michael.

"Good morning, Fiona," Richard said.

"To you as well, Richard."

"And to you, Master Donovan. Good morning." *Master Donovan.* He had said it with such genuine warmth and affection. Michael didn't know how to respond.

"And to you as well, Master Larrabee."

Richard laughed and shook his head, placing his hand to his chest. "No, please; in this, you are far more the master."

What was going on? Could it be that Richard Larrabee was flirting with him? He had suspected slightly the afternoon before, and many times before that, but this... this seemed to be altogether different. "All right, then," Michael settled.

"Miss Fiona," Carter said, standing to the left of Richard and making a slight bow.

"Oh, please, Carter Mayland, don't you dare bow to me," she laughed, and touched his shoulder. Carter seemed hurt for just a moment, as if he had just been rejected—but upon the touch of her hand, Carter realized he had not been dismissed at all. He smiled brightly as he lifted himself back up, never letting go of her gaze. "You both are very kind."

"And brazen. Please do not forget brazen," Richard said to her.

"Certainly not," Fiona responded with a chuckle.

"We were hoping to escort you both into class." Michael was stunned. He couldn't believe this. Why was Richard Larrabee being so forward, especially if he truly did have affection for him? It was dangerous and sinful. It was absolutely wrong, and nothing good could come from it if anyone noticed.

"I suppose that would be fine. Wouldn't it, Michael?" Fiona's voice called him from his stupor, and he nodded a little hastily.

"Yes, of course." Richard smiled at him and tilted his head just a little, a slight, nearly unnoticeable bow to him as Michael and Fiona walked. The eager young men followed their strides but slightly held back, as if they were there to guard, and Fiona and Michael were the ones to lead.

V

THEY WALKED INTO MR. Upton's classroom and once again made their way towards the back of the class, taking desks nearest to the windows. For the first time ever—though Fiona would have never known this—Richard and Carter sat with them, taking desks next to them both. Carter and Richard had always sat towards the front of the room, but now, here they were, as if nothing that had been before mattered any longer. It was as if they had been spelled by them both.

They were all talking, all but Michael, who could only sit there and smile, watching it all, and everything seemed so far away and distant. Their voices, and whatever it was that was being discussed, were like sounds being heard from under the water. Here was Richard Larrabee, his classmate, the boy he had grown up with, whose home was only a few blocks down the hill from his own. The boy he had thought of often through the years was now talking to him and giving him his company. It was like something out of a dream, and he worried that perhaps it was a dream, another dream from which he could not wake.

Everything seemed to be right, to be perfect, as if nothing could hinder it. Then the whispered gasps of the classroom commanded his attention and brought him back to reality.

Marjorie Hampton walked in, along with Esther Smith and Kaitlin Fairchild. Marjorie's head was wrapped in a silken purple scarf, and her head was hung low in shame. The three girls looked at them, and their eyes all seemed to focus on Fiona. Marjorie's eyes grew wide in fear, but the other two girls held nothing but contempt on their faces. They made their way down the aisle, Marjorie taking a seat in the empty desk at the front of the room, but Esther and Kaitlin continued walking, making their way towards them, making their way towards Fiona, until they were both standing over her.

"You did this. We know that you did," Esther accused.

"How could you do something so cruel? You truly are a wicked girl." At that, Carter stood as if to defend her honor. Richard shook his head, but Fiona just sat there and looked at them without even blinking.

"And what makes you think I did something to her? I didn't even touch her."

Esther folded her arms across her chest, and Kaitlin laughed. "Because you're a witch. Your family sold their souls to the devil long before you were born. Father Kieran told us. And every generation after has already had their souls claimed, including yours. You can't be good and righteous for the Lord, even if you tried. You're evil. Black and pure, straight to your very core."

"That's enough of that!" Carter exclaimed defiantly. They looked at him, stunned, and Michael suddenly noticed that a crowd had gathered in the room. All of the students were standing and looking at them.

"And if I'm so dangerous, if I'm so evil and sinister as you say, then why is it that you are standing here in front of me, daring to make these accusations to my face?"

The two girls looked at one another, the question casting a shadow of fear on their faces. "I'll tell you why," Fiona began, standing now and resting her hands on her desktop. "Because you know that it's nonsense. You know that if I was really as you say, you wouldn't even dare approach me for fear of what I might do. But you know deep down, some part of you, that I have done nothing and I am not what you say.

"Maybe you should consider science. Perhaps simple genetics will explain what happened to your friend. I am not the fault you are looking for."

"We know you did it," Esther said defiantly.

"Then I suggest you back away fast, because if I truly am to blame—if I truly am what you say I am, if I truly have that power—then I would get as far away from me as possible. Because if it's true, then what I did to your friend is harmless compared to what it is I could do."

They all looked at her shocked, even Carter, who seemed to wonder for just a moment. Michael wanted to hide his shock, but he could not. This was something he had not expected, but nonetheless he admired. She had a courage that he wished he could possess. She was willing to throw caution to the wind and just be who she was, uncompromising and defiant. She refused to give in to the times or "keep her place" as so many women did in 1908.

Fiona sat back down and refused to look away from the girls. Once again she would not even blink, and Esther and Kaitlin slowly backed away from her, moving back down the aisle and taking their seat next to their shawled friend.

"Are you all right?" Carter asked.

"I am, yes. I'm sorry; I just got so angry." Michael wanted to hug his friend, but that was just something you dared not to do. It was an inappropriate display for any man, no matter how old, to show such closeness and affection to a woman, especially when so young.

"I think you were brilliant." It was Richard who said this, and they were all surprised.

Fiona laughed. "Well, it's nice to know I've got a fan."

Carter cleared his throat in an exaggerated manner. "Do not forget about me, Fiona."

She smiled at him, warm and serene. She cared for him. If she had not had any inkling towards him when they first met yesterday, he could see that it was slowly growing inside of her, blossoming like a young flower in the warm sun.

"And I know Michael is, without question," Richard said.

"Yes, as Richard said, you were brilliant." He wanted to talk to her alone, to speak in private of what had occurred and what was the truth about her and her family, but he also knew that to ask of her such a thing meant inviting the same kind of questioning. To let down the same walls and give the same honesty. How could he ask Fiona Blackmoore to be so vulnerable, to be so transparent, as if she were made of glass, unless he was willing and able to do the same?

"Don't worry," Fiona said suddenly, placing her hand on his arm and giving it a gentle shake of reassurance. "You and I will talk. When the time is right." He thought Carter and Richard had heard her, but they had not, and when he looked at her she was looking at them. Her hands were on her desk, her fingers holding lightly to her books.

Had he imagined it? Had he imagined her words—her touch? But he was certain of both, and none of this made any sense. *'All right,'* he said in his head, just in case she had, and just in case she would hear him again. For a moment there was nothing, then from the corner of her eye, Fiona looked at him and grinned.

Mathematics seemed to go on forever. It was the subject Michael hated the most, not that he was bad at it—quite the contrary; with his education in music, math seemed to come easy to him. But it was so boring, not like playing the violin, which he would often think about instead of algebra equations—but now, music was not at the forefront of his mind.

What grasped him now and took hold was Richard Larrabee sitting in front of him, the back of his head, the tiny hairs that ran along the back of his neck on the olive skin. Wondering what it would feel like to touch that hair, that skin, to run his fingers along the back of it, to feel the warmth and the soft of his flesh.

There was nothing he wanted more at this moment than to touch him, to just reach out when no one was looking. That was all he wanted, to touch him, to be touched by him, to hope that maybe Richard would turn around and smile at him as if thinking the same, or wanting the same. He just wanted so badly to feel that kind of affection, to feel that acknowledgment, to just feel his heart quicken and his body become alive.

But as he sat there looking at him, looking at that beautiful olive skin, he remembered that body burning on the pyre. He could recall the smell and taste of that flesh burning, and he thought he would vomit all over his desk, right then and there. He cupped his hand to his mouth and swallowed hard, trying to force it down, to push the sensation back into the pit of his stomach where it belonged.

He could not understand everything that was happening to him. He couldn't grasp it. There was no sense to be made of this darkness, this horror that seemed to make itself at home in his life. He wanted to understand where it was coming from, and he wondered if he was slowly starting to lose his mind. Michael tried to focus on Mr. Upton and his hand moving across the blackboard, writing out equation after equation for them to solve.

But then there was the music. It was calling to him. It was summoning him and there was an urge, a sudden need, to get up from his desk and return to his home, to sneak in and move up to his room unnoticed, simply to play that violin—that black instrument with its silver strings, that thing that knew his desires and knew how to fulfill them.

He wondered if anything else would ever do to him what the violin did to him. He wondered if there would be anything else that could take the place of the music. There seemed to be no answer, and there seemed to be no reprieve from what was happening to him. He had been able to ignore his desires for so long by throwing himself into the music.

The violin had once been able to take him far from all of that, but now it seemed to do the opposite. It seemed that the violin was making him meet those wants—those desires—head-on, and there was no escape. All there was was agony and ecstasy, all wrapped into one destructively glorious package.

He feared that the world might burn all around him, or that inky black water would consume everything at his feet, and he would be to blame for it all. That he was the one at the heart of all evil, that he was the one who made everything sinful. Perhaps Fiona Blackmoore wasn't the witch. Perhaps it was he, Michael Donovan, who had given his soul to the devil the moment he first took up the instrument as a five-year-old boy.

If that was the case, then he didn't know what to do. Here he was, playing the devil's instrument, as it was so often called, and lusting after the beautiful guy in school from the prominent family—just as prominent as his own—and fraternizing with a rumored witch. Maybe it all came from him.

Maybe this was all his creation, and they served his whim. Maybe what had happened to Marjorie was his doing. Maybe he had cursed her for whispering about his friend. Maybe it wasn't Fiona at all; maybe it was his anger and his will that caused her hair to fall out from her head.

Perhaps it had been him this entire time. As class continued, as they spent the last twenty minutes of the hour dedicated to math, he began to wonder if he could solve the equation of his own life, or if this was it. Perhaps it was an equation he could not work out. Perhaps it was something he could not solve.

Maybe there was no choice but to go with it, to bow to it and let it do its work. Maybe his destiny was to serve the devil till the very end, and stop fighting it. Perhaps there was no goodness inside of him to claim. Was that the truth? Was that the undeniable truth of it all: that he was doomed? That he had in fact sold his soul before he actually knew what it meant, and there was no reprieve and no way to save himself? He wanted to find the answer. He wanted it to be untrue. He wanted it to all be something as simple as an overactive imagination. Too much reading and too much religion. But neither thing was certain. The only thing that was, was that Michael Donovan felt like he was losing his mind.

BY LUNCH THEY WERE all ready to relax in the commons. The first half of the day had seemed to go on forever, but now it was over. They could relax, they could eat their lunch, and they could talk freely amongst themselves.

Richard and Carter smiled and shook hands with their friends as they moved through the school to the common room, but they did not join them. The two young men stayed with Fiona and Michael, and when they walked in all heads turned to their attention. This seemed like celebrity, or simple infamy. Was it Fiona Blackmoore, or was it the fact that Richard Larrabee and Carter Mayland were hanging with them suddenly? Did it really matter?

They slipped effortlessly into a table and Richard took his place next to Michael, and Carter found a home next to Fiona, whom he could not stop looking at.

"Do you mind if I sit next to you? I could move if you'd like."

Fiona looked at Carter and shook her head. "No, you're fine."

Michael looked at Richard and he smiled a dumb smile, a smile that seemed to express nothing but utter and simple happiness. He knew he didn't have to ask, and he wasn't going to. He seemed aware of the fact that there was no place else Michael wanted him than right there next to him, and Richard very obviously wanted the same thing.

"You know, my parents talk about your skill with the violin all of the time. I grew up listening to it."

Michael looked at him, embarrassed by such a thing. "I'm sorry you had to listen to that."

Richard shook his head. "No, I'm sorry I haven't seen you play before. I've heard you, though."

Michael's eyes grew wide. "You have?"

He nodded. "I've walked past your street more than once and have heard your music coming from inside. It's amazing. It's your music that always brought me back to your street whenever I felt the need for a stroll. Hoping that I would be able to hear you play."

"Why have you never told me before?" He shrugged. "I would have always welcomed you to come over and listen." Michael knew this was a lie the moment he said it, but he wanted to believe it. The truth of it was if Richard Larrabee had suddenly knocked on his door or approached him out of the blue in school and asked to hear him play, he would have been scared and mumbled something stupid and incoherent before walking away.

"I just didn't feel it was my place. I've never had the courage, really, I guess. I don't really know. It just seemed like I'd be intruding." Michael had never thought of that before, but perhaps he was onto something. Maybe he would have felt as if Richard was intruding on him in some way. Though he had always wanted and hoped for attention from the young Larrabee, there was something terrifying in the idea of actually getting it. Until now. Until Fiona Blackmoore.

Maybe it was that now that he had a friend, a confidant, a sense of not being completely on his own, that he could find ease in letting someone else enter his orbit. "Well, whenever you want, just let me know."

Richard smiled. "Well, what about this afternoon?"

Michael wanted to say yes, was about to say yes, when suddenly the dark eyes of Marsilio Merrin flashed across his mind, and he knew that he could not. "Today, no. Unfortunately, I have lessons today."

"Lessons? From my understanding, you don't need any. You could be a teacher of music yourself." Michael had always known this and felt this way, but there was no arguing with his parents, and he did not want to seem arrogant in any way, especially not in front of Richard.

"I have been told I need to work on my control. My form is just fine, but my control is lacking. I broke the strings on my violin the other night because I was playing too hard. I need to learn how not to play so forcefully."

Richard laughed. "I don't think there's a problem with playing anything too hard... you have to; otherwise how can you be the best?"

"With violin, it is a fine line. Some of the best music is created when you let go... but if you don't control your instrument it can control you, and that's when it becomes a problem."

Richard grinned, resting his elbow on the table and resting his cheek on his fist, his eyes seeming to glisten in the light. For just a moment, Michael wasn't even sure that he was breathing.

"I don't think there's anything wrong with being controlled by your instrument...." His other arm dropped onto the bench, and his hand seemed to move ever so closer to Michael's leg, brushing up against him. "Sometimes the best feeling is when your instrument takes control."

Michael's mouth fell open, but no words would come out. There it was; that touch, the feeling of Richards' fingers caressing the side of his leg, and his copper eyes seemed to shine like two pennies in the sunlight.

Those fingers moved along the side of his leg gently and slowly, and there was a moment where everything seemed to stop and nothing else existed—nothing else mattered. Not the people around him, not the whispers of gossip about his friend and her family, not the strict rules of his father, not the looming reality of Marsilio Merrin and his music lessons. Just this moment, this amazing connection he was feeling to Richard. If he could have died right then and there, he would have, and Michael would have done so happy and content.

It was the smallest amount of affection, the subtlest touch, and yet in this moment, it was all he could have ever hoped for.

"Well, some other time then," Richard said, still keeping his hand in place against Michael's leg. His erection was growing in his BVDs, threatening to burst free.

"Absolutely. Next time I don't have lessons. I'll let you know."

"So, who wants to go to the beach after school?" Carter's question got their attention, and Richard moved his hand away suddenly.

"Well, Michael can't; he has lessons," Richard said with a veiled tone of disappointment.

"I'd love to. I think that would be fun. You could show me something to do in this town." Michael looked at Fiona and frowned. He had hoped that she would walk with him back home, but then he was the one held with obligations, not them.

"I'm for it. I've been itching to go for the past couple of weeks!" Richard exclaimed.

"Great, then it's settled." Michael seemed to sober suddenly, as if the moment with Richard had been a fog, a haze that had cast itself over him but had now suddenly lifted, burnt off by the sun.

"Well," he said, standing. "If you'll excuse me, I need to use the restroom before we return to class." He turned from them and walked without looking back, without waiting to see if they would object. It wasn't their job to object or try to console him. It wasn't their life; it wasn't their obligations.

In the past, he wouldn't have cared. He had never had friends or been invited out to the beach. Sure, he had known that's what everyone did when the season became warm, but he had never had any interest in doing anything other than playing his violin. But now... now he did have reason, and it turned his stomach and felt like a bee's sting deep inside to have to be excluded.

But he knew that all that really mattered was the music anyway. Sure, he was upset now, but he knew once he had instrument in hand it would all be okay. The hurt and the anger would leave him; it would be expelled from him by the power of the music. The violin would summon it, would pull it out of him like a priest performing an exorcism.

He found comfort in that knowledge. Knowing that no matter what, the music would always be there to take him away from it all. To free him from the things that he feared he was missing out on. The music always comforted him and reminded him that with it, there was no need for anything else.

"ARE YOU OKAY?" FIONA asked him. She was leaning over to him and speaking in a whisper. Michael didn't know what to say, wasn't sure how to express something that he felt was so stupid. He felt as if he would sound like a whining child that was crying because he didn't get the toy he wanted. "Whatever it is, you can tell me."

Michael sighed. "Yeah, it's just I hate that I can't go with you guys to the beach. It just seems like I always have obligations. Like I always have things that I have to do that are not of my own choice, and I have to obey."

Fiona offered a comforting smile and there was sympathy, and even understanding, in her eyes. "I know how that is. There are things, things in this world that are beyond us, things that are set out for us and no matter what, we have no choice but to obey them."

Michael looked at Richard, who was writing in his notebook. The essay assignment for the day was a reflection thus far on the failures of Faust. It seemed right now the only failure that Michael could see was in being so blinded by desire and a need to have the world that he was willing to give up his immortal soul just to have it. But then, that was the entire point of the story of Faust.

"It's because you're so close to the one thing you want, and yet the world around you seems to be taking you away from it." He looked at her, stunned. Her eyes moved from his face to the back of Richard's head. Did she know? Was she telling him that she knew his dark secret, that she knew what burned within his heart? That she knew what made him ache, what had made him ache for so long?

"I guess, yes, that's it. That's it exactly." There was no need for her to say "I know." She was well aware of how it ached. She knew that he burned for Richard, that everything inside of him had pined for his classmate, had yearned for him. He just wanted to spend time with him, time outside of these walls, away from the eyes of everyone else. A chance for both of them to express what was inside. The thing that they both seemed to share, the desire that seemed to be exactly the same.

"It'll come, Michael, I promise you. You just have to be patient. Now, let's finish our work before we're both given marks for the day." Michael sighed and gave a nod, running his hand through his hair and picking his pencil up and putting it to paper once again, focusing on Dr. Faust and the dilemma of his immortal soul—much, as it seemed, like the dilemma of his very own.

VI

AT THE END OF THE DAY, they all walked out of class. At this point they had all learned to ignore the whispers and the stares. It had taken a lot less time than Michael had thought it would, but the four of them seemed to form this kind of unit. It was a feeling he had sensed the day before, and when they felt the warmth of the sun, standing there at the top of the steps, the afternoon heat beckoning to them, he realized that whatever anyone thought or what anyone said didn't matter. All that mattered was that they were all enjoying the company of one another.

The air was rich of salt from the bay and fragrance of the flowers around them. Flowers that were not seen, as there were none on campus, but from the houses all around them, their gardens were in full bloom and their perfume was everywhere. If only he could stand here and take in this moment forever. The four of them on this cement, Carter and Richard taking off their jackets and stretching their arms, and the light from the peridot necklace around Fiona's neck glittering in the sunlight.

"Shall we go?" Carter asked.

"Let's!" Fiona responded. Carter extended his arm and she took it, following him down the steps.

Richard and Michael looked at them, and to one another. Michael knew that Richard wished that he could do the same. But it was not for them. It was not allowed. Such behavior would bring about more condemnation than an accusation of witchcraft.

"You know what I'm thinking—what I'm feeling," Richard said to him suddenly, having leaned into him. He spoke so quietly so that Michael had to tilt his head to hear him.

"If it's anything even close to what I am, then I understand completely."

Richard smiled at him. "Would you stay close to me? Allow me to walk so close to you that we can imagine that our hands are touching? That our arms are locked as one?"

Michael looked at him and tried to search for words, something that was poignant and adequate that he could say, but there was nothing. There were no words on this thing, this unspoken declaration and coded expression of their feelings, that left them both elated and melancholic.

"Yes." The smile on both of their faces had no definition. Michael had never smiled this way before, and he was certain that Richard hadn't either. They stepped off the steps, making their way down the long walk, and that walk seemed to stretch for miles. Richard and Michael moved close to one another, so close that they could barely feel the air pass between them. There was barely a separation as they just walked in stride with one another.

Fiona and Carter were some steps ahead, but it didn't matter. Let Carter and Fiona be happy and content, locked arm and arm, moving through the world with the freedom granted to them for being a man and a woman. They were happy just for what they could get.

Richard and Michael both wished for more. To feel their hands clasp together, for their fingers to interlock, to feel the warmth and the sweat, to feel flesh upon flesh, but for now they would have to make do. Richard wanted to escort Michael like a gentleman would, and Michael knew this, because Michael wanted it too. But if this was all they could have, just this time to walk together as close as possible without the actual pleasure of touch, then they would take it.

He wanted to tell Richard so many things, but he didn't know how. As they made their way across the bridge into Fairhaven and saw Dianaca Castle looming on the hillside, along with the spire of Sacred Heart, Michael thought of home. He thought of his violin and his new instructor waiting for him, and he felt as if he would cry. As if he would fall to the ground right then and there and cry out for freedom, for a chance to suspend time and linger as long as possible with Richard Larrabee.

He wanted to skip his lessons; he wanted to forget about returning home to the manor on the hill with its garden and enormous orchard. He just wanted to abandon all of it and go with Richard and the rest of his friends. To go to the beach and languish in the sun and laugh, and roll up the legs of his trousers and run into the freezing waters of Bellingham Bay.

There was much more to life than just his lessons and the music at the moment, and that thing was Richard. That one thing that carried more weight and held more importance than his violin, more value than the music was spending time with Richard Larrabee, of confessing what was deep inside of his heart.

"If only you were coming with us...."

Michael looked at him and sighed. "I know. Trust me when I tell you, I wish I was too."

Richard stretched his arm out slightly, just enough to brush it quickly against Michael's. "And trust me when I tell you that if you could, I would have found a moment to steal you away to the edge of the water, away from everyone else, and confess to you everything that I have wanted to for so long."

Michael grinned. "And trust in me when I tell you, Richard Larrabee, that I want nothing more than to hear those words, and that I've wanted to tell you the same. It has been inside of me for so long, and for so long I have wondered if perhaps you felt the same."

They were nearing Harris and once they did, Michael would have to continue on to Knox, while the three of them went the opposite way down to the water. He had never dreaded a street corner more than at this very moment.

"I don't want to part, but I want you to know, Master Donovan, that I have and I will tell you so when the opportunity comes, and I know it will come. I know it will be soon, even if I have to move heaven and earth to make it happen, I will, and I will tell you these things—we will tell each other these things! This is a promise to you."

Michael knew Richard's words to be true. He nodded and wanted so much to wrap his arms around him, to touch the firm width of his backside and kiss his lips.

It burned inside of him; the want in his heart, the desire and the need. Everything inside of his body was pulling him towards Richard, but he couldn't give in and neither would Richard. Not at that moment, standing on the corner of the street in front of all of those people in those shops, moving in and out with all of their packages, and sitting in cafes drinking cups of coffee or glasses of wine. No, all of that would have to wait.

"Goodbye, my friend. I will see you in the morning," Fiona said to him, kissing him lightly on the cheek.

"Yes," Michael smiled, and Carter waived.

"Till tomorrow, Master Donovan." Richard bowed his head once again; just enough for Michael to notice and for Michael to return it.

"I'll see you tomorrow, Richard." He stood there and watched them go, making their way down Harris and towards the bay. Michael felt everything inside of him shrink away, and he wanted to stand there until they grew so small in form that they were like gnats, until they were nothing but distant specks in the sun.

He turned and looked up to the hill, towards the direction of his home, and he knew that it was waiting for him, calling to him—that violin, resting in the red arm chair in his room. Summoning him to forget everything, and to come and play.

The violin was missing him, and now he was missing it. He looked at them once more and sighed. They were now exactly as small as he thought they would be—and inside, at this very moment, that's how they felt: small and unimportant. They were nothing more than distant memories and shadows of desires of things that he had long ago given up, things that had all been replaced with music and the singing on the strings against the deftness and skill of his bow.

VII

HE STOOD THERE ON THE street staring at his home, the turret of his parents' room to the left of him on the second floor, reaching out beyond the apple trees. The light purple of the wood promised a sense of joy coupled with the white trim of the great Victorian.

He looked over to his window above the roof of the porch, and it was as if he could feel his violin waiting for him, as if it were not an instrument at all, inanimate, but a living, breathing person—a specter standing in his room at the window, looking down at him.

He sighed and pushed open the wrought iron gate and walked up the flagstone path the seemed like a serpent's tongue sticking out between the neatly-groomed orchard on either side and spread out an acre to the right side. He smelled the fragrant flowers and thought of how sickly sweet it was in the fall, when the apples would be littered all over the grass and rot.

That was the most wonderful and intoxicating smell, those rotting apples, mixed with the mossy damp of the rain. All of that was so far away now, memories of the past and a premonition of how things would be in the fall, but for now everything was fresh and alive and in the prime of youth. As he continued towards the steps of the front porch, he thought about Fiona and Carter and Richard, and all the fun he was sure they were having at the moment. He wondered then if he was even missed. He missed them. That was certain, and this sense of doom, as if he would never see them again, began to haunt him. He wasn't certain where it was coming from, but he felt as if the moment he walked inside of his home and closed the front door, he would be locked away from them forever.

There was no point in thinking of such things, and he knew this. He knew that there was no reason for it. It wasn't like he wouldn't be going to school the next morning; it wasn't like he wouldn't see their smiling faces or hear their words. Richard had all but confessed very plainly that he felt deeply for him—as deeply as he felt for Richard—and of course the young Larrabee would be just as eager and yearning to see him.

He moved slowly up those wood steps and heard the laughter from beyond the walls. He knew that his new teacher was here, waiting for him to begin their lessons; he also knew that his mother was charmed by him. His stomach seemed to turn at this. There was a gnawing fear inside of him, and yet what was it? What was disturbing him about his mother Claudette getting on with Marsilio Merrin? Did he fear that, just like him, his mother harbored secret desires, desires beyond their home and his father?

Michael didn't much care for his father as a person most of the time, but he did love him, and knew how much his father worshipped his mother, though often it was hard for him to show it. But there had been moments, moments in private, that Michael had seen this love and affection pour out of Jasper Donovan for his wife—and Michael suddenly feared that somehow Marsilio Merrin would take it all away.

He turned the brass knob with its ornate fleur-de-lis ornamentation and walked inside, staring at his reflection in the glass in the middle of the door.

The first floor was filled with the music of the phonograph, and the vases were filled throughout the house with all of the fresh and abundant flowers of his mother's garden. Nellie came to him immediately from the dining room and took his bag and jacket from him. He thanked her as she gave a nod and made her way down the hall, a look of slight dismay on her face.

"There you are!" his mother said to him, sitting in the black Chesterfield in the front room, her beautiful face beaming as she looked at him. To her left, sitting in the sofa in front of the large picture window, was Marsilio, dressed in the same black satin suit as before, with a deep wine-red tie around his neck, the jacket open and showing the black vest with its gold buttons.

"Took a longer stride home, I imagine...." He met Marsilio's face and was unnerved by that beautiful grin, a grin that said he knew so much more than he would ever reveal. He stirred desire inside of Michael once again, and it was as if, somehow, there was a way in which his new teacher knew this, and made no move to hide this from Michael.

"It was such a wonderfully beautiful day, I felt the need to linger in it for a little longer. To clear my head." They both nodded and his mother stood, smoothing out the front of her emerald gown of velvet.

"Well," she began, making her way towards him and kissing him on the cheek, "I'll leave you to your lessons; I'll be in the garden reading if you need me." He nodded, and Marsilio bowed. "And Michael?"

"Yes?"

"Try to be gentle. He's a nice man, and your father is paying him a lot of money." Michael nodded, and she disappeared down the hall and to the back of the house, yelling for Nellie to follow her out with some lemonade.

"So, Master Donovan, let's –"

"It's Michael."

"I beg your pardon?"

"Just call me Michael." There was something about being called Master Donovan by anyone else other than Richard that upset him. It was as if, from that first moment that Richard had called him that in the morning, it now belonged to him. It was Richard's name for him—though formally, he was referred by that title at parties and by the staff. But from Marsilio he would not have it. He did not want to hear it from this man's lips. And it seemed that once again, Marsilio Merrin knew something of this that he wasn't saying, because that terrible and knowing grin spread across his beautiful face.

"Very well, Michael. And you can call me –"

"Mr. Merrin."

Marsilio laughed, a deep-throated laugh the reverberated inside of Michael's body like a strong engine. "Whatever you like."

Michael gave a nod and moved towards the steps, refusing to take his eyes off of the man. "If you'll excuse me, I need to grab my violin."

As he placed his hand on the rail and began to lift his foot to the step, Marsilio shook his head. "Not to worry, your mother had Nellie bring it down shortly after I arrived." Michael sighed and moved into the front parlor and to the music room, Marsilio's hand outstretched formally as he passed.

There it was, sitting in the wooden chair with the harp carved into its back, waiting for him. His dangerous friend. His friend that cried out all of his feelings. Marsilio went to grab it for him, but Michael rushed him and snatched it from the chair quickly.

"Don't worry, I got it." Marsilio nodded and stood silently as Michael opened the case and removed the violin from its case. He looked at that varnish, so dark that its red could only be seen in that high midday sun. The strings glistened and seemed so delicate and almost invisible, like the webs of a spider.

He placed it under his chin and kept his eyes on Marsilio, those dark eyes that looked so eager, as if starving, absolutely hungry to hear the strings cry out. Michael had never seen anyone have such intensity for music—not even Michael had starved so much—as if there was something more to all of this, a bigger plan, a plan that he was somehow a part of and yet did not know his role.

"Begin."

"What would you like me to play?"

"Whatever you wish. Whatever your heart wishes to say." He had never been told this before. In the past, his instructors had always had him play specific pieces, something they had already prepared.

"Any composition by any composer?"

Marsilio sighed and shook his head. "No, Michael, I want you to play freely; I want you to play what's inside. Let's be honest, shall we? You are beyond simple instruction. You know how to play the pieces of others; you have been doing it for years. Why would I teach you to play something you already know? This is about learning control, and to first learn to control your instrument you need to let it free, to grow and experience release."

Michael blushed and looked away from him.

"Don't be embarrassed. Let the music move you. Let it take you to wherever you want to go. No matter how far away, no matter with whom. Let that dance take you."

Dance. He thought of the fire and the body and the devils. He swallowed hard and closed his eyes, placing chin to rest and bow to strings, and then he began to play.

It came out slow and melodic, moving with a serene calm, thinking about the beginning of his day, his moments stolen with Richard. And as he continued, moving through the confrontation in class and the courage of Fiona's words, the music picked up in pace, crying out against accusation, and then moved into a harmony of hope as he stood on those steps with Richard. It continued until he remembered nearing Harris Street, then it changed, became sullen, almost detached, as if drifting away and running out of steam.

Then he felt the hot breath on him and the hands, strong hands take hold of his sides. "Stand straighter. Arch your shoulders back and let it take you away...." Marsilio was right in his ear, the hot of his breath on his skin, and the smell of it something musky and enticing, but also sulfuric, like a burnt match. It was a smell that was intoxicating.

"Feel the music; feel the violin reach deep inside of you... to your darkest places, and go with it." He tried to hold onto the memories of the day, but those images changed, began to flash away the faster he moved his bow. Those draped dancers emerged once again from the black water, and those fires once again burned the dead flesh.

"Yes," Marsilio purred. "That's it. Keep with that." Michael played faster and faster; his violin felt hot and his body moved, swaying with the rhythm, locked in place by his teacher's hands. "Play!" Those flames grew brighter and that hallow in the woods became darker in the night around him, and as the devils emerged from the ooze and played with him, he could feel his cock begin to grow stiff between his legs, and he didn't care. He didn't worry, and Marsilio's hands continued to move, making their way down the sides of his legs, curving to the front of his thighs, and soon those hands were pressed against his dick.

"Keep playing." The sweat formed on his head and hands and arms, and he was dampening his shirt, and he didn't care. Marsilio's fingers wrapped around his shaft and began to stroke him slowly.

"Oh, my...." His words trailed off. The fire was so intense, and the dancers sheathed in black drapery moved ritualistically around him and raised their hands to the night sky as that body continued to burn. Then beautiful naked bodies, both male and female, seemed to rise from those flames. Their flesh glistened with sweat and blood slipped down that flesh, over nipples and down abdomens and to their organs between their legs. But their heads were not human heads; their heads were the heads of bucks with long antlers, and cats with fierce dripping fangs.

"Keep playing...." He felt everything inside begin to give as the sensation of orgasm rode up through his legs as Marsilio was stroking him faster, whispering in his ear: "Keep going," and he did. He had never felt another male hand on his body, had never had his cock touched like this, and he couldn't stop. He didn't want it to stop. Marsilio was working him as he worked the violin, and just as the explosion seemed imminent, Marsilio suddenly stopped. Not releasing his hand, but kept it in pace.

"Now, slow it down...." And Michael did. "Feel what I'm doing to your instrument... feel how I take care of it... how I stop it from releasing... from letting it all go." Michael nodded and let out a great sigh, leaning his body against Marsilio's. "Feel me support you... feel me take care of you and control the rhythm of your body. Make your violin do the same... make it do for you, what I am making you do for me."

Michael was swaying and shivering against Marsilio's strong body. He cooled his violin and the melody slowed, and Marsilio continued to stroke him once again, slowly pumping his throbbing cock. "That's it, beautiful Michael... that's it...." And then Marsilio began to pump him harder once again, and Michael's speed picked up and they were once again in unison. And soon that sensation came up once again, riding up in his legs.

It was then that Marsilio slipped his hand beneath his trousers, inside his briefs. His hot hand and fingers cupped the flesh of his cock and continued to pump him, and Michael continued to play until he couldn't take it anymore. He stopped his bowing without a screech and the cum came out of him in a great rush, a fount like he had never felt, and it went everywhere. It was over Marsilio's fingers and his underwear, and in the pubic hair and mixing with the sweat on his balls, which Marsilio gently massaged.

"That was perfect, my beautiful Michael. I told you I would help you." Michael couldn't speak. His body was filled with the most delicious sensations, and Marsilio just held him. They were standing in that wood now, amongst those dancers and demons, and Michael didn't care. If this was what hell felt like, if this is what his body would feel in exchange for his immortal soul, then he never wanted it back.

"Yes."

"And do you want to always feel this way, Michael? Do you always want to know this?"

Michael whimpered into Marsilio's ear.

"Then allow me to instruct you always and I promise you, I will always give you such pleasures, such sounds, such music."

Michael nodded. "Yes...."

Marsilio pulled his hand out of his trousers and brought it to Michael's face, turning his head back and tilting it so their lips met, their tongues touched, and the semen on his fingers found its way onto both of their lips and tongues. They licked it, just as they both tasted the salt of one another's skin.

"Forever and ever, my beautiful Michael."

"Forever...."

MICHAEL SEEMED TO COME out of a daze, and he was slouched in his music chair, alone. The sweat was dripping off of him, and there was the stain of his orgasm on the front of his pants, and he could smell only sulfur. He was alone. Marsilio Merrin was nowhere to be found, as if he had never been there. It was just he and his violin, resting perfectly in his hand.

"Hello?" he called out. But there was no one. "Mr. Merrin?" he asked again, but only his voice answered him.

"Master Donovan?" Nellie came towards him and he stood quickly, placing his violin in front of his stained crotch, and smooth back his mess of dark brown hair.

"I'm fine, Nellie." The sun had set, and the lamps were glowing throughout the front parlor. How much time had passed? He was certain that he had only started playing fifteen minutes earlier, but it would seem that the rest of afternoon had left him, and now it was the coming dark that found him in that chair instead.

"Oh, good. Might I say, you made the most interesting music. It was like nothing this house has ever heard before. Your mother and I spent two hours in the garden, just absolutely amazed."

Two hours? How could that be?

"Uh, thank you."

Nellie smiled gently. "You're welcome; I can't wait to hear it again the day after tomorrow."

"The day after tomorrow?"

She nodded. "Why, yes—your next lesson, sir."

"Oh, right. Yes, I forgot myself for a moment." He began to make his way past her, catching his reflection in the mirror. There seemed to be something different, something in his eyes and face he couldn't place, though he was sure she didn't notice.

"Please change for dinner."

Michael nodded. "Yes, I'll be down in a few moments."

Michael raced up the steps, past the portraits on the walls, and threw himself into his room, slamming the door behind him. The sun was burning pink and violet beyond the window of his room. He wondered where Marsilio Merrin had gone, and how time had moved so fast. How had he not known him to leave?

The shock and left-over passion quickly began to melt away and fill with sorrow as he remembered Richard Larrabee, and he felt overcome with the sense of betrayal. What had he done? What had he allowed to happen? He had to be losing his mind. That couldn't have happened. He had to have imagined it. And right in front of his teacher.

It wasn't real. Couldn't have been. Nothing like that would ever occur. But he knew it was. Though he couldn't explain it, he knew that it was, that it had all happened. And he knew that it could not happen again, no matter what. This would be erased, and he would make it known to Marsilio Merrin. He would not be taken advantage of again. Never. He belonged to Richard. His heart only bore one name, and it was Richard's.

VIII

ONCE AGAIN HE HAD THOSE dreams, those frightful visions of that witches' sabbat. That was the only thing he could think to call it, and yet if those were witches, they were not witches like Fiona. Those beings were dark and served evil things, things that he had read in history, the legends that fueled the inquisition. The Burning Times, as they were called—and the fevered fears and accusations that ran rampant and sent twenty to death in Salem, Massachusetts.

He wanted to tell Fiona everything that was plaguing him. He wanted to confess it all and hope that she could explain it to him, that she could make sense of it for him, and perhaps ease his troubled mind. Perhaps she would tell him that these were nothing more than fears and his subconscious concocting these things. There had to be some sort of answer.

He used to give little credence to the idea of the supernatural. Witches and demons, and dark things with grave power, seemed all a grim fairytale told to children in the dark of night on Halloween. This was something else entirely now, though; this was something that felt all too real. And if it was like this, then there had to be something more, something deeper, at the root of it all.

He was late to class. He had overslept, though his parents had both been out by the time he emerged—his father Jasper at the lumber mill, and his mother out to a breakfast with the

South Hill Society ladies. When he saw Nellie, she assured him that she would say nothing of his tardiness.

When he finally stepped in class, he found the desk next to Fiona empty. He hastily apologized to Mr. Upton for his being late, but given that this was the first time that this had ever happened, his teacher forgave it with little word.

"What happened to you this morning? I waited." He looked at her and saw the concern all over her beautiful face, and he shrugged. "We all waited." Richard's face had lit up when he walked into the room, and their eyes had stayed locked on one another from the classroom door to the desk. His head turned and followed him as he moved past and sat down in the desk behind him.

"I overslept. I was so worn out from practice yesterday, I guess. I don't know." Fiona nodded but seemed not to accept this, as if knowing there was more to it. It seemed that sometimes Fiona could penetrate his mind and read everything that was there with such clarity, and at other times it was as if she could hear or see nothing, however it worked. He was puzzled.

"I was worried," Richard whispered to him.

Michael looked at him and took in the deep beauty of his face, and smiled softly. "I'm all right. I'm sorry. But the good news is I don't have practice today. I'm free." Richard smiled at him brightly and gave a nod before turning back around to face the front of the class.

"I think we need to talk. Very soon," Fiona whispered. He looked at her, and he could see it in her eyes that she meant to tell him everything and that it was time that he did the same.

"I would like that very much." She let her head tilt ever so slightly, and brushed those auburn locks over her shoulder. She was beautiful in white linen and black stockings, her sleeves short and resting just past her shoulder blades. "When?"

"Tonight. Tonight we will speak." Tonight? How would they manage that? He had never met anyone in the night before. Would he sneak out of his house? How could he do that when the night staff was always roaming the halls and keeping the home safe from possible prowlers?

"Do not worry about that." There it was again. She had heard his thoughts again. It was dizzying. Truly dizzying. He couldn't make sense of anything that was happening in his life anymore. And the touch, the burning lips and strong feeling of Marsilio Merrin rushed through him, and turned him inside out with a great sense of guilt.

AS BEFORE, THEY SPENT the afternoon outside on the lawn reading from *Faust*. The four of them sat slightly apart from everyone else, and after what happened the last time, the class seemed to want to keep their distance from Fiona.

Michael wondered if he was the only one who noticed this. Perhaps it was because he always felt as if he were on the outside looking in: he understood the other three just seemed to be absorbed in their books, and Carter and Richard only seemed concerned with making sure they stayed as close to Fiona and Michael as possible without arousing any certain suspicion. Though by this time Michael had also taken notice that suspicion had already been aroused in others, he was certain that everyone suspected that both boys were enamored of Fiona—that none would have ventured to guess that two of the boys were enamored with each other.

By the end of the day, they all once again agreed to go to the beach. Fiona, Carter, and Richard had had so much fun the afternoon before and they wanted to return, and it meant more now that Michael was free to go as well.

He wished that the day had gone with little incident, but the rumors had started to spread through the halls of Fairhaven by the end of the day that Fiona had hexed Marjorie Hampton, and everyone was certain that she had bewitched Carter and Richard's hearts and minds to her will—for how else could be explained all their attentions? The other girls burned with hatred towards Fiona, and this was now matched with a jealousy over wanting claim on Carter and Richard, and finding that now both boys were unavailable.

When it came to Michael and his role in all of this, no one suspected anything. They had always thought him strange—mostly arrogant and inflated with ego over his skill, and that he came from such a well-respected and prominent family. It had always been obvious to them that Michael felt no need to try to befriend anyone because he felt himself apart and more interesting than anyone else at Fairhaven.

Everyone now only spoke to this rumored and made-up arrogance and "greater than" attitude that made him befriend Fiona Blackmoore. That he found her shocking and diabolical reputation appealing, and more interesting than anything that his schoolmates had to offer.

All of this was untrue, of course. Michael never saw himself as greater or more interesting than any of his classmates. He truthfully had just held little interest in putting in the effort to get to know them or spend time with him, when everything he had ever done—all of his energy and free time—had been devoted to his music. Besides, he wasn't the one who had approached Fiona; she had opened the doors of communication with him. If she hadn't, well, Michael knew that he wouldn't have put in the time or energy to get to know her either.

But as for he and Richard, there were no suspicions, no rumors, and no one had ever seen anything to raise question. Part of him was relieved by all of this. The last thing he wanted was to put him and Richard in danger of being discovered, but at the same time it also stung him, because it meant that what existed between them was of no notice—that he was of no notice. He might as well have been invisible at this point.

They walked in the way they had before, in the same fashion, only this time they all walked together as a unit. The sun felt nice, and when the boys took off their jackets, Richard offered to carry his. They couldn't walk hand-in-hand or arm-in-arm, but Richard could carry his jacket for him, and Michael was glowing inside at this gesture.

When they reached Harris, standing on the corner surrounded by brick citadels and lamp-posts on either side, they waited for a trolley and a few horse-drawn buggies to pass by before crossing the dirt road and back onto the flagstone walk. They made their way down, past the shops and past the wide fields of tall grass, reaching the entrance to Fairhaven Park. The sixteen-acre grounds featured a beautiful rose garden, which was a favorite of the ladies of the Cooperative Society, as well as the ornate pavilion, and the wading pool and petting zoo were a favorite of many of the children.

But this they would pass and continue on to the beach at the park's very edge.

The beach insofar was mostly a grassy patch of land and rocks. There was no sand, just grass and the thicket of birch trees that acted as a wall. But this was nice, and when they sat their book-bags down on the grass, Richard and Carter kicked off their shoes and rolled up their sleeves, revealing their strong and beautiful arms.

Michael and Fiona looked at them both with hunger and desire. They craved the both of them in such a carnal way, a way that only seemed more prominent after what had occurred the day before with Marsilio—or what hadn't occurred, whatever the truth of it really was.

"That's a good idea." Michael slipped off his patent leather shoes carefully, followed by his socks. As he went to undo the cuffs of his shirt and roll up the sleeves, Richard walked over to him, their eyes meeting. The heat of his body seemed to be emanating from him like a radiator.

"Let me help you; it can be tricky." Michael blushed as Richard reached down and took hold of his sleeves, his fingers grazing his arms and lingering a little bit longer than would be normal, before gently and meticulously rolling up the cotton to his elbows.

They stared at one another so deeply, and Michael's heart seemed to be beating so fast that he feared it would burst out of his chest at any moment, bathing Richard Larrabee in a hot, wet crimson spray.

"Thank you."

Richard sighed, "You're very welcome, Master Donovan." There it was: *Master Donovan*. It only sounded right coming from Richard; of that Michael was now certain, and if Marsilio Merrin ever addressed him that way again, he would smash that violin over his skull. "You ready to go into the water?" Michael looked over Richard's shoulder and saw that Carter and Fiona were already splashing around in the glittering, cool bay. It was as if they were kicking up diamonds or the purest gold, and it rained down like sparks in the sun.

"I'll beat you to it!" And with that Michael took off, laughing as he ran into the freezing water, Richard chasing right behind.

They were all screaming out in laughter and excitement, kicking water at one another, and Fiona and Michael began jumping up and down and dancing in the water. Michael had never felt this kind of sublime freedom. He had never felt this young before. Many children their age—the poorer ones—were already deep into marriages and families, but not them. They were in the senior class, and they would have the chance to go off to university, and maybe carve a life for themselves outside of this town.

Maybe, just maybe, Michael thought, he and Richard could somehow form a life somewhere, perhaps Paris or Berlin. Someplace far from everyone. Maybe New York. Anything was possible.

The world seemed to be nothing but possibilities to him in this moment. Being in this water, playing around carefree, was the greatest moment so far in all his seventeen years—next to his first meeting with the violin and his moments stolen with Richard.

Richard reached out and took his arm suddenly, and drew his ear close to his lips. "Can we go and speak in private?" Michael turned and looked at him, looked into those amazing eyes, and nodded. Those eyes that seemed to hold him steadfast and in place in this world; he would agree to go anywhere with him.

They treaded out of the water and back up onto the grass, Richard leading Michael towards the cluster of birch trees beyond the grass, back towards the direction of town. They said nothing, just walked. Michael kept his eyes focused on the back of Richard's head.

"What is it?" he asked as soon as they had stepped into those trees, obscured from anyone's sight.

"Michael, I do not believe in condemnation, and I do not believe that feeling, that love and passion—any of it—is wrong or sinful, or a sickness. If that were true, then that would mean the only real sickness would be love itself, and everyone would be ill. Everyone would be committed. And perhaps then everyone should be."

Michael nodded, trying to catch his breath and resisting the urge to put his hand to his chest to try to hold his heart in place. "I agree."

"Then you must agree that there is something so great and deep between us, and you must know that I carry such affection for you, and that I have for quite some time.

"I have never tried to rationalize it away or try to seek some sort of help for it, because I don't think that it is something that needs to be helped, and I have often felt that you felt the same. Whenever our eyes met, I could feel that we had the same deep affection for one another. The only reason I have never approached it sooner is that in this world—in these times that we live in—there is no easy way to confess feelings for one's own sex without risking being locked up in some state sanitarium."

Richard stretched out his left arm and took hold of the trunk of one of those skinny birch trees.

"In this, too, we are in agreement," Michael replied, moving closer to Richard, who was grinning and sighing and shaking his head.

"If you only understood the power of what you do to me."

Michael smirked and looked to the ground quickly, only to have Richard's bent index finger gently nudge his head up by his chin.

"I have wanted you for so long, Michael Donovan. To touch your face, to touch your hands, to hold you close to my chest, to let you hear my heart beating for you, to imagine what it would be like to lie down with you, to feel your body, to pet your hair...." His hand grazed the side of Michael's cheek gently and traced the line of his jaw. "To kiss your lips with my own." And there it was:

they were drawing closer, his thumb touching Michael's soft lip, bringing his head closer and closer.

"It's all I've wanted as well..." Michael said while closing his eyes, and Richard was doing the same.

"Then let's fight it no longer. Let's give in to our hearts and give in to the love that we both have felt for so long...." And then there was the meeting of their lips, Richard's hand on the back of Michael's head holding him in place. First it was just air that passed between their open mouths, and then the tongues followed, slipping past them and massaging one another. It was slow and gentle, and for a moment they pulled away and looked at one another, smiling and laughing, trying to catch their breath.

Their hearts were beating so fast and then they came together again, bodies slamming hard against one another, pushing backs against trees and almost wrestling as they kissed. They felt their erections grow stiff and strong between their legs, drilling against their thighs.

This was music; this was the melody. This was how it was supposed to be and they couldn't stop. No matter what they did, they could not stop. Not at this moment, when all the stars in the heavens seemed to explode and set the world before them on fire.

Fire.

He was flooded once again with the memory of those visions, and he thought that somewhere in the distance beyond these birch trees, he could hear them chanting. But then it faded with the taste of Richard's mouth, the press of his weight against his chest, as he held him in place against a tree.

Michael pushed him back and jumped up, wrapping his legs around Richard's waist, and Richard cupped his buttocks and steadied him. They continued to kiss, continued to take in the scent of each other.

Michael let go and touched back to the ground and they looked at one another, now holding tight to each other's hands and fighting the urge to keep on kissing.

"What do we do now?" Michael asked him, their breath labored.

"We get far away from here. We leave Fairhaven; we leave Bellingham, all of it. We go and leave this place, and make a life for ourselves somewhere else. I don't care about any of this! All I care about is you. As long as we're together, who cares about the rest?"

Michael thought on this, thought of everything in his life, and he agreed. "Yes! Damn it all to hell!" They laughed.

"Michael!" Fiona called out. "Michael and Richard, where are you two?"

"Be right there!" he shouted back, never taking his eyes off of Richard. "And what of our friends?"

Richard shrugged. "I don't know if I could ever confess this all to Carter, and maybe I never will be able to, but perhaps Fiona would be safe. She seems as if she would keep this confidence, and if not... well, then that's okay. We'll discover a new circle of friends out there, in the great cities of this country—of this world!"

Richard and Michael laughed again, and continued to try to catch their breath. "All right, when shall we go?"

Richard thought for a moment, then spoke. "We can slip out on May Day. It's only a week's wait; we can leave when everyone is at the May Day festival for the crowning of the May Queen."

Were they really going to do this? Michael couldn't believe it. Yes, of course he would talk to Fiona and tell her everything. He had to now, and he knew that she wouldn't care, and that she would support them both. He wanted her to tell him their future, and he wanted to make sure that Fiona would always know how to find them—that she would come and visit them both.

When they emerged from the trees, Fiona and Carter were lying on the grass, staring up at the sun. No ordinary young South Hill woman would have been caught alone with one gentleman, let alone three, without a proper escort. But Fiona didn't care for such things, and he somehow knew that her family didn't care either.

She turned her head towards their emerging forms, and she and Michael locked eyes and she smiled. She knew; she had to know. She had to already know everything. Of this he was certain. And soon—that very night, however it was done—he was going to confess everything to her, and their souls would be cemented together forever as one.

"Took you guys long enough; what were you doing?" Carter asked.

"Honestly?" Carter nodded. "I had to take a piss, and I asked Michael to play look-out. I would have asked you, but I didn't want to interrupt your fun."

"Thanks for sharing, especially in front of a lady."

Fiona laughed. "Oh, please, like I care. Pee behind as many trees as you want; as long as I have this radiant sun, I couldn't really care about anything else!"

They spent the rest of the afternoon on that grass, soaking up the warmth of the sun and staring at the light dancing on the cool waters. They saw the boats in the distances and the smoke from the lumber mills—his father's lumber mills. Everywhere they looked, there was something that belonged to their families: the Fairhaven Hotel and Citizen's National Bank, both of which belonged to Richard's father, the railroad and the mines on Sehome Hill also belonging to him, and this very park that they were languishing in.

The Maylands owned four law firms: two in Seattle, one in Manhattan, and one in downtown Bellingham. There wasn't a strip of property along the bay that did not belong to Michael's family, and though it hadn't happened yet, eventually the newly-arrived Blackmoores were going to lay claim on parts of the city as well. They could only be kept out for so long.

Were they really going to walk away from all of this? Did Richard really mean to do this? And with what money? That was the even greater question. Michael had a trust that he would access when he was eighteen and an inheritance that would become his officially at twenty-one, but he knew that would all be thrown out the window once they ran off, and once all of the pieces to the puzzle were put together.

It would only be a matter of a day or two after May Day that it would be deduced that Michael and Richard had run off together, that there was something horribly disgraceful going on between them, and that they had gone to live a sinful and debauched life.

Were they really going to risk bringing ruin to their families? To their mothers? Richard's mother had always seemed nice, and Michael practically worshipped Claudette—but then, what to do when the heart wants what it wants?

Michael wanted to be able to speak to his mother, to be able to tell her everything that was going on, but he knew he couldn't. Though she loved him, she wouldn't understand; how could she? And she would probably think them both sick of the mind and have him locked away, filled with drugs and kept in a padded cell where he would never play a violin or touch Richard Larrabee ever again.

Richard was right. They had to leave. They had to get away, or else deny their hearts and stay as far away from one another as possible. That was not an option; leaving was the only way. If they could slip out, if they could just board the train for parts east or even south, like California, then so be it. Maybe they could find their own fortune in gold, or gambling. Rumor had it Richard was brilliant at blackjack.

It made him smile.

As they made their way out of the park, walking back up to their homes on the hill, Michael looked at Dianaca Castle and thought of the White City Amusement Park that was owned by them: one of the most popular weekend destinations on the north shore of Lake Whatcom. That was where The May Day Festival would end, after the coronation parade in Fairhaven Park, with the maypole being danced around the 177-foot flag-pole.

While everyone was eating hot dogs and ice cream and riding the roller coaster and Ferris wheel, and enjoying music in the dance hall or retiring to the rooms at the Silver Beach Hotel, Michael and Richard would slip out into the night and begin their lives anew and unknown.

IX

THEY HAD PARTED WAYS with Richard at Twelfth and Harris, as his family occupied the rooms of the Fairhaven Hotel, and Carter went along with him to work on their studies. They had shared knowing glances with each other, a secret goodbye which went unnoticed by Carter, who was too busy kissing the top of Fiona's left hand.

The two of them walked the rest of the way back up the hill in silence, partly as they were so complacent in the dimming afternoon, having been subdued by the warmth of the sun. And then there was the fact that they both had so much to say, so much to talk about—but this wasn't the time. They knew that if they began to speak, then all of those things, those things that could not be discussed in the light of day, would pour out.

They both knew that they needed the concealment of the night and the observance of the stars to open that door and let the confessions of their hearts—their deepest secrets—come tumbling out of their mouths. They needed the night to take those secrets and carry them away to its blackest shadows.

If they looked towards downtown Bellingham, it was almost covered in the smoke of his father's business. It was as if, even though Fairhaven had eventually become incorporated with the city of Bellingham, it was still separated by these Fairhaven industrial barons.

"Tonight I will come to you; in the dark you will know when I am here. You will know, and you will know where to meet me,"

Fiona had said to him, standing outside of the gate of her home, which neighbored the looming giant of Dianaca Castle. He had nodded and she had kissed him on the cheek again, leaving him with a smile before slipping away in a flurry of satin and thick auburn locks, the heels of her boots echoing in the early twilight.

IN HIS ROOM MICHAEL sat, trying to focus on his notes for science at the pine secretary opposite his bed. His parents were downstairs, having dinner with Gregory and Martha Mayland—without Carter, who had stayed at the Fairhaven Hotel with Richard. It was an adult-only dinner, and he was not going to be required to perform tonight. This relieved him as he was already so anxious for Fiona's meeting, and the idea of touching that instrument made him absolutely nervous.

That instrument.

He looked at it sitting in that armchair once again, inside its sleek polished case as if it were a body in a casket. Yes, a casket. That thing was a creature of the night. It was as any vampire or any wraith, needing the bed of the dead to keep it from the healing and cleansing powers of the sun.

Looking at it was like looking at a cake that he was starving for but trying to resist. Everything inside of him was buzzing and urging him to get up and go to it and play it. He felt as if he were thirsting for it. His mouth felt dry and the sweat began to bead, and the organ between his legs began to rise and stiffen.

"I can't," he told himself. He needed to focus on his work. He knew that once he played he would go someplace else, and see things that would horrify and repulse him—and yet this thing, those visions, invited him to see and explore things that he had never thought possible. Gruesome and terrible, yes, but hard to deny, hard to pull away from it or to deny its allure. It wanted him and it wanted to show him that dark forest, to dance with those devils.

He wanted to explore that forest.

It made him want to go through the thicket, far from that fire, and venture further into its unknown. He wanted to step through that earth, tread those black waters that seemed to flow out of the ground like blood from a wound. He wanted to move deeper and deeper into that night, and see what monsters truly lurked.

"Do your work!" He shook these thoughts away from him and focused back on his chemistry book. He was trying to focus on the table of elements perfected by Dmitri Mendeleev in 1869. They had a large test on it the following day and he needed to learn all of them, and at the moment he had only memorized forty.

He looked at it again.

Though it was sitting there in that chair, locked away in its coffin, he could hear its strings being plucked. The aroma of the cake, warm and sugary-sweet. It was calling to him, and the sweat was slipping down his forehead.

He wiped his brow with his sleeve and pushed his dark hair back, feeling how slick it was with his perspiration. "Why can't you just leave me be?" he asked the thing. This was crazy, he knew. He was mad to be talking to an inanimate object, but he was no longer certain of its lifeless nature.

This thing seemed to be alive, felt as if it were pumping blood through its tiny wooden crevices. When he touched it, when he played it, it was always so warm, filled with its own life. There was nothing ordinary about that violin. There was nothing simple to it, and it had not been crafted by any old violin-maker.

He thought of Marsilio. Thought of his hands, his lips, his sulfur-like perfume, and it made his knees buckle.

He tried to focus, but his mind and his body, working as one strong force, would not let him. He was an addict to this stringed beast, and the only thing that would cure him—the only thing that would make him feel better, and stop the ache inside—was to play.

Michael stood and walked over to the chair on the other side of the room. His legs threatened to let go and bring him to the floor; he was shaking so violently.

He felt dry and he undid the top two buttons of his collar and began to rub his sweaty throat, feeling how dry everything was inside of his mouth. The closer to it he got, the more he salivated. If he hit the floor and had to crawl to it, he would. And he thought then, what a sight that would be, to see a seventeen-year-old boy crawling helplessly towards a violin.

He had heard of drug fiends, so warped from opiates that they could barely control themselves, and moved about like wild beasts. Well, at this moment he felt as if that was exactly what he was: a wild beast. A dangerous and primitive thing that had no sense of control or decency or morality. He was a hunter; he was a rabid, feral thing.

He was hungry.

He heard the music and laughter beneath him. Were they all still in the dining room, or had they all moved into the front parlor? Were they still eating, or almost done with their evening? What was going on? What was it that they were all doing?

He wanted to know. He did not want to be disturbed.

Closer and closer he came to it, until he was looming over that chair and casting it in his spindly shadow.

Where was Fiona? Why was she not here for him?

He reached for it, and he could not believe that his hands were shaking. The closer he got to it, the more his hands shook, until he snapped open each latch and began to pull it open.

'*Michael.*' He heard Fiona's voice and a flash of her in the far side of the orchard, in the middle of all of those trees by the natural pond. A sudden sense of relief came over him, and he let out a deep breath. This relief was like cool water and he was once again able to compose himself, and forget about that infernal instrument.

He looked at himself in the mirror and smoothed back his hair. His eyes, dark and deep, seemed as if his sockets were hallowed and that his skin was wasting away.

He cleared his throat and was about to button his shirt back up at the neck, but in the end decided against this. There was no need to be so formal. He grabbed his jacket and threw it on, slipping out of his room and moving down the steps.

For a moment he wasn't sure how he would slip out, as the stairs would surely creak against the weight of him, but then he spied the windows above the landing and slid one of them open carefully. After he had gotten out onto the roof above the back door, he brought the window down and placed a tiny pebble in the corner of the sill, just enough to keep it cracked so that he could lift it again—but not enough that, at a glance from the stairs walking by, it would appear to be open.

He moved to the ten-foot maple tree and made his way down, knowing that he would be able to get back up with a similar amount of ease.

The night was crisp, and the air was fragrant with his mother's abundance of roses and lavender. He moved under the fir arbor, which was covered in grape vines, and made his way down the flagstone path and through the courtyard, which was home to all of those beautiful roses of all colors. He moved past the wrought-iron table and chairs, past the gurgling mermaid fountain, and to the rustic fence that led out into the lush apple orchard.

The only illumination was the night sky and those lamps burning from inside the house, which cast their light through those windows. He knew beyond the fence he would have to rely on the moon and the stars and his own knowledge of the orchard—which was an acre-and-a-half of manicured trees, but no less like a forest of emerald leaves, and fruit budding on the bough.

He was quiet when opening the gate, knowing that its hinge creaked if opened too fast, and he closed it slowly behind him. The grass was fresh and he could smell the cool water of the pond. He moved towards its direction now, moving between each tree, which was all lined in a mismatched beauty. The apples, still green and firm, brushed against him and the night called out with owls and bats.

He had never found the orchard so haunted, so terrifying as he did in this moment, and he feared that perhaps he would stumble upon those beings in black, dancing under the moonlight.

He couldn't wait to be away from all of this. To leave with Richard and never see this place again. He wanted to call out to Fiona, to let her know that was near, but he knew that she was aware of him, and he did not want to alert anyone inside his home. He feared that even now, this far from the house, his parents would hear him and all would be lost.

He took those steps carefully, and soon he was near the pond. There she was, dressed in a long black velvet coat, her familiar black boots, and her thick hair cascading down her back. The moon lit her fair face, and her eyes were large and full of warmth. Even in the dark he could see them, as if she had the reflective eyes of a cat, refusing all light instead of absorbing it.

"I wondered how long it would take you to get here," she said to him with a grin.

He chuckled and shook his head. "It's not exactly simple getting away from my parents. But they have the Maylands over, so we should be fine."

Fiona walked over to him and took his hand, leading him to the bench his family had placed along the pond. "How are you doing?"

"I guess I've been better."

She seemed to understand this, and as she turned to him there was nothing but care and sympathy across her beautiful face. "I understand. I hope that tonight I will be able to help alleviate some of the things that trouble you."

They sat there for a moment in silence, listening to the night, looking at the moon shining in the clear water. He didn't seem to know where to start, how to begin. He had hoped for such a conversation with her the past few days, but now that it was here, it all seemed impossible, something that was no longer tangible. He wondered if the silence would overcome them both and nothing would be revealed, no truth would be illuminated.

"What are you?" The question came out of his mouth before he could think, before he could actually form the question in a polite way, and he worried that he had offended her.

"Just a girl, just as you are a boy."

Michael sighed. "But that's not entirely true, is it?"

Fiona nodded, understanding what he meant. "I suppose you're right. I'm not exactly like you, but I am still just a girl."

"And a witch." Again it had come out in a way that seemed accusatory, and again he worried that he had injured her.

Fiona closed her eyes and took a deep breath, before opening them and looking deep into his own with such earnest compassion. "I am." There it was: the admittance, the truth of her nature. Now he wanted to press her, to ask her so many questions, but he knew that he didn't need to; these things would now come all on their own.

"I am a witch. I come from a family of witches, a great coven, but we are not the only witches, and I promise you, we are good. We do not worship the being that you would refer to as the Devil, or Satan, or whatever names your religion chooses to call him."

"Then what? Did your family not sell their soul—your soul?"

She laughed quietly and to herself. "In the old world, in ancient times, there were many gods, and there was a great goddess who ruled supreme amongst my ancestors back in Ireland. But at night... at night there was a terrible god. A god who craved blood, a god who commanded fierce, dark creatures—creatures you may call demons—and if we did not appease him, we would suffer the brutal attacks by these creatures.

"My family began to give him this blood. We did sacrifice those we captured, and even the willing from our own tribe. But when we finally left the moor, when we began to learn the written word, we did not take this thing with us. We left him there, and we thought that we had become free of him.

"But there are things—powers beyond this world that you can't see, things that still served this beast—and at times, these beings, these agents of this dark god would come for us, try to kill us, to make us pay the price for our leaving. Some Blackmoores have been lost at the hands of this thing. But we continued to go on and continued to thrive, first in New Orleans and now here, and all over the western world."

He listened to this with the greatest respect. Before Fiona Blackmoore had entered his life, he would have dismissed such things as delusions and he would have called them out as such. But now he knew better.

"Where does your power come from? What things do you do? What can you do?"

Fiona looked at him and sighed. "Well, we don't fly on broomsticks. But there are things... charms, hexes, enchantments; these things we can do. I can hear thoughts... it comes and goes. The only time I can hear yours are when you specifically want to talk to me or reach out to me. But your random thoughts are still your own.

"There are other things I can do, that we all can do. We can talk with spirits—even some, like my mother, can command the very dead to do her bidding. But you have to understand, my family doesn't run around doing these things whenever we wish, and the majority of our days are just spent living, just as you do. Eating dinner, going to concerts, working, starting businesses, and reading. We don't gather in great numbers around a fire or cauldron and conjure spirits to dance with. Not as we did in New Orleans."

He had never been to New Orleans, but he had read about it and often imagined it, imagined its tropical beauty and what its humid air would feel like.

"What do you mean?"

"In New Orleans my family would dance with the slaves and Free People of Color, and we would draw the sacred symbols of the African gods and dance and enter trances and be horses for the gods."

Horses. The word thrilled him. "What do you mean, horses?"

"The gods sometimes choose to enter a devotee and ride him for brief periods of time. The horse gives his body to the god, and the god gets to exist, contained for a moment inside a human body—to taste food and drink and smoke as a human would, and speak to the people and give blessings and tell their futures.

Then the god leaves, and often the horse has no knowledge of what took place while the god was in control.

"They would say, you go to church to talk to God; we go to church to become God."

All of this was so thrilling. It sounded like some great adventure, a crossing of the bridge between worlds, and he wondered if Fiona had ever done it.

"No, I have not. I never danced in Congo Square and I never saw the things my mother saw, or my uncle Jeremiah. I was telling the truth when I said I was sent away to school in France; it was in part to keep me safe, and to have me become a woman of the world. I did not return from France until my family moved here, to start again with a newly amassed fortune of our own.

"Little did we know, a family just like ours—a family that was so terribly dangerous and served that dark god of the wood—would be right in the same place, that we would neighbor them."

Michael gasped. "Who do you mean?"

He followed her eyes; beyond the trees to the right of them was the tall turret of Dianaca Castle with its English lattice windows illuminated by faint firelight. "But the Dianacas have been here since the beginning. They are such a well-respected family."

She shook her head. "That means nothing. They are diabolical and murderous. They serve the Dark God of the Wood, and they would give this thing the world. There are reasons, many reasons they came here to these shores to help found this town, and that is because this city runs on powerful energy currents. Everything, from where churches to cemeteries are placed, were all done so on the powerful currents of these lines.

"They are up to something terrible, and they did not count on us moving here. I'm not even sure they knew specifically about us, for there are witch families all over the world.

"Every single witch in this world comes from a family like ours. Not all know their families. Some are alone, perhaps orphaned and never knew, or their families have long stopped practicing, and they are coming into their powers without guidance.

"Some of these families are large; some are very small clans. Many are poor; some are rich and come from all types of education, or no formal education at all. Some witches are good; some are bad. They are all races, and all of them have their own traditions, and love and are loved by their own gods.

"Some serve many; some serve just one. Some serve no gods at all, or call them something else. But all witches come to it from their bloodline, and their blood is what stirs and awakens them and calls to them.

"Some follow; some don't. Many practice their craft and many try to avoid it, but they still cannot control the outbursts of phenomenon that sometimes occurs simply because of a heightened emotional reaction."

"And the Dianacas are evil?"

Fiona nodded assuredly. "Very evil. Perhaps not all of them, but the ones in that house, the ones who occupy that home and are rarely ever seen... there is no good amongst them. We have no idea what they are up to, and we do not discuss it. We just go about our day-to-day lives and keep our guard up."

Michael sighed and looked up into that night sky, looked at all of those stars and that beautiful moon. He realized there were so many more things to this world than he could ever comprehend, and he felt so small in all of it, so vulnerable.

"Do not worry, my wonderful friend; I will keep you safe." Fiona took hold of his hand and squeezed it tight, lifting it into their vision. "No matter what, I will never abandon you to the evils of this world or the one you cannot see." He smiled at this, and then he was suddenly sad, remembering that in a week he would be leaving all of this behind for good.

Michael looked to the left and saw the tall arched roof of the two-story white Federal manor of the Maylands, just beyond his orchard. "And what of Carter?"

She followed his eyes to his rooftop. It hadn't even dawned on Michael before that Carter and Fiona lived across the street from one another. "I will never tell him these things. In the end there are so many other things, so many other terrible things that plague my life, that to let Carter be a part of it—to risk him like that—would endanger his life in a way that it never would with you."

He wasn't sure what she meant by that, and he could tell by the way she spoke, and the heartbroken look on her face, that he shouldn't press it. It was hers alone, and he knew that it was a secret too painful to share.

"Well, I thank you for telling me. And do not worry; I will keep your secret close."

"And I will keep yours."

He looked at her, knowing what she meant, but he still couldn't confess it on his own. "What do you mean?"

She laughed and patted his hand before moving hers into her lap. "You and Richard Larrabee, my love! Of course I know; I've known since that first day when you two looked at one another. I glimpsed into both of your hearts and saw how much you both so desperately wanted to talk to one another. So I gave him a little push. Just a bit of suggestion to be brave and come speak to you, beyond simple salutations and greetings."

"So he is not bewitched?"

Fiona laughed and shook her head. "Oh, lord, no! I would never take away a person's free will like that. I merely made him think my voice was his own inside of his head, and convinced with much urgency that he needed to cast all fear and doubt aside and come speak to you, to break the silence and pursue what was in his heart."

Michael breathed a sigh of relief. He had been so worried that Richard was only enamored of him because of Fiona's divine intervention. To hear that this was not the case, that truly Richard did love him—had loved him for so long—made the decision to leave all the more definite.

"You know," he began, swallowing hard. "He asked me to run away with him. To leave with him and start our lives together in a few days."

Fiona's eyes began to become glassy with the sheen of welling tears, which she quickly wiped away with both her hands. "Go on, please."

"Well, we are going to sneak away during the May Day festival while everyone is gone. We both wanted to tell you. I wanted to tell you because I need to know you will always be in my life, that you will come to see us wherever we end up, as we may never be able to come back here."

Fiona smiled and laughed and nodded her head enthusiastically while wiping the tears from her face once again. "Of course I will! Of course I will!" He smiled and realized that he was crying as well. They reached out for one another and embraced with fierce abandon. "I will always be with you, and I will always come to see you both and spend time with you. No matter where you are in the world!"

"Really?"

She put her soft hand to his cheek, and Michael kissed Fiona's open palm. "Of course. I made you a promise, didn't I? A promise that I will always be there for you, that I will always protect you."

"Yes, yes, you did."

"Here." Fiona reached around her neck and pulled off that peridot necklace, all of its lime gems glittering in the light, and she slipped it on over his head and tucked it into his shirt. "If ever you need me, no matter what, just hold tightly to this and I will hear your call, and I shall come. I will be there with the speed of hummingbirds' wings in flight!"

He wanted to object, to tell his friend that he could not accept such a thing, but he knew that she could easily replace it with something far more expensive and gorgeous. This was something else. This was enchanted—if he could even believe that he was admitting that such a thing was true—and that he needed to accept it without question.

"I will keep it safe and wear it always. I promise, Fiona, I will never take it off!"

She smiled and kissed him on both cheeks. "I know. And please, now that you know the things that you know, you must never let on that you do. You must forget them, push them far from your mind. If anything out there, any of these creatures and horrid people, knew that you were aware of the truth—that you had knowledge of me, my family—all of them, they would come for you.

"You must bury it deep and forget it all. Do you understand me, Michael? Please!"

He nodded. "I will, Fiona. I swear it on our friendship, I will!"

"Dinner is almost done," she said, standing, looking back at his house. Michael turned to look, and when he turned back to face her, Fiona was gone—as if she had never been there in the first place—and he was all alone in the night.

Michael took hold of the necklace and looked at it, spinning it in his fingers to see it in the light: this beautiful necklace, which he had to keep close to his heart and hidden from the world. He thought of all that he had learned tonight, and realized that he had not told his friend everything, not all that he had wanted to. He had never told her about the violin or the visions, and now that he knew everything that she had revealed to him—all of these secrets—he thought again on the vision of that forest. As an owl called out, he began to fear.

He made his way back to his home quickly, seeing it large and comforting in the dark.

Just beyond the trees, he told himself as he continued to rush, fearing those demons would come again.

The closer he got to the gate that led into the courtyard, the more he cursed himself for not telling Fiona. He hurried through the courtyard, seeing his family and the Maylands through the window in the music room at the back, sitting in chairs and drinking sherry. He bent down as to make sure that he would not be seen, and shimmied back up the maple tree and onto the roof.

He stood and looked down at the orchard and the bright moon and the great form of Dianaca Castle, and noticed a figure standing on the second floor balcony above the carriageway. He shivered and slid the window open quietly and slipped back inside, carefully closing it behind him once again. Michael crept back up the stairs silently and into his bedroom, hoping to be able to cast away everything and continue back with forced concentration of his studies.

Leaving the world of magic and witches and ghouls behind, Michael put pen to paper and focused his eyes on that table, returning once again to the world of science and material things, casting everything else back into shadows. Deep shadows, far away and in the back of his mind.

X

THERE IT WAS AGAIN. *The music. That music that wouldn't stop no matter what he did, no matter how much he put his hands to his ears and tried to force them out of his head. It would not be denied, along with the voices of their chants and the screaming of those strings, filling the night sky as they continued to dance.*

"Bagabi Laca Bachabe. Lamac Cahi Achababe. Karrelyos. Lamac Lamec Bachalyas. Cabahagy Sabalyos. Baryolos. Lagoz Atha Cabyolas. Samahac et Famyolas. Harrahya."

The flames kept growing—kept rising. His eyes took in their glow, just as he took in the forms of those beings dancing. Watching their movements, he couldn't help but feel like he could sway with them, that he could move right along with them and give into the music just as they were.

"Bagabi Laca Bachabe...." *The ground bled with that black liquid, and it no longer mattered to him that it was all the way up to his ankles, or that it was filling his shoes and making his feet feel heavy, and that he was sinking in this ink.*

He watched as once again those beautiful naked bodies—covered in sweat, grease, and blood, with their animal heads rose from that water and began to writhe and gyrate and wrap around each other like serpents on the vine. They were intoxicating and spellbinding, and everything about them made Michael's heart race. The desire to join them in this orgy thrilled him and made his pulse quicken in a way he had never felt before.

"What is happening to me?" *He thought of Richard; he thought of Fiona and the necklace around his throat. He thought of taking hold of it and seeing if he could call her, if she could hear his cries and come rescue him from this infernal dense.*

He reached for the necklace with his hand and found it gone from his neck. What happened to it? Where could it have gone? He couldn't remember taking it off, nor could he imagine that it had fallen off—but perhaps it had, and he just hadn't noticed. Either way, he knew that he was screwed. There was no way to summon his powerful friend, to enlist her divine aid and bring him back home.

Everything now seemed so far away from him. He watched the thick black vapors from the burning flesh rise from the pyre and reach towards the heavens, moving like a cyclone towards that large moon. What a moon it was! Large and yellow in a way that he had never seen it. It was not silver and crisp, but rich and almost illusion in that midnight tapestry, bejeweled with the luminescence of stars.

He wondered, if he uncovered his ears and listened to their words, if they would have some effect on him. If he took in the chanting and tried to decipher what it was that they were actually saying, if they would be able to slip inside of his head and begin to make him think and see awful things. But how could they make him see anything more appalling than what was already happening before him, right before his very eyes?

He decided to tread through the inky black and get closer to their fire, to get as close to these beings without being noticed.

The inky thick was heavy, and it took all of the strength that he possessed to move through it—and yet these beings, these demons and these witches, navigated through it as if it were nothing. Perhaps they were weightless; perhaps they were suspended above the ground. He simply could not tell for sure.

No, they were not floating. They were in that ooze, and they were splashing in it and moving through it. Perhaps it was because of the nature of what they were that they were not constrained by it as Michael was. The closer he got to them, the more he could see how garish the demons were with their twisted maniacal faces—some of them missing eyes, others with spikes piercing through their faces. Their flesh was like the leathery membrane of a squid, and their veins were visible under the grayish-white of their skin.

Some had horns and claws and those bird-like feet, and others had ears that were long and pointed at the tips, with fierce animal-like eyes—or no eyes at all, just emptied hollows in their sockets. The witches in their black airy fabric danced around them and touched them and caressed those leathery faces with their hands, and licked their fingers and other parts of their bodies.

Michael was shaken to his very core, and though repulsed, he could not look away. This macabre ball, this dance of death, was hypnotic and commanded his attention.

The chanting continued, and as he came closer to them and their fire in the clearing, he watched as once again that dark, lanky figure rose up from the flames and bowed to them all. He beckoned them with hands to continue their chants, and his dark eyes seemed to glow, the reflection of those flames clear in them. Michael could see from the distance where he stood amongst the trees that the whites of this man's eyes were gone, just the black that filled his sockets, and he put his bow to his violin once again and played.

Michael was certain that he knew the face of this man; he was trying to put it together. It was so handsome, with the black hair on his chin and the matching hair with the window's peak that crowned him.

"Who could you be?" he whispered. He watched as one of the dancers dipped their hands into the flames and took hold of that charred head, and with a mighty pull it was removed from the neck

and lifted into the air. The head was black and smoking, and bits of ashen flesh fell from it as the head was then smashed against a stone at the foot of the pyre, and the skull was cracked open like an eggshell.

The head was once again raised into the air. The tall maestro sat down his violin and took hold of that head, offering a nod before bringing it to his lips and revealing a mouth full of vicious wolf-like teeth, which he shoved into the exposed brain.

Michael felt his stomach turn and begin to force everything inside of him out as this beast devoured the brain. Michael put his hand to his mouth and turned quickly, trying to get as far away from them as he could, to disappear once again into that dark.

The liquid was even thicker now, and he was getting through it at a snail's pace. "I have to get out of here!" *He kept forcing himself through, but then he was brought to a halt. He fought hard to free his legs, but there was no movement. He tried again, with more force this time, and he wobbled, losing balance and falling forward, falling into that black ooze. Michael threw his hands up in front of his face and braced for impact. His body splashed into it, and he felt it thick and warm, felt it envelop his body and absorb him in its black embrace.*

MICHAEL'S EYES FLUTTERED open and he was relieved to find himself staring at his vaulted ceiling, to hear the birds chirp outside his window and to see the cool blue light of morning brighten his room.

These dreams have to stop, he thought to himself. He knew now that it was more, much more than just the result of an overactive imagination or anxieties over everything that had taken place in the recent days. This had all started the night before Marsilio had arrived with the new violin. The vision he had

had when he last played to an audience and that masked figure, which he was now certain was the same maestro of the woods. Could it be that the evil being that Fiona had told him about—the "Dark God of the Wood," as she had called him—was reaching out to him, to use him in some diabolic plot against his friend and her family?

Well, if that was the case, he wasn't going to let it get him, and he surely wasn't going to let this thing get a hold of one that he loved so dearly. But he had to tell Fiona. He knew that now, and nothing could stop him from doing it. He had to tell her what was happening, what had been happening to him, and he was confident that she would know how to put a stop to these demonic visitations.

He stood and stretched and yawned. As eyes fell on that infernal violin, he suddenly felt its pull again, and he knew that this thing, this instrument, was something evil. He could feel the dark energy radiating off of it, and he was filled with nothing but contempt and revulsion for the thing.

This was not his. It was not a part of him; his violin was gone. His violin was sacrificed for this black thing to be placed into his hands, to be played by his skill and to summon those beasts from hell.

"Well, I am done playing you," he said to it. He knew that it could hear him; he knew that it was a living thing and that it was aware of every word he said and every move he made. It wanted to control him, and he needed to find a way to destroy it.

Michael walked to his closet and began getting ready for school. He thought for a moment that he might bring the instrument with him, but there was something in him that didn't trust it, even in its case. There was something about it that made him worry that if he brought it to school, its invisible tentacle-like energy would somehow reach out and grasp everyone around him.

"I know what you're capable of," he said to it. He felt that with the playing of this instrument, he would be able to ensnare the hearts and minds of everyone who heard him play. Perhaps even make those around him obey him, but he also suspected that that would be an illusion to make him play it more and more, that illusion of control and power that really trapped those poor souls who heard the music of those strings to serve the dark being. He knew that he would be handing them over to this creature, and in turn this creature would use all those entranced to bring harm to the Blackmoores.

Well, that wasn't going to happen. He would keep it here, locked in his room forever. He would never let another soul, no person out there in the world, hear its fiendish sound, its hauntingly ethereal voice. No, this could not happen.

"I am never going to play you again. Do you understand me? I know you can, and you... you dark thing, you can take my proclamation to the ears of that dark one. I will not play you!"

Michael dressed himself in gray cotton pants, a white linen shirt, and gray suspenders. He rolled the sleeves to his upper biceps and put on a black wool cap. He looked himself in the mirror, and satisfied and excited to see Richard, he made his way out of his room and down the stairs, clutching tightly to the necklace through his shirt, breathing a sigh of relief that it was there.

His mother was sitting at the dining table in her usual place next to the fireplace on the right, next to the head of the table, where once again his father was absent.

"Good morning, darling," she said to him, her beautiful and gentle face beaming with her usual smile. "I hope you didn't feel too left out last night."

Michael smiled and shook his head. "No, Mother. It was fine, really; I had so much studying to get done. I was glad to be without the distraction." Claudette Donovan clasped his hand and gave it a light squeeze as he sat down in the chair across from her. She was a vision, with her thick mane pulled up above her like a crown, and her white linen blouse tucked in her long black skirt. A beautiful diamond ivy bracelet was clasped around her left wrist, and at her throat was a large cameo of Aphrodite framed by tiny diamond facets.

"Well, that's wonderful, my love." Michael nodded and cleared his throat, preparing to speak, when Nellie came into the room pushing a buffet cart with fresh coffee, juice, and a plate of French toast and a bottle of champagne.

"Shh..." his mother said, taking the champagne and pouring both herself and Michael a glass. "Don't breathe a word of this to your father. I felt like being naughty, and it's no fun doing so when you're by yourself."

Michael loved his mother so much. There was nothing but absolute kindness inside of her, and for just a moment he thought of telling her all that had occurred between Richard and himself, just confessing his soul to his mother right then and there. But then the fear of losing what they had between them, not getting to enjoy these last days with her for what they were before he left for good, prevented him from saying more.

"I won't." He cleared his throat once more to signal to Claudette that he needed her attention, and she gave it to him quickly and quite earnestly.

"What is it, dear? What do you need to tell me?"

"I can't play that violin." She looked at him, but said nothing. "It just will not do. I don't like it; it doesn't feel right to me, and I feel I must have my own instrument, one that I choose for myself. I will gladly give it back to Mr. Merrin, but I cannot play that thing! Not one note more!" He hadn't meant to say this with such a forceful tone, but it could not be helped. He could think of no other way to express the importance of his feelings and to get across the fact that he would not budge on it.

"Are you sure? It is such a beauty, and when your father saw it he said he never wanted to see you play anything else because it would never measure up."

He nodded. "Yes. I am, and I will not play it. And unless I can pick out a violin of my own, from my own violin dealer, I will not play ever again. I cannot be forced, and no one can force me to play anything if I do not want to."

Claudette sighed. It was a sigh of understanding. "I was afraid of this."

His eyes grew wide. "You were?"

She nodded. "Of course I was. I had a worry that it might not suit you. A musician's instrument is personal to him, and it should be something that feels as if it is an extension of yourself. I had a feeling that you may reject it. It's all right."

"I don't want to stop playing. But I cannot play that thing. It doesn't feel right, and the music feels foreign to me when I hear it coming from those strings. I have to feel as if I know it, and I do not know that thing!" He was pointing towards the stairs. His mother rose and went to a silver snuff box on the mantle, beneath the portrait of Queen Victoria standing in a regal parlor, dressed in a large dark green satin gown and a lace veil spilling down the back of her head.

She came back and handed her son a handful of bills. He was not going to count it in front of her and appear to be greedy or ungrateful, but he knew that it was several hundred dollar bills that she had just given to him.

"If what you need costs more, then I want you to put it on our credit. Just get the one that pleases you. The finest you can find. I want you to be happy, and I do not want you to ever stop. No matter what happens in your life, and whether you play for a crowd or no one but yourself, I want you to use your gift, and I want you to be happy doing it."

Michael's eyes welled with tears, tears that he quickly wiped away with the backs of his hands. "I will. Thank you." He kissed her fiercely on the cheek.

"You are my greatest joy," she said. "Now, please, let us get as drunk as can be before you have to go to school!" Michael laughed and nodded. He and his mother raised their glasses to one another and took a big drink, thinking only of the bubbles and happier times. Michael was going to miss these moments with his mother, and so he was determined to savor every single one of them until he had to leave, and they would be no more than memories to comfort him on nights when he may feel alone. Perhaps he would wrap himself in these memories while they were at parties, or while he or Richard were working and separated from one another on end.

He didn't really know how to work. He knew this, and he wondered what was Richard skilled at? He supposed they would just have to find out when they got to wherever it was that they were going. He was glad that no matter what, they would have each other—and perhaps over time his mother, at the very least, would come around to the direction his life had taken. She would come to understand that her son was no different from the boy she had always known; only she would realize that she knew him all the better.

But that was far into the future, and for now he would just have to do what was best for him, and hope for another outcome in the future.

XI

HE STOOD OUTSIDE THE black wrought-iron gate of the Blackmoore home, keeping his eyes focused on the large oak front doors with their covered glass windows. The front yard was lush with imported banana trees with wax-like leaves, a lush variety of flowers and the strong oak trees with their brilliant green radiance. He had never been beyond this gate, and he was extremely curious, especially after the other night, to see what was beyond the doors.

The house, he knew, was a long single story that looked like a bungalow, but spilled down the hillside at the back. Before the Blackmoores, the front yard had been barren, with the exception of the oak trees—but it seemed, after the arrival of the family, this tropical paradise erupted from the earth as if it had always been there.

The neighborhood had been consumed with talk of displays of gaudiness when all of this greenery had arrived. For Michael, they had just been plants, nothing more and nothing less, but for the rest of the residents of South Hill, it showed a lack of humility and class. Michael figured that perhaps the Blackmoores had brought these tropical plants as a way to bring a little of the lush tropical landscape of New Orleans to the wild green of Washington.

The front door opened and Fiona emerged, wearing a slim dress made of ivory silk with a black jacket of lace, which was breezy and draped down to her ankles. On her head was a large black brimmed hat filled with plumes of black-and-white ostrich feathers, and accentuating the low-cut neckline was a new necklace. It was three tiers of amber that seemed like honey in the sun, the longest string hanging past her abdomen and the smallest resting delicately above her small but perky breasts. She smiled at him as soon as she saw him, and glided towards him as if she were walking on the air itself.

"Good morning," he said to her, opening the gate for her to pass.

"Well, good morning to you, *Monsieur* Donovan."

He gave a laugh. "And to you, *Mademoiselle* Blackmoore." He tipped his wool cap to her and they began to make their usual walk down Knox.

"So, my darling, what are your plans for today?"

"I have music lessons again." He frowned. "But before that, I need to get a new violin."

She looked at him, perplexed. "But don't you have a new violin from your instructor?"

He nodded. "I can't use it. It doesn't feel right. I don't like it." He thought that it would seem odd to her, but to his surprise the look on her face seemed to be filled with suspicion.

"What's wrong with it?"

"I suppose it has no soul—or better yet, it has the wrong soul." He was waiting for another perplexed reaction, but there was none. "Is that even possible? For an instrument to have a soul, I mean?"

She seemed to think on this for a moment—not on the answer, but it seemed she was thinking about how to answer. "If someone puts a soul into it, yes, yes, it's possible."

He stopped and looked at her. His face was expressing a very real fear, a fear that he knew she could see. "What do you mean?"

"If someone—a witch, perhaps—decided to summon a spirit or entity and place it into an object, that object could be a vessel for something dark and unnatural, and it could then reach out to whoever was in possession of it, and begin to possess them."

Michael began to wonder if he should tell her what had been happening to him. A part of himself told him that he would just sound crazy if he started talking about living violins, but then he had to remind himself that Fiona had revealed to him the night before at the pond, in the middle of the orchard, under the moonlight, that she was a witch.

She had proven it, and he knew it was true. That had to give him the confidence to tell her and to trust in their relationship, and to know that she would never doubt him. "It's true. I never would."

He nodded and took a deep breath and began to unveil the whole mystery, everything that had been terrifying him and keeping him up at night.

As they walked he told her of the forest and the demons, and the witches in black and the naked orgy of beautiful sweaty bodies covered in that black grease, and the animal heads that crowned their necks. He told her of the seductive violinist and the way he had first seen him, in that palace hall in the vision, that had caused the breaking of his strings in the first place.

He told her of how this violin seemed to speak to him, to get hot and pulsate with life, how he craved it though he didn't want it, as if it were some kind of drug that had gotten into his system and which he now could not avoid.

All of this she listened to patiently, absorbing all of his words and nodding with an understanding that relieved him immensely. "I fear for my life—my very soul," he said with a defeated sigh.

"I will not let anything happen to your soul. But you have made the right decision in forsaking that infernal thing. You must never play it again. I suspect that every time you play it, it is taking more and more of yourself away, and replacing the empty spaces with its own malefic intentions."

Malefic. He did not like this word. He did not like malice. He understood what she meant in the context with which she used it. In the old days, in the times of the burning, they referred to witchcraft as Malice. Malice was more than a feeling; it was more than intent to commit an act of viciousness against another. Malice was a thing in itself. Malice was an actual instrument, a tool that could be used against another, or just for personal gain. Malice was an invisible yet no less physical force that could reshape the whole world.

"So you will support me today as I find a new instrument?"

Fiona nodded. "And I'd also like to accompany you at your lessons today; I'd like to meet this Marsilio Merrin for myself." He looked at her, and a great wave of relief washed over him. He did not tell her of the experience he had had at their first lesson the other day, but he did not want to be alone with his new teacher.

"I'd be so happy if you did." They smiled at one another and continued their walk to the school looking at the beauty of the morning and the ships in the harbor, the both of them trying to expel their own worries from their minds.

THROUGHOUT THE DAY, Michael and Richard kept their eyes on one another. Fiona and Richard traded places so that she could sit across from Carter, and Richard could sit next to Michael. Carter seemed completely ignorant of all of this, believing it was only for the benefit of him and Fiona to be able to be closer.

That suited the three of them just fine.

Richard looked at Michael and cocked his head towards the door and whispered "washroom" with a grin. Michael nodded and raised his hand, asking for permission to go, to which Mr. Upton agreed.

Michael looked back at Richard as he opened the door and slipped out, making his way down the quiet hall and towards the closest lavatory. He slipped in and breathed a sigh of relief to find it empty. It didn't take long for Richard to come in after him, smiling as he closed the door and turned the lock.

"What is it?" Michael asked him, leaning against one of the porcelain sinks.

"I had to touch you; I had to kiss you." Richard moved onto him, casting Michael in his shadow. They looked deep into each other's eyes, and Michael could feel himself growing between his legs. As their lips met, the two of them were taken over by a frenzied hunger that could not be abated.

They were on the tiled floor, not caring about the dirt from the hundreds of feet that crossed it dozens of times throughout the day. They didn't care about the cold, or the possibility of people trying to get in. They were overcome with their need for each other, for the way they craved the taste of their flesh—the taste of their hot, moist mouths.

Their hands fumbled under shirts, lifting them from off their bodies without bothering to unbutton them. They ran their tongues along each other's throats, dragged them down the cavity of their chests, and teased each other's nipples. Michael gripped Richard's hard hot cock on the outside of his tented trousers and squeezed playfully and gave him a tug, and Richard did the same.

"I love you, Michael Donovan!" Richard said to him, with labored breaths, and the sweat began to bead. Michael looked up at him and grinned, Richard's cock in his hand, his eyes wide with hunger.

"I love you, too." They kissed again, their tongues wet and tangled. Michael unbuttoned his pants and pulled that thick strong cock out from his briefs. It was darker than the rest of Richard's olive skin, and it looked beautiful with its perfect mushroom head. Michael licked his lips and stroked it, his palm sliding up and down that warm satin skin.

He began to kiss it, and Richard's dick quivered with excitement. Michael liked the taste of him, and began to slide his tongue up and down that shaft, getting it nice and slick before opening his mouth and taking Richard all the way down his throat.

"My god!" Richard declared before giving way to a deep sigh. He placed his hand on Michael's head and began to guide him gently, back and forth on his cock, all the while stroking Michael's own strong organ. He wanted it; he wanted to taste him, just as Michael tasted him. "Hold on," he directed Michael onto his back and leaned over him, feeding his cock back down his throat, and began to pull out Michael's.

He licked his lips and kissed the head a few times before taking his lover deep into his mouth, sliding his tongue up and down Michael's shaft.

They sucked each other for several minutes, while Richard began to slip his fingers past his boyfriend's balls and between the warm sweaty space under his legs. There he found the entrance to his hole and began to slowly insert his fingers, feeling inside the moist, hot rectum.

He pulled his dick outside of Michael's mouth and moved in front of him, removing his pants and underwear completely, lifting Michael's legs over his shoulders. He smiled as he spat a couple of times on his hand and then added it to the slick of saliva that was already on his cock. Michael took a deep breath as Richard guided his way in, stopping for just a moment as Michael winced in pain, only to nod to him, letting him know that it was okay. He placed his hands on Richard's plump, firm buttocks, giving him a squeeze and urging him to keep going.

Soon they were moving in a rhythm. Richard and Michael looked at one another, the sweat glistening on their bodies, their breath heavy, their hearts racing. Michael nodded in reassurance and smiled in delight, and Richard leaned forward and kissed him. That kiss was hot and quick. It was strong, and Richard kept fucking him, the both of them conscious of their own voices, doing whatever they could not to scream out.

Richard felt it move up in his body in waves, and he loved the look of Michael under him, loved to see the pleasure on his face, pleasure that he was giving him. He stroked Michael's cock faster and faster, until his own orgasm rode up through his legs, causing him to clench his buttocks and spill his seed in his boyfriend's insides.

"Oh," Michael let out, and before his own orgasm erupted, Richard quickly took him in his mouth and swallowed the hot sticky sperm that shot out of Michael and down his throat.

Richard fell on top of him, spent, and still deep inside. Their skin hot and glistening.

"I can't wait to leave here," he said, his breath hot and close to his ear. "Everything is ready. Since I'm eighteen, I have access to my inheritance: $450,000 at my disposal. I've already booked us the train—our own deluxe car from here to San Francisco."

Michael looked at him and smiled wide, the look of excitement and surprise all over his face. "Really?"

Richard lifted his head and looked down at him. "Yes, really. I hope you still want to go through with this."

Michael nodded, and they kissed hard and fast. "Good, 'cause I want us to start our lives, as quickly as possible. We leave on the 8:00pm train."

"This is going to be perfect." They laid there for a few more minutes, kissing and listening to the quiet pulse of their heartbeats. Michael felt like nothing could touch him; nothing evil could hold sway over his world, and together with Richard and his new violin, they were going to begin anew. Get a home and travel the world. Nothing was going to stop him; nothing could harm him. It was going to be perfect. No longer a nightmare, but a sweet dream, a dream that was birthing—hatching like a baby bird—into a beautiful reality.

THE REST OF THE DAY went by with little event. Fiona and Carter continued to be wrapped up in each other, and Richard and Michael kept exchanging their secret knowing glances. At the end of the day when they walked out, all of four them decided to board the trolley car into downtown with Michael to obtain his new violin.

They boarded the trolley and road it through State Street into downtown, which had been previously called New Whatcom before the integration. They passed his father's pulp mill and lumber yard, the smoke rising from the stacks and filling much of the sky in black. The trolley stopped just before Railroad Avenue, and the four of them hopped off and made their way through the congestion of the city, arriving at *The Cat & The Fiddle*.

They walked in, and the door knocked the bell that hung above the frame, alerting the elderly shop keeper with his wire spectacles and lighting his aged face with a smile.

"Master Donovan!" he said with glee. "How can I help you?"

Michael looked around, his three companions staring at the various violins that hung on the wall. "I need a new instrument. My violin broke." The old man nodded. "It needs to be exquisite. I have about a thousand dollars; if it costs more, you can put it on my family's credit. But I need the best."

"I have just the thing! Newly acquired." He put his finger up in the air, telling him to wait just a moment. The old man disappeared into the back workshop and then reemerged with a beautiful polished Stradivarius. "It's from 1791." He handed it over to Michael, along with the bow.

"And it's authentic? Not something from the Sears and Roebuck catalog?"

The old man shook his head. "This is authentic. I've appraised it myself. Try it."

Michael placed it under his chin and began to play an aria by Paganini. The bow moved effortlessly across the strings, and the music poured out of him in a way he had almost forgotten. Since the destruction of his old violin and the gifting of the new one, he had lost what it meant to actually be in control of the music, to be in control of his form and the instrument itself. He thought of the strangeness in the fact that Marsilio Merrin had come around and given him the new violin under the pretense of teaching him control—and yet, since receiving and playing the new violin, he had felt as if control was the one thing he was missing.

That violin played him; he did not play it, and now, with this beautiful Stradivarius, he was reminded once again what it meant to play an instrument that was just an instrument. He knew that he would never, under any circumstances, touch that accursed black thing ever again.

"I'll take it. How much?"

"Well...." The old man began to wring his hands together. "It's certainly not a steal."

"How much?" Michael pressed.

"$12,000, sir."

Michael looked at it once again, inspecting it, and then nodded. "I'll take it." He pulled out the wad of hundreds that was folded neatly and held in a sterling silver Tiffany's clip. "Charge the rest to my father's credit."

The old man nodded and took the cash hungrily. "I will indeed. Enjoy it, Master Donovan."

Michael nodded and turned around, facing his companions for the first time and realizing they were staring at him with awestruck faces.

"What?" They all shook their heads.

"You play magnificently!" Fiona exclaimed.

"Yes," Carter echoed.

"I've heard you before, from the block, but to see it... there are no words!" Richard's eyes were glassy with tears. Michael smiled and bowed to them graciously.

"I am so glad!" The old shopkeeper returned with the violin in a new case, and placed it in a bag before handing it to Michael.

"We want to hear more!" his three friends shouted. Michael thought on this for a moment and was about to object, when he thought of Marsilio Merrin and all of his lessons. Michael was suddenly overcome with how devilishly delightful it would be to bring his friends and lover to his lessons, and how much he knew that it would upset his new teacher—especially on the second lesson.

"Then come with me; Fiona was already going to follow. You can come to my lesson and get a real show!" He turned and nodded to the old man, who graciously returned it. Then they made their way out of his shop and back to the trolley to watch his scheme unfold.

THE TROLLEY MADE ITS way through Eleventh Street and into Fairhaven, rocking along and stopping here and there to pick up or drop off passengers. The trolley turned on Harris Avenue and continued its journey. Michael reached out for the cord and pulled it, chiming for the machine to stop. They got off at the base of Fifteenth Street, took a left, making their way up the steep hill towards Knox Avenue.

Richard politely carried Michael's violin, and Carter allowed Fiona to hold onto his arm as they made their way up the hill. It was hot, and they were grateful for the moments that they passed under the shade of the trees, and were greeted with a cool sea breeze that was perfumed with the scents of all the private gardens that surrounded them.

"I remember when you used to live there," Michael said, pointing to the forest-green Victorian along Fifteenth, sheltered by spruce and cypress. Its second-floor veranda was decorated with moons and stars cut out of the wood of the guardrail.

"Yes, I loved that home. It was such a wonderful house to grow up in. But," he sighed. "Father wanted something bigger and better to match the accomplishments that our family has achieved."

"And I'm sure it'll be a grand place," Fiona said. Richard looked at her, and she winked at him. He understood that wink. She knew the truth, and she was happy for them and she knew that he would most likely never see the new home once it was completed. "But better to have memories attached to one place and spend these last remaining years in a hotel, not getting attached to something else that you will just have to say goodbye to anyways."

Carter looked at her quizzically.

"When you go off to university, I mean."

Carter nodded, accepting this, and he and Michael each breathed a sigh of relief that he didn't raise any additional questions.

"Yes, it is for the best," Richard agreed, smiling at Michael, who blushed and looked away.

They crossed the street at Knox, both he and Fiona refusing to look at Dianaca Castle, though Carter commented on how beautiful it was. The two of them mumbled in what he must have taken as agreement. As they neared his home, his stomach began to twist into knots, nervous about Marsilio and Richard meeting, but he knew this was the right decision. His new teacher needed to see that he was spoken for, and that what had transpired between them—which he was now certain had actually happened—was wrong and could not happen again.

They reached the gate and Michael took a long deep breath before opening it and making his way up the front walk beneath the shade of the trees, his companions close behind. They all walked up the steps, their shoes thudding on the wood. He smiled nervously as he opened the front door and walked inside, welcoming his friends to his home.

"OH, DARLING, YOU BROUGHT some friends; did you forget that you had lessons?" Michael looked at his mother, who was sitting in her usual chair with her hair pulled back from her face. Marsilio was sitting in the sofa next to her, holding a saucer of tea.

"No, I invited them to come see me play. I've never had the opportunity to play for friends before."

Claudette's face seemed to light up at this. For so long, her son had shown no interest in playing to an audience. "Well, that's wonderful."

Marsilio's face seemed to harden, and he eyed Michael with a glare that seemed like daggers directed towards him. "I don't know if that's such a good idea," he said, clearing his throat.

"Why's that?"

Marsilio stood and smoothed out his usual black trousers. "Because your control is unsteady."

"I think his control is just fine," Richard stated assuredly.

"And who are you?"

Richard stepped forward and extended his hand. "Richard Larrabee, son of Charles and Frances Larrabee." Claudette's face was beaming.

"It's a pleasure," Marsilio responded curtly, refusing to take his hand.

"Hi, there, I'm Carter Mayland." Again, Claudette began to smile. Michael could tell that his mother was happy to see him fraternizing with such esteemed company.

"And I'm Fiona." She curtsied, but refused to give her last name. Michael understood why; she worried that Claudette Donovan would become hysterical at the knowledge of a Blackmoore being in her home.

"Fiona..." his mother said, looking Fiona up and down.

She nodded. "That's right."

Claudette continued to inspect her, holding her glass of sherry. "As in, Fiona Blackmoore?"

They all looked at each other, and Michael's heart began to race. "That is correct."

"Well, that's just wonderful!"

Michael let go a sigh of relief. He also took notice to the way in which Marsilio seemed to tense up as soon as she confirmed her identity. "It is?" he asked his mother.

"Yes! I never take to idle gossip, and I have been dying to have a consultation with your mother, Aria." Michael had never thought his mother would have any curiosity with communing with spirits, but then, his mother always seemed to surprise him. "I think a little concert would be just wonderful!"

Marsilio cleared his throat. "I'm not so certain –"

Claudette waved her hand in dismissal. "Nonsense; if my son wants to play for an audience, then so be it. He's not an amateur; he's played for hundreds of people many times! I'd say this is actually a step in the right direction!" She placed her hand on Marsilio's forearm. "You have done such a wonderful job, and only with one instruction.

"I have really felt it was just my son's apprehension with playing for others that caused him to have his slip, which I did relay to my husband. Your job may be finished very soon, and then you can get back to teaching those who really need it."

Marsilio was taken aback by this, and Michael was stunned. He knew his mother; he knew the meanings behind her words and the way she said things. It was quiet obvious to him now that Claudette Donovan was not a fan of Marsilio Merrin, and most likely had never supported the idea of Michael receiving a teacher.

He thought back on all of those interactions between Marsilio and his mother, and he realized that—as with any woman of her position in 1908—she was being hospitable to him because she had to, not because she actually wanted to.

"I see...." Marsilio cleared his throat again, and his words trailed off.

"Is that your new instrument?" Claudette asked.

"New instrument?"

Michael smirked at Marsilio. "Why yes, Mother, it is."

"Oh, let me see!" She stood and walked towards Richard, who smiled kindly, and Michael thought it was humorous to see his mother's cheeks become flushed.

Richard removed it from the brown paper bag and handed it to Michael's mother.

She delicately carried the case with her back to her chair and took a seat. She flipped the latches and opened the case, looking at the beautiful violin in the afternoon sun. "Oh, Michael!"

"It's a 1791 Stradivarius."

"Once again, with all due respect, I must object to this." They all looked at Marsilio, whose black eyes seemed all the more fierce and unnatural to Michael.

"And why is that?" he asked.

"Because, Michael –"

"Excuse me, sir," Fiona interjected.

"Yes? Fiona, is it?" Marsilio seemed to be seething.

"Fiona Blackmoore, yes, and you should be addressing him by his title. You are staff, after all." Michael couldn't believe it. He had never known Fiona to seem so proper or entitled. But from the sideways glance, he realized that she had other intentions.

"Fine." He folded his arms across that strong, flat chest. "Because, *Master* Donovan, I brought you a very priceless and beautiful one-of-a-kind violin." Unlike the last time, this time he didn't mind being called "Master." It held a different connotation now.

"Oh, yes, that." Michael turned and made his way up the stairs towards his bedroom, breathing a sigh of relief that he could now, finally, be rid of the damned thing.

He walked in and grabbed it from his chair. He felt its hum, its pull, calling to him and enticing him to remove it from its case and play it. But he would do no such thing. He did not want it, and he felt as if it knew what he meant to do—that it was aware and understood what was happening, and it was trying desperately to fight against it.

"Shut up," he said to it, making his way back down the stairs and smiling at Marsilio Merrin, who no longer looked beautiful or elegant when compared to Richard.

He reached the floor and handed the violin back to Marsilio. "I won't be needing this. I just don't feel comfortable with it." Marsilio stared at it, and Michael moved closer to him, urging him to take it. "I just don't feel it suits me. It's a beautiful instrument, sir, but it just is not the right one for me. I'm sure that once we have concluded our business, you will be able to find a student far more deserving and a better fit for such a beast."

"A beast?" Marsilio asked.

"Yes; in fact, it is quite the creature, sir. I mean, truly it is beautiful—but I have only always felt at home with a Stradivarius, and I can really only effectively play that to my fullest potential. You understand, don't you?"

Marsilio shook his head. "I do not think there is another more deserving of this instrument and everything it promises than you, *Master* Donovan." He said the title with such disdain. This was completely different from their last encounter, when there was such a deep intimacy between them that it seemed it would take over everything and burn away everything else.

There was a clear, smoldering anger underneath all of this. Everything Marsilio said was filled with so much hate that Michael could only think of one word to describe it.

Malice.

He shuddered. "I think that if you look hard enough, you will find plenty of idiot savants in Bellingham who could do it justice, sir."

"Well, if this is your wish. I certainly do not want you to feel uncomfortable or out of sorts." Michael knew that Marsilio meant nothing that he had just said. This was all formality. He hoped that after today, Marsilio Merrin would be out of his life for good.

"Fantastic. Mother?" He turned his gaze to Claudette, who stood at attention.

"Yes, my darling?"

Michael felt like the master of his home. This must be what his father felt, he was certain: this sense of power and control of his domain and everyone who was in it.

"Would you please have Nellie put together refreshments for our guests?"

Claudette smiled and walked over to him. "Of course, my darling." She kissed him on the forehead and disappeared down the hall.

"Now, if you, my wonderful friends, would please take a seat, I will play for you."

They all nodded, and Michael winked at Richard, who quickly returned it. They all made themselves comfortable on the sofa and Michael looked at his violin in its open case on the coffee table. "Fiona, if you wouldn't mind."

"Oh, it's all right." Marsilio began to reach for it.

"No." Fiona grabbed it by its neck before he could. They seemed to stare at each other hard. "I got it. You just get ready to instruct." She walked over and handed the Stradivarius to Michael. They looked at each other, and Michael understood now. She didn't trust Marsilio Merrin. There was something deep within him that she didn't like. Perhaps she had used her divine skills to see inside of him, to see what he was up to.

"Thank you," Michael said to her. There was something in her eyes, something that told him that she was aware that not all was right, that there was something darker going on—something poisonous that had moved into his life.

"You're very welcome, darling." She smiled and returned to her seat, slipping between Marsilio and the coffee table. "Excuse me, sir."

"I beg your pardon," he responded. It seemed to have come out like a hiss, and Michael didn't like it. He wanted Marsilio out of his house. "Paganini's Violin Concerto Number One, whenever you're ready!" he ordered, commanding the silence from the entire house.

"Very well," Michael looked at his friends once more and began to play, fearing what would happen.

At first there was nothing, just the music and his home and his friends who watched him. The music was controlled and smooth, and his stance firm. He felt as if he could relax, finally relax and not be *en garde*. There was a peace inside of him, an overwhelming peace, and the promise of his future—his future with Richard, and all that that entailed—was just on the horizon.

In this moment, his destiny wasn't something to be feared. It was no longer something that threatened of a life held captive to someone else's plans. For the first time, everything was going to be the way he wanted it to be. It was going to be the way that he dreamed, the way that he envisioned. He could build his future, dream by dream, as one would erect a building brick by brick. It was going to be perfect.

"Harder, Master Donovan!" Marsilio shouted. He didn't understand why he wanted him to attack the piece with such ferocity, especially since the solo was delicate and poetic. It commanded pause and reflection. It was the changing of the seasons, the leaves lush and green, then slowly withering to hues of gold, before falling from their branches in rot and landing on the grass.

It was the apples falling to the wet earth in the orchard. It was the snow that came and covered it all in its white embrace, hardening it, killing everything in nature: Black Death for the botanical world.

The music was spring arriving with the beaming and radiant sun. It warmed the earth and melted that snow, and that snow, then in its liquid state, nourished the dead earth and coaxed it to bloom once again.

The allegro ushered in summer, and gallantly it answered the call, heating the ground and burning with a passion and promise of longer days and shorter nights.

The concerto could banish the darkness; it was that powerful, that strong, and needed to be respected.

"Harder!" he commanded once again. Michael continued to play, but he would not do as was asked. He feared breaking his strings once again and having to play that horrid thing that Marsilio had brought him, that awful and beautiful thing.

He began to drift, to think of nothing, and the world seemed far away from him. Everything seemed cold, distant, and there was no light behind his lids, no hint of sun.

Michael stopped playing and opened his eyes.

HIS WORDS CAUGHT IN his throat, and he was finding it almost entirely impossible to breathe. The front parlor was gone, his house was gone, and everything was night. There were trees and a moon that seemed red—a red as deep as blood—and the air was cold. Summer had gone, and the grass glistened with frost. He noticed that under the blood-red moon, the blades of grass and leaves seemed bejeweled with rubies.

He was in the orchard. He knew it. He was close enough to the pond now to see that that was exactly where he was, and its water was not crisp, clean, and tranquil. It was cobalt, and hot and bubbling.

"How did I get here?" he asked aloud, seeing his breath form in front of him. He turned his head back towards the direction of his house, and it seemed so far away—so much further than it had ever been. It seemed as if it would take hours to make his way back to it. "What's going on?"

There was no sound. No animals, no owls or bats or crickets or toads, just this dark orchard with fruit that was rotting all around him, but did not fall to the earth. "Fiona... Richard?" He called out for them, but only his own voice answered him.

Though there was nothing else in sight, he knew that he wasn't alone. He could feel it in the air, in the darkness between the trees, somewhere that he could not see. There was another presence, another entity with him, watching him.

"Oh, fuck me!" He began to make his way cautiously back to his house, feeling for his necklace and finding it this time around his neck, not missing like it had been before, when he was amongst that hellish black sabbat. He reached in for it, rubbing his fingers on the peridot gems, thinking only of Fiona, calling to her, using his thoughts to reach his house, to penetrate this dark night that he knew could not be real, and bring his friend to him.

"All alone...." He stopped, and his heart began to pound in his ears. The voice seemed neither male nor female, but held some sort of space in between, and it was amused. The melody in which it sang out was filled with absolute glee.

"Who's there?"

Again came the laughter that seemed to surround him.

"All alone with no help of your own...." Again it sang to him as one would sing when speaking to a small babe or a pet.

"Fiona!" he cried out, clutching tightly to his necklace. *No matter where you are, I will come to you*, she had said to him, and he needed this to be true, now more than ever.

"All alone...." The voice seemed to be getting closer, closing in on the space around him. "All mine... all his...."

"Fiona!"

Another laugh, and then the stirring of the wind around him, its speed increasing as those branches began to slam into each other, throwing those decaying apples all over the place. He looked up to that moon to see it begin to darken, eclipsed by the sun. The red glow around him was being replaced with a black drape that was covering everything in sight.

He resolved himself to the fact that he was going to die. He knew there was no way out of this predicament, and there was no getting back to the house. He felt helpless, small, and he allowed the weight of this hopelessness to render him weak and force him to the grass beneath him.

"Michael!" He heard her, and his heart jumped just as he jumped to his feet, and standing in front of him was Fiona. Her dress billowed in the wind, and her hair seemed black in this darkness and was wild in the wind. She had her arm outstretched to him, and that necklace, that collection of delicate ambers around her throat, seemed to be glowing like candlelight.

"Fiona!" He got to his feet and began to run, avoiding tree limbs and those hurling apples that were knocking against his body and hitting his face.

"Michael, let's go!"

Yes, escape. "Fiona!" he screamed again.

"You cannot leave here! You can never leave!" the voice shrieked in objection. "You shall die here, and your blood shall unlock the door and set Him free!" Michael threw his arm up, and it broke against a wild branch. It stung and hit the side of his head upon impact, but he didn't care. He made it to her; he took Fiona's hand and held steadfast to it.

"Hold tight to me, and don't let go!" she ordered. Fiona raised her other hand and held it out, palm open, in front of her. "Darkness, abate; I seal your fate, trapped in this place between time and space. You shall not move, and you shall not pass!"

Michael closed his eyes and clung to his friend, convinced they were going to die.

"Away from here and out of sight, we leave this place at the speed of light!" There was a great howling, and he wasn't sure if it was the presence or the wind, but he kept his eyes closed. It seemed as if the world around them was spinning, moving quickly around them, and he had no idea what was going to happen or where it would end.

HE OPENED HIS EYES and was shocked to find himself standing once again in the front parlor before his friends. The sun was bright, though beginning to set, and radiating warmth through the large window. Richard and Carter were there, and they seemed in awe of his playing. They each had smiles on their faces. He then looked to Fiona, who sat directly across from where he stood. He could see by the look on her face, the intense gaze that she gave him, that what had happened—whatever it was, wherever they had been, whatever world—had been real.

For a moment they just stared at one another, and then, slowly, Fiona's eyes moved from him and up towards Marsilio Merrin. He slowly turned his attention to his music teacher, and there was a dark fire that seemed to burn in those black eyes; though human, there was a primal, almost beast-like visage that seemed to twist his features. Although, it was nothing that anyone else seemed to notice.

"That was brilliant, darling!" Claudette said, standing to her feet and clapping. Richard and Carter followed suit, and Richard's face was glowing with pride in his lover's skill. But Fiona and Michael did not notice. They could not take their eyes off of Marsilio Merrin. Nothing else seemed to exist in this moment. As if Marsilio knew this, he winked to Michael quickly, almost as if he hadn't at all—and then he, too, began to applaud.

"*Bellissimo!*" he repeated over and over again. Michael composed himself and bowed, and cautiously Fiona stood and began to clap as well, only reluctantly moving her gaze away from Marsilio.

"Thank you; thank you all," Michael said, continuing to bow. "I have not felt so much pleasure in playing in so long, and I am so humbled and elated to play for an audience... whatever stumbling blocks there were before me, hindering me, not just a week ago, have all seemed to vanish." He looked to his mother, and she nodded in agreement and understanding.

"We must have you perform at the concert hall at White City on May Day!" his mother declared. Michael looked to Richard and Fiona nervously, and they both returned it. It seemed as if Richard was thinking, and then—as if struck by a lightning idea—he began to nod.

"Yes," Michael agreed wearily. "Yes, I think that would be a splendid idea!"

Claudette walked over and placed her hands on his cheeks, and kissed her son on the forehead. "Excellent!"

"Well, I don't know..." Marsilio said. They all turned their attention back to him.

"And why is that, sir?" Michael asked.

Marsilio sighed before responding. "I do not think that you are ready, and your lessons are not finished yet –"

Claudette stopped him. "Oh, I do apologize, Mr. Merrin, but it seems that whatever was plaguing my son and causing his impotence has passed. In no small part to you, no doubt. But I don't think we will need your services any longer."

Marsilio seemed to be searching for some kind of retort. "We have a contract for two months, Madam."

Claudette sighed. "I know." She reached for her pink satin purse, the color of a carnation's petals, and began to remove her check-book. "And that is why I am still going to honor our price." They all watched as she wrote him a banknote for a thousand dollars and handed it to him with a gentle smile on her face.

"There; that should settle you until you find another position, and Mr. Donovan and myself will be sure to promote your services to everyone we know. And I'm sure Michael will be happy to do the same."

She looked at her son, and he gave a slow nod. He could tell that his mother was desperate to get Marsilio out of her house. "Yes, of course. It would be my honor, pleasure, and duty to do this. You have helped me in more ways than you could ever know."

Marsilio looked at their faces, and a shadow of utter defeat seemed to fall over him. "Very well, then." He grabbed his black bowler cap and that mysterious black instrument—that "beast," as Michael now referred to it—and bowed to everyone. "I thank you for your hospitality, and for the opportunity to help reinvigorate and inspire such a virtuoso as Michael Donovan to rediscover his passion."

He walked over to Michael and outstretched his hand. Michael looked at it briefly and then took it. His grip was strong, and he pulled Michael close to him with such force that his lips were just grazing the shell of his ear.

"Until we meet again." Michael's heart was pounding. His eyes, which were looking at their locked hands, grew wide in fear as he watched Marsilio's thumbnail begin to grow, to elongate right before his eyes. It became a glassy, talon-like point, and punctured the surface of skin between the thumb and index finger. It broke the flesh and the blood slipped out like a crimson tear drop.

Michael jerked his hand away and Marsilio smiled, bringing that nail, now painted with a drop of his blood, to his lips and stuck it in his mouth, tasting Michael and closing his eyes in a sort of swoon of pleasure.

"I will see you soon enough." He turned and bowed to them all. Michael realized that none of them had noticed, and the wound looked to be nothing more than a scratch.

Michael forced a smile and wave at the unnatural Marsilio Merrin as he opened the front door and walked out, whistling as he made his way down the steps of the porch and through the trees along the walk. Michael didn't relax or breathe again until he heard the front gate swing open and shut once more, the whistling fading into the distance.

"Well," his mother began, "I am certainly glad to be rid of him. How about a glass of champagne to celebrate my son's triumphant return?"

"Thank you, Mrs. Donovan; that would be delightful!" Fiona responded, trying to mask the look of concern on her face.

"Yes, please, Mother. I could definitely use a glass!"

Claudette looked to Richard and Carter, who also nodded in agreement. "All right, I will be back."

They all smiled to her as she left, disappearing once again down the back hall. Michael was glad to be rid of Marsilio Merrin and that violin of his, which had done nothing but cause him trouble from the day it had first been placed into his hands.

"So, do you really think you are prepared to play in front of such a large audience?" Carter asked him, sitting as close to Fiona as he could without seeming inappropriate.

"Of course. It will be good for me, I think—and to have all of you there, supporting me, I don't see how I could fail." He looked to Richard.

"Of course," Richard said. They both knew this was never going to happen. They would devise some excuse, of course, some plan, but this concert would never be. Everyone, he knew, would worry and wonder to his absence. Perhaps, he figured, they would think he was overcome with nerves and was unable to go through it. Maybe they would whisper that Michael Donovan was too full of himself and felt that he was too good for the city and that he didn't need to bother with entertaining them, that they were undeserving of his brilliance.

Either way, he didn't care. All he cared about was getting as far away from Fairhaven and South Hill as quickly as possible.

"Well, I am certainly looking forward to it," Fiona said.

"As am I," Carter echoed.

"Well, thank you." They heard the tinkling of glasses, and Claudette returned with a tray laid with flute glasses. Behind her was Nellie, who carried a sterling silver ice bucket that was sweating from all of the ice. In her other hand was a bottle of Veuve Clicquot and a white linen towel.

"Here we go, darlings," Claudette said, setting down the tray of glasses and taking her seat in her usual throne-like Chesterfield at the head of the room. Michael took a seat in the blue velvet club chair closest to Richard, and they all cheered when Nellie popped the cork and the frothy liquid gold began to pour out. She laughed and poured the glasses.

"And, Nellie, won't you please have a toast with us?" his mother asked.

Nellie looked at them all; her kind face was filled with affection and surprise. "But I haven't a glass." They all smiled when she took stock and noticed that there was indeed an extra glass on the tray.

"Yes, please. It would not be the same for me if you didn't," Michael said to her.

"Very well." She poured herself a glass, and they all lifted them into the air.

"To my brilliant son, and to his wonderful and otherworldly talent!"

"Here, here!" They all cheered and were about to drink when Michael stopped them.

"I would like to salute all of you. To my mother, who has always stood by my side and refused to let me give up. To Nellie, for always putting up with me when I can be an absolute brat!"

They all laughed.

"And to the three of you." He turned to his friends and looked at them, the warmth and beauty of their faces, the light that seemed to radiate in their eyes, and he could not help but feel the immense wave of love that seemed to wash over him, to cover him in its embrace.

"From the wisdom you hold, Fiona, to the carefree humor that you, Carter, exhibit in every moment of your life." And then he turned to Richard and locked eyes with him. They were now holding each other in place, and it seemed as if it was pouring out of them and that anyone would be able to notice, but he didn't care. What would be the point? He was happy. He was happy and he was grateful, and he wanted to cherish what he had and give it his appreciation.

"And to you, Richard, I wish that I could say something short and simple, but I am at a loss of words because it isn't so simple. I want to thank you for your fearlessness; you have shown me how not to be fearful myself.

"You have shown me how to confront every challenge, even if that challenge is inside of myself, and to rise above it, and for that I thank you from the bottom of my heart!" He raised his glass once again and they all followed suit, giving a "here, here" before they all took a sip of their champagne.

He was happy. Sublimely happy. Everything was going to change, he knew, and soon he and Richard would be far from here, and perhaps—with the exception of Fiona Blackmoore—he would never see any of these people ever again.

He knew he had to treasure these moments and take them in for what they were. He had to note every detail, every smile, every laugh, every joke made, and he had to lock them away and keep them safe. He never wanted to lose this memory; he wanted this moment to be as fresh and as real in twenty years as it was in this very moment.

They were all in the middle of discussing the concert, and getting it arranged with the Dianacas, when the door opened and in walked his father Jasper. He seemed at first surprised, then quickly overcome with displeasure with the guests that occupied his front room.

"Darling, you're home!"

He looked to his wife, but his face did not soften. It was stern and like stone. "I do live here." He turned his attention to Nellie, who had been seated on one of the sofas. She quickly sat the champagne glass on the coffee table—so quickly, in fact, that she had almost broke it. She moved to him and curtsied.

"Your coat and hat, sir?" She held out her hands. The look in his eyes was a look of utter displeasure with her.

"Thank you," he said, practically throwing them into her arms and forcing her to stumble back slightly.

"Darling, don't be cross; we were celebrating!" Claudette said again.

"Celebrating? Celebrating what?"

Michael stood and turned, meeting with his father's gaze. "To my triumph." He looked his son up and down, examining him, as if trying to measure the change in him, or how to cut him down.

"Your triumph over what? From where I stand, you still seem just as insecure and impotent," he growled.

Michael laughed. "No, Father. To my triumph over all of those things that have held me back, like the doubts of others," he said pointedly. "And to my no longer needing your instructor or his inferior violin. I will be performing at the White City May Day Festival for the entire city. It will be glorious."

Jasper folded his arms across his chest and grunted. "And you have accomplished this so quickly, after one lesson?"

"Yes, Father, I have. You can doubt it if you wish, but you will see in a week's time. I will rise from the ashes and flames of your doubt, and I will conquer this city. Like the Pied-Piper, they will be entranced and willing to follow me into whatever world I paint for them!"

His father said nothing. Michael could tell that he was mulling his son's words in his head, examining his declaration, just as he was now examining the people in his room.

"And might I ask who all of you are?"

"I'm Richard Larrabee, sir; you and I have met." Jasper's attitude seemed to shift. It took him a moment, but he did realize that Charles Larrabee's son was indeed standing before him, and companion to his son. Michael could see the pride that began to take over his face, softening it from its stony resolve.

"Ah, yes, and of course I know you." He turned his attention to Carter. "Master Mayland, how are you, son?"

Carter shook his hand and nodded. "I am fine, sir."

It was then that Jasper's eyes fell on Fiona. He looked at her, examined her face, her eyes, her clothes, the sophisticated air that seemed to surround her, and the relaxed and feline movement of her body. Michael knew that he was trying to place her features with people that he associated with, but he could not.

"And you?" he said to her, moving closer and casting her in his shadow.

"Fiona Blackmoore." He took two steps back and looked her up and down, taking her in now. There was a very subtle shadow of fear that fell on his face, and he drew his lips back in a controlled anger.

"A Blackmoore, a Blackmoore in my house?!" He looked to his wife and then his son. "Some *Gibson Girl* under my roof?!" Michael had to stifle a laugh. They all did, even his mother. A Gibson Girl was the epitome of the new woman. Confident, sexually alluring, beautiful and thin—a woman who wore dresses without hoops or corsets. She knew how to control men with her wiles, and dared to drink in the same cigar parlors as the men that longed to entertain her.

As far as Michael was concerned, that definitely described Fiona Blackmoore.

"Jeepers! I had no idea I was courting a Gibson Girl! How lucky am I?" Carter said with a laugh.

"Darling, Fiona Blackmoore is lovely, and she has been a wonderful and supportive friend to our son. They all have." Claudette walked over to her husband and placed her hand on his shoulder. "Please, just let them celebrate, and you come with me; I'll fix you a scotch and you can have your cigar."

Jasper refused to look at her. "You bring the devil into this house!" he said to Michael, glaring at him with terror and disapproval. "The devil on to all that this family has built? That I have built for you! For your future!" He was in a quiet rage.

"Father, she is not the devil; she has nothing to do with the devil. She's a girl who likes to read, to listen to music—my music. Who supports me and wants to be my friend. It is all nonsense. Idle gossip!" Michael fired back.

"And what of the Hampton girl? Are you trying to tell me that this girl had nothing to do with her hair loss?"

Michael nodded. "Yes, Father. Science is finding new things about our bodies all of the time. I have no doubt that it was caused by something she inherited."

He sighed and shook his head. "It's been a long day, and I am tired. Please, see your friends out." Michael nodded and watched his father move to the stairs, his wife leading the way.

"Well, that was quite the turn of events," Carter said.

"Yes, I'm so sorry, Fiona," Michael said to her.

She shrugged and gave a dismissal with her hand. "Oh, please; as if I haven't heard far worse. Your cranky father will not get me twisted into a bunch of knots, I promise you."

"I should be getting back to the hotel for dinner anyways," Richard said. Michael looked at him and nodded sullenly.

"Yes, I should be getting home too," Carter repeated.

"Well, thank you all for coming." He smiled and led them to the front door, holding it open and smiling as they walked past him. Carter placed his hand on his shoulder and gave him a pat, and Fiona followed him out.

"We will speak," she said to him as she kissed him on the cheek.

"Yes," he replied with a nod.

Richard was the last to leave, his hand brushing against Michael's, brushing against the prick by Marsilio that Michael had almost forgotten entirely.

"Till tomorrow, and soon to our future!" Richard said with a smile, looking to see that Carter wasn't looking, and then he kissed Michael quickly on the lips. Michael placed his hand over Richard's heart and felt it pound against him.

"To our new life!" Michael responded. Richard Larrabee nodded and took hold of that hand and brought it to his lips, kissing the inside of his palm and then his fingers, before racing down the steps and joining his friends.

"I'm dating a Gibson Girl!" Carter shouted, he and Fiona laughing as they all ran down the street. Michael stood there and sighed, looking at the setting sun over the waters, the sky now ablaze in pink and orange and violet and green. It was the most beautiful sunset that he could recall seeing in such a long time.

Everything was different now, better. And no matter what happened, he would be with the one he loved, carving a place for themselves in the world. He only hoped that the week would pass by as if sands through an hour glass, fast and barely tangible.

THE EVENING PASSED into night, and Michael did not see his father for the rest of the evening. At times he heard him in his study on the second floor, complaining to his wife about Fiona Blackmoore being in his home. Claudette was constantly reassuring him that it was all right, that she had meant no harm, and that she had been polite, gracious and a proper young lady.

Michael sat there in the front parlor, watching the light fade and the house become darker and darker as the sun was all but extinguished by the night. He heard Nellie and the other cooks in the kitchen preparing dinner, but this was all distant now. He thought about all that had transpired, and the evil that had taken hold, the evil that had taken him from his home and brought him into his dark and foreboding orchard.

He thought of the voice and the malice and the delight in its own evil, and began to think that it was Marsilio Merrin himself. He thought of the talon that had grown from his thumb and pierced his skin and drawn blood. He thought of that smile, and the way in which Marsilio had tasted him and had enjoyed his flavor.

He jumped with a start when he heard the light knock on his front door. Michael stood and made his way to the door with cautious steps. He was afraid that Marsilio would be there on the other side, coming to finish whatever infernal plan that he had started.

As he neared the door he saw the svelte silhouette on the other side of the lace curtain, and was overcome with relief when he realized that it was Fiona.

"Hi," he said to her. Her eyes were wide, and she looked frantic. She was clutching to her necklace, and cocked her head to the left to have him join her outside. He looked behind him, knowing his parents were still upstairs and had not heard her knocking. Michael walked out and closed the door gingerly behind him. "What happened?"

She shook her head and walked over to the wicker love seat that sat in front of the picture window. "This is terrible, Michael, truly terrible. I don't know if I brought this on you or not, and if I have I am so sorry."

Michael took a seat next to her, and put his hand over hers and gave it a squeeze. "It'll be all right. I'm sure of it. He's gone."

"That Marsilio Merrin—I hate to even say his name aloud—he is not human. He is not a witch. He is something else. Something diabolical."

Michael was overcome with fear, and he began to shake despite himself. "Something else?"

Fiona nodded. "That place, that orchard... it was yours. We were between time and space. We call it the astral plane; the world between this one and the next. The mirrored world. There is a plan, a great evil plan unfolding."

"What can we do? Can we do anything?"

She placed her hand on his cheek. Her eyes were so large and radiant, and though she tried to calm him, to look assured, he could see the fear and the uncertainty all over her face. "I will find a way, Michael. I will keep you safe. Just be careful, and watch your back. Never let your guard down. You only have a few more days here, and then you will be gone from this place for good.

"Whatever you do, trust no one but your parents and the three of us." She stood and he held her hand a little too long than was acceptable, before letting go.

"And what do you want me to do if I see Merrin?"

She had just reached his steps when she stopped and turned to look at him. "Run." And with that she made her way quickly down the steps and back to her house at the end of the block.

Michael stood and wrapped his arms around himself, looking over the porch and the courtyard, looking at the canopy of trees of the apple orchard, and a chill came over him.

Would he die? Would this be the end of him? Was this his unknowing dues that he had to give to the devil? Was the dark lord coming to collect for the gift of the music that he had given Michael?

He wanted to believe that his music came from the angels, but the angels played the harp and the devils played the violin. Had he sold his soul when he was a child, he wondered again, and was it now time to repay the Lord of Darkness for this gift?

He figured, while looking at those trees—seeing the spot where he knew the pond to be—that yes, the devil was coming for him, that devil did want his dues, but he was going to fight like hell to refuse him.

Michael sighed, and a single tear slid down his cheek. He didn't bother to wipe it away. He let it come. He'd let all of the tears fall, and he would fight with every last breath, with every ounce of strength he had inside of himself, to fight this collection of debt. He was finally going to live, and nothing—no god of heaven or beast of hell—was going to take that from him.

No matter what, he was determined to live.

XII

THE WEEK HAD PASSED with little incident. The nightmare visions had stopped, and his father had long ago given up his tirade over a Blackmoore in his home. He and Richard had been busy making their plans. They would never write them in notes for fear of discovery, but after school, often when his mother was busy downstairs and his father gone at work, they would talk quietly in Michael's room, naked in bed, tracing the journey across the flesh of each other's bodies.

Often Michael would play his violin for Richard in between bouts of making love in hushed whispers of pleasure. Great Baroque pieces, songs of the lovers. They were both blissfully happy, and as the days passed into nights, and the nights once again moved into days, and continued on, soon the time had come.

"Michael...." He was sitting on his bed, going through all of his clothes and packing his trunks as quietly as he could, when he heard Fiona call his name. He looked around and saw nothing. "Michael." There it was again. He heard a rapping at his window over the roof of the front porch, and to his amazement Fiona was standing there, waiting for him to come.

He smiled and walked over. She returned his smile, and Michael quietly lifted the frame. "How'd you get up here?"

"I came to get you. Come with me."

He looked at her, perplexed. "Out there?"

Fiona nodded. "Yes."

"But I'm sure I will fall."

She shook her head. "Oh, come now, don't be a coward. You know I wouldn't let anything happen to you." He looked around his room for just a moment before nodding. He slipped out onto the roof, not bothering to bring his jacket as it was too warm still. He stood and took a deep breath, looking at the clear velvet night sky with its diamond-like stars and the brilliant white of the almost full moon.

Fiona looked elegant in her pearl satin dress with short sleeves that draped her body effortlessly. She smiled and extended her hand to his.

"What do you want to do?" he asked her.

"I want you to trust me and take my hand. We're going to jump." His eyes grew wide and he shook his head. "Michael Donovan, after all this time, you're not going to just trust me and do as I say?" He knew that she was right. She had always been there, and she had never let him down. In the short time that they had known each other, Fiona Blackmoore had demonstrated that he could trust her with his life.

"Very well," he said with a sigh. He took hold of her hand and then they both leapt from the roof. They came down slowly, gliding as if they had not jumped at all, but instead had taken to the skies and were now making their return to the earth after a long night soaring through the heavens.

"How did you do that?"

Fiona laughed. "I'm a witch, remember? There isn't much I can't do."

"What now?" he asked her, looking around the yard and the night sky.

"Now you meet the rest of my family."

Her family. He had always wondered about them, and wondered about the inside of their home, and what the rest of the

Blackmoores were like. He was on his way to find out and he was awash of wonder, excitement, and dread.

THROUGH THE LUSH TROPICAL leaves he could see lights piercing the darkness, and there was music coming from a victrola inside the house. "Are you guys having a party?" he asked.

"Um...." She pushed the gate open. "Sort of." She walked in and then stepped aside to allow him entrance. The front courtyard smelled delicious. There were lilies and jasmine and lavender. There were lush lilacs and roses and cherry blossoms. The flagstone path that led to the front door was newly swept, and coupled with the heat, Michael imagined that this was what New Orleans had been like.

"Not exactly, but close," she answered him aloud. There was no front porch, just a five-foot wall of packed stone on either side of the door and in front of the house, making a sort of courtyard. The oak door's window was no longer covered by that lace curtain, and he could see inside the home. It had a long front hall that went to the other end of the house, and the floor was a glossy pine. The furniture was all ornate Louis XV, and there were oil lamps as well as electrical Tiffany lamps throughout the house.

"Don't be nervous," she said to him as she opened the door.

"Easy for you to say," he said with a chuckle.

"I guess so."

They walked into the house, and Michael was overwhelmed. There were gorgeous, rich oil portraits hanging from every wall, regal men and women and children. All of them were similar in their looks, in their expressions and eyes. On ornate end tables there were framed photographic portraits of people with the same eerie, otherworldly look in their gazes.

"Are these all Blackmoores?" he asked her.

Fiona looked at them and nodded. "Yes. Most of them are born; others are Blackmoores by name only."

"Because they were married in?" Fiona nodded. They stepped into a great double parlor with beautiful stained glass windows and oak wainscoting throughout. There was a great marble fireplace to the left, perhaps six feet in height, and its fire was burning bright in the room. The only other light came from two corner lamps, which only gently penetrated the rest of the darkness.

"I want you to meet my mother and uncle." Michael nodded and followed her through the great room and towards a door to the right at the back of the house. They were now in a great dining room looking out on the countryside below the hill. It was as if they were looking into a valley. The moon shone down on all of those stately Victorians and the hillside on the other end of Fairhaven, where the electric lights of White City could be seen twinkling like fairies in the night.

They moved through another door and now they were in a grand kitchen with a large Aga and two large ice boxes. This kitchen was certainly larger than his own, and it smelled of herbs and flowers. He had never smelled a fragrance as intoxicating as what he was smelling at this very moment. He felt delirious.

Fiona led him through another door to the right and they were in a grand library. Shelves reached from the floor to the ceiling, and there was a large round oak table in the middle of the room. There were candles and large statues of saints standing in corners. Around their necks and at their feet were what seemed to be carpets of flowers, and candles of different colors also burned around their feet.

Before them were large French doors that were opened up onto a courtyard of brick and flagstone, and in the middle there was a great fire that burned brightly. There were even more candles burning on jutted shelves of stone on the walls of this courtyard.

There, standing before the fire, was a beautiful raven-haired woman with the same eyes as Fiona, standing before them, wearing a sheer black robe with small delicate sleeves. He could see her nakedness beneath this and he averted his eyes, flushed with embarrassment.

The man had that same black hair, long, reaching to his chin, and his face was extremely handsome, with vibrant blue eyes and strong cheekbones. His mutton-chops framed his jaw, and his body was fit and lean. He was obviously older, perhaps fifty, though he didn't look it, and he was without clothing, save for that same draping of sheer black fabric, which was wrapped around his waist. Michael could see the dark hairs that blanketed his thick sizeable cock, and despite what was happening before him, he could feel a tinge of lust rise inside of him.

"Michael, this is my mother, Aria." He looked back to the beautiful, nearly-naked woman who seemed more like a goddess, and gave a polite if not awkward bow. "And this is my uncle, Jeremiah Blackmoore." Michael turned to him and bowed once again.

"What is going on?" Michael asked. "Why am I here?"

"Do not be alarmed," Aria began; her voice was gentle, sweet, and motherly. "My daughter has told me what is going on, everything that has been happening, and of your plans to run away from here with your lover tomorrow night."

Michael looked at his friend, not sure if he was fine with this or upset with her for telling. "Don't be upset with her. We want to help you; we want to use what power we have to get you and Richard out of Fairhaven safely."

"And how are you going to do that?"

Fiona sighed and took him by the arm. "Take off your clothes."

He looked at her; it was as if his jaw had hit the floor. "I beg your pardon?"

Fiona laughed. "Don't be difficult. You need to be free of all earthly restraints. You need to be unhindered and one with the universe. It is May Eve, the night before Beltane. When the Goddess makes love to her consort and child, the great God, and they give birth to the bounties of the earth. Tomorrow night is the Great Rite, and we want to use this power to place a powerful protection around you, one so strong that these evils—which have targeted you, for whatever reason—will not be able to succeed!"

Michael was reluctant, but after a moment he sighed in defeat and began removing his clothes, save for the necklace, which he refused to take off.

There he stood, naked, his body exposed to these people that he had never met before, surrounded by burning flames and the light of the nearly full moon.

Aria drew both her arms up to the night sky, along with Jeremiah and Fiona, while Michael stood there, unsure if he was supposed to do the same—but in the end he didn't. He watched then as Aria withdrew a sharp black-handled dagger from a sheath around her slender right thigh.

"Queen of the moon, Queen of the sun, Queen of the heavens, Queen of the stars, Queen of the waters, Queen of the earth. Bring to us the Child of Promise!"

She handed the blade to Jeremiah who took it and raised it high into the air. "It is the Great Mother who gives birth to him; it is the Lord of Life who is born again. Darkness and tears are set aside when the sun shall come up early."

The blade was then passed over the flames and handed to Fiona, who did the same as her grandfather and mother had before. "Golden sun of the mountains, illuminate the land, light up the world, illuminate the seas and the rivers, sorrows be laid, joy to the world!" Fiona handed the blade back to her mother, who once again held it high above her head.

"Blessed be the Great Goddess, without beginning, without end, everlasting to eternity—blessed be!" they finished in unison. Michael watched in enthralled horror as Aria Blackmoore drew the blade across her palm and then passed it on to her brother and daughter, who did the same. They extended their hands over the flames and thrust their blood into that fire, which seemed to rise higher, and its color changed to a pink hue.

"Great Hecate, accept our witches' blood, the blood you give us. Take our blood and grant us our request. From your throne in the other realm, Queen of Heaven-Queen of Hell, harken to our spell. By moonlight and starlight, bend the axis of the world on this night. Place your protection on this boy and those he loves, enchant the amulet around his neck, protect him, Hecate! Protect him!"

The necklace seemed as if it was glowing, and each stone was beginning to get hot and burn against his skin. He let out a cry, but refused to take it off.

"Deliver him from those with evil intentions. Keep him safe! Keep him safe; do not let them succeed in their plot against him!" The stones burned with such unyielding heat that it brought him to his hands and knees, but he refused to take it off. No matter how much it burned.

"Don't ever take it off, Michael!" Fiona cried out to him, though she now seemed so far away, a distant ghost. "Don't ever take it off!" she screamed again.

He was floating in a dark, weightless sea. There was a peace and a quiet. Everything was so far away: his parents, his violin, the moon and the night. All of it was someplace beneath him and in the past. The present was sparse and endless. It was serene.

MICHAEL'S EYES POPPED open and he was surprised to find himself in his bed, dressed in his clothes, the sweat beading on his forehead. He looked around and saw his window closed, his two steamer trunks packed and locked. He wondered if perhaps he had actually fallen asleep and dreamed the whole thing. He was certain that that had to be it.

"How ridiculous," he said with a laugh. He stood and turned on a lamp, walking over to his floor-length mirror. He unbuttoned his shirt, preparing to get ready for bed, when the sight of tiny little red indentations, like burns, lined his chest and matched precisely with the position of the peridot gems.

"So it was real..." he said with a grin. He felt better now, knowing he hadn't imagined it, and that the Blackmoores really had used their powers to protect him and Richard—that they would be okay, and by the setting sun they would be boarding a train safely, leaving all of this hellfire and horror behind. They were going to be able to start that new life, the life that they knew that they deserved, and everything would be right with the world.

Once they were away from here, nothing would ever harm them again. He finished undressing and crawled under the covers naked, loving the feeling of the silk sheet over his smooth skin. As he closed his eyes he imagined that the sheet was Richard, that it was his strong, warm body enveloping him in sensuous pleasure, lulling him safely into a dreamless slumber.

There were no nightmares. There were no witches in black dancing or devils playing violins, or bodies burning on a pyre. There was only the quiet empty black of sleep.

XIII

MICHAEL WAS UP EARLY, as soon as he heard the rooster crow down the block and the golden sun filled his room with its light. He stretched and sat up, his brown eyes looking at the walls with their paper of blue flowers, the furniture, the various paintings of his favorite composers staring at him with grins that seemed to be in on a secret joke, and the fresh bouquet of peonies that seemed to him like radiant pink fire balls.

He looked down at his black steamer trunks with their gold locks, and the reality of the day hit him in a way that it had never before. He was probably never going to see this room—any of these things—ever again.

It pained him. It was slight, and not overwhelming enough to give him any second thoughts of his and Richard's plan. But knowing that there just wasn't a place for someone like him, who felt and loved the way that he did, in this world of his—this world that he had only ever known his entire life—caused him to grieve.

He wasn't going to be able to say goodbye to his parents—though his father, who had always been distant and removed from his life, wasn't something that hurt him too much. But not being able to say goodbye to his mother... well, that was the thing that broke his heart; that was the thing that made the tears catch in his throat so he had to swallow them down.

He moved quickly; every movement expressed an excitement, an impatience to get through the day. He showered quickly, not choosing to linger under the hot water as was so often his custom, and the ritual of shaving was committed with less care than was safe. After getting dressed in a pair of soft black breeches which reached to the knees and were worn with black stockings and low black leather shoes, and rolling up the sleeves on his white-and-black striped button shirt to his elbows, Michael walked into the dining room to join his mother and father for breakfast.

Since his father's meeting with his friends, Michael and Jasper hadn't exchanged much conversation with one another, and this morning seemed to be no different. His father sat at the head of the table, his brows furrowed, and his eyes stern and fixed on the special May Day Festival edition of The Bellingham Herald. Last year's queen, Patricia Knickerbocker, graced the front page in black-and-white. A large crown of various stars made of roses and carnations sat in her mess of light curls, and her smile seemed sickly sweet with her innocent-looking eyes.

Michael was happy that he would not have to be at this year's crowning, or the festival at all for that matter. He smirked at the fact that while everyone was gone, while the entire population of Fairhaven would be up at the White City Amusement Park, he and Richard would be together, in their own private deluxe rail car, on their way to San Francisco.

"Are you excited to be playing for the whole city tonight?"

Michael turned and looked at his mother. She was so beautiful in her white cotton dress with powder blue lace. She had her mane of brown hair pulled back from her face and in a great wave it cascaded down her back. "Oh, yes; yes, of course I am." He offered her a smile.

"And will your friends be coming to support you?" his father asked him, not bothering to lift his eyes from his paper.

"Yes, I believe they will be."

Jasper Donovan lifted his eyes from the newsprint to meet his son's face. "No doubt that Blackmoore girl will be one of them."

Michael gave a nod and let out an exasperated sigh. "Yes, Father, she will be there, along with Richard Larrabee and Carter Mayland. They will all be there to support me, as friends often do for one another."

Jasper shook his head. "You know, I don't know why you give in to such nonsense. You're not just anyone. You're a Donovan. You have a certain place in this city. You have to think of your future in this town, and that is greatly impacted by the company you keep."

Michael threw his head back and laughed. "Nonsense? The only one who is giving in to any nonsense is you, Father. All of this slanderous talk of witches and devils. The Blackmoores are fine people. You say so because of what others say, and because Aria Blackmoore runs the spiritualist church—but if it is so wrong, then why do so many of the people in this city, the same ones who say such horrible things, seek out audience with her? It's because people are excited by it, and they all know, deep down, that the Blackmoores are no more harmful than anyone else."

His father continued to stare at him. Michael had never given such an impassioned speech to his father before. He would have never dared it, but now—now that he was leaving—he feared nothing.

"Hm, point taken, my boy." He said this with a cool even tone, and then turned his attention back to his paper and continued reading. Michael no longer existed for him, and he knew this. Jasper Donovan had always found everything else more interesting than his son, and this was no less true than right now.

"Excuse me; I need to practice." He stood, rolling his eyes as soon as he had turned his back to his father, and began walking to the stairs in the front hall.

"Are you going to be coming with us to the park for the parade walk this afternoon and the crowning at sunset?"

Michael shook his head, not bothering to turn around, knowing that he would start to cry if he looked at his mother's beautiful face again. "No. I just need to practice. I'll see you before I get on stage."

He turned and began to make his way to the stairs, when he glimpsed a tall shadow down the hall to his left outside the back door. He thought of Marsilio, and his heart began to race. He had tried to keep his now-former music teacher and all of those horrible visions out of his head, and now it was all coming to him, replaying once again on the screen of his mind.

It can't be, he said to himself.

Slowly he walked down the hall, the floorboards creaking beneath his feet as he passed the piano that sat against the wall, and the portrait of their home that had been painted shortly after it had been completed. His heartbeats seemed like thunder in his ears as he neared that door at the back of the house.

He slipped his finger under the lace curtain on the little window and glanced out, hoping not to be noticed. There was that short chocolate hair and olive skin, and a smile spread on his face as his worry was replaced with joy. He opened the door gently and smiled wide as soon as Richard's head turned, and those copper eyes met his and his lips spread into a wide smile.

"What are you doing here?" he asked, slipping out and closing the door behind him.

Richard took hold of his hand and began to lead him under the arbor with its lush green leaves and the grapes that had seemed to fatten overnight, little round jewels of juice that glistened ruby in the morning sun. "I had to see you; I had to make sure that this was real, that we are really doing this!" They leaned against the wood siding of the house, between the two windows of the music room. He was dressed in dark gray trousers and a white shirt and black bowler cap with a satin ribbon wrapped around the brim.

"Yes; yes, we are. This is really happening. We are going to be leaving here forever!" Michael replied, placing one hand on the side of Richard's face; the other he pressed into the cavity of his firm chest. "We are going to begin our lives together!"

Richard's breath escaped his smiling face, warm and sweet, and they kissed. The passion moving through them, their eyes closed as their tongues wrapped together in their mouths. "I will come for you as soon as the sun sets. Everyone in the village will be gone; it will be empty, and I will have a taxi waiting to take us to the train."

Michael nodded and chuckled, kissing him again. "Yes, and then this will all be a distant memory." Richard nodded and held his body close to his.

They looked at the flagstone courtyard and the array of flowers that bloomed around them, seeming to explode with all of their brilliance. Michael had never thought that the garden had looked as beautiful as it did in this moment. The morning sun, warm on their faces, seemed to mean something more: a promise of a new life, a new dawn, a chance to blossom just as those flowers were, to become the young men that they were always meant to be.

Richard took Michael's hands to his lips and kissed the tops of his fingers. "Just a few more hours, and then we will never have to see this place again!"

Michael nodded, and Richard kissed him hard and fast on the lips before running to the gate at the back of the house and disappearing down the lane.

MICHAEL SPENT THE DAY in his room playing all the music he could think of to try to pass the time. It was nothing composed by someone else, nothing that anyone would know; it was simply what moved him, expressing everything inside of his heart that he couldn't say out loud.

In the music, he was telling his mother everything; he was declaring his love for Richard Larrabee to his father, and he was saying goodbye. They called to him from the front hall when they were leaving, telling him that they would see him at the concert hall later, and he responded with his music. He couldn't say anything to them, and he couldn't see them out. It would have sabotaged everything, and he knew it.

He needed this time to himself, to his music, and as the sun moved across his walls, moving from morning to afternoon and afternoon into early evening, he let the tears come. He let them slip down his face, knowing that the time had come: he would never stand here in front of his window as he had done a thousand times throughout his life, and play to that setting sun. It was over now; it was time to stop playing and take his bow. The pink and orange of the sky was giving way to hues of light green, purple, and deep velvet blue.

It was time to go.

HE WAS GLAD THE HOUSE was empty, Nellie and the other staff having been relieved of their posts for the night so that they could all go to the festival. He dragged the first trunk along the floor and used all of his strength to lift it and begin carrying the thing down the steps. He had just reached the landing when the doorbell rang throughout the house, and he looked to see Richard on the other side of the glass.

"Good, he can help me get these out of the house!" He raced down the steps and pulled open the door, seeing Richard standing there, a smile on his face. Behind him on the street, the carriage was waiting to take them to the train.

"Are you ready, Master Donovan?"

Michael laughed and nodded. "Just help me get my trunks."

"Of course." Michael moved aside, and just as Richard began to enter into the house a long, slender black form, with long claw hands, seeming to be made of smoke, swept in from the right, and Richard was gone in an instant.

"Richard!" Michael screamed. He stepped out onto the porch and saw Richard and this monstrous thing ascend quickly over the courtyard and over the trees, before disappearing into the middle of the orchard.

Michael raced back into his house, running down the hall and out the back door. "No! Richard!" he screamed over and over, racing through the courtyard, nearly tripping over the table and chairs. He burst through the gate that led into the orchard, and was overcome with darkness. The branches of those apple trees hit him hard across his face, but he didn't care. He knew that he needed to get to the pond. That was where Richard was, and his stomach began to twist into sickening knots as the memories of those visions came back to him.

He reached into his shirt and pulled the necklace out, gripping it tightly in his hands. "Fiona, I need you! Fiona, please help me! I need you!" he yelled between great bleating sobs.

When he reached the clearing in the middle of the orchard, he felt as if the entirety of his breath had been knocked out of him.

There, standing on the other side of the pond, was Richard, his shirt ripped into shreds on his body, barely hanging on. He was struggling to break free of the iron grip that held tight to his throat. Long, talon-like nails pressed into his flesh, and a tall slender body in a long black velvet frock coat stood behind him.

He looked up into that face, and it was a face he knew all too well: it was the face of Marsilio Merrin, but that face was different. It was vicious and twisted, almost beastly. The lips were drawn back, and long gleaming teeth, like the jaws of a wolf, beset his face. His eyes were no longer black, but burning hot red embers in his sockets.

"Let him go!" Michael demanded, finding the courage deep within him to speak.

"You dare!" Marsilio hissed. "You order nothing!"

"Michael, run!" Richard spat out, obviously being strangled by Marsilio's grip.

"Please," Michael cried. "Please let him go; please don't hurt him."

Marsilio laughed, and his laughter seemed to boom around them. "I don't want to have to hurt him, but I will. I will if you don't do as I say. Do you understand?" Michael looked from him to Richard's face, the way in which he fought in vain for his freedom. He knew that he had no choice.

"What do you want?"

"Play!" With his other hand, Marsilio threw that violin case at Michael's feet, and it was then that he understood: he was going to play for an audience after all, just not to any audience he could have ever imagined.

Michael stared at the black case before him resting in the grass. "If I play this, you will let him go?"

Marsilio nodded. "Yes...." Michael looked around him and prayed that Fiona had heard him and that she would get to them soon, before whatever it was that Marsilio was planning would come to fruition.

"Very well." He reached down and popped open that case, looking at that black creature with its strings that glistened in the twilight and silver of the rising moon, and he picked it up and placed it to his chin. "What do you want me to play?"

Marsilio grinned. "Whatever it tells you to play."

Michael looked at Richard one last time and mouthed "I'm sorry" before placing bow against strings and closed his eyes, letting the music play and the strings sing.

The wind seemed to pick up around them, and the world—which had been so warm—was now turning into bitter cold and getting darker. He continued to play; he knew that Marsilio was telling him to play faster, to play harder, like he always had. Michael realized that he had been training him for this moment, whatever it was.

He felt something reach for him; something moved out of that violin and took hold of him and refused to let go. It was making him play now; he knew this, and he wouldn't have been able to stop if he tried. He was no longer in control, and this music—whatever it was that was coming from his hands—was not controlling him either. The only thing that was in control was the violin itself.

"Yes!" Marsilio let out. Michael opened his eyes and saw that the light of the moon was changing; its silver-white light was being replaced with something else, a crimson glow that was igniting everything around them.

"Michael, stop! Run!" Richard yelled. But he couldn't stop. He couldn't make the bow rest. It would not be separated from the strings. Michael looked and saw that large moon covered in a ruby wash, and the winds began to rip the leaves from the branches and the branches from the trunks, littering the edge of the pond with them.

Before him the pond began to heat, to boil and change, and soon its clear waters were thick and black—black like his visions, and he understood: hell itself was erupting from the earth. Several long clawed hands shot out from the thick tar and dug into the ground at the edges of the pond, and bodies began to pull themselves out of the tar. It was those witches that had been cloaked in their hoods and robes. They were emerging from this very pit, and began to struggle to their feet, before dancing around Marsilio and Richard, and that infernal black pit.

"Tonight it comes!" And then, those little monstrous demons—those beings, which in his visions had always been playing the fiddles—began to emerge from the tar itself. They began to take those branches, and with a speed that was impossible for any human, they began to stack them together intricately, until they had a large crude pyre standing at the head of the pond in front of Marsilio and Richard.

Michael understood. This was happening; this was real, and now he feared Richard Larrabee would be that body on the pyre. "Please, don't!" Michael called out. Marsilio stared at him with those burning eyes but said nothing, and Richard continued to struggle.

The next things to emerge were those naked creatures with the animal heads; the stags and the cats and now wolves on lean greasy naked flesh rising from the tar. "Keep playing!" Marsilio commanded.

Michael wanted to stop, but he couldn't, and he was afraid that if he did, Richard would be killed.

"Michael, stop!" It was Fiona, her voice behind him, and at her command, the violin seemed to lose its power and he stopped playing.

"And here she is!" Marsilio laughed.

Michael turned and looked at his best friend. She was dressed in a deep plum satin gown with black lace and crystals on the sleeves, and that amber necklace was certainly glowing now, he was sure of it, and her eyes seemed like those of a cat, reflecting the crimson light of the moon. "Let him go!" she demanded.

"And you think I will bend so easily to you, witch?!" he spat out.

Fiona moved quickly towards Michael, one hand at her side and the other clutching her necklace. "You will because I command it!"

He laughed. "What power do you have?"

Fiona shot her hand up into the air, and the sky seemed to crackle around them. "This!" She threw her hand down towards her side, and as soon as she did, a white-hot flash of lightning came from the heavens and struck Marsilio in the face, miraculously missing Richard, and throwing Marsilio back far across the field.

"Now, Richard!" she screamed. Richard got to his feet and began running towards them, charging through those creatures that tried to stop him, and those witches of the pit that attempted to get their hands around him. It was no use. He moved with the same skill he used on the field, forcing them away from him.

"Richard!" Michael yelled. Richard got to him and they were just about to embrace, when suddenly Michael felt hands around him, and it was as if the world were spinning. He felt disoriented and out of sorts. It took him a moment to get his bearings and realize that he was now in Marsilio's grip, and before him was the pyre. Those devils and witches were clapping and cheering all around him.

He saw over them the stunned and horror-stricken faces of Richard and Fiona on the other side of the pond. "You see," Marsilio began, "you were just the bait for the witch—you who lived in this house, this house above this nexus, and this powerful convergence of energy that we can use as a vehicle for the Dark One to gain strength. Tonight, we will use the power of Beltane; we will corrupt the Great Marriage of the Goddess and her consort, and use it to bring about the dark god, the one who craves Blackmoore blood, who demands them and their power!"

"Let him go!" Fiona yelled. Richard stood helpless and unable to speak. His eyes seemed to be looking everywhere, taking it all in, while at the same time trying to figure out how to rescue Michael and keep him safe. "I'm here now; let him go!" Fiona yelled again.

"Stupid girl, don't you get it? You've already lost; you cannot even win this. To make this work, we first had to break your heart, to get you to use your power. To complete the final task, we had to make sure first that the blood moon would rise, and we got that with the first sacrifice."

Michael looked up into Marsilio's face, realizing only now that some of the flesh had been burnt away from his skull by that bolt of lightning.

"What do you mean?" Fiona asked him.

"Have you seen Carter Mayland today?" Marsilio asked her with a grin.

"No," Fiona said, shaking her head and refusing his words.

"Yes, his blood flowed not fifteen minutes ago, and the moon was washed in his blood, and now your heart is broken." Fiona shook her head over and over again, refusing to believe it, refusing to accept his words as truth. "And now...." Marsilio threw his hand over the pyre, and it burst into flames—great hot flames that stung Michael's face. "The final act."

"No!" Fiona and Richard screamed in unison, as Marsilio drew the long sharp nail of his index finger swiftly across Michael's throat. "NO!"

Michael began to choke as the blood poured out from his neck. It sprayed the flames, and he watched as he came closer and closer to those flames. Then he was watching as his body fell into the fire, as he seemed to slip out of his own backside.

Richard and Fiona were staring at him, and then down at his body burning in the pyre, and then back into his face.

"Don't you get it? If you hadn't come, the Dark God of the Wood could never leave." He turned to Michael and took hold of his hand. "And my prize is you! Your soul is mine, and your music is my reward. You will play for me, and you shall play for him in his dark court. The witches who serve him will dance to your music, and the witches who fight him...." He fixed his gaze back on Fiona. "Well, your music will be the last thing they hear before they die!"

"No!" Fiona screamed.

"But either way, this boy is mine!"

"NEVER!" Fiona shot her right hand into the air and closed her eyes, taking a deep breath before slamming it down, with her palm open, onto the earth.

From her hand came a great ring of flames that spread out and scorched the earth, and quickly consumed all of those witches and devils that had been dancing and cheering, though they did not harm Richard. A few of those witches jumped back into that pond and vanished beneath its surface, but the rest were like ashen logs scorched in a fireplace—and if they were touched, they would collapse into nothingness.

The ground was black and smoking, and for a moment Marsilio did nothing, and Michael realized that he was a ghost. Everything was hot, and yet he was cold, and his body was desperate for that warmth. He looked at his hands and they were white—like marble—and nothing felt real, not even the fabric of his clothes.

"I will kill you myself, witch, in his glory!" Marsilio snapped his fingers, and the trees burst into flames around them. "I will watch you burn!" The flames from all of those trees shot across the burnt earth from their roots, great fireballs speeding towards Fiona and Richard.

"Move!" Fiona used one hand and threw it into Richard's chest, and he blew back several feet through the air, and Fiona rose high into the sky, avoiding the inferno.

"From the darkest depths, from the infinite sky," Fiona began, placing her hands across her chest and looking down at them, her eyes fierce and filled with rage—an all-consuming pain and hate that was directed for Marsilio. "From the celestial realms and infinite hells, I conjure thee. Serpents from the astral plane twist and coil and give him pain."

Marsilio began to move uncomfortably, and started shifting his weight and wincing in obvious anguish. He released Michael and fell to his knees.

"No!" he cried out. They watched as his mouth was forced open and he began to gag, and out of his throat came thick black serpents with glowing red eyes and silvery-sharp razor-backs like dragons, bits of flesh clinging to their ends from slicing his stomach and throat on their way out.

"Hecate, bring your fearsome winds, made of ghosts and rains of infernal hosts!" It was then that the sky began to erupt again with that lightning, and the winds came faster and stronger than before, bringing with them harsh rains that attacked those burning trees and reduced them to wet and blackened smoke.

"Great Hecate, open the earth and take this demon! Take him and keep him deep within, never to see the sun or moon again!" It was then that the ground beneath Marsilio and Michael began to split and break open, and Marsilio struggled and tried to keep his balance, but the earth wanted him back.

"Fiona!" Michael yelled, falling into the earth right along with Marsilio Merrin. "Fiona! Don't let me go with him!"

She looked down and they both could see that peridot necklace glowing green and bright on his charred, dead body.

She descended down to the earth, closer and closer to Michael's body; his hand outstretched and directed towards his eviscerated carcass.

"If there be no heaven, then there is no hell; in between is where you shall dwell. Here with me, forever you'll be. Michael Donovan, you shall not leave!"

The last thing he saw was the broken-hearted smile on his best friend's face, and the tears in Richard's eyes. "I'm sorry!" he yelled to him, hoping that he would be heard.

"Michael!" Richard called out to him. He was running towards him now, tripping on branches and crashing through those charred bodies. "Michael, don't leave me!" he yelled again.

"Richard...." He was drifting now, as if he were falling back into a dark black tunnel—some calm, quiet, peaceful well—and all he could see were the forms of Richard and Fiona getting smaller. He threw out his hand for him, and Richard did the same, trying to grab him, trying to take hold of him and keep him in place. But they couldn't touch, and Richard's fingers slipped right through his.

"Michael! Stay with me!" Richard pleaded, the tears glistening in the light of the once-again silver moon.

"Goodbye..." he managed with a gasp before everything was black, before the world was suddenly quiet and there was nothing left but the stillness and the weightlessness of eternity.

Cry Havoc

*The belly filled, the dance begins; for after they
have devoured meats either fleeting and illusory
or most hateful and abominable every demon leads
the witch who was his neighbour at the table beneath
the accursed tree, and there, one facing toward center
of the dance, next toward the outside, and so on for all,
they dance in round, stamping and capering with movements
the most indecent and obscene that they are capable of.*
-TABLEAU DE L'INCONSTANCE des mauvais anges et demons

Chapter: Nineteen

TIME MEANT NOTHING: just numbers that changed on a digital clock, blinking in and out, or the hands of a watch moving forward but never backwards. There was the constant beeping of the machines, and the nurses came in and out periodically to check on the quiet, unmoving Trevor, who floated someplace in a world of dreams, lost in the abyss of the subconscious mind. He had gotten used to the sound of the beeping. At first, it had bothered him way too much; it had been an annoyance that he could not ignore. In the beginning he had found himself grunting and moaning in the middle of the night, trying to get some sleep, no matter how little—though, really, how much sleep would he have gotten anyways?

A week had passed, and the world was still dark. The news outlets could talk of nothing else, and Braxton had given up on the news a long time ago. He could see enough of the chaos outside of the hospital's windows. He hadn't been home in days. The downtown sky was still burning orange, and plumes of black smoke only added to the oppressive dark.

Braxton hadn't left Trevor's bedside since they had arrived, and though he had been able to shower and bathe in the en-suite bath, he hadn't done so for fear of Trevor's condition worsening the minute he left him. As it stood now, Braxton put off using the restroom for as long as he could, waiting until his organs seemed to be squeezing together so tightly that it felt as if they would rupture his insides and he would fill with blood and other fluids, and die slowly and excruciatingly.

He hadn't been back to the apartment and he had no idea if, in the ensuing disorder, their building was even still standing—or if it was a burning ruin, a shell of stone and empty insides, a skeleton without intestine and veins. The fact of the matter was, he didn't really care either way. The only thing that mattered was keeping vigil over Trevor and making sure he was there the second he woke up, that his face was the first that he saw when he opened his eyes.

Braxton yawned and rubbed his face with his hands, feeling the oils that leaked from the pores and the beard that had begun to thicken on his face. He felt dirty and needed to shave and shower. He knew this, just as he knew he needed to change his clothes. He hadn't changed since the attack, and the blood was dried into the cotton fibers. It was his blood and Trevor's, blood that was the same, mixed together like a crude painting, a splattering like a Jackson Pollack canvas.

His eyes were red and burned from the lack of sleep and the constant crying. He was exhausted, and at times he would find himself shaking. His nerves were rattled, and his body ached from that chair. The doctors and nurses and everyone else tried to convince him to go home and change, to get some rest and something to eat. He felt weak, and moving his legs—even his arms—took a concerted effort that he had never experienced before.

He had no idea what was going on with his band, and he had no idea what was going on with J.T., who until this point had always been there. His best friend and confidant was now keeping his distance. Even Cheri hadn't heard from him. He felt awful. He had brought J.T. into this hidden world, this world of witches and monsters, and had asked him to break the law for him and his comatose lover. He was ridden with guilt over J.T., over Cheri, who had finally found someone to love, someone to love her for exactly who she was—and he had probably taken that away from her. He wouldn't have been surprised in the slightest if Cheri hated them as well.

He stood and stretched, letting out a great yawn as he walked over to the large windows. He focused his eyes on the lights of the skyscrapers and the blossoming flames that now lived between them. Sirens sounded out in pockets of the city around him, and the streets—which had always been so busy with the white dots of headlights—were now almost always empty.

He wondered when it would all end, when it would all go back to normal and the moon would leave the sun, and the sky would become blue once again, and the radiant light would chase away the never-ending night.

Kathryn and Francesca would come throughout the day to check on him and bring him food in various takeout boxes and containers from every restaurant they ate at, but in the end they would find their way to the trash. He couldn't eat. He didn't want to eat. Not while the love of his life laid in the hospital bed, suffering in silence.

"What did you do to bring this?" he asked aloud. He looked over his shoulder at Trevor's serene face, only marred by the healing cuts from the bits of glass. Trevor had been stitched up in so many places he could have come out looking like Frankenstein's monster, but in the end it could not detract from his beauty, and that beauty pained Braxton's heart all the more.

Kathryn had said this darkness was caused by something Trevor had done, a spell he had worked against someone who was a member of the witch clan who now reigned over the Conclave. And who was this family, and how did Trevor know this person? All of these unknowns, and the only one who had any answers slumbered and might never wake again.

Don't think that! he told himself. He had to believe—with everything that he had inside, all of the faith that he could muster—that this was temporary, and that any second now Trevor would wake and ask what had happened and where he was, just as it always seemed to happen in the movies.

He wanted to know who this person was that Trevor had apparently worked his witchcraft against, and beat the living hell out of them. He wanted to find out who this ruling family was so he could demand that they make everything right again, and make Trevor wake up. He wanted to know who was behind the wraiths that had ambushed them in their home, and kill them slowly.

He imagined what tortures he could devise, and what damage he could inflict with his bare hands on the assholes who were behind it. He wanted to go out there and break things and burn things alongside everyone else on the street. He wanted to bring pain to something, or someone. He imagined going out and picking fights with the rabble, just to make someone feel what he was feeling. He wanted to crush something, to tear something apart, and he wanted it to hurt.

He found himself more and more accustomed to violent thoughts, dark daydreams of inflicting pain. He was not unfamiliar with imaginings like these, but now—with Trevor laying there, his mind someplace far away—there was nothing but these thoughts of savagery to bring him solace.

He imagined that with his power he could rip lampposts from the concrete and hurl them through windows with a flick of his wrist. He envisioned throwing a glance at a moving cop car and making it flip over or send bodies through the air and impale them on the tree branches that lined the street and littered

Westlake Center. He envisioned watching with diabolical satisfaction as their blood sputtered from their mouths and spilled
from their open wounds, painting the trunks red and pooling on
the ground.

He would never do these things: the reality of such violence
at his hands was sickening. And yet, to imagine them, to give
some kind of voice to the rage he felt inside, was therapeutic. It
made him feel better, even if for just a moment, to imagine punishing the world for not mourning his love as he was mourning
him.

He gave a long sigh and shook his head, dismissing it all, and
made his way back to the chair at Trevor's bedside. He fell into
it quickly, and it skirted back a little across the linoleum floor.
Braxton smoothed Trevor's forehead with his thumb and took
hold of his limp hand, kissing his fingers as the tears came once
again, praying silently that he would move those fingers—or better still, open his eyes and look at him once more with a gaze that
told him everything would be okay.

CHERI STARED AT THE clock on her Louis XIV nightstand
with its distressed silver varnish, watching time move slowly.
Classes at the university had been canceled due to the disorder
and the concern for the safety of students and staff. That had
been fine with her, as she didn't feel like leaving her apartment
anyways.

The events of seven days ago kept replaying in her head. The
chaos, the trip to the hospital, walking into that room to find
her best friend hooked up to all of those wires and tubes, bruised
and lacerated, unconscious and unmoving. The distraught look
on Braxton's face, his own injuries and the despair, the look of
utter helplessness in Kathryn's eyes, and the defeat that seemed

to hang heavy on Francesca. Lastly, there was everything that had occurred with J.T.—the reveal of everything that they had tried to keep him in the dark about for his own safety.

He had been ignorant of demons and ghosts and witches with arcane powers. He had known nothing of a world that existed on the other side of the mirror, interwoven into the tapestry of the mundane universe. He had now been given the truth, and the reality that he had always known had been destroyed, replaced with the fact that the monsters of his childhood—the terrible creature under the bed, the beast that lived in the closet—were all there, waiting to emerge from that dark abyss and snatch him from his bed, to take him away into their netherworld and tear his soul apart.

Cheri rolled over and looked up at the ceiling, staring at the tiny crevices in the plaster, and counting them as one would try to count the endless and all-knowing stars. Those silent, celestial hosts of heaven that watched on mankind and yet, like documentarians, observed without interfering, only taking the chronological record of events to be preserved in some alternate timespace.

She was angry with those stars, angry with their stoicism, and their refusal to show their power and commit some sort of miracle to right the world once again.

In the dark she fumbled for her sterling silver cigarette case and her matching lighter. She grunted when she almost knocked down her open bottle of malbec, only to remember it wouldn't have mattered as she had already consumed it. She popped open the case and removed a cigarette, feeling in the dark for the end of the filter to make sure she was putting the correct end between her lips. She sparked her lighter and watched as the flame briefly illuminated her room, which had been completely hidden from all light by the thick drapes that covered her walls of glass.

She grimaced at the shadows that danced across the walls, cast from the Louis XIV arm chair and vanity table. She glimpsed the flat screen on the matching dresser from the corner of her eye, and the door to her closet.

She drew from her cigarette, and it was all gone in a second as soon as she closed her lighter, throwing her in that complete darkness once again. She watched in mild amusement as the red burn of the cigarette briefly brought life back to the room with a dim red glow, and then it was gone once again.

Cheri found this darkness soothing. She always noticed that in a room devoid of all light—no matter how small that room—the complete thick of black could make it feel as if there was no end, no walls or doors or pieces of furniture. The darkness was immense. There seemed to be secrets in the dark, a hidden knowledge, and in these times, Cheri had always imagined getting up and walking in that darkness. And if you believed, the walls would disappear and you could just keep going, perhaps finding yourself in another world altogether.

The tears came again, and she sat up and wiped them away, the blanket falling to her stomach, revealing her naked breasts.

Shit.

Cheri climbed out of the bed and took another drag from her cigarette, stretching and stumbling naked to the windows. She closed her eyes and pushed back the drapes, which slid across the iron rod, hoping that when she opened them again, the sun would be there to greet her.

Of course. She leaned forward and rested her forehead against the cool glass, looking at the smoke and glow of fires before her. Pike Street was empty, save for a few vandals and abandoned vehicles and broken glass. A cop car moved slowly up the street, its lights flashing as it came closer to her building and then drove past her building towards Boren Avenue.

After they had told J.T. the truth, he had gotten up, stunned, and left the room. Cheri had tried to go with him, but he had brushed her off and told her that he needed to be alone for a moment. He never came back, and he had never returned any of her calls or texts. She didn't know where he was, or what was going on inside of his head. She didn't know if he was even still alive.

She had stayed at the hospital by Trevor's side for two days, and then finally decided to go home and change. But having heard nothing from J.T. for those two days, Cheri fell apart as soon as she made it inside her apartment, and could only get as far as her bar and her bed to drink herself into a stupor.

Cheri knew she needed to get back to the hospital. She knew that Trevor needed her—that Braxton needed her, that there was something much bigger than her relationship going on—but at the moment she just couldn't find the strength. She just couldn't make it into the shower. She had drunk so much wine that she had thrown up all over her clothes, and after she had taken them off, she had found it impossible to bother with putting something else on.

Her parents had called more than once to check on her. She knew that Kathryn had come by at some point, but she hadn't bothered to let her in; she just couldn't deal with anyone. As long as Braxton didn't call, she knew that Trevor was still alive, and that was enough for her.

Cheri tilted her head over her shoulder. Her head throbbed and she looked at the gleaming screen of her phone, reflecting the lights that spilled in through the parted drapes. She wanted to call J.T. She hoped that if she did, he would answer. She knew he probably wouldn't, and she told herself repeatedly to leave it alone.

She had done all that she could, and now the ball was in his court. But the urge to hear his voice, and beg for him to come over to talk with her was too much to take, and she finally walked over to her phone and picked it up.

There was his number. She had called him thirty-five times. She knew that it was excessive, but she no longer cared. She figured he'd have to deal with her eventually, even if it was to tell her to fuck off. She just wanted some kind of response, some kind of blip, a signal of some kind that he was okay and that he was still alive.

She stared at his number for several seconds before finally selecting it and giving it a ring. Her heart beat hard in her chest; she could hear it in her ears and feel it pump that blood fast, hoping and praying that he would answer her call.

J.T. SAT IN THE STUDIO and stared at his phone, a part of him aching to answer the call, desperate to hear Cheri's voice, to whisper words of love and to comfort her and ease her troubled heart. But he knew he wasn't ready for all of that. He was still trying to come to terms with everything that had been revealed to him, to wrap his head around the fact that witches were real, that ghosts really did exist, and that terrible, evil creatures really did walk the earth amongst mankind.

All of those things that he had believed to be myths, tales told at campfires to scare children were truth, and that all the rumors and legends he had heard about the Blackmoores growing up—and had dismissed as superstition—were more than just a tale to be told.

He knew Braxton was suffering, that he was lost deep within a labyrinth of pain and despair and crippling heartbreak. At first he had felt nothing but resentment towards all of them, and he was even certain that he now hated Braxton, that their band would be over, and that he would never want to see him again.

But as the days and nights passed, all consumed by the eternal darkness of the hidden sun, his anger moved into guilt and pain.

Braxton had confessed everything to him: growing up with his strange ability to see things just by touching objects or people, and then how, upon the fatal confrontation with his father Eric, a new and much greater power had emerged, a power that could destroy windows and fry a person's brain, a power that had ended up claiming his father's life.

It broke his heart to think that Braxton Volaverunt had gone through life weighted by so much tragedy and confusion about who he was and where this power came from—only to discover that Eric had known all along and had tried to keep it from his son, that the truth of where he came from had claimed his mother's life, and in the end took his last remaining parent from him as well. All he had now was this new family that he was distantly related to, and the friendship of Cheri and himself to fill the void in Braxton's heart.

He strummed absentmindedly on his guitar, trying to work on the arrangement for a new song, but there was too much in his head already—all of this new information that he had to process. His chestnut eyes looked muddy, and they were red from lack of sleep. He knew that until he confronted all of this and made the decision to deal with it and move forward, he would not be getting any rest any time soon.

He got on the web and looked up a florist and gave them a call, not even sure if they would answer, given everything that was going on outside.

The other end picked up and he placed an order for a bouquet of chrysanthemums and dahlias, and a simple card that just said his name to go along with it. "Yes, and that needs to be delivered to room 1035. The patient's name is Trevor Blackmoore." He gave his credit card over the phone and thanked the florist.

"Is everything all right?" J.T. looked up from his phone, startled, and was greeted by a grin on Joshua Dianaca's face. His icy eyes seemed wide with curiosity. He stood in the doorframe dressed in blue jeans and a green-and-black flannel shirt, his Rolex reflecting the light overhead.

"Yeah, just sending some flowers to a friend at Swedish."

Joshua nodded slowly and made his way in the room, closer to J.T. "I'm so sorry; is that why Braxton has been gone?"

J.T. nodded and felt the tears catch in his throat. "Yeah, it's his boyfriend, Trevor –"

"Blackmoore?"

"Yeah, they were both injured a week ago when these riots started, Trevor worse than Braxton. Trevor's in a coma." Joshua seemed to express nothing. There was what appeared to be a flash of shock, quick and fleeting as if it were imagined, and then Joshua took a look at his cell phone.

"Well, give him my best when you talk to him; I have a meeting to get to. Why don't you go home? No sense in being here right now." J.T. said nothing and only stared at Joshua as he watched him pivot on his heel and make his way back out of the studio, and disappear down the hall.

"Yeah, no problem," he replied. J.T. returned his pick to the strings of his guitar and began to strum once again, hoping to drown out his thoughts with the sonic waves of melody.

KATHRYN AND FRANCESCA hadn't been able to get into the penthouse for a week, ever since the riots had erupted as soon as the sun was devoured by the moon. Fourth Avenue between Pike and Pine Street had been blocked off by police after they had forced the rioters out of Westlake Park, which had in the beginning been their base camp.

As soon as she had heard on the television in their corner suite of the *Mayflower Park Hotel*—with its gold walls and pristine crown molding—that the police were opening it back up for the residences of the Seaboard building, who had been evacuated from their apartments by the end of the first night, Kathryn had shot up from the sofa and woke Francesca, telling her that they could get into the apartment and inspect the damage.

Kathryn stood in the elevator, tapping her black suede Louboutin on the floor, her arms folded tightly across her chest, her body hugged by her DVF wrap dress, with a gold and diamond chain belted around her waist and black stockings underneath. She watched it pass the floors impatiently, wanting to get inside of the apartment and light a cigarette.

"What do you think we'll find—you know, aside from thousands of dollars in repairs for everything broken?"

Kathryn shook her head, brushing her lush auburn strands from her face. "I'm hoping that we will be able to sense something from those wraiths, a way to discover where they came from, and also connect with it so we can detect that energy pattern in the future."

"Right!" Francesca had never been that adept in her witchcraft. She hadn't really followed the faith and learnt the spells and rituals.

In Rome as a teen in the '90s, she had been recovering from the loss of her mother to the Legacy by shamelessly flirting and dating numerous boys with beautiful names like Paolo and Antonio, boys who took her on the backs of their scooters and gave her cigarettes and joints, falling desperately in love with her.

She had never interested herself with learning spells and ceremonies, beyond the occasional love charm or spell for gambling when she'd jet off to Monte Carlo. She enjoyed her innate abilities, being able to move objects with her mind, to glimpse the future and past, and to start fires with her intent.

As a result, Francesca was always learning new ways in which to focus that power with a specific goal.

The door slid open and the two women stepped out and stood in the small foyer facing the front door. They looked at one another and felt their hearts pound as Kathryn pushed the door open, not having bothered to close it in the ensuing panic of getting Trevor to the emergency room as quickly as possible.

As the door swung open, the apartment revealed all of the aftermath. The windows were blown out and there were bits and shards of glass all over the hardwood floors, glittering from the flames and streets lights that shone outside. The hoots and hollering of the rioters filled the silence of the home.

"Jesus," Francesca let out, her blue eyes wide, and her mouth hanging open in a slight gasp. She walked further down the front hall, careful as she stepped over broken furniture pieces and broken dishes. She was dressed in black Tommy Hilfiger equestrian boots, black leggings, and a thigh-length fitted red, yellow, and orange flannel shirt. She gathered her cherry-red hair between her fingers and brought it over her right shoulder, letting the damage percolate in her head. It looked like a war zone, and in truth it was. Though they had won that battle, it had not been without its consequences.

Near the windows that looked out on Pike, there was the dark stain of dried blood—Trevor's blood—on the floor, and that piece of glass lay near, stained with the same red-brown mess.

"Thank God we have insurance."

She looked at Kathryn and nodded. "Yeah, no kidding." They could feel the leftover residue, the energy that seemed alien and fragmented everything around them. It just felt off, a scent left behind by an animal after it shit on the ground or pissed in order to mark its territory. "Do you feel that?"

Kathryn nodded slowly as they began to make their way down the hall towards the bedrooms and study. "It's their imprint. We need to find where it is the strongest, and then we will hopefully be able to connect with it and discover its source."

"And you don't think that the attack and the eclipse are one in the same?" Francesca asked as they found their way, entering the study as if having been pulled into it by some invisible cord.

"No, I don't. I think this eclipse is related to whatever it was that my son did to piss off the Conclave. But I think these wraiths; they came from someplace else... something that only used the eclipse to its advantage to launch an attack."

"Any ideas?"

"Well," Kathryn began, stopping in the center of the room and looking at Francesca, who had stopped moving as well. "It was obviously in service of the Dark God, but as for who sent it? It could be anyone."

"The Dianacas?"

Kathryn nodded. "That I wouldn't doubt."

They closed their eyes and spread their arms out slightly, taking each breath long and deep, allowing themselves to focus on nothing but the foreign energy that lingered all around them, taking note of what it felt like—the sense of dread, of overwhelming terror, as if it could manifest itself into your worst fears or your own shames and crimes.

Kathryn had never felt anything like this before, and she knew that the apartment would have to be cleansed as well as repaired before Trevor and Braxton moved back in. She would put them up in a suite at the W Hotel, and get the place cleaned up and new furniture bought. Kathryn didn't really care; it was all of the items that Tom had picked out after he decided to redecorate the family penthouse.

Even a spirit that took his form had been enough for her. She didn't care that the furniture and glassware was destroyed, or the lamps were broken. Let it be part of the rubble; let it be the ruin and collateral damage of the invasion. As she looked around and took stock of it all, she felt satisfied that now, nothing of Tom Preston remained and he could not haunt her.

In the depths of the ethereal abyss, she felt something coming towards her. A presence was nearing her, slowly coming closer and closer, as if it was right behind her, creeping up on her as if it wanted to take her by surprise. Her head throbbed, and she felt heavy. Perhaps it had not come up on her at all; perhaps, she surmised, she was the hunter, the predator, and she was coming for it.

'*Amduscias...*' she heard the sexless voice whisper. What was it? A name? Was it the name of the Dark God of the wood? The name of the person who had sent these vagabond spirits to her son and Braxton?

Francesca suddenly called out and it drew Kathryn back from her trance. She opened her eyes quickly to see Francesca looking not at her, but to the left of them. She turned her head to find a boy standing there staring at them. He was an attractive young man, perhaps no more than eighteen, with a strong, lean build and chestnut hair that hung in his black eyes. He was dressed in a white shirt stained with blood. His marble-like skin was carved at the chest with what must have been deep and fatal wounds and they created an intricate symbol that she could not discern completely through the torn white cotton. This young man looked familiar to her, though she couldn't place him and was too terror-stricken to try to search her memory for the reason why.

He lifted his arm slowly and directed his fingers to the both of them, his lips parting. '*Amduscias...*' he said, just as the voice had in her mind.

"What does that mean?" Kathryn asked the dead boy. "What does it mean?" she repeated, and he was gone. In the blink of an eye, an inhale or exhale of breath, he had vanished, and they were once again alone in the study.

"Who was he, and what was he saying?"

Kathryn shook her head. "Amduscias, whatever that means."

"I heard that before I opened my eyes," Francesca said, taking a look at her watch.

"Me too." They turned and began to make their way back towards the front room.

"What should we do?"

Kathryn gave a sigh. "I think we need to go to the hospital and get Braxton to come to dinner, however we do it. We need to get him out of that room so he can get some fresh air and a change of scenery!"

Francesca agreed. Braxton had not been taking care of himself at all, and though he never left the room, and they spent many hours there every day, it was as if he were a ghost—as if he were just a shadow, a sense of something that lingered but was no longer there.

He rarely spoke more than a word, and he kept his eyes focused on Trevor's sleeping face and his fingers wrapped around those seemingly lifeless hands. He was crumbling inside. He was withering like a plant, and soon he would petrify and break, being reduced to dust.

"I just don't understand how this happened."

"What we need to be more concerned with is the fact that it will be *Samhain* in a couple of days. The veil between the worlds continues to thin, and whatever was behind this attack, I feel that they are just getting started.

"You're right. It slipped my mind that Halloween was so close."

"The most important Sabbat of the year, and the most dangerous—whatever *this* was, it's just starting, I think." They walked back out into the foyer and this time, Kathryn was sure to close the door behind them and lock it, mulling all that they had just discovered in her head, analyzing it and desperate to figure out their next move.

They both hoped, though they would never share it aloud, that when they walked in they would find Trevor awake and ready to leave the hospital. It was a wish that they felt whenever they got up to get coffee from the cafeteria or the Starbucks down in the lobby, or whenever they got up to use the restroom or go get something to eat. It was a wish that had never come true.

Though they knew it was better to just let it go and stop hoping, to silence those wishes, they could not. They all needed Trevor to be okay. They needed his heart, his understanding, his determination, and his refusal to give up. Without him, everything felt cold. Everything seemed hopeless, and Braxton continued to decay in silence like a body in the earth, an animal along the side of the road, a dead bird, the insides being devoured by the maggots and worms and the flies that laid their eggs.

ELISABETH SAT IN ONE of those beige armchairs with the cream stripes in the great room, her crisp blue eyes skimming through the latest issue of *Vogue*, dressed in denim skinny jeans and a v-neck white tee, her black curls pulled back in a ponytail. The penthouse was dark, save for the two lamps lit on either end table. A week had passed since the eclipse, and the attack she had waged on the Blackmoores. She had hoped to kill the chosen ones, whoever they were, but in the end she was aware that they still lived. She could feel it. They had survived her assault, and she was trying to figure out another way to wage a second attack.

The thirty-first of October was getting closer—only two more days—and without the chosen ones out of the way, without the spilling of Blackmoore blood, the Dark God could not rise. The Reckoning had not been attempted in a century, and unless the sacrifice of three could be made, it would fail once again, just as it had in 1908. Her family had ruled Fairhaven society, and had used the church to manipulate the people of the fishing port—and later, the rest of Bellingham—into a frenzy of religious fervor and superstition. They had served the Dark God for centuries, after her ancestors migrated from Italy to England in the sixteenth century.

He had called to them from the other side of what would become the Irish channel, and they had answered his call. They had heard the soft whimpered cries for help, his promises of power and fortune, and the story of his desertion by the clan of the Black Moors, who had left him isolated and alone in the abandoned woods.

He needed flesh and blood, and their leaving two centuries earlier had left him starved and trapped within the roots and soil, and only the spilling of Blackmoore blood on the ancient feast nights of Samhain and Beltane could set him free to wreak havoc and eradicate the Blackmoores for their betrayal, and bestow the rewards of the New Kingdom on all of those witches who praised his glory and sang his name.

The Dianacas would finally get their revenge on the family that drove them from their great manor on South Hill, forcing them to abandon it in the dead of night and never to be able to return again. They had tried to hold on to the property, but the Blackmoores had seen to it that if they even stepped foot on the grounds of Dianaca Castle, they would very quickly fall prey to the very same plague that the Dark God had inflicted on the Christian world. In the end they had to sell the property, and now it was a Bed and Breakfast.

The plan had been simple enough: to stop the chosen ones, to kill them, and then their younger cousin Victoria and her friend Melanie Porter would lure the naïve Mary-Margaret Blackmoore to her death. The Dark God would rise once again, and lay waste to all those who denied him.

But the chosen ones still lived, and Mary-Margaret hadn't been seen for days. And since the eclipse—the eclipse she knew was caused by the rules of the Conclave and the pandemonium that had ensued throughout the world as a result—classes at all schools had been canceled, and people everywhere had been urged to stay indoors.

He'll kill us if we fail. She knew this. She knew that no matter how loyal her family had been, no matter how dedicated that they had been to serving the Dark God after all this time, he still had ways of reaching them. He still had the power to command infernal beasts that could come for them, emerging from the shadows like weeds that pushed their way through the earth and the cracks in the pavement, to decimate them and annihilate the Dianacas in one fell swoop—and time was running out.

The elevator opened beyond the front door. The lock clicked, and she heard the front door skirt across the marble floor.

"Success!" Joshua yelled, walking quickly through the foyer. "Success!" He appeared before her, his breathing quick and his eyes erratic.

"What are you going on about?" she asked him, only briefly looking at her brother before turning her attention back to her magazine.

"I have discovered the names of the chosen ones." Elisabeth lifted her eyes slowly and searched Joshua's face for any sign of insincerity. There was none to be found. His smile was wide with childish excitement, and his eyes were set on her with an earnest desire to confess what he had learned.

"How do you know this?" She sat the Vogue face down in her lap and gave Joshua her full attention.

"Well, you know that new band I just signed to Arcadia?"

She nodded. "The Vomiting Gorillas?"

"Spit Monkeys."

"Right, the Spit Monkeys."

Joshua rolled his eyes. "Anyways, the bassist is this guy named Braxton Volaverunt –"

"Why does that name sound familiar?"

"See, I wondered the same thing. Then I remembered that in the nineteenth century, before the Blackmoores left New Orleans, Katy Blackmoore moved to Spain and married an aristocrat named Antonio Volaverunt, infecting the Volaverunts from her line with Blackmoore blood and creating a fourteenth witch family."

"That's right...." Elisabeth was recalling the time when she was a young girl of twelve, hearing this story for the first time from her grandmother Geraldine back in Sussex.

"Oh, this only gets better. You see, Katy Volaverunt ended up returning to New Orleans a year later, and to try to escape the fate that was placed upon her family, she gave the Blackmoores several fortunes in exchange for being left alone. But the universe will not be deterred, and in the end, Katy's descendants found themselves in Bellingham, along with the other Blackmoores. I have no idea if they know or not; I'm going to assume not, as Braxton Volaverunt is romantically involved with none other than Trevor Blackmoore, son of Kathryn Blackmoore and Sheffield Burges."

Elisabeth's heart began to race and the same eager smile spread across her face. "Really? That is better."

"Oh, the best-the absolute best—Trevor Blackmoore is in a coma at Swedish. Apparently hurt during the riots, which I'm sure is only a lie, as I am certain it was your spell that put him there; all we have to do is get to him when he's alone in the room. He's defenseless!"

"Ripe for the picking." Elisabeth stood and walked over to the sliding glass doors that led to the balcony, staring out at the never-ending darkness and the smoke and flames that burst around them between the stone citadels, and the various residents of those buildings who stood there looking out at the same destruction.

These lives that would soon be bowing to the Dark God, and the lives of those witches and non-witches alike, who had been hunted down and eradicated for some false religion with their one god and their mythological devil, would be avenged.

Paradise would be made on earth, and once again the witches would reign supreme, and those zealots would be forced to serve them and pay penance for the hundreds of thousands of lives lost to the Christian Church during the Burning Times, the Crusades, and the Inquisition.

"I've already called Victoria and told her everything, including his room number. She will call us when she gets into the city so we can do our bit to help her get him out of the hospital. Who needs Mary-Margaret when we have the son of Kathryn Blackmoore? The direct line to Sarafeene and Malachey!"

It was too perfect. Finally, they would accomplish what Fiona Blackmoore had thwarted a century before. This time, they would succeed.

The entire world was cast in the darkness of witches, and the veil between the worlds was getting thinner every day, allowing for more and more spirits to come through, and it was with this power that The Reckoning would be performed, and the Dark God of the Wood would rise once again and begin to build his kingdom. No other witch would be able to oppose him, and no other god would be able to stop him.

They would make the goddess bow to her metaphysical knees before him, as he would rise in flesh and blood and they would still be ether, invisible and intangible. As he gathered those beating hearts brought before him, ripped from the bloody casing of skin and bone and the delicious blood that he would use to drink down those hearts, the Dark God would restore the world to the way it was before the Jews came from the east with their one male warrior god who sought to condemn and destroy all others.

"And how, dear brother, did you find out all of this?"

Joshua laughed. "I just happened to walk in on the phone call of one of the other band mates ordering flowers for Trevor's room."

They stared at each other for just a moment before she and Joshua erupted in a fit of laughter. The time had finally come and the heavens would soon rain down fire, and the stars themselves would hide.

BRAXTON YAWNED AND leaned back in the chair by Trevor's bedside, stretching out and shaking his head. He took a look at his watch. It was 8:30pm, and he hadn't attempted to eat anything since the night before. He looked at the moving lines of the heart monitor and the rate of pulse, and sighed.

He looked down at his boyfriend, lying there under those thin powder-blue covers and white sheet, his slender body draped in an unflattering matching blue hospital gown with streaks of pink and purple. It made him think of the label for *L.A. Looks* hairspray and mousse, which he used to use religiously when he was a kid.

"What is going on in there?" he asked, rubbing Trevor's scarred forehead with his thumb, and then running his fingers through that soft red hair. "Why won't you wake up?" He felt the tears, and this time he did not choke them back. He let them come; he let them fill his onyx eyes and slip down his cheeks, his face reddening from the crying.

Through his blurred vision Trevor looked all the more ethereal under the lights that shone down on him from the wall a few feet above him. It was much better to have those lights on, versus the harsh white fluorescents on the ceiling overhead.

"I'm so lost without you, Trevor. I don't know what I'm going to do—how I'm going to go on if you don't wake up. Please, baby, don't leave me all alone; I can't do it without you!" His crying grew from a soft murmur to great bleating sobs that echoed off of every wall. He didn't care. He couldn't care. He was a man lost and broken, a man without direction, and without Trevor he didn't see the point in going on. He saw no reason to live if he had to do so in a world without him.

He heard steps. They were delicate and fast, heels clicking on the linoleum, and then there were soft arms embracing him, pulling him close to a warm body and full breasts, the fragrance of vanilla and jasmine. It made Braxton think of summers down at Bellingham Bay skipping rocks into the cool green waters of the Pacific.

"Braxton, it's okay; it's okay," Francesca was saying to him, holding him close and kissing his forehead, trying to soothe him with her words. "He'll wake up; I promise he will." Braxton shook his head, pulling himself away from her and wiping his tears away with the palms of his hands.

"Oh, God," he said, sniffling and wiping his nose with a piece of Kleenex on the nightstand. He looked to see Kathryn standing on the other side of the bed, Trevor lying between them, her blue eyes gentle, and a sympathetic smile rested on her face.

"I like to think that he can hear you," she said, reaching her hand out across Trevor's sleeping body and wrapping her fingers around his hand. "That out of all of us, it's you that he can hear and that he's making his way back to you. He just needs to keep hearing your voice."

Braxton wanted to believe her. He wanted so desperately to think that what she said was true, but as the days and nights pressed on—unchanging, always dark—there was no longer the strength to believe. Now, there was only the begging and the pleading with the heavens that Trevor would open his eyes again.

"When is the last time you ate anything, sweetie?" Francesca asked him, her hand resting on her hip.

"Um, not since—not since last night." They both shook their heads.

"C'mon." Kathryn tossed him a Barney's bag. "We stopped by the apartment; we were finally able to get in. I grabbed a change of clothes for you. Get into that bathroom, put on these clean clothes and brush your teeth, because your breath is really starting to stink!" She smiled, and Braxton couldn't help but return it to his future mother-in-law—which is how he had begun to see Kathryn, as he knew that one day she would be.

He took the bag and walked into the bathroom, switching on the light and squinting immediately, as the darkness erupted with that harsh white illumination.

"Fuck!" he called out, blinking a few times to adjust his eyes. He stuck his hand in the bag and pulled out a clean pair of black boxer-briefs, a fresh pair of dark denim 5'11s, and a black cashmere sweater. He didn't want to leave Trevor, and as he removed his clothes, seeing the weight he had begun to lose—the beginning protrusion of his ribs, and the almost frail-like stance of his body—he realized that if he didn't get out of there, at least for a little while, he would soon find himself a patient of the hospital as well.

After showering, brushing his teeth, and changing, Braxton walked out of the bathroom and turned out the light above Trevor's head, kissing him on the lips and forehead.

"Sweet dreams, kiddo," he said, kissing him one last time and placing his hand over his heart, paying the wires little mind. "I'll be back."

The three of them walked slowly out of the suite and closed the door behind them, grateful in knowing that Trevor would be safe while they were gone.

Chapter: Twenty

LIST was located on First Avenue between Bell Street and Blanchard, a narrow restaurant and bar that sat nearly thirty people, and could fit more during the warmer months on the front patio with its steel railings that sectioned it off from the streets. The inside was surrounded with mirrors, and hanging from the ceiling were candy-red neo-classic chandeliers—as if formed from melted Jolly Ranchers—and straight down a narrow hall with black and white neo-classic designed wallpaper were two restrooms. On the right side was the narrow bar, and the place was packed, even in the midst of all of the uncertain and never-ending darkness outside.

Braxton figured, even with all that was going on, people still needed to eat and drink. They sat at their table nearest to the wall, waiting for their food and sharing a bottle of *Barbera Fontanafredda*, a red wine from the *Piemonte* region—a wine that Kathryn had thought would pair well with her grilled pheasant and his and Francesca's grilled top sirloin.

"I am glad you came to dinner," Kathryn said, her eyes looking at him over the rim of her wine glass.

"Well, I don't think I really had a choice at this point. You guys would have made me go one way or another." He offered a slight smile, and Francesca nodded in agreement.

"It was getting to that point, for sure," Francesca responded.

"It's important that you get some fresh air and move about. Trevor wouldn't want you wasting away and giving up life entirely. Not for him."

Braxton looked at Kathryn for just a moment and then dropped his eyes to the base of his wine glass. He began to spin it slowly by the stem, which was pinched between his fingers.

"Without him, there is no life." His heart continued to ache. The pain never seemed to cease, and though Trevor was not dead in the ground, it did not lessen the feeling of loss—as if he had already been interred in the family mausoleum along with all of those other decaying Blackmoores.

"No, he's not. That is why you have to keep going on. He lives. He will open his eyes again, Braxton; he will come out of this. I promise you. We just have to wait for him to find his way back," Kathryn remarked with a gentle smile.

"I know this isn't over. The warnings we received have assured me of that much." The two women sat up and leaned closer towards him over the table as to not be overheard.

"What warnings, Braxton?" Francesca asked him, keeping her voice hushed.

"This boy, probably around the same age as myself and Trevor. Brown hair, white shirt, the usual dead-black eyes; he came to Trevor a couple of times—I don't really know how many—and told us that they're coming."

"That what's coming?" Kathryn asked, tucking her bangs behind her right ear.

He thought for just a moment, trying to recall the dead boy's words. "The Soul Wanderers." Kathryn's eyes grew wide, and Francesca turned to look at her with the same questioning that Braxton had as well.

"You're certain he called them 'The Soul Wanderers?'"

He nodded. "Who are they?"

Kathryn was about to go on when their plates of food arrived and their server, a young woman with blonde curls and a couple of tattoos, refilled their glasses and smiled coyly at Braxton. Kathryn took a bite of her perfectly-grilled pheasant and chased it down with a sip of wine before continuing. "That is the name of the agents—the witches—of the Dark God of the Moor."

Braxton's steak knife scraped across his plate. "Seriously?"

Kathryn nodded.

"I don't know anything about this," Francesca stated.

"That's because you were more interested in bewitching Italian boys and expats growing up, and you didn't have Queen Mab or Fiona constantly talking about the Legacy."

"You mean the curse?" Braxton asked.

Kathryn shook her head. "The Legacy means two things. It can refer to the curse, but it is also what we call the family history. The Legacy is everything that makes us who we are, and the Soul Wanderers are a part of that legacy."

"So, who are they specifically?"

"There are witches in this world who serve Him, and they have spent countless centuries trying to bring him into being. After we left the Moor, abandoning that deity and his name in the twelfth century, it was not even assumed that this being would be so driven to be worshipped that he would summon other witches across the world to go into His service, promising power and the vengeance on the Christian world for all of their crimes against us, and those they accused of being us.

"Though pagans and other accused heretics were driven into hiding and butchered during the Inquisition and the Crusades—and even earlier, at the great rise of Christianity in the fourth century—it was, more often than not, just innocent men, women, and children who were seen as undesirable.

"But with this war waged by the Christians, witches did die, and the great gods and goddesses of the world were stamped out and reduced to devils and demons, to manipulate the faithful of the old ways into abandoning their deities and wash themselves in the blood of the lamb. Those who did not convert, those who kept to the old ways, were eradicated. Tortured to death—or at least near death—and finally burnt alive.

"Hundreds of thousands, as I'm sure you know and have learned in school, were eventually killed during the witch trials. In some European villages and cities, whole populations of women, and even cats, were eradicated. The Black Death had already emerged by this time as well, and this of course only continued to fuel the fear of us, and also a fear of vampires and werewolves."

"And the Soul Wanderers?" Francesca asked, taking a bite of her steak.

"They were the name of the coven of the Dark God. He promised them vengeance, and as a result of this vengeance and the proof of his power, they offered their souls to him so that he may one day come into corporeal form. You see, he brought the plague with the rats and fleas that carried it and wiped out most of Europe. Witches were unaffected by this plague, and as the ravaging of the Black Death killed numbers equal to those who had already been executed for the crimes of paganism and heresy, many witches gave their allegiance to him."

"So...." Braxton took another bite of his steak and enjoyed the warm, fragrant, spiced and bloody meat. "How did they get their name? Which, by the way, sounds kind of lame."

Kathryn laughed. "I suppose it does. The rituals they perform are little known. But their goal is to bring the Dark God into flesh, allowing him to become a living God—like the legend of Christ—and walk amongst the people, and rule the earthly realm. From what we do know, they have committed their bodies to being a living host to the Dark God, and once they die, for whatever reason, their souls become wraiths—not simple spirits, for the spirits of witches contain great power—and their souls wander, so to speak, waiting to be used in his service."

"So, then, why haven't they succeeded?"

Kathryn shrugged. "Because we have always been there to stop them. You see, once we figured out what was going on—and more so, that when it was realized that this Dark God was so intrinsically tied to our family that we had the power to destroy him, that his goals of the flesh could be stopped by us—he began sending his followers to try to kill us, hunting Blackmoores whenever they could find us. Every time they have tried to raise him—which has only been a handful of times, as far as I know—they have failed.

"The Soul Wanderers only have one goal, one mission that they serve, and that is to bring the Dark God forward. To offer the world to him, and make what they believe will be a paradise for witches. But we were the first to discover him and feed him and give him power and strength, and we know that all this deity wants is human flesh and human blood, and the same of witches as well.

"With the resulting witch persecutions at the end of the fourteenth century and the three hundred years that followed, the Dark God was able to build his army, and feed from those who were blamed. Witches were blamed for the Black Death—for the very thing that He created as an act of vengeance in exchange for their loyalty—and he gained that power, and at the same time acquired more servants.

"This deity is a petty deity, one that wishes to tether itself to a body that it can exist in. You see, it is too powerful to keep all of itself inside a body, but like the Christ story, it can implant itself into flesh and walk around while still existing in the ethereal world."

"And how are we supposed to get rid of it?" Francesca asked.

Kathryn shrugged at her cousin and poured herself more wine. "I don't really know if it can be. It's a God. It's deity. It has unfathomable power. I think the best we can do is what we've always been doing, which is prevent him from getting a body."

"You know, we saw the boy earlier," Francesca said to Braxton.

"You did?"

The women nodded. "Yes, he appeared in the penthouse and spoke to us," Francesca answered.

"What did he say?" Braxton asked excitedly.

"He simply said 'Amduscias.' Not sure what that means, though," Replied Kathryn.

"Anything else?"

"Nothing."

"I don't like any of this. When do these attempts happen?" Francesca asked her cousin.

"The only one I know for sure is on May first, Beltane. I know that because in 1908 Fiona stopped it from happening."

"Really?"

"Yes. I also have just realized something else, something that did not dawn on me until this very moment, but I know who that dead boy is."

Braxton and Francesca's eyes grew wide, as if they would burst from their sockets. "Who?"

"My uncle, Carter Mayland; he died years before my father was born. He was murdered—sacrificed—by Jonathan Marker. A picture of him sits on the wall in the front hall back home. I haven't actually looked at it in so long that it did not even strike me when he appeared to us. But it came to me just now. It was him; I am certain of it!"

Kathryn threw back her wine and looked beyond Braxton's shoulder at her own reflection in the mirror behind him. Her eyes seemed dark and sullen, and her face seemed older—from the lack of sleep, no doubt, and the constant worry was making itself visible all over her face.

"He must be tied to all of this—tied to what's happened to Trevor. Maybe we can contact him?" Braxton suggested.

"It could be possible, Kathryn. He didn't die because of the Legacy; he could come through on his own, I'm sure." Kathryn seemed to be pondering all of this. The idea of trying to summon her dead uncle, an uncle she had never met and whose life she had only the vaguest knowledge of, seemed presumptuous and even rude.

He had appeared to give warning, so perhaps he was trying to help them all, but she knew that he could also be one of those wraiths, one of those dead witches who now had to serve the Dark God. Kathryn knew that either way, they had to try. They had to do whatever they could to find out if there was some more specific and diabolical scheme behind the attack.

Was it simply another attempt by these agents of the God to try to eradicate the Blackmoores, or was it something worse? Were they going to try to bring forth the Dark God once again?

"We should get back to Trevor," Kathryn said, and Braxton nodded and finished his wine quickly, eager to get the bill and get back to the hospital, where he could once again keep watch over his comatose love.

THE HOSPITAL WAS IN chaos when they arrived, and Braxton, Kathryn, and Francesca raced into the nearest elevator, not at all prepared for what they found. Patients in their beds were calling for assistance, and nurses and doctors from the other floors were now scrambling around them to try and wake the plethora of sleeping orderlies all around them.

"What the hell is going on?" Doctors and nurses were slapping the sleeping staff, trying to wake them, and there were even men and women lying haphazardly on the floors. Vials of blood and plastic cups with pills and liquid medicine were everywhere. It seemed as if they had come under a great sleep all at once, and were now as comatose as Trevor was.

"There is a patient missing," they heard one of the female nurses say to one of the female doctors. "Everyone is accounted for except for the patient in 1035." They all looked at each other and Braxton began to shake his head in disbelief.

"Trevor!" he called out as they raced down the hall, the three of them jumping over the slumbering bodies. "Trevor!" They turned the corner and entered the room, and everything looked to be in place, except for one thing—and that was Trevor's empty bed.

"What the hell happened?!" Francesca asked.

"No, no, no!" Braxton began to sob and raced to the sheets, clutching them, smelling them and crying into them.

"Where the hell is my son?!" Kathryn screamed at one of the nurses who had just walked into the room, a young Korean girl who looked at Kathryn like a deer caught in headlights about to be hit.

"I don't know; none of us know what's happened up here."

"My son is fucking gone! Did anyone see anything?"

The nurse shook her head.

"Security tapes?" Francesca asked.

"I'll get the doctor," she said to them.

"Yeah, you better get the fucking doctor!" Braxton yelled behind her.

"We'll find him; we'll find him. I know we will!" Francesca said. She went to Braxton and attempted to put her arms around him, but he pushed her back forcefully.

"Don't touch me! Don't fucking touch me! No one touch me!" He stumbled back and began to beat his fists on the bed over and over again, gasping for air as he cried.

"I'm Dr. Wheeler." Braxton looked up at the man in the white lab coat. He was a lean man, just over six foot, with short brown hair that was receding at both sides. His skin was tanned, the kind of tan that only someone who vacationed in warmer climates a few times a year would have.

"Dr. Wheeler, what is going on and what the hell has happened to my fucking son?"

"That's what we're trying to figure out."

"Well, check the footage on your fucking cameras," Kathryn barked.

"We have..." he said with a defeated sigh.

"And?" Kathryn was becoming increasingly impatient.

"And we don't know. Everything is fine, and then everyone just seems to drop to the floor, or on the nurse's station, or wherever they are standing or sitting at the time. It makes no sense. One of the elevators open and two nurses drop to the floor as soon as they step out. We checked every camera on the floor.

"Your son is not shown leaving the room on his own or by someone else at all. The only other strange thing that happens is that a few minutes after the elevators first opened, the elevator is requested from this floor, but there is no one standing in front of them, but we know for sure that it was requested from here. You can see the button light up as if someone pressed it, but there is no one there."

"Where the fuck is he?!" Braxton shouted. He curled his fingers into his palms and began digging them into his flesh. He felt the cyclone of heat move through his body, rising like a hot flash, and make its way up the back of his neck and made his ears hot.

He released his fists and as soon as he did, that heat moved out of him and the windows that surrounded them exploded, glass falling to the streets. The lights above their heads blew out with a spark as the fluorescent bulbs rained down around them, forcing Kathryn, Francesca, and the doctor to throw their arms up over their heads and duck for cover. The electrical equipment in the room blew up as well, shooting sparks and smoke before catching fire.

"What the fuck?!" Dr. Wheeler let out, surveying the damage.

Francesca raced over to Braxton and grabbed his arm, pulling him forcefully towards the door. "Whatever is going on in this hospital is your mess! *We're* going to find my cousin!" Francesca said to Dr. Wheeler. "And you," she whispered into Braxton's ear. "Get your shit under control. We need to find Trevor!"

Kathryn brushed the bits of glass off of her black coat, and gathered the bag she had brought the clothes for Braxton in, as well as the bag which had Trevor's belongings in it from the day he was admitted. She said nothing as she brushed past the doctor, slamming her shoulder into his and refusing to apologize.

Whatever happened to Trevor, she knew that he was taken, and she was certain that a glamour had been performed to make sure the abduction—and therefore the abductors—went unseen.

"We'll find him. We will. I promise you," Francesca was saying to Braxton over and over again, hoping that he would believe it and be able to calm down.

"How?" he asked, sniffling and defeated.

"We need to go back home. Back to Bellingham."

Braxton looked at Kathryn, startled, and fiercely shook his head. "We can't leave. We can't. What if he's here, in Seattle?" Kathryn shook her head. "How can you know?"

"I can't explain it. It's just a feeling I have. My intuition tells me to go back to Bellingham; if we have any chance of finding him—of saving him—then we have to go back there." Braxton wanted to argue, but he was too tired, and every second spent arguing was another second lost.

As they entered the parking garage, Braxton removed his cell phone and stared at it for several seconds, knowing that he was going to have to call Cheri and J.T. and tell them what happened. If either one would even answer their phone. Cheri and J.T. had both just disappeared. He knew that Cheri was at home and most likely okay, but as for J.T.? He knew nothing.

A dark thought began to creep on him, a fear that perhaps something had happened to J.T., something terrible and final. What if it was too late and J.T. could not be saved? Braxton began to cry again, a fresh set of tears that spilled down his face as they made their way out of the parking garage in the limo, Kathryn's young driver keeping his eyes steady on the road.

Braxton stared at the bags of belongings that rested on the floor in front of Kathryn's feet. Both of those bags contained bloodstained clothes. Blood that belonged to Trevor, blood he feared would spill again. As they merged onto I-5 North, Braxton opened his phonebook and selected Cheri's number, swallowing those tears hard as the line began to ring, part of him hoping that he would get her voicemail instead.

CHERI HAD BEEN SITTING on the floor of her bedroom. Her butt was itching from the carpet, and she wasn't quite sure how she had gotten down there in the first place. She figured she must have passed out again at some point, but the only thing she could remember was going to her bathroom to throw up in the toilet. It took her a moment to realize she had never made it that far.

Her nostrils filled with the sour and acidic stench, and though she couldn't feel it, she knew that she had either thrown up on herself or on her floor. This was embarrassing. Even though she was all alone, it was enough to humiliate her.

"Jesus." She began to crawl over to the edge of her bed, walking on all fours and ignoring the itching feeling her carpet gave her on her knees. Her head throbbed, and all she wanted was to lie down again, or take another drink, but she knew that she couldn't.

She was a total train wreck, and people needed her. Braxton and Trevor were counting on her. She knew this. She knew that despite not hearing from J.T., despite everything that was going on out in the world beyond the protection of her windows, she needed to be there for her best friends.

Get it together.

She placed her hands on top of her mattress and began to lift herself from off the floor, trying to steady herself and ignore the aching throb that was going on inside her skull.

Her cell phone rang again, lighting up the dark with its pale blue light. She was going to ignore it as she had always done, but from the edge of her bed she could see Braxton's picture smiling back at her from the screen. She quickly raced over to the phone, grabbing it from off of her nightstand and putting it to her ear.

"Braxton?" She heard him sobbing on the other end of the line. "Braxton, what is it? What's happened?" She feared the worst. This was the phone call she had dreaded. She had known that as long as she hadn't heard from him that everything was okay. Trevor was the same. If he was calling, then that meant that there had been a change—and by the sounds of his crying, she knew that it wasn't a call to tell her that he had woken up.

"He's gone!"

Her heart felt as if it had ceased to beat, and her breath caught in her throat. "What do you mean, gone?"

"He's gone. They took him!"

He wasn't making any sense.

"Who took him?"

"I don't know; something bad, something that had the power to put all the staff on his floor to sleep, and take him out of his room and out of the hospital without being seen on the cameras."

She was searching her mind to try to come up with a way that that was even possible. But she remembered that she had seen many impossible things, and had seen Trevor and Braxton do many impossible things. "You mean, like witches?"

"I don't know! I don't know!"

She was already digging around her drawers for a pair of jeans. "Okay, okay; where are you now?"

"I'm in the car with Kathryn and Francesca. We're going back to Bellingham. Kathryn is certain he is no longer in Seattle. I just don't know; I don't know." She pulled on a pair of black skinnies, and was already going through the racks in her closet for a shirt. She found a black cardigan and began putting it on over her naked breasts, buttoning it up to her cleavage.

"Okay, I'll meet you there. I'm on my way now."

"Okay...."

"And, Braxton, we'll find him. I promise you. He can handle himself; you have to remember that. He's so much stronger than all of us." Braxton said "thank you" and then hung up the phone.

"SHIT!" She pulled on a pair of black knee-high boots and decided to text J.T., letting him know that there was an emergency and that she was heading straight over to his house.

He needed to be with Braxton, and he had been the one desperate to be let in on their secret. He had pushed it and pushed it, and despite the methods which brought him into the truth, the fact of the matter was that he had gotten what he wanted. Now he needed to step up and prove that he had been worthy of being let in, and that he was worthy of her trust and her love.

She was done punishing herself, and she was going to make him face her. She was going to make him confront everything that he was avoiding. If he wanted out that was fine, but he was going to have to do it to her face.

SHE HAD DRIVEN LIKE a bat out of hell down I-5, and when she took the exit on Northeast Fiftieth Street to get to his house, she almost sideswiped a Mini Cooper with her Fiat. She now stood outside of his home, a two story Craftsman with white trim and cream siding. The light was on in his room on the second floor to the left above the awning, and she could hear the music of his guitar coming from the other side of the plate glass window.

Cheri took a deep breath and walked up the concrete path to the wood porch, noting absentmindedly that the ivy needed to be trimmed back, as it was threatening to take over the porch. Her hand was shaking as she pressed the bell and looked through the red, orange, and yellow stained glass window that was in the top center of the door.

She impatiently tapped her foot on the floorboards and looked at the time on her phone. She was only going to give it a couple more minutes, and then she was going to give up and leave without him.

Luckily it didn't come to that.

She watched him move down the stairs with heavy steps, and as he neared the door she could see that he was tired and had had little sleep. *Good*, she thought, *let him be a wreck.*

"Hey, what's the emergency?" He was dressed in a pair of gray jeans and a black-and-red diamond-patterned sweater, and when she looked into those honey eyes she saw how red and strained they were. She saw the bags under his lids, and all she wanted to do was wrap her arms around him and cover him in kisses and tell him that she loved him and that everything would be okay—but she knew that she could not.

"I've missed you too," she said to him. Her tone was melancholic, and she let her eyes drop to his feet.

"I'm sorry." She looked back up at him. "That was not how I meant to open this up. It just came out when I saw you. What I meant to say is, I'm a dick. I shouldn't have taken off on you. There was just so much to take in –"

"I know."

"And I needed to process it. The longer I let it go, though, the harder it was to swallow my pride and admit that I should have talked it out with you and with Braxton.

"I realize now that you were honest. Trevor told me the truth almost two months ago when we moved here. That night at the Melting Pot; I just didn't want to believe it. It's still so hard to believe." They stared at each other for a moment, the light from the foyer spilling onto the wood of the porch like paint behind him, and casting J.T. in shadow.

He reached his left hand out to her, and for a moment she hesitated—shaking as much as she was—but in the end she let him take her hand into his, entwining his fingers with her own.

"Thank you."

He smiled warmly. "I really am sorry."

"I love you, J.T."

"I love you too, Cheri, more than anything." He pulled her close, crushing her gingerly against his body and wrapping his arms around her. She had missed these arms. She had missed the smell of him, the feel of his warmth, and for a moment she thought of nothing but him. She thought of nothing but the soft moist feel of his lips, and she wanted to stay like this forever—but then the memory of Braxton's tears and the panic in his voice brought her back. She pulled away from J.T., still holding onto his hand, but her face had once again grown dark.

"Trevor's been taken."

"What?" J.T. was shaking his head. She could tell that he was trying to understand how.

"He was taken right out of his room. Braxton is a mess; he needs you. I need you." He said nothing. His face registered no response, and she was feeling herself slowly being taken over with disappointment.

"Witches?" he finally asked, breaking the silence that had rested between them.

"I don't know. I think so, but it could be something worse. Something that I couldn't possibly dream of, though I've already seen ghosts and reanimated corpses possessed by complete evil, so I take that back. At this point I could imagine that it is every terrifying thing we ever grew up being afraid was under our beds."

"Where?"

"Braxton is with Kathryn and Francesca; they're on their way to the 'Ham right now, and so am I. I came here to see if you would go with me, if you will help us save Trevor." J.T. seemed to be weighing it all, as if debating if he wanted to be a part of all of this or not. She didn't have the time for this. "I have to go."

"Then let's go." He smiled at her and pulled the door shut behind him, checking the pockets of his jeans to feel for his keys and his wallet. Cheri smiled as they walked quickly back to her car. With J.T. by her side, she once again felt as if she could take on anything. She would have gone and faced down the armies of hell no matter what, but with him next to her, she was more certain that she could win.

They got into her car and Cheri quickly threw back a few ibuprofens and chased them down with an iced mocha. She knew that she was going to have to step on it; she only hoped that the universe would be looking out for her and prevent them from getting pulled over—or worse yet, into an accident.

"Buckle up!" she said as she made a sharp U-turn and sped back towards the exit to the interstate, nervous about going back, dreading the very idea of returning to Bellingham—and worse still, to set foot back in Fairhaven, back to all of those ghosts and lost lives cut tragically short by dark powers that seemed insurmountable in their will.

Chapter: Twenty-One

THE LIGHTS MOVED OVER him. He could see them flashing from beyond his eyelids, lights that did not simply go in and out, but passed over his face as if they were scanning him. He felt weak, and his head throbbed. He could barely hold onto consciousness, but he was trying. He heard voices and smelled leather right by his nose. It was the smell of a car.

How could he be in a car? The last thing he remembered was going to the hospital and bleeding everywhere and Braxton crying and screaming at him to hold on and to not leave him. Was he still in that car?

"Yes, we have him. He's in the backseat right now."

Trevor began to open his eyes, and the first thing to greet him was the bright piercing orange of street lights moving over him fast, and then he began to make out the profile of the girl to his right, who was sitting in the passenger seat. She couldn't have been any older than he was. She had thick dark curls which seemed to be brown, though they could have very easily been black, and her eyes were round and large and looked to be brown—though, again, they could have been dark green.

He tried to see if he could garner anything from the girl in the driver's seat, the girl who was talking on the phone, but aside from her refined English accent, he could gauge nothing else about her. She was right in front of him, and the back of her seat was casting him in shadow.

"We'll get her too. I'm not, cousin; I told you I could do it." He was beginning to drift again. He was trying to stay awake and alert, but it was obvious that there were drugs in his system. Had they drugged him, or had he been in a hospital? He wasn't sure. But as they continued to drive quickly down what he figured was the freeway, the lights passing overhead, orange and then darkness and glowing flash of orange once again, Trevor's eyes closed, and he was soon drifting on a slumbering sea.

'*Come back... come back...*' the voice said to her. It was somewhere in the black distance, as if on the other side of a door. She could hear it calling her to it. The voice was Michael's. She knew that it was his. She had become so familiar with it, living like a phantom in his own life, watching his memories and his heartaches, and the reasons he came to be what he was now: a ghost trapped inside the house that he had been birthed in, the place that had been his prison till the very end of his days.

A place he had never gotten to leave, and a world on the other side of the wall that he never got to see, and a future with the man that he loved that would never be fulfilled. All of those hopes and dreams burnt away by the raging hellfire and the music of the violin.

Mary-Margaret opened her eyes. She was back in her room, lying in her bed with the covers brought up to her chest and tucked neatly around her. The world was still dark. How had she gotten up here? She knew that she had been down in the music room. That was where she had picked up his violin and connected with the shattered spirit of Michael Donovan.

"What time is it?" she asked. She felt slightly dizzy as she attempted to sit up and prop the pillows behind her.

"It's ten o'clock, dear." She looked over to see Queen Mab sitting in that arm chair, the same armchair that had been home to the cursed violin, and she realized that all of the future in this room had belonged to Michael in his days of flesh. "But the better question would be to ask what day it is."

Mary-Margaret furrowed her brows and gave Mabel a quizzical look. "What day it is?"

Mabel nodded. "Yes, dear." She reached out and switched on the elaborate brass floor lamp, which illuminated the bedroom but also cast shadows in places the light could not directly touch. She was dressed in black silk palazzo pants and a matching silk blouse, which was tucked into the waist of her pants, and there, hanging around her neck and shimmering in the light was that three-tiered amber necklace—the necklace that had belonged to Fiona Blackmoore, after she had given her peridot necklace to Michael to try to keep him safe.

"What do you mean?"

Mabel shook her head and sighed. Her legs were crossed, and she began to wiggle the foot that was draped over her right knee. The black satin pump fascinated her in this moment, though Mary-Margaret wasn't exactly certain why the light dancing across the fabric was so captivating. She figured perhaps it had to do with being back in the present.

"It's the twenty-ninth of October. You've been asleep for a week!"

She shook her head in disbelief. "How can that be?"

"I found you on the floor of the music room, Michael's violin by your side. I had to call Jared—Kathryn's driver—to come help me get you upstairs." Mabel removed a black Nat Sherman from her cigarette case and placed it between her lips. Her gray eyes narrowed towards it, and Mary-Margaret watched as the end suddenly sparked to life with nothing more than the old woman's will.

"Michael...."

Mabel took another drag from her cigarette and nodded. "Yes, Michael. What did he show you?"

Mary was trying to recall. She felt as if she were navigating through a thick fog. She knew that she remembered everything: Marsilio Merrin, Fiona, Carter Mayland, and Richard Larrabee, but it was all jumbled with what was going on now.

"Um, his life. He showed me his life. The events that led him to be in this house—haunting it. He said it would prepare me for what is to come, that I'll somehow know how to help stop it."

She was confused by all of this. What was coming? Had it already happened? She had not been approached by some demonic and seductive music teacher, and aside from Rebecca, no new person had come into her life. Certainly Michael couldn't have been warning her against her girlfriend? Rebecca was the first person outside from her family-especially her sister-that she had ever come to love. The idea of that being wrong, that it could be bad, was a possibility too unbearable to face.

"Well, maybe then whatever he has told you will help now." Darkness began to cast itself on Mabel's face, and Mary-Margaret's heart began to race.

"What do you mean?"

Mabel got up from the chair and quickly made her way to Mary-Margaret's bedside.

"There's been... well, there's been an attack –"

"An attack?"

Mabel nodded. "Yes, the afternoon that this infernal eclipse started, Trevor and Braxton were attacked. They were attacked by spirits called wraiths. They can take any form, usually settling on the form that will be the most upsetting to the victim. They can cause physical harm, though it is impossible to cause physical harm to them.

"Trevor was injured very badly and taken to the hospital. It would seem though, that tonight, while Braxton was out to dinner with Kathryn and Francesca, something or someone came in and took Trevor from his hospital bed."

A tear slipped down Mabel's aged face.

"What?"

She nodded and wiped the tear from her cheek. "Yes. He's gone. Nothing showed up on the security cameras, and every staff member on Trevor's floor was spelled into a deep sleep. Kathryn and the others are driving up here right now. We need to try to find him."

Mary-Margaret threw her comforter off of her body, grateful to see that she was dressed in her slip. Queen Mab stood and assisted Mary out of the bed. Mary yawned and stretched out her body, trying to shake the lethargy of the past seven days.

"We'll find him. I'm going to shower and change and get my bearings on everything. We'll figure it out. I promise, Queen Mab, the answer has to be in whatever it was that Michael showed me."

"I hope you're right. I fear that if we cannot find him—if we fail—then it will mean the end to us all."

SHE STOOD IN THE SHOWER, letting the warm water and soap run down her naked flesh, running the loofah all over her stomach, arms, and legs. She thought over everything that she had seen in Michael's past, and as everything became more cognitive and clear, and she could string the thread from one memory to the other until the sequence of events was once again in place, she began searching the details for what it could be that connected her journey into Michael Donovan's past with Trevor Blackmoore's present.

"Michael, I wish you would just tell me," she said aloud, hoping that the spirit would appear on the other side of the frosted glass, a lean male shadow that could give her answers. "Is there a wolf in sheep's clothing? Is it Rebecca? Are you trying to tell me that she is behind this?"

Still nothing, not even a minimal sign that the spirit had heard her. "Goddamn it!" She shut off the water and wrung her hair out in her hands, listening as the water landed on the porcelain floor. She opened the glass door and stepped out, staring at her own reflection in the mirror. Her fiery red hair and her sharp green eyes seemed to radiate in the light, and she sighed as she realized that Michael would not be coming to her.

Mary moved out into the hall and made her way back into her room—Fiona's room, and before that, it had been Michael's room. Nothing had been changed since the time that he had been alive, hiding away in here, dreaming of railways.

"I'm so sorry for everything that happened to you. I'm sorry that you are trapped here. I'm sorry you never got your chance to be with Richard. I'm sorry that everything was taken from you. I'm sorry that my family did this to you, Michael. But you are a part of this family. I don't know if you can hear me or not. I think you can. Unless you are in some other realm now, but I need you to help me if you can; I need you to tell me why you showed me these things, and what it all means!"

She stood there in the middle of the room, her hair dripping on the floorboards and her svelte frame covered in her soft terrycloth white towel. She listened to the silence, hoping to hear something—perhaps the music of his violin, or to see the quivering of a shadow that was out of place with the rest of the shadows cast in the room—but there was nothing, and the only thing to answer her back was the silence.

Chapter: Twenty-Two

THE LIMO WOUND AROUND the jagged dark cliffside, surrounded by those monstrous guard-like evergreens that encased the city of Bellingham down below and seemed almost like a million spires warding off invading armies, as if they were in some medieval, faraway land in the wilds of eastern Europe.

Braxton once again thought of Dracula and the nightmarish land of Transylvania, and the terrible mouth-like walls of the Carpathians, which to him had always seemed like a village that existed within the jaws of the devil himself.

The time away from Bellingham living in Seattle, with all of its day-to-day freedoms and activities and complete normalcy—outside of recent events—made coming back home all the more unsettling. He could see Bellingham for all that it was. Its mystery and darkness, its strange energy that seemed to linger above it like a cloud of fog that blanketed the city, though there was no real fog in sight.

He could see the orange glow of fire coming from the direction of Red Square at the university, but save for that, there was nothing. The city was dark. There were no sirens, no sense of chaos, and as they took the Fairhaven Parkway exit, dipping down into those trees and making their way through the city towards Fifteenth Street, he could feel everything inside of himself twist into unbearably painful knots.

"It is quite different," Kathryn said with a sigh, looking out of the window at the houses they passed and the glowing Jack o' Lanterns on old wood porches and sitting on tables in front windows. There was a return to the past here. These old houses and tree-lined streets, looking skeletal without their leaves, their branches looking like horrible and garish claw-like fingers ready to descend on these houses and begin ripping them apart.

"Yeah," Braxton agreed. "Really different."

"I suppose it's the superstition. The spiritualist beliefs that run through this town, the ghosts." She looked at Braxton and smirked. "The witches." The three of them shook their heads as they continued the drive, getting closer to Fairhaven, and then at Fifteenth Street the car made a right and continued straight ahead. Soon they were making their way up the hill, the amber glow of the windows of Dianaca Castle coming into view.

"Shit!" He buckled over and hugged his stomach. He felt as if a hand had somehow found its way inside of him and was gripping his intestines and giving them a tight squeeze.

"Are you all right?!" Francesca asked, quickly placing her hand on his back and giving him a gentle rub to try to sooth him.

He began to nod, and noticed the sweat that was dripping from his nose and forehead. He sat back and wiped his face with his hands. "Yeah, I'm fine... I'm fine. I don't know what that was...." He thought for a moment, searching his thoughts, trying to connect what he was feeling to what it could actually mean, and then finally it did dawn on him, and his heart began to race. "Trevor is here! You're right! He is in Bellingham. I know it!"

Braxton wanted to stop the limo and hop out and begin scouring the city for Trevor, but he knew that that would be pointless and just waste more time. He had no way of knowing where Trevor was, or even how to find him. That kind of witchcraft was beyond him, and he needed help, the kind of help that only these Blackmoore women could give.

"We'll find him. If you felt him, then he is still alive. If he were dead, you would know." Kathryn's voice grew sullen, and she averted her gaze out of the window once again. "I'm sure we all would...." Her words trailed off as they took another right on Knox and drove halfway up the block to the stately Blackmoore home.

Beyond the white gate was the now bright red door on the two-story Federal with its column-like molding on either side of that door. The dark green shutters and drape-covered windows looked ominous amongst the naked oak trees that filled the front yard.

He remembered how growing up, the kids in school used to be afraid of this house, and he was certain that none of that had changed. Superstition died hard in Fairhaven, and the Black-moores would always instill suspicion and fear. He was now a part of that, and he wasn't sure if he had gotten used to it.

He had not been the subject of rumors and strange glances growing up, but as soon as he had gotten together with Trevor, as soon as he had gone public and become part of this family—this family that was in fact his own—he noticed that he had begun to be looked at differently, and even avoided by many of his class-mates for the rest of the year.

J.T. hadn't abandoned him, though, and for that he had been relieved and grateful. But then, his best friend had never believed in the rumors and superstitions that surrounded the fami-ly—that was, until now. He had finally seen it all for himself, firsthand, and Braxton knew that J.T. could never be the same again. No matter what happened, his life was forever changed.

Braxton could really use his best friend right now.

He had been happy to get out and not return for a while. He and Trevor had talked about hosting Christmas at the apartment in the city, and having all of the family come there so they could stay away. They had planned to avoid Bellingham until the following August, but now here they were, back in the lion's den.

The car pulled up along the curb. Kathryn grabbed the two bags full of clothes and handed them to Jared as soon as the young driver opened the door and helped her outside. The three of them stood on the sidewalk, looking up at the house, its comforting eeriness and its halls void of ghosts and for a moment Braxton released a sigh of relief. But they could all feel the dawning of something else, a battle that was being waged once again.

It moved through the nighttime sky and seemed to envelop the home and curl around them with its invisible embrace, moving into their bodies with each inhale of breath, swirling in their systems and causing their blood to run cold.

Kathryn hugged herself and shuddered. "We're home."

Chapter: Twenty-Three

BLACK ROBES EVERYWHERE. Garments as black as ink covering these lithe forms dancing around the burning body, their faces covered by loose fabric that hung from the conical crowns on their heads. They moved in unison, in circles to rhythms of drums and those ghastly violins that screamed hellish melody. They could not be stopped as frantic as they moved, casting this circle and chanting.

What was it that they were saying? He couldn't make it out and he didn't want to watch, but he was unable to turn away, and the smell of that putrid flesh burning filled his nostrils and went down into his lungs so that he was choking on it. It was the most horrendous thing that had ever occurred. It was the worst feeling, this flesh in his lungs, and he was gasping for air and it was burning his eyes so much so that he began to cry, to try to eradicate what was infecting them, this flesh of the deceased that was making its way in.

It seemed as if the earth around them began to bleed, as thick tar-like liquid oozed up from each crevice, between each mossy patch of grass and uneven earth. They continued to dance faster and faster as the demons played. Their pointed ears, their naked bodies with long claw-like hands and their monstrous faces and horns that were thrown back with maniacal laughter as they played, and these shadow figures danced around the burning body.

HE HIT SOMETHING WITH a thud. Could it be the ground? His eyelids fluttered, and he knew that he was being taken out of the vehicle that he had been lying in for the longest time.

"Careful!" the girl with the accent spat out.

"Sorry! Like it matters, though; look at him!" He caught a glimpse of stars and clouds, the darkness of trees that stretched out on the edge of his vision, and the locks of hair that hung down on either side and tickled his face.

"Ugh...." He tried to speak, tried to move his arms, but he had barely enough strength to move a finger.

THIS BLACK RIVER MADE its way out from the roots of that central pyre and flowed around them, so that they were all ankle-deep in a midnight river, and it continued to flow, to make its way between gravestones that stood uniformly around them.

His eyes grew wide and his mouth fell open in fear as he watched in horrified silence as a dark figure, tall and lean, rose up from the black river before his very eyes, its hands emerging from the earth first, those sharp nails digging into the ground and the black mess and pulling itself up.

At first, this figure was covered in it, his body shiny and slick as it reflected in those burning flames—but that water, that black oil, slipped off of him slowly and the figure began to take form. His eyes were inky wells that gleamed, and his body was naked and thin, with open sores and exposed muscle tissue and veins, but as that tar-like substance slipped down his body, it began to repair the rot and make the skin new again.

"WE HAVE TO GET HIM inside quickly, before he has a chance to come to!" They got him to his feet and draped his arms over their shoulders. He could smell their perfume and feel the soft of their hair kissing his cheeks. He was stumbling, despite them carrying him. They dragged him up a set of three steps, and then he glimpsed one of the girl's hands reach out and stick a key into the lock of a door.

HE TRIED NOT TO LOOK into the eyes, those eyes that were beset in a handsome face, those eyes that between them was a narrow, somewhat pointed nose, a strong angular jaw and dimpled chin, his hair long and black, framing his face, and he grinned with diabolical satisfaction.

The black figures around him fell silent and bowed before this naked man with his lean muscular frame. His skin glistened in the firelight of the pyre and their burning torches.

THE DOOR CREAKED, AND there was more darkness. "Where do we put him?" the girl without an accent asked.

The girl with the accent grunted. "In here; put him in here, and grab that chair!" He was trying to see where he was, to take in his surroundings. He glimpsed light from the outside cast itself on hardwood, which creaked beneath the weight of their feet. To the left he saw what appeared to be a fireplace with a mantle of found stone, and what seemed to be a Victorian sofa partially draped with a sheet.

"PLEASE, LET ME GO!" he pleaded, but they all seemed not to hear him. "Please let me go home." And then the naked man who had risen from the earth turned, and with those fierce eyes acknowledged him and smiled.

"HERE." A WOOD CHAIR—PERHAPS it was a dining chair with a short back—was placed in front of him. The girl with the accent used all of her strength to get him into it, letting out a "*humph*" as she pushed him onto the seat.

Trevor blinked and saw the girl with the accent walk out of his view, and then there was a clanking sound, followed with the sound of something heavy skirting across the floor, dragging with a scratch as it came into view.

"Wha...?" His head rolled as he found it impossible to keep it up, and his eyes kept fluttering.

"Shh...." She placed her hand to the side of his face and gave it a pat. "It's no use."

"*BAGABI LACA BACHABE. Lamac Cahi Achababe. Karrelyos. Lamac Lamec Bachalyas. Cabahagy Sabalyos. Baryolos. Lagoz Atha Cabyolas. Samahac et Famyolas. Harrahya.*"

The flames kept growing-kept rising and his eyes took in the glow, just as he took in the forms of those beings dancing. Watching their movements, he knew that they were doing something great and ancient, something that he had been especially chosen for.

"HOLD HIM BACK!" THE girl with the accent commanded. The other girl complied, placing her hands on Trevor's shoulders and pulling him forcefully against the back of the chair.

"Please..." he muttered. Neither girl answered him, and soon he realized that the girl with the accent—the girl who was obviously the leader of this plot—was binding him with the chain, wrapping it around him and strapping him to the chair. "Please, stop..." he tried to plead once more. Again, there was no answer.

"There we are, now," the leader said, fastening the chain with a lock and giving it a tug to ensure that he was unable to get free from the chair. "Sit tight, Blackmoore." She stood and ruffled his hair with her hand before pushing his head back and slapping him once again on the cheek. "Your time will come soon!"

He heard them laughing as they walked away, the sound of their boot heels fading in the distance.

"Braxton...."

HIS EYES POPPED OPEN and he sat up in the dark, staring at the pocket doors that led to the ballroom-turned-office and the black grand piano that stood in the corner of the room at an angle. The window behind the piano bench was cracked open and a breeze blew in, disturbing those satin drapes and carrying Trevor's voice.

Braxton heard him. Even in the dreamless slumber, he had heard his voice calling to him, pleading for him to save him. Trevor was alive. There was hope, and perhaps Trevor was out of his coma. Perhaps he was awake, and could soon reach him again and tell him where he was. His shirt and face and neck were covered in sweat. His hair was dripping with it, and he wiped it all away and pushed his bangs back from his face.

Braxton turned and planted his feet firmly on the floor and rested his face in his hands, his elbows balancing on the tops of his knees.

"Fuck!" He felt helpless. What was he supposed to do? How was he supposed to find Trevor? And what horrible things were being done to him? Was he okay, or was he being tortured?

The idea of someone inflicting pain on Trevor—the thought of someone abusing him and taking pleasure in it—made his heart race and made him anxious. He wanted to do something, hurt something. He knew that if they didn't find him soon, he would begin using his witchcraft to tear Bellingham apart.

"Braxton?" He looked up to see Kathryn walk into the great room from the foyer, her hand resting on the frame, the other holding a glass of scotch. She smiled softly at him; her thick auburn hair reflected the hall light, giving her a halo. She had changed out of her wrap dress, and boots and was now covered in a black silk robe, her diamond rings glittering in the light.

"Sorry, I fell asleep."

Kathryn shook her head. "No need to apologize." She turned to look back over her shoulder for just a moment, before looking back at him with a grin. "You have guests." He looked at her, perplexed, and then he saw Cheri and J.T. emerge from around the corner with smiles on their faces, though he could visibly see the pain and regret behind those smiles and in their eyes.

"I'm sorry man," J.T. said as he made his way towards him. Braxton stood and opened his arms. They hugged and patted each other firmly twice on the back.

"It's okay," he offered through tears.

"I should have been there."

Braxton shook his head. "You just found all of this scary shit out-"

"Yeah, it was like I suddenly woke up in an episode of *Buffy* or *The X-Files* or something. Definitely not easy." The two of them snickered.

"Yeah, that's how I felt last Christmas when I found out."

"I wish you could have felt like you could tell me." J.T. shook his head and sighed. The guilt was heavy, and seemed as if it were pushing his best friend to the ground. He didn't want J.T. to feel like this, but he knew that guilt was something that only the guilty could work through. No matter what he said, no matter how much he protested, he could not make J.T.'s guilt go away for him.

"I know. There were so many times that I wanted to, but to bring you into all of this—to make this a part of your world, to put you in this kind of danger—well, I just couldn't do it to you, and honestly I wish it hadn't happened."

"Yeah," J.T. agreed with a sigh. "But I'm glad it did, and I'm glad I was able to help."

"Me too."

"I'm sorry too, Braxton," Cheri began, walking over to him, the tears spilling down her face, making her brown eyes look like melted chocolate. "I shouldn't have left the hospital; I shouldn't have gone home. I should have made myself go back."

"No." He moved over to her and wrapped his arms around her, holding Cheri close to him and breathing in the smell of her. It was obvious that she had just recently bathed. "You were dealing with a lot. We've caused so much heartache in your life. This family and everything that comes with it has asked so much of you; I understand needing to hide away."

Cheri shook her head and cried harder. "But had I stayed, had I not left the hospital, had I been there with Trevor –"

"Then whoever or whatever took him would have either put you in the same sleep as everyone else on that floor, or they would have killed you. Either way, they were going to take him—whoever they are—they were just waiting for their moment."

Cheri nodded and took a couple of deep breaths. "I know, I know..." She wiped the tears from her eyes and took a few more calming breaths.

"So, do we have any idea who took him or why?" Braxton looked over to Kathryn, standing there in the entryway, her face cast in grievous shadow.

She shook her head and threw back the rest of her scotch. "No, we don't." She pivoted on her bare feet and disappeared back down the hall. They glimpsed her phantom-like figure once more as she passed the other entryway and vanished into the kitchen.

"We'll find him. I know we will," Cheri said to him.

Braxton turned and looked at her and gave a deep and hopeless sigh. "I hope so..." he said. "I hope so...."

Chapter: Twenty-Four

`

There was a dull hum as he moved, slipping past trees and headstones. He was trying to outwit the burning prisms that slipped through the mist. He stopped, caught off-guard by the darkened figure of a cloaked woman, her face covered by a hood, paying him no mind. She moved apart from the present, and he knew that she was one of the dead. Not ever an entity that lived a life, but one that was made up of thousands of lifetimes. She was an essence formed from the very pieces of the hundreds that lay beneath the earth.

She was Bayview's guardian. She watched over the souls; her business was not the living, except for only when they trespassed—and at night, a human being's presence was certainly that.

His skin crawled as he watched her, forgetting those ominous, burning orbs that glided through the mist—wondering only about this shadowed woman, and what she may or may not do. His foot gave, his knee popping his leg straight, a lone twig snapping beneath his foot. He turned and came face-to-face with a quick black form: the face withered, the nose narrow, the mouth rotting away. From beneath her hood, her yarn-like, purple-silver hair billowed, but it was those empty sockets—black and endless, hollow in her skull—that took him by surprise and sent him into darkness.

TREVOR'S EYES OPENED, and everything around him came into focus. He saw the large picture window directly in front of him, and the darkness that still seemed to encompass the outside world beyond the shadowed thick of evergreen trees and bushes that obstructed the view of the other side. He didn't know if he was in the middle of a neighborhood or some rural town.

He saw the peeling wallpaper of pansies that at some point had been a vibrant blue against white, but was now pale and dingy and looked as if someone had spent years pissing all over it. The place smelled like a second-hand shop, musty and sour and slightly damp, and the chandelier in the middle of the room was broken and hung for dear life from three remaining wires.

He could now see the two girls who were on their knees before him on the scratched-up hardwood. It was obvious they hadn't realized that he had come to, and they were busy tracing something in white chalk around him. One of the women, who was directly in front of him, had straight shoulder-length light brown hair and her petite body was dressed in tight blue jeans, a black silk collared button-up with the sleeves rolled up to her elbows, and black riding boots on her feet. The other girl, who was to the right of him, had thick dark chocolate curls and alabaster skin, also dressed in blue jeans and sand-colored riding boots with gold buckles, a blue, black, and red flannel shirt, with a long gold and diamond strung necklace around her neck.

They were both chanting quietly, and he could barely make it out. *Shit!* He realized that he was barefoot and dressed in nothing more than his underwear and a hospital gown. *How did I get here?*

He followed the thick chain that was wrapped around him with his eyes, and finally fell on the lock that kept him there. Trevor took a deep breath and focused his sight only on that lock and began to enter a trance-like state, trying to summon his witchcraft, trying to connect with it and feel it cyclone inside of him, trying to feel that familiar heat. But it was no use. Nothing came. He gave it three more attempts, and still there was nothing.

How can this be? He began to thrash about and the two women, who were only a few years older than him—perhaps twenty-two or twenty-three years old—both looked up at him, startled, but that surprise quickly shifted into a grimace.

"Look who's awake!" The woman with the dark brown hair—the one with the English accent—knocked him hard across the face with her forearm.

"Bitch!" Trevor yelled. The hit caused him to bite in to the inside of his cheek, and his mouth began filling with the metallic taste of blood.

"Shut it, fag!" the other one ordered, slapping him across the face. Trevor spat a stream of blood at the English woman's feet. She stepped away in disgust, and then grinned.

"Well, my darling Blackmoore, you just made this a whole hell of a lot easier!" She leaned down and rested her open left hand six inches over the spot of blood and spit. "I was going to cut you till you bled, but now I don't have to."

She began to mutter incantations in a language he had never heard and as she did, the floor beneath his feet began to get hot, as if the floorboards were heated and turned up to their highest possible setting. Trevor closed his eyes and clenched his teeth, throwing his head back as he was singed by the heat.

"FUCK!" he let out, and tried to lift his feet off the ground. After a few seconds of excruciating heat that seemed like an eternity, everything went back to normal and the floor beneath him was once again cool.

"Just in case you think about getting loose or trying to use any of those powers of yours, this circle will keep you in place until it's time!" she smirked, and her eyes burned with a cool fire.

His face and chest was dripping with sweat, and his hazel eyes looked forest-green and luminescent with his tears. "Time for—for what?"

"Oh, sweetie." The woman with the accent took hold of his chin between her fingers and tilted his face up to look directly into hers. She was beautiful; that was certain, but as vicious as a viper, and he was sure that her blood must run black and thick like venom. "For your family to finally make amends for their betrayal of Him, those centuries ago...."

Trevor's eyes grew wide with understanding. "The Dark God...."

She smirked and nodded slowly. "That's right... he will rise tomorrow night, and you will be his first." She directed her gaze over his head, smiling at the other woman behind him. "Sweet dreams!" She yanked her hand away from his chin hard and walked away from him, disappearing around the corner into the foyer. The girl behind him laughed and followed suit, walking confidently with a sway of her hips.

"Braxton...." He hung his head and let the tears slip silently down his face.

He would not cry out; he would not give the two women the satisfaction of hearing him suffer, or taste his fear. But he was afraid; there was no escaping that fact, just as he knew there was no escaping this ruined and rotting house, or the chair and chains that kept him bound and helpless inside the chalked circle—which, he realized, was in the shape of a six-pointed star. The circle that surrounded it was lined with archaic symbols that he couldn't decipher, though he knew that it didn't really matter. As long as he was in that circle, he was as defenseless as a swine about to be slaughtered.

BRAXTON SAT UP IN TREVOR'S childhood bed, the white linen pillows propped up against the antique mahogany headboard, the lower half of his naked body covered in sheets, and his arms were crossed over his raised knees.

"Trevor..." he said softly, hoping that perhaps he would be able to hear him, as he was certain that he was able to hear his boyfriend.

Braxton reached for a cigarette from the pack on the nightstand and lit it with his purple Bic, taking in the first inhale and releasing it back out slowly. His black liquid eyes were large and pained, and his beautiful Botticelli-like face was covered in a scattering of tiny black hairs.

"C'mon, baby, just give me something to work with...." He seemed to be begging the empty air, or perhaps spirits that he hoped could take up his plea and give some divine intervention. He held his cigarette between his cushion lips and slid the window up from the sill.

"Braxton?" Cheri called from the other side of the bedroom door.

"Yeah," he said, ashing his cigarette into the crystal dish. "You can come in." The old white wood door creaked as it skirted across the floor, and Cheri came in, dressed in a midnight-blue thigh-length slip that he assumed she must have borrowed from Kathryn. She and J.T. had slept over instead of going home to their respective parents' houses. They had figured that in the end it would have been too much trouble to try to come up with some excuse for showing up in Bellingham without notice in the middle of the night.

Cheri ached for him. She could see the loss and anguish in those absorbent and endless inky wells. Though he had always been the more confident—the more aware and assertive, between him and Trevor—in this moment Braxton's face seemed to hint at the pre-teen boy she had first encountered in the seventh grade. "How are you holding up?"

Braxton ran his right hand through his thick glossy black hair, pushing it back from his face over the top of his head.

"Like I'm going to die." She nodded and Braxton handed her a cigarette without asking, which she took without thanking him for it. There was no need. "How are you?"

Cheri could feel the tears, but she quickly choked them back. "Uh, like shit. Still." She took her first drag and then closed her eyes as she let it back out. "I can't lose him. I've lost so many already, you know?"

Braxton nodded.

"I know there was a lot of pain for those five years, but before that, it wasn't all bad, and the four of us—Christian, Greg, and Trevor—we made a unit. We were bound together since we were small, and though in the later years there was a lot of pain and a lot of betrayal, and in the end, so much death, it didn't take away from our history. It didn't take away from a time when we were still innocent. Without Trevor, that's all gone."

She wasn't sure if it was selfish of her to talk like this, or if it would piss him off to hear about Christian and Greg and those years before and after the separation—or, as she had begun to refer to that time, B.B. and A.B. (Before Braxton and After Braxton).

"He's the last connection to my own innocence, whatever's left of it." Braxton added. "So, I guess I'm saying I get it." He offered an understanding smile and she returned it.

"Knock, knock," Francesca said. She was gripping the door with one hand and holding onto the glass knob with the other. She was dressed in a gray tank top and tight black leggings, her thick cherry hair pulled back from her face and wrapped up in a loose bundle, held in place by a plastic tortoise shell clip. "I figured we could use this...." She was holding up what obviously appeared to be a joint.

"I don't think we need to sit around getting baked," Braxton said with a snort.

"Oh, yes we do!" she said with a grin, padding across the floor with her bare feet, taking a seat on the bed between him and Cheri.

"And that's not all..." Kathryn said, appearing behind them in the door, holding a bottle and three crystal sherry glasses. She was wearing the same black silk robe, which was opened, and her slender body was draped in a matching slip that swept the floor.

J.T. followed behind her, dressed in green flannel pajama pants and a plain white tee, his eyes sleepy. He held two mugs of coffee in his hands, one of which he gave to Cheri, and planted a kiss on her cheek before taking a seat in the green satin arm chair in the corner of the room.

"What is that?" Braxton asked.

"This," Kathryn began, holding up the bottle and offering glasses to him and Francesca, "is our very own absinthe."

She began pouring shots of the chartreuse liquid into each glass.

"It has a stronger concentration of wormwood as well as a drop of one extra special ingredient, which would most likely kill anyone who wasn't us." He gave her a quizzical look.

"It's datura... the herb used by witches of long ago in a salve that they would rub over their bodies, so that their spirits could rise up and meet at the sabbats, invisible to the eyes of others."

"And this," Francesca began, lifting the thick and pungent joint to his eyes before placing it between her own lips and sparking it up with his lighter. "This is marijuana laced with wormwood oil and belladonna."

Braxton watched as she took it in and held it for a moment before letting it out and passing it to Kathryn, who did the same.

"And what is this supposed to do?" he asked, as Kathryn let out the smoke and passed the joint to him.

"This..." Francesca began. "This is going to help us connect our power, and hopefully find Trevor." Braxton looked over at Cheri and J.T.; their eyes were transfixed on the whole ritual that was beginning to take place before their eyes.

"Here," Kathryn said, removing a folded piece of paper from the pocket of her robe and handing it to him. "Say this with us before we take the shot." He opened the paper and held up the glass.

They closed their eyes for just a moment, summoning that familiar power, feeling their bodies inflame with that tingling heat. They then opened their eyes slowly, and Braxton held up the paper so he could read it.

"As above, so below; as within, so without; as the universe, so the soul!" they said in unison, and threw back their glasses. The usual licorice flavor of the absinthe was mixed with something that was sickly sweet and slightly bitter.

It went down quick and he could feel it make the journey down his throat and into his stomach, and from the inside it felt as if it had instantly erupted into what he imagined was a bright glowing green flame that spread throughout his entire body.

"Now smoke this, and count to three every time before letting it back out, and every time you do, imagine Trevor," Francesca ordered.

Braxton complied, thinking only of Trevor's face: his slightly narrow nose and that chiseled angular jaw, the deep red of his short hair, and those hazel eyes with their hues of brown, green, and gold. He envisioned his wide and infectious smile and dimples, and the slight natural curls in his hair.

With each intake of the "witches' pot," as he had decided to call it, Trevor came more and more into focus. His lean but muscular body and arms, perfectly smooth and hairless, the pink of his nipples, and the soft sparse mat of hair that poked out from beneath the elastic band of his underwear. Those lips of his, soft and moist, and how much he enjoyed kissing them.

The three of them continued to pass the joint until there was nothing left, and each time it felt as if they were rising further and further from their bodies, detaching from the flesh and stepping out of themselves.

Braxton saw blackness, and then the lights of stars of all different and vibrant colors that seemed to move all around him. He was weightless, and yet he had direction. He was going to something. He knew that he was. Something was pulling him closer and closer to it, refusing to let him go.

HE QUICKLY FOUND HIMSELF surrounded by gravestones and bodies cloaked in garments of black, their faces covered. They danced around a great fire and encircling them were burning torches, and Trevor was being held in place before that fire with a blade to his throat. He was naked, save for a tiny pair of athletic shorts, and his bare flesh had strange symbols carved into it, and the blood seeped down his sweaty body. Tears slipped down his face, even as he fought and struggled to get free.

Braxton wanted to go to him, to save him, and yet he couldn't move. He could do nothing, and he knew that he was just a visitor here, an alien apparition that could affect nothing.

"This holy night, he shall hear our call." The one with the knife to his throat began to speak. It was a young woman, and she had an English accent. "Now that the veil between the worlds is the thinnest, we shall spill the blood and set him free.

"We offer him the body beneath the earth, the body that has been dedicated willingly to Him, and from this earth He shall rise and rule and decimate the witches who betrayed Him!"

The earth seemed to be forcing tar out from its soil, and in the pyre that burned before them was a body in the flames. A body with a face that was not yet gone. He knew that face. How was it that he knew the face of the body that burned? He focused on that face, and the head suddenly rolled to its side. Its crisp green eyes met with his and the mouth fell open, and he realized then that the body belonged to Mary-Margaret.

"The Devil shall come for his witches...." She proclaimed in strained agony.

BRAXTON OPENED HIS eyes. He was lying on his side along with Francesca and Kathryn, who too opened their eyes, and they all sat up and looked around at one another.

"Did you see it?" Braxton asked. They nodded.

"What did you see? Tell us!" Cheri asked.

"Yeah, what happened?" J.T. added.

Kathryn ran her hands through her hair and gave the thick auburn mess a shake. "They have him. The Soul Wanderers."

"The who?" J.T. asked.

"The Soul Wanderers. It's the name given to the witches who follow the Dark God of the Wood, the thing that wants to kill our family," Braxton answered, taking another cigarette and handing one to Kathryn.

She lit them both with her mind.

"Um, so explain this to me. I mean, Cheri kind of filled me in, but I'm still really confused." They all turned their attention to Kathryn, who sighed and began to tell the Legacy to J.T., explaining everything from the beginning. From the days back in the sixth century, when they had finally arrived on the shores of Ireland after their hundreds-of-years-long journey from India and central Europe and the Mediterranean; the sacred woods on the edge of the Moors, and the rise of the Dark God, and his massacre and demand of blood and hearts.

She spoke of the abandonment of the God in the twelfth century, and how he had become weak without followers and used what remaining strength he had to reach out to all of the other witches, who were in hiding and reeling from the rise of Christianity, and the promise of vengeance with the Bubonic Plague if they pledged to give their allegiance to him after the devastation.

She explained how from that plague the Burning Times had emerged, and with each witch that was actually put to death, he grew stronger from their power. She told him about the family's eventual arrival in New Orleans in the eighteenth century and the curse that was laid upon the family, causing them to kill any who they exchanged sexual fluids with. All of this J.T. listened to with eager ears.

She spoke of the history of the Soul Wanderers, once again explaining how they got their name, and their goal of bringing forth the Dark God of the Wood, whose name was lost to time—though she was certain that his followers knew it. She explained how these agents of the God would come for them all, but especially for Trevor and Braxton, and that their mission was to erase the Blackmoores from off the face of the earth, committing the family to the annals of the past.

"And so you think these Soul Wanderers are going to try to use Trevor to raise this Dark God?" J.T. asked, and they all nodded.

"Yes, and I think the three of us can agree that from what we saw they are going to try to do this tomorrow night." Braxton and Francesca nodded.

"They said 'when the veil between the worlds is the thinnest.' That would be Halloween," Francesca stated.

"What did they look like?" Cheri asked.

"Well, they were... I don't know how else to describe them other than to say they looked like they were wearing the robes and hoods of the Ku Klux Klan, but they were all in black instead of white," Braxton responded.

"Yes," Kathryn added. "They dress like dark phantoms, one with the night and shadowed world. They are souls in service of Him."

J.T. shook his head. "And where did this happen?"

"In a cemetery..." Braxton said with a sigh.

"It had to be Bayview," Kathryn mused.

"Yes, and that girl on the burning pyre..." Francesca seemed to be searching her memory.

"It was Mary-Margaret," Braxton interjected.

"Mary-Margaret?" Kathryn asked. "Are you sure?"

Braxton took a long drag from his cigarette, savoring the taste of the mentholated nicotine before nodding. "Yeah, I got a good look at her face, just before she warned me with the prophecy."

They all looked at each other, and it seemed as if the room had grown cold, a sudden chill that caused the five of them to hug their bodies for warmth.

"We need to talk to her right away," Kathryn proclaimed, and they all nodded.

"Yeah." Braxton finished his smoke and smashed it in the crystal ashtray. "Before it's too late."

Chapter: Twenty-Five

MARY-MARGARET STOOD on the corner of Eleventh and Harris Avenue, holding her phone in her hands and reading through all of the missed texts and phone calls from Rebecca.

They moved from one degree to the other, the first being simple enough messages asking what she was up to, or if she wanted to get dinner later; the next wave grew worried, asking if she was upset about something or angry with Rebecca, and the final wave moved into panic, asking if everything was okay.

She listened to the voicemails, messages filled with worry, heartache and pain. Rebecca told her that she had stopped by the house a couple of times but there had been no answer. She worried that perhaps Mary had been involved in an accident in this never-ending darkness.

The last voicemail, which was tinged with the sound of tears and exhaustion, said that she would be going to Seattle for a few days to check on her grandmother.

Shit! Mary-Margaret had been hoping to reunite with her girlfriend and garner some comfort from her in the midst of all of this uncertainty.

She sighed and made her way into *Tony's Coffee House*, a local roaster attached to the *Harris Avenue Café*, in a charming hundred-year-old brick building with regal green columns and fire-engine-red trim around the picture windows, and English-lattice pane glass above them. The name of the coffee shop was painted on the glass, and after a long night of recovery and trying to decipher the reason behind Michael's reveal, she was glad to see that Tony's was open for a morning cup of coffee, despite the fact that it looked like the middle of the night outside.

The coffee house was still full of people busying themselves with their usual routine, and others staring out into that forever dark and expressing a visible hopelessness on their faces. She knew that these people were missing the sun, which most people never seem to think about when growing up under the constant cover of clouds—but the sun always shone, even through the constant nebulous.

She tugged on the sleeves of her black cable-knit turtleneck with her palms and folded her arms across her chest, tapping the screen of her phone with her thumb. Her red hair looked wild, and she realized she probably should have brushed it before she left.

She had just thrown on a pair of blue jeans, black suede buckle knee-high boots, and this turtleneck before racing out of the house. She needed to get out and clear her head; she needed the solitude that only being around a bunch of strangers could give.

"Hi, what can I get you?" a cute brunette girl asked. She was wearing a black *Tony's Coffee* tee, and her skin was a dark olive with a scattering of delicate moles. She seemed tired, and Mary-Margaret figured it was because of the eclipse that was throwing her—and probably everyone else in the world—off.

She stood there, tapping her feet on the old hardwood floor, and looked over the menu. She had been more prone to drinking large amounts of black tea throughout her life, only recently having become an avid coffee drinker since first moving to the States back at the end of the summer.

"A latte, I suppose…." She had only ever had mochas before, but the combination of espresso and steamed milk seemed simple and manageable.

"This eclipse is just crazy, isn't it?" the barista asked her.

Mary frowned and nodded. "Yeah, it is."

The barista sighed and shook her head in defeat. "I just don't get it. It makes no sense. An eclipse lasting for eight days now? I stopped watching or listening to the news because it's all anyone talks about and scientists all over the world can't seem to figure it out, and the religious nuts keep talking about the end days, and they're calling it a sign of the Anti-Christ and blaming him."

"And what do you think all of this is?"

The girl shrugged. "I don't want to think about it. Maybe it is the end of the world. But I don't think it's the fault of some antichrist… there was no antichrist when the dinosaurs were wiped out, but it was certainly the end of the world as that world was, and the same goes with the Ice Age. That was much older than Christianity or the Bible."

Mary nodded and handed the girl a five-dollar bill. "So you think this is something older?"

The barista thought for a moment. "Don't you? I mean, eclipses? That's ancient omens… that's the anger-of-the-gods-type shit."

"Maybe," Mary responded, taking her first sip of the latte and realizing it desperately needed sugar to sweeten its bitter bite. "Maybe it is."

She thanked the girl and went over to the bar against the wall to add some sugar before finding a table in the corner next to one of those front windows, where she could look out onto those eerie and foreboding streets. She unlocked her phone with a swipe of her finger and quickly went to calling Rebecca, hoping that she still had a girlfriend after her week-long radio silence.

"What in the hell happened to you?! Are you all right?!"

Mary felt joy and relief as soon as she heard Rebecca's voice panicked on the other end. "Yeah, I'm fine. I'm sorry. My aunt got really ill and it was just chaos, and I didn't know if I should tell you or not, and I felt guilty at the idea of dragging you into it."

She hated having to lie, but she knew that she couldn't tell her the truth. Rebecca at the least wouldn't believe her and would think she was crazy, or at the worst, she would believe every word and want nothing to do with her.

"Oh, thank God." Rebecca's words trailed off for just a moment. "I was afraid that I had done something, or that something horrible had happened to you."

"No, no." Mary took another sip of her coffee and her head began to hang low, wishing she could tell her everything.

"Well, in the future, please, babe, tell me when there's an emergency. Hell, tell me when you buy a new toothbrush or a can of soup, just don't go dark on me like that!"

Mary hated to admit that she felt good hearing the worry. It made her feel wanted. It made her realize that she really was valued and treasured by another person. "I will, I promise."

"Thank you." She could hear Rebecca's smile through the phone.

"So, Seattle, huh?"

"Yeah, my grandmother took a slip down the stairs –"

"Oh my God!"

"No, no. She's okay, this time; I just want to make sure she really is okay before I return. She's been doing great and is moving a little slower, but you know, it's good just to make sure."

Mary nodded and picked at the skin on her nail bed. "Yeah, I'm glad she has you; looks like we're both wrapped up with family stuff."

"I know, but I should be back up in a couple of days, and then I'm never letting you go for anything."

She smiled at the thought of being with Rebecca again, the thought of smelling her hair against her face or the feel of her soft skin, and kissing her satin lips. "I'll be waiting."

"I love you."

It caught Mary by surprise and her heart felt as if it had paused. Her hand began to shake and she realized that aside from her family, she had never said those words to another person. She hadn't even felt love for anyone outside of her family, but she realized that she was feeling it now.

"I love you too," she said, and with that they hung up and Mary sat there in the wood chair. Forgetting for the moment about anything other than the way Rebecca's voice sounded when she said those three words to her.

"I LOVE YOU, HUH?" BENJAMIN said, sitting in one of the red-and-white neo classic pattern arm chairs, opposite the pearl-white sofa that Rebecca was sitting on, in the drawing room of the first floor of the Tramer Estate in the Seattle highlands. The room was filled with a mix of East Asian and English furniture, the walls the color of custard, and a great white marble fireplace burned opposite of them.

He was holding a glass of rioja, dressed in a navy V-neck tee and black jeans. His neck-length dishwater-blond hair, which he normally had pulled back into a bun, was loose and framing his face, which was now sprouting a thin beard.

"Yeah, I do love her," Rebecca replied. She was dressed in a burgundy silk blouse, which was tucked into a heather-gray pencil skirt.

"But you hate that you can't tell her the truth?"

She looked at her younger brother and gave him a sullen nod. "Of course I do. It would make everything so much easier. To be able to tell her that I know exactly who she is, and that I am just like her."

Benjamin's face seemed to fall in a sad understanding. "But you can't because we are the family in charge of the Laws of the Conclave."

Rebecca tapped her nail against the empty wine glass and sighed. "Yeah, and so now we both have to lie to each other. The same lie, over the same thing."

Benjamin reached out for the bottle and offered more wine to his sister. Rebecca held out her glass, and he filled it to the brim and then topped off his own. "Trevor's gone."

She looked at her brother, confused. "What do you mean, he's gone?"

"I went to his hospital room last night. I wanted to check on him. I've been doing that a lot –"

"Benjamin..."

"I just wanted to make sure he was okay. I overheard his friend, Cheri Hannifin, explaining to our Gay Lit professor the day after the eclipse, before classes were canceled. She said that he was injured in the initial riots and was at Swedish in a coma. So I've been going to see how he's doing. His boyfriend Braxton was always there, so I never went in, but last night at the hospital, the place was insane. I mean, utter hell, and I overheard nurses talking.

"The whole floor mysteriously fell asleep at the same time, and all of the patients were accounted for—all but Trevor Blackmoore. They were worried that his family would file suit against the hospital." He looked away from her, as if trying to hide the worry from his sister's eyes, but she could see it as plainly as she could see the glass of wine in his hand.

"Kidnapped?"

Benjamin looked back at his sister and nodded. "The place was full of magic. I could feel it thick in the air."

"You think it's the Soul Wanderers, don't you?"

He sighed. "Yeah, I do. I think they've taken him, and I believe they are going to attempt The Reckoning."

Rebecca could not deny the fear that began to rise in her. She wanted to leave and get back to Mary-Margaret as quickly as possible. "You care about him, don't you?" Benjamin only stared at her. "You have very real feelings for him."

There were tears in his eyes, and for the first time since they were kids, Rebecca watched amazed that he did not try to choke them back or wipe them away.

He closed his eyes and let the saline slip down his face. "Yeah, I do. I know he does not feel the same. I know he's with Braxton, but it doesn't stop how I feel. It doesn't stop me for wanting him to be happy and okay."

"But we can't interfere. You know this. The rules of the chosen family are simple. Once a family is put in charge of the Conclave, they have to be neutral. We are to uphold the laws that were set after the trials. True witches must stay in the shadows, and we must exact the consequences of those laws on any who violates them."

Benjamin stood and shook his head in disagreement. "But the Dark God? The Reckoning? That in itself would destroy the Laws as soon as He is given flesh!"

"I know, but he is a deity. He gives us power as much as any other God or Goddess. If a God or Goddess makes itself known and exacts its judgment, then that is the will."

"But we don't serve him. Of all the deities our family has followed and worshiped, He is not one of them and never has been. I don't want to see the world enslaved, and if he rises, then we will surely be punished, along with all of the other witches throughout the world who have refused to bow to him."

"That is true, grandson." They both turned to see their grandmother Virginia standing in the entryway, her weight supported by her ivory cane, and her frail body dressed in that wedding gown that she never took off. "So, what do you do?"

He looked from her to his sister and back at his grandmother and shrugged. "I don't know... I just wish I knew how to help him."

Virginia Tramer moved towards them, walking crooked through the room. "But, you see, this eclipse is his punishment. Trevor will be helpless as long as the sun hides."

"What do you mean?" Rebecca asked.

"The young Blackmoore worked a spell against you, Benjamin. You must have felt it."

He began to scan his memory for any instance that he could recall, and then a flash of the party came back to him, and the sudden fever that seemed to take over him as soon as he had touched Trevor.

"You're right, he did. But I don't care! What do you mean, this eclipse is his punishment?"

"It's a Binding. As long as the sun hides, he cannot use his witchcraft."

Rebecca sighed. "But why this eclipse? It's unnatural, and is certainly something that would draw attention to something otherworldly."

"Because it alerts witches the world over that the Laws have been violated; it's just the nature of the Binding."

Benjamin shook his head. "Then why isn't history littered with events like this?"

Virginia laughed. "My dear, in this whole wide world, with billions of people—and out of those billions, thousands are witches, and only one bloodline every thirteen years—what do you think the likelihood of a witch working a spell against another witch who happens to be one of the ruling bloodlines at the time? I'd say this may very well be only the second or third time since The Conclave's existence that this has happened."

"But when does it end? There certainly has to be a timeline? The world can't simply just stay dark forever?"

His grandmother maneuvered her way into the chair that Benjamin had been occupying, giving an exhausted sigh as she sat down. "It lasts for thirteen days and thirteen nights. Each day for each bloodline and for every year the family rules."

Rebecca sat her glass down on the table and ran her fingers through her thick locks. "But if the Soul Wanderers are going to use Trevor to attempt The Reckoning, then Trevor will be helpless. Tomorrow night is Halloween. I doubt they are just going to keep him until May."

"But," their grandmother began, lifting her dress and removing a flask from the garter around her leg and taking a swig from the aged bourbon. "We are the ruling bloodline; we cannot interfere with anything they do –"

"But if we don't, they will give flesh to a being who craves worship and blood –" Benjamin protested, but Virginia shook her head.

"And we, along with the other witches who do not serve that goal, will deal with it then."

"But, the only ones who can stop Him are the Blackmoores. They were the first to bow to him; it was from their blood that he first drank, and their heart that he first consumed and then began to crave more," Rebecca said. Benjamin nodded furiously in agreement.

"But you cannot interfere."

"Not with them..." Benjamin said. They both looked at him and saw that he was deep in thought, devising a scheme.

"What are you thinking?" Rebecca asked her brother.

"We end the Binding. We give Trevor back his power." He grinned, and Rebecca turned to her grandmother.

"Is that even possible?" she asked.

"There might be a way...." Virginia took another swig of her flask. "Tomorrow night, at sunset, when the doors between the worlds become as passable as a beaded curtain in one of those hippie communes, we may be able to break the Binding."

Benjamin and Rebecca's faces lit up, and eager grins spread across their lips.

"What do we have to do?" Benjamin asked his grandmother.

Virginia put her flask back under her dress and stood. He offered to help her up, but she brushed him off with her hand. "Give me some time. I do not even know for certain if we can. As I said, this never has really happened in all these centuries. In the end it may not work, or we could pay a consequence for trying to do so."

"I don't care," Benjamin said.

His grandmother smiled at him warmly. "Are you certain this is something you want to risk?"

He nodded. "As long as he's safe, I'll pay any price."

"My sweet boy, you finally love with all your heart and do not run from it, and yet it is for one who does not feel the same."

Benjamin's eyes filled with more tears, and Virginia began to shake her head and make her way back out of the drawing room into the long, expansive front hall. "Ain't love grand...?"

Yeah, he thought, his heart crestfallen, *yeah, it is.*

Chapter: Twenty-Six

MABEL SAT IN HER DINING room, sipping coffee from a white porcelain tea cup painted with delicate pink roses. She missed the sunlight and was sick of this darkness. She was grateful to be wealthy, as the need to keep the lights on constantly was surely going to result in a very high electric bill. She let her graying blonde hair hang freely down her back, instead of putting it up behind her head as she so often wore it. Her beautifully thin and aged face was cast in worry and fear for her great-nephew.

"Where could he be?" she asked aloud—perhaps to the silence of her old home, or to the spirit who inhabited it. But she hadn't heard or seen Michael in days, not since he had done what he had to Mary-Margaret, who was now also missing. Mabel had waited to speak with her the night before, but after her shower Mary had never come downstairs, and she was gone by the time Mabel had woken up.

The air was thick with an otherworldly coldness, a disturbance, and a sense of something moving invisible throughout the world. The veil between the realm of the living and the realm of the spirits was thinning, and the disembodied dead were making their way through the city. She could feel them and sometimes hear them when her windows were open. Some were angry and muttering words of vengeance; others were mournful, heartbroken souls crying out for lost loves, families that were still alive; and others searching for something left behind.

The night before, while waiting for Mary-Margaret to emerge from her room and tell her all of what she had been shown, Mabel nearly screamed out in terror as she saw a figure pass by the large window that faced her front yard. It was a tall, lanky female with a dirty dress of white lace.

Her eyes were the usual black, cool pools, and her translucent white flesh was thin and rotting, exposing parts of her jaw and cheekbone. Her long, frail hands and fingers were almost completely devoid of flesh, and as she glided through the yard she tapped her bone-fingers together, making a hollow *knock* over and over again in steady rhythm.

As used to the dead as Mabel was, she was still often terrified by them. Knowing them and conversing with them never negated their ability to summon paralyzing fear in her. In truth, Michael Donovan was the only spirit who, due to a lifetime of knowing him, could not scare her.

She was dressed in a rich plum satin gown with medium-thin sleeves, and delicate beadwork of purple agate that lined the trim of the breasts and waist.

She stuck her cigarette into her mother's black cigarette holder and struck a match from the box next to her on the table. She felt her heart sink as she took in the vision of an eight-year-old Trevor Blackmoore running to the Christmas tree that always stood in front of the bay windows of the dining room, eager to play Santa and hand out the gifts to everyone else, happy to see everyone else's faces light up at the piles of brightly-wrapped packages and gift bags that he brought them.

She shook the memory and resolved herself to finding him. She wanted answers, and if she couldn't speak to Mary, then she would do what she could. She was tired of waiting, and she was tired of the silence that now filled the hallways and rooms of her great home.

"Michael!" she called out, her voice booming throughout the house. "Michael Donovan, I'm not asking, I'm demanding!" She started to rap her nails on the tabletop, staring out through the pocket doors which were pushed back into their slots in the walls, seeing the front parlor lit with the Tiffany lamps which cast shadows in corners, and from the satin sofas and armchairs. The great fireplace that faced her was burning brightly, and the glow of the flames were dancing on the floorboards.

"Michael!" she called again, listening to the silence for a few moments, feeling the frustration with the spirit begin to build and preparing to give up, when the lamps began to flicker before blinking out entirely, leaving only the glow of the fireplace to light the front room.

She watched as he emerged from the darkness of the music room around the corner, his skin reflecting the light just as his black eyes did. His handsome face looked somber and his form flickering, just as the flames in the hearth were flickering.

'*I do not know where he is...*' Michael declared, breaking the silence that existed between them.

"But you know what is happening? They're attempting to bring him back, aren't they? And they're going to use Trevor to do it." Michael dropped his gaze from her. "That's it, isn't it?"

'*He will not be the only one....*'

She thought for a moment, and Mary-Margaret's face flashed across her mind. "You think they will try to use her as well? That's why you showed her whatever it is that you showed her, isn't it?"

The spirit gave a slow, confirming nod.

"What did you show her, Michael?"

'*I showed her what happened to me....*'

"What happened to you...?"

He nodded again. '*Yes, I was a part of the sacrifice; I was the bait to lure your mother to try to bring about the rise of the Dark God....*'

"She never told me this." Mabel was confused. She had never known why Michael was in the house, why he haunted the rooms, other than that he had lived in it before the Blackmoores moved in. Her mother had never told her that she was tied to Michael, that she had known him in life—or why, though completely aware of each other, Mabel had never seen her mother interact with Michael, or Michael with her.

'*Too much pain and bitterness...*' he responded.

"What do you mean? How are you and my mother connected to all of this?" He began to fade from her, his form melting back into the shadows from which he had emerged. The lamps flickered on once again, returning light to the front room of the house.

"Michael!" she called again, three more times, but it was no use. She knew that he had slipped back into the ether, returning to whatever in-between world of the invisible where he dwelled.

HE STARTED WAKING UP again, his head throbbing as he began to take in the sounds around him. Noises taking place in other parts of this house. He could feel that the drugs had finally worn off completely, having coursed through his system. He really had to piss.

Trevor opened his eyes and saw a series of white seven-day candles burning in their glasses and stacked on a stool a few feet away from him. He stared at those flames and tried to connect with them, to focus on them and summon his witchcraft, but there was nothing. That tingling wave of heat did not rise, and the more he tried, the more the sweat began to seep from his pores.

"What are you doing?" the young woman with the accent asked him, catching him off-guard. She was dressed in a knee-length black dress with three-quarter sleeves, and a pair of black open-toed stilettos on her feet.

"Nothing," he replied through exasperated breath.

"Don't try any tricks. That circle you're in ensures that you can't do anything."

He had figured as much but had to be certain, and having her now confirm it, he felt an immense wave of defeat and hopelessness wash over him. "I have to pee," he said to her. The young woman smirked and walked over to him, her steps exaggerated and arrogant.

She knelt down and let her eyes meet with his, and then she gave a brief and condescending chuckle.

"Then piss yourself!" She stood up straight again and walked behind him, around the perimeter of the circle before disappearing into another part of the house, her heels echoing off the walls as they clicked on the hardwood.

"What am I going to do?" he asked, feeling the despair begin to overpower him. He thought of Braxton's near-black eyes and his beautiful face. His smile and the one desire to see him and kiss him once again, and realized that he may never.

The tears came and he struggled hard to get free from the chains, but it was impossible. There was no moving, and his bladder felt as if it were being squeezed. He hadn't bathed and he could smell the stink of his skin from the sweat that soaked through the hospital gown. He pissed himself without meaning to; it was warm and was soaked up by the cotton of his underwear.

It didn't matter to him now. They were probably going to get away with killing him. There was no escape, and unless by some divine miracle—some holy intervention—he wasn't going to see the sun or the faces of those he loved ever again. There wasn't going to be any goodbye, any chance to touch that face or kiss those lips or smell that skin ever again.

This was it. This was his fate. He had been bested, and the darkness had won. All he could do now was sit in his filth and wait.

"Braxton, I'm sorry...."

"ALL RIGHT, THANKS FOR understanding, Joshua." Braxton hung up his phone and looked at J.T. "He said not to worry. We can postpone the show." Braxton was dressed in a ratted and worn-through black Guns N Roses tee featuring the cover for the album *Appetite for Destruction*. It had belonged to an ex of Kathryn's back in the '80s when she was living in L.A., and she told him that he could keep it. She no longer needed to hold on-to it.

J.T. let out a sigh of relief. He sat in the sofa next to Cheri, dressed in the same clothes as the night before. "Oh, thank God! I seriously thought he was going to say we were in violation of our contract or something."

"No. He was cool about it. He said he'll get the show rescheduled, maybe around the New Year. He said just to focus on recovering. I can't do much with a fractured arm anyways." They were all gathered in the front parlor of Mabel's house, waiting on Mary-Margaret to arrive.

"Do we have any idea where she is?" Francesca asked, draped in a knee-length light gray cashmere cardigan and dark blue denim jeans, her cherry-red hair hanging wildly down her back and over her breasts.

She took a sip of espresso and looked at her elderly cousin, who was sitting in the red satin armchair in front of the long narrow window next to the left side of the fireplace mantle.

"No. She never came downstairs last night. I figured she was still recovering from her... journey. She slipped out before I got up this morning. I don't know where she is, and she hasn't answered her phone."

J.T. shook his head and stood up, taking leave of his place next to Cheri on the sofa. He walked over to the painting of the crude stone cottage with its thatched roof. "Kilcommon..." he read the gold inscription that was fixed to the frame aloud.

"Yes, that is where the family established itself after we left the Moor. The cottage is still on the grounds on the edge of Broadhaven Bay, though after we acquired great wealth in the mid-nineteenth century, we purchased surrounding lands and built a great limestone mansion, which we named Blackmoore Hall. There's a painting of it above the upright piano against the wall down the corridor."

He glanced around the banister of the staircase and saw the large oil painting spotlighted by a tiny gallery light fixed into the wall above it. He made his way over to it, inspecting it.

Blackmoore Hall stood three stories over a visible sunken basement. Four columns—two on each side of the large front entry—stood proud atop a mild incline of steps centered on a single-bay breakfront. Above this portico was a large Venetian window. There were seven chimney pipes—fourteen in total—on each wing of the mansion, and J.T. could be certain that one could get lost for days in such a great home.

"And who lives there now?"

"Mary-Margaret and her sister Natalie were born and raised in Blackmoore Hall, and their younger brother and father—as well as a few cousins—still reside in the manor," Kathryn responded. She was dressed in a forest-green Athletic-style sweatshirt made of chenille, and jeans the same blue as Francesca's.

"More cousins?" Braxton asked. "I don't remember more cousins at the funeral."

Kathryn nodded. "That's because they're so superstitious and religious over there and, like Mary-Margaret in the beginning, run from their witchcraft. They believe that if they stay away from anything involving our family or the shadows that fall on us, they will be saved from the Dark God of the Wood. The only reason Seamus was at the funeral was because he and his brother Malachey had been close to their older cousin growing up."

"Oh, does Trevor know about these other cousins?" Saying his name seemed to strike Braxton hard in the gut and force all of the breath out of him. He hadn't thought about it before actually saying his name, and now he was wishing that he hadn't.

"No," Kathryn said, her voice falling and her eyes hanging low. "No I never told him because he never met them... and now I'm afraid he'll never get to know." She sniffled and wiped her eyes quickly with her fingers.

Cheri reached her hand out and put it over Kathryn's. She looked into Cheri's brown eyes and smiled gently, opening her hand to hers and giving it a squeeze. "We'll find him."

"I know." She gave a quick and tight squeeze to her son's childhood friend. "I know we will." Kathryn thought she looked elegant in the plum cashmere off-the-shoulder sweater-dress that she had loaned her along with a pair of black tights.

"I just wish we knew where Mary-Margaret was, or that she would get back here. Especially if she knows what's going on!"

Braxton hit the arm of the sofa hard with his open hand. "I can't stand this much longer!"

"Do we have any idea where she could have gone?" Cheri asked, looking to Mabel.

The old woman sighed and shook her head. "Truth be told, Mary has been very distant since she got here. I know she was seeing someone –"

"We met her," Cheri interjected.

"That's right," Braxton added. "Rebecca something...."

"Wait, she's dating a woman?" Francesca asked. "How very pot calling the kettle black."

Kathryn said nothing.

"Yeah, she apologized for her behavior, though," Braxton replied.

"Well, that doesn't matter now. We have no way of finding this woman and I highly doubt, with everything that Mary has just gone through, that she's with her," Mabel stated. "I'm sure she is alone."

"So she really went through this channeling or whatever with the Michael kid who haunts this house?" J.T. asked. His eyes expressed unease as he looked around the room.

Mabel nodded. "She was out for a week; I found her on the floor right in there." Her eyes moved to the right, directing them to look through the open pocket door of the music room. "She was on the floor, out cold. I tried waking her, but she would not move. As soon as I touched her I could feel that she was someplace else. She was accessing Michael's memories."

"And we have no idea what he showed her?" Kathryn asked.

Mabel shook her head. "No. He has never shown me his life. I have asked him, but he will not tell me."

Kathryn stood and walked into the music room, going to the bar in the corner in front of the back window next to the servant's door, and poured herself a scotch. "Spirits speak in riddles more than they speak in plain truth."

"And there's no way to make him tell us?" J.T. asked.

"Oh, there are ways," Kathryn responded, pouring more glasses for all of them. "But it would violate a spirit who has been a part of our lives for so long, and who has done nothing but watch out for us and try to guide us. To force him to speak would fracture that relationship."

She began bringing the glasses to everyone. "And it would be the worst way to repay him for that loyalty."

"Where is he now?" Braxton asked, swallowing the stiff amber drink. "Queen Mab?"

She looked at him and shrugged. "He's somewhere in the ether. He is still here; he cannot leave, but he is between worlds. Somewhere in the shadows. I do not know where that is or what that looks like, but he is always here."

J.T.'s body went rigid and he turned his head slowly to the door, looking out of the window into that dark daytime world. "It seems like someone just walked across the porch...."

Mabel stood, her satin dress scrapping across the floor as she looked out of the picture window behind Kathryn and Cheri. "That's because someone did. The veil between the worlds continues to thin. Spirits are everywhere, roaming, making their way through the living realm." J.T. looked at her. "People are almost always so caught up in their day to day lives that they simply never notice it. But it's always like this this time of year. You have just had too many distractions in your life to pay attention."

"This just keeps getting more unsettling and even scarier the further we go down this rabbit hole," he added.

"Oh, my dear boy," Mabel said to him with a compassionate gaze. "We're not even at the end of the rabbit hole, and there are more blood-curdling things to come. I can promise you that."

J.T. tried to shake the fear away and made his way back to the sofa next to Cheri, taking her hand and squeezing it tightly.

"Don't worry," Cheri said to him. "I'll protect you."

"But in the end we may not survive any of this," he responded.

Braxton shook his head and ran his hands through his hair, pulling his bangs away from his face. "We will, and we will find Trevor.

"I will rip this entire city apart, and when I find these bastards, they will wish they had died quickly, because I'm going to make it hurt. I'm going to give them a pain that they could have never imagined!"

"You don't want to kill them," Francesca said with a grin. "You want to make them suffer."

He nodded. "A fucking suffering they can't even begin to comprehend."

J.T.'s eyes grew wide and his mouth fell open in a slight gasp. He had never seen this kind of rage in his friend before. Not in all their years together had he seen such fire burn in his onyx eyes. Cheri had seen, though. She remembered that fierce rage from the times that she had talked shit to him when they were growing up, and she had seen it when he and Trevor had saved her from Tom Preston and his death-punch. She knew it, and she knew the damage that he could do.

She had seen Trevor's witchcraft the day the world had gone dark, and she knew that if Trevor had been capable of all of that when scared for his friend's safety, she could only scarcely begin to imagine the kind of power their witchcraft could have when they were angry.

Good, she thought to herself. *Let these bastards find out. I hope I get to hear them beg for their fucking lives.*

MARY-MARGARET LOOKED at her watch; it was just after two. She had spent the entire morning at Tony's, replaying everything that Michael had shown her over and over again. It was the house. It had been a vortex.

The city had been formed on vortexes by the Dianacas.

They had built it for that purpose, and that purpose was to bring flesh to the Dark God. Queen Mab's home was on one of these vortexes. Marsilio had killed Michael Donovan to help open this vortex. But there had been a sacrifice before that. It had been Carter Mayland—Trevor's great uncle, the older brother that Kathryn's father, Trevor Mayland, had never known.

But there was something else, something that dawned on her as she finally turned up Fifteenth Street, passing the darkened front yards of those old Victorians, lined with ominous oak trees pierced only by the faint yellowish glow of porch lights and lamps behind windows.

There were going to be three sacrifices.

"Shit!" She stopped as she began to piece the puzzle together.

"Carter Mayland had been the first sacrifice to bring about the blood moon. Michael had been the sacrifice to saturate the earth to bring forth the Dark God, and he was chosen as bait for Fiona Blackmoore. She was intended to be the third sacrifice, the offering to the Dark God to devour her heart and drink it down with her blood!"

She felt the hairs on her arms stand on end, and she folded them tightly across her chest, desperate to make it back to the house and tell Queen Mab everything that she had figured out.

The neighborhood was quiet, save for her footsteps, and yet she could feel a thickness all around, as if she were in the middle of a crowded department store. From the corner of her eyes she glimpsed figures moving out of synch with the rest of the world.

She knew they were all spirits making their way through the living plane and taking advantage of the thinning veil.

As a child they had carved turnips, as was tradition, and lined them all along the front steps and between the giant pillars and in all of the windows of Blackmoore Hall, to ward off all of the ghosts that roamed the 12,500 acres of land. She crossed herself and wished now that she had one of those Jack o' Lanterns to light her way and keep her safe until she made it inside.

She was almost to the top of the steep hill when she suddenly heard a rustling sound behind her. She stopped, her heart pounding in her chest, her knees trying to buckle—to force her to the ground.

"Shit...." She turned around slowly and breathed a quick sigh of relief as she saw nothing but the dark hill and Mill Avenue below. "Thank Go–"

A hand took firm hold of her left arm from behind, and another hand moved over her mouth. She tried to kick and break free just as another figure—draped in flowing black, with a large pointed conical hood with a covered face, with the exception of two holes for the eyes—stepped out quickly from around one of those oaks and took hold of her waist.

"Sleep," the figure who held her from behind said to her. It was a female voice. A voice with an accent. A voice that she was sure she recognized.

Before she could figure it out, before she could piece the puzzle together or perhaps devise a way to break free from their grasp, a great emptiness washed over her and then there was nothing, just the unconscious slumber void of dreams as they quickly carried her body off into the black Escalade that was parked across the street.

Chapter: Twenty-Seven

THEY HAD SAT THERE, waiting impatiently for Mary-Margaret to return, as the clock on the wall continued to chime. The passing of the hours could be heard by the constant ticking of the hands. They had tried to keep themselves busy. They read books and the paper and spoke of memories of Trevor, trying to keep the hope of his well-being alive by recalling those memories and trying not to allow themselves to think the worst. But now it was once again night—though one would never know it anymore, given that the world was cast in forever darkness.

Braxton looked at the hour; it was almost seven. "This is ridiculous. I'm going to go find her," he said suddenly. He grabbed his coat, the Dolce & Gabbana that Trevor had purchased for him weeks ago, slipping his arm into the sleeve frantically. He wanted to rip off the sling. He was told he had to keep it on for three weeks, and then come back in for a checkup, but it was getting to the point that it didn't matter to him anymore. He was sure he could just deal with the pain.

He had just neared the front door, about to turn the ornate brass knob, when Cheri spoke up. "I'm coming with you." She stood and walked over to him, throwing her head to the side to toss back her chocolate hair.

"Me too," Francesca added. "You guys stay here in case we miss her, and you can fill her in." Kathryn, Mabel, and J.T. nodded.

"Let's go," Braxton commanded as he opened the door. The crisp night air greeted them along with the sickly sweet perfume of rotting apples and spice from the chimneys from the houses around them.

They could feel the spirits that surrounded them, moving in the road and on the sidewalks, passing between houses and their windows. Even Cheri, who had no such abilities, had never forgotten the feeling of Jonathan Marker masquerading as Christian in her home that Christmas before. That same familiarity, that same unnatural sensation of being in the company of something that could not immediately be seen, lingered all around them.

"We don't even know which way to go," Francesca said, pulling her cardigan tight around her and holding it in place with her folded arms.

They stood on the sidewalk, looking each direction. Something in Braxton told him to head left down Fifteenth Street and make their way towards Knox Avenue.

"C'mon." He cocked his head and began to walk at a quick pace, the two women tailing behind him.

"Do you think she went into Fairhaven?" Cheri asked. They were all listening to the night, keeping their ears open to the darkness. They could hear the waves of the bay in the distance, see the boats glisten along the water, their lights dancing on the sea, and then there were mournful and almost hushed cries—cries they knew belonged to the dead.

"I don't know. I just feel something-something pulling me in this direction," Braxton answered.

"I feel it as well," Francesca said. "This is definitely her route. I can feel the lingering of her energy. It's in the air still, though it's fading. If we're quick, we can hopefully get to her before it dissipates completely."

They reached the corner of the block, standing juxtaposed to Knox Avenue. Across the street Dianaca Castle loomed, eerie and silent, save for the lights that shone through the English-lattice panes of glass. The empty lot next to it on the left had once belonged to the Blackmoores before it was brought down in flames after Michael Donovan's murder and Kathryn's home three houses up from them on the same side of the street.

"Let's cross," Braxton said.

They followed him to the other side of the road, making their way around the corner to continue down the hill on Fifteenth towards Mill Avenue, when Braxton suddenly came to a halt between two large oaks.

"What is it?" Cheri asked. "Why are we stopping?"

"She was here. Recently here," Francesca answered.

"It's been a few hours now, I'm sure, but her presence is stronger than where it was when we left the house," Braxton added. He bent his knees and crouched down to the concrete, closing his eyes and summoning his witchcraft. He placed his open palm to the sidewalk and felt a sudden jolt of kinetic energy move out invisible through his hands and into the ground.

Then, as if in a circle, it looped back into him and rushed through his arm and up his shoulders and neck, moving into his brain.

The visions rushed him fast and fierce.

He saw Mary-Margaret on the sidewalk, making her way up to the top of the hill, on her way back to the manor; he saw her stop and turn, and then suddenly quick hands took hold of her and covered her mouth.

He saw the terrifying and phantom-like black figure come at her in flowing fabrics, and a face covered and a head crowned with a conical point. It was wearing the same thing as the figures dancing in the vision they had had after smoking the witch's pot.

He saw her try to struggle and then fall limp, and finally he watched as she was dragged away quickly and quietly across the street and into a vehicle.

"FUCK!" He stood up quickly.

"What is it? What did you see?" Francesca asked.

"They took her! They fucking took her!" He kicked at the stone wall that lined the hillside of Dianaca Castle and ripped the sling off of his arm and threw it to the ground. "They fucking got her too!"

"What do we do? How are we going to find them now?" Cheri asked.

"I don't know...." Francesca was shaking her head. She wanted to stand there and cry. She wanted to do nothing but grieve for everything and everyone, but she knew that she could not.

They were Blackmoores, and Blackmoores had no time to give up in the middle of a crisis. Blackmoores fought back, and they fought hard. It was how they survived. They were a clan built on that strength and that need to carry on and thrive.

"Queen Mab will know what to do, I'm sure. C'mon." She took hold of Braxton's shoulder. "Let's get back to the house and tell them what happened."

The three of them turned around and made their way back quickly to the house, running down the street, deserted of all other living things but teeming with the long-ago dead. Time was running out, and they all knew it.

They had until the following night to get Trevor and Mary-Margaret back safely, otherwise everything would be lost and this world would be made into a hell on earth where the Dark God of the Moor, the bloodthirsty deity—along with those witches who had served him faithfully and turned their backs on all other life-giving and balance-keeping gods and goddesses—would rule, and that was not an option.

"GOD, I HOPE THEY FIND her..." Kathryn said, pacing back and forth in the dining room, wringing her hands together as J.T. and Mabel sat at the grand table, watching her with an equal amount of anxiety.

"I fear the worst," Mabel said, dealing her tarot cards over and over again and getting nothing. "I keep casting dead cards. Whoever or whatever has him has done something to make it so I cannot get any sense of him," she said, lighting her fourth cigarette and handing one to Kathryn, and offering one to J.T., who finally accepted and lit up, smoking it quickly and impatiently.

"As do I," Kathryn added. "I'm at my wits' end. My little boy is out there and I feel so fucking helpless!" She took off her diamond tennis bracelet and threw it hard to the floor, its glittering fragments scattering everywhere. The front door opened, creaking as it moved across the floor. The three of them came in, looking saddened and exhausted.

"What happened?" J.T. asked, standing quickly at the sight of their hopeless faces.

"They took her. They took her right off the sidewalk. She was on her way back home. It would have been a few hours ago. I saw everything," Braxton said.

"What did you see?" Kathryn asked.

He walked into the front room, grabbing a pad of paper and a pen off the bureau, and returned to the dining table. He began to sketch the robed figure he had seen in his vision. They stared at him silently, and after he finished he lifted the paper for them all to see, and Mabel and Kathryn gave a gasp.

"Do you recognize them?" Francesca asked her cousins.

"Those are the ritual robes of the Soul Wanderers. They do mean to sacrifice them and complete The Reckoning," Mabel said.

"No, that's not fucking happening!" Braxton said defiantly.

"You're right. It won't," Kathryn added, holding her hand to her hip. "Enough screwing around; Braxton, go back to the house and get the bag of Trevor's things from the hospital. Now!"

Braxton looked at her and nodded.

"My keys are in my purse."

"I've got my copy with me," he responded, pulling his keys from his pocket and holding them to her face.

"Good. Go now! We don't have a moment more to waste!" Braxton took off, racing down the hall and out the back door, moving up the walk and through the ancient wood swinging gate, running as fast as he could down the alley and back to the sprawling federal at the end of the block.

He opened the gate to the back courtyard, passing the carriage house and opening the back door into the manor.

The house was as silent as the grave, and as he moved through it, met with the faces of those dead Blackmoores and Maylands, and the sounds of the floorboards crying out beneath his steps, he located the bag sitting next the staircase in the foyer.

The glimpse of Trevor's bloodied shirt caught him instantly and his knees buckled and brought him to the floor, he began to cry out in great heavy sobs. He knew this was pointless; it wasn't benefiting anything, and the longer he stayed on this floor, gasping for air and choking hard on his never-ending tears, would only delay finding Trevor.

"Oh, God." He sniffled and wiped the tears from his face, sweating now from his crying and gripping the banister to bring himself back up to his feet. Braxton took hold of the bag and turned, preparing to make his way down the hall and to the back door, when suddenly that young man with the black eyes and handsome face and chestnut hair stood before him. Radiating what seemed to be a soft bluish glow as he stood in the hall between him and the door.

Braxton had only seen these spirits in his visions. He had never seen them take corporeal form as Trevor saw them, but now here this spirit was: looking at him and forcing Braxton to look at him, forcing Braxton to acknowledge that he saw him, that he was bearing witness to his existence.

"Who are you?" Braxton asked, trying not to show the fear that he was feeling inside. The boy turned his head towards the wall with all of those daguerreotypes and lifted his finger to a portrait hanging there. The same face as the ghost that stood before him stared back in silver resin.

"You're him?"

The spirit nodded.

'*Carter Mayland...*' the spirit finally answered.

"You're—you're Kathryn's uncle, the one who died in this house before her father Trevor was born." The spirit nodded. "Jonathan Marker killed you."

'*Sacrificed...*' the boy answered back. '*Killed in the name of the Dark God, to bring him back....*'

Braxton's heart was pounding, and his body shook all over. "You have been trying to warn Trevor, haven't you? You knew they would try The Reckoning again...."

The ghost nodded. '*I have....*'

"What do we do?" he asked, his voice going up a decibel at the mere idea of getting some sort of help from the ghost.

'*They must sacrifice three....*'

"Three?"

The ghost nodded again. '*One to make the moon run with blood, another to feed the earth to open the door for Him to come forth, and a third to feed Him....*'

Braxton gripped tightly to the hospital bag with Trevor's belongings.

"Trevor and Mary-Margaret."

'*Save them. Save them both. Protect my family as I failed to do....*' The spirit slowly began to fade. '*Protect them, save them, do what I could not do for Fiona....*'

The ghost who in life had been Carter Mayland faded from the hall right before Braxton's eyes, as if he had never been there, leaving Braxton alone once again in the immense old house with nothing to bear witness other than those dead faces and the shadows that covered every room.

BRAXTON MADE IT BACK to the house, practically slamming the door into the wall as he made his way through the hall to the front of the house. They were all still sitting in the dining room, standing quickly as soon as they saw him.

"What happened?" Kathryn asked. "You look like you've seen a ghost!"

Braxton was panting, trying to catch his breath, and it wasn't until he was still that he realized how shaken he was by the visitation. "You could say that," he said between quickened breaths. "Carter Mayland came to me."

"Carter Mayland?" Mabel asked.

He nodded. "Yeah. He's been appearing to Trevor off and on since August. Right before we moved. He told me that he was used as a part of the sacrifice for The Reckoning back when he was alive, that he couldn't stop it or help Fiona."

Kathryn turned to look at her aunt. "Did you know any of this?"

Mabel shook her head. "No. My mother never told me that she even knew Carter Mayland. She never mentioned any involvement with him or Michael Donovan."

"Well, she was, and it definitely went down. He said that there has to be a sacrifice of three, and we know that they have Trevor and Mary-Margaret now."

Braxton sat the plastic bag containing those bloody clothes on the tabletop. "He confirmed it takes one to make the moon run with blood, the second to feed the ground, and a third to feed the Dark God once he rises."

"Oh, God..." Cheri let out with a gasp.

"Whatever we're going to do to find them, we need to do it now!" Braxton concluded.

Kathryn walked over to him and placed her hand warmly on Braxton's shoulder. "And we will, right now."

She looked over to Mabel and Francesca, who both stood and walked out of the dining room. Mabel disappeared through the kitchen and back down the hall, and Kathryn, Braxton, Cheri, and J.T. followed Francesca into the front room, switching off all the lights one by one, with the exception of a brass floor lamp with a linen shade that stood next to the great fireplace in the parlor.

"What are we going to do?" J.T. asked. He was visibly wary of whatever it was that was going to take place.

"We're going to call the Hunt to find him..." Mabel said from behind, walking back into the parlor to join them. In her hand was a bushel of dried stems with a cluster of purple petals.

"The Hunt?" Cheri asked.

"That's right," Mabel answered back. Francesca was already stacking fresh logs into the hearth, a bed of newspaper between them and underneath. She struck a match and began lighting the various pieces of newsprint and stood, proceeding to switch off the final lamp.

The flames were dim, and they were all nearly hidden by darkness. Kathryn stood in front of the slowly growing flames and was as still as a statue, then with a deep breath she blew the air out of her mouth in the direction of those flames. They instantly ignited, a great burst of fire that quickly consumed the logs and illuminated the front room at once, the light now dancing reflectively in their eyes.

Mabel came forward with those dried flowers and tossed them into the flames, their smoke and perfume filling the room and traveling up through the chimney.

"By wolfsbane I lure you here, hounds of Hecate, Queen of Night. Bring your beasts to us to collect our prey, to chase them down and trap them in their cave...."

Mabel bent down and reached into the hospital bag, removing the shirt that Trevor had been wearing the night of the attack. It was torn along where the glass had entered into his side, and the mess of blood was now a dried red-brown.

She tossed it quickly onto the flames. "Infernal hounds of the Hunt, take his scent and track him down, lead the chase and guide our way, bring us to our intended prey!" They all stood there and watched it burn; they were silent as those flames consumed the bloodied shirt quickly, carrying the smoke and ash up through the shaft and out into the night sky.

"What now?" J.T. asked.

Kathryn turned to him, her arms folded across her chest. "You'll see."

The night broke out with howls. Howling from every dog on South Hill, it seemed. It became more and more numerous and louder, as the call of the canines continued to summon others.

Cheri, J.T., and even Braxton were held in eerie suspense as the gooseflesh began to spread across their arms. Then they heard a loud pitter-patter on the steps outside on the porch, followed by barking and scratching at the front door.

"Oh, Jesus!" Cheri let out as they all turned their attention to the front door. Mabel walked over to it and turned the knob, and as soon as she opened it, a great strong Doberman with cropped ears and a blue studded collar came into the house and began circling them around the room and barking loudly as it brushed against them.

"Amazing!" Braxton let out. The Doberman nudged them at their legs, making its way back towards the front door, then stopping, turning around and barking.

"Go!" Mabel commanded. "You must follow it. It will take you to Trevor!" Without missing a beat, they moved quickly out of the parlor and towards the front door, the great dog leading the way. Once outside, they saw even more dogs running down Sixteenth Street towards Knox. German Shepherds, Beagles, Terriers, Huskies, even Chihuahuas; any dog that lived in South Hill seemed to find a way out of their homes and yards and began charging like an army through the neighborhood.

I'm coming, Trev, Braxton said as loud as he could with his thoughts, hoping that he would hear him. *I'm coming to save you; we're gonna save you both!*

TREVOR HAD BEEN ASLEEP. It was all he could do. They weren't feeding him and they were barely giving him water, and now his underwear was soiled in piss and shit. He had tried to hold it after the first time he pissed himself, but his body was cleansing itself of all of the crap that had been put into him while he was in the hospital.

He felt embarrassed and ashamed at the state of himself, and the more the hours passed, the less hope he had that he would get out of this alive. He could not summon his witchcraft, and he was too weak to fight any other way. This circle drawn on the floor saw to that.

He was trapped in this dark old house, which obviously had not been lived in for ages and had holes in the ceiling. Much of the hardwood was rotted, and there were many loose floorboards. The smell of his waste was sickening and he tried his best not to breathe it in.

He was hungry and his throat was parched, and his captors moved about one floor above him. He wasn't certain what they were doing. He could only hear their occasional whispers, and unless they came to give him a sip or two of water from a dirty glass with a straw, he was otherwise constantly left alone to his thoughts.

He gathered enough to know that they were going to use him to somehow raise the Dark God, though he wasn't sure exactly what that entailed. Was he to be a sacrifice, or were they saving him to give to the Dark God himself? He couldn't be certain, and at this point it didn't seem to matter anymore anyways. The chains that held him to the chair were tight and constricted his breathing; in fact, it hurt to breathe. With every breath that he took, the heaving of his chest constricted the chains and caused him pain.

"No hope..." he whispered to himself. "No, hope...." His eyes began to close; he began to fade once again in his exhaustion, when the quiet night suddenly erupted into the howls of dogs. At first it was a few sparse howls, which then began to culminate in numerous howls, followed with barking.

Through the open picture window several feet in front of him, he could see shadowed forms move past the front of the house quickly. It became all the more numerous and the howling and barking all the more frantic.

His captors stopped whatever it was that they were doing and raced downstairs, their feet pounding down the steps as they raced into the room. The two girls looked out that large window and then turned back to him, and then back to the window. "What the fuck is happening?" the girl without the accent asked, her brown eyes wide with anxious uncertainty.

"They fucking found us!" the other woman said to her, looking around frantically.

"What the fuck are we going to do, Victoria?!" The front of the house was surrounded with dogs: dogs that were howling, dogs that were barking, dogs that were now scratching at the front door, clawing and growling and trying to get in.

Finally... Trevor thought to himself, unable to fight the grin that was spreading across his face at the sense of relief that was washing over him like cool water being dumped on his head. *Finally....*

"We need to get out of here!" said the woman with the accent—the one named Victoria—to the other girl. "Go upstairs, Melanie, and gather everything up! Hurry!" Victoria barked. "I'll take care of these two!"

These two? Trevor maneuvered his neck, beginning to look around him. He could see no one in front of him or at his sides, but as he got his neck craned enough over his shoulder he saw from the corner of his eye another body, a female with long red hair lying helpless in a similar circle.

"Mary-Margaret!"

Something hard hit him on the back of the head. There was a flash of white across his eyes and a stinging shock of pain as he was struck one more time, sending him into black.

BRAXTON, KATHRYN, FRANCESCA, Cheri, and J.T. ran
fast, following the neighborhood dogs. They had been led across
Knox Avenue, towards the empty lot that had once been home
to the original Blackmoore house, and here there was a somewhat steep and overgrown trail that led down the hillside towards Mill Avenue. The dogs were ahead of them and behind
them, and moved at their sides and between their feet, barking
loudly as they crashed into branches and overgrown ivy and
loose earth.

They were careful to keep their balance as they raced down
the hill with their hearts pounding in their ears. When they got
halfway down the ridge, between Knox and Mill Avenue, they
stopped to see dozens of dogs gathered in front of a dilapidated
two story Victorian farm house with weathered yellow paint and
white trim. It was set back amongst trees, and several of the windows were broken and the porch was visibly rotted.

"They're here?" Cheri asked.

"I had no idea this place even existed," Kathryn said.

"I've never seen it either," Cheri confirmed. The dogs were
scratching at the front door and pacing the porch and jumping
up against the large front picture window to the left of the entrance, eager to get inside.

"Let's go!" Braxton ordered. They made their way quickly to
the front steps, feeling for a steady place to put their feet and
holding on to the railing, careful not to break the steps. Braxton placed his hand on the door knob and gave it a turn. It was
a thick pine door and would not budge easily, despite the farm-
house's disrepair. "Locked!"

He closed his eyes and summoned that tingling cyclone of
power, and when he opened his eyes again that great familiar
heat rushed out of him and the front door imploded into pieces

of wood and glass, scattering all throughout the front of the house.

The dogs rushed in and began barking and charging through the various rooms of the old house. The five of them walked in carefully, Cheri and J.T. hanging behind the three witches, unsure of what would greet them once inside the ruin.

They took a left and moved immediately into the large double parlor, seeing sparse pieces of furniture draped in sheets, and lamps without shades or bulbs. Cobwebs hung from the pine beams that stretched like great arms across the ceiling and there were holes in the rotted footboards. The air was odorous with a stale and putrid stench, something akin to a cat's little box when it hasn't been cleaned for weeks.

"What the fuck?" Kathryn questioned with a mix of shock and revulsion.

Braxton, who had been standing in front of a great fireplace with recently burned candles on the mantle, turned to see what she was looking at. There in the middle of the room towards the back was an empty chair that had been knocked over.

It was within a circle drawn in chalk, with various words in some other language writ along the ring and a large six-pointed star in the center.

There was a smell, a smell of feces and ammonia which came directly from that circle—and was a fresher, separate smell from what they were met with when they first walked in. There were visible stains on the floor, one of which looked very much like blood.

Beyond this was another circle with those same symbols, and the various hounds were sniffing and pacing them both. "What is this?" Cheri asked, hugging herself tightly as she tried to take in what it was that they were seeing.

"It's a witch's seal. It protects whatever is within the circle..." Kathryn answered back.

"Protects?" J.T. asked, confounded.

"Yes, but that can also mean—intending on how it is used—to protect those outside of the circle from whatever is within the circle. If Trevor and Mary-Margaret were in these circles, which I'm certain they were, it was to protect the people who took them from their power."

"So, like a magical jail cell?" Braxton suggested.

"Exactly," Kathryn said, looking around the room and trying to avoid the dogs running frantically throughout the house.

"There's no one here!" Francesca announced, appearing from around the corner after having come downstairs. "I've checked everywhere. They're gone. They must have gotten out of here just before we arrived. The dogs must have alerted them."

"God fucking damn it!" Braxton yelled. "What the fuck are we going to do?" The house around them began to shake, and dust and bits of ceiling fell around them as the house itself seemed to moan and growl.

"Please don't do that again," J.T. said, looking around the room wearily.

"That wasn't me..." Braxton responded. It happened again, and this time the foundation moved as if struck by an earthquake. The dogs began to cry out and race towards the front door, and more and more pieces of the ceiling, including those beams, began to rip apart and fall around them, crashing through the floors, which had been made weak by decades of termites and saturation from animal urine and droppings.

They moved quickly back out of the house, jumping off the porch and landing in the grass. The dogs quickly ran back into the darkness, returning to their respective homes. As the five of them got back up to their feet and backed away safely from the house, they watched as the old and abandoned Victorian fell apart and came crashing to the earth in a pile of dust and rubble.

They coughed and brushed the bits of debris off of their clothes. "What the hell just happened?" Cheri asked.

Francesca shook her head. "They must have worked a spell on the house to try to kill us."

Braxton and Kathryn had tears in their eyes and he once again fell to the ground, just as he had done in the foyer of Kathryn's home, sobbing uncontrollably and gasping for breath.

"It'll be okay," J.T. said to him, placing his hands on his forearms. "It'll be okay."

"No, don't touch me!" Braxton tore away from him and stumbled to his feet, wiping the tears from his eyes. "We're running out of time!"

The sky was full of stars that glittered, and in those stars Braxton sought some sort of solace, some sort of answer, some sort of assurance that it would all work out. But there was none. There was only the silence of the night, the distant sound of cars, and the occasional cry of bats and owls in the nighttime sky.

He had never noticed the moon since the eclipse had happened. He had never realized, in all of the chaos around them, that at night the moon still shone. It still let out its silvery illumination, and in the hours of night the world was indeed back to normal; it was only in the daytime when that moon remained, forever passing and keeping its place in front of the sun, that mankind seemed to have been abandoned by their omnipotent god.

It was a crescent now, a great pointed thing, like the crown of the goddess Selene herself, and this moon—this realization of its light—gave him a sudden sense of hope, a sudden feeling that not all was lost.

"What are you looking at?" Cheri asked him, walking up slowly from behind.

"The moon." They all looked up and gasped. They had all been as ignorant of it as Braxton had been. Here it was now, its radiant light washing everything in its bluish-white hue, and giving a sense of hope to Braxton, Kathryn, and Francesca.

"The moon has to run with blood. That means that whatever this ritual entails, they will not do anything until the moon reaches its apex in the sky," Braxton said with a weary smile.

"Time is still on our side," Kathryn concluded. "We will stop them. Whatever it takes."

Halloween

Fear not the sound like wind in the trees;
It is only their call that comes on the breeze;
Fear not the shudder that seems to pass:
It is only the tread of their feet on the grass;
Fear not the drip of the bough as you stoop:
It is only the touch of their hands that grope-
For the year's on the turn, and it's All Souls' night,
When the dead can yearn and the dead can smite.
-FROM *All Souls* by Edith Wharton, Stanza II

And now that they rise and walk in the cold,
Let us warm their blood and give youth to the old.
Let them see us and hear us, and say: "Ah, thus
In the prime of the year it went with us!"
Till their lips draw close, and so long unkist,
Forget they are mist that mingles with mist!
For the year's on the turn, and it's All Souls' night,
When the dead can burn and the dead can smite.
-FROM *All Souls* by Edith Wharton, Stanza IV

Chapter: Twenty-Eight

"DAMN IT, SHE'S STILL not answering!" Rebecca slammed her phone down on the black and-gray-granite of the large island in the middle of the professional kitchen of the Tramer Estate, a room filled with white cabinets and butter-cream walls with white crown molding.

There was a large stainless steel gas stove and double ovens next to each other, and the backsplash was golden-and-white mosaic tile beneath a large and discreet hood-range that resembled the mantel of a fireplace. Above her hung three sconce lamps spread out along the length of the island, and the two large six-paned windows looked out on the side garden.

"Still?" Benjamin asked her. She shook her head. He was sitting at the large breakfast table under a wrought-iron chandelier, with bulbs designed to look like flames glowing above his head.

Rebecca turned to face her brother, unable to mask the worry that was all over her face. Her brown hair was pulled back in a ponytail, and she wore a pair of black cotton lounging pants and a black tank top.

"I barely got any sleep last night. I just kept tossing and turning and looking at my phone, hoping for something. But there has been no answer, and now her phone just goes straight to voicemail...."

"Well, it's not even 6:30; maybe she's not awake yet."

She could tell by the look on her younger brother's face that he didn't believe it, even while he was saying it.

Rebecca took a sip from her coffee and sighed. "I think something happened to her. I know it. Just like it did to Trevor."

Benjamin rubbed his eyes and ran his hands through his hair, which hung loose and reached the nape of his neck. He was dressed in black basketball shorts and no shirt, and his eyes were red from lack of sleep.

"Tonight's the night. If they're going to go through with The Reckoning, it'll happen tonight." His voice shook as he said this.

"And we don't even know where this is happening, or how we can help!" Benjamin nodded. "Have you seen Grandma Virgie?" Rebecca asked.

"Not since yesterday." They were both visibly anxious and alone in this great house, feeling disconnected and far away from everything else; they were even more aware of their fears and insecurities.

It was the emptiness of the rooms and the vastness of the mansion, free of distractions in this early morning darkness that made Rebecca and Benjamin feel minuscule and powerless, as if they were once again children feeling shut out of the grown-up world, left to their rooms on the east wing of the manor, while the family kept them out of knowing things that they had believed they were too young to know.

They didn't like this feeling. Benjamin and Rebecca had never been ones to settle on keeping their place, or sit idly by while everything else happened around them, unable to affect or change anything. Their grandmother Virginia had always affectionately accused them of being "wicked little witches" because they were always eavesdropping on conversations, or witnessing her working spells for people that they should not have seen.

Once—though now it was nothing more than a fragment of memory with details neither one of them could recall—they had crept downstairs late at night, hearing faint humming and indiscernible chanting taking place deep in the cellar of the mansion.

They had followed a dim spill of light from the door behind the grand staircase, and as they descended each step, getting closer and closer to the cold stone floor below, they had witnessed their grandmother standing before a table alit with candles, and in the middle of the table was the slowly-decaying head of a man.

His eyes were open and looked dim, completely vacant of any life. The skin was gray and there were white maggots crawling slowly over that flesh. Rebecca had felt sick when she watched one of those maggots fall out of the left nostril and land on her grandmother's hand.

They both remembered watching her pick up two long needles, which she whispered over as she passed them six times into the candle flames. Then quickly she shoved those hot needles into the middle of the eyes and the dead man's closed mouth fell open, and a great wailing erupted from lungs and vocal chords it no longer possessed.

They had both screamed in terror and the last thing they both could remember was their grandmother, dressed in her aged bridal gown, moving to them almost as if she were a great shadow, the queen of phantoms herself, sending them back into dreams.

Benjamin and Rebecca had thought on occasion to bring it up, to ask their grandmother what she had been doing that night, what kind of magic was she working when they had snuck up on her as children, but there was a part of them both that didn't want to know.

They both knew that now that they were adults, Virginia Tramer would most likely tell them the truth about anything they wanted to know, but they weren't certain if this was one of those things. It seemed dark, primitive, treading into an infernal territory that contained the beasts of hell itself.

Witchcraft wasn't always pretty. They had both known this. Some spells required the use of ingredients that would sicken and terrify many, but working with human parts—flesh, bones, appendages—these things were mostly unknown and very rarely ever applied.

Rebecca and Benjamin both knew that whatever it was that their grandmother had been doing, it was extreme and for a very important reason, a reason that they perhaps were better off staying in the dark about.

"I'm tired of waiting!" She dumped the rest of her coffee down the sink and sat the empty blue mug on the counter, rapping her nails against the granite.

"Waiting is all we can do right now. Wherever she is, Grandma Virgie is finding a way for us to help." Benjamin got up from the chair at the table and walked over to the window, looking out at the pitch-black garden and the lights of the city twinkling on the other side of the water.

"And if she can't?" Rebecca asked, turning to face her brother, staring at his handsome and perfectly-chiseled profile.

He continued to look out into the darkness and sighed. "C'mon, let's get the pumpkins and start carving them up. We gotta get them lit and placed at all of the entrances of the house before the veil thins completely." He faced her and offered a smile.

"Yeah," she smiled back. "We also need to get all of the mirrors covered before anything tries to come through." She stretched her arms above her head and yawned. "We already have enough to worry about as it is; the last thing we need is unwanted houseguests."

CHERI SAT ON THE STOOL in her kitchen, smoking her tenth cigarette of the morning and staring at the report of Teri's death, which was front page news of the Bellingham Herald's Christmas Eve edition.

She couldn't believe it: her friend Teri was dead. Someone had murdered her, ripped her to pieces, and she was left with more questions.

"Everyone around me is dying; everyone I know is being taken from me. What's going on; what have I done?" Cheri had no answers, and she was further confounded by the fact that her parents would not be returning home until late into the night.

It didn't seem right that at this time of year, it would become a season of death. Lives so young, lives terribly unlived, were being taken, as if God were harvesting his human garden for the winter's hibernation.

If this was the cost, if this was the price of her redemption, then she didn't want it—not if it meant the loss of so many souls. She sighed, just as the house creaked and the steps of a stranger could be heard behind her.

"Hello?" she called out, her brown eyes searching the kitchen and entryways, attempting to discern the source of the sudden footfalls.

Again it happened.

"Who's there? Motherfucker, you had better answer me!" Her heart was pounding now, slamming in the cavity of her chest, her breath erratic. "Stop it!" The cabinet doors began to fly open, drawers beginning to slam and door hinges beginning to rattle.

"Shit!" Cheri jumped from the stool and fell to the floor, throwing herself between some drawers and the fridge. "Stop it!" she screamed louder, clutching her hands to her ears, attempting to block out the noise, her eyes filling with tears.

'Cheri....' *She looked up to see Christian staring at her. Her voice was dead in her throat as she looked at the sight before her. Christian with his face gray and decaying, withered, bones visible; blood ebbed and membrane caked on falling skin, his sockets empty.*

CHERI SAT UP IN BED with a start. Her heart was racing, and the sweat beaded down her face and made her hair sticky and damp.

"Jesus!" She ran her hand through the sweaty strands and shook them from her fingers, feeling the sticky moisture of her perspiration between her fingers.

She looked next to her and saw that J.T. was no longer in bed. They had slept over at Queen Mab's house after the failed rescue attempt, agreeing that it was safer for all of them if they were under one roof. It was too dangerous to be separated, given what had happened to Mary-Margaret.

There was no telling who the Soul Wanderers intended to be their third sacrifice—and if it was planned to be one of them... well, as long as they were together, they could possibly prevent The Reckoning from even happening.

She and J.T. slept in Magdalene's old room. It was the first door at the top of the stairs, and inside the walls were painted a deep red and were papered with blown-up black-and-white images of Sid Vicious and Johnny Rotten.

There was the face of a young Debbie Harry, her eyes and lips large and seductive. They were everywhere, all of these images, from the floor all the way up to the ceiling: the coolest room of any '80s teen. There was Robert Smith of the Cure, Iggy Pop twisted backwards like a serpent, Siouxsie Sioux with her black lips and eyes and garish hair, the Velvet Underground, U2, Depeche Mode, and the New York Dolls.

It had been amazing to see. How she had gotten images like this blown up so large and made into wallpaper, she had no idea, as she wasn't certain if they had had that kind of technology back in the '80s, though it was obvious they must have, given this room and all of these black-and-white rock stars.

"What time is it?" she asked aloud with a yawn. She reached out for her cell phone on the nightstand to her right and lit up her screen. A selfie of her and Trevor smiled back at her, and immediately she felt as if her heart had dropped quickly into the pit of her stomach, deep down to a place where it could never be recovered.

"8:30!" She threw off the covers and flipped on the lamp that sat on an art deco vanity from the 1930s. The room lit up and illuminated a picture of Stevie Nicks on stage singing in front of a microphone, along with a dried rose and a long black shawl with purple and red embroidered flowers on it. Cheri was almost certain that it was safe to assume both the flower and scarf had come from the songstress personally.

Cheri quickly pulled on the forest green yoga pants that Kathryn had loaned her to sleep in. She threw on one of Trevor's old blue GAP sweatshirts and made her way out of the room and down the stairs, hearing all of their voices inside the dining room.

"Good morning!" Kathryn said to her. She and J.T. were sitting at the table with large heirloom pumpkins of pale orange and dim white in front of them, their tops open and their guts in bowls.

"Morning..." she said, looking around visibly confused. Francesca walked out holding another pumpkin in her hand, dressed in gray sweats and a white crewneck tee. "What is going on here?"

There were pumpkins all over the great oak dining table and on the floor under the bay windows: pumpkins of all sizes, from large to small, waiting to be hollowed out and carved into.

"We've got thirty-seven pumpkins to carve and not much time to do it," J.T. said to her with a grin from the other side of his rather large white gourd.

"Okay... but why?"

"Because, my dear," Kathryn began answering, wiping the orange stringy membrane off of her fingers. "We need to get these lit before evening. Every minute that passes, the veil between the worlds becomes thinner and thinner, and more and more spirits will be coming through. And many of those will be the ghosts of people who were not the most shining example of humanity in life, and in death are now just forces driven with pure evil.

"The Jack o' Lanterns keep them at bay and will protect this home from them trying to get in. But, every entrance needs to have a lantern in it. That's every window and at the doors."

Cheri pinched the top of her nose between her eyes and shook her head. "I need coffee...."

"There's coffee in the kitchen; Queen Mab and Braxton are in there," Francesca told her with a smile as she shoved her knife straight through the crown of the pumpkin.

"Yo!" Braxton yelled out from the kitchen. Cheri smiled and walked in. He was sitting on the kitchen counter next to the sink, in a burgundy v-neck tee and green-and-black checkered boxer-briefs with white piping, shoveling a spoonful of Wheaties into his mouth.

"Good morning, dear," Mabel said to her. She was in a soft cotton nightgown patterned with gardenias, and her long fingers were turning through the pages of a big book that seemed to have been written in hand.

"What is that?" Cheri asked her.

"It's our family's spell book. It's been passed down for generations, since 1340. It was started by Linyeve Blackmoore. All the spells and rituals and recipes are all very European up until the eighteenth century, and then it changes with Sarafeene Blackmoore after her arrival in New Orleans and learning all of that Voodoo, and then there is a shift again when Kathryn took her copy with her to Los Angeles in 1987 and discovered Santeria.

"When she finally returned home she copied everything she had learned into this book, which is the original."

Cheri was fascinated by all of this. Trevor and Braxton were lucky to come from such a rich and woven bloodline. She only knew as far back as her relatives' arrival here in the nineteenth century, after the Hannifins came from Ireland—but before that time, she knew nothing.

This was intricate—intact—held together by a strength and involvement and dedication that ensured the Blackmoores were never without an understanding of their roots and where their power came from. It was the thing that ensured that they would be able to go on fighting and face down any threat that could come for them.

"How did you sleep?" Braxton asked Cheri.

She smiled at him and shook her head. "I was going to ask you the same thing," she said to him.

"Well," Braxton responded, taking another spoonful of his cereal, "I asked you first."

Cheri poured herself a cup of coffee from the pot and added three cubes of sugar and a little cream to what she liked to call 'black gold.' "Um, fine, I guess. Just not the best dreams."

"I know what you mean..." Braxton sighed. "But we just gotta stay focused." He rubbed the crusted sleep that was still in the corners of his lids and brushed his fingers across his naked thigh.

"Yeah." She took a sip of her coffee and looked at him. His beautiful face was visibly broken, those inky eyes red and luminous with what seemed to be a never-ending veil of tears.

She just wanted him to be okay.

She wanted to find Trevor and stop this ritual from taking place, so that they could all get back to their lives and return to some sense of normalcy. As she glimpsed the world through the window above the sink, she also thought about how much she wished to see daylight again, even a thick overcast—just something other than this endless night.

"Braxton, my dear?" Mabel asked, still not looking up from the pages of that great book.

"Yeah?"

"When you're done with your breakfast, could you please go to the hutch at the top of stairs that leads down to the cellar and remove all of the black fabric in there, and get all of the mirrors and glass cabinets covered?"

He nodded. "On it!" he said with his mouth mid-chew.

He hopped down from the counter and put the bowl and spoon in the sink and walked out of the door and into the hall.

"Why are you doing that?" Cheri asked.

"Because...." Mabel finally lifted her head from that book and turned to face her. "When someone dies, you should always cover your mirrors and any other reflective surface with black cloth so that the dead do not get trapped in the glass. And on Samhain—or Halloween—we cover them so that no spirits can use them to come through and make their home with us here."

"Really?" Mabel nodded. "That's crazy!"

"I suppose it is," said Mabel. "And also very dangerous. For witches it can be especially dangerous, as the dead, eager and desperate to make contact with the living, will often come to us in droves, striving to be heard and helped."

"Well," Cheri said, grabbing a knife from the block on the white marble countertop. "I suppose I should get carving."

TREVOR OPENED HIS EYES. Everything was cold and damp and firm. He was lying on his side, and he still couldn't move as he was bound in those same chains from before. He had no idea how long he had been out, but his head throbbed and he could tell that he was lying on stone of some kind.

There was a dim glow; it was barely enough to see by, but it would do. He cocked his head up and saw that there was an alcove in a stone wall, and in that alcove was a candle almost brunt down to the quick, and he gathered quickly that he was in some kind of basement or cellar.

He was cold and he could hear water dripping annoyingly somewhere in a corner, and the floor was nothing but bare stone. He could see the white around him and knew that he was once again in that circle. As he wiggled himself up, he noticed there was another body across from him in a similar circle. It took him a moment, but then he remembered that before he had been struck on the head, he had realized that they also held his cousin captive.

"Mary-Margaret!" he yelled at her. She was lying there, still and unbound in that circle. "Mary-Margaret!" he yelled again at her. "Wake up, it's Trevor! We have to get out of here!" Still nothing. "Come on, get up!"

After a few minutes of trying, he finally gave up and stopped struggling to get off the cold ground. What was the point? He couldn't move, his cousin was out cold, and the circle he was in seemed to prevent him from being able to do anything.

"C'mon, Braxton... please find me...."

Chapter: Twenty-Nine

"FOUND IT!" MABEL EXCLAIMED. She had been in the kitchen going through the book for most of the morning and into the afternoon, and now that it was pushing close to 4:00pm, she finally emerged with a smile on her face.

"What did you find?" Francesca asked, looking up from the screen of her phone.

"There's a note in here from Linyeve Blackmoore about the first Reckoning in 1350. We were right that it must be done when the moon is at its apex in the sky, and it must always be a full or waxing moon, but never waning or new, and the moon must be seen. The light cannot be obstructed because once the moon runs red; the light must shine down on the place where He will rise."

They all looked at her. "The place where He will rise?" Braxton asked.

"Yes."

"So." Kathryn stood and placed her hand on her hip. "The light of the blood moon must shine down clearly on the spot that he will rise up from. We know that this is going to take place in a cemetery—has to be Bayview—and they will have to use the remains of a deceased Soul Wanderer to give him a home. If we can get the jump on them and figure out how to obstruct the moon in the sky tonight, we may have a chance!"

"Uh...." J.T. looked at all of them sheepishly. "Unless you can, like, create a storm, I don't see how you're going to cover the moon."

Francesca smirked. "That's exactly what we're going to do. Don't you know anything about witches?"

"But, I mean, how are you going to do that?" he asked. It was obvious to all of them that he was still trying to wrap his head around everything that was happening. This world, that he had always thought was regulated to fairy tales and stories told around a campfire, was in fact very real and very dangerous.

Kathryn shook her head. "Don't worry about the how. We just need to get ready. The moon is starting to come into view."

TREVOR HEARD A DOOR open somewhere in the distance, and then footfalls on stone steps. The candle was now out and he was no longer certain of the time, but he assumed it was late. The temperature had dropped significantly since he was last conscious, and now he was shivering and the candle was nearly out.

Silently before him figures cloaked in layers of flowing black fabric with covered faces and pointed crowns moved about—emerging, it seemed, from the very shadows themselves, like phantoms made up of black smoke. They said nothing as two of them picked up his cousin off of the ground. Before he could react, before he could try to plea once more for his cousin to wake up, they came down upon him and threw a hood over his face, casting him in complete darkness.

"Let me fucking go!" he demanded, trying to fight them as they worked to lift him off the ground. "Fucking let me go, you fucking pieces of shit!" He was hit hard quite suddenly across his face. "Fucking inbred trash!" he spat back, and again he was struck on the head several more times.

"Stop hitting me, you shit. You fucking pathetic cowards!" They hit him again, but he refused to go down. "Let me go!"

"Shut it!" he heard a voice with an English accent order him. It was a male voice, and it was the last thing he heard before he was struck with a strong blow across the face, knocking him out cold.

BRAXTON STARED AT THE picture of himself and Trevor at their senior prom, standing on top of the piano in the hall. It had been a while since he had looked at it. They looked happy, he and Trevor. Their smiles were filled with a joy and a sense of promise and hope, despite having already faced down Tom Preston, or the fact that he had already killed his father with a power at the time he was unaware that he even had.

Though they had mourned the deaths of Christian Vasquez and Brighton Blackmoore, he and Trevor had been happy and excited for the future and all of the opportunities it would bring to them.

They had been eager to get out of Bellingham, away from the rumors and the superstition, and even the ancient oak-lined streets and the antiquated mansions that sat on them. Seattle was supposed to be their escape, their chance to start anew and build the kind of life that they had wanted to live, free from everything that threated to cast a shadow over them.

Funny, he thought to himself, *now here we are; we've ended up right where we began.* Braxton was dressed in a pair of black jeans and that same Guns N Roses tee as before, with a plain black hoodie zipped up to the sternum. He tapped the floorboards in an old pair of steel-toed black boots that he had left at Kathryn's months ago, when he had temporarily moved in after his father's death.

His black hair was parted at the hairline on the left and slicked back. Around his neck was Trevor's confirmation rosary; its ruby-and-black diamond beads glittered in the light of the Tiffany lamp and danced on the walls.

The great staircase moaned, and Braxton turned and looked up into Kathryn's face. She was descending the stairs in black jeans, her black leather equestrian boots, and a black jersey-knit boat-neck tee, her usual three-tiered pearl necklace hanging delicately around her throat. Her thick auburn mane seemed to shimmer in the light.

"Are you ready?"

Braxton looked back at the picture of he and Trevor holding tightly to each other in front of a backdrop of Picasso's Starry Night; he had Trevor bent backwards in a style the old MGM musicals would have admired.

"Yeah, let's get my boyfriend back."

"Sounds good!"

They turned to see J.T. and Cheri standing there, with Francesca close behind. J.T. had borrowed a pair of Braxton's jeans and a black sweatshirt from the collection that had been left behind. Cheri wore black leggings and a pair of suede booties and a black-and-gray flannel shirt. One of Kathryn's pea coats was draped over her right arm, and her hair was pulled back in a bun.

"Are you sure you want to go with us?" Francesca asked from behind. She looked almost completely identical to Kathryn, except she wore a white tank top under a black hoodie, and her bright cherry-red hair was pulled back and clipped loosely at the crown of her head.

"This is going to be dangerous... and there's no telling what they can do," Kathryn said to Cheri and J.T.

They both shook their heads. "I can't leave Trevor alone in this. He's my best friend; he's already saved my life, and it's my turn to save his," Cheri added.

"Yeah," J.T. began, "I won't feel all right with myself if I let something happen to Trevor, and I may have been able to make a difference had I not stayed behind. I don't want that kind of guilt. Besides...." He reached out and placed his hand on Braxton's shoulder. "I can't let my best friend go into the unknown alone. I think he's had to do enough of that already."

Braxton grinned, but he could not mask the fear he felt inside for their safety. J.T. and Cheri weren't as they were; they had no power, no otherworldly abilities to affect and manipulate the world around them. Who knew what things these Soul Wanderers could do, or what this Dark God could do if he achieved flesh.

No. He couldn't even think of that. He couldn't consider something so awful. They weren't going to let that happen, and Trevor and Mary-Margaret were going to get out of this safe and sound—no matter what.

"All right," they heard Mabel say as she made her way behind them at the top of the stairs that led down to the cellar. "Everything is ready. At eight on the dot, I will perform the spell. The moon will have just reached its apex, which means they will have already reached Bayview, and you'll be able to get to them before they have a chance to escape."

She was spinning her amber beads between her fingers. Her aged face was painted in dark blue mascara and her lips were rouged in the color of dried blood, and her nails were painted the same.

"How long should the spell last?" Kathryn asked her aunt.

"It should last the whole night, as long as they don't realize a spell has been worked against them." They all looked at each other, and each of their faces mirrored the same uneasiness.

Aside from the occasional car that had gone by, the world outside the front door was eerily quiet. Not a single child in costume had attempted to come to their door, or anyone else's.

Unsure if there would be, Mabel still had Cheri and Braxton get a couple of bowls of candy together to be set outside on the porch in case any children did come—but the last time Braxton had checked, the bowls still sat in the same place, completely untouched.

"There's no turning back from here..." Kathryn said, grabbing her black Burberry trench coat with its gleaming gold buttons, the collar popped up and revealing the signature novacheck pattern underneath. "I don't know what's going to happen, and there is a chance some of us—or perhaps even all of us—will die, or that Trevor or Mary-Margaret, or both of them, could be dead. It's a possibility we have to prepare ourselves for.

"If that is the case, God forbid, then we need to focus on switching gears and stopping them from raising the Dark God. If they do, then everything—this world, the people in it—it'll all be gone."

Braxton didn't want to think about the possibility of them failing or finding that they had killed Trevor. Just vaguely entertaining that idea was filling him with a rage he had never quite known before. He would grasp this rage; he would take hold of it and let it fuel him; let it drive him to do what he needed to do. He would find his power—his strength—in that rage, and he would use it to tear them limb from limb.

"Let's go," Braxton said. He embraced Mabel tightly and she kissed him on the cheek.

"May the gods guide you, and may they direct your hand and lend you their power," she whispered to him.

"Thank you," he replied.

They made their way to the front door, opening it and smelling the damp dead leaves and the spice of the fireplaces that burned in the houses and filled the sky with the plumes of their smoke. The streets were crowded with the invisible bodies of the dead.

They moved through them, and though they were only briefly seen by Kathryn, Francesca, and Braxton from the corner of their eyes, they could feel them everywhere. They moved through yards and past windows, and they glimpsed a couple of them skirt away from any house alit with pumpkins.

They descended the steps that led from the front walkway to the sidewalk, and there, parked along the curb in front of the house, was Jared standing in front of Kathryn's black limo.

"Bayview Cemetery," she said to him as they piled into the back of the car. "Don't drop us off at the gate; find a spot near the corner of Lakeway and Woburn, and then park the car further down Woburn."

Jared nodded and closed the door behind her.

"Here we go..." Braxton said. Taking deep breaths and trying to steady himself and praying silently that everything would go as planned, that Queen Mab would be able to bring about the clouds, that Trevor and Mary-Margaret would still be alive, and that they would be able to save them and stop The Reckoning.

At this point nothing was certain, and as the car wound down Knox Avenue, making its way towards Bill McDonald Parkway, he felt everything inside of him twist into knots. The closer they got to the campus of Mariner High School, Braxton couldn't help but remember everything that they had all been through together in vivid detail.

He couldn't lose Trevor. Losing him was not an option, and considering the idea of living in a world without him was just not possible. Trevor was alive. He could feel it. His blood seemed to sing with his name, and Braxton knew that if something had happened to Trevor, if he had been killed, he would know it. He would have felt it as if it were happening to him. He was certain of this. There was nothing else in this world that he was more aware of than Trevor, and everything about Trevor.

They were going to find him and save him, and as soon as he was out of harm's way, Braxton was going to kill them all, one by one, until there weren't any Soul Wanderers left.

The thought of it made him grin.

Chapter: Thirty

REBECCA AND BENJAMIN had spent most of the day and evening in the drawing room, reading books, playing on their phones, checking the news, and doing whatever else they could think of to try to keep themselves busy. They had watched the hours pass by and waited anxiously for their Grandmother Virginia to return to the house.

It was now a quarter-till-eight.

"This is getting ridiculous. We may already be too late. We have to do something," Benjamin said. He stood up quickly from the black leather mid-century club chair and walked over to the bar, dressed in blue jeans and a deep green hoodie with nothing underneath.

"I know, but what are we going to do?" Rebecca asked, her hand resting on her hip. She had straightened her hair and was standing in the corner next to the window, trying to keep her eye on the drive. She hadn't changed out of the clothes she had slept in.

"I don't fucking know!" Benjamin screamed, throwing the bottle of scotch to the ground after he had poured himself and his sister a glass.

"Ben..." Rebecca said with a compassionate sigh. They were both so terribly on edge that it felt as if their skin was crawling. She was still trying to get used to the fact that her brother was in love with someone, and that that someone was Trevor Blackmoore.

She felt awful for him that those feelings would never be reciprocated, but she knew—as everyone eventually comes to know—that love never runs smooth, and more often than not, we fall for those who are always out of reach. It is only in those rare occasions that one gets lucky enough to find someone who returns those affections.

"If you're going to destroy my home, I hope that you plan on at least cleaning it up."

They turned to see Virginia standing in the doorway, a bemused smirk on her face. Her eyes were cool and knowing, like she had a secret she was about to let them in on.

"Well? Did you find a way for us to break the Binding?" Benjamin asked her.

She nodded. "I absolutely did. It will not be easy though, and I don't want you to think that it will be as simple as lighting some candles, burning some herbs, and chanting a spell."

Benjamin shook his head. "Of course not."

Virginia folded her arms and nodded. Her tattered wedding gown looked all the more dingy and faded in the lamplight. "Good. This kind of magic is old and powerful and demands a payment. A payment only you can make."

"I understand," he said to her. "I just want to get this done. I want to save Trevor any way I can." Virginia moved closer to him and placed her hand on his face. She looked on him with such love and devotion, and they all understood that the price he was about to pay could very well do more harm to him than good.

"You have no idea," she said to him. "Both of you." She looked over her grandson's shoulder and stared at Rebecca. "Follow me." And they did, back out into the long front hall, past the ornate benches and potted palms and ferns in the large china vases, and the great mirrors and yards of curtain panels that lined the immense windows.

They walked past the grand white marble staircase with its black iron railing, and turned towards the back door behind it. The door that led to the cellar: that place that had seemed as if it had existed in some seductive and nightmarish vision of witches around a blazing fire, summoning their imps and assorted familiars to do their bidding.

This had been a place that she and Benjamin had both avoided, a door they had both refused to go near, though they would never tell each other. And now here they were, watching their grandmother on her cane unlock the door and make her way down the stone steps in the dark, as if they were entering the very bowels of hell.

MABEL SAT IN THE CIRCLE she had drawn around her with coarse sea salt, her eyes closed. The light from the various candles that sat on her large wood table that stood three feet off of the ground cast large shadows on the stone walls. A stick of witch hazel incense burned on the simple wooden holder, and an ornate gilded fan sat on the top of the altar, along with a jar full of goose feathers.

She summoned her witchcraft, felt it seem to start in her toes, like a dozen tiny cyclones that seemed to grow and rise up through her legs and up through her gut. Finally, it ignited like cool fire throughout her body, causing her skin to break out in gooseflesh. When she opened her eyes, the faces of the various saints that hung on the walls in vivid painted detail and the statues that held post at the left and right of the altar seemed to come to life and even blink at her.

"Taken from far off, darkest Hecate, hear my call, queen of witches—wielder of storms, bring the clouds to this clear sky!" She reached out for the jar and quickly dumped the feathers out on the altar. Then, grabbing the fan, she began to move it slowly over the feathers—gradually building in strength each time.

"By sunlight, and moonlight, by shimmering stars, hide the moon from our sights!" The feathers blew everywhere, spinning and falling all around her as if it were snowing. She felt that great power rush out of her, as if it escaped from her eyes and past her lips and through her hands and out into the world.

Her heart raced and her body was filled with that usual tingling sensation, and she began to feel light-headed. She fell backwards to the floor and looked up at the ceiling, a grin spread wide across her face and she let out a euphoric laugh.

"So shall it be...."

"FROM THE DARKEST DEPTHS, from the infinite sky," Fiona began, placing her hands across her chest and looking down at them, her eyes fierce and filled with rage—an all-consuming pain and hate that was directed at Marsilio. "From the celestial realms and infinite hells, I conjure thee. Serpents from the astral plane, twist and coil and give him pain."

Marsilio began to move uncomfortably, and started shifting his weight and wincing in obvious anguish. He released Michael and fell to his knees.

"No!" he cried out. They watched as his mouth was forced open and he began to gag, and out of his throat came thick black serpents with glowing red eyes and silvery-sharp razor-backs like dragons, bits of flesh clinging to their ends from slicing his stomach and throat on their way out.

"Hecate, bring your fearsome winds, made of ghosts and rains of infernal hosts!" It was then that the sky began to erupt again with that lightning, and the winds came faster and stronger than before,

bringing with them harsh rains that attacked those burning trees and reduced them to wet and blackened smoke.

"Great Hecate, open the earth and take this demon! Take him and keep him deep within, never to see the sun or moon again!" It was then that the ground beneath Marsilio and Michael began to split and break open, and Marsilio struggled and tried to keep his balance, but the earth wanted him back.

TREVOR'S HEAD ROLLED from side to side as he came to. He was being dragged across earthen terrain, and it was cold out. He was bare, save for a clean pair of shorts that they must have put on him while he was out and he knew that they had washed his body clean of all of the piss and excrement.

His head was still covered with the hood, and though he wanted to try to fight—to attempt to break free once more—he knew that it would only lead to them knocking him out once again, and that was the last thing he wanted.

He had seen Michael Donovan and his great-grandmother Fiona as a young woman fighting a demon. Where this came from, this memory, he did not know—but he knew that it was real. His mind had not feverishly created it in his dreams; what he had seen had really happened, and he knew that there was a reason he had been shown this vision. Someone was trying to help him—some otherworldly thing was giving him a clue how to fight back.

They were humming. It was something melodic, and in a deep vibratory baritone, and if evil had a sound, this was the sound evil would make. His feet dragged upon loose earth and got caught on grass. He tried to summon his witchcraft, to use his mind to reach out to Braxton, but there was no use. There was nothing he could summon, and everything inside still lay dormant.

Had they put some kind of amulet on him to keep him from using his powers? He felt nothing knocking against his chest, but that didn't mean there wasn't something attached to him all the same.

They stopped.

He was pulled up to his feet and pressed against someone's body, his wrists held in place by the strong of someone's grip.

What's happening now? He refused to fight back, and thought it better to pretend to be weak. The hood was removed quickly from his head, and yet still he did not open his eyes. It wasn't until he allowed two hard slaps across his face before he finally opened them.

He saw all of those robed figures with their hidden faces, like a gothic branch of the KKK but with better quality fabrics, standing before him. Some of them were holding torches, and all around them were headstones and the clear night sky over head.

"What the…?" He looked down and saw a natural puddle of water from a dip in the ground at his feet. A strong, rather large, solidly-built male held him naked—save for the '70s-style athletic shorts which barely covered the tops of his thighs.

"Behold the glory of this night!" one of the figures—another male—said to him, a long sharp dagger gleamed in the light.

"Behold!" the others called out. From what he could see, there were at least twenty of them, and they were all cloaked and standing like phantoms amidst the gravestones.

"Tonight we shall perform The Reckoning and bring Him forth. Tonight we shall take back the world that was once ours, and the world will quake and fall before His feet, and the stars themselves will hide!" another said.

It was an older woman with the same English accent, whose voice was so similar to that of the one named Victoria, that Trevor was almost certain that they were related.

"No!" Trevor yelled, and was met with a slap across the face. It stung, and he liked it. There was something in that slap that recharged him; it jolted him and brought new life into his system, and reinvigorated him to keep fighting.

"Yes!" the man said. "We shall open the earth and from the depths He shall emerge, and you will be the first thing he tastes!"

Trevor shook his head and struggled against the man who held him.

"Bring the bell!"

Trevor watched one of those figures turn around and pick up a shovel from off the ground. The figure then walked over to a grave with a name he could not make out in the dark, and watched as the figure began to dig.

Trevor took note of the roads around him. Everything was empty: not a single car drove past, not a single child in costume made an appearance. It had to be everything with the eclipse. He figured all of the uncertainty, chaos, and lack of sunlight had made it so that almost everyone preferred to stay indoors.

"You see, Blackmoore, you are all alone…" the man holding him whispered into his ear. He sounded to be in his late thirties to early forties. "No one is coming for you. No one can stop this."

Trevor shook his head and continued to struggle. "Say whatever you want; just don't breathe on me, dude!" Trevor spat back.

"Fucking shit!" the man said, and slapped him across the face. The figure who had been digging returned with a bell caked in earth, and covered with various planetary symbols that Trevor recognized from his family's older books on witchcraft.

"Kept for seven days and nights in the grave of the one you wish to summon," the older woman with the accent said. "Kept in the grave of a Soul Wanderer, and it will bring back that body, that body which will play host to the Dark God!"

"Praise Him!" they all shouted.

"And he shall reward us for our service and for the gift of your flesh and beating heart!"

Trevor shook his head. He had to get away. He needed to break free and find help.

Mary-Margaret!

He looked around, trying to crane his neck to see behind him. And then he saw her, being held in the arms of another one of those robed witches, holding her naked against his chest. She was still out cold.

"He will rise and bring justice to our kind. He will decimate those who persecuted us, and He will punish the witches who stood against him!"

"You guys know you sound like nut jobs, right?" Trevor asked.

"I'm going to enjoy watching you die..." she said to him.

Trevor glared at her, staring hard into those eye-holes. "We'll see."

"Victoria! The summoning of the blood!" Trevor watched the figure he knew now to be Victoria turn and face the figure that had dug up the bell.

"We don't have a third," the girl with the shovel said to her. The voice was familiar to Trevor, and he knew that it was the one named Melanie. Victoria took hold of Melanie with one hand and with the other she tore off the hood, exposing her shocked face.

"Sorry, Melanie, but I've moved on." Victoria quickly brought a blade across her throat. It happened so fast that Trevor hadn't even noticed where the blade came from, and Melanie had been just as ignorant.

"Shh..." Victoria said while she held her, the blood pouring like a river into the puddle of water, turning it black with its mess.

"On sacred land, the time is at hand." The woman with the English accent, along with the male who held that dagger, began, their arms outstretched towards the clear, star-filled sky.

"Make the moon run red, open the doors and give him new life in the dedicated dead!" Trevor caught sight of that waxing moon, a large crescent that was changing, slowly turning a deep crimson right before his eyes.

"Bagabi Laca Bachabe. Lamac Cahi Achababe. Karrelyos. Lamac Lamec Bachalyas. Cabahagy Sabalyos. Baryolos. Lagoz Atha Cabyolas. Samahac et Famyolas. Harrahya." They began to chant, moving around in circles, dancing as that puddle began to turn thick and black. He had seen this, and this black liquid began to rise higher and higher and start to slowly spill out over the puddle's edge.

"Shit!" Sharp, talon-like hands emerged from that water and began to pull out large pieces of wood from underneath. Several long, similar hands came out of that water from every direction, stacking the pieces of wood intricately, like a Jenga puzzle.

"Bagabi Laca Bachabe. Lamac Cahi Achababe. Karrelyos. Lamac Lamec Bachalyas. Cabahagy Sabalyos. Baryolos. Lagoz Atha Cabyolas. Samahac et Famyolas. Harrahya." They continued to chant, and then those creatures began to pull themselves out of the water.

They were fit bodies, some lean male naked forms, and the women were lithe with soft breasts. Unlike their bodies, their heads were not at all human. They were beasts: goats with long curled horns, bucks with enormous antlers, ravens and wolves and cats. They groped each other, feeling their naked flesh and smearing that black water, and then they began to dance around with the rest of the coven.

"Behold his coming glory!" the man who held him said.

Quickly and unexpectedly a fog crept in, rolling across the uneven lawn. The dancing began to slow as this fog, that seemed almost as if it were thick smoke, covered the cemetery and the clear sky above. That blood-red moon was suddenly being consumed by thick, dark clouds.

"No!" they all began to shout, and those beasts—those devils of the pit—began to howl out like the beasts they were. The grip of the man who held Trevor loosened just enough that Trevor was able to force his arms down and shove his elbow hard into the man's gut.

"That's for the slap!" Trevor drove his knee into the man's face and pushed him back.

"Where is he?!" Victoria shouted. The fog was so thick that you could barely see five inches in front of your face. He could see their torches, and knew that almost all of them were gathered in front of him.

Trevor ran backwards, stumbling through the fog and the dark, seeing the orange streetlights in the distance, on the other side of the cemetery's lawn. He ran to those lights, knowing that they were behind him. He heard the humanoid beasts growling behind him, and he could hear the footfalls of the others as they chased him.

He didn't think that he could run any faster, the earth kicking up beneath his feet, navigating through thick dark, the air chilly and the fertile soil evident of the rain that had just fallen. The thick monuments stood like silent guards watching him pass. The sweat beaded down his face and glistened on his naked chest.

This was Bayview; this was where Christian Vasquez and Greg Sheer lay beneath the earth, being devoured by worms and maggots. The fog was thick and the air was crisp as he ran, knowing that if he stopped, they would catch up.

He turned and spied numerous burning orbs moving towards him in succession, like fairies in the Halloween night: desperate to lure a weary traveler or awaken the slumbering dead.

There was a dull hum as he moved, slipping past trees and headstones. He was trying to outwit the burning prisms that slipped through the mist. He stopped, caught off-guard by the darkened figure of a cloaked woman, her face covered by a hood, paying him no mind. She moved apart from the present, and he knew that she was one of the dead. Not ever an entity that lived a life, but one that was made up of thousands of lifetimes. She was an essence formed from the very pieces of the hundreds that lay beneath the earth.

She was Bayview's guardian. She watched over the souls; her business was not the living, except for only when they trespassed—and at night, a human being's presence was certainly that.

His skin crawled as he watched her, forgetting those ominous, burning orbs that glided through the mist—wondering only about this shadowed woman, and what she may or may not do. His foot gave, his knee popping his leg straight, a lone twig snapping beneath his foot. He turned and came face-to-face with a quick black form: the face withered, the nose narrow, the mouth rotting away. From beneath her hood, her yarn-like, purple-silver hair billowed, but it was those empty sockets—black and endless, hollow in her skull—that took him by surprise and sent him into darkness.

THE LIMO DROVE UP LAKEWAY, and the five of them said nothing. They kept their eyes focused outside of the tinted windows, watched with relief as everything became consumed with fog. When they looked out of the sun roof, they each grinned subtly at the sight of the clouds that overtook the night sky.

The car stopped right on the edge of the cemetery, and the five of them carefully stepped out, not bothering to wait for Jared to open it for them. They said nothing as they stood there. They could see faint glowing light dance around in the far distance of the cemetery. It was so deep in that if one wasn't looking for it, it would have been easily missed by anyone.

There was no one out. They had only passed five cars the entire way there, and now the sidewalks and the roads were all empty. There was no one. All of the houses across the street had their lights on and their curtains drawn. Not even the occasional cop car (which could normally be seen in this area at night) was anywhere to be found.

They said nothing as they made their way into the cemetery, following those distant, glowing orbs to help them to navigate the thick. They were so close, and the closer they got, moving between the headstones and stepping over uneven ground, they could sense the thick crowds of wandering spirits, lost and many not understanding what was really happening.

We're coming, babe! he thought as loud as he could. *We're coming....* The fog was unseeable, and the air grew colder the deeper into Bayview they got. The last time Braxton or Cheri had been here was Greg's funeral, which he had only attended out of deference to Trevor and the history that he and Cheri had shared with him.

Braxton had hoped he would never have to come here again, that he would never again have to walk over these bodies and sense the misery and sorrow that hovered over this place like an invisible net.

They were so close now. The flames were brighter and the shadowed outline of moving bodies could be seen, coming much more easily into view.

Hold on, babe, just hold on....

TREVOR OPENED HIS EYES. He was once again held in place by the same man as before.

"Thought you could get away?" he growled.

"Well, I figured it was worth a try," he smirked.

"Smartass!" The man yanked him hard, giving him a firm shake. "We'll see how smart that mouth of yours is once you've watched your cousin die!"

Trevor looked through the fog, and there, between him and that puddle, was his cousin Mary-Margaret, lying naked atop that pyre of wood that had been constructed by those beasts.

"Mary!" he yelled.

"She can't hear you. She's under a spell. She won't awaken until it's time for her screams to sing Him into flesh!" the man said to her.

"We can't do anything with all this fog and these clouds!" he heard Victoria complain to one of the figures.

"Yes, I know that!" another male with the same accent hissed back. *As long as the moon is hidden from view, He cannot rise....* Trevor closed his eyes and prayed that the clouds would not dissipate.

BRAXTON, KATHRYN, AND Francesca clasped their hands together and their witchcraft stirred, moving throughout their bodies and up through their lungs. They took a deep breath through their noses and whispered, "Reveal," letting the air out as if they were blowing on something hot. The thick fog blew away as if forced by a great wind, and they all stood around in stunned silence.

There was Mary-Margaret naked and asleep, her body lying on top of what appeared to Braxton to be a crudely-made altar. On the other side of her was Trevor, dressed in nothing but little blue shorts, his body writhing and struggling against one of those cloaked figures who held him in place.

On the ground next to a black, tar-like puddle was the body of a girl face-down in the pool. She was dressed in the same robes, but her head was no longer covered with a hood.

"What the fuck are those?!?" J.T. asked. All around them were the Soul Wanderers in their ritual garb, and then there were other naked things that crawled around and made guttural screeches. Their bodies were human, but they had the heads, hands, and feet of beasts, and hissed at the five of them.

"Braxton!" Trevor screamed, and the man who held him struck him across the face.

"Trevor!" Braxton charged ahead, and Kathryn and Francesca were quick to follow. The Soul Wanderers and those beasts charged at them. Braxton took his fist and popped one of the figures hard in the face, and he quickly brought his foot into the gut of another who came at him.

One of those humanoids with a raven's head came at Kathryn, and she outstretched her hand and clenched it together. The creature's head bent sharply and unnaturally, and even in the chaos the bones of its neck could be heard breaking as it fell dead to the wet ground.

"Stop them! Offer their lives and blood for Him!" shouted the man with the dagger. Francesca threw her arms out and three of the Soul Wanderers were sent backwards several feet through the air.

"Get away from my son!" Kathryn shouted. She set her eyes on one of those torches and the flame ignited fast and fierce, sparking on the figure's robes and instantly igniting the person in flames. Kathryn then focused those flames and they continued to spark, catching four more quickly.

They were running and screaming all around them. There was complete disorder and Braxton was so close to Trevor. Another one of those creatures, one with the body of a man and the head of an elk came for him, and Braxton focused, thinking only of the pain he wanted to cause, and the creature snapped backwards; its limbs bending and twisting as it howled in pain and fell to the ground.

"Braxton!" Trevor called out again, struggling to get free. There was complete disarray and there were flames and smoke everywhere, and the night sky was filling with the cries of these beasts and burning bodies.

"Trevor!" He was close to the puddle, which instinct told him to avoid. He just had to get Mary-Margaret off of the pyre and get Trevor loose. All he needed was a clear path. One of those Soul Wanderers charged him, brandishing a knife, and was about to shove it into Braxton's gut, when out of nowhere he heard J.T. howling angrily and jumping between them, throwing the robed figure to the ground.

"Get-the-fuck-off-of-my-boy!" He punched the figure repeatedly, and got hold of the knife and shoved it deep into the figure's chest. Braxton had never thought J.T. had the capability to kill, but in this instance he was glad that he did.

"Enough!" the older woman with the accent yelled. She slammed her foot on the ground and the earth shook violent and fierce, sending them to their feet. Braxton looked up to see the woman race over to Trevor and place a dagger to his throat.

"No!" they all yelled.

"Get up!" she commanded. "Get on your feet! All of you!" They reluctantly agreed, and the remaining humanoid beasts took hold of the five of them. The creatures sniffed them and licked their necks and faces with their tongues. "You shall witness his resurrection, and you shall feed him and strengthen him, and pay the price for abandoning him all those centuries ago!"

She took the blade and dug it into Trevor's flesh. She began to carve various symbols in his skin, and he grimaced and cried out in pain as his blood slipped effortlessly out of the wounds and began to soak into the earth.

"Stop!" Cheri pleaded with the woman who held him. "Please stop!"

"Look upon them, my young Blackmoore; look upon their faces and take comfort that they will be the last thing you see, and that they will still live." She continued to carve. "Be grateful that you shall be devoured first, that He shall consume you and you will not have to witness your loved ones being torn apart and skinned. Be grateful that I am so merciful!"

"Fuck you, bitch!" He spat on her face.

"Charming till the end..." the woman laughed. "Light her!" One of the other Soul Wanderers picked up one of those burning torches and placed it at the foot of the pyre. It began to burn, slowly climbing up the dead wood and making its way to the slumbering Mary-Margaret.

"And as for these clouds," another Englishman said, lifting his hand into the air. "This is nothing. This is a parlor trick!" The clouds began to roll, to move quickly across the night sky and the stars. That bright crimson crescent came back into view, shining down on them and bathing them in its wine-colored glow.

The Englishwoman returned the knife to Trevor's throat. "And from beneath us he shall rise!"

Chapter: Thirty-One

THE CELLAR WAS JUST as Benjamin and Rebecca had re-membered it. There were various dried plants hanging from the beams above their heads, and there were shelves with U.V. lights over living herbs and numerous flowers, and bookcases upon bookcases filled with books. There were candles burning every-where: on sconces and candelabras, burning on end-tables and sitting in the cellar windowsills, and roaring in a large stone hearth.

The floor beneath them was cold but dry, and before them in the center of the room was the giant table from their memory: the table where the corpse-head had sat, where it had opened its mouth and cried out with hellish torment. There were candles placed strategically around the table, and an iron cauldron was placed in the middle, along with a razor-sharp steel blade and a jar of large, black shiny spiders, which fought to be on top of one another.

"Gather 'round..." Virginia ordered, and they did, taking their places around the table. She looked up into her grandson's eyes, taking hold of the jar of spiders and raising the glass over the cauldron.

"Now, you come to this with the strongest heart, do you?"

Benjamin nodded.

"And you wish to give what you must in order to break the Binding tonight—to break the punishment of the Conclave and release Trevor Blackmoore from his chains?"

Benjamin nodded without hesitation. "I do. More than any-thing."

"Very well," Virginia said to him, turning the jar of large, vi-cious-looking spiders on its side. "So begins this magic spell!" She dropped the jar into the cauldron, and it shattered in two.

"Hold out your arms!" she ordered, and Benjamin did. His grandmother quickly lifted the blade and sliced it deep across the veins in his wrists, and blood poured out quickly, spilling into the cauldron.

"Fuck!" Benjamin let out, and Rebecca could not help but look in horror at what their grandmother had just done.

"Now, think of Trevor, only of Trevor; stick your hands into the cauldron and repeat: 'Ties that bind, I now unwind; set him free, the price is mine.' Do not think of anything else, no mat-ter what happens. If you do, you will bleed to death and you will die!"

Benjamin thought clearly of Trevor's mischievous and play-ful smirk, his short and messy dark red hair, his tanned skin and bright hazel eyes. He pictured how soft his skin looked, and the defined shoulders and lean chest. He could see those soft lips so clearly that for a moment he thought he might actually be able to kiss them, and he shoved his bleeding arms into the cauldron.

"Ties that bind, I now unwind; set him free, the price is mine!" he repeated over and over. The world seemed to be spin-ning, and then he felt those spiders latch onto him and crawl up his arms.

He kept seeing Trevor in his mind and kept chanting, refus-ing to pay attention to the excruciating pain, though he knew that those spiders had stretched out the flesh and muscle tissue and were burrowing themselves deep into his skin.

He felt them crawling up his arms from under the flesh, us-ing his veins to make their way to his heart and into his brain.

He wanted to cry out in pain, he wanted to take his arms out of that pot, but he refused. He held tight to the memory of Trevor's smile and the all-consuming love he felt for him, and how much he wanted to see him again, to speak to him and know that he was safe.

The more this desire burned inside, the more he could feel those spiders crawling around under his skin and sinking their fangs into his heart and at the back of his brain. "Ties that bind, I now unwind; set him free, the price is mine!"

"Keeping chanting!" his grandmother shouted somewhere far off in the distance, someplace far from the fiery stinging venom of these arachnids and their quest for his blood.

He could feel his balance leaving him and his legs suddenly gave out, and the pain inside of his heart and brain was so intense that he could no longer stand it.

"Fuck!" He fell to the ground and doubled over in pain and began to heave, and as he did, those spiders fell out of his mouth and onto the ground.

They were thick, and he could feel them pressing against the walls of his esophagus as they crawled out and then proceeded to run quickly into the fireplace against the wall behind him, making their way willingly to their demise.

"It is done," Virginia said.

Benjamin looked at his wrists, and all that was left were two small scars that were already scabbing over. "That's it?" He tried to get himself to his feet, but lost his balance. "That wasn't so bad," he said sarcastically.

Rebecca rushed to his side and helped her brother up off of the floor. "What was the price?" she asked.

"He will die before Trevor Blackmoore's feet. The last face he will see is the face of the one he loves."

Benjamin and Rebecca looked at each other. He wished that he could have said that he still would have agreed to do it, even if he knew the price. But he wasn't certain. Did he trade his life for Trevor's? And in the end, would Trevor be the one to kill him? It seemed like it.

"It's all up to Trevor now..." Virginia said, the flames dancing in her cold eyes. "If he survives this, I suggest you think about what the best thing for you will be." She began to make her way to the stairs of the cellar, relying on her cane.

"Because your life is now tied to his... forever."

Chapter: Thirty-Two

"MARY-MARGARET!" TREVOR screamed as the flames climbed higher and higher, consuming the wood and inching closer and closer to her naked flesh. Her eyes popped open, and she began to scream wildly and sit up on the wood, looking at the flames consuming her.

"Ring the bell and bring Him into flesh! Amduscias!" the woman screamed. The one he knew to be Victoria began to ring the bell, and its music was loud and reverberated all around them, filling their ears with its silvery cry.

"No!" Trevor cried out, just as the sky cracked with lighting, and the winds around them began to stir.

"Trevor!" Mary-Margaret screamed, bringing her body tightly into itself, trying desperately to keep herself from the licking flames. There was a strange sensation, as if he had just received a shot of adrenaline straight into his heart, and everything inside of Trevor was finally awakened and alive. He felt that great tingling heat—that witchcraft—building, compressing like water within a pot, forcing the lid to begin to rattle.

"Let me go!" And that power rushed out of him, that great force moved out of his body and blew everyone back. The beasts and the Soul Wanderers all fell to the earth, and the woman who held him was forced to the ground.

"Now!" Kathryn screamed, and she and Braxton and Francesca looked up to the heavens, which had filled quickly once again with those clouds and cracked with thunder and the white hot flash of lightning. They brought their eyes back down to the ground and the lightning followed them, striking the earth and hitting many of the remaining witches and those creatures.

Mary-Margaret closed her eyes and outstretched her arms, feeling that power, embracing it for the first time, accepting who she was and where she had come from. She thought of Fiona and how she had used the fire to cleanse the earth when she had fought to try to save Michael, and to stop the demon Marsilio Merrin.

She spread out her arms through the flames, no longer fearing them. They receded down the pyre and shot across the earth, igniting that black puddle and catching those creatures in the flames. Trevor raced towards her and they took hold of each other's hands, gripping them as tightly as possible, feeling the shared power of their blood, and the strength of Fiona Blackmoore's words a century ago.

"No!" someone yelled. The handful of Soul Wanderers began to back away, to retreat into the thick woods behind the cemetery.

Trevor and Mary-Margaret locked eyes on all of them and began to speak Fiona's words. "Hecate, bring your fearsome winds, made of ghosts and rains of infernal hosts!" The sky ignited again with that lightning, and the winds came faster and stronger than before, knocking the trees together, ripping their highest branches from the trunks and sending them through the air.

"Great Hecate, open the earth and take them back. Take them and keep them deep within, never to see the sun or moon again!"

The ground split open around them, upheaving graves and forcing some of the coffins into view.

There was chaos everywhere, and those creatures—those humanoid demons—cried out in despair as they struggled to keep on their feet, digging their claws into the ground as they slipped into the open earth.

"You motherfucker!" the one named Victoria screamed. She charged them with one of those daggers, her black robes billowing around her, the hooded cowl having fallen off her head. "I will not let you win!"

"Victoria! No!" one of those Englishmen called out.

Braxton ran in front of Trevor and held out his hand. "Pain!" he shouted, directing his hand down, feeling his hate and anger and need for vengeance begin to consume him.

She fell to the wet earth and her arms bent back unnaturally, causing the bones to break and rip out through her flesh.

She screamed out, and the dagger fell to the ground. There seemed to be a black fire raging in Braxton's eyes as he stepped closer to her. He knelt down so that his eyes met hers, taking the knife into his left hand and taking hold of her throat with his right, forcing her to look into his eyes.

"You messed with the wrong fucking witch!" He took the blade and shoved it deep between her breasts, breaking through the bone, and then with all of his strength, Braxton brought that blade up between her clavicles and tore it out of her neck.

The blood sprayed hot and red. Braxton cocked his head towards that burning black puddle, and the body of Victoria flew back into it and disappeared beneath the flames and thick inky water.

They turned around, prepared to keep fighting, but found that aside from bodies on the ground and the demons that were burning down into that same black liquid; they were the only ones there.

"Where'd they go?" Cheri asked. She was hugging tightly to J.T., who had some cuts on his face. Cheri's leggings and her coat were torn, but they were otherwise okay.

"Whatever pit they crawled out of..." Francesca said, wiping the dirt and blood off of her arms. Trevor looked at Braxton, looked into those dark eyes and that perfectly beautiful face, and began to cry. Without missing a beat, Braxton opened his arms and Trevor fell into them, the two sobbing hard against each other.

There was no need for words. No words would have sufficed. They both had lived with the fear that they would never see each other again, that they would never be able to inhale the scent of their skin, or kiss each other's lips and taste the familiarity of their mouths.

They had come very close to never feeling their bodies pressed against one another, and the reality of that threat—now that it had passed—was leaving them in the great waves of these tears.

"I love you..." Braxton whispered into his ear between fevered kisses.

Trevor gasped for breath. "I love you too...." They weren't sure how long they stood there, wrapped in each other's embrace as the bodies burned around them. The smoke and smell of that smoldering flesh, coupled with the putrid rot of those creatures, filled the night sky.

They had left before the police arrived, Francesca having retrieved that bell from off of the ground. The sirens could be seen coming in the distance, their lights flashing blue and white on all of the trees.

There were people standing outside on their lawns and on the sidewalks, finally emerging from their homes since the disorder of the eclipse had taken hold a week before.

MARCUS JAMES

"So," Cheri began, looking at Trevor as they slipped back into the limo, which had been parked along Woburn Street. "You nearly died and saved the world... what do you want to do now?"

Trevor turned and looked at her; she was grinning playfully at him, and he returned it. "Actually, I could really go for some food right now. I'm starving."

Trevor grabbed the bottle of scotch that sat on the bar and drank it straight, not bothering to pour it in a glass. "Anyone else?" he asked, holding it up.

"I think I could use that," Mary-Margaret replied. She looked exhausted, and cold as she pulled Kathryn's trench coat tight around her body. They all did, and it reflected in their eyes and could be seen in the flash of orange streetlight outside on their faces as they drove.

"By all means." Trevor handed her the bottle and watched with mild amusement as she began to take down the scotch in great big sips. "As for the food?" Trevor turned his head to the right, staring into Braxton's deep black eyes.

"Anything you want," he said to him, placing his arm around Trevor's neck and bringing his forehead to his lips. "Anything," he whispered. The only thing that had meaning was this moment, and being together, all of them, intact and stronger than before.

They had faced down demons and the possible rising of the Dark God. They had come face-to-face with the Soul Wanderers, and through all of it, they had learned something about themselves.

They weren't strong because of some primal need to survive; they were strong because of their primal need to win and to do what was right. There was darkness deep inside each one of them. They were capable of horrific things, and Trevor knew that they could do so much more.

The difference between his family and those other witches was that they were aware of the dark things that they were capable of, and the kind of power that they had—but they still chose to be better, to make the difficult choice.

There was no drive for vengeance against the entire world, and there was no wish to enslave others. That, to Trevor, was the real evil: the desire to force others to bend to your whims, to strip people of their free will, of their ability to make choices, and to make those choices for them, regardless of what it did to them.

As the limo continued to drive, past the lights of downtown and all of the homes that stood on the hillside buried in trees, Trevor thought of how everything had changed. He was a different person—they all were. Too much had happened since Christmas of last year. The threat was real now, in ways it had never been before—not since Fiona had faced it down alone at the age of seventeen back in 1908, losing Michael Donovan and Carter Mayland in the process.

As they descended off of the freeway and into the tree-lined neighborhoods of South Hill, Trevor grinned at all of the Jack o' Lanterns that smiled at him from their porch stoops and front room windows. The sun would come again; he could feel it. The darkness had passed with all of the terrors of the night.

Just as those spirits he glimpsed wandering the streets, spirits as solid to him as everyone in the limo was, the moon would go right along with them, fading in the bright light of the coming day.

Epilogue

A WEEK HAD PASSED, and the sun had in fact come again. The morning of November first, All Soul's Day, the sun had come blazing bright and golden on a cloudless sky.

People emerged from their homes, walking out into the sun, lying in the grass, going for walks throughout the neighborhoods, or reading in lawn chairs and patio furniture. Whatever anyone could do to stay out and enjoy the light, they were going to do it. People were treating it like it was summertime, though it was only fifty degrees.

The news was still trying to explain it, and scientists couldn't figure it out. NASA was still trying to come up with an answer. They wouldn't find an answer, of course, and Trevor surmised that in a couple of weeks, the media and news outlets would move on anyways. Conversations about it would begin to fade, as people tend to rationalize away what they cannot explain.

Before they had returned home to Seattle, they all explained to him everything that he had missed, all of the stuff that had happened, and what had caused the eclipse. He was told about the Conclave, this secret tribunal of selected witches, and that the eclipse and his loss of his powers had to do with a spell he worked against a member of the Conclave.

He had lied and said he didn't know who it was, or that he even remembered casting a spell. He didn't want to make matters worse before getting a chance to speak with Benjamin Tramer himself.

Mary-Margaret was excited to finish her semester, but would not be completing the year. She had nearly cried when she finally got ahold of Rebecca on the phone, and they instantly began discussing taking a sabbatical to travel Europe without any distractions.

Trevor realized that Rebecca was the sister that Benjamin had been talking to him about on that first day of class, but he decided against telling her. They were not supposed to know about who the ruling family was and who was not—and as far as Trevor knew, Rebecca had yet to tell Mary-Margaret that she was even a witch.

Trevor and Braxton spent their first week back living in a suite at the W Hotel in downtown, while the apartment was getting redone. Trevor didn't mind living in the 1,000-square-foot suite on the twenty-fourth floor of the hotel, but he was eager to get back into his own bed and be amongst his own familiar things.

Braxton and J.T. were spending more time with each other, outside of practice, finally being able to share everything. There were no more secrets between them, and the relief was evident on Braxton's face.

He no longer had to keep his best friend in the dark, and he could actually tell him all of his worries and fears without finding ways to word them so that J.T. wouldn't know what he was actually talking about.

Cheri was her usual proactive self, delving back into her studies and trying to catch up on everything she had missed, while filling the in-between times with shopping excursions and happy hours. There was now only one more door to close, and Trevor was eager to do it while Braxton was at the studio.

He had called Benjamin Tramer and told him to meet him at the freeway park at the Convention Center. He didn't tell him why, other than that they needed to talk. He had agreed, and his tone had lacked the usual smugness that Trevor had come to expect from him.

Trevor stood in the middle of the deserted path of pavement, looking at all of those leafless branches, seeing their paper-like decay of colors on the grass. He was dressed in blue jeans and a gray sweatshirt with a white crew-neck tee underneath, looking at his watch occasionally, but mostly just standing there with his eyes closed, smelling the crisp autumn air tinged with the smells of the city and the salt of the sea, and feeling the sunlight on his face.

A part of him had to fight the urge to spread his arms out and spin. The city was for the most part back to normal, though some of the businesses still had their broken windows covered with big sheets of wood.

"Hey."

He opened his eyes and saw Benjamin standing there. He had on a blue-and-red flannel shirt with the sleeves rolled up to his elbows, brick-red skinny jeans, and black suede lace-up boots on his feet. His dirty-blond hair was pulled back from his face in its usual bun, and his golden eyes seemed sad, as if he had been stricken with some sort of terrible grief that he could not move on from.

Trevor knew that kind of grief intimately; he knew what it looked like on the face, as he had seen it many times staring back at him in his own reflection. "Are you okay?"

Benjamin nodded. "Yeah, I'm fine. I'm just tired... trying to get caught up on the work we've missed."

Trevor smiled. "Yeah, I know how that is." Benjamin gave a slight smirk, and Trevor felt the faintest hint of butterflies, and he blushed in spite of himself.

"I heard what happened to you, getting injured and all...." Trevor averted his gaze. "I'm glad to see you're okay."

Trevor shook his head and took a deep breath. "I know."

"Good, I was afraid you'd think I didn't care or something –"

"No," Trevor interjected. "I mean, I know." He looked at Benjamin, and the revelation flashed over his face quickly. "About you and your sister, and about the Conclave."

Benjamin began to shift his weight nervously from one foot to the other. "So, what... um, what are you going to do?"

"Nothing." He hadn't even been certain of what his course of action was going to be until he was face to face with Benjamin and could look into his eyes. Now that he saw them, and saw the genuine worry and the fear at being discovered, he realized that he needed to keep his secret.

"You mean...?"

Trevor nodded. "Your secret's safe with me." They smiled at one another, a warm smile that expressed relief.

"Why would you do that?" Benjamin asked him, sweeping his foot back and forth across the concrete.

"Because I think you had something to do with ending the Binding and giving me my powers back." Benjamin said nothing, but the look on his face—the way his eyes grew at this idea—told Trevor that he was right. "What I want to know is, why?"

"Why what?" Benjamin kept his eyes locked with Trevor's.

"Why did you do it? You could have let the Binding run its course; why did you break it? It couldn't have been easy to break a hex that is centuries old."

Benjamin began to move closer to him, and with each step, Trevor's heart began to pound. "No, it wasn't."

"But then why –"

"Would you have done it?" Benjamin interjected, placing his index finger to Trevor's lips. "Would you have risked anything for Braxton if he was in the same situation, and you were the only one who could do it?"

Trevor nodded. "Of course."

"That's why," Benjamin said, placing his hands on Trevor's forearms and holding him in place. "I did it for the same reason."

Trevor frowned and nodded slowly. He understood. He understood completely, because everything that he was, everything that he could ever want or hope to be, was wrapped up inside of Braxton Volaverunt.

"Take care of yourself, Trevor Blackmoore." Benjamin closed his eyes and pulled Trevor close to him, placing his lips to his forehead. Trevor felt the tears drip from Benjamin's eyes and onto his cheeks.

"I will...."

Benjamin pulled himself away from Trevor and smiled at him, not bothering to wipe the tears from his eyes. "You know, in the old days, today would be the New Year. I suppose in a way it still is... for people like us."

Trevor fought hard to keep his own tears at bay, standing there in the middle of the park, watching Benjamin begin to step back from him.

"I suppose it is."

"Happy New Year, Trevor Blackmoore." He began to walk away. It was slow and deliberate, and Trevor wondered if he would ever see Benjamin Tramer again.

They still had school, but he had a feeling he would not be seeing Benjamin on campus ever again.

"Happy New Year to you, too!" he shouted through the tears that he could no longer hold back. Benjamin turned around one last time and smiled at him, before disappearing around a corner.

He wanted to stand there for as long as he could. Alone in the cold and the sun, letting the tears fall. Perhaps it was the goodbye; perhaps it was whatever sacrifice Benjamin had made to save him and release him from the Binding, or maybe it was simply the constant stream of goodbyes that seemed to make up his life.

But watching Benjamin go felt akin to someone dying, and he needed to mourn, alone, just for a few moments, just until the tears stopped.

AN HOUR LATER, HE WALKED through the door of their suite. The city and the water was bright and glittering in the evening sun. There, splayed out on the modern blue velvet sofa, flipping through the channels on the big forty-two-inch plasma television on the living room wall, was Braxton, dressed in those loose Jnco's he seemed to somehow keep from falling apart after all of these years, and a gray cotton tank top with a screen-print of an American Flag upside down, made to look as if it had been spray-painted in black.

He turned and locked eyes with Trevor, those wonderfully large and liquid onyx eyes, and he knew that everything would be okay. That smile spread wide on that devilishly handsome face, and Braxton pressed the mute button and sat the remote on the glass coffee table.

"You okay?" he asked.

Trevor nodded and made his way over to the sofa. Braxton sat up and opened his arm to him, letting Trevor rest his head on the usual place on his chest, just above his heart. "You know, I heard you."

Braxton shook his head, trying to think of what Trevor was talking about. "What?"

"At the hospital... when I was in the coma." He sat up so that their eyes could meet. "I don't know where I was. There was no world full of dead boyfriends or deceased family members, but there was your voice. In the empty void, there was your voice."

He smiled at him and Braxton returned it, his eyes beginning to fill with tears, and he nodded and tried to fight back the sobs. "You heard me?" He barely made it through those cries.

"In the emptiness, you were the only thing I heard. You were the only thing that reminded me that I was still alive." Trevor extended his hands and wiped Braxton's tears gently with his thumb.

"When I heard your voice, I would be aware—for just a moment—long enough to keep me fighting."

Braxton nodded hard and took Trevor's face into his hands and brought him to his lips, kissing him over and over again. Kissing him through the tears and through the fear and the loss, kissing him through the memories of blood and broken glass and fires, and dead fathers, and children being buried beneath the earth.

He kissed him for the promise of always hearing each other. No matter how deep the darkness or how terrifying the terrain. No matter the threat, no matter the evil, they would always find a way back to each other.

"I'll always hear you," Trevor said to him, unable to fight back his own tears.

"And so will I," Braxton responded. He brought Trevor up on to his lap, his legs straddling him, his arms wrapped around Braxton's neck while he cupped Trevor's butt with his hands. They looked deep into each other's eyes, eyes that they had looked into since they were both kids, eyes that had always made them feel safe and protected from the world, eyes that could see into each other's souls.

"I'm going to ask you to marry me one day; you know that, right?" Braxton smirked.

Trevor laughed and shook his head.

"No?" Braxton asked, poking him on the side with his finger. "No?" he asked again, followed by another poke.

"We're too young..." Trevor said, kissing him on the lips.

"For now," Braxton agreed with a nod. "For now."

"But," Trevor said, staring deep into his dark eyes and brushing back that stylish black hair, admiring the golden luster of his olive skin, and the beautiful coloring of his tattoo sleeve. "Don't wait too long to ask me."

Braxton smiled wide, his white teeth gleaming in the evening light, his breaths deep and labored, expressing the peace that he felt in this moment with Trevor. "Never."

They stayed that way for a long time, until the sun finally set and the lights of all of those windows in all of those skyscrapers lit up the twilight sky, and the only thing that could be seen along the water were the ferries going back and forth from the islands.

There was no point in moving. There was no point in turning on lights or ordering food, or sending texts or making phone calls. The only thing that mattered was this moment, right here, together, held in place and anchored by their souls, adrift in a sea of one another.

The evil would come again, as it always did, and there would be more battles to face, more blood to be shed, and likely more lives lost. It would always be coming, but for now, in this moment, they would just stay right here, on this sofa on their last night in this suite—kissing and waiting till the morning, making sure that the sun came up again and chased away the dark.

It was one of the best nights they had ever had.

It was perfect.

An exclusive preview of the next novel in The Blackmoore Legacy...

THE

BECKONING

ONE

Coming soon from Candiano Books

Halloween

HE KNEW THESE STREETS. Knew them like the back of his hand, had run them every morning for the past two years, following their cracked and sometimes uneven terrain, snaking up and down never-ending hills and amazing vistas. His neighborhood streets, Fillmore and Pierce behind him, and Scott Street just ahead of him, and somehow—some way and for a reason he did not understand—he was standing on his block, Green Street, with no memory of how he got there.

No. Standing wasn't right. He had no limbs and there was no sensation of ground. No sidewalk beneath his feet that he could feel. No bone, no clothing, no weight; no sense of himself other than what he could see, and that he was aware of it and knew it.

The sky was black and the branches of trees were made garish by orange streetlights. It was late—the middle of the night—he knew this. But it was about all he knew, for the answer to the question to how he had ended up outside in the first place still had yet to be answered.

He heard a door open, an old thing that creaked on its hinges and cried out in the quiet dark. He looked to his left, spying one of those numerous Sears & Roebuck Queen Anne Victorians (the twenty-foot-by-one-hundred-foot houses that the city was infamous for, and that could be ordered for a few thousand dollars from the iconic department store over a century ago) painted white and cream. From under its porch, a young girl with red hair and peach skin emerged from the shadows, barefoot and padding down the concrete steps in nothing but a powder-blue night gown.

"...Take his hand and go inside, for The Beckoning One is coming by. Pure as petals they will be—all the girls that he will need..." she sang to herself, walking quickly up the street towards Scott, passing dark windows and still cars parked along the curbs, and trash cans waiting to be emptied.

He was following her. He wasn't sure how he was doing it, as he felt no ground beneath his feet, and yet he could smell the fresh bay air, the constant damp at this time of year, and all of the other random odors that lingered in every crevice and wafted in the air as brief as a ghost.

This city was full of ghosts, and he knew a lot about them himself.

From the bay windows of all of those Victorians, the numerous apartments—also Victorian with stacked turrets that went on for many stories, and the later Spanish-style with their picture windows and stucco exteriors—he spied glowing pumpkins carved with a kaleidoscope of faces, and strings of ghost lights in windows and wrapped around banisters, decorations that would be taken down and put back into boxes to rest in the dark for another year.

All about them was silence, and the city had never felt so dead.

"...Past the green and deep in the trees—this is where he will be..." she continued to sing, her voice gentle and adolescent.

Her song carried on the wind and to his ears, a cheerful melody, much like a nursery rhyme. Her hair lit up like a spark under orange streetlight, and she walked uninhibited, not at all concerned at the possibility of stepping on broken glass or a used needle. She must have been ten or eleven, but not any older than that.

Where was she going?

There was no ground, there was no breathing, and yet he followed right behind her, as if he were the camera lens of some immersive virtual reality documentary. He went where she went, and yet he could not speak; he could not intercede. He could not even draw conscious thought. He could form no words; he could only watch and go along with a sort of awareness that was rooted in some yet-unknown mystery of his mind.

She crossed Divisadero Street, not bothering to look for cars. In the end there were none to be had, as everything was deserted—barren—a city that was still asleep. Normally it was the most serene time to walk the city. Those wee hours when everything was quiet, the streets sparse and clean, and no sound but delivery trucks and garbage collectors going about their routines, when they were afforded the opportunity to maneuver the narrow streets and intimidating and often near-impossible hills, free of the congestion of the waking world.

This time though, there was nothing. It was still too early for all of that but too late for anyone to be up, except for the beasts and the creatures of the night. That time after bar close but before the trucks that were the eeriest and the most dangerous. The time before early morning commuters and dog walkers; this time when it was just potential predators and possible prey.

And now this young girl.

She took a right on Lyon Street, traversing the border of the Presidio, the former military post-now-park that would be filled with dozens of joggers in just a couple of hours, continuing to sing her rhyme absent-mindedly, not at all hindered by her bare feet.

The dark grew the further down the hill they went, passing rows of spike-like trees that appeared jagged and razor-sharp against the night sky. At first he thought it was a glitch in the system—whatever it was that was happening to make him see whatever it was that he had been seeing and doing, for the dark appeared to be growing, consuming more and more of the environment around them, and it took him a moment to realize that the streetlamps were blinking out, along with porch lights and traffic lights.

Every light the little girl passed blinked out, sending everything into shadows—shadows of different hues—different layers, all draping atop of each other; draping over everything that surrounded them.

Deeper into this dark they went, and the girl kept singing.

"Darkness falls and you can't run—children wait for The Beckoning One..."

The fog began to roll in, thick and white, slipping between trees, houses, and cars. Traveling up the streets and crossing the intersections, drawing closer and closer to them, until it was consuming her and everything around her.

He worried that he would somehow lose sight of the girl, but this did not happen. She was taking him with her, deep into the mist, into the dark, where no light burned and where they would be hidden from another person's view.

There was music. An old tune. He knew it. He had grown up hearing it. He was trying to place it. It was a smooth tenor of a man, singing a song warning kids against the bogeyman and how to fend him off.

Where was it coming from?

Everything was dark, and yet he could still make her out. He could still make out the surroundings. The high Greco-Roman colonnades and the inky, nighttime waters of the lagoon, the abundance of foliage and exotic plants, and in the center, the rotunda, reminiscent of the great ruins of the ancient world and that now looked like an eerie graveyard, like those gothic Victorian cemeteries in the United Kingdom and Ireland, a decaying and haunted place—a monument to a withered and antiquated time.

The Palace of Fine Arts. What was she doing here? Where was the music coming from?

It was getting closer. The girl stepped along the path, into the garden and between the columns, making her way to that remnant of the city's triumph over earthquakes and fires that could have decimated her every single time. But the city had risen more triumphant, and this had been a show of that—an intended teardown for the 1915 Panama-Pacific Exposition that became a prized relic for a city that treasured its old things.

Hush, Hush, Hush, here comes the bogeyman...

That song; where could that song be coming from?

The girl got closer and closer to the austere columns, and the rotunda was draped in shadows, casting down the cornices and spilling across the sleek floor. The song echoed from within, traveling up and making its way back down again from the domed ceiling.

In the middle of the rotunda was an old crank phonograph, its needle dancing along the thirty-eight, and the tenor's voice was coming out of that flower-shaped horn. Everything inside of him wanted to recoil, to get away from there, but the girl was his tether, and the girl was taking more and more steps towards it.

He wasn't dreaming. He knew that he wasn't. He knew what dreams felt like, and they didn't feel like this. Whatever *this* was, it was brand new.

Weird things in general weren't new to him. Not when a person came from a family like his. A family that could do things: great things and horrendous things, things that were deadly and terrifying; the things of nightmares and the fright of any fire-and-brimstone heart.

He had always chalked up the strange things that happened in his life to being who he was and where he came from. What he didn't like was not being able to have control over it, and right now, he had absolutely no control over what was going on.

She got closer to the phonograph, still humming her song, when suddenly the crank stopped and the tenor went silent mid-chorus.

"...Stay with him forever more...just walk through his open door," she finished.

A ghastly cackle—slowed down and much more drawn out— followed by a feral shriek, filled the black of the rotunda in some sort of deranged pleasure. The girl turned her head towards it, her hazel eyes wide as they peered into the pitch that surrounded her, and her mouth fell into what seemed to be the start of a scream.

A long, corpse-gray arm, connected to a hand with boney twig fingers—the middle and ring fingers being the longest by several inches, and that were capped with talon-like black nails—suddenly shot out of the gloom and ripped into the girls' chest, hooking her in a spray of blood and torn cotton, pulling her back into the impenetrable dark, while the other clawed-hand scooped up the phonograph, dragging it back into the shadows.

'Blackmoore...' the voice hissed in a high singsong, before devolving back into that animal shriek and unnerving cackle. 'Marcel... Blackmoore....'

Wages of love and sin, and at its heart: the Devil

"...You must know, therefore, that men grow bewitched when they look continuously straight into the eyes of another and that the eyes of the two fasten themselves strongly to one another, and light of eye also to light of eye; mind then joining to mind and carrying flashes to it and fixing them upon it."

—*Philosophie Occulte, Book I,* Cornelius Agrippa

ONE

HIS STOMACH HAD TWISTED and turned into knots the entire walk from his studio apartment on Capitol Hill down to the freeway park on Union Street, behind the convention center. He hadn't expected the phone call from Trevor. He had not anticipated the sound of his voice on the other end of the line, secretive and earnest, as if he didn't want Braxton to hear him make that phone call to him in the first place.

It had made his heart race and his palms sweat. He had agreed—a little too hurriedly—a little too eager, but he had been caught off guard by Trevor's voice—his desire to see him—that he gave away his hand without even realizing it.

Benjamin Tramer had been laying back on his bed, his honey eyes staring up at the white plaster medallion in the middle of the ceiling from which a large 1920's flush light with a domed-white drum-shade hung from its center, his sculpted body covered only in white briefs, and the sunlight coming through the plate-glass windows danced on the golden hairs of his chest.

His dishwater blond locks were pulled back from his face in a loose bun, and his seductive lips and angular jaw were framed by a growing dark blond beard that was not quite-yet full.

He was smoking his third joint while trying to recover from the spell he had performed a week earlier on Halloween night—the spell ending the Binding that had caused Trevor to be so vulnerable and nearly resulted in him getting killed and the Dark God of the Wood being set free—when the call came in.

He wouldn't have gotten out of that bed for anybody. His body ached all over and the inside of his throat felt completely torn up and there was the ever-present sensation of those Impish spiders crawling up through his esophagus and forcing him to heave them out onto the cellar floor of his grandmother's home.

He wasn't going anywhere.

And then Trevor called and he found himself quickly picking up a pair of already-worn brick-red skinny jeans off of the floor, a fresh pair of socks, a blue-and-red flannel shirt—also on the floor—and stuffing his feet into a pair of black suede lace-up boots as he stumbled to get his bearings.

He pulled open the large white pocket doors that separated his bedroom from the living room—with its bay windows to his left, and straight ahead, a kitchen so small, that sometimes he felt as if he could barely fit into it, let alone fit two people—and grabbed his keys, rushing into the narrow but long foyer and out into the hall of the third floor, quickly locking the door behind him.

He had walked at a brisk pace down Pike Street, trying to imagine what it could be that Trevor would want with him, and why he had sounded so secretive and deliberate? The glistening steel and glass citadels of Seattle's skyline were capped in low-hanging clouds and bright sun. Horns honked and the cries of seagulls could occasionally be heard rising above the sounds of an active city; a city that was recovering from the apocalyptic-like chaos of the past couple of weeks.

The closer he got to that large glass sky bridge high above the street, the more his hands began to fidget in his pocket. He took a left and made his way into the tunnel connecting Pike to Union via the Convention Center, bringing him closer and closer to the staircase on Seventh Avenue: that great wall of concrete that led up to the urban park that intersected with the freeway.

Benjamin walked up the steps slowly, trying to steady his breathing and his racing heart. He felt a wave of elation move over him as he began to ascend those final concrete steps, spying Trevor Blackmoore standing in the middle of the path, a maple tree with golden-red leaves looming over him, the autumn sun reflecting in his mess of wine-red hair.

His eyes were closed, and his lean body was dressed in a pair of blue jeans and a gray sweatshirt with a white crew-neck tee underneath it. His sneakers shuffled against the concrete as he waited.

He smiled. He couldn't help it. Trevor looked beautiful there in the sun. He could tell that Trevor was appreciating the fact that he was still alive. That he was able to breathe in the city and the damp and that he was able to look at the leaves and feel the sun on his face again.

Benjamin could have stood there all day, just watching him. He had never felt so taken by someone before. He had prided himself in his abilities to separate emotions from sex—from desire. He had inherited that from his father Jasper, and it was about the only thing he had inherited from a man who was otherwise an aloof authoritarian figure who only barked orders and yelled about tradition. A man who wasn't a witch, but a devil in his own right, and who preferred to live in plausible deniability when it came to his children and his wife's family.

Trevor Blackmoore had torn that all away. He had come in and like the powerful swipe of a grizzly's claws, he had ripped through that wall that divided the two, and let them run rampant.

He had tried to ignore it. He had tried to deny it, to push it away, and stay focused on just making contact with him and discovering how aware Trevor was of what he was, and maybe eventually, what he knew of the Dark God of the Wood.

Benjamin had always been used to his looks and his charm disarming those he spoke to, and as a result, had always been able to get his way. But Trevor Blackmoore had been different. He had responded to his devil-may-care flirtations with the cool reserve of someone who had been used to guys like him, and he wasn't going to tolerate any of it.

It had put him at a disadvantage—one that had kept growing the more and more he thought about, looked at, and spoke to Trevor. His resolve had fascinated Benjamin, his silence—his mastery over his own obvious attractions to him, the challenge Trevor presented in just getting close to him; to get one ounce of warmth and vulnerability from him. It all had been enough to turn in on itself and develop into a desperate obsession that festered deep in Benjamin's heart.

Trevor turned slowly, his eyes still closed, and he was soon facing Benjamin. He stopped. Faces perfectly aligned, and Trevor seemed to respond to his presence, as if when they lined up with one another, it had moved him like a ghost passing through.

"Hey," he said.

Trevor opened his eyes, and those russet green eyes looked particularly bright the way they caught the sun. His lids grew wide and then his face immediately turned sullen.

"Are you okay?" he asked.

Benjamin nodded. "Yeah, I'm fine. I'm just tired..." he lied. "Trying to get caught up on the work we've missed."

He thought about the week-long eclipse that was the result of the Binding on Trevor. He could tell by the slow nod that Trevor was thinking about the same thing, though they would never talk about it.

He smiled. "Yeah, I know how that is."

Benjamin gave Trevor a slight smirk in response. "I heard what happened to you, getting injured and all..." Trevor averted his gaze from him. "I'm glad to see you're okay," Benjamin finished.

Trevor sighed and took a deep breath, shaking his head in what he could only conceive of as disappointment.

"I know," he finally said.

"Good," Benjamin responded. "I was afraid you'd think I didn't care or something—"

"No," Trevor interjected. "I mean, I know." Benjamin's eyes grew wide, and he thought of his sister. He thought of his family back in Boston, and the rules of engagement if discovered. "About you and your sister, and about the Conclave."

Benjamin began to shift his weight nervously from one foot to the other. "So, what... um, what are you going to do?"

Benjamin should have already killed Trevor by now. The rules of protecting the coven in charge was that if a witch discovered their identity, then that witch was not allowed to live. There was too much risk to the governing family to permit that kind of knowledge from getting out.

"Nothing."

He had to stifle a visible gasp. "You mean...?"

Trevor gave a gentle smile and nodded. "Your secret's safe with me."

Benjamin returned the smile and swept his foot back and forth across the pavement. "Why would you do that?"

"Because," he grinned sheepishly, "I think you had something to do with ending the Binding and giving me my powers back."

Benjamin tried to keep his face still. He said nothing, would not even nod—he didn't know how to answer or if he should. And yet he knew that the look in his eyes was giving him away.

"What I want to know is, why?" Trevor finally asked.

Benjamin's palms began to sweat and he stuffed them quickly into the front pockets of his jeans, but he kept his eyes locked with Trevor's, determined to hold him in place. "Why what?"

"Why did you do it? You could have let the Binding run its course; why did you break it? It couldn't have been easy to break a hex that is centuries old."

The question of why. It was always the most impossible to answer honestly, because doing so would expose the truth—the real motivation behind every thought and deed, the inner workings of the human soul. The physiology of human needs—desires—ambitions; the ego. It was all there. All wrapped up within the answer to why.

"No, it wasn't."

"But then why—"

"Would you have done it?" he interjected, placing his finger to Trevor's soft, pink lips and silencing him. He decided to take a chance and just go ahead with it, letting it all out come-what-may. However it all turned out, it really didn't seem to matter. He was thinking about leaving anyways. He needed to.

Ending the Binding meant tying his life to Trevor's and when he died, it would be in front of Trevor—or possibly by Trevor. The actual way it would happen wasn't clear, as a spell's consequences rarely were; besides, Trevor was in love with someone else. It wasn't good for him to stay in Seattle either way.

"Would you have risked anything for Braxton if he was in the same situation, and you were the only one who could do it?"

Trevor nodded and responded without hesitation. "Of course."

"That's why," Benjamin said, reaching out for Trevor's forearms and wrapping his hands around them, massaging his fingers into his skin and trying to choke back the tears that were catching in his throat.

The realization of his words and the depth of his feelings were dawning on Trevor. He could see it in the way his shoulders relaxed and his stance softened. He could see it in the tears that began to glisten along the brim of Trevor's eyes. Trevor was understanding and desperately searching for a way to respond. A way that would make sense and that would spare them both the pain of more truth—of more honesty.

Benjamin's insides quaked as he held him, wanting to risk even more—to dare even more—but too terrified to try. "I did it for the same reason."

HIS EYES OPENED SLOWLY, the whirring of the plane's engines bringing him out of a gin-and-Robaxin-induced sleep. He didn't need them; he just enjoyed muscle relaxers for plane rides and a Tuesday night in on occasion. He hadn't dreamed. It was just a sleep full of memories playing on loop—memories that brought him to catching a three in-the-afternoon flight out of SeaTac the next day in the first place.

He needed to get out of Seattle. He needed to get away from Trevor Blackmoore and the consuming ache and need that he was feeling for him, and to get away from the intense jealousy towards Trevor's boyfriend, Braxton Volaverunt. The envy was thick and tar-like. It was tar that was hot and filled with bits of broken glass, gravel, and twigs that moved through his veins and into his heart as thick and slowly as possible, strangling him on its pungency.

The temptation to harm Trevor's partner was getting to be too much to bear, and Benjamin wasn't certain how much longer he could go on for and not resort to acts of malice. He tried to avoid using witchcraft as much as possible in his life to get his way. Learning to accept life on life's terms when he could easily turn the course was a daily struggle. It always had been, and his feelings for Trevor—no matter how unrequited and how aware of that he was—were getting too strong, too desperate and suffocating to ignore anymore.

He needed to get free from it. He needed to put a whole country between him and the witch who stole his heart: the witch who would be the death of him.

Benjamin Tramer wanted to live. He wanted that more than anything else, and nothing was more important than that—especially a love that couldn't be returned, no matter how much he wished for it. He wasn't going to attempt any sort of love spell on the kid. That wasn't his style anyways, so why risk dying for it?

He sat curled up in his first-class seat, his feet propped up, his black peacoat pulled around him, his mop of dirty-blond hair sticking out from under a gray knit-cap, and his eyes crusted over with sleep, feeling the effects of the pills wearing off.

"Fuck." Benjamin shook his head and reached for the third airline-sized bottle of *Tanqueray* stuffed into the pocket of the seat in front of him and quickly twisted off the black cap, putting it to his lips and swallowing it quickly.

There was no one in the seat next to him, and aside from a portly twelve-year-old boy with semi-rimless glasses watching *Iron Man* on the screen, the first class cabin—along with business class behind him—was quiet. It was dark and most of the travelers were fast asleep, all of them hoping to wake up once the plane started to descend.

He checked the map on the screen, watching the animated plane make its way over New York and felt the nausea take hold. His parents didn't even know he was coming home.

When he had returned from his meeting with Trevor—finally pulling him close and kissing him on the forehead before saying goodbye, allowing Trevor to see his tears and to feel them and to know them, and know that they belonged to him and him alone—he stopped into the Eagle, a gay leather bar in the classic sense, evoking the seediness of the Seventies and pre-AIDS gay liberation.

It was a narrow two-story place with black walls, red and blue lighting, sticky black floors, and a bathroom with a trough urinal that had hosted more than its fair share of casual sex. It was a dark place where anything could happen, and it usually did. A place where Benjamin had seen—and even taken part in—a fair share of debauchery over the past two years.

Benjamin had ignored the discriminating glances and the salacious grins as he walked up to the bar and ordered himself a shot of whiskey, followed with another, and another—all of which the handsome bartender with the trimmed brown goatee and muscular, shirtless body was more than happy to provide.

He would have fucked him.

He would have left there with the guy or banged him in the bathroom or out on the enclosed back deck where all sorts of sucking and fucking went on, amidst patrons puffing on cigarettes, smoking weed, and enjoying their drinks.

But then Trevor Blackmoore happened, and the first time he had fucked a guy after a couple of weeks of knowing Trevor had made him feel sick afterwards, as if he had committed some sort of sin—some sort of terrible infidelity against Trevor. He tried to explain it away, tried to remind himself that Trevor was already with someone and that Trevor had never given him any sort of impression that there could be something more between them. Trevor was to be watched. Contact was to be made, and information was to be gathered and that was supposed to be the end of it.

Trevor had gotten under his skin before he had even realized it, and that passion had grown and infected everything else. He hadn't even bothered to try hooking up after that—and now, he didn't want to.

By the time he had left the Eagle he had been shit-faced and angry. By the time he walked through the door of his studio, stripping off his shirt and tripping onto the floor to get his boots and jeans off, Benjamin knew without a doubt that he had to get out and put as much space between them as he could. Sometimes it wasn't about running away; sometimes it was about saving yourself, and that's what he was doing: saving himself.

His rent was already paid up for the year—he could ride it out or terminate it early and pay the fee, still having money coming back to him in the end, or he could do something else.

He liked the place. Its hardwood floors, the elegant molding and nine-foot ceilings, the decent-sized living area looking over the Mercedes dealership and the apartments across the street with windows he couldn't avoid looking into. Along with a view of *The Honey Hole*—a bar and sandwich shop that he had become addicted to over the years and that was now part of his Wednesday night ritual, and he could see *Edge of the Circle Books*, which was the occult shop next door with its giant black cloth pentacle in the window.

He liked the old pocket doors that split the room. The manager of the building had told him that it was not a true bedroom and that it had been intended as a sleeping/living space, and the front room with the bay windows had been designated as the dining area—which he could see—but that most just forsook a dining area in preference of having a separate sleeping space. It was what Benjamin had ended up doing as well.

He had enjoyed the apartment, and even though he had recently found himself spending more and more time at his grandmother Virginia's estate up in the Highlands, an area that was twelve miles north of downtown, he had no desire to ever leave the apartment.

But now all of that was up in the air.

The cabin lights came back on with blazing intensity, stirring the slumbering passengers as the voice of the middle-aged woman with the kindly Southern drawl came on the intercom, announcing that they were making their final descent into the city and that they were due to arrive at Boston-Logan International Airport in the next fifteen minutes.

Benjamin's golden eyes glanced out of the window. The dark surfaces of the Charles River and Boston Harbor danced with the orange-and-white lights of the city's fluorescents, twinkling from the streets and office windows of her towers, and like a jewel it glittered in the night.

He tore his eyes away from the window and closed them, taking a deep breath and holding it. He needed to steady his nerves. He was returning home—to Tramer ground-zero since the family's arrival in 1680—where he would have to deal with not only his father's constant disappointment, the family's blue blood legacy and expectations—but also three generations of cousins who lived in the townhouse, which was more like a compound for the Tramers of Boston than anything else.

The family had come to the colony seeking refuge from a Europe hell-bent on eradicating witches; they were bankers who took a gamble on the new colonies and their foundations of freedom and opportunity. They had left for the New World with the taste of smoke and charred flesh in their lungs and the image of one of their own burning and writhing in agony, while spitting curses at her persecutors, her King, and the God of the people.

The family had always stayed together. His father had had to accept that when he married his mother, Finley Tramer, in 1976. She wasn't going to leave the house, and her cousins weren't going to leave it either. That's the way it had always worked, and he was going to have to face all of it. All of that would be waiting for him, and with a slew of judgments and unwanted opinions as to why he was back and his inability to follow through with anything.

Benjamin sighed and dug around for the final bottle of airplane gin. It was already close to midnight, but he knew that wouldn't matter. His parents were sure to still be up, along with his cousins Simone and Tyler—though there was a good chance Simone would be at a party with friends and the other would be in his room playing the latest *Grand Theft Auto* with his Lacrosse buddies while drinking champagne smuggled from the wine cellar and passing the bong around.

"Found you, you bastard!" he whispered as he pulled the blue bottle out and devoured its contents in one swig. He should have gone someplace else, and he could still. He could get off the plane, grab his luggage, and then turn around and pick any other place, but he didn't like not having a plan. He hated the idea of just trying to settle on something.

He needed to know what he was doing next. He had just up-and-left everything. He wasn't going to be returning to school—that much he did know—and he had no idea what he would do with his place.

In the end, he needed to go home. He needed to pause and take a breath and sort out his options, and that's what home was for. That was the whole point of it. It didn't always work out like that, not for everybody, but at its core, that's what the concept of home always was—a refuge in familiar lands, surrounded by those who loved you and stood by you, despite the differences that existed.

Stumbling home from the bar the night before had felt foreign to him. He had felt like a stranger in a strange land. The sidewalks he walked—sidewalks that he had treaded so many hundreds of times—suddenly felt alien to him. Nothing was familiar anymore, and when he woke up passed out on the floor just as the sky was paling to dawn, he realized that that feeling was still there, and made worse by his pounding headache.

You have to go home, he reminded himself with a somber nod, looking at his reflection in the porthole window. *You have to go and figure your shit out. You have to go and try to breathe. You have to try to extract him from your veins. You know he isn't good for you. You know this....*

As he finally remembered to put his seat belt back on and gather the empty bottles for the flight attendant coming his way with a white plastic garbage bag in tow, Benjamin looked down at those two scratches across his wrist—the only remnants of those hellish spiders that had burrowed under his skin and crawled throughout his body, infecting him with their curse as they devoured the Binding that had been placed on Trevor for whatever spell he had tried to work on him—and shook his head.

He hoped that it was worth it. He hoped that he wouldn't regret his decision at some point. At the moment, he didn't. Despite it all, he still didn't. He had done it all for love; he had willingly put a potential expiration date on his life, and he was okay with that because it meant that Trevor lived.

For a second there, he hadn't been certain that he would have still gone through with it knowing the price he would pay—but in the end, he knew that he would have still made the same choice. He couldn't see Trevor die. He couldn't go through life knowing that Trevor was dead and he could have stopped it, or in knowing that it even had something to do with him.

A flash of Trevor turning slowly in the sun with closed eyes ignited across the screen of his mind, and Benjamin could feel the tears begin to catch in his throat. He swallowed them down and looked back out into the night, at that city beneath him, and he was so much closer to it now, as if he could reach out and touch those rooftops and telephone posts.

The details of cars and trees, of people moving on the wet streets, and the coming airstrip—it made everything inside of him tremble. *Take a deep breath, man,* he told himself. *Just breathe... you don't have to stay here forever.*

As the wheels came down and made contact with the pavement—screeching across it like a bullet—he imagined it not stopping. He envisioned the plane charging ahead and spearing other jets making their way in and out. He smiled at this thought; after all, if he was smeared all over the runway, then he wouldn't have to worry about facing his parents or dying at Trevor's feet. Either way, it felt like a win.

About the Author

MARCUS JAMES IS THE author of eight novels, has been a featured writer for Seattle Gay News. He has contributed to a dozen short story anthologies with Alyson Books. He lives in the Pacific Northwest with his husband and their Staffordshire Terrier Nikita. He is 35 years old.

Find him on facebook: @MJameswriter
Follow him on twitter: @MJamesbooks
Instagram: @marcusjamesauthor
www.marcusjamesbooks.com

Made in the USA
Columbia, SC
08 January 2020